A SEASON OF CLOUDS

When only your past can save your future

ALEX GERRICK

A Season of Clouds: When only your past can save your future

ISBN: 978-1-922644-17-6 (Paperback)
978-1-922644-18-3 (eBook)

NATIONAL LIBRARY OF AUSTRALIA
A catalogue record for this book is available from the National Library of Australia

Editor: Jason Martin
Cover Design: Ocean Reeve Publishing
Design and Typeset: Ocean Reeve Publishing
Printed in Australia by Ocean Reeve Publishing and Clark & Mackay Printers

Published by Alex Gerrick and Ocean Reeve Publishing
www.oceanreevepublishing.com

Ocean REEVE PUBLISHING

Dedicated to Richard.

Friendship consists in forgetting what one gives and remembering what one receives.

—Alexandre Dumas

Author's Note

A *Season of Clouds* is a work of fiction written as a personal memoir. Although inspired by my own long journey through PTSD and mental illness, the book's other main characters are fictional, with no connection to any real person. Like all works of fiction, it is set within the background of the real world, but any reference to an actual place or person or entity is purely for this purpose.

Who in the world am I? Ah, that's the great puzzle.

—Lewis Carroll, *Alice in Wonderland*

An excerpt from *The Search for Martina*

By Greta Schumacher
Preston Press © 2046

Kiama, New South Wales, Australia

The old man she had come all this way to see was found slumped in a wheelchair, his empty thoughts lost inside the distant waves that crashed mercilessly against the ruins of an abandoned lighthouse. Although in another time he had walked in the footsteps of the rich and powerful, the man's only companion that day was a tiny grey sparrow, which somehow burrowed its way through a tightly clipped rose bush before perching itself on top of the steel railing next to him.

From where she was standing near the water fountain, it seemed as if the old man was challenging the world to one final duel. But as the afternoon shadows crept menacingly towards his bony legs, she understood better than anyone that his long-forgotten secrets would always find a way to protect him.

The woman slowly turned her head towards the bird pond and watched carefully while the other residents of the nursing home went about their daily routine. There appeared to be a mutual understanding among them—a pact, if you like—that the old man must not be disturbed under any circumstances. As such, they rustled silently in between their deck chairs, chattering softly to each other in excited whispers, determined not to interfere with his daily rite of contrition. Their servitude only strengthened the woman's desire to have him accept her into his heart.

She cautiously took several steps closer towards him and was immediately intrigued by the undeniable allure of his presence. Admittedly, she had been a restless teenager that day in Potsdam, Germany, all those years ago and, therefore, paid scant attention to the

grey-haired man sitting in the corner of the café playing with his iPhone. Now in her mid-forties, fighting her own battle with middle age, she jealously marvelled at the radiance of his Mediterranean skin, the raw texture of his dark, hollow eyes, and the feline dexterity of his long, wrinkly hands. Her mother once said that he resembled a famous Hollywood actor, but she could never remember who. Regardless, it was not hard to imagine that he was the same man who stole her heart in London all those years ago.

As trumpets of fear pounded against her chest, the woman somehow found the courage to kneel beside him, her lips searching for those simple words she had practised so diligently that morning in front of her hotel room mirror. Although she was certain that he could hear the gentle ebb and flow of her breathing, he continued to ignore her, his arms glued to the woollen shawl covering his lap, that endless gaze never losing its intensity.

The head nurse, overcome by her enduring affection for the old man, had warned the woman when they spoke over the phone last week. She explained to her about his good days and bad days, about his long periods of silence, and his dark, fractious moods. He was slowly slipping away and, more than anything, she wanted him to die with some dignity. Only his wife was allowed to visit him now. Perhaps it would be best for everyone if the woman returned to Austria.

Without being overly rude, she had merely laughed at such a suggestion, for that option had been discarded weeks ago. After all, it was his wife who had invited her to meet with him. Surely the head nurse knew this. Hadn't she read the newspapers or followed the hashtag on social media? Everyone familiar with her story understood why she had come to Australia: why she alone had the power to absolve this man, Alex Gerrick, of his sins.

Deep beneath her blue cotton blouse, her skin itched and burned. It was a family trait that only reappeared when she was extremely nervous. 'Mister Gerrick,' she began, hoping that her strong German accent wouldn't confuse him. 'My name is Greta Schumacher, and I have travelled from Austria to meet you.'

For some reason, Greta had always imagined that at this very moment, Alex would unscramble his brain just for her and then leap from his wheelchair into her arms. So when things didn't quite go to plan, the desolation of his ongoing silence only succeeded in breaking her heart.

'Mister Gerrick,' she repeated, this time more firmly, 'I want to help you.' Of course, Greta knew that this was nothing more than a bare-faced lie—the only person she wanted to help was herself because everything about this obsession was tearing her apart. It had destroyed Greta's marriage to the man she still loved and alienated a proud and doting mother from her precious children. Overnight, before she even had

time to understand the consequences of her behaviour, Greta had become a parody of the woman her family once admired. The only thing that now sustained her was a steadfast commitment to her mother's dying wish.

'I am Eleanor's daughter.' She pressed her face closer to him to see whether there was any reaction, even a mild flicker of recognition. 'Do you understand? My mother was Eleanor Kuhn—the Austrian woman you met in London in 1999.'

She waited impatiently for a response, her nose twitching at the smell of fresh eucalyptus that clung to her scarf. Then out of the corner of her eye, something caught her attention.

Yes! Right there! His legs! They are moving!

Greta's moment of jubilation, however, was remarkably short-lived. The puffing of his cheeks, the trembling of his hands, that peculiar dilation of his eyes, suddenly convinced her that Alex was having a stroke.

By Christ, that dreadful head nurse will blame me—just you wait and see.

Suddenly, Alex's brittle fingers managed to grasp the side of his wheelchair, and he slowly cranked his neck around to face her. 'Eleanor? From Salzburg?'

Oh my God! He remembers her!

'Yes, Mister Gerrick,' she replied, gripping herself ever so tightly so she didn't fall on top of him. 'Before she died, I promised her that I would come to Australia to find you. Your wife and I have been corresponding for nearly three months.'

'My wife. She is a wonderful person, is she not?'

'Yes, she is.'

His mouth began to tremble—a warning sign, perhaps, that he could slide back into purgatory at any moment. 'Mum wanted me to pass on a message,' she continued. 'And to give you a present.'

Alex's eyes circled curiously around her face before they lifted upwards to admire a flock of screeching cockatoos flying high above them. For some reason, their raucous symphony seemed to energise him.

'You are beautiful like your mother,' he said softly.

'Thank you,' she gushed.

'My condolences for your loss. She was a lovely woman.' He sounded very genuine. 'May I ask how?'

'Ovarian cancer. Nine months ago.'

He quietly absorbed this information. 'Poor darling,' he finally said. 'She saved me; did you know? They all saved me in the end.'

'Who did? Who saved you?'

'Those remarkable women I met overseas. Marlena, Lottie, Eleanor, Danielle, and Sally. And one must not forget, Delilah! Please never forget Delilah!'

'Delilah? Sally?' Greta replied to Alex, but mostly to herself. Her mum had divulged every intricate detail of the story before she died, and Greta had become a walking encyclopaedia on the topic.

Of course, there was Aunty Danielle: everything had begun with Aunty Danielle and her story about a picnic in Stratford-Upon-Avon. Then there was her mother's meeting with a Dutch woman called Lottie, who met Alex in Greece, and Danielle's phone call to an Italian lawyer called Marlena, who told her about a massive fight on the island of Samos involving a young man from Florence. But apart from the main character in this drama, the woman from Alex's past that connected everything back to this very moment in time, her mother never mentioned any of those other names. Perhaps Alex's dementia had invented new characters into his story?

'I can tell that you are confused,' Alex said quietly. 'Your mother would not have known about Sally and Delilah, for I met both of them well after my Lost Week.'

'Your Lost Week?'

'Yes, I wrote about this in my book.'

Droplets of sweat pierced her tired eyes. 'You mean *Season of Thunder?* The book you wrote about your parents. It was a bestseller.'

Try as he might, Alex refused to despair at her ignorance. 'No, not that book. I mean the book I wrote about my own life. I never finished it, you see. There was one chapter I could never write.'

A book? There is another book? 'May I ask—'

He didn't allow Greta to finish her sentence. Rather, he quietly pointed to the ocean with his index finger, inviting her to guide his wheelchair further along the freshly cut lawn until he called a halt beneath the shade of a weeping willow.

'I know why you have come.' He stared at Greta. 'It's about her. Danielle told your mum about our conversation, didn't she?'

'Yes, she did,' Greta nodded. 'Before Mum died, she and Danielle discovered something that they wanted you to know.'

'You are wasting your time,' Alex shook his head. 'Nothing can ever remove the guilt. I accepted that a long time ago. Perhaps you should as well.'

'But I can help you,' she implored. 'If you only allow me the chance to explain.'

He found a way to smile at her. 'What do you do for a living, Eleanor Kuhn's daughter?'

'I'm a writer.'

'Yes, of course you are. And what are you writing about, my dear?'

Greta coughed nervously in the direction of the sea. She had not expected this level of scrutiny. Not from him, anyway. 'I'm writing a book about Danielle and my mother.'

'And you think that I can validate your story?'

'I don't know what you mean.'

'There must be something that you want from me?'

'I just want to put things right.'

He laughed at Greta in a way he once laughed at her mother. 'If there is one thing I have learnt in my life, it's that the world is full of well-intentioned people hoping to put things right. Whether they have the capacity to succeed or not is a different matter. In fact, I usually find that their arrogance only makes things worse. But I'm far too old for such platitudes now.'

She blinked wildly at him. 'My apologies, but you must believe me. I truly didn't know that you wrote another book before today.'

He said nothing for the time being. Instead, they remained locked together in an imaginary embrace while the afternoon sun snarled at their faces.

'You need to talk to Brother Rojo,' he finally revealed.

'Brother Rojo? Does he work here at the nursing home?'

'You really *don't* understand, do you?' he said politely.

'Not everything, no.'

'Then perhaps I will help you, just like Brother Rojo once helped me.'

A gust of wind tugged furiously at a lock of Alex's thick grey hair. 'I have told one of the nurses where I hide all my valuables. Her name is Mary. She can be a right pain sometimes with her fussing and dithering, but I like her very much. Tell her that I have agreed to lend you my book—she will find it for you.'

Greta wriggled her toes in shock. 'Are you sure you want me to read it?'

'You're writing your own version of these events, are you not? If I'm to be a part of your story, I at least want it to be factual. An old man never enjoys being falsely accused of things he never did, especially when he doesn't have much time to repair the damage to his reputation.'

She didn't know what to say. This wasn't how it was meant to be.

'But my offer is subject to one condition,' he demanded. 'Promise me that you will read it carefully. Remove the chains around your heart, just like your mother and Danielle would have done. And when you have finished, if you still think I should hear your story, I will listen to what you have to say.'

'I promise.' What else could she do other than give a dying man his wish?

Just like she had given her mother.

'Good,' he growled, pushing his arms out towards her. 'Now, leave me alone before I get cranky and change my mind.'

She hurried back to the front office to search for Mary. Not for the first time in her life, Greta Schumacher was tormented by the deceitfulness of her vanity.

It's not fair! There can't be another book! There just can't be!

What about mine? What about all my work—all the sacrifices that I have made?

Do I have to rewrite it now? Will my publisher even give me more time?

If I had known there was another book, I would never have come.

Twenty minutes later, Mary watched Greta as she stumbled down a deserted footpath towards her hire car, Alex's laced manuscript tucked tightly beneath her armpit. Greta Schumacher hadn't realised it yet but hidden within those old, dusty pages lay the pathway to her redemption. By the time she finished reading the book just before dawn, everything she had thought she knew about the world would explode around her.

On the day she discovered the secret of the Clouds.

A SEASON OF CLOUDS

As initially read by Greta Schumacher

Prologue

Ringo Bingo the Clown

It all began with the colour yellow or—more specifically—that song about a yellow submarine I often heard playing on the family radio. It made me so happy, but I didn't know why. Each new morning, as I lost myself within the corridors of my lonely imagination, its unrelenting magic carried me to new worlds beyond my comprehension. Then one warm, sunny afternoon during a hastily arranged game of hide and seek, I casually asked the girl with the droopy eyes and the harelip who lived across the street whether she also liked the song. 'Oh yes!' she loudly screamed over and over again in my ear until I begged her to stop. Only when I promised to give her the last of my Marella jubes did she explain in between more of her piffling little screams that the man who sang my favourite song was called Ringo and that she was madly in love with him and his three best friends—John, Paul, and George.

So when a scary-looking clown suddenly appeared at my bedside several nights later, resplendent in yellow trousers, a yellow paisley shirt, rotten, jagged yellow teeth, and shrunken yellow eyes, what was I supposed to think? I asked him very politely if his name was Ringo, and he replied, 'No, little boy. It's Ringo Bingo!' No matter how often he would pursue me with his other disguises during my life, I would only ever know him as Ringo Bingo the Clown and nothing else.

Sadly, our friendship—if you could call it one—never really progressed as I would have liked. For a start, he never wanted to play cowboys and Indians, and his twisted extra leg meant that he wasn't into ball sports. Furthermore, I found his constant hissing, farting, and feeble discussions about taking over the world rather irritating.

Thankfully, on the night before my fifth birthday, common sense prevailed, and Ringo Bingo and I finally struck a deal to end our association once and for all. In exchange for unlimited access to my nightmares, Ringo Bingo promised that he would never revisit me unless, of course, something awfully bad happened in my life. While some might argue that there had to be a catch, that it was never wise for children my age to negotiate with nefarious scoundrels like Ringo Bingo, in the final analysis, we were both delightfully proud of our work.

After all, why would a little boy like me choose to have a hideous-looking clown with an evil grin as their regular companion, day after day, night after night, for all of eternity? And Ringo Bingo was so excited by the scrumptious delights he might find swirling inside my head that when I finally got to shake his hand, it snapped right off from the rest of his arm.

This might surprise you but, despite his insidious ways, in the beginning, I didn't find Ringo Bingo particularly scary. Okay, that might be a slight exaggeration. If I'm honest, Ringo Bingo wasn't someone you necessarily wanted to see practising his cartwheels next to your bed during the middle of the night.

But neither did Ringo Bingo scare the pants off me like, say, the Carter twins from next door, who threatened every day to up-end me, headfirst, into a large bucket of cow poo. I mean, what could be scarier than being upended, headfirst, into a large bucket of cow poo?

No, Ringo Bingo was more like that snotty-nosed kid from kindergarten who always wanted first pick of the best toys and then bullied you when he didn't get his way. In the bigger scheme of things, thrashing out deals with scary clowns like Ringo Bingo was no different from any other odious chore that little boys had to deal with every day, like eating mashed potatoes or making your bed. As with most bullies, I was sure that once I gave Ringo Bingo what he wanted, he would leave me alone and pick on someone else.

However, this was where my contract with Ringo Bingo became rather unstuck. You see, everything was predicated by the not-so-unreasonable expectation that my life would always resemble a huge bowl of ice cream with caramel topping; that nothing bad would ever happen to me as long as I took the righteous path to salvation. But there was only one problem with this theory: it was absolute cobblers. For no-one in the history of the galaxy attracted more misfortune than I did.

To illustrate this further, two days after my fifth birthday, I was shot in my left arm, just below the elbow, while playing cowboys and Indians by myself in the front yard of our house. I know what you must be thinking: *how could this possibly have happened to a five-year-old boy in Australia?* But it did; I'm gratefully still here to tell you.

It was three o'clock in the afternoon, and I was about to shoot Chief Sitting Bull square between the eyes with my plastic toy rifle when suddenly, the crazy little bugger started firing back with real bullets. Luckily, my older brother Charlie was home on leave from national service, and he initiated a daring rescue operation before Chief Sitting Bull and his evil hordes could finish me off.

'Bahahaha,' laughed Ringo Bingo in the hospital later that night after completing an excruciating long rendition of his favourite song, 'This Old Man'. 'What sort of person would sneak up on a little boy while he was playing cowboys and Indians and shoot him with a .22 calibre rifle?'

That was a damn good question, I decided, *even for an evil, dim-witted clown dressed entirely in yellow like Ringo Bingo.*

Although he soon left my bedside for his other nightly commitments, it didn't take long before he returned to torment me a second time. Three months later, after I fell into the deep end of the public swimming pool in Mudgee, Ringo Bingo suddenly materialised next to me in a ridiculously tight yellow bathing costume and persuaded me to hold his hand as we slowly sank to the bottom together.

'Look, I can breathe underwater, Alex!' boasted Ringo Bingo, in that squeaky, high-pitched voice that I would learn to despise so much. 'Isn't this peachy? I bet you an extra-large packet of Smarties that *you* can't do that!'

As much as I tried to prove him wrong, all I could feel were the gallons of water gushing into my tiny lungs, sapping away every last drop of air inside of me, while Ringo Bingo sat cross-legged on the bottom, laughing and laughing it up like the arrogant little turd he would always be.

Then on the day of my first holy communion, hours after that horrible thing with the older girl that I never talked about (until I met Sally), I found Ringo Bingo jumping up and down at the end of my bed as if it were the Carter twins' brand-new trampoline.

'You lucky, lucky bastard,' he whistled happily, in between more perverted verses of 'This Old Man'. 'If only I had met a girl like that when I was just a young whippersnapper of an evil clown!'

Well, Ringo Bingo, you can take your sordid wish and shove it right where it hurts. Because what that girl just did to me should never happen to any kid. Understand?

Ringo Bingo and I were then reacquainted the following year, on the day that I collapsed in our lounge room from a rare form of hernia that almost killed me. My testicles had grown into mini-grapefruits, I will have you know, and walking around with those things wasn't for the faint-hearted.

Our family doctor, who just happened to be Bettie Scott's uncle, explained that my parents had caused my condition. 'They spoil you way too much,' he announced to me after tucking away his stethoscope, not realising that I was secretly in love with his niece.

'It is pretty hard to imagine how your parents spoiling you too much can somehow initiate a process inside your body that makes your testicles grow into mini-grapefruits,' observed Ringo Bingo after I woke up from my first operation. I had to admit that, on this occasion, he made a very valid point.

But, putting aside Doctor Scott's dubious diagnosis for the time being, I proposed to Ringo Bingo, while the other patients in the post-operation ward were fast asleep, that this whole agreement with him was an absolute sham. What was the purpose of him visiting me only *after* something awfully bad happened in my life? Surely, this was not the intent of the deal we negotiated.

'Doesn't it make more sense, Ringo Bingo, if instead, you visit me *before* something awfully bad happens in my life? This way, I can then prepare myself for whatever calamity is about to fall upon me.'

If Ringo Bingo had a chin, I'm sure he would have scratched it in deep contemplation. Instead, he did three backward summersaults with a mid-air twist and then farted out a row of yellow balloons from his colossal backside. 'That's a damn fine idea,' he said with a grin so vast that he could have swallowed a cat or two completely whole. 'Oh yes, that's such a dandy idea!

'What's more, because I visit your nightmares so often, I know what scares you into tiny little smithereens! So how does this sound? I will no longer appear to you as a clown, but rather, whatever happens to frighten you most at the time! This is the perfect outcome for both of us! Win-win and all that!'

As a confused nine-year-old boy who had just survived major surgery, I really didn't appreciate the gravity of the situation. But the implications were indeed frightening because, inadvertently, I had given Ringo Bingo permission to do whatever he pleased, whenever he wanted. For instance, if I happened to have a nightmare about a ferocious ten-foot gorilla in a pink dress chasing me with a machete, Ringo Bingo would then appear to me as a ferocious ten-foot gorilla in a pink dress chasing me with a machete. *Do you see what I mean?*

'Yes indeedy, Mister Speedy.' Ringo Bingo laughed hysterically before he mysteriously disappeared for the next thirty years. 'Think of all the different ways I can screw with your head when you get older!'

Although I initially applauded his decision to seek newer pastures, Ringo Bingo's self-imposed exile didn't fool me at all—not one little bit, because he was never too far away from my thoughts, always lurking in the background, making things up as he went along, waiting to strike at a time of his choosing.

Of course, I didn't discount the possibility that Ringo Bingo had perished, as all imaginary friends did at some point during one's childhood. But, if that indeed rang true, how could you explain everything that happened to me in Greece during my holiday in 1995? Surely only Ringo Bingo possessed all the heinous qualities needed to orchestrate so much chaos and confusion in my life? (And what about that whole thing with … No, it wasn't him, I still liked to pretend after all these years.)

It would have been far too easy to blame this all on my overactive imagination but, just before I attempted suicide four years later in the seaside town of Bateman's Bay, I became convinced that a strange, hairy man with yellow eyes, wearing a yellow sweater and twirling around a yellow umbrella was following me in the shadows all day. Then, several months later, when Eleanor and I experienced our very own foray into the supernatural while attending *The Phantom of the Opera* together in London, I swore that the old lady wearing a yellow dress in the seat in front of us was singing 'This Old Man' throughout the whole ordeal.

No, this was all part of Ringo Bingo's warped sense of humour, don't you see? He loved to tease me with these tantalising titbits left scattered before me like breadcrumbs on the pathway to my self-destruction. My only option was to bunker down beneath my sheets at night and prepare myself for our next showdown.

Eighteen months quietly passed without incident until finally, on a hot, humid morning in January 2001, my patience was duly rewarded, and Ringo Bingo made his triumphant return into my life, just like I always knew he would.

On the day I was detained at gunpoint during a military coup in Manila, months after I had bid my tragic farewell to Sally, I woke up to see her rotting corpse lying beside me in bed, blood cascading down her porcelain cheeks from two bottomless pits where her eyes had once been. *Yes, you thought long and hard about this, didn't you, Ringo Bingo? Very impressive, indeed.*

Tragically, Ringo Bingo paid me one final visit after Manila: on the day my best friend, Jack, was killed in a light plane crash in June 2011. For whatever devious reasons known only to him, Ringo Bingo didn't present himself until the exact hour of Jack's death.

Just after midday, I found myself alone inside a lift at Parliament House, where I worked as the chief of staff to the Cabinet Secretary, when suddenly the ceiling above me rattled violently out of control. For one nerve-racking moment, I wondered whether I was about to freefall into oblivion, and my last resting place would be some narrow, concrete tomb that my family and friends would never find. Thankfully, the excruciating noise quickly abated, and the lift door then opened before me.

That's when I saw her. The little girl from Mindanao: the one that I wasn't able to save. Her dirty little fingers were still grasping that torn teddy bear as if it was the only friend she would ever have. *Boo hiss, Ringo Bingo! That cuts way too close to the bone. How much lower can you get?*

However, one shouldn't be surprised by the intricate nature of his skulduggery. After all, Ringo Bingo was merely keeping the promise he had made to me all those years ago when my testicles blew up like mini-grapefruits. For he understood better than anyone the things that scared me the most. And he knew—God how he knew—that there was still so much more to come, so many more prizes for him to collect along the way, until he claimed the ultimate jackpot: you know, the *grand prix* of nightmares.

But only on a beautiful autumn morning in March 2016, hours before the Spiders betrayed me, did Ringo Bingo finally reveal his true calling. Because the form he chose to take for my pleasure, floating as it was, high above my bedroom window, was neither a clown dressed in yellow, nor Sally, nor the little girl from Mindanao, nor Jack, nor even a ten-foot gorilla wearing a pink dress.

Instead, it was the one person whose name I dared not whisper, the one person whose vengeful memories had pursued me relentlessly across time itself.

Martina!

Part One

Strangers on a Ferry

Reginald Crump

Athens
Early May 1995

Some would later say that my story had all the hallmarks of a Greek tragedy. Therefore, it was deliciously ironic that the seeds that led to my downfall were first sown by Dumbo, the bumbling reception clerk at the Hotel Hellas in Athens.

'That will be two hundred American dollars, sir,' he demanded in his annoying, artificially clipped English. 'Will that be cash or credit card?' As I foraged inside my backpack, I suddenly realised why I had taken such an instant dislike to him: he had one too many teeth, and I had always disliked people with one too many teeth.

'Here, take this,' I sneered back at him. With a casual snap of my wrist, I flicked my Visa card across the recently polished reception desk and tried to counter his vacuous gaze with some mental arithmetic. *Let's work this out.* I had about a thousand Australian dollars left on my card, another five hundred dollars in traveller's cheques, and eighty dollars in my wallet. That left me roughly two hundred dollars a day before my overdue army reserve pay rocketed into my savings account next week.

Excellent! More than enough cash to support my debauched lifestyle for a few more days. But to be safe, it might have to be fish and chips for dinner tonight. The nagging pangs of hunger that had bubbled away inside of me since I landed in Athens an hour ago started to vibrate hard against my teeth, and for the tenth night in a row, the sombre reality hit: I had hardly eaten anything other than fish and chips since my new girlfriend, Rachel, departed for her European tour.

'Thank you, Mister Jerrick,' Dumbo said with a grin, handing me back my card. He shuffled around some paper on his desk as if it meant something important before he finally remembered to hand me my room key.

'It's "Gerrick" actually,' I said, offering him a fake smile. 'With a G.' A deliberate pause. 'Like in the word *Goose*.'

I received nothing in return other than the dimmest of dim smiles. The lights were definitely on, but the building had been vacated an awfully long time ago. 'Never mind.'

'Oh, by the way, you have a visitor, Mister Gerrick,' Dumbo proudly announced, using the proper pronunciation of my surname this time to piss me off. He pointed to an obscure figure in the corner of the lobby.

'His name is Reginald Crump from our head office, and he is here to welcome you to Athens formally.' Dumbo stood on his tip toes to try to give the impression that he was actually taller than he was. 'That's "Crump", by the way, with a C.'

Admittedly, not a bad comeback—even for a right bell end like Dumbo. But rather than waste another one of my brilliantly witty retorts on such an unworthy foe, I turned my attention to this man who called himself Reginald Crump.

My initial impression was that he looked like one of those fat embassy officials you might have occasionally seen in a 1960s spy movie. You know, the guy who always greeted our hero at the start of the film in some exotic location, warned him about imminent danger, which of course our hero only chose to ignore anyway, and then faded into his favourite bottle of Scotch for the rest of the movie.

Reginald Crump was either in his late forties or early fifties, with a tub of lard for a belly and a huge bald patch in the middle of his hilariously bulbous head. Narrow beads of sweat cascaded down his bloated, ruddy face. This wasn't surprising, given the sweltering heat and the ridiculous cream safari suit he was wearing.

I growled at Dumbo just for the hell of it, reached for my backpack, and stomped over to where Reginald Crump was sitting. His enormously plump hand was clutching at a glass of wine while his cat-like eyes darted hopefully towards a pretty young Greek girl in a short denim skirt. Apart from her rather generous cleavage, our delightful Mister Crump seemed totally oblivious to anything else inside the hotel. A sure sign, you might say, that he took his job very seriously.

'Excuse me, Mister Clump?' I interrupted.

Reginald Crump offered me a tormented frown. 'It's Crump, actually. With a—oh, forget it.'

'I'm sorry,' I replied, trying very hard not to mean it. 'I was told by the reception clerk that you wanted to see me?'

Reginald Crump carefully placed his glass on a table and reached for a black leather briefcase. His movements were deliberate and precise as if he suspected someone was secretly filming him.

'Yes, of course. Your name?'

For the next three weeks, Jemima and I never left each other's side. We cycled together through the solemn battlefields of Belgium, climbed the rusty steps of the Eiffel Tower, danced together at the Moulin Rouge, and burrowed our way along the cold, windy alleyways of Liverpool. Things between us started to get very serious until she developed an irrational hatred for my new West Indian friends. Unfortunately, we argued so much about them I had no choice other than to stick her at the bottom of my backpack, somewhere between my dirty socks and jocks, to keep her quiet.

But since we had arrived in Athens, the time for reconciliation had come. So, I dusted off the loose threads from her pale beak, readjusted that silly light-blue hat, and stood her upright on one of my pillows, reinforcing how special I thought she was. However, her indignant black eyes gave away her mood immediately.

You bastard! I thought there was something special between us. How dare you force me to spend the last two days next to those disgusting army socks. Have you any idea how badly they reek? That's no way to treat a classy female toy like me.

'Oh, stop your whining, Jemima. You just wouldn't shut up about my friends, so I had to take drastic action. Why can't you move on and enjoy this beautiful hotel room with me?'

You did make a good choice with the hotel; I will give you that.

'Of course I did, Jemima.'

Even though this was only my second overseas trip and the first for ten years, I had developed the perfect routine for my travels. Whenever I arrived in a new city, I always stayed at a four-star hotel on the first night. This enabled me to get my bearings, access the knowledge of hotel staff, and take advantage of the better-quality services and facilities that were usually on offer. You know: the things that you wouldn't usually find at a youth hostel or a cheap tourist hotel, like maps, a proper iron, a washing machine, and a hair dryer. Besides, I could be a terrible snob as well. As much as I loved being a backpacker, I also enjoyed that extra bit of luxury that a hotel like this offered. *Why should I be ashamed of that?*

You are the self-professed working-class hero, chum, not me!

'I'm having a shower now, Jemima. Don't do anything I wouldn't do.'

There is little chance of that with you here, so do me a favour: try not to walk around with nothing on. It's disgusting!

Once I finished my shower, I snatched a pair of crumpled blue jeans from my backpack. Despite all the minor irritations of an overseas holiday, like wearing the same clothes for days on end, I loved every minute of this lifestyle. Some believed that travel broadened the mind, but for me, this trip represented a new beginning: an opportunity to leave behind the remnants of a wasted life.

Even as a young teenager, trapped in my small, stuffy bedroom where I grew up in the Queensland industrial town of Gladstone, I often dreamt about exciting and dangerous adventures in faraway places. Sometimes I pretended to be an international man of mystery, hunting down devious Russian spies and ruthless terrorists like Carlos the Jackal across the major cities of Europe. Then, long before Indiana Jones hit our screens, I was an archaeologist discovering stolen Nazi treasure in the steamy jungles of the Amazon. After the darkness had taken away my childhood, my imaginary world was the only thing that sheltered me from the madness of our family life.

By the time I reached my last year of high school, my desire to see the world had become an irresistible force that I could no longer contain. While my friends focused on girls, parties, and looking cool, I spent my spare time plotting how to leave Gladstone and start a new life.

The plan I formulated was a simple one. I would go to Brisbane and study arts and law at the University of Queensland. After graduation, I would apply for the foreign service and become a diplomat. All I wanted was a future full of exotic countries, cocktail parties, and beautiful women.

In my final year of school, I coasted towards a tertiary entrance score that would secure my chosen course. I trembled with excitement when the time came to apply for university officially. But just when I had my pen and University of Queensland application ready to sign, my father suddenly dropped a major bombshell.

'You're not going to Brisbane, Alex. You are going to Rockhampton to study business at the local college of advanced education.'

Rockhampton? Seriously? I want to attend a prestigious university in Brisbane, not a college of advanced education. And business? I have no ambition to become an accountant or a computer programmer. My interests are history, politics, and international affairs, not balance sheets and computer algorithms.

I was devastated by this news, but there was nothing more that I could have done. You didn't contradict your Yugoslavian father when you were a skinny seventeen-year-old kid living at home.

If I had been smart about it, I should have just bit my tongue, done my three years in Rockhampton, graduated with good marks, and then pursued my dreams far away from my father's interference. But I didn't possess the emotional maturity or common sense to figure that out for myself. Instead, I had the freedom to enjoy being a young man on campus.

'Make the best out of a bad opportunity,' some spaced-out lecturer with a porn-star moustache suggested to me during orientation week.

As a result, I mixed with the wrong crowd, drank way too much, and focused on playing soccer. I may have been one of the team's stars, but I failed most of my subjects as a result. Three years later, I found myself working as a lowly paid travel clerk in Brisbane, with no degree, no self-confidence, and no real prospects for the future. The dream of being a diplomat was but a faded memory.

While I wasted my life away booking unhappy, boring people on unhappy, boring cruises, I applied for every interstate job I could find to escape my self-induced malaise. In late 1984, following months of endless rejection slips, I finally received an offer to join the Australian Public Service in Canberra. Without really thinking about the implications, I jumped at the chance to start a new career, while my parents—who had retired to Brisbane—were relieved that their wayward son had a new direction in his life.

My first job in the public service as a pay clerk—imprisoned inside some drab, grey office stuck in the outer suburbs of Canberra—quickly developed into another epic disaster. Despite my lack of skills, university education, or any other redeeming qualities, I convinced myself that the duties of a pay clerk were way beneath me. Before too long, I proudly became the worst pay clerk in the history of the public sector.

Over several months, I racked up an impressive list of failures. I lost somebody's file, screwed up some bigwig's pay rise, turned up to work half-drunk, and then got caught cheating on my flexitime sheet. But rather than buckle down and take stock of my life, I foolishly took out a bank loan for an overseas holiday that I couldn't afford to pay and then spent most of it moping over a girl.

When I returned home, the girl dumped me (come to think of it, were we even going out?), and I sensationally morphed into a self-entitled loser. A few weeks later, I got drunk at the office Christmas party and made a snide comment to one of my co-workers. In the ensuing fight, he accidentally smashed a glass into my right eye. That night, the duty doctor at the emergency ward warned me that I was fortunate not to lose my sight.

The following Monday, word of my misadventures quickly spread across the department, and my superiors finally gave me an official warning. If my work performance and behaviour didn't rapidly improve within the next month, I faced instant dismissal. I was fast riding down Last Chance Avenue.

Fortunately, a low-level job became available in our Brisbane office, so I applied on compassionate grounds, citing my father's sudden financial woes as the excuse I needed to return to Queensland. For once, luck was on my side, and I somehow won the job.

When I stepped off the bus in Brisbane just before Easter 1986, I was at a shallow point in my life. *How could everything have gone so wrong for me?* Six years before, I had been head prefect and president of the student council at school; a young man tipped to succeed in life by his teachers and peers. Now I was nothing more than a meaningless shitkicker in a public service graveyard, badly in debt and out of hope, while most of my friends were getting married or buying their first home.

It would have been easy to blame such a fall from grace on the failure to realise my childhood dream, but that was far too convenient. For there was an emptiness inside of me that I couldn't explain: an inability to achieve personal happiness no matter what I did. I was nothing more than an outsider, an anomaly, who belonged nowhere and amounted to nothing.

I prised open the balcony door guarding my hotel room and walked outside. The oppressive Athens heat lashed against my clammy skin. After leaving the cold, windy streets of London behind me, I had seemingly landed on a completely different planet.

I took a deep, rueful breath and stared into the golden lights of the Parthenon as they streaked recklessly across an impenetrable night sky. I had come to Athens for a reason: to explore an ancient world that continued to inspire my thirst for knowledge. But instead of being grateful for this incredible opportunity, I was standing there knee-deep in despair, fretting aimlessly about my past. Wasn't that so bloody typical?

Despite myself, I gulped down a burst of hot air and began to revisit those first few wasteful years in Brisbane. Man, the disasters kept tumbling out almost every day: my father's financial problems, his cancer, and subsequent death, several crises of self-confidence, and then my failed marriage. When it rained for me, it bloody well poured. But almost overnight, I found a way to break free from this vicious cycle, transforming myself from a no-hoper with no prospects into a hardworking young professional on the rise. All thanks to a documentary I watched one night about the American Civil War general Ulysses S Grant.

Here was a guy who had failed at everything, an alcoholic and a grifter, but who, at the time of his country's greatest peril, triumphed over his frailties and became a national hero. Something about his story resonated with my sense of justice: that you could defeat any shitty little hand given to you if you believed in your ability and never gave up. Indeed, Grant's famous quote, 'Lick'em tomorrow', quickly became my new personal creed.

Slowly but surely, I built myself a new life. While I continued to dance between the raindrops, I found a way to hide that ever-present emptiness into a forbidden corner of my brain. Whenever my irrational thoughts started to overwhelm me, I ruthlessly eliminated them one by one before they could do any further damage to my rehabilitation.

Emboldened by a new sense of enlightenment, I soon returned to university and completed my business studies before commencing a part-time arts degree, majoring in politics and history. It was important to give myself every opportunity to expand my mind and fulfil my academic potential.

My career started to prosper as well. After succeeding in several different jobs and graduating as an army reserve officer, I finally possessed an impressive array of skills that I could sell to prospective employers. New job opportunities began to emerge every day.

Then, one Saturday afternoon, in the middle of a ferocious Brisbane thunderstorm, the Spiders paid me a visit at my home.

'We have been watching you for some time,' Funnel Web Spider had admitted. 'You are finally starting to realise your potential. That's good, Alex. That's very good.'

For reasons I dared not imagine, they immediately decided that I had a part to play in their depraved schemes.

They taught me what to do.

They taught me what to say.

They taught me how to dress.

Then, when I thought I knew everything there was to know, they taught me how to lie.

Provoked by their unruly demands, I eventually returned to Canberra, where I found work as a senior policy adviser in my chosen field of industrial relations. Just as the Spiders had predicted, people in high places quickly began to take notice of me.

What did my boss say before I left for my holiday? 'Alex, you are going to have a great career. If you work hard enough, I see no reason why you can't make it to the Senior Executive Service.'

'She was right, of course,' Rachel had said to me during a late-afternoon stroll along the Royal Mile in Edinburgh. 'You have been an outsider for far too long, and this is your time to shine.'

Her words tingled along my arm, and I realised that she had somehow found a way to share that precious moment with me.

'Thank you, Rachel,' I whispered into the night breeze.

I haven't met this girl yet, but she sounds so much more intelligent than you!

I walked back into the room, grabbed my sports jacket, and expertly threw it on top of Jemima's head. 'Now I remember why I stuck you at the bottom of my backpack.'

Arsehole!

I flung on the Loch Ness monster T-shirt Rachel recently bought me in Inverness and soon found myself inside a slow-moving lift accompanied by an elderly Greek couple who, despite my presence, were pawing at each other with the audacity of high school teenagers. Their geriatric high jinks disturbingly made me think about Rachel and our burgeoning relationship once again.

When my marriage ended last year, the prospect of dating other women was the furthest thing from my mind. I had embarked on that holiday to expunge all the hurt and driftwood from my system and rewire my brain for that next relationship.

But three days after arriving in London, I met Rachel on a bus tour to Canterbury Cathedral. Given that she was the only other Australian on board, we connected immediately and spent the whole day hanging out together. We soon discovered that we also had mutual friends in Canberra and then laughed at how small the world was. Later that night, over dessert in an Italian restaurant, we decided to travel together for a while before sneaking in that obligatory first kiss.

We officially became boyfriend and girlfriend during three wonderful days in Brighton. For the next month, we traversed far and wide across the UK in style, never staying in one place too long and never overthinking the future. Before she left for her tour, we both agreed that things needed to get a lot more serious between us when we returned to Australia. Rest assured, I had been counting down the days before we would see each other again in London the following week.

As I magically connected with her dancing blue eyes, I wondered what the future held for the two of us when we finished our holidays. Starting a new relationship was never easy. There were so many things that I needed to organise before I could enjoy myself again. I had a divorce to finalise, I had to find an apartment, and I would have to explain to people that I had a new woman in my life. Most importantly, Rachel lived in Sydney, so we needed to figure out pretty quickly how to make a long-distance relationship work. What did that mean for me in the long term? Who the hell knew? There was even a possibility that I would have to leave Canberra again.

Yes, Canberra. Canberra. Canberra? Hang on a minute! Canberra! How in the hell did he know that? Canberra!

As soon as we made it to the ground floor, I rudely pushed the Greek couple aside and stomped towards reception. Dumbo was still behind the counter, preoccupied with stapling a receipt onto a piece of paper. It was not an onerous task by any means, but for Dumbo, it was like splitting the atom. And if anyone shouldn't be allowed to split the atom, it was Dumbo. When he looked up and suddenly saw my loathsome face staring wide-eyed at him, he spiralled around in fright and then tripped over his feet.

'Can I help you, sir?' he growled as he hobbled to the counter.

'You checked me in tonight, remember?'

'Yes, and what a privilege it was, too,' he replied sarcastically. 'So what is the problem now? Don't you like your room?'

'No, my room is fine. It's that man, though—the one who came to welcome me to Athens. Reginald Crump? From the company?'

'What about him?'

'How often does he come to the hotel?'

'Why do you want to know? Do you need to speak to him?'

'Maybe I do. When is he due to return?'

'Tomorrow morning, I imagine. But I am sure he will have other guests to attend to as well. You can't expect him to drop everything just for you. If you need assistance with a tour booking, I can give you the company's general number. Besides …' He stopped for a moment to interrogate his tiny brain and almost lost an index finger up his squashed little nose.

'Besides what?' I pressed him further.

'The strange thing is, I never met Mister Crump before today. Normally the company sends Mister Browne to greet our guests, but he was sick.' He paused to reflect some more, blinked his eyes, and then added: 'That was what I was told, anyway.'

I could feel the skin on my face tug at my cheekbones, so I pointed to Dumbo's computer terminal. 'Can you please check something for me?'

He muttered a few uncomplimentary words in Greek that even I understood but eventually accepted that the guest had to come first—even if that guest was an uncouth Australian loudmouth wearing a ridiculous Loch Ness monster T-shirt. He dazzled me with a couple of quick keystrokes and then glared into his screen.

'The name is Gardner, correct? Room 315?'

'No, you jackass. It's Gerrick, Room 1015.'

If I had been Dumbo, I would have thrown his stapler right at my head. But credit where credit was due: he somehow managed to keep his cool before politely gesturing to his computer with a bony finger.

'I now have your details on the screen. What would you like to know?'

I thrust my nose towards his chair. 'That initial booking that I made through a London travel agency last week—can you tell me whether I provided the consultant with my Australian address?'

Dumbo carefully scrutinised the data in front of him. I could tell that he genuinely wanted to help, even if his sole motivation was to get rid of me as soon as he could.

'No, the original booking only contained your name, flight details, and passport number. You will recall that I took all of your details, such as your home address and telephone number when you checked into the hotel.'

I burped out some stale air. 'Just as I thought.'

'What does this all have to do with Mister Crump?' asked Dumbo curiously.

What indeed. My head suddenly felt way too heavy for the rest of my body. *I'm tired, I'm hungry, and I've got a raging headache. And I now have some fat English geezer stalking me in a strange, foreign city.*

'When Crump introduced himself to me tonight,' I began to explain, 'he knew that I lived in Australia's capital city, Canberra. How did he know this if I only provided that information to you several minutes earlier?'

'I-I-I … am not sure,' Dumbo stuttered, trying to find an explanation where indeed one didn't exist. To avoid further embarrassment, he arched his back, pumped out his shoulders, and pretended that he was in complete control of the situation.

'I should speak to my manager,' he said with an air of defiance.

'Yes, perhaps you should,' I replied angrily. 'You can tell your manager from me that I was a travel consultant for two years, and none of this makes any sense. I want to know how Crump got hold of my personal information before this hotel even did. I don't care how you do it, but I expect to have an answer when I return from dinner.'

I scanned the lobby one last time for any tell-tale signs of Reginald Crump before disappearing into the waiting night.

Marco

Athens
May 1995

'No, no, no!' I cried out in exasperation at the young Japanese couple who had just asked me to take their photo. 'Behind you, behind you!' I furiously rotated my spare hand in a clockwise direction in the grim hope that they would soon glance over their shoulders, where, only several feet away, the marble columns of the Parthenon loomed menacingly above us like a family of ancient giants.

At first, the husband found my frustration mildly amusing, until he suddenly admonished me with a polite wag of his finger, as if he had finally unmasked my devious plan to fool him and his wife out of the greatest photo of their lives. That would be the one of them standing next to a broken information panel containing a large black and white print of the Parthenon when, if they only took the time to turn around, they could have seen the real thing in technicolour.

We bantered aimlessly for several more minutes before I got jacked with the whole thing and squeezed off a couple of photos to keep them happy.

Satisfied that I wasn't about to abscond with their life's work, the couple celebrated this momentous event by hugging, kissing, and generally slurping all over each other. After all, it wasn't every day you travelled halfway across the world to have a photo taken of you and your partner standing next to another photo.

Once he had safely extracted his tongue from the back of his wife's throat, the husband snatched his ridiculously expensive monstrosity from my hands and pointed to my own flimsy little camera bag to see whether he could return the favour.

'No thanks,' I replied facetiously, even though we both knew that neither he nor his wife could understand a single word I was saying. 'I'm saving my film for our trip to the toilet block.'

'Yes, yes—toilet block!' the husband enthused, while his wife rewarded my sarcasm with an approving smile. I shook my head in despair before wandering off to find a quiet place where I could rejoice in their lunacy.

I eventually found myself standing next to a pile of broken rocks scattered expertly around a pool of muddy rainwater. Tiny droplets of perspiration trickled down my sunburned nose, so I reached into my pocket for a tattered old handkerchief that I always kept with me for such emergencies. After smoothing out my tangled hair, I peered out towards the endless horizon which sweltered beneath a red, burning sun.

There it is! Athens! City of the Gods! I casually flicked at a lone mosquito that had been following me all morning and marvelled once again at the endless tapestry of white ceilings that swept across the shimmering metropolis below me. Trapped inside this perfect moment in time, I begged Athena to reward my never-ending devotion to her by sharing with me the endless secrets of the immortals.

When she cruelly denied my latest request, I summoned the power of my prolific imagination and magically transformed myself into a fire-breathing warrior with wings, a close depiction, perhaps, of Icarus from Greek mythology. Free at last, I began to soar high above the sun-drenched fields that surrounded the Acropolis in search of a legendary pool of ambrosia that would surely deliver me everlasting life.

My quest soon led to a lonely grove of olive trees that swayed gently to the rhythm of an afternoon breeze. As I emerged into an open field, I was welcomed by a guard of muscular *hoplites,* who averted their eyes to my presence before thanking the gods for my safe arrival. Their captain, a sculptured brute with a jagged scar tattooed across his hairless chest, somehow found the courage to raise his head and then beseeched me to follow him up a rocky path that would take us to a temple built in my honour.

Many great people craved my audience, he informed me, including Plato, Socrates, and Aristotle. But before I could ascertain whether Alexander the Great would also be in attendance, the captain clapped his hands several times, after which a party of young maidens, dressed in finely cut silk gowns, carelessly wandered through selected gaps in the surrounding tree line. Chosen for my pleasure by Aphrodite herself, these beautiful creatures danced seductively to the tune of a mystical lyre until they all dropped to their knees and laid their expensive ivory bangles in front of me as proof of their virtue. I swallowed the lump in my throat and then …

'Holy shit!'

A rock suddenly came flying through the air and smacked 'Icarus' square on the jaw, hurtling him back to the twentieth century. I opened my eyes and stared down at a group of giggling school children, who quickly found refuge behind their dopey teacher in the vain hope that his huge backside would protect them from my looming vengeance. When I ordered these little devils to reveal their guilt-ridden little faces, they screamed out in abject terror and then scattered away like frightened mice in a thousand different directions. My pride felt obliged to chase after them, or at least give the teacher a piece of my mind. But my lips began to crack, my throat began to sting, so I decided to dispense with my Slavic thirst for revenge for the time being and reached for my mineral water instead.

I heard more commotion behind me and watched as our intrepid Greek tour guide finally succeeded in getting the attention of the Japanese husband and wife, both of whom were still happily admiring their beloved information panel.

'The bus will leave in ten minutes,' he warned them. I still had things to do, so to avoid his gaze, I dropped to my knees and hopped along a dusty path until I reached the viewing wall located behind the Parthenon temple.

Lost within a sea of excited tourists, I slowly lifted my head until my chin was bobbing over the side of the ledge. Once I had acclimatised my eyes to the raging sunlight, I deftly removed my trusty little Canon camera from its bag. I began to manoeuvre the lens several times from this awkward position until I was satisfied that a perfect photo of the Athens skyline lay within my grasp. I rattled off maybe four or five snaps in quick succession and then looked out into the distance one last time. *I will be back one day*, I promised myself.

Just after midday, our tour bus made its final stop at Syntagma Square, located in the heart of central Athens. I was soon bouncing down a crowded footpath, pondering how I would spend the rest of my afternoon.

I decided that treating myself to a nutritious lunch would be a good start, given all the fast food I had been eating lately. After that, I would kill a few hours exploring the historic Plaka district on foot before collecting my backpack from the Hellas later in the afternoon. From there, I would walk the short distance to the Hotel Adelphi, where I had a room booked for the next two nights.

As I shuffled past a row of ice-cream vendors jammed with people seeking temporary refuge from the stifling heat, my mind wandered back to that one thing I had tried to ignore all morning. Just for dramatic effect, I was calling it the 'Reginald Crump Affair'.

I was still greatly troubled by last night's events, especially when no-one at the hotel took my concerns seriously. Sure, the night manager agreed to see me when I returned from dinner. But despite the night manager's never-ending smile and tobacco-filled breath, it was clear from the discussion he later had with Dumbo that he thought I was some crazed mass murderer from Australia who had escaped from a mental asylum. I eventually left reception frustrated by his careless indifference to my plight, much to Dumbo's lasting joy.

However, I had woken up that morning with a steely determination to solve this mystery before I left for my tour of the Acropolis. After my ritual morning shower, I produced Reginald Crump's business card from my wallet and called his number. Following ten unanswered rings, I was automatically transferred to a standard company voicemail.

Bugger it. I'm not going to leave a message, for that would put the onus on Reginald Crump to call me back. Who knew if he ever would? No, I'll try again after breakfast when I know that the company will be open for business.

I wandered downstairs to the hotel restaurant and devoured a delicious feta omelette. When I returned to my room an hour later, I sat on the bed and decided to give Reginald Crump one more call. But after five unanswered rings, I was transferred to another voicemail account belonging to a woman called Edna Krajicek. Exasperated, I angrily slammed the phone down, gathered my things, and finalised my bill at reception.

After I secured my backpack with the concierge, I began to prowl around the lobby for several more minutes, doing nothing beneficial to advance my cause before deciding to grab a local newspaper from a nearby stand. Of course, I couldn't read a single word of Greek, but that was all part of my ruse to catch Reginald Crump in the act. With feline precision, I slithered into the same leather chair he had sat in the previous night and unfurled my newly acquired newspaper around my head. For a moment, I thought seriously about cutting two small holes into the paper to accommodate my beady little eyes but quickly realised that this was too ridiculous even for me. Regardless, I sat patiently on the chair for the next hour, waiting for Reginald Crump to blunder his way into the hotel lobby.

But of course, the joke was on me. The concierge, a naturally suspicious fellow, soon wandered over and politely asked me why I had been reading the same page of my newspaper for the last thirty minutes. When I couldn't think of a logical reason, we both agreed that it was time for me to join my prepaid tour of the Acropolis.

Back at Syntagma Square, I obtained a free city guide from a corner tourist booth and checked out some local restaurants. I sifted through several options before settling on a quaint little café barely a stone's throw away, which offered an impressive array of local cuisine, as well as an outstanding view of the Greek parliament building.

To counter the wild afternoon heat, I found a table under the shade of a huge pink umbrella and slapped on some sunscreen from a small tube that I kept hidden inside my camera bag. A Greek waiter with huge curly sideburns soon arrived to take my order. I initially tried to follow his bullet-paced Greek as he blabbed out the specials of the day, but to his disappointment, I ended up ordering a *kotopita* (a Greek chicken pie) and a salad from the main menu instead.

He seemed annoyed at first that I had wasted his precious time, but he soon returned with a small plate of bread and a resigned smile. I politely thanked him in jumbled Greek before turning to watch the endless stream of people swarming across Syntagma Square in their lunchtime rush.

'Ah, Mister Gerrick, how nice to see you again. Remember, if you need any assistance during your stay in Athens, please don't hesitate to call me.'

My body froze as soon as I heard that familiar English accent. *It can't be, surely?* I managed to contort my neck into various insane positions in an attempt to locate the source of that voice before making a simple left turn towards the table next to me. And there I was, staring right into the face of a beaming Reginald Crump.

'It's you!' My words ricocheted off a couple of nearby buildings before whistling straight back through my hair. 'Why are you following me, Crump?'

Reginald Crump stuffed one final cabbage roll into his vulpine mouth.

'Come now, Mister Gerrick,' he replied after wiping his sweaty forehead with a napkin. 'Following you? I mean, how utterly ludicrous.'

'You expect me to believe that this is just a coincidence?'

'I don't know what you are talking about,' he said, laughing. 'I am simply enjoying the warm Athens sunshine and this wonderful food.' He brushed away some loose crumbs from that same safari suit he was wearing the previous day and then slid out of his chair.

'Where are you going?' I asked. 'I want to—'

'Can't waste time chatting, Mister Gerrick. I have things to do, people to see. I'm a terribly busy man, I will have you know. Enjoy your lunch!'

'No, wait!' I screamed at him as he pumped his ridiculous billiard table legs towards the Syntagma Square metro station. 'I need to talk to you.'

'Give me a call—you have my number,' he shouted back.

'I've already called you twice today, but you never answer your phone.'

'I'm a terribly busy man, I will have you know,' he repeated. 'But keep trying!'

'Come back here, Crump!'

Everything happened so quickly. I leapt upwards from my chair, with every intention of rugby tackling Reginald Crump onto the bitumen pavement. But for some reason, my feet didn't want to follow my brain. Before I could comprehend the extent of my clumsiness, I found myself lying horizontally on the ground, my hands gripping my knees in agony.

'You know, there are laws against this!' I cried out.

'Have a nice day, Mister Gerrick!' Reginald Crump bellowed from the other side of the street. He clicked his heels together in one last act of defiance before disappearing down a nearby set of stairs.

Incredibly, once he was out of sight, the feeling immediately returned to my legs.

How bloody weird is that?

I lifted myself back onto my chair and turned to face the centre of the café, where I expected to see a thousand eyes staring in my direction. But no—there wasn't even a passing interest in my predicament. Indeed, most of the café's patrons were either immersed in their conversations or wolfing down their lunches. No-one even had the common courtesy to ask for my wellbeing. *I mean, someone throw me a bone here.*

A young waitress placed my lunch on the table. When I neglected to thank her, she scratched her little nose and said something to me I couldn't understand in Greek.

'Do you speak English?' I replied hopefully.

'A little,' she nodded. 'Are you okay, sir? You don't look very well.'

I ignored her question for the time being—mainly because I was an arsehole—but pointed to the empty dishes on Reginald Crump's recently occupied table. 'The man who just left. Does he come here often?'

'I am terribly sorry, sir, but I didn't pay any attention to him.'

Now, there's a surprise. Can anyone in this damn city tell me anything about Reginald Crump at all?

What's more, my chicken pie was bloody awful. It took several bottles of sparkling water to finally relieve the foul aftertaste of fermented flour inside my mouth. Once I flushed everything out of my system, I picked at my little bowl of salad and a leftover piece of dry bread. Yes, my altercation with Reginald Crump had ruined my entire afternoon.

I was just about to swallow my last cherry tomato when a local policeman, dressed magnificently in a bright new blue uniform, casually strolled past my table and raised his baton to acknowledge the English-speaking waitress. His sudden arrival gave me a crazy idea. What if I called him over, and with the help of the waitress, explained to him that a fat English sexual pervert was stalking me? *Yes! Let's get a posse together and arrest this geezer right now!* Only when Reginald Crump was rotting in jail would I be able to relax and enjoy the rest of my holiday.

But so often in life, there had to be a spoiler, and, on that occasion, it was something called common sense. Because, you see, serious holes in my plan became evident as soon as I began to workshop my impending conversation with the policeman in my mind.

So, Mister Gerrick, what is the nature of Reginald Crump's alleged crime?

Well, it's like this, Mister Policeman: I am not sure whether he has done anything illegal or not, but if you must know, he is a smug, obnoxious prick, and he makes my skin crawl.

Well, Mister Gerrick, even within the boundaries of your warped little mind, you can't just arrest someone for being obnoxious. God knows, if that were the case, most of my family would now be in jail.

But he knew that I lived in Canberra. How do you explain that, Mister Policeman?

Yes, so you have said. But I am sure that there is a logical explanation for this if you just give him the benefit of another phone call.

But why is he following me, Mister Policeman?

Following you? What proof do you have of that, Mister Gerrick? Zilch. Zero. None. And tell me this: how did he predict that you would pick this café, out of all the places you could have chosen in central Athens to have lunch today? As you said yourself, he was finishing his meal when you finalised your order, which means, of course, that he was at the café long before you ever arrived.

No. Just like Dumbo and the night manager before him, the policeman's reaction would have been one of derision.

My thoughts turned to that lovely Greek woman I recently met in Brussels. Angelina was her name.

'Make sure you take control of Athens,' she said to me as we sculled down those exquisite Belgian beers together. 'Don't let Athens take control of you.'

She was a smart one, that Angelina, and a Liverpool fan, no less. And with no-one else in this city willing to help me, she was the only Greek person I was inclined to trust at that moment in time. I was taking one hell of a gamble, but I took her sage advice and finally left these absurd events behind me at the restaurant.

I happily spent the next two hours exploring the elegant streets of the Plaka. I took in a coffee here, an ice cream there, and stepped in dog shit everywhere. When I finally returned to the Hellas, I noticed that Dumbo had commenced his afternoon shift, and I felt the inexorable urge to get under his skin one last time.

But before I could enact my deviously concocted plan—which may or may not have involved dropping his mobile phone into the lobby aquarium—a huge party of tourists jumped off a large blue bus and invaded reception, each demanding to be checked into their rooms immediately. The sheer look of terror on Dumbo's pimply face suggested that sorting this lot out was punishment enough for him. Finally satisfied that I had won our duel, I slung my backpack over my shoulders, smiled at the security camera, and began my short walk to my new hotel.

The owner was a towering Greek man in his early fifties called Spiro, who proudly sported an overly bushy moustache and a pot belly made in hell. At first, he paid no interest in me as he methodically processed the paperwork associated with my booking. But once he examined my passport, everything about his sullen demeanour suddenly changed.

'Oh, you are Australian!' he roared out in almost perfect English.

'Am I? My God, I should have checked my passport earlier.'

'My mother and sister live in Melbourne! You might know them?'

'Quite possibly. I know lots of people in Melbourne.' Like, about two.

He thumped his hands on the reception desk and called out to his wife. 'Selene! Come quickly! This man is from Australia, and he might know Mama and Calliope!'

Out of nowhere, a huge woman with bowling pins for arms suddenly crashed through a side entrance and stampeded towards me at a million miles an hour. Self-preservation was the only thing on my mind. With the agility of a drunken gnat, I removed my jacket and cunningly turned it into a matador's cape in a feeble attempt to protect my sorry arse from her outraged fury.

'Ole!' I cried out several times in desperation as I tried to manoeuvre her out the front door. But just when I thought she was about to trample all over me, she abruptly stopped inches away from my terrified face and thrust something underneath my nose.

'Eat, eat,' the woman insisted as she flaunted her latest batch of baklava.

As I happily munched away, grateful that my life was no longer in danger, Spiro proudly held up his appointment book.

'You are in luck; I give you our best room. It is on the top floor, and you will love it!'

To be fair, he pretty much did, and I pretty much do. For eighty Australian dollars a night, it was an absolute bargain. Okay, the furniture was old and rickety, and I needed to kick the television a few times before I could get a clear picture on CNN. But the queen-size bed was remarkably soft, the air conditioning worked, and to top it off, Spiro threw in half a dozen cans of local beer into the bar fridge for free.

I grabbed a late-afternoon nap and woke up just after six-thirty. Spiro recommended a pizza restaurant just around the corner, and once again, he was the main man. I ordered the hot salami special in broken Greek and washed it down with a jug of lemonade. The tiny Greek waitress with the safety pin through her nose smuggled me a free slice of *galaktoboureko*—which is an unnecessarily long name for a custard pie—and I finished the evening with a game of pinball at a local parlour.

When I returned to the Adelphi, Spiro lectured me about finding a nice Greek girl to marry and then suggested I take in a night view of Athens from the hotel rooftop.

That wasn't a bad idea, I decided. Not the part about marrying a nice Greek girl, but that night-time view of Athens. So I detoured via my room, collected my biography of the German field marshal, Erwin Rommel, grabbed a few cans of beer, and then jogged to the top of the building.

Spiro was absolutely on fire: the view was indeed spectacular, and the cool evening breeze was pleasantly refreshing. I found myself a chair next to the balcony rail, cracked open a coldie, and then lost myself in my book.

Ten minutes later, my solitude was interrupted by a minor racket developing outside. I turned my head sideways to find four people emerging from the stairwell, engaged in animated discussion. One was a handsome man in his early thirties, with a three-day growth glued onto his sunburned face and a shock of dark brown curly hair that extended to his shoulders. His fierce blue eyes inspected me inquisitively before he quickly ushered his companions, all women in their early twenties, towards a spare table to my right.

'Hi there,' he said in excellent English. 'Do you mind if we join you?'

'How could I?' I smiled, pissed that my tranquillity had been interrupted.

'Thank you.' He muttered something to his friends in what I assumed to be Italian. One of the girls pulled out a bottle of chianti and four wine glasses from a plastic bag. The man then produced a pen knife from his pocket, ripped out the cork, and then carefully filled the glasses in four equal portions. There was some more animated chatter between them before the man finally gathered up his chair in exasperation and dropped it several feet away from where I was sitting.

'Cheers,' he said as he lifted his wine glass towards me.

'*Saluti*,' I replied in butchered Italian.

'Well done!' he said with a laugh. 'My name is Marco, from Florence in Italy.'

He offered me his hand, and I shook it firmly. '"Marco from Florence in Italy." That's an exceptionally long name. If you must know, mine is "Alex from Canberra in Australia".'

Despite the promise of a new friendship, Marco ignored my juvenile sense of humour a little bit too easily for my liking. 'Hey girls!' he yelled out excitedly to his three companions. 'This is Alex.' He grabbed me firmly by the wrist and pointed them out individually. 'This is Sophia, this is Dominica, and this is Marcella.' I did my best to make them feel welcome by offering them a friendly wave and a smile. It worked an absolute charm, too. Well …

They at first collectively responded with some low-key grumbling—never a good sign—before each of them took turns to stare coldly at me with varying degrees of disdain and hostility. Okay, the one called Marcella tried to lift her arm in a hopeless attempt to wave back at me but then gave up when she realised that everyone else had lost interest as well.

Marco rubbed the stubble on his chin. 'Sorry,' he bemoaned, rightly embarrassed, 'but they are not very nice girls.'

'Fuck you, arsehole!' roared out Sophia, and the other two simultaneously gave him the middle finger in support.

'You see what I have to put up with?' he asked mournfully.

'I'm sure they are just very tired,' is all I could say.

We soon began talking. I learnt that Marco was a photographer who worked for an illustrious travel magazine. Like me, he was thirty-two years old. Unlike me, he was committed to a lifestyle that never saw him in one place for more than a month. Marco admitted, somewhat sadly, that there was no place he called home anymore, although he still had parents who doted on him whenever he returned to Florence.

Marco supplemented his photography income during winter by doubling up as a ski instructor in the Austrian Alps. When his contract there ended, he usually spent the month of April holidaying in the Greek Islands with a close group of friends before they all scattered for their summer jobs. That year, the group had set up camp on the historic island of Samos, close to the Turkish coast.

As Marco refilled his glass, I took a moment to inspect his striking features. You had to be envious of the guy, you really did. Unbelievably good-looking, charismatic, worldly, and living a lifestyle that most men my age could barely imagine. For the second time in twenty-four hours, I started to question the mistakes I had made in my own life. But this was neither the time nor the place to drown in self-pity.

'And what's the story with them?' I asked Marco as I flicked my head towards the three girls.

'It's all a bit complicated.'

'I gathered that. That's why I'm dying to know.'

He placed his wine glass next to his chair and moved closer towards me. 'Well, it's like this,' he began in an extra-low whisper. 'You see, I have been intimate with all three girls, but they only found out earlier this afternoon.'

'I thought as much.' I smiled. 'Had they met each other before today?'

'I should imagine so,' Marco admitted. 'Sophia and Dominica are cousins, while Marcella is their best friend.'

'Wow, that's one for the books,' I whistled. I scooped up another beer from the ground before giving Marco a solid pat on the thigh. 'Well, my friend, we have a saying in Australia that I think summarises your situation perfectly: "You're in deep shit, mate".'

'I think they want to kill me,' agreed Marco.

'You have got that right, you bastard!' screamed out Dominica.

Her incisive contribution to our conversation provided Marco and me with the perfect opportunity to shuffle further along the railing. We then gazed out together into the pristine night sky.

'Athens is incredible, is it not?' asked Marco.

'Yes, it's everything I imagined it to be.'

'So, what are your plans for the next few days?'

'More sightseeing tomorrow, I guess. On Sunday, I will probably travel to one of the islands.'

'Really? Which one?'

I tried to remember the list of names I had memorised from a travel brochure before boarding the plane at London Heathrow, but under pressure from Marco's inquisitive gaze, I could only come up with Santorini and Naxos.

Marco screwed up his face to look serious.

'No good?' I asked, genuinely interested in his views.

'Santorini is far too windy at this time of year, and Naxos doesn't get rocking until later in the month. Have you thought about Samos?'

'Not really,' I admitted. I remembered seeing an article about Samos in one of those useless airline magazines on the flight to Athens, but I had fallen asleep halfway through the opening sentence. That bloody hangover again, you see.

'You would love it,' Marco promised. 'You are into history, right? Then you couldn't come to a better place for that. Did you know that Pythagoras was born there?'

'Really? Wow!' *Who the hell was Pythagoras again?*

'Samos is only a short ferry ride to Kuşadası in Turkey. When you arrive, you can jump on a bus, and an hour later, you are in Ephesus.'

Ephesus. Now that's a coincidence. I watched a fascinating TV documentary about Ephesus just before I left Australia. It looked like a pretty cool place. And didn't Sting once play a concert there? Yes, Marco's proposal might have some merit after all.

'That could work,' I said carefully. 'Maybe I will consult the Oracle of Delphi tonight and let you know what she says later.'

'By all means,' Marco replied, smiling. 'Coincidently, I'm returning to Samos on Sunday afternoon. If you come with me, I can show you around the island and introduce you to some of my friends. I think they will be fascinated by you.'

I laughed loudly. 'Nothing is fascinating about me, pal. Trust me.'

'You sell yourself short, Alex,' he replied, and I wanted to believe him. 'In fact, I have a special friend who you should meet. Her name is Martina, and I think you would both get along famously.'

I quickly realised where he wanted to go with this, so I held my hand up in protest. 'I already have a girlfriend, mate. But thanks for thinking of me.'

'If you say so.'

We talked some more, mostly about football, Italian politics, and, of course, women. Meanwhile, the three girls continued to plot, curse, and cry out as if they were having their own private conversation with the devil himself. The longer Marco and I talked, the more I knew that he was deliberately prolonging our conversation to avoid whatever evil torments were about to come his way.

Not that I could blame him, mind you. Given the circumstances, I wouldn't have wanted the three of them to be responsible for the future of my testicles either. More to the point, the way Marcella kept staring at me with her dead fish eyes suggested that I was on her shit-list too, even if it was just by association. *Sorry, Marco—I think you are one cool guy and all, but you're on your own with this one.*

I finished my last beer, complained about a headache that I didn't have, and announced that I was going to bed. Marco turned into a bottomless pile of quivering goo when I jumped out of my seat to leave, but we both agreed that if he survived the night without getting slaughtered, we would meet for breakfast to discuss my final decision about Sunday. After we exchanged a series of meaningless high fives, I made no promises to him about Samos, and he made no promises to me about surviving the night.

However, as I walked back to my room, the strange kinship that had developed between the two of us stirred within me a tide of excitement that I had not felt for some time. Our connection inexorably plunged me headfirst into Marco's unique world—one that contained every hope and dream I had ever wished for myself. The desire to face my lost ambitions on a faraway island with a group of strangers was something I couldn't possibly deny myself. For a hopeless romantic like me, there was only ever one decision I could make.

The Party

Athens
May 1995

I was sitting inside the hotel dining room, swallowing endless cups of black coffee, waiting for Marco to join me. Selene suddenly appeared at my table with a huge white plate consisting of twenty fried eggs and half a pig's worth of bacon.

'You must eat more; you are far too skinny,' she insisted while waving a carving knife disturbingly close to my throat.

I plunged backwards to escape instant decapitation and then noticed that most of the other guests in the dining room were staring enviously at the size of my breakfast portion compared to their pathetic morsels.

'Any chance I can order the big breakfast instead?' I asked Selene.

'You want me to cook you more food?' she growled. 'It is not enough?'

'No, just kidding. I wouldn't want you to massacre another five pigs just for me.'

My sense of humour went right over her head while her knife alarmingly got closer to mine. 'All the eggs on your plate come from our very own special chicken,' she boasted.

'What, all of them?' I asked incredulously. 'That must be one helluva bird. Is it still alive?'

'Yes, of course,' promised Selene. A young Chinese woman sitting at an adjacent table was making a huge song and dance about her burnt toast, so Selene flicked the hair away from her horns and angrily stomped knife-first towards her.

Meanwhile, an Australian couple sitting near the door dared to question the favouritism I was receiving.

'Hey,' the boyfriend/husband yelled at me. 'What gives? Why are *you* so bloody special?'

'I might know Mama and Calliope, that's why,' I roared back at him. 'So back off, mate.'

He muttered something uncomplimentary about my parentage, which I merely passed off as unfounded jealousy, before I began to attack my obscene banquet with relish. To my sheer delight, Marco marched across the dining room floor towards me like a victorious Roman consul in full plumage.

'You survived!' I greeted him with a firm handshake, just to make sure it was him. 'For a moment there, I thought you weren't going to make it.'

He laughed rather too loudly, and I suddenly tasted his cheap cologne on my toast. 'I sorted it all out, Alex. They fly back to Italy this morning—one big, happy family.'

'How the hell did you manage that?' I asked while negotiating a huge gob-full of bacon. 'When I left you last night, you were about to be castrated with several pink lady razor blades.'

'Alex, have you ever had sex with …'

I dropped my cutlery and threw my hands up in violent protest. 'Hold it right there! Way too much information, mate. I can guess what happened, so please spare me the sordid details—until at least the next time you see me drunk.'

Marco laughed once more and poured himself a glass of water. Selene had finished slicing the Chinese girl in half and, when she saw Marco, began to go weak at her concrete knees. She casually dropped the knife onto the floor before bounding towards us at supersonic speed.

'Marco, you scallywag, you haven't said hello to me since you arrived!' She reached out and grabbed one of his rosy cheeks between her humungous fingers. 'You are such a naughty boy.'

'You don't know the half of it,' I said.

She quickly ignored me and looked Marco right in the eye. 'Who were those awful women who left the hotel this morning? They are not worthy of you, Marco. I tell you again to marry a nice Greek girl!'

I seriously began to wonder whether there were any single Greek girls left in Athens, given the ease with which people seemed to be offering them out to complete strangers.

Marco released one of his smouldering smiles at Selene, and she was mesmerised by its intensity. Heck, I was mesmerised as well, and I was one of the straightest guys on the planet.

'The only Greek girl I want to marry is already taken. I have to wait for Spiro to die first.'

I didn't wish to be overly critical, but really, Marco? *Have you any shame?*

'I can kill him if you like,' pleaded Selene. 'It's going to happen sooner or later, anyway.'

Marco shook his head sadly. 'No, you can't do that. For if you did, they would jail you for life. And then where would I be without you?'

A collective groan, led by yours truly, spiralled across the dining room, but neither Marco nor Selene seemed to care.

'What would you like for breakfast, my darling?' she asked, taking out her notebook and pencil.

Marco pointed to my plate. 'I will have what he's having,' he smiled. 'And a coffee, please.'

'I will get you a larger plate,' she said, nodding excitedly.

'A larger plate?' I spluttered into my coffee mug. 'There is already enough food on mine to feed the three hundred Spartans at Thermopylae!'

Selene ignored me again and rushed off to the kitchen to prepare breakfast for her future toy boy husband.

Marco slapped me on the back. 'Just before I forget—Marcella asked me to send you her regards.'

'Really?' I replied. 'And the other girls?'

'No, they didn't like you very much.'

I tried to smile anyway. 'There you go. That Marcella, she is one crazy gal. I always knew that behind those pointed talons, she had a thing for me.'

Like everyone else that morning, Marco decided to ignore me as well. 'So, Alex,' he began, in between sips of water, 'have you decided about Samos?'

I pointed to my travel guide, which was sitting next to the pepper shaker. 'Had a good read, and I must admit it sounds like a terrific place. Did you know that Pythagoras was born there?'

Marco looked confused but nodded anyway. 'I take it that's a yes?'

'I'm going to regret this, but yeah, I'm all yours, mate.'

Marco clapped his hands. 'Excellent news, my friend. You will have a terrific time, I'm sure of it. Lots of great people to meet, endless bottles of ouzo to drink, and the best food you will ever taste!'

He pulled out a card from his trouser pocket and placed it in front of me.

'Go and see my friend Maria. She runs a travel agency just around the corner from here. Get her to book you a business-class seat on the ferry from Piraeus for Sunday afternoon. It might be a little more expensive than a regular ticket, but you will thank me by the time we reach Samos.'

'You're the boss.'

'Don't worry about accommodation just yet. There are plenty of good places to stay at the main port, and the best deals are usually found at the ferry terminal when you arrive.'

I placed the card in my shirt pocket and thanked Marco for his advice.

'And another tip about life on Samos,' he said. 'Travel light, my friend. Buy yourself a small carry bag and take what you need for the next few days. Spiro has a storeroom here, and he will look after your luggage until you return.'

'Okay,' I nodded. It wasn't often that I allowed a total stranger to control my life, but I was utterly under Marco's spell by that stage. The coolest guy at school had picked me to be his best friend, and my ego loved every minute of it.

'One last thing,' said Marco, as he produced yet another card. 'A friend of mine, Scott Farmer, is holding a party tonight at one of the hotels in the city. The address is on the card. I spoke to him this morning, and he is happy for you to attend. I would consider it an honour if you joined me as my guest.'

I shuffled uncomfortably in my seat. You see, I usually disliked parties. Pretending to be nice to people I didn't really know and dancing the night away to washed-up disco music wasn't my idea of having fun. But what choice did I have? Marco had gone out on a limb for me, and I couldn't offend him now.

'It sounds like an upmarket affair.' I chose my words carefully, reading the address on the card. 'I don't have the clothes for something like this.'

'Nonsense,' he retorted. 'People will dress casually, trust me. Come as you are, just like the Nirvana song says. You will be fine.'

After he finished his coffee, Marco announced that he had left something in his room and then, bizarrely, never returned. Meanwhile, I had become convinced that Selene's maniacal attempts to fatten me up were a precursor to some ancient Greek sacrificial ritual. While she wasn't looking, I donned several different disguises to confuse her—my one of the chicken an absolute triumph—before escaping the hotel via the rear door. Once I obtained my bearings, I stared out into the grey morning mist and began looking for the travel agency.

It took fifteen minutes of walking around in circles before I finally located the correct address. I explained to the girl at the front counter in English that I needed to speak to Maria and immediately a pretty woman in her late twenties appeared from behind a computer terminal. Unsurprisingly, she gushed as soon as I mentioned Marco's name. *Oh dear, not another one!*

After Maria interrogated me for any juicy gossip about the Italian super stud, she studiously tapped into her computer. Within minutes, I was booked on the cheapest return business-class fare to Samos available. Like any good travel agent, Maria then asked me whether I needed anything else for my trip, and I mentioned my desire to visit Ephesus.

She made a couple of quick phone calls, screamed down the receiver at someone she didn't like, and eventually found a combined ferry/bus tour for Tuesday at a very special price. Because I was a friend of her dear Marco, she even threw me an extra ticket on the house, just in case I wanted to take him with me. I thanked her profusely for her kindness and naïvely promised that I would get Marco to give her a call.

With time to kill, I loitered around the centre of Athens before I took an ominous detour through the bewildering side streets of the famous Monastiraki flea market. Within minutes, I found myself trapped within an eclectic maze of boutique stores and novelty shops that sold everything from juiced-up stereo systems to tiny plastic figurines of the Parthenon. I soon realised that the only way I could escape this madhouse alive was to buy something—anything. So, with total disregard for my safety, I picked out a white designer shirt from an obscure little corner stall and then purchased a blue carry bag at a souvenir outlet run by some obnoxious hipster wearing a fake Manchester United tracksuit.

Back at the Adelphi, Spiro tackled me in the lobby and lectured me again about being single. When I explained to him that I had a girlfriend and that I didn't need to meet his forty-year-old unmarried cousin Ariadne, the topic of conversation turned to my upcoming trip to Samos. He generously agreed to keep my backpack in storage until the end of next week without me even asking.

However, the quid pro quo was that I had to listen intently while he shared his colourful observations about Turkey. I was able to escape his clutches only after I promised him that I would say a prayer for his excellent health and that of Selene and the chicken when I visited some obscure chapel in Ephesus that he recommended to me.

After preparing for the event, I headed back downstairs, where Spiro convinced me that the best way to get to the hotel was by train. He drew a couple of stickmen and some squiggly lines that I couldn't make out on a piece of paper, made me repeat back to him at least five times the name of the station where I needed to disembark, and then sent me on my way.

I was soon holding grimly onto a safety bar inside a packed train carriage, with an older man's sauerkraut breath splashing across my face. Thankfully, I had one more stop to endure before I flung myself onto a deserted platform and went in search of an exit sign. When I eventually stumbled out into the real world, a passing truck angrily spewed out a stream of exhaust fumes in my direction, and I began to cough wildly until half a lung was hanging out of my mouth.

A street vendor selling his wares from a nearby booth called out to me in passable English. 'Are you okay, sir?'

'Water, please,' I replied, almost choking. He pulled out a plastic bottle from his tiny fridge and made a joke about how he could tell I was English, even though I was Australian. I played along with him until I flicked the empty bottle into a nearby bin.

'How far away am I from the Golden Archway Hotel?'

'Two blocks that way.' He pointed further up the road.

I dropped him a few extra drachmas for his trouble and then pushed my way back onto the pavement. It was only then that I noticed a dishevelled figure slumped in front of me.

It was an old woman, maybe in her late seventies. She was sitting on top of a tattered old blanket, her skeletal fingers locked together in front of her. Her thin, scraggly hair reminded me of the brown spaghetti one could buy in health stores, and her face was covered in deathly streaks of grey. When she saw me, she hissed through her broken front teeth and gestured towards a single coin half-buried beneath her blanket.

Beggars were commonplace throughout Europe, and although I once pitied them, a couple of recent bad encounters with the Gypsies meant that I was mostly immune to their travails. But there was something about this woman's pathetic desolation that tugged at my heartstrings. Maybe it was because she was similar in age to my own mother. Or perhaps it was because I couldn't equate the old woman's poverty with the decadent party I was about to attend. Whatever my reasons—pure or artificial—I reached for my wallet while the old woman furiously whimpered in my face.

'No!' the street vendor shouted at me as he jumped out from behind his booth. 'You must not give her money. If you do, every other beggar in the neighbourhood will want to take advantage of your generosity as well. Begging in this city is a way of life for some.' To emphasise his point, he poked his finger towards the next set of traffic lights, where I could see a group of desperate beggars maltreating some other unfortunate tourists.

'But—'

'No "buts", English. Let me handle this.' On that occasion, I actually did what I was told, and with a timid spin of my fingers, I slid the money back into my pocket. When the old woman realised that I had betrayed her, she threw her hands above her head and began to wail loudly into the night.

But I was too much of a coward to come to her rescue. As soon as the vendor started to lecture her, I used it as an excuse to barge my way into a large group of teenagers standing at a pedestrian crossing. With the old woman's cries still echoing behind me, I shamefully hid within the group's protective shell until we all crossed the road together.

Minutes later, I arrived at the Golden Archway Hotel. My lungs were aching, and my new shirt was covered in sweat. I found a bathroom near reception and splashed cold water over my tomato-red face for several minutes. Once I had sufficiently cooled down, I followed the signs to the function room, where the party was in full swing. A valet at the front door, dressed in what can only be described as some sort of traditional Greek military attire, greeted me with a cheeky smile.

'I'm a friend of Marco Tropozzi,' I explained in slow-motion English.

'No worries, squire,' he replied in the strongest East End London accent I've ever heard. 'Come on in and get yourself a playground stink.'

'A what?'

'A playground stink, matey,' he said again, laughing. 'You know, a drink! Mister T and Mister F are currently in a private meeting. Go inside, get yourself a beer, and relax! They both should be out soon.'

I took one last look at the ridiculous fez he was wearing before wandering into a large ballroom. Its decor immediately reminded me of some obscure set from an old Vincent Price horror movie. The room's dark-blue walls were stained and peeling, and the massive chandelier that guarded the centre of the dance floor must have been hanging by its last thread of cable. A curious smell of camphor wafted past my nose, and I watched with amusement as a burly man in a white skivvy tripped over a loose clump of electrical wire.

On the surface, it seemed a strange place to hold a party for a bunch of middle-class yuppies. But hey, it actually worked! There were so many pleasant distractions on offer to make you forget about the decrepit state of the room.

For a start, the food was prepared to mouth-watering perfection, and the complimentary wines would usually be absurdly over-priced if you had to purchase them in a restaurant. A four-piece band played an upbeat version of 'Hotel California', and the female waitresses were incredibly cute and attentive.

One of them welcomed me to the party, and I expertly whisked a glass of rum-filled punch from her tray. With a drink in hand, I took the opportunity to appraise the people around me. Most were hovering inside that twenty-five-to-thirty-five age group, I decided. Marco was right too: it really was a casual, dress-down affair, and no-one seemed to care what others were wearing. Indeed, compared to some, I looked surprisingly cool and sophisticated.

'Oh my God, it's you!' cried out a honey-blonde woman in her late twenties. It took a moment for me to register that her hawkish blue eyes were targeted right at my nose.

'No, it's not,' I reliably informed her. 'It's me.'

She rushed over in a mad panic, grabbed my elbow, and then kissed me on the cheek. 'You awful, awful man,' she admonished me in a soft, drunk English accent. 'When did you arrive back in Athens?'

'Er, Thursday night?'

'And you expect me to believe that you haven't had time to call me?'

'Was I supposed to call you?' I asked curiously.

'Of course you were. What sort of question is that?'

Well, that's it! I am not copping this! How dare she accuse me of deliberately snubbing her when we've never actually met before now?

'I've been terribly busy,' I replied testily. 'Cut me some slack, will you?'

'Okay, you are forgiven,' she blurted out, taking another sip from her cask of wine. 'But I simply won't put up with your tomfoolery again. Do you understand?'

'Listen, I'm—'

'Hey, Cassandra!' she yelled out to a friend. 'Look who it is!'

A slender African-English woman of similar age danced across the shiny floor with all the panache of a failed ballerina. She somehow managed to land safely next to her friend without even spilling a drop from her glass of champagne.

'Oh my God, it's him!'

It took me about ten minutes before I realised that the man they had me confused with was called Robert. Now, I never actually got to meet Robert, but at that point in proceedings, I could only feel sorry for him that he was somehow connected with these two utter nutjobs.

In quick succession, we covered off Mary's skiing accident in Switzerland, Doug's botched vasectomy, and whether or not Tony permed his pet Burmese cat. It was all pretty savage stuff, but worse was to follow.

'What do you think about Tommy and Josie having a baby?' asked Tammy, the blonde girl.

'Are they characters on *Melrose Place*?' I replied hopefully.

'No, silly. Tommy and Josie from the embassy.'

'Oh, that Tommy and Josie,' I offered, trying to keep a straight face. 'Didn't Tommy want kids?'

'No, he wants Josie to have an abortion,' Cassandra sneered at me.

'Okay, so he doesn't want kids then,' I snorted back at her, not really caring whether he did or didn't.

'Who are we talking about again?' Tammy asked through her alcoholic haze.

I grabbed an English-speaking waitress by the arm, who had been busily serving people some weird-looking green stuff on dry biscuits.

'Excuse me, miss, but does the hotel keep any cans of petrol?'

She used her spare hand to scratch her chin. 'I will have to check with the manager, but I'm not sure that we do. May I ask why you need petrol?'

'I just want to pour some over my head, that's all. And if you could also find me a box of matches, I would be eternally grateful.'

Luckily, I was saved by Marco, who literally appeared out of thin air.

'There you are,' he said with a mischievous grin. 'Enjoying yourself?'

'Things are definitely about to heat up,' I replied.

Marco glanced at the two girls. 'Excuse me, ladies, but I need to borrow this man for a short while.'

Cassandra really didn't hear Marco at all because she had somehow fallen asleep standing up. On the other hand, Tammy seemed disturbingly transfixed by a large moth flying around in circles near a fluorescent lamp.

'Bye, Rrrrobert, see you sssoon,' she slurred once she returned to her own version of reality.

'Robert?' Marco quizzed me when we were out of earshot.

'Don't even ask,' is all I could say.

He guided me across to the other side of the ballroom, where I was introduced to a tall, angular man with fuzzy sideburns and a marine-style crewcut.

'Hey, Scott—this is my friend, Alex.'

Scott offered me his hand, which was deliberately limp and soft. He slowly looked me up and down and then smacked his lips. That was when Alex realised that Scott was gay, while Scott hoped that Alex was gay. Look, being hit on by another man didn't worry me—if you must know, I had several gay friends, and I enjoyed their company. However, something about Scott's cold reptilian eyes unnerved me, regardless of his sexuality, and I didn't want to give him the slightest hint that I was interested in him.

'Ah, you must be the Australian that Marco told me about today.' He turned to his Italian friend. 'You never said he looks like Richard Hunte.'

Marco shrugged his shoulders. 'What was I thinking?'

Okay, perhaps I should have mentioned this Richard Hunte thing long before now. But to be honest, after all these years, I still found the whole thing embarrassing.

Maybe I did have a vague resemblance to the famous Hollywood actor if you really wanted to stretch the limits of your imagination. After all, we both had dark brown hair, deep-set, brown eyes and walked around as if we owned the world. On the flip side, I was almost a foot taller than Richard, while his superbly muscular physique completely dwarfed my somewhat skinny frame. Yet despite these differences, I was regularly subjected to bouts of unexplained hysteria where I was mistaken for Richard's deranged twin brother.

'And what brings you to my party tonight, Richard?' Scott asked, testing the waters in an especially suggestive tone.

To obtain maximum impact, I had to pitch my response with a certain *élan*. 'The coloured balloons, mainly,' I casually replied, rolling my eyes at the ceiling.

Marco tried hard to keep a straight face, while in a moment of divine intervention, a party of young women wandered right past our noses.

'I wouldn't mind one of those either,' I said, as I smiled at a striking fake blonde with a striking fake tan.

Even before I finished my sentence, I could see the fierce indignation erupt across Scott's pale cheeks. He obviously didn't enjoy being rebuffed by one of his potential victims. Without saying a word, Scott formally withdrew his interest in me and began talking to some bald guy in leather pants. *Man, that was pretty special;* I congratulated myself.

'Okay, Richard Hunte.' Marco tugged at my arm. 'Perhaps we should get you out of here before he changes his mind.'

'I'm not sure if I like your friend very much,' I muttered.

We soon found ourselves entrenched in the main bar area, after which Marco gleefully introduced me to his American colleagues from the travel magazine. As we busily moved from one person to the next, I realised that Marco loved the novelty of having an Australian for a friend. It was as if my presence provided him with a convenient excuse to meet new people, even though a man of his dripping charisma didn't need one. For the first time since last night, I wondered whether Marco's motives were always entirely pure. Marco soon began to chat up a gorgeous young American woman who must have either been a swimsuit model or maybe, well, a swimsuit model. At the same time, I became stranded with an overly talkative couple in their thirties from Texas.

They seemed friendly enough, and at first, I was mildly interested in their tales about the rough-and-tumble world of the Texan oil industry. But the inevitable happened, and soon I was drawn into the type of farcical conversation that some Americans seemed to enjoy with us Australians. You know: how was it that I could speak such good English? Did kangaroos really jump down the main street of Sydney? Could koala bears actually eat you?

Then came this doozy.

'Do you have supermarkets in Australia?' the woman asked excitedly.

'No,' I replied, as forlornly as I could. 'We usually wait for the ships to come in on the weekend, and then we go down to the docks to barter for food.'

'Oh, really?'

Get me out of here! I politely explained that I needed to use the bathroom and then navigated my way through several randy couples heading for the dance floor.

This had to be the most bizarre party I had ever attended. In the space of an hour, I had been accosted by the Slosh Sisters, hit on by the party's gay host, and wasted valuable oxygen on the dumbest couple in history.

Could this party get any weirder?

'Are you having a good time, Mister Gerrick?' asked Reginald Crump as he munched away on some corn chips.

Of course. I had to ask, didn't I?

'Jesus Christ,' I blasphemed, more loudly than I should. 'What the hell are you doing here, Crump?'

Reginald Crump took his time to finish his mouthful of food before releasing one of those annoying grins. I noticed for the first time that he was holding a brown walking stick with his left hand.

'You don't seem all that happy to see me, Mister Gerrick.'

'Just answer the question.'

He pointed a chubby finger towards Scott, who was still engrossed in deep conversation with Leather-Pants Man.

'Mister Farmer and I are old friends from way back. Whenever he throws one of his parties, I just have to drop everything.'

'Do you always wear that same disgusting safari suit?' I asked pointedly.

Reginald Crump stared down at me. 'You seem very upset, Mister Gerrick. Is something the matter?'

All I could do was laugh at him. 'It might have something to do with the fact that everywhere I go in Athens, you seem to be right behind me.'

Reginald Crump shook his ridiculous Easter Island head. 'Like I told you yesterday, pure coincidence.'

'Okay then. Explain to me; how did you—'

'Well, I can't stand here gossiping all night,' Reginald Crump said. 'I have things to do—'

'And people to see,' I interrupted him. 'Yes, I have heard it all before. Like yesterday, at Syntagma Square? Remember?'

'I hardly think—'

'Stop screwing with me, Crump.' The intensity of my tone startled even me.

Reginald Crump pretended to be offended. 'My goodness, I'm here to help you, Mister Gerrick, not—as you put it—to screw with you.'

'I don't need or want your help.'

'Everyone can use some help in their lives, Mister Gerrick. Just like the baby crying for its mother's milk or the blind man crossing the road or the old woman begging for money on the sidewalk.'

'What did you say?'

'You have my number, Mister Gerrick.' Reginald Crump pushed himself towards an empty table before edging the toe cap of his shoe into the floorboard. 'Oh, and one more thing,' he added before bending deep into his walking stick. 'It's not too late to cancel your trip to Samos.'

What the hell? 'How do you know about Samos? And why on earth would I cancel my trip?' I demanded.

'You are not ready.'

'Not ready? Not ready for what?'

'Goodnight, now.'

That's it! He is not getting away from me this time! However, just as I pushed my hands out to grab his shoulders, every thought inside my head exploded into an obscure haze. Just like at the restaurant, I found myself flat down on my stomach, lying between a row of plastic chairs while Reginald Crump's wobbly, fat arse walked straight out the main door.

What the hell is going on? Who is this guy? Did he really say that about the old woman? And how in God's name did he know about Samos?

I picked myself up, brushed myself down, and stole a cold beer from a nearby table to soothe my frazzled nerves. I needed some answers, so I saw an opportunity to grab Scott's attention while Leather-Pants Man was distracted by someone on the dance floor.

'Excuse me, Scott'—I squeezed next to him—'but can I ask you something?'

Farmer's stare was suitably disdainful, the type one reserves for a person who had previously offended them.

'What is it now?'

'Do you know some guy called Reginald Crump?'

'What are you talking about? Who is Reginald Crump?'

'Never mind.' I decided not to pursue it any further, especially when the obnoxious prick turned his back on me.

'Fuck you too, Scott,' I screamed into the music. I ducked and weaved between several warm bodies, stretching my head above the crowd to scan the dance floor for Marco. But neither he nor the American girl was anywhere to be seen, and I didn't have to be a rocket scientist to figure out what they were doing.

What an absolute disaster this party had turned out to be! Marco was shagging a swimsuit model in some fancy hotel room while I was stuck inside an episode of the *Twilight Zone*. Well, my obligations to him had indeed been met, so it was time to get the hell out of Dodge.

I crawled to the entrance door undetected, where my pal, the cockney valet, was adjusting that silly fez.

'Had enough then, squire?'

I pointed to my stomach. 'Feeling a bit queasy, actually. Can you tell Marco that I've gone home and that I'll see him tomorrow?'

'Will do, matey.' He winked. 'Yet, somehow, I don't think he'll be returning tonight.'

I marched out into the hotel courtyard, where the cool evening breeze tousled my hair. *Thank God that is over! If I ever see that damn hotel again, it will be too soon.* With the night still relatively young, I considered grabbing a light supper back in Syntagma Square. But I reminded myself that I was taking a ferry ride to the end of the world the next day so perhaps a hot bath, a cup of tea, and a good night's sleep was the best therapy for what had been a wasted few hours.

However, before I jumped into a taxi, there was one more thing I had to do. I carefully pulled out a twenty-dollar American note from my wallet and shuffled back towards the train station. By now, the streets were full of drunken partygoers, and I immediately became disoriented by their unwelcome presence.

Where was the old woman sitting again? I thought it was here. Or was it over there? Wasn't she occupying that little square near the lamp post? The street vendor was still serving customers, so I would ask him. I waited for a couple of teenagers to buy some cigarettes and then dropped my hands onto the counter.

'Hello, it's me again.' I greeted him with a fake smile.

'Ah, English, how are you? Have you had a good night?'

'It has been a real eye-opener,' I told him. 'But I wonder if you could help me. Do you know where I can find the old woman? Remember, the one who was begging for money earlier this evening?'

He immediately offered me one of those harangued looks that could only mean bad news. 'They took her, my friend.'

'They took her? Who did?'

'The ambulance men. She became sick just after you left, and I think she may have died.'

On the ferry ride to Samos, I would try to remember what had come first: the initial shock of this news or the spasm of pain that descended deep into my bowels.

'What's wrong, English? Are you feeling unwell?'

Am I feeling unwell?

I suddenly reeled backwards from the counter, doubled over in pain, my hands gripping my stomach. Every scrap of food that I had eaten burrowed its way through my oesophagus. With nowhere sensible to go, I dropped to the ground and crawled sideways towards the street kerb, which seemed a perfectly good place from which to retch into the gutter.

The vendor, and a group of young girls casually waiting for a taxi, rushed to my side. One of the girls pulled out the handkerchief from my pocket and delicately started to wipe away the specks of vomit from my lips. A bottle of water was slapped hard against my face in case

I needed a drink, but I had become too distracted by a figure standing on the opposite side of the street to bother.

To my horror, Reginald Crump was sitting magically on top of his walking stick, watching the madness of the night engulf me. As I became increasingly transfixed by his remorseless stare, I gradually noticed something different about his demeanour. For when his eyes found a pathway to connect with mine, they were alight with an unforgiving sadness, and I realised that I, rather than the old woman, was the cause of such relentless sorrow. Satisfied that I finally understood my place in the universe, Reginald Crump doffed his white fedora in my direction, flicked out his walking stick, and allowed himself to be consumed by the surrounding darkness.

Martina

Samos Island
May 1995

'*Prosochí parakaló*,' the ferry announcer cried. 'Welcome to Hydra Ferries, taking you to the Greek Islands. To ensure that your trip is a safe one, all prisoners are kindly requested to listen to this safety briefing.'

A group of elderly Australian tourists sitting diagonally opposite me smirked quizzically at each other before they all broke out together in raucous laughter. Meanwhile, an animated conversation in Greek between the announcer and her supervisor began to play out over the ferry intercom for everyone to hear. Suitably rebuked, the announcer finally tapped the microphone several times and started to correct her previous message.

'*Prosochí parakaló*. Welcome to Hydra Ferries, taking you to the Greek Islands. To ensure that your trip is a safe one, all *passengers* are kindly requested to listen to this safety briefing.'

One of the Australians, a feisty old guy with teacup eyes, worked himself into a panicked frown. 'Do you think this boat is safe, cobber?' he quietly leaned towards me so his wife couldn't hear our conversation.

'I'll let you know once we are safely on board the life raft,' I replied bleakly.

Marco appeared from the other side of the business deck and buried himself in the empty chair next to me.

'How are you going, Alex? Feeling any better?'

Ever since my vomiting fit last night, my stomach had gone into Delhi-belly overdrive. I was unable to keep any food down, or more precisely, any food in. Even the anti-diarrhoea tablets that I'd been sucking down all night like candy corn refused to help.

But when all seemed lost, enter Selene the Magnificent. Although I suspected that her cooking was the real cause of my current intestinal predicament, she conjured up some unearthly concoction full of baking powder, bat wings, toad skins, and scores of other dubious ingredients, then forced me to drink it under pain of death. Actually, if I had my time again, I probably would have taken my chances with death rather than subjecting myself to the drink's putrid aroma.

'I'm fine,' I reassured Marco. 'Selene's magic potion seems to be working. I'll be back to my old self by the time we get to Samos.'

'First a headache on Friday night, and now your stomach. You need to look after yourself better.'

'Perhaps Spiro is right.' I said. 'It's time for me to settle down with Cousin Ariadne.'

Marco laughed. 'At least you haven't lost your sense of humour.' He watched while a young couple sauntered down a passageway towards the business-class bar. 'Listen, I am off to have a few quiet drinks. Why don't you get some rest, and I will check up on you later? It's a long journey to Samos—about fourteen hours—so we have plenty of time to talk during the night.'

'Okay, Marco.' I nodded wearily before he disappeared behind a glass partition. I felt like a prick for even thinking this, but a few hours away from Marco was not such a bad idea. He was terrific company, to be sure, but if the train ride from Athens to Piraeus that afternoon taught me one thing, it was that Marco's favourite topic of conversation was usually himself. If I'd had to hear one more lurid detail about his depraved night with the American girl, there was a real chance that I would have thrown him out the window into an oncoming train.

I picked up my Rommel biography from my carry bag and tried to make myself comfortable. *Maybe I was too harsh on Marco,* I reflected, just as the Germans started bombing the crap out of Tobruk. Okay, the previous night he introduced me to his slimy friend, used me as an excuse to meet some beautiful American woman, abandoned me at a party that I never wanted to attend in the first place, and then that morning, had made me pay for his rail ticket to Piraeus after he ran out of money.

But, to be fair—he was remarkably understanding when I threw up over his new alligator-leather shoes. Furthermore, he gained many brownie points by convincing me to purchase a business-class ticket for this trip. I mean, the canvas seats were so much cosier than the cracked plastic buckets found below in economy class. When you saw how tightly they were all crammed in together like deranged sardines, I reckoned the extra space my ticket provided was alone worth a train fare to Piraeus.

I struggled with a few more pages of my book before I closed my eyes and descended into an arcane world that was silent and peaceful: where stomach cramps and diarrhoea didn't exist and where Selene was forbidden to boil water.

The sound of the ocean smashing into the side of the ferry woke me up several hours later. It was pitch black outside, and everything was eerily quiet. Even the seagulls had seemingly gone to bed. I checked to see whether my stomach was still firmly attached to the rest of my body and decided that I felt so much better for my nap. So I tucked my travel bag underneath my seat, made sure that I didn't tread on any sleeping Australians, and shuffled off to find Marco.

The unmistakable sound of his bawdy laughter led me straight into a smoke-filled cabin. There he was, holding court in the centre of the room, happily surrounded by fifty-seven different women. When he noticed me from afar, he released a drunken howl, which caused his new companions to stare in my direction as if I was a circus freak.

'Alex, buy yourself a drink and get your skinny butt over here.'

Rarely in my life had I received such a heartfelt yet worrying invitation. Alcohol was off the agenda, of course, so I ordered a lemon squash instead and forced my way back through the crowd until I reached Marco's chair. He immediately pulled me into his side, shook me around a few times until my head started to spin, and then pretended to kiss me.

'Listen, everyone! Who do you think my friend looks like?'

'No, Marco, please,' I begged him. I could already feel the blood rush through my hollow cheeks while the entire room carefully considered his question.

'Can we just get on with it?' some haughty little French princess demanded through five layers of mascara.

'I give up,' her equally indignant friend yelled out. 'What about the Grim Reaper?'

'Richard Hunte,' a voice cried out from the back of the room. We all turned to face an attractive woman in her mid-twenties with long, silky blonde hair, sitting at a table with two older people, presumably her parents. I had experienced enough European accents by that stage to work out that she was Dutch. Emboldened by the fact that she was the centre of attention, the woman casually lifted her glass of wine to acknowledge everyone and then cleared her throat.

'Isn't it obvious?'

'No bloody way,' derided the French woman. A look of utter disdain was stamped onto her polyester face. 'You are seriously on drugs, lady.'

Marco decided it was time to play peacemaker. After all, everything up to that point was squarely his fault, so it was only fair that he had to mediate rising tensions between France and the Netherlands.

'Yes, Richard Hunte! Exactly! Well done!' He laughed at the Dutch girl. 'You are the winner!'

The mood in the bar nosedived into an ear-splitting competition between those who agreed with Marco and those who didn't. I really couldn't make out which side prosecuted their case the loudest, but I consoled myself with the thought that at least half of the people there didn't think I was a total loser.

With Marco's ill-conceived scheme to raise my onboard profile officially deemed an abysmal failure, I decided to check out the Dutch girl, ahem, just to make sure that she was okay. After all, it had been an incredibly stressful ten seconds for her. As I confidently strode towards her table, her beaming, fluorescent smile immediately confirmed that I had made the right decision.

As I'd suspected, what we had here was a mother, father, and daughter from Amsterdam. The girl's name was Lottie, and she worked as an accountant for a cruise line company in Athens. Her mum, Nina, and her dad, Frankie, had come to Greece to visit Lottie, they told me, because they missed their precious youngest daughter terribly.

After being exposed to Marco's immoral decadence for much of the day, that was a refreshingly innocent comment to make, and I instantly warmed to the entire family. They all seemed like intelligent, humble people who deeply cared for each other.

Lottie and her parents were on their way to visit Ephesus, which had been on the family's bucket list for years. It didn't take long to work out that we would all be on the same bus tour together come Tuesday morning.

I wasn't sure how it happened, but Lottie and I soon became separated from the rest of the crowd, and we found ourselves deeply immersed in some pithy conversation about Paris. To be honest, I was far more fascinated with Lottie's dreamy blue eyes than anything to do with the Eiffel Tower but, sometimes in life, you are called upon to take one for the team.

As luck would have it, she was definitely my type as well: attractive, sexy, intelligent, funny, and any other cliche one might wish to add at this point. I was rather clueless when it came to the whole 'does she like me' bit—you see, I never really progressed past Grade 3—but even I could work out from the delicate flicking of her hair that maybe, just maybe, Lottie wished that her parents would rock off to sleep.

By the time I decided to risk a glass of wine, and then another, and then another, and maybe then another, any pretence to what was happening quickly dissipated. Given that our knees were locked permanently together, there was little doubt that our pheromones had escaped and were jumping wildly out of control. Once they met in no-man's-land, bingo—we would have a real-life situation, folks!

Needless to say, the more we exchanged dreamy smiles and dirty thoughts, the more I considered my feelings for Rachel. I realised that I needed to remove myself from the shooting gallery before I did something stupid. But I was confronted with a problem that most young men were never trained to deal with: how to distract the attention of a beautiful woman away from you? Luckily, I was aware of a ready-made solution: you found the most attractive man in the room and then begged for his help.

Of course, Marco didn't need much convincing. As soon as the word 'blonde' escaped my shameful lips, he picked up my distress signal and groggily weaved his way towards us, knocking over a chair or three in the process. He arrogantly brushed me aside, somehow managed to introduce himself to Lottie without falling over, and then effortlessly pinned her up against the wall. In the meantime, I quietly slumped next to Frankie, who was bemoaning the current state of the Dutch national football team to a couple of uninterested Germans.

Several minutes later, I finally found the courage to drift an eye in Lottie's direction. There she was, waiting for me with a very precise 'Why the hell did you do that?' stare. I innocently shrugged my shoulders at her before resuming my animated conversation with Frankie.

The night bumbled along aimlessly until Lottie finally extricated herself from Marco's slimy clutches and sidled off to bed. Nina soon followed her daughter, while Frankie bought Marco and me another drink for the road. When Frankie joined his family soon afterwards, Marco grabbed me by the arm and reliably informed me that he was 'in' with Lottie.

I couldn't really see that happening, but I indulged his fantasies, nevertheless. After all, he had come to my aid at the time of my greatest peril. With Lottie safely out of the way, I spent the next few hours flittering in and out of several pointless conversations with several pointless people while watching Marco slowly drink himself into a benign stupor.

When the barman finally threw me an enraged grunt, suggesting that Marco was on his last warning, I caught his elbow and quietly guided him back to the business-class deck. Once tucked safely in his seat, I placed a pillow under his head and blew him a kiss goodnight. He muttered something rude in Italian, but before I could say 'Rip Van Marco', he turned into Rip Van Winkle. Satisfied that I had done my good deed for the day, I flopped myself back into my seat, decided that no, it was not a good idea to wake up Lottie, and then gratefully joined Marco in the world of dreams.

The bellowing sound of a foghorn made me jump, and I was welcomed to a new day by a grinning Marco standing over me.

'Time to wake up, handsome,' he demanded. 'Your beauty sleep is officially over, and we are about to arrive in Samos.'

I stared at him with utter contempt. 'Aren't you just a little bit hungover?' I asked tersely as I wiped the gunk away from my eyes. 'I had to practically carry you to bed, you were that drunk.'

'You did such a good job of it too,' he said, smiling at my naïvety. 'I feel like a thousand lira this morning.'

'A thousand lira? That's actually not a lot of money.'

'True, but us photographers like to do things on the cheap.'

'I will remember that next time,' I replied facetiously. It was obvious that I had been thoroughly had, but I wasn't sure how.

We were greeted at the port of Vathy by a hot, cloudless day. I ripped off my jumper and felt the sun's burning rays pinch at the back of my T-shirt. Marco escorted me down the gangway towards a group of waiting onlookers.

'Those people over there are all here to sell you a room. Don't accept anything for more than fifty American dollars a night. And make sure they offer you breakfast.'

'Sure thing.'

Marco made me turn towards the street that ran parallel to the ferry terminal.

'You see that big white building to my left with the two travel agencies? Directly opposite, there is a little side street where you will find an outdoor café. My friends and I usually meet there just before lunch. Get yourself a room, have a shower, and join us when you are ready.'

We exchanged some more tedious high fives before I was set upon by a gaggle of rabid hawkers. Amid this confusion, I looked across to my left and saw Lottie cajoling her parents, together with their luggage, down the gangway. I wondered for a fleeting moment if they would consider allowing me to stay with them just for a night.

'Mister, mister,' a young teenage boy screamed out at me. 'You want room? You want room?'

I inspected his slender frame and puppy dog eyes and decided that he looked honest enough.

'How far away?' I asked him, gesturing to the street in front of us.

'Just down the road, just down the road,' he promised.

'How much?'

'Forty American dollars a night or equivalent in drachma. We take cash or credit card. And we have the best breakfast on all of Samos. The best!'

The best? That's a rather big claim. But as someone who loved his breakfast, how could I say no?

'Alright, kid, you have a deal. Two nights, okay? Lead on.'

When he heard my offer, he danced in front of me with unbridled joy.

'Good choice, mister. Good choice. If you need anything, just ask. I can wash your socks, shine your shoes, cut your hair.'

Somehow, I couldn't see myself allowing this kid to do any of those things, but I smiled nevertheless and followed him idly down the road. Minutes later, we arrived at a freshly painted detached house, guarded on either side by a pair of handsome-looking citrus trees. A skinny black cat slept peacefully on the verandah, and a plastic chime swayed gently above the entrance door.

'Please come inside,' the boy said. We walked into something resembling a reception area where we were joined by his mother—Samos' intricate replica of Selene.

When this enormous woman shook my hand to welcome me, she nearly yanked my shoulder straight out of its socket. I quickly paid her two nights' accommodation in advance and waited for her son to escort me to my room to avoid further physical damage.

Once I was safely inside, I sneaked in a well-earned shower and then somehow managed to cut a jagged line through my chin while shaving. It took thirty minutes of shrieking and cursing before I triumphantly found a way to stem the bleeding. Not to be deterred, I threw on a clean T-shirt, blow-dried my hair, and wandered off to meet Marco. I eventually found him relaxing outside in the sunshine with several other young people, sipping on a coffee. Once he recognised me through his purple sunnies, he immediately demanded that I join their table before machine-gunning out the names of his friends:

'This is Karl from Vienna.

'This is Julia from Berne.

'This is Tom from Tunbridge Wells.

'This is Kitty from Portsmouth.

'This is Franco from Milan.

'This is Marlena from Bari.'

I greeted them all with my customary fake enthusiasm while they each contrived to welcome me in their own perfunctory way.

With formalities over, I looked across to the table next to us and noticed a young woman sitting by herself, deeply committed to an extra-thick novel. Her long tanned legs were stretched arrogantly across the chair in front of her. She must have felt the ferocity of my staring because she lifted her eyes to consider me, intentionally screwed up her face, and then dropped her head back into her book.

Some women exude a fierce sexual intensity that can destroy an entire room within seconds, and I could tell already that she was one of these accursed creatures. Her chocolate-brown hair was thick and lustrous and fell simply past her slim shoulders: a perfect match, you would think, for her dark olive skin, high Slavic cheekbones, and liquid black eyes.

Yet, there was an undefined quality that extended beyond her natural beauty—an aura, I guess, that encircled her like a halo you might see in a religious fresco. I could feel her life force cut a swathe right through me, and I prayed to God that this woman wasn't Martina, who Marco thought would be such a good match for me.

'And that lovely specimen over there, ignoring us as usual, is Martina from Sarajevo.'

Of course she is.

I turned to Marco for some brotherly intervention, but his only reaction was to laugh in my face. It was as if he always knew that meeting Martina would elicit such a pathetic response.

'Say hello to Alex, Martina,' he called to her, with a hint of expectation in his voice.

'Hello,' she replied coldly, without even bothering to lift her head.

'Martina has people issues,' Marco joked, while Karl and Tom laughed in unison.

'Leave her alone, Marco,' snarled Marlena. 'You are always picking on her.'

Marco rolled his eyes at being admonished before firing Marlena a conciliatory grin. After everyone was civil to each other again, I ordered myself a coffee and started to chat with Marco's friends while trying hard to avert my eyes from Martina's table.

Out of this motley crew, I decided that I liked Franco and Marlena the best. Karl and Julia seemed to be too obsessed with each other to allow anyone else into their world, especially a stranger like me. On the other hand, Tom and Kitty were the archetypal upper-class English couple struggling to cope with the silver spoons wedged up their entitled arses and their natural aversion to us crude, convict Australians.

They tried hard to engage with me at first, but we all decided very soon that we didn't have much in common. I graciously allowed them to get distracted by the share prices quoted in Tom's week-old copy of the *London Times* before turning my attention to the Italian couple.

Thankfully, they were happy-go-lucky people, comfortable with their own lives and their relationship. Franco was Marco's roommate at university and ran a small but profitable surveying business. On the other hand, Marlena confessed to being a loafer but loved dancing, drawing, and other arty-farty hobbies, while working three days a week as a legal secretary. We spent the time talking about Australia, Milan, the *Godfather* movies (Franco and I agreed that number two was the better film, but Marlena swore by the original), and the virtues of a Mediterranean climate.

Despite my initial reservations, I was actually enjoying myself. Franco and Marlena were great company. The early afternoon sun was pleasantly warm. The pizza I was devouring was mouth-tingling delicious. Reginald Crump was no doubt stalking some other fool in Athens. And Martina continued to ignore everyone around her, including me. What could possibly go wrong in this Aegean paradise?

'Martina,' Marco suddenly called out, 'why don't you take the jeep and drive Alex down to Pythagoreio so he can have a look around?'

'Argh!' A piece of salami suddenly became wedged in my throat, and Franco quickly thumped me on the back several times to prevent me from choking. Meanwhile, Martina muttered something to herself in Serbian, slammed her book down on the table, and whacked Marco with a salacious frown.

'If I must.'

She pulled out a set of keys from her back pocket, jingled them in front of everyone for dramatic effect, and then stared down at me with those 'don't fuck with me' eyes.

'Are you coming?' she asked loudly so that the whole world could appreciate her displeasure.

I considered this brazenly seductive woman with those incredibly short cut-off jeans and her very tight low-cut blouse and decided that I didn't want to go anywhere near her by myself.

'I am sure Martina has better things to do today other than being my tour guide,' I offered to no-one in particular.

'Nonsense,' said Marco. He offered me a crude wink. 'Once she gets over her usual hissy fit, I'm confident that you will find her very compliant.'

Karl and Tom smirked into their coffees while Marlena warned Franco not to join them by pre-emptively smacking him on the arm.

Martina ignored everyone and pointed to a small roofless jeep parked in front of the café.

'That's our dune buggy over there,' she explained to me coldly. 'Now get in!'

There was clearly no way out for me. My only option was to see this through to the end, pretend to have a good time, and then kneecap Marco once we returned to Vathy. Five minutes later, I found myself alone with Martina in a dilapidated old jeep that could barely reach thirty miles an hour.

Apart from a constant stream of swear words, which I presumed were solely for my benefit, Martina said extraordinarily little at first. In any case, I was more preoccupied with how my six-foot-four-inch frame was going to fit into a very tight front passenger seat. My knees were bunched up so close to my face that I could practically swallow them.

Pretty soon, I started to contort myself into a zillion different positions in a feeble attempt to get more comfortable. Martina finally noticed my distress and produced the closest thing to a smile I had seen from her that day without it actually being one.

'There is a small lever under the seat,' she explained. 'Pull it up a notch and then lean back hard.'

I followed her instructions, and, to my relief, I felt the seat tumble backwards by a few inches. It was not a perfect solution by any means, but at least it allowed me to stretch my legs out just a little more.

'Thank you,' I replied timidly. 'I'm afraid that cars like this were not built with tall people in mind.'

'Well, I am five foot ten, and I don't have any problems.'

Not exactly the friendliest of responses, but at least she was talking to me. I decided to push my luck a little further, given that we were manacled together for the rest of the afternoon.

'Thank you for showing me around. I really appreciate it. But I hope that I haven't spoiled your plans for the day.'

Martina produced another one of her trademark grunts.

'Marco rang on Saturday to tell me that I was taking you for a drive this afternoon. So you see, I wasn't allowed to have any other plans.'

Bloody Marco. I should have figured that out during lunch: the back-handed sniggers, the hidden glances between him and his male friends. Talk about my naïvety.

'I wasn't aware that he called you on Saturday,' I replied truthfully. 'It's almost like he is deliberately setting me up.'

I paused for a moment as we drifted past an old woman pulling at a goat on the side of the road.

'Is he deliberately setting me up?' I finally asked her.

'Of course he is,' replied Martina. 'Are you that stupid?'

'Yes, I probably am.' I calmly faced her derision head-on. 'Look, none of this was my idea. I have come to Samos purely to see the sights, nothing more. I don't want you to feel uncomfortable around me just because of Marco's game-playing.'

'Don't worry, I won't. You seem harmless enough.'

Harmless!? What the hell did she mean by that?

My eyes diverted back to the winding road in front of me, and they just happened to gloss over Martina's bare legs in the process. I am talking about, like, two seconds. It wasn't even intentional; her legs were just, well, there. Where else was I supposed to look? But of course, Martina was extremely multi-skilled and was able to watch me like a hawk while driving simultaneously.

'If you want to admire my legs, you could at least do the decent thing and ask for my permission first. Like you should have done back at the café.'

I silently groaned. This girl was determined to turn my afternoon into some sort of Alfred Hitchcock psychodrama.

'I'm sorry. It wasn't intentional.'

'I don't mind you looking, but just be honest about it.'

She lifted up her right leg and plopped it down on top of the gear box compartment that separated our two bodies to make her point.

'There you go, have another look. They are nice, are they not?'

They were more than just nice; they were frigging amazing; in fact, she was frigging amazing. But of course, she knew that already and knew that I knew that too.

'Yes, they are,' I gulped. 'You are a beautiful woman, and if this were Australia, I probably would be horse-whipped alive just for saying that.'

'Lucky for you, then, this isn't Australia,' she said with a crude twist of her mouth. She returned her leg to its previous position and then allowed a minute or so of awkward silence to brood between us.

'Do you have a girl, Mister Australian Man?' she finally asked.

'My name is Alex, and yes, I do.' I explained to her about Rachel, her tour and how we had planned to meet again in London the following week.

'Sounds a bit odd to me,' reflected Martina, without taking her eyes off the road. 'If you really want to be with someone, I can't see the point of travelling separately. Maybe your relationship is not as strong as you think?'

'It's perfectly fine, thank you,' I replied through gritted teeth. I could tell Martina was playing with me, as a cat does with an injured mouse, flicking her paw out whenever she felt like it just to see how I might respond. I wondered how many other men in her life she had cruelly tortured like this.

'When did you first meet Marco?' I asked her, hoping to God that we could quickly change the topic.

She didn't respond at first, as if she needed to clarify the exact facts for herself.

'Last June in Santorini,' she finally revealed. 'We decided to hang around each other for the summer, and then I travelled with him to Austria for the ski season.'

'You're actually a couple, then?' I asked her quizzically, not really sure whether I would like the answer that she was about to give me.

Martina sensed the irritation in my voice but decided that this was not the time or place to eviscerate me. It was almost as if she believed that I deserved the courtesy of a proper explanation.

'Depends on who you ask, I guess. I like to refer to Marco as my fuck buddy; he likes to call me his girlfriend. But there are no emotional bonds between us, put it that way. We just like having sex with each other when we feel the need.'

I was sure that she wanted me to react somehow, but I wouldn't give her the satisfaction. Unfortunately, that only encouraged her to probe my feelings further. 'You don't approve the nature of our relationship?'

I began to laugh. 'I didn't even know that you had a relationship until three seconds ago.'

'Well, now you know.'

Yes, now I know, but it still doesn't make any sense.

'Look, Martina, I follow one basic rule. I never judge someone's private life, so what you do is your business.'

'That is a good rule to have,' Martina wryly observed. 'But if that is the case, why are you acting like a jealous schoolboy?'

Man, this one really is a prize, gold standard piece of work.

'I am not jealous. I just don't understand, given the nature of your, um, friendship, why Marco has spent the last three days trying to set me up with you.'

We had reached the outskirts of Pythagoreio and Martina began to pound her horn at a slow-moving car in front of us.

'Fucking tourists!' she screamed out to the entire island, forgetting that she was one herself. Once she released every ounce of her rage at the world, she tilted her head back towards me.

'It's all to do with his ego. Marco loves the thought of passing me onto his friends to tell him afterwards how superior he is to them in bed. The man is a complete narcissist.'

I was, at first, too revolted by what she had just said to respond in any meaningful way. Look, I was no angel: Jesus, I had done some thoroughly rotten things in the pursuit of uncomplicated sex. But I would never have dreamt of using a woman in that way. Never.

'When you say he shares you with his friends, do you also mean the other men back at the café?' It was none of my business, but I desperately needed to understand Marco's motivation for bringing me to Samos.

Martina seemed happy enough to reply.

'Yes, I had sex with both Karl and Tom back in Austria,' she admitted, almost too casually. 'Marco was very insistent that this should happen before we came to Samos. He wanted to make some point—I am not sure exactly what. It's all about who has the power in that group, and Marco is desperate to have it.'

'And Franco?' I pressed further, pushing my luck.

'No. I have too much respect for Marlena to ever go behind her back. We are not friends, you see, but she is always nice to me. Unlike those other two cows, especially that toffee-nosed little bitch, Kitty.'

'What does all this have to do with me?' I persisted, not interested in what she thought about the other girls. 'I did nothing more than have a few drinks with the guy at our hotel in Athens before he invited me to Samos, and I am no threat to him or his friends.'

'I have no idea, and I don't want to know either. Maybe because you are Australian? Who knows with Marco? My point is: don't pester me with your problems. Take it up with him yourself.'

I suddenly felt clouds of anger rise from the soles of my feet. What sort of man would encourage a woman to sleep with his friends so that he could exert his authority over them? And why would an intelligent, beautiful woman like Martina allow Marco to manipulate her in that way?

Martina somehow did an excellent job of reading my mind. 'I thought you said you didn't judge people, Mister Australian Man?'

Before I had a chance to respond, she spotted the entrance to a tourist lookout and manoeuvred the car into the side of the road. She turned off the engine and stretched herself across the steering wheel so that she could look me straight in the eye.

'You might ask yourself why I choose to hang around such a self-serving bastard like Marco? Well, first of all, you have to give it to him. He is a great fuck. The best I have ever had. What girl would want to give that up so easily, hey?'

'As I said before, it's none of my business.'

'You protest way too much,' she snarled back at me. 'So you are now going to shut up while I tell you everything. To put it bluntly, I have nowhere else to go. My house in Sarajevo is nothing but rubble, and my parents are refugees living in some shithole camp in Germany. Furthermore, my brother managed to get himself killed fighting for a cause that never accepted him. Until my next job starts in Chios this weekend, Marco and his stupid friends are all I have. Does that explain the situation for you, Mister Australian Man?'

'Call me Alex,' I repeated for her benefit. Given the circumstances, this might have seemed a peculiar thing to say, but when someone was lopping off your head, it always paid to keep your words to a bare minimum.

'No, I won't call you that at all. You will be nothing to me other than Mister Australian Man. I don't want to know your name. In fact, I don't want to know anything about you. That would suggest a form of intimacy when none exists whatsoever. I will never see you again after Wednesday, and that suits me fine. Am I making myself clear?'

'Perfectly,' I swallowed.

One might predict that after such an unpleasant exchange and my discovery of Marco's clumsy attempt at a prostitution racket, the rest of my afternoon in Pythagoreio would have been a catastrophic disaster. But I ended up having a fantastic time. To her credit, as soon as we entered this beautiful ancient seaport, Martina's entire demeanour changed, and she miraculously evolved into the most incredible tour guide the world had ever seen.

While I tried to figure out which of her ten personalities was driving the car at any one time, Martina created for me, over the next three hours, a mesmerising journey through the island's imposing history. With her foot permanently glued to the accelerator, she raced through a slew of cluttered alleyways, simultaneously introducing me to the deeds of Pythagoras and the equally famous resident of Samos, the philosopher Epicurus.

After she answered every one of my needless questions, we explored the Eupalinian aqueduct, one of the great engineering feats of the ancient world. We then marvelled at the astonishing Temple of Hera. Everything was undertaken at the speed of sound as if we were involved in some interstellar race against time itself. When we arrived at

Pythagoreio Harbour just after four-thirty to enjoy a coffee and some baklava, both of us were thoroughly exhausted.

As she silently munched on her dessert, Martina became obsessed with a luxury yacht moored in the harbour, and I used this time to admire her exquisite beauty. A few hours earlier, I wanted nothing more to do with this woman. She was an evil, mythical siren from Homer's *Odyssey,* who thought it perfectly fine to tear out a man's heart, trample all over it with both feet and then turn it into stone just for good measure.

But somewhere between the Temple of Hera and this little café by the sea, I came to a realisation that I thought would have been impossible several hours earlier: I bloody well liked her! Beneath that dark, crass exterior was an intelligent and charismatic young woman with a latent softness that could be strangely disarming.

'What the fuck are you looking at now, you filthy little pervert?' she barked at me.

'Nothing.' I apologised, admiring her latent softness once again.

I slapped at an irritating fly that had been doing laps around my head for the last five minutes, and in the process, accidentally ripped off the tiny scab on my chin. As a result of my clumsiness, tiny estuaries of blood began to flow down my neck and chest. *Man, I am so frigging hopeless.* I grabbed a napkin to compress my wound, but something came bounding out in front of me and snatched it out of my hand.

Martina dipped the napkin into her glass of water and then pushed it down firmly against my face.

'I can do that, thank you very much,' I sulked ungratefully.

'Oh, stop acting like a spoilt little child,' she growled.

'I can if I want to.'

'Is it because I just called you a filthy little pervert?'

'You're getting warm.'

When I stared at the bright red streaks dripping off her hands, she added: 'I am a nurse, so I think I can handle a tiny squirt of blood.'

Martina increased the pressure on my wound and then moved her head closer to mine. I was sure that she was about to kiss me, and I struggled with the whole concept of how I would respond if she did.

'You have beautiful brown eyes; has anyone ever told you that?'

'Not lately, no. Most new people I meet seem more preoccupied with my vast array of sexual deviancies.'

'They are quite remarkable. Some silly girl could easily get lost in them.'

'I will remember that next time you threaten to gouge them out.'

Okay, Martina didn't kiss me after all but instead produced the widest smile I had seen for years, which I guessed was the next best thing. It completely changed the structure of her face, and for a moment, I was staring at a completely different woman.

'What are your plans for tomorrow?' she finally asked once the bleeding on my chin stopped.

'Well, if I survive your attempts to shoot me at dawn, I have booked a tour to Ephesus. I was going to ask Marco to come with me, but I'm not so sure that I would appreciate his company right now.'

I'm dropping a big hint here, Martina. Why don't you come with me instead?

'Well, screw him then,' she growled. 'Why don't I come with you instead?'

Bingo! Alex, you absolute legend!

'Jeez—I don't know whether that would work,' I teased her. 'I mean, I wouldn't want you to think that there is any form of intimacy between us now, would I?'

She laughed and called me a cheeky bastard but somehow stopped short from smashing me over the head with an empty chair.

'I am not sure why, but I like you, Alex. Very much. Perhaps it's because you remind me of a labrador puppy I had when I was a little girl. Big brown eyes and totally clueless, but kinda cute in a clumsy, dim-witted sort of way.'

'Shucks. That's one of the nicest things anyone has ever said to me.'

We paid our bill and walked back to the jeep in silence. Martina was just about to start the engine when she pushed her hands away from the steering wheel and considered me with a raised eyebrow.

'Did you notice that I called you Alex just before at the café?'

'Well, now that you mention it, yes, I did. It was a rather pleasant change from some of the other names you have been calling me this afternoon.'

'You mean, Mister Australian Man?'

'No, I mean "filthy little pervert".'

She pretended to check that her foot was still firmly on the clutch before deciding that the best way to seal my forgiveness was through a wet kiss on the cheek.

'There, happy now?' she asked.

'I will have to think about it some more, of course, but it's definitely a step in the right direction.'

That made her laugh, and I felt good about that.

'You know what, Alex? I think our short time together will be quite interesting.'

Just as she finished her sentence, a lonely white dove flew innocently above our heads—a sign perhaps, that at last, Martina and I had found a commonality between us.

Ephesus

Samos Island and Ephesus
May 1995

When we returned to Vathy, Martina begged me to join her for a walk along her favourite beach so that we could watch my first sunset in Samos together. 'It's the most incredible thing you will ever see,' she promised me.

A wise man once told me that walking next to a beautiful woman on a secluded beach at sunset can often lead to all manner of strife for the unsuspecting male. But I was confident that what had developed between us that afternoon was nothing more than a curious friendship that was doomed to expire within forty-eight hours. So, rather than contemplating a roll in the hay, I found myself barefoot, with my jeans rolled up above my ankles, enjoying the feeling of sand between my toes.

Our initial conversation during the walk involved fishing or, more precisely, the tastiest fish in the world to eat. I reckoned it had to be barbecued barramundi, a native Australian fish whose name completely perplexed Martina. She, on the other hand, swore by an oven-grilled sole with a twist of lemon. Once I allowed her to win on that one, she began to tease me that while she could speak perfect English, I was unable to string three coherent words of Serbo-Croatian together.

Although I laughed at her clever jibes, my immediate fear was that this would inevitably lead to a discussion about the current war in the former Yugoslavia: a topic I desperately wanted to avoid with her. Here I was, an Australian of Croatian lineage, strongly opposed to Serbian nationalism from the peaceful luxury of my Canberra lounge room, standing next to a Bosnian Serb who had experienced firsthand the horrors of that awful conflict.

I didn't want to assume some ill-conceived moral authority on the issue, given my firm views. After all, I had enough arguments about the war with several Serbian friends in Canberra to last me a lifetime. Nevertheless, I wanted to avoid offending the delicate balance that existed between us if Martina indeed proved to be an ultra–Serbian nationalist. You see, I was simply incapable of keeping my mouth shut.

Sure enough, Martina soon made an offhand comment about how the new state of Croatia was deliberately changing the pronunciation of some words to make them sound less Serbian. Before I could offer an opinion, she pressed me for my views about the war. I tried to be diplomatic at first and talked about being isolated from world events in Australia, but she saw right through me and ordered me to drop the bullshit.

So I told her the truth: that I supported an independent Croatia, that I believed the Serbian president, Slobodan Milosevic, should be charged with war crimes, and that the United Nations had become an utter joke. There! When I finished spluttering out these disjointed thoughts, Martina grovelled towards me and, surprisingly, gave me another kiss on the cheek.

'Thank you for being so honest with me,' she said. 'I disagree with you about Croatia, but independence is a reality now, and so there is no point opposing it anymore. But you are right about Milosevic and those useless bastards from the UN.'

We arrived at a tiny cove near the bottom of a rocky headland. Every morning for the last fortnight, Martina had come here to pray and feed the hungry seagulls with her daily gift of bread. After we waded through a series of rock pools, Martina pointed to a dry escarpment that she promised would protect us from the rising tide. When we reached the summit, she invited me to sit down next to her; our outstretched legs dangled precariously towards a red-tinted horizon. This was the perfect place to hear a confession, so I wasn't surprised at all when Martina suddenly decided to reveal her life story to me.

Despite the savagery of the war, Martina was an immensely proud Serbian, although she suspected that there was a sliver of Hungarian in her background as well. She was born into a medical family twenty-six years ago: her father was a prominent surgeon, and her mother, a much-loved local midwife. Her older brother, Draga, was completing his last year of medicine before he quit his studies to join the Serbian Army.

Her parents retired in 1990 and moved to the Dalmatian coast, leaving Draga and Martina to manage the family home in Sarajevo. Theirs was a typical sibling relationship: sometimes they fought like cats and dogs; more often than not, they laughed at each other's eccentricities and always offered a shoulder to cry on whenever one of them had a shitty day. They worked hard, saved what money they could, and made plans to visit their beloved parents later in the year. But little did Martina realise during those initial hot, sultry weeks of June 1991 that an oncoming apocalypse was about to engulf her and her entire family.

The fall of European communism, which began in 1989 upon the tearing down of the Berlin wall, precipitated a torturous unravelling of the Yugoslavian state. As the 'winds of change' emboldened a new generation of political activism, it also encouraged an outpouring of nationalistic fervour that Europe had not witnessed since World War II. While Slobodan Milosevic agitated for greater Serbian hegemony in the region, some of Yugoslavia's key states and principalities openly prepared to leave the federation.

Both Slovenia and Croatia formally declared their independence on 25 June 1991. Although the Serbian-led Yugoslavian army briefly invaded Slovenia, an agreement for the country's autonomy was soon reached. But Belgrade never intended to afford Croatia the same luxury. After all, the Serbian minority living in Croatia had rights, too, and they needed to be protected at all costs. Sadly, the internecine rivalries and religious bitterness that had guided the destiny of both races for centuries had been unleashed, and vicious fighting broke out across the country.

Martina's parents were suddenly trapped inside the Serbian enclave in Zadar, with no immediate prospect of returning to Sarajevo. Although Draga despised Milosevic, his close friends convinced him that all Serbians living in Croatia and Bosnia faced the genuine possibility of genocide just like in World War II. The only solution was to join the army and fight!

Martina desperately pleaded with Draga to reconsider his decision. After the siblings had a terrible fight one fateful morning in July 1991, Draga left university that same day, and Martina never saw him again. A year later, she received the news from a mutual friend that her brother was killed by Croatian militia during the savage fighting around Vukovar.

By late 1991, Martina's parents were at breaking point. Conditions in Zadar were deteriorating rapidly as the Croatian Army tightened its grip around the enclave. As former medical practitioners, they did what they could to help the sick and vulnerable. When their local hospital ran out of antibiotics, her parents made the courageous decision to purchase more supplies in Šibenik, an hour's drive to the south. But, minutes after leaving their sanctuary, they were apprehended by Croatian police, beaten, tortured, and then detained at Split's infamous Lora prison camp.

Following a negotiated ceasefire in early 1992, Martina's parents were finally released and driven back to Zadar. During that journey, they were warned by a gruesome Croatian policeman that if he ever saw them again, they would be shot as spies. For the next few months, her mum and dad desperately tried to return to Sarajevo, but every attempt frustratingly ended in failure. When Bosnia received international recognition of its own independence in April 1992, a brutal siege of the city commenced, closing the door to any reunion between parents and daughter.

A year later, the Croatian Army decided to renew its operations in the Zadar area. Martina's parents were once again caught in the crossfire. One evening, under cover of darkness and with mortars exploding all around them, they jumped into an old army lorry and somehow escaped to the Serbian stronghold of Knin. With the help of the Red Cross and some influential friends in the medical community, they were eventually granted temporary asylum in Germany, where they remained in detention until a final decision was made on their future. Although she could write to them, Martina hadn't seen her parents for over four years.

I wasn't sure why, but Martina was less forthright about her own experiences in Sarajevo. What I could piece together was that she worked as a nurse in a hospital during the worst days of the siege and witnessed far too many people die on the operating table. The family house was destroyed during a relentless artillery attack in May 1993, and Martina eventually escaped to Vienna several months later, taking with her only a passport, her nursing qualifications, and a change of clothes. Since then, she had alternated between Austria and Greece, picking up nursing work wherever she could. She hoped to save enough money to help her parents re-establish their lives once their status in Germany was determined.

'I don't know what to say,' I finally said. 'That is such a sad story. Personally, I think you must be the bravest girl I have ever met.'

Such a hackneyed remark was worth at least one cuddle, and predictably, Martina and I were soon embracing. When we finally managed to disconnect ourselves, she wiped her salty eyes with a tissue.

'There are thousands of Serbian families who have suffered terrible injustices in this war,' she said sadly. 'Maybe when you get back to Australia, you might encourage people to see all sides of this story, not just the one spun by the international media.'

'Of course; I will,' I promised her. Her incredible story had indeed changed my previously one-sided perspective on the conflict.

However, the whole exchange had a major 'spoil the rest of the evening' feel to it. For a selfish prick like me, this had to be avoided with extreme prejudice. So it was time to lighten up the mood between us just a notch.

'But there is one small problem with your request. I am not sure whether anyone back in Australia would listen to a filthy little pervert like me.'

Luckily, Martina responded with a beautifully crafted smile.

'That will be a major problem for you, I agree.' She laughed. 'Perhaps we should spend tomorrow fixing the many flaws in your personality rather than going to Ephesus?'

Touché!

We arrived at the café just before eight-thirty, and by then, our stomachs were rumbling loudly into the night. All the gang were back as well—or did they ever leave?—and their jaws collectively dropped in amazement as they watched us waltz down the pavement arm in arm.

'Excuse me,' interrupted Franco. 'Are you the same two people who left this place together earlier today? If not, where are they now, and what have you done with them?'

Martina politely told Franco to bugger off while Marlena and I laughed in sympathy.

'Well, well,' sniggered Marco as he suddenly appeared from behind a stack of chairs. 'You never cease to amaze me, do you?'

I wasn't sure whether Marco's question was directed at me, Martina, or both of us, but as soon as I saw him, my hackles began to rise. After listening to Martina's life story on the beach, my growing disregard for Marco had only intensified. *How dare this worthless piece of crap exploit Martina's tragic vulnerability in the way that he does?*

Martina picked up on my 'I'm not pleased to see you' vibe and dug her thumb into the middle of my back. It was her way of warning me to shut up.

'Whenever I do try to surprise you, Marco,' she retorted, 'you are usually too busy looking at yourself in the mirror to take any notice.'

Marco's eyes betrayed an unspoken fury that I had not seen from him before. For a moment, I was genuinely concerned that things might get out of hand. But to my relief, he finally released one of his deep, guttural laughs and then joined Tom and Kitty at their table without saying another word.

Martina and I ordered some dinner and the night slowly moved forward without further incident. While I was attacking a lobster, Marco insisted that I join him later at a party, but I politely declined, citing tiredness and my early morning start. He was disappointed with me at first but then appeared genuine when he wished us well for our trip to Ephesus. Despite his newfound sincerity, Martina and I were hugely relieved when he left the café several minutes later, with Tom, Karl, and their girlfriends loyally in tow.

After the obligatory coffees, Franco and Marlena invited us back to their unit to play Monopoly and drink more wine. Before I knew it, I was half-drunk and wrestling with Martina on a patch of prickly carpet when, for the second time that night, she landed on the three hotels I had built on Mayfair. We were laughing so much that Marlena, at one point, threatened to pour cold water over us if we didn't stop.

Just after midnight, I dashed to the bathroom, only to find Martina fast asleep on the sofa when I returned. I tiptoed across the creaking floor, collected a loose woollen blanket lying on top of the kitchen table, and gently placed it over her naked legs. I took a step backwards and pondered her smouldering beauty, wishing that I could somehow permanently replicate this image inside my head.

'She often passes out like this without warning,' whispered Marlena, who suddenly appeared beside me.

She gave my shoulder a reassuring rub. 'I will take care of her from here.'

'Thank you for being so kind to her,' I whispered back.

Marlena sadly shook her head at me, the mournful expression of an older sister who was about to give her younger brother some crucial bit of life advice.

'Franco and I have never seen Martina as happy as she was tonight. It was amazing—like she was a different person. So, well done, you.'

'All I did was treat her like a real person and not as a sex object,' the alcohol inside of me replied. 'Some other people might consider doing the same.'

Yes, I was having a dig at her boyfriend's best friend, but I suspected that Marlena was far too clever to take the bait.

'Just be careful, Alex,' she warned. 'Martina is a woman who lives in a very lonely place at the end of the rainbow. I doubt that anyone will be able to catch her when she eventually falls, not even someone as caring as you.'

'Sure thing,' I replied guardedly before we slipped into another goodnight hug.

I woke up at the bottom of my hotel bed six hours later with one of those thumping, alcohol-induced headaches I always hated. After swallowing some painkillers, I suddenly remembered that the best breakfast in Samos was waiting for me. Not wishing to miss out on that mouth-watering feast, I jumped into some clothes and danced excitedly towards the dining room.

But when I stumbled through the front entrance, I found the room empty: not a single living soul anywhere to be seen. Undeterred, I walked up and down the polished floor several times to make sure that I hadn't imagined things. I quickly concluded that no-one had eaten there in days, for everything around me was picture-perfect pristine. Not a tablecloth had been removed, not a chair had been drawn, not a window had been opened. This sucked big-time, but I wasn't going to give up on the best breakfast in Samos without a fight. I began to call out in my most depraved voice to see whether anyone else in the hotel was awake. But the only response I received was from a half-mangled cuckoo clock, ticking idly away in the corner of the room.

That confirmed it; there was no-one else there but me: no guests, no waiters, no skinny kids, no cooks, no super-fat Selene replicas. No-one. Even the frigging cat had disappeared. What conclusion could I reach other than I had been totally duped? Begrudgingly, I tramped back to my room, vowing to wring that little kid's scrawny neck whenever I saw him next.

I collected my camera, sunglasses, and passport just before eight o'clock and jumped outside to meet Martina. There she was, waiting for me, casually leaning against a citrus tree.

She was dressed in a tight-fitting, light-blue pair of jeans and a pink T-shirt, while her hair was scrunched up into a bun.

'Well, if it isn't Sleeping Beauty,' I teased before kissing her on the cheek. 'I trust you aren't going to pike out on me like you did last night?'

'Depends how bored I get with you.' She grinned. Now that the inevitable repartee had commenced, we wandered down to the ferry terminal, where we would first catch a bus to Pythagoreio and then a ferry to Kuşadası. It was a great day for a morning, and a scent of intrigue filled the air. If I was brutally honest, there was no other place in the world I wanted to be at that moment than in Samos, with this beguiling Bosnian woman beside me. *I'm so sorry, Rachel.*

As we waited to board the bus, I noticed that Lottie and her parents were talking to the driver, and I wondered whether we should say hello to them. I still felt terrible about the other night on the ferry, and I wanted to make it up to Lottie somehow. But when I went searching for Martina, I found her standing next to a nearby vending machine, threatening a young family of four with the blunt end of her daypack.

'What was that about?' I asked when she returned grim-faced, carrying two bottles of mineral water.

'Those arseholes back there couldn't decide what they wanted,' she fumed. 'So I gave them a piece of my mind.'

I tried to reason with her. 'They are just a harmless young family, Martina.'

'So? What do I fucking care?'

I briefly gazed back at Lottie before watching Martina offer her latest antagonists a series of middle fingers. Okay, a change of plan was required. Maybe introducing Martina to Lottie and her parents wasn't such a good idea after all. In fact, how about we just stayed the hell away from them for the rest of the day? That way, no-one would end up getting unnecessarily maimed.

We took our seats right on eight-thirty, and happily, the first part of our trip was largely forgettable. But somewhere on a barren stretch of road, just outside of Pythagoreio, I carelessly told Martina about my breakfast experience. For some reason, she found the whole notion of me being conned by some skinny Greek kid absolutely hysterical. Her wild laughter soon curled its way down the aisle at lightning speed before circulating ominously around a particular family from the Netherlands who just happened to be sitting right behind us.

Of course, to put the icing on the cake, when we boarded the ferry half an hour later, that very same family from the Netherlands decided to select a row of seats directly opposite from the ones that Martina and I had just chosen for ourselves. *So much for spending the day incognito.*

When we were well out to sea, Martina suddenly bumped my arm with her elbow and pointed discreetly at Nina.

'That woman over there is acting very strange,' she whispered. 'I swear that she wants to kill me.'

'I think you will find that she probably does,' I muttered. 'But don't worry; I'm way further up the queue than you are.'

'What do you mean by that?' asked Martina. I reluctantly explained to her how I flirted with Lottie on the ferry to Samos, my last-minute decision to withdraw from hostilities, and Marco's brave intervention.

Martina was, at first, incredibly understanding. 'She is pretty hot; I will give her that. Definitely Marco's type as well. Although, anything with two legs and a vagina usually is.'

'I will bear that in mind,' I noted unhappily.

'But let's talk about you for a moment, shall we?' Martina insisted through her thick red lips. *I'm not going to like this, am I?* 'For someone in a serious relationship, you sure do throw yourself about.'

'That's very unfair,' I said. 'Besides, you are not exactly helping the situation either, with all of your dirty talk and innuendo.'

'Well, maybe I should,' she replied with a smile that had been conjured up inside a charnel house.

Oh God, what is she going to do now?

It didn't take me long to find out. Before I could intervene, Martina jumped up from her seat, pinned both of my thighs together with her hands, and thumped herself down on top of my lap.

'What the hell are you doing, Martina?' I growled at her.

'Oh, Alex,' she moaned loudly. 'Last night was simply amazing. I orgasmed so many times, I had to crawl to the bathroom on my knees just to have a shower.'

Everyone on the ferry immediately stopped what they were doing and began to stare at my swollen head and the beautiful, crazy woman sitting on top of me.

'For God's sake, stop it,' I whispered into Martina's ear. 'You're embarrassing me.'

My eyes darted across the wooden deck just in time to see Nina's eyes combust out of her sockets. Lottie, meanwhile, was trying awfully hard not to laugh by swallowing down hard on her cheeks.

But Martina had only begun to humiliate me. Seeing that she had a captive audience, she gripped me tightly around the back of my neck and started panting into my ear.

'Can we have a threesome tonight, Alex?' she cried out. 'Please? You can choose a woman from this ferry if you like? Perhaps a blonde? Yes, a blonde, Dutch girl would be ideal!'

Lottie's brave fight ended abruptly. She initially tried to hide her stifled giggling by bending down to stare at her toes but then collapsed into raucous fits of laughter when she accidentally bumped her head on her knees.

Unfortunately, this drew an instant riposte from Nina. She glared at her daughter with a combination of anger and revulsion, while poor Frankie did his best to defuse the situation by putting a comforting arm around his wife.

But Nina was having none of it. Frazzled beyond repair, she pushed her husband away—almost knocking him overboard—and then belted out a long-winded diatribe at her red-faced daughter. In the space of three minutes, Martina had turned a happy family unit into a war zone.

After safely negotiating passport control at Kuşadası, I turned to Martina and poked her in the arm.

'Next time you pull a stunt on me like that, I will, I will—'

'You will what? Bend me over your knee and spank me?' she asked.

'If that's what it takes to teach you a lesson, yes.'

'Um, I think I could possibly enjoy that,' she replied.

'You're incorrigible.'

'And you wouldn't have it any other way.'

Our first stop on the road to Ephesus was some sleazy carpet emporium just outside of Kuşadası. None of us really understood the point of this diversion when we were herded off the bus, but it then became abundantly clear that being harangued by Turkish carpet sellers was all part of the tour.

However, the time spent in that awful place didn't completely go to waste: Martina soon rushed to the bathroom while I saw an opening to apologise to Lottie. She was standing wistfully by herself next to a rack of carpets while her parents were preoccupied with some swarthy Turkish salesperson.

'Hi there,' I grovelled with all the snake-oil charm I could muster.

'Hey,' Lottie snapped back at me.

'Look, what happened on the ferry before? The thing that you have to understand about my friend is that she is completely off her rocker.'

'If you must know,' Lottie replied, 'I was extremely impressed with her acting skills. Has she ever considered a career in the movies?'

'That wouldn't work, I'm afraid. All those people telling her what to do? She doesn't respond very well to authority, you see. Anyway, I hope we didn't get you into too much trouble with your parents.'

Lottie allowed herself a mild grin. 'Forget about it. Mum goes loopy when she thinks she has a reason to be offended, and I'm used to it by now, trust me. But I should add at this point that she thinks you are lower than a garden worm.'

I shrugged my shoulders. 'Aww—she is way too kind. But it would upset me very much if her daughter felt the same way.' I wasn't sure whether that was meant to be a question or a statement.

'No, you're pretty much harmless.'

'Of course I am.'

'Is there anything else?'

'I just want to explain about the other night.'

'You really don't have to, Alex.'

'No, I really do.'

'Fine. But make it quick before my mum comes back and hits you over the head with a roll of carpet.'

'I really enjoyed your company, Lottie. So much, in fact, that I momentarily forgot that I had a girlfriend. I then felt guilty that I was leading you on and betraying her trust, so I decided to walk away before I made a complete fool out of myself. My behaviour was appalling, especially how I pushed Marco onto you like that.'

'Yes, he was indeed an interesting person, just like your little friend, the porn queen over there. It's tough having a conversation with a man when his eyes are locked onto your breasts for the entire time.'

'I agree that Marco is a proper creep, and that's why I am now offering you an apology.'

Lottie gently touched my arm. 'Look, I am cool about it. So stop worrying, okay? But can I offer you a bit of friendly advice?'

'Sure.'

'Next time you decide to hit on a girl, you might wish to mention upfront that you are in a relationship. In my case, it would have prevented a lot of confusion afterwards.'

We talked some more, and I invited her to the café, where there would be a small party to celebrate Franco's birthday. She agreed to come if I promised to shield her from Marco. Nina then stomped around the corner towards us, so I reluctantly dropped to my knees and crawled away to safety.

When I reached Martina, she torpedoed Lottie with a wicked frown. 'What did Little Miss Muffet want?' she asked cattily.

'She wanted to know whether you ever considered an acting career.'

'Funny she should ask,' she replied. 'I thought long and hard about it during my last year of high school. I certainly have the stunning looks for it, of course.'

'Of course.'

'But having to deal with all those directors and screenwriters? I am not sure if you have noticed or not, but I don't respond all that well to authority.'

'No, I haven't noticed, Martina. But that's a damn shame. Because you know, you do have the looks for it.'

'Without question.'

We soon managed to escape the decrepit sweatshop without any casualties. Half an hour later, Martina and I found ourselves walking down a dusty marble street, deep within the ancient ruins of Ephesus. Despite our volatile Slavic temperaments and general pigheadedness, we somehow negotiated a six-point ceasefire agreement for how the two of us would explore this incredible ancient city in the limited time that we had. In quick succession, we visited the Temple of Artemis, the Celsus Library, St Luke's grave, and the Ephesus Museum of Archaeology. Both of us were having such a wonderful time, and I didn't want the day ever to end. Then I had to go and spoil it all by opening my big mouth at the Ephesus amphitheatre.

'Isn't this place amazing?' I reflected after guzzling down some water.

Martina considered the ancient steps of the theatre below us with a twist of her neck and then lost herself inside some mystic prism that only she could enter.

'It's awesome,' she replied after returning to planet Earth. 'I am so glad that you begged me to come with you.'

I nodded wearily but decided that I didn't have the energy or the inclination to bite back. Instead, I tried to impress Martina with my recently acquired knowledge of Ephesus.

'Just think. Alexander the Great, Julius Caesar, Mark Anthony, and Cleopatra all visited this place when it was a thriving city.'

'These ruins must hold many secrets,' Martina observed while unscrewing the top from her own bottle of water.

'No,' I replied firmly. 'Secrets belong to men and women, not places or objects. What you see is simply a consequence of history's failure to stop those secrets from ever being revealed.'

Mistake number one.

Martina swallowed some water and followed the early afternoon sun with her fierce black eyes. '"Secrets, silent, stony sit in the dark palaces of both our hearts: secrets weary of their tyranny: tyrants willing to be dethroned."'

'Ah, James Joyce—*Ulysses*,' I said, smiling.

'Very good, smart-arse.' Martina laughed. 'Okay then, let's see if you know this one: "Three may keep a secret, if two of them are dead".'

I scanned my brain for those tiny baubles of useless information that I usually kept hidden away for trivia nights, but nothing came readily to mind.

'No, you got me on this one.'

'Benjamin Franklin,' she said.

'Ah, the great man,' I replied.

'I always loved books that were shrouded in secrets.'

'What was your favourite?' I asked curiously.

Mistake number two.

Her answer was spontaneous. '*Strangers on a Train,* by Patricia Highsmith.'

'Didn't Alfred Hitchcock do a movie with the same name?'

'Yes, he did. The movie was based on the book.'

'I see.'

'The story always fascinated me, even as a little girl,' she continued. 'I love the whole idea of two complete strangers meeting by chance and then sharing their innermost thoughts with each other.'

I could see where Martina wanted to go with that, and if I had my time all over again, I would have changed the subject right about then. But no, all I did was indulge her fantasies even further.

'We are also two strangers who have met purely by chance. Strangers on a ferry, you might say.'

Mistake number three.

'Yes, we are,' replied Martina. '*Strangers on a Ferry.* How cool!' She reached across to caress my knee, and millions of electrons whizzed through my body.

'You are leaving tomorrow, and we will never see each other again. But before we say our goodbyes, I want to take something from you as a memento of our short time together.'

'What did you have in mind?'

Mistake number four.

'You tell me your biggest secret, and I will tell you mine. This way, we will own a piece of each other's heart forever.'

'Wouldn't it be easier if I just gave you my business card instead?'

Martina wasn't impressed. 'Stop being such a smart-arse, Alex. It doesn't sit well with your sensitive side, and I like that side of your personality so much better.'

I should have been flattered in a way, but even so, I still felt thoroughly defeated by her logic.

'Are you really sure you want to do this?'

'Of course; I do. Why else would I suggest it?' She lifted my arm and pulled me closer towards her until our faces were almost touching.

'Listen, you scallywag, either you share a secret with me now, or as soon as we get back to Samos, you throw me on my bed and fuck me senseless all night, girlfriend or no girlfriend. Your choice, mister, but either way, I am getting a piece of you.'

'You know, in another time, they would have burned you as a witch.'

'I doubt it. No-one would ever have caught me.'

'Why do I have to go first?' I asked, wondering if I would survive this ordeal unscathed.

'Because I said so, that's why. It has to be something important, too. I don't want to hear that you had a crush on your high school English teacher or something trivial like that.'

Which was an absolute bugger if you thought about it because I actually *did* have a crush on my high school English teacher. Miss Taylor was her name. What's more, with nothing else to offer Martina, I was banking on her being my big secret. But now that she had been cruelly ruled out, what else did I have?

Well, there was that time I kissed Libbie Moore at the movies in Year 5 while her boyfriend was playing football. Or maybe that day, I stole my first *Penthouse* magazine from the corner store. Or perhaps when I smuggled a can of beer into Grade 9 camp and then blamed it on another classmate.

'How about this?' I offered. 'I never read the same book twice.'

Martina bludgeoned me with her Satanic eyes. 'Are you trying to be funny? I said it must be something substantial.'

'Do you know how hard it is to convince people that I've only read *American Psycho* once?'

'Alex!'

'Okay, I think you will like this one. Just before I left Australia for this trip, I was staying at a friend's place when I suddenly developed an unbelievably bad case of haemorrhoids. My friend suggested that I use some special gel he had in his bathroom, but somehow I got the tubes mixed up and ended up using heat cream on myself instead.'

'You are really starting to piss me off,' Martina snapped.

'Maybe we should consider plan B after all,' I sighed. 'How about I take you back to your place, fuck you senseless all night, as you poignantly suggested, and then I will arrange for my castration when I return to Athens on Thursday. This way, I can save considerable time before I meet up with Rachel next week.'

Despite herself, Martina laughed. 'You can be such an idiot.'

'I'm just finding this very hard,' I replied truthfully. 'If you must know, I have lived a life full of lies. But they all belong to the same bucket of nonsense that you continue to reject. Nothing I say is going to please you.'

'Rubbish! There must be one big secret you have never shared with anyone before. Everyone has something, Alex.'

I truly hoped that Martina couldn't hear the banging inside my chest. *You are right, clever girl: everyone indeed has something.* For me, it was that terrible thing that happened when I was eight years old in Kandos. A sordid affair that destroyed my childhood without me even realising it. But I had no intention of succumbing to its wrath, not even for Martina.

'My father passed away in 1990,' I suddenly began. 'Things between us had been strained in the year leading up to his illness. But he was still my father, and I was compelled to visit him before he died.'

My mind wandered back to that day five years ago in Brisbane. I saw myself walk into the hospital where my father lay stricken with cancer, gripped with a fear that I dare not describe. Even at that point, I wasn't sure what I would say to him, especially when both of us knew that there was not enough time left for either of us to tell each other what we really felt.

As I walked past reception, I desperately wanted to turn around and go home. Any residual emotions I had for my father disappeared a long time ago, and I saw little reason to reconcile my relationship with him now, just because he was about to die.

But I somehow took control of my fears and kept moving. As I approached the ward where he would spend his final hours, I felt like the empty child who was visiting the abandoned home of his birth. There was no sadness within me, just a sense of relief that my hypocrisy would soon be over.

For I had experienced firsthand the impact of my father's deceptions. He had recently caused so much hurt, anger, and regret within our family that my heart was devoid of pity, even when I saw that he was consumed with excruciating pain.

It wasn't my responsibility to absolve him for his sins or to make excuses for his actions. I had already expended far too much time trying to justify his life within my own conscience. It was due to the war. It was the loss of his family. It was because he was a new Australian. No, enough was enough. As I sat next to the skeletal imitation that was once my robust and handsome father, I refused to tell him that I understood his motives because I didn't and probably never would. But I knew as he prepared to leave this world, my forgiveness was what he craved from me more than anything else.

After ten minutes of needless small talk, I left him for the last time. There were no goodbyes, no apologies, no admissions of guilt, just a handshake with impending death. I felt nothing other than a desire to leave the hospital as fast as possible and never turn back. And I never did, to my ongoing shame. Not even to shed a solitary tear for his passing.

'You never cried when your father died?' Martina repeated back to me. I had been so absorbed with self-reflection that it just occurred to me that she had been sitting next to me all that time.

'Terrible, isn't it? The funny thing is, I have never cried since. I don't know why, but I just can't cry anymore.'

'Sweet Lord,' said Martina, her lips shining in the sun. Was it possible that I had finally succeeded in shocking her?

'So that's my big secret. Do you now think any less of me?'

Martina looked strangely sympathetic. 'No, I don't,' she reassured me. 'I just escaped from a war where sons and fathers killed each other over a piece of bread. Your situation is trivial by comparison.'

'I suppose you're right,' I admitted. 'Perhaps you should have been a philosopher, not a nurse.'

'They are one and the same profession.' She smiled.

I allowed her to rest her head momentarily on my shoulder before she eventually pulled away to follow a beam of light reflecting off my camera.

'Okay, Martina. Let's get this over and done with. Your turn now.'

Mistake number five.

She, at first, pretended not to hear me, and I began to wonder whether she regretted this whole stupid thing. *Well, too bad, gorgeous. This was your idea, and you have to keep your side of the bargain. There is no way I'm going to release you from your obligations now.*

'Come on, Martina—spit it out,' I demanded. 'What is your big secret?'

Nothing I had experienced in my pitiful life so far prepared me for her response.

'Three years ago,' she began, wiping away her forgotten tears, 'I was gang-raped by Serbian soldiers.'

My Miss Sarajevo

Canberra
March 2016

In late 1995, the same year I visited Greece, the Irish rock band U2, performing as 'Passengers', released a single called 'Miss Sarajevo'. It was the title song from a documentary made two years earlier by an American filmmaker named Bill Carter, whose work brought to world attention the realities of underground life in Sarajevo during the height of the Bosnian War.

The heroine of this uplifting tale was a wonderfully precocious seventeen-year-old blonde Bosnian girl, Inela Nogić, who won a beauty contest held in the city during the height of the siege. The documentary poignantly demonstrated the resilience of Sarajevo's downtrodden population and how the small things in life could sometimes give hope to people suffering great duress.

Despite an impressive body of work amassed across almost four decades, including two of the greatest albums of all time, *The Joshua Tree* and *Achtung Baby!*, Miss Sarajevo quickly became my favourite U2 song. Bono's delicate vocals, the Edge's beautifully refined guitar mix and, of course, the decisive intervention of the world's greatest-ever opera singer, Luciano Pavarotti, all combined to turn a simple anti-war message into a musical masterpiece. The song projected, for me, a perfect blend of pop art, urban poetry, and operatic tragedy.

But sometimes, the things you love the most in life find a way to disappoint you. And so it was, twenty years later, that Miss Sarajevo and I finally parted company for the last time. Such was the intensity of our breakup that I temporarily erased every other U2 song from my Apple devices just for spite.

Of course, with every relationship breakdown, there came a time when you asked yourself the usual questions. What happened? How did we get it so hopelessly wrong?

At first, I decided that the song had become a metaphor for my past: a constant reminder of how I once abandoned a young woman from Sarajevo when she needed me the most. But it soon became apparent during those bitter, sleepless nights that there had to be something else: a missing clue that I hadn't yet found.

This mystery would continue to confound me for weeks; even Roy, my therapist, was lost for answers. No matter how hard I tried, I couldn't understand why I felt so betrayed by one beautiful song.

Then, early one Sunday morning, as I listened to the autumn winds howl outside my bedroom window, everything slowly began to make sense. My emotional detachment had nothing to do with the song – indeed, its purity still offered hope to many people who had battled oppression, violence, and cruelty during the Bosnian conflict. Rather, it was me who had changed. For those last droplets of hope I had jealously guarded for years had inexplicably disappeared, to be replaced by a new, unedifying emotion—resentment. Yes: the resentment I felt for my current predicament. The resentment I felt for the Spiders. The resentment I felt for the mistakes of my past. The resentment I felt for a song that immortalised a beauty contest in Sarajevo.

Because you see, I had a secret: one that I never shared with anyone until now. Within the halls of another existence, I knew of a far more compelling story from the Bosnian War: a story that was destined to become nothing more than a passing rainstorm caught within the winds of time.

That story belonged to Martina.

Cursed forever to be my very own Miss Sarajevo.

*

Ephesus
May 1995

'I am sorry,' Martina whispered. 'I didn't mean to embarrass you, but tomorrow will be the third anniversary. It has been on my mind all week.'

'My God, please don't apologise, Martina,' I replied softly. 'I am simply devastated for you, and I don't know what to say.'

'You don't need to say anything, Alex.'

'It's just that I've never met a woman before who has been raped.'

Yeah, I know—what a thoroughly heartless thing to say. But in my defence, a thousand different emotions were swirling inside my head.

'Jesus.' Martina pursed her lips indignantly. 'Would it have been easier for you if I had a red sign painted on my forehead?'

'That's very unfair, Martina,' I said, even though it really wasn't.

She squeezed my hand to signify a truce, and we both waited until a group of German tourists walked past us.

'I wanted to tell you last night on the beach,' she admitted. 'However, you had to make me laugh instead.'

'And all this nonsense about sharing secrets? It was just a way of getting me to hear your story, wasn't it?'

Martina smiled. 'I never waste an opportunity, Alex.'

'Yeah, right.' For the second time that day, I had been tricked by a total stranger, which pissed me off no end. I picked up a loose stone and tossed it down an adjacent set of steps. 'I understand why you felt the need to confide in someone, Martina. But why me? Why not Marlena, who, by the way, adores you?'

'For some reason, I feel more comfortable talking about this to a man. Whether you like it or not, you are the nicest man I have met in a long time.'

'You don't even know me.'

'What is that supposed to mean?'

I didn't want to hurt her feelings; I really didn't. But neither did I want her to make a terrible mistake.

'Look, I'm not the person that you think I am. In fact, if you want to know the truth, I am a complete arsehole. For instance, I have a new girlfriend who cares about me very much, but I spent most of the ferry ride from Piraeus salivating over another woman. And don't think that I haven't spent every spare second wondering what you look like stark naked.'

'I would be disappointed if you didn't.' She managed to smile. 'Aren't all men supposed to think like that?'

'Only the selfish ones.'

'You are too hard on yourself,' she berated me. 'I have spent most of my life dealing with arseholes, and you're nothing like any of them. That you can express your feelings to a stranger makes you different from any other man I have met. Besides, who I decide to trust is my business, not yours.'

I blew out some air just to demonstrate my utter exasperation with her. 'What I'm trying to say, Martina, is that I'm not sure if I can help you. I'm leaving tomorrow, and you will be back right where you started before we ever met. Alone and dealing with this horrible secret by yourself.'

'Why don't you listen to my story first before you jump to such conclusions?'

Martina had me where she wanted me, and we both knew it. There was nothing more I could do other than sit back and listen.

'Okay.' I finally admitted defeat. 'Tell me your story.'

It all started with a panicked phone call from her mother late one Sunday evening. Her older sister Ana—Martina's beloved aunty—lived by herself in a Serbian-occupied village just outside of Sarajevo. Martina's mother had been trying to contact her for over a week now, but the phone line was always engaged. Ana had an ongoing heart condition, and Martina's mum was very concerned that something may have happened to her, especially if she hadn't replenished her medication before the fighting commenced. Could Martina drive out there the next day after work and see if she was okay?

Martina tried to make her mum understand that Sarajevo was under siege and almost entirely surrounded by the Serbian Army. Furthermore, the violence had escalated to unimaginable levels. Several days prior, the Serbs had partitioned the city in half, prompting a brutal counterattack from Bosnian forces and local gang members. Martina explained that she had been working nonstop for the previous three days as the dead and the wounded continued to pile up inside her hospital. This beautiful, historic city, which had once hosted the Winter Olympics, had become a scene from Dante's *Inferno*.

Given that every inch of ground was critical to victory, each side had carefully constructed roadblocks to control the movement of people to and from the city. Martina was genuinely scared about being detained and falling into the hands of the wrong people, for already there were rumours about mass rapes and other brutalities. She promised her mother she would do what she could before her phone went dead.

The next day, Martina's on-again-off-again boyfriend, Branco, convinced her that he had found a safe route into her Aunt's village. As he marked out directions on Martina's map with a black felt pen, Branco reassured her that no self-respecting Serbian soldier would ever touch a young Serbian girl like her. But when Martina begged Branco to come with her for male protection, he made up some sob story about a bad back, and they fell into yet another argument that often blighted their volatile relationship.

Martina obtained permission to leave work early that afternoon, despite a truckload of casualties arriving just after lunchtime. She did what she could to help out her colleagues in the emergency theatre before setting out on her journey just before five o'clock. The spring days were longer, and Martina worked out that everything being equal, she would be safely back inside the family house in Sarajevo by sunset.

At first, everything went according to plan. Okay, the streets were eerily empty, and the black billowing smoke that peppered the skyline was a stark reminder of the incessant fighting, but despite a heavy military presence all around her, she managed to reach the outer suburbs of Sarajevo unmolested. For once, that arsehole Branco had been right.

Martina had divided the trip into four phases: Sarajevo to the outer suburbs, the outer suburbs to Aunty Ana's house, Aunty Ana's house back to Sarajevo, Sarajevo to Martina's house. With the first phase completed, Martina allowed herself a welcome sigh of relief. With the radio blaring Madonna's greatest hits in the background, she even managed to recite a thankyou prayer to the baby Jesus for looking after her so far. But somewhere on the way to heaven, her prayer must have lost its way because after turning down a detour that Branco promised would be safe, she drove straight into a military roadblock.

Martina had no choice but to pull over to the side of the road. A burly soldier carrying a semiautomatic rifle appeared at her window and ordered her to get out of the car. One glance at his soulless face made her recoil in terror, for he was the embodiment of evil: right from his polished boots to his peculiar mohawk haircut. Her only hope was that his uniform clearly confirmed him to be a soldier of the Army of the Republic of Serbia. Martina clung to Branco's reassuring words that a Serbian soldier would never harm a Serbian civilian, and she did her best to remain calm.

The soldier demanded to see Martina's driver's licence, and she politely asked his permission to collect it from her handbag. When he gruffly nodded his head, she frantically rummaged through her belongings before the horrible reality smacked her right in the face. *Oh God, I left my license on Branco's kitchen table this morning during our argument! You imbecile! What am I going to do now?*

The soldier sensed her panic, but he was not the type to show her any compassion. 'You are a filthy Bosniak spy,' he shouted at her. *Bosniak*, Martina explained to me, was the term commonly used for a Bosnian Muslim.

'You're wrong!' she insisted. 'I am a Bosnian Serb, and I work as a nurse in Sarajevo. My brother is in the Serbian army. Please believe me.'

'Filthy Bosniak whores are only good for one thing,' he ignored her. This thoroughly obnoxious assessment was obviously indoctrinated into him during basic training. He caught her by the arm and almost wrenched it off with one savage yank of his wrist. Martina screamed out for her life, hoping that someone would hear her desperate cries for help. Unfortunately for her, the only people who responded were a small cadre of Serbian soldiers who suddenly appeared from behind the roadblock.

'What do we have here?' asked a muscular young sergeant with a half-crescent scar mashed across his nose. He was not much older than Martina, but they belonged to different worlds.

'A Bosniak spy, sergeant!' screamed out the bald soldier.

Martina knew that she had to do something quickly, or else these thugs would rape her. The terror she felt upon this realisation was indescribable. Her one chance of escape was to create a diversion and make a dash for her car. She whispered out another prayer, and with all her strength, kicked out one of her long legs, smashing the hard stub of her heel into the flabby soft tissue surrounding the soldier's knee.

'Take that, you bastard!' she screamed, as the soldier comically jumped about on one leg as if he had just invented a new Serbian folk dance. While the other soldiers began to laugh at their friend's misfortune, Martina spun around, her feet chugging aimlessly in the mud, her eyes glued to her car, which was agonisingly only several feet away. But hang on. Why wasn't she moving? It might have had something to do with the fact that the sergeant had seized her by the hair and was pulling her back towards him. She screamed, she scratched, she fought for her fucking life, but to no avail. You see, the sergeant had subjugated far more worthy opponents than Martina during his career. When she was close enough to smell his garlic breath on her face, she begged him, through an avalanche of tears, to let her go.

However, God decided a long time ago that humans couldn't negotiate with wild animals. Rather than take pity on her, the sergeant slowly raised his rifle to the horizontal. He smiled at Martina at first, a deathly, pale grin that amplified every hatred he had ever collected in his life, and then viciously smashed the butt of his rifle into her unprotected stomach.

Martina doubled over in agony, her lungs bursting into flames. For one crazy second, she wondered whether or not she should take her next breath. But her procrastination simply made it so much easier for the sergeant to kick Martina's feet from underneath her. She plummeted straight to the ground, her head smacking against the edge of a sharp rock. The last thing Martina remembered before she descended into a bottomless void was the sergeant ordering his men to 'take the slut back to the farm'.

Martina regained consciousness fifteen minutes later in the back of an army lorry. She remembered the reference to a farm and prayed that she would meet someone there in authority who believed her story. Once again, she did her best to remain calm before the truck came to a sudden halt and two grimy-looking soldiers pulled her outside.

It was on a muddy driveway leading to a farm in the middle of nowhere that the first of the rapes occurred. The youngest of the soldiers, barely eighteen himself, pushed Martina onto the ground. Both men made time to avail themselves of the obligatory verbal insults, suggesting that Martina was nothing more than a worthless whore who deserved to be raped before they each forced her to perform a sexual act on them.

Once satisfied with the results of their brutal attack, the two men reconstituted their respective zippers and exemplified their undoubted courage by spitting in her face. When Martina tried to wipe away the gobbles of phlegm dripping off her chin, the young boy threw her back onto the ground and launched several punches into her unprotected ribs.

'Dirty Bosniak slut,' he roared at her once again. They then lifted Martina by the arms and dragged her across the ground until they reached a small barn guarded by a pair of grinning soldiers.

'We have another Muslim whore for you,' the older soldier explained. 'This one is a real beauty, too.'

One of the guards roughly seized Martina by the hair and lifted her head to his eye level so that he could thoroughly inspect the new goods.

'Man, she is damn pretty. So much nicer than the four pigs we have inside.'

'Hands off her, Lukic,' the eighteen-year-old soldier barked. 'She is for our use later this evening. Sergeant's orders.'

They shoved Martina into the barn and forced her to sit next to four frightened women, who were all huddled together near a small tractor. She collapsed backwards into a pile of straw and watched helplessly while blood from her head poured onto the new designer jeans that she had only bought a few weeks before.

When the guards finally left the barn, two Bosniak women crawled over to Martina and did what they could to comfort her. One of them ripped off a piece of material from her very own shirt and started to wipe away the dried blood from Martina's face. The other woman realised that Martina had been sexually assaulted and wrapped her spindly arms around her shoulders to stop her from going into shock. They sat together like that for the next hour until Martina regained some semblance of composure.

The women explained to Martina that a Serbian military unit had come to their village earlier in the day and ordered all Muslim females under the age of forty to congregate in a small park. Even girls as young as twelve were not exempt; anyone foolhardy enough to intervene was immediately dispatched to their graves. The woman with the spindly arms described in vivid detail the terrible atrocities she had witnessed that morning, including a father being forced at gunpoint to rape one of his own teenage daughters in front of the entire village.

Just before lunch, the captured women were divided equally and then herded into four separate trucks. With some twenty passengers on board, the vehicle arrived at this farm site just after two o'clock. During the afternoon, various soldiers had intermittently wandered into the barn at their leisure to select whatever woman tickled their fancy. The four there with Martina were the only women left from those original twenty prisoners.

'Sometimes it is a virtue not to be all that good-looking,' laughed one of the other women, totally insensitive to Martina's plight.

Just as she finished her sentence, the barn door crashed open, and four filthy soldiers barged their way inside. Without uttering a single word, they each snatched their selected

Bosniak woman from the ground and tossed them over their shoulders as if they were nothing more than a slab of meat they had just purchased from a butcher. For the rest of her life, Martina would never forget the sheer terror of their screams as they were carried out into the waiting darkness.

But Martina did not have time to reflect upon the fate of her companions. Just as one group of subhumans left with their cargo intact, a new group arrived to reacquaint themselves with the tempestuous young woman they had met only hours before. Yes, it was the sergeant, his bedraggled lot of filthy psychopaths and several bottles of *rakija*.

Afterwards, Martina tried to calculate how many men had violated her. She recalled seeing at least six soldiers with the sergeant when they initially entered the barn but was pretty certain that others joined the party later in the night. All told, she believed that more than a dozen men were involved in her assault.

When Martina realised what was about to happen, her first reaction was to push herself up onto her feet and run towards the open door. But one of the soldiers expertly caught her by the neck as she tried to sprint past him and then drove her onto a large blanket that had been laid out on the ground just for her. Before she could scream and scream again, an orchestra of laughing hands was tugging at her jeans, silk top, and undergarments.

Once her clothes had been completely removed, the sergeant stood above her face and nudged the side of her buttocks with his steel-capped boot.

'Welcome to hell, my sweet little Bosniak princess,' he smiled as his eyes greedily inspected her naked body. 'For the glory of the Serbian nation, I now declare you the property of its brave soldiers. Hopefully, by the end of your time with us this evening, your stomach will be venerated with the seed of a future Chetnik warrior.'

It started. Each of the soldiers took their turn, and when they finished, they rejuvenated themselves by gulping down vast quantities of *rakija* before starting all over again on her, sometimes in pairs, sometimes in groups of three or four. Martina did what she could to struggle and fight, but she soon realised that this only made these monsters more excited. In the end, she decided that the best way of denying them any pleasure was to close her eyes, wander off into a distant world where she was safe with her family, and just let them do to her what they wanted.

Consequently, Martina lost all track of time during her horrendous attack, although she assumed that it lasted for about five hours. She remembered finally falling asleep after midnight, covered head to toe in dirt, blood, and male excretion. A few hours later, the soldier who originally stopped Martina at the roadblock returned to the barn drunk as a monkey and wanted to go another round with her. When he couldn't perform, he completely lost the plot and aimed a series of savage kicks into her groin, breasts, and head. It was at that point that Martina was convinced she was going to die and started to recite the Lord's Prayer in between her cries of pain.

That lonely recital probably saved her life. Another soldier entered the barn and just happened to hear Martina praying amongst the kicking and the screaming. When his limited brains cells finally made the connection, he pulled his colleague away from Martina's body before he could do any more damage to her.

'What are you doing, Bozic?' yelled the bald soldier. 'She is just a worthless piece of Muslim filth.'

'How many Muslims do you know recite the Lord's Prayer when they are getting the shit kicked out of them, you ignoramus? She is not a Bozniak; she is a fucking Serbian!'

'I guess we screwed up, then,' was the final sum of the bald soldier's idiotic response.

Just like that, Martina's horrific ordeal had come to an end.

After the Philippines, when I finally solved the riddle behind the Season of Clouds, I would try to banish all thoughts about Martina and what happened to her during that awful night. But the only feeling I had at that moment was one of unimaginable sadness for a beautiful young woman whose life was needlessly destroyed. So I gathered her delicate body into my arms and held her tightly until a strand of her hair tickled my face.

'I hope those bastards rot in hell for what they did to you.'

'It's my battle, Alex, not yours,' she replied softly. 'But, yes—eternal damnation is far too good for them.'

'I simply cannot believe that it was your own people who did this to you.'

She lifted her slim shoulders in response. 'In hindsight, it was simply a terrible case of mistaken identity. But the perpetrators could have easily been Croatians or Bosniaks. Genocidal rape and murder are common occurrences in Bosnia every day. Some men in this world, regardless of nationality or background, are inherently evil. War allows these creatures to don uniforms and commit awful crimes in the name of their country.'

'They were not men; they were animals.' Before Martina could reply, I leaned across her body, gently cupped her soft face with my palms, and kissed her on the lips. It was not done to elicit any sexual response but to show Martina that I genuinely cared about her.

'Thank you,' Martina whispered. 'I needed that.'

'I know you did.'

'What would your girlfriend say?'

'If you don't tell her, I won't.'

She dropped her head against my shoulder blade, and we sat quietly like that for several more minutes.

'What did you do afterwards?' I finally asked her. 'Did you report the crime to anyone?'

Martina offered me a sardonic smile. 'Once those idiots realised that I was a Serbian, everything changed. Some clean-cut officer type walked into the barn and placed a blanket around me. He led me back to the farmhouse, where he forced me to take a long, hot shower to wipe away the evidence. After I dried myself, he threw some fresh clothes in my direction and told me to get dressed.'

'Jesus Christ.'

'Oh, it gets better,' Martina growled. 'I have just been raped, sodomised, spat on, beaten, kicked, and called a whore at least a thousand times. I have two broken ribs, three teeth knocked out, a badly torn anus, and a nose that looks like a watermelon. So what does this weedy little prick do? He asks me to join him for breakfast! You know, like we are a new couple waking up together for the first time.'

'I don't believe it.'

'Over a cup of tea, he apologises to me on behalf of the army and suggests that sometimes terrible mistakes happen in warfare. He reassures me that the soldier who tried to kick the shit out of me in the barn will be suitably punished. Unfortunately, he is less clear about the other dozen or so men who have just violated every fissure of my body.'

'What did you do then?'

'I just wanted to go home, so I kept my mouth shut,' she said. 'We engaged in some more meaningless chitchat before he arranged for me to be returned to my car. The officious little prick also provided me with an escort to ensure that there were no more 'misunderstandings,' as he put it, with some of his soldiers. When I returned to Sarajevo, I went straight to the hospital where I worked, told people that I had been ambushed by drug addicts outside of my home, and then collapsed into the arms of a doctor. I was in intensive care for about a week but never told anyone the real truth about what happened to me. I was far too petrified. To this day, I still don't know how I got out of that place alive.'

I caressed Martina's arm, and for a moment, she seemed at peace with herself.

'Some story, huh?'

'Yeah, some story,' I replied.

'Any more questions?' Martina asked me curtly as if she was hosting a show and tell presentation.

'Just the obvious one. Why didn't you tell people the truth? I don't understand. Those bastards needed to pay for their crimes.'

'Let me give you an insight on how things work in Bosnia,' Martina growled. 'Aunty Ana, God bless her golden heart, was alive after all. Her telephone line had been cut, nothing more. My idiot ex-boyfriend finally grew the balls to find her and then took her to see me while I was still recovering in the hospital. Do you know what she said to me when I started to explain that I had been raped by Serbian soldiers?' She did not wait for me to reply. '"Don't be silly, Martina. Serbian men don't rape women. It's just Muslim propaganda".'

If Martina expected me to be shocked, I wasn't. My mother often repeated this very same mantra whenever I had the temerity to mention the mass rapes in her former country.

'That's just the older generation refusing to admit fault with their culture. However, that should not prevent you from seeking justice.'

'You don't understand, Alex. You have spent far too much time living in Australia. There is no such thing as justice in Bosnia anymore. Where would I take my complaint? The Bosniaks? They couldn't give a damn that a Serbian girl was gang-raped except to support Islamic propaganda. And the Serbs? You didn't rat on your own kind, ever. If I had made a formal complaint to the Serbian Army, my death warrant, and that of my family, would have been signed virtually overnight.'

'Your war is now over, Martina: you don't intend to return to Bosnia any time soon. So what is stopping you now? The United Nations recently said that they will prosecute war crimes, especially those committed against civilians.'

'Those idiots?' she sneered at me. 'You said yourself how hopeless they are. Days after I escaped Bosnia in '93, I was briefly interviewed by some snooty little English tart from the UN Peacekeeping Force. All airs and graces she was as if I were somehow personally responsible for my own gang rape. Wanted to know how much of a fight I put up! Can you believe that? I am still waiting for her to call me back.' Martina took my hand. 'All I want to do is help my parents and figure out where to live for the next few years. At the moment, I am just a street urchin, looking for somewhere to sleep. I will follow through with the UN once everything else in my life is resolved. But until then, they can all screw themselves.'

'What about you personally? Have you fully recovered from your ordeal?'

Yes, I know. Another puerile, typically male thing to say, and I regretted it immediately. But Martina refused to take offence.

'Following the rape, my first concern was getting pregnant or contracting AIDS. Thankfully, I received a clean bill of health, although it is unlikely that I will ever be able to have children. Those animals did terrible damage to my insides.'

I squeezed her tightly. 'I am so sorry, Martina.'

'Don't be, Alex. The last thing I want to do is bring a child into this screwed-up world.'

'No-one would begrudge you that.'

'Possibly not,' she replied. 'But then again, you have never met my mother. She still harbours dreams about fifteen grandchildren. And with Draga dead ...'

She began to choke on her words, so I pulled her closer towards me.

'We don't have to talk about this anymore, Martina.'

'No, let me finish,' she pleaded with me after taking a deep breath. 'Time is a great healer, of course, and I try to live the best life I can. But there was a period when I got lost inside the darkness and never wanted to come out again.'

'Meaning?'

'Meaning that in the weeks following the rape, I attempted suicide on three occasions.'

Oh, dear God.

'Have you spoken about this to anyone?'

'Only you.'

'No, I don't mean that. I am talking about a real professional, someone who is an expert in trauma.'

'I have tried several psychiatrists, but I could never get past the first meeting. They always wanted me to remember; I just wanted to forget.'

'I understand, Martina—I really do. But you can't live like this forever.'

Martina brushed away a stray dandelion from my face. 'As I told you before, I have my priorities. For the moment, I am determined to stay alive for the sake of my parents. With Draga gone, I'm all they have.'

'There has to be another way,' I offered firmly. 'People need to know your story.'

'Perhaps in the future. Who knows, you and I might even write a book about it one day?' She smiled at the thought. 'But until then, this is the life I have to live.'

I bit into my tongue. 'What about Marco?' I asked Martina.

'What about him?'

'Does he know?'

'I have already explained that to you,' she licked her lips. 'You are the only person with whom I have shared the full story.'

'That's not what I am asking, Martina.'

I could tell that I had hit a raw nerve.

'I am sure he suspects something,' she replied icily. 'It is impossible to hide the scars on my body, do you understand? And he likes to do certain things to me.'

'Like what?'

'Alex.'

'Like what, Martina?'

'You know, handcuffs, bondage, that sort of thing.'

As soon as Martina completed her sentence, waves of undefined anger spiralled down the back of my spine. They magically flipped me onto my side, and I stared at Martina's blank face.

'That sick bastard. I'll fucking kill him!'

'Alex!' she screamed at me. A flock of seagulls pecking at a discarded chip packet scrambled away in fright, and several tourists arched their heads towards us.

'You will do no such thing,' she ordered, lowering her voice. 'My relationship with Marco is my business, not yours.'

Maybe so, but that Croatian red mist wasn't so understanding.

'Can't you see how he is using you?'

'What do you mean?' she asked.

'You said yesterday that the reason he palms you off to other men is to satisfy his ego. That's not why he does it at all. He does it purely because it turns him on. He is raping you all over again, without the legal consequences, and then asking his friends to join him.'

'You are wrong,' she fired back at me. 'Rape isn't about sex: it's about power and control.'

'Of course it is. But tell me this—do you enjoy being with a pig like Marco?'

'What if I do?'

The age difference between us was only six years, but suddenly I felt like a lost traveller from another generation.

'Let's just drop it,' I insisted.

Martina stamped her foot angrily on the ground until I agreed to meet her eyes.

'You find it abnormal that I can enjoy sex again, don't you?'

'I never said that.'

'But that's what you were thinking—admit it.'

I remained silent, not wishing to commit myself to anything.

'Listen to me, Alex,' Martina snarled. 'This may sound absurd to you, but those bastards did me a favour that night. They made me realise that when you have control, you never have to fear anything. Why should I worry about the men I sleep with when I have the power to make that choice? You see, I enjoy sex because it helps me reassert my authority over life after what happened. I will never allow men like those soldiers, or Marco, to take that choice away from me again.'

I wanted to make the point that this was precisely what she was doing, but I decided to let it go for the time being, more for my own sanity than anything else. It was Martina who'd hoodwinked me into this discussion with all this sharing secrets bullshit. If she didn't want to listen to me, why should I bother?

After all, I didn't ask to share in her pain; that was purely her decision. In a week, she would meet some other guy in Chios willing to indulge her excuses. Women like Martina always had a never-ending supply of men waiting to replace the last one. But not this little black duck. This whole situation was way over my pay grade. All I wanted to do was find a reason to get out of there.

Deliverance arrived in the form of an elderly New Zealand couple who interrupted our conversation to remind us that the tour bus would be returning to Kuşadası at three o'clock. This immediately caused Martina to flap around in a mild panic because she desperately wanted to see the Temple of Hadrian before we departed. While she studied our map for directions, I wandered off to take some last-minute photos of the amphitheatre, grateful that the madness of the previous half-hour had finally come to an end.

I positioned myself on the highest row of steps I could find and then steadily worked through a logical sequence of interlocking shots that guided me around the theatre's narrow circumference. Only when I reached the last frame of the series did I see Martina's unwanted intrusion in the corner of my right eye, madly waving her hands around in the air.

'You're ruining my photo, Martina,' I shouted at her, my patience wearing thin. But my mouth and my finger had become so outrageously out of sync that I ended up hitting the camera button by mistake anyway.

'Damn it! I have to take another photo now!'

'Oh, suck it up, drama queen!' she said, laughing.

*

Canberra
March 2016

Oh, suck it up, drama queen! Those words rattled inside my head one more time. She had been right; I really did act like a drama queen that afternoon.

I walked into my study and picked up the photo album that had been gathering dust on top of an old wooden bookshelf. As I slowly turned the pages, I regretted that I had allowed my fears to erase so many memories of that holiday.

Westminster Abbey. Canterbury Cathedral. Tower of London. Stonehenge. The Roman ruins in Bath. Loch Ness. Edinburgh Castle. The Eiffel Tower. Notre Dame Cathedral. The Arc de Triomphe. Ypres. Waterloo. All monuments to the man I would one day become.

But this was hardly the time to bask in my lost memories, for my purpose that day wasn't to reminisce about what was but to unlock the chains of what would be. Like it or not, I always knew that this photo album contained my last chance for salvation.

There it is. The Ephesus Amphitheatre. Thankfully, I never threw it away.

I lifted the thin veil of plastic that protected the photo from the vagaries of time. Once I carefully extracted it from the sticky blue tack, I laid it out on my desk and took a step back to consider its raw power.

Like most things in my life, I got it so horribly wrong in Ephesus. Places and objects did hide secrets, after all. This one photo, through an accident of time, revealed the biggest secret of them all.

The woman who brought me where I am today. Martina.

I gently manoeuvred my index finger along the contours of the photo. Maybe if I prayed hard enough, the image would come to life, and I could finally beg Martina for her forgiveness. But deep within my soul, I knew it was far too late for such miracles. The only thing I could offer her were the tears that began to drop with perfect symmetry across her crumpled face—the tears that reflected the guilt I had carried on behalf of the world.

For though her tragedy had confounded the ages, no-one ever knew the extent of her pain.

No-one, that is, except for me.

Pandemonium

Samos Island
May 1995

I decided not to attend Franco's birthday party as soon as we boarded the bus in Ephesus later that afternoon. There had been a slow build-up to this decision for several hours. From the moment we departed the amphitheatre, I could sense that something unnatural was happening to me.

It reminded me of a dream I had recently. I was lying on a beach, in the middle of a beautiful tropical island, enjoying the warm sunshine, when a gigantic crab sprang from a nearby rock pool and pinned me to the ground. Before I could scream for help, it laid several eggs deep inside my throat. Slowly but surely, I began to feel the evil growing inside of me until my stomach started to bloat, my head started to spin, and the next thing I knew, a gruesome monster was ripping a hole through the middle of my intestines.

Crazy stuff, to be sure. But there was no better way to describe how I felt. For some reason, Martina's story had torn its way into my bloodstream, consuming me with an interminable fear that I couldn't explain.

The ferry ride back to Samos only added to my deteriorating mood. The afternoon was beautiful and clear when we left Kuşadası's golden shores. But as soon as we chugged into open water, our journey suddenly turned into a scene from the *Poseidon Adventure*. From out of nowhere, our boat was swamped by the swell from hell, and we were soon tossing from side to side like an out-of-control roller-coaster ride.

I came from a long line of seafarers, so living it rough on the sea was in my genes. I rarely, if ever, suffered seasickness. Unfortunately, this didn't apply to the other sixty passengers on the boat, apart from Martina. Pretty soon, she and I had a front-row seat to the largest synchronised mass vomit in history.

If there was one small consolation, it enabled me to see the other side of Martina's bewildering personality. Whatever else we might have said about the Underworld's favourite nurse, she maintained a natural desire to help people in distress. Although it was virtually impossible to stand upright in a vessel that obviously wanted to capsize as much as this one did, Martina was immediately on her feet, busily lurching from one side of the cabin to the other, providing support and comfort to anyone who needed it.

She was incredibly kind to Nina, whose face had become so alarmingly green you could quickly run a lawnmower over it and collect the cuttings. The girl who had deliberately mocked the same woman that morning with her outrageous antics placed a soothing arm around her shoulders while wiping diced carrot from her lap with nothing more than a solitary tissue.

At the height of our peril, I became mortally offended when no-one wanted to take up my offer to hold hands and sing 'There's Got to be a Morning After'. But as soon as we approached the Samos shoreline, the tossing and vomiting magically stopped, and the sea returned to a bygone era of tranquillity.

'Thank you for travelling with Ephesus Ferries,' beamed the immaculately groomed hostess as everyone staggered off the boat in varying degrees of atrophy. 'We hope you enjoyed your visit today.'

On the ride home, Martina sat next to Nina to look after her, while Lottie joined me at the back of the bus.

'The porn queen actually has some redeeming qualities after all,' said Lottie. 'She is full of surprises.'

'That's one way of putting it,' is all I could say. I watched closely as the blood magically returned to Lottie's beautiful, pale face. 'How are you feeling after surviving the tidal wave?'

'I'm well enough. But poor Mum, though: she gets seasick at home just walking over the local bridge.' We both tried hard not to laugh and then spent the rest of the trip making flirtatious small talk.

When we disembarked the bus in Vathy, Lottie and I were greeted by the unlikely sight of Nina and Martina hugging each other like old friends. Nina even managed to tap me on the arm as she walked past, in an effort, I assumed, to reinforce that, while I was still very much a bottom feeder, all was forgiven.

Everyone from the bus eventually disappeared until Lottie, Martina, and I were left standing by ourselves next to a park bench.

'Do you still want me to come to the party tonight?' Lottie asked hopefully. I could tell by the irrational excitement in her voice that she desperately needed a night away from her parents.

'Yes!' screamed out Martina. 'Please come, Lottie! It will be so much fun!'

Of course it would be fun. Things usually were when I wasn't around.

'Actually, guys,' I coughed tentatively, 'I might give tonight a miss. I'm not feeling particularly well, and I need a good night sleep. Perhaps we can all catch up for breakfast in the morning?'

Martina looked crestfallen.

Lottie looked confused.

Alex looked petrified.

'If I remember correctly,' Lottie snorted, her closed fists dangling dangerously beside her hips, 'you were the one who asked me to come out tonight. You even said you would protect me from Marvin.'

'That's Marco,' Martina corrected matter-of-factly. She succeeded in jabbing her finger deep into my soft flesh. 'And you promised me this morning that you would spend every remaining minute you have on Samos with me!'

'Every minute? I actually said that?'

'Yes, you did. Liar.'

I quickly scrutinised the creased faces of both women for any hint of violence. She might have looked like a model from a Rembrandt painting, but Lottie's fingernails were dangerously long and mischievously sharp, and I could definitely see them being used to scratch out an eye or two. As for Martina, well, did I even have to guess? There would have been no constraints with her. Shoes, belts, nailfiles, perfume bottles—virtually anything she could get her hands on.

'Okay, you win,' I conceded rather pathetically. 'I will go, but only for a few hours.'

The café was overflowing with patrons by the time we arrived, but we somehow managed to secure our favourite outside table. Not unexpectedly, this just happened to be as far away as possible from Marco, who, true to form, had moved inside to chat up some Swiss girl with blonde pigtails. For competing reasons, this development suited all three of us, and we soon relaxed with a couple of bottles of Riesling and a large plate of seafood.

Disturbingly, Martina—the porn queen—and Lottie—Little Miss Muffet—promptly fell into their own private conversation while I was left as a mere passenger on the sidelines. My only role now, it seemed, was to nod occasionally at some obscure comment either of them made about Ephesus. On the one occasion I interrupted Martina to correct her about something she had just said about the amphitheatre, both girls collectively gave me the evil eye and told me to shut up. If someone could explain to me how the female mind worked, this was probably a good a time as any.

We were soon joined at the table by Franco, the birthday boy, and the wonderfully elegant Marlena, and this became an ideal excuse to indulge in more wine. With a bottle in one hand, a glass in the other, and my natural charm and wit all around me, any subversive thoughts I had about Lottie and Martina's booming friendship were soon forgotten.

At some point during the night, Lottie hived off to another table to talk to some German guy named Dieter, while Martina, Marlena, and Julia dragged themselves into a women-only conversation about having babies. With everyone suitably distracted, I decided that it was the perfect time to return to the safety of my hotel room.

But as soon as I withdrew my legs from beneath the table, my conscience got the better of me, and I briefly stopped to consider whether it was rather impolite for a gentleman to leave without first saying goodbye. Unfortunately, by the time I realised that I wasn't really a gentleman, that one crucial millisecond of hesitation proved costly.

The catalyst for most disasters usually derived from some nondescript event that didn't seem all that important at the time. On this occasion, it would be some clumsy sod spilling red wine all over my white T-shirt.

'You should wash that out now, or it will stain,' suggested stickybeak Martina.

'Sure,' I mumbled, disgruntled that my plan had been shredded.

The nearest bathroom was inside the café, so I slowly made my way through a line of intoxicated bodies before I finally reached my destination. By pure coincidence, the bathroom door squeaked open and out popped Marco, looking snappy as always in a black heavy-metal T-shirt and dark-blue jeans. When he recognised me through his alcoholic haze, his eyes lit up, and he threw an arm around my chest.

'Alex,' he slurred, 'I have hardly seen you these last two days.'

On a scale of drunkenness out of ten, Marco was operating at a seven or an eight, while I was hovering around a five. This didn't excuse in any way what was about to happen, but it didn't necessarily help, either.

'You wanted me to spend time with Martina, so I have,' I replied coldly.

'I am so happy that you eventually saw things my way.'

'I bet you are.'

My sarcasm soared right past Marco's dopey face. Indeed, his only reaction was to tug at my arm some more.

'Is tonight the big night?' he pondered excitedly, his mouth crumbling into an imbecilic grin.

'What do you mean?' I asked, despite already knowing the answer.

'What do I mean? Are you crazy? Are you going to fuck Martina tonight or what?'

'You'd like that, wouldn't you?'

By now, the monster inside of me was tugging wildly at the walls of my stomach.

I am ready to come out, Alex, it howled angrily at me.

'Can I give you one bit of advice before you do the deed?' Marco whispered. 'She is a real screamer, that one. Can blow the ceiling down on top of you if you are not careful. But there is one good way to shut her up.' He laughed as if what he said next would be the funniest thing he said in his life. 'Just do what comes naturally. Understand? Because she gives the best head ever, my friend.'

Remarkably, despite such an offensive, derogatory comment directed at a woman I actually cared about; I somehow found a way to remain unreasonably calm. 'No doubt she does. And I am sure if you ask those Serbian soldiers, they will probably agree with you.'

Marco's mouth dropped into his chest. 'What do you mean? What Serbian soldiers?'

'The ones that gang-raped her, you fucking bastard!'

The monster had clawed its way well and truly to the surface.

Marco's tiny brain somehow tried to compute this new piece of information.

'She was gang-raped?' he finally said. 'Really?'

I squeezed my hands in front of his face. 'Give me a break, Marco. You're not trying to tell me that you never suspected anything?'

'I had an inkling that something happened to her during the war,' he said, with a carefree nod of his head.

'You had an inkling?' I suddenly shrieked at the top of my voice.

Everyone inside the café watched while the monster exploded headfirst out of my stomach.

'You thought there was something wrong, but you never bothered to find out what?'

Marco tried to touch my arm in a futile attempt to calm me down. 'Look, we don't have that type of relationship. We shag. We drink. We eat. That's about it. Deep conversations are not our cup of tea.'

I bent my face towards him so that our eyes were directly lined up. 'Yet that didn't stop you from pimping Martina around to other men like Tom, Karl, and God knows who else.'

'She told you that?' he asked.

'Yes. Do you deny it?'

'No, Alex—'

I didn't let him finish. Maybe I should have allowed him to explain, but by then, the monster had ripped a hole in me the size of a crater, and all it cared about was satisfying its thirst for vengeance.

'The way that I see it, Marco, this makes you no better than the scum who gang-raped her.'

It might sound crazy, but I immediately regretted saying those words. Sure, Marco was a proper arsehole whose immoral and decadent views about women contradicted any concept of ordinary decency. But to have compared him with the brutes who had violently abused Martina was not only unfair but also unnecessarily provocative.

I could offer several reasons for my stupidity: alcohol, my mental state, or the distress I felt about Martina's story. But in the end, it was none of those things. You see, Marco would forever be one of those guys who romped through life, never having to be accountable for his actions. As soon as he did something wrong, all he had to do was flex those biceps, push out that astonishing smile, and suddenly, everything would be forgiven. It was guys like me who ultimately suffered the consequences of other men's poor behaviour and never got anything in return. No, just this once, Marco needed to take responsibility for his relationship with Martina, and I refused to do it for him anymore.

Unsurprisingly, Marco didn't quite see it my way. It took several seconds for my words to sink past the barriers created by several hours of nonstop drinking. But once they did, his face turned into a lump of incandescent rage. He quickly pushed me up against the wall with his muscular forearms and twisted my left arm behind my neck.

'How dare you speak to me like that, you fucking bastard!' he bellowed. 'You don't know anything about Martina and me'.

'I know enough to realise that you treat her like shit.'

Marco did what all cowards did when they had an advantage over you. He raised his fist menacingly, and when I was not looking for a millisecond, whacked me hard across the cheekbone. Surprisingly, it didn't hurt very much. In fact, it felt a lot like being hit with wet lettuce. At this stage of my life, years of constant army reserve work ensured that I was in good physical shape.

With a natural fighter's instinct I didn't realise I possessed, I quickly released myself from Marco's sterile grip and jabbed him with a well-timed uppercut to his exposed jaw, causing him to reel backwards into a table. It was not an especially hard punch, but the way he carried on, you swear he had just been hit by a world heavyweight champion.

'You bastard, I will get you for that,' Marco moaned. He steadied himself onto his rubbery legs and prepared his body for another lunge at my head. But before he could execute his next plan, a pair of sturdy arms grasped him around the shoulders and pulled him away from me.

'What the hell is going on here?' demanded Franco.

'Why don't you ask Marco how he just hit me with a cheap shot?' I snarled back at him.

'You deserved it!' Marco shouted at me. 'I go out of my way to invite you to Samos, to introduce you to my friends and show you a good time. And this is how you repay me?'

I laughed hysterically into his smug, clueless face. 'You take me for a fool, Marco. This was never about me. Rather, it was about you wanting to big-note yourself with Martina and your friends. Everything in your life is about satisfying your pathetic ego.'

Marco attempted to struggle out of Franco's iron grip, while the owner of the café threatened to kick us out if we didn't all calm down.

'You are way out of line, Alex,' said Franco coldly. At first, I was taken back by the ferocity of his words. I thought more of him, to be honest, especially after last night when we all bonded together over Monopoly. But I shouldn't have been that surprised: birds of a feather and all that.

'Trust a couple of piss-weak wankers to stick together,' I growled at them.

'Leave now, Alex,' demanded Franco, his eyes bulging. 'You are not welcome here anymore.' He lifted his shoulders at me aggressively, signalling that he was also willing to use force himself if necessary to get his way. Given that whole 'two versus one thing', it was time to reconsider my options.

Admitting defeat, I dropped my head in despair and turned to walk outside, suitably humiliated by my impotence. You might think that Marco would have taken the win provided to him by Franco and shut the hell up, but that was never going to be his style.

'You don't belong in our world, Alex,' he announced to the entire bar.

Fortunately, I wasn't about to let that slide without a smart-arse riposte. 'You know, Marco,' I roared back at him, 'in the short time I have known you, that's the only sensible thing I have ever heard you say.'

'Well, go then,' he screamed. 'Go back to that pathetic desk job of yours and never come back. You dumb Australian bastard.'

An English skinhead type, spoiling for a fight, offered to help me out if I decided to take offence at Marco's latest insult. I thanked him for his trouble, told him to enjoy his beer, and then hustled my way back through the noisy crowd.

By now, word had passed around about an altercation inside the café. When everyone saw me storm outside into the courtyard with Marco and Franco following in hot pursuit, the dots all began to join.

'Alex, what is going on?' asked Martina when I returned to our table. I immediately looked across towards Lottie and sent her a whispered SOS while Dieter madly tried to regain her attention.

'I'm leaving, Martina,' I replied, holding my cheek. 'Unfortunately, your boyfriend and I no longer see eye to eye on the state of the world.'

'What did you say to him, Alex?' Before I could answer her question, she collected her handbag from the ground and stood up to join me.

'Where the hell do you think you are going, Martina?' Marco howled when he reached our table.

'I'm going with Alex,' she said firmly.

'You want to leave with that fucking loser?'

'That's what you always wanted, Marco, wasn't it? What was the conversation we had the other day? That I needed a raw Australian inside of me? You sick bastard.'

Marlena reached out and touched Martina on the arm. 'Please don't, sweetheart.'

She glared back at Marlena. 'No, I am sick of this shit. You all sit here with your fake smiles and fake tans and pretend that Marco is fucking God or something. None of you seem to care that he is a vile human being without one shred of decency.'

'If that's the case,' interrupted Marco, 'why have you hung around me like a bad smell for the last year? You disrespectful little bitch!'

It was good for him that he was standing behind Julia and Marlena, given that even I wouldn't dare jump across their table to hit him.

'I have often asked myself that very same question,' said Martina. 'But it doesn't matter anymore. We are through, Marco, and I never want to see your stupid face again.'

It was painstakingly obvious that Marco didn't like women breaking up with him, especially in front of his friends, because as soon as Martina did, he childishly stamped his feet several times on the ground. 'Well, go then, see if I care! You are nothing more to me than a cheap whore!'

The situation quickly descended into total bedlam. Ironically, it was the usually calm and collected Lottie who initiated the next phase of the drama. When she heard Marco's latest insult, she bounced up from her seat and positioned herself directly in his line of sight.

Marco initially studied her with a quizzical stare, as if he had forgotten that he tried to hit on this very same woman only forty-eight hours earlier. 'What the hell are you looking at?' he raged at her.

Lottie pointed one of her sharp fingernails right at his face. Man, she looked so beautiful, yet so dangerous. 'I have always wanted to know what a total prick looks like. Thank you for showing me.'

Dieter, who I worked out was one of Marco's best friends, told Lottie to shut her mouth and sit back down. I couldn't imagine that his intervention would go down too well with her, and she didn't disappoint me. Smiling to herself, Lottie calmly ambled back to her table, as ordered, but then picked up her own wine glass and poured the remaining contents right over Dieter's crotch. 'That's what I think of you and your pathetic attempts to get me into bed.'

'You filthy little whore,' he screamed at Lottie as if he was obliged to follow Marco's use of that word. Luckily, he scampered off to the bathroom before Lottie could contemplate her next vengeful move.

'Why don't you all just get out of here!' shrieked Kitty, who suddenly appeared at the table with Tom behind her. 'None of us like any of you!'

Okay, if we were all going to revert to kindergarten, then I would throw my hat in the ring as well and declare that I didn't particularly like Kitty. Neither was I overly sympathetic to that overweening, Chelsea-supporting boyfriend of hers. But when it came to hating Kitty, Martina was in a league of her own and what happened next brought this to a whole new level.

'You should ask Tom what he thinks of me,' she began with an evil smirk.

No, Martina, please don't do it.

'What do you mean by that?' demanded Kitty, although she must have suspected something.

'Well, a few weeks ago in Vienna, when I was on top of Tom in bed, he kept yelling out, "I love you, Martina, I love you!"'

It was one of those moments that belonged to the ages. Everything went totally still, while everyone tried to pretend that they didn't just hear what they actually just heard.

Kitty's woozy blue eyes dilated straight out of her head, and she tossed her hand away from Tom's grasp. 'Is this true, you bastard?'

'Which part?' was Tom's somewhat dopey reply.

That simply nailed it for Kitty. She reached over for Marlena's glass of champagne, embraced it with both hands, and then smashed it deftly on top of Tom's head. The daft bugger just stood there in total confusion as fragments of glass and streams of bubbly rippled down his face.

'This is all your fault, Martina,' Julia reassured us as she rushed over to put her arm around her distressed friend.

'Oh, enough from you, sweet cheeks,' retorted Martina. 'You should ask your own boyfriend how much he enjoyed banging me from behind in your Athens hotel room.'

For the love of God, here we go again.

As soon as Julia processed this life-changing bit of information, she released herself from Kitty's arms and unleashed a wild scream in Karl's direction, who by now was trying to help clean up the mess that was Tom's face.

'I was drunk,' admitted Karl in front of all of us, somehow expecting that this excuse was actually going to curry favour with Julia.

Look, I wasn't a cruel person, but neither did I have any sympathy for what happened next. Yes, I really didn't like Julia all that much; but really, what idiot wore high heels in the middle of a mountainous island like Samos anyway?

When she heard her boyfriend's solemn plea for understanding, Julia picked up her skirt and dashed clumsily through the collection of tables in front of us, presumably on a mission to break down in the private comfort of her bedroom. But once she reached the footpath, she tripped over one of her heels and undertook a series of superbly timed half-pikes before landing serenely next to a garbage bin. To make matters worse, I could hear the snap of her left leg even from where I was standing.

'I've broken my ankle!' she cried out in agony while simultaneously checking whether her expensive new lipstick had just tumbled down a nearby drain.

Lottie placed a hand around Martina's waist. 'Listen, gorgeous, if you have slept with anyone else here, I'd probably keep that to myself for the time being.'

Despite the unfolding chaos, Martina's immediate instinct was to rush over to where Julia was lying prostrate on the ground to provide her with first aid. But Julia was made of sterner stuff.

'Get away from me, you horrible person!' she screeched at Martina as she clutched her injured ankle. She momentarily stared into an oncoming raincloud before screaming out: 'Karl! Karl! Please help me!'

We all took a step back and created some space for Karl to reach his soon to be ex-girlfriend. As he kneeled on the ground, trying to calm her down, Franco moved to wedge himself between me and Marco, Tom, and Kitty.

'This is my last warning to all three of you,' he announced. 'Go away and never show your faces here again.'

If that guaranteed the end of 'high noon', then so be it. But of course, Marlena, a quiet observer up to this point, had to deliver those immortal words.

'Who gives you the right to make that decision, Franco?'

You could cut the air with a knife. The happiest couple on this whole damn island was about to enter the gates of Hades together.

'What are you talking about, Marlena?' Franco sneered. 'You're not taking their side, are you?'

Marlena was only about five foot four and very slender, but as soon as she stood up to face Franco head-on, he started to shake in his boots. Her face was flushed red with anger, and her sea-blue eyes were filled with venom.

'Well, I'm certainly not taking his side,' Marlena pointed at Marco. She stared fiercely into Marco's cowering eyes. 'Just for the record, everything Martina said before is true. The callous way that you treat her and every other woman you get your filthy hands on just disgusts me.'

Lottie tugged at my shirt. 'I didn't see that coming,' she whispered to me.

'This is not going to end well,' I promised her.

Indeed, Marco's watermelon head bulged at Marlena in anger. 'I expect nothing less from a whiny little bitch like you,' he thundered. 'How Franco puts up with your endless complaining every day is beyond me.'

We all looked at Marco, then Marlena, and then Franco.

Marlena raised her fist at her boyfriend. 'Are you just going to stand there and let him speak to me like that?'

I could tell that Franco was conflicted. He had to make that one decision that every man dreaded: choosing between your best friend and girlfriend. I had been there, done that, and it wasn't something I ever hoped to do again. There were never any winners in these situations, only years of regret and recrimination. *So choose wisely, Franco, because if you don't, your life will be screwed forever.*

'Apologise to Marco,' Franco ordered Marlena, even though it was obvious to everyone that he regretted his words before he even finished the sentence. But it was far too late for him to turn back now, and we could only collectively shake our heads in disbelief.

'I see,' Marlena replied calmly. Her voice betrayed no sense of surprise or disappointment at Franco's remarks. Instead, she searched for Martina's hand and coaxed her onto the footpath. 'Let's get you back to your hotel room, sweetheart,' she said softly.

'Did you hear what I said, Marlena?' Franco demanded more aggressively, as if emboldened by Marco's approving smile.

I gave it some serious thought and decided that this was the perfect time to escalate the situation further. Without concern for my safety—or anyone else's, for that matter—I stepped into the space that existed between Franco and the girls and shouted loudly into his face. 'How can you treat Marlena like that, you dickhead? You don't deserve a woman like her!' Yes, that was me all over—the perfect man for a crisis!

The roles had, peculiarly, flipped and this time it was Marco's turn to stop Franco from turning me into his personal tea towel.

'Easy, my friend. He is only a bit player in this circus.' He pointed the finger at Martina. 'It's that fucking Bosnian bitch over there. Mark my words; she has poisoned everyone against us.' He stepped back onto the footpath and summoned all the contempt and hatred he could find within himself. There was absolutely no other rational way to explain why he said what he said next.

'I am glad those Serbian soldiers raped you,' he shouted so loudly that the entire café could clearly hear him. 'I hope you think about them every night.'

As I began to contemplate the best way of separating his head from his torso, Martina reached across with her open palm and slapped me hard on the very same cheek that Marco had hit just minutes before.

'You didn't! How could you?' she hollered at me.

'Which question would you like me to answer first?' I asked her, checking to see if all of my teeth were still intact.

Martina exploded into tears, and Marlena placed a solitary arm around her shoulders.

'It's not what you think, Martina,' I pleaded with her. 'Please let me explain.'

'Not now, Alex!' Marlena barked at me. 'Just help me get Martina back to her hotel room.'

The four of us began to march down the road in single file, Marco's ongoing abuse constantly ringing in our ears wherever we turned. Marlena took the lead, followed by an overly distraught Martina behind her, while Lottie casually joined me at the end of the queue with all the other slithering nightcrawlers.

'Very impressive, Alex,' she said, in between stifled giggles. 'In the space of fifteen minutes, you started two fights, helped destroy four relationships as well as several long-term friendships, and also contributed to a girl breaking her leg. What's next?'

'I'm not sure,' I replied glumly. 'Perhaps I'll visit Santorini tomorrow and see what damage I can do out there.'

Much to her credit, Lottie clapped her hands in support and encouraged me to follow my dream.

The Promise

Samos Island
May 1995

Martina's hotel room smelt of freshly picked roses, but that did nothing to alleviate our sullen mood. Once we were all inside, Lottie encouraged Martina to sit on a small, moth-bitten couch, together with several boxes of tissues and a flick-knife, while Marlena made her a cup of tea. Meanwhile, I had been relegated to the kitchen, along with the used dishes, the sour milk, and an overly concerned cockroach and told by Marlena, or Lottie, or Martina—or perhaps all three women—to keep my mouth shut.

'I don't want to stay on Samos a minute longer than I have to,' Martina sobbed in between sips of tea. 'I will leave on the morning ferry to Chios.'

'Good idea,' agreed Marlena. 'We will help you pack.'

'There's no need,' said Martina. 'Most of my belongings are in storage. I just need to throw some clothes and toiletries into a suitcase.'

That was music to my ears. 'Well, now that's all settled,' I muttered from behind the fridge. 'I should really get going.'

'You're not going anywhere,' Marlena barked at me. 'If I know Marco, he will turn up here later tonight, extremely drunk, demanding to see Martina. God knows what he will do to her if he gets the chance.'

'I think Martina should decide whether she wants me to stay or not,' I replied sternly.

'Of course I want you to stay, Alex,' she cried.

I turned to Lottie for some moral support, but all she did was offer me another one of her impertinent grins. *Man, she really does enjoy seeing me squirm. What do you do in your spare time, honey? Pull wings off butterflies?*

'Good—that's settled,' said Marlena. 'In the meantime, I should get back to the café and see if I still have a boyfriend.'

Martina and Marlena performed a bizarre mid-air hug that defied every known principle of aerodynamics. 'I love you, sweetheart,' said Marlena, wiping a tear from Martina's fragile cheek. 'I will say goodbye to you in the morning at the terminal.'

Marlena then frogmarched me back into the kitchen. 'And as for you—you better look after her, or you will have me to answer to. Understood?'

'Understood,' I gulped nervously.

Once Marlena left, Lottie tried to keep us entertained with her hilarious impersonation of Dieter before announcing that she had to leave as well. Her parents would be worried about her—the usual feigned excuses. She gave Martina a reassuring hug and then allowed me to escort her to the door.

'You really know how to show a girl a good time.' She grinned. 'Let's do this again real soon.'

'Do you want me to walk you home?'

Lottie laughed in my face. 'Don't take this the wrong way, but I would feel a lot safer if I walked home by myself.'

She was smart enough, though, to work out from my extra-stooped shoulders that I had, indeed, taken it the wrong way.

'Oh, stop sulking,' she reprimanded me. 'We are staying in the apartment block next door, so it will barely take me thirty seconds.'

'Sure.' I sulked just a little more.

Despite herself, Lottie edged closer towards me. 'Assuming that Franco, Martina, Tom, Kitty, Marlena, Karl, and Marco don't end up killing you tonight,' she began, 'how about we meet tomorrow afternoon at the ferry terminal for a coffee before you leave for Piraeus. A deal?'

I mumbled back an undignified 'Yes,' and she kissed me on the cheek just for good measure, leaving a smidgin of her musky perfume laced across my sweat-stained shirt. Long after she left, its lingering presence was a constant reminder of my deepening attraction to her.

Once I closed the door behind Lottie, I walked back into the living room where Martina had strategically set up her forces in front of the sofa, ready to strike at the whim of her command.

'What do you have to say for yourself, Alex?' she asked.

Bloody hell. Was this day ever going to end?

I adroitly bypassed the obstacle course that she had laid out before me and calmly outlined the events that led to my fight with Marco. When I finished my story, she finally ordered the Alsatians to bed and offered me her own stymied version of an apology.

'I should not have slapped you,' she conceded, her crazy black eyes darting across her face. 'I hope we can put this behind us.'

'It's forgotten already.'

'Even though we both know that I should have cut off your balls and fed them to a tiger shark,' she added.

'You have every reason to be angry with me. I betrayed your confidence, and that was unforgivable.'

Martina wiped her nose again and then tossed a selection of used tissues into a nearby bin. 'I know that you were trying to protect me, and for that, I am incredibly grateful. But I warned you this afternoon to leave it alone.'

'I couldn't, don't you understand?' I pleaded with her. 'The way he talked about you, the way he treated you. I was unable to control my anger any longer.'

'You should have tried harder.'

'I couldn't let him talk about you like that, I just couldn't. You … me … I just don't know.'

'I heard you the first time, Alex.'

'I just can't let them talk about you like that … I can't let them do that to you … I just can't.'

That definitely was me talking, but then again, how could I be sure? For I was standing high above my body, watching some other guy who looked like me juggle hand grenades in the air. Before I could make any sense of the situation, I was writhing on the ground, watching my tears trickle down my skinny arms.

'Oh my God, Alex, what's wrong? Why are you crying?'

I am crying. What the hell is she talking about? I never cry. Didn't I explain this to her in Ephesus?

Martina quickly tucked her hands underneath my armpits and somehow found the strength to drag me back onto the couch. 'What's wrong, Alex?' she seemed to repeat over and over again. 'Please stop crying.'

Yes, stop crying, you goddamn loser.

She managed to pull my body towards her, and I greedily squeezed my head in between her heaving breasts.

'How could God let those things happen to you?' I cried. 'It is so unfair. I just don't understand any of it.'

Martina gently rubbed the bottom of my scalp until, by a stroke of alchemy, the two of us completely ran out of tears at the same time.

'I am so sorry, Martina,' I whispered. 'I don't know what came over me. I haven't been myself since we left Ephesus.'

Martina placed a finger to my lips. 'We don't need to talk about this anymore, Alex. Just come to bed with me. This is our time.' Somewhere in the back of my mind, I couldn't help but wonder whether this was always her intention.

Our mouths were only several seconds apart, but it was long enough for me to realise that I had reached a pivotal juncture in my life. Everything changed if I proceeded with this kiss or went the next step and made love to her. My relationship with Rachel, my career, my friendships, the Spiders, the whole box and dice. Because if I succumbed to Martina's advances now, I would become completely intoxicated by her world and never want to leave.

No, I cannot destroy what I have worked so hard to keep.

I suddenly pulled myself away from her confused face, realising how close I had come to total self-annihilation.

'I'm sorry,' was the only explanation I could find. 'But I can't do this.'

At first, Martina appeared to take my rejection surprisingly well. 'I understand, Alex,' she insisted before reaching out for her multi-barrel shotgun.

'It would be a betrayal,' I reassured her.

'Yes, it would be,' she said calmly, after releasing a cartridge into the chamber. 'But who would you be betraying? Rachel or Lottie?'

'I don't know what you mean.'

'Oh, knock it off, lover boy,' she replied scornfully. 'I see the way that you look at Lottie. It's not the same way you look at me. And I would bet a million American dollars that it wouldn't be the same way you look at Rachel, either.'

'That's nonsense,' I protested. 'You can't possibly know how I feel about these things.'

'Then you're a bigger liar than I thought you were.'

I could cope with being abused, punched, and slapped, but I wasn't going to sit there and have my integrity questioned as well. Fuck everyone: it was time for me to leave.

'Please don't go,' Martina begged. 'I don't want to be alone tonight.'

I couldn't be bothered arguing with her any longer, so I reluctantly agreed to stay. We shared a mutually soothing pot of tea before Martina convinced me that the safest place for us to hide from Marco was anywhere but her hotel room. After a flustered search in her bedroom, I stole a woollen blanket from a cupboard, and she soon led me through a maze of cobbled streets until we arrived at an old, secluded pontoon camouflaged by a circle of citrus trees.

'Marco will never find us here,' Martina promised me. She pointed to an old wooden bench that directly overlooked the ocean below us and invited me to sit down next to her. The midnight winds that had swelled from the south began to roar ominously towards us, forcing Martina to unravel her blanket over our legs. Once she snuggled her body next to mine, Martina rested her head on my shoulder, and we sat quietly like this while a trillion stars twinkled carelessly above us.

'Do you enjoy being in the army?' she suddenly asked. After everything that had occurred that night her question caught me completely off guard.

'Let's make sure that I have properly understood you,' I said. 'I reveal your darkest secret to your boyfriend, he and I fight, you break up with him, you then slap me across the face, I reject your sexual advances, and now you want to know whether I enjoy being in the army?'

'Yeah, that's right.' Martina looked at me hopefully.

I figured that the easiest thing to do at that point was to simply comply with her wishes. So I explained to her that I was only an army reserve officer, who served approximately seventy days a year. My obligations were much different than those of a full-time soldier.

'I do enjoy it,' I admitted. 'It keeps me fit, and I love being outdoors.'

'But if Australia went to war, would you have to fight?' she asked.

'In some circumstances, yes.'

'Could you do it, then?'

'Do what?'

'Could you hurt a woman, like how those animals hurt me?'

My skin went cold. *Why on earth would she ask me such a question?*

'How am I supposed to answer that?'

She looked surprised at my response. 'You mean to say that you don't know whether you could hurt a woman or not?'

'That's not what I meant at all, Martina. I just don't do hypotheticals.'

'Personally, I don't think you could hurt anyone,' she insisted.

'If that makes you feel better, fine.'

'But it's worrying that you couldn't give me a direct answer.'

Oh, for Pete's sake. 'Can any of us predict what we will do in the future?'

'I know the evil that exists within some men. But I don't see it in you.'

'Then why ask me the question in the first place?' I responded irritably.

'I have my reasons.'

'Do you want to tell me what they are? Because I'm not even sure why we are talking about this.'

'I want to understand how you think about yourself.'

'Oh, sweet Lord, save me,' I cried out into the night.

We collapsed into yet another awkward silence before we began to giggle at each other's pettiness. I used this latest outbreak of laughter to explain a few things to her.

'As you know, the situation in Yugoslavia during the Second World War was a highly complex one,' I began. 'While various local guerrilla groups fought against the Germans and Italians, they also fought against each other. My Father often found himself fighting both the Nazis and the local communists at the same time. The horror of his wartime experiences never left him until the day he died.'

'I'm so sorry, Alex.'

'Dad was a big shot, too,' I continued. 'He worked for the British as a spy and led a guerrilla brigade during the closing days of the war.'

'Did he ever discuss things with you?'

A good question. I thought back to those times when it was just the two of us in the lounge room, watching some old war movie together on television. How often did I want to ask him about his exploits? How many times did I want to know what it felt like to walk into battle? But whenever I tried to raise these issues with him, something always prevented me from going further.

Except for that one occasion.

'We were watching this B-grade movie one night,' I continued. 'It was set in wartime Yugoslavia and portrayed the local guerrillas as rabid Nazi sympathisers, complete with long, flowing beards, riding beautiful white stallions into battle. My father could barely control his rage.'

'I saw that movie too,' said Martina. 'It was total rubbish.'

'After he calmed down, I finally summoned the courage to ask him about the war.'

'And what did he say?'

I somehow played out that night in my head.

'Please, Dad, tell me,' I asked him with those inquisitive teenage eyes. 'I need to understand what you did in the war.'

He looked at me with an air of resignation, as if he knew that this was one conversation with me he could no longer avoid.

'There is an evil that exists within every man that only reveals itself during wartime,' he said solemnly. 'I pray, my son, that you never have to find this out for yourself.'

'He was right,' Martina replied. 'As I said to you this afternoon, war turns ordinary men into vicious killers and rapists.'

'Ordinary men,' I whispered at the wind. 'My father was indeed an ordinary man, yet he lived his entire life running away from a war that he never understood. As a result, I have spent most of my life determined not to follow him down that same path.'

'That doesn't mean that you are capable of doing bad things, Alex,' Martina said. 'We are all born different. We all make different choices.'

'If that's true, then why do I always feel so scared about everything?'

Martina gently stroked my prickly face. Unlike before in the hotel room, her touch was not sexual, but one that exhibited a resolute kindness.

'Maybe it's because you are hiding something,' she replied.

'You are not going to bring up Lottie again, are you?'

She shook her head vigorously and, for some reason, that made me very afraid. 'It's about what happened this afternoon in Ephesus. That stuff about not crying when your father died was never your big secret, was it? You were going to say something else, but you changed your mind at the very last moment.'

'How could you possibly know that?' I snarled.

'I could see the fear in your eyes.'

I drifted my head towards the sea so she couldn't bear witness to my latest batch of tears.

Who in God's name was this woman?

Why couldn't she leave me alone?

'You owe me a secret, Alex,' said Martina.

'Some secrets should remain locked away forever.'

'But I told you mine.'

As if I needed reminding.

'That was your choice, Martina. I didn't force you to tell me your story. In fact, it would have been better for both of us if you hadn't.'

'That's very cruel.' She glared at me.

'Cruelty works both ways, Martina. Your insistence that I tell you something that I don't want to discuss is also rather cruel, don't you think?'

'I am just concerned for you, Alex,' Martina retorted. 'If you choose to ignore your past, it will only catch up with you once you get older.'

'That's a bit rich coming from you,' I replied. 'The woman who won't discuss her rape with anyone except for some dumb Australian she meets by chance on an obscure Greek island.' My belligerence had gone too far this time, but I was over this shit for one night.

Martina silently stared into my eyes. Never had she looked so beautiful, so vulnerable, as she did at that point. 'I don't want you to experience the same pain that I have been forced to endure every day for the last three years.' She began to cry. 'I lost hope a long time ago, but there is still some for you.'

'Please don't say that, Martina.' I threw myself into her arms until her tears tore into my sweat-stained shirt.

As befitting of such a crazy, fucked-up day, we remained locked together like this for over an hour, her head resting quietly on the nape of my neck, my face draped inside her wild, tangled hair. Inside this tiny microcosm of despair, nothing else in the world mattered to me more than this strange, tormented woman. As I sat trapped within her bosom, I never felt as close to another person in my life as I did right then. It was as if we each possessed one half of the same soul and after all these years of searching, destiny had at last found a way to bring our pieces together. It was a thoroughly surreal experience that would haunt me for decades to come.

Just after one-thirty, Martina reassured me that it was safe to return to her room. Marco, if she knew him at all, would either be screwing some other woman or snoring loudly in his bed. She wanted to pack her things and have a quick nap before she caught her ferry in the morning.

We walked back into town in total silence, both knowing that our brief but tempestuous time together was about to come to an end. When we arrived at the front gate of her hotel, we did our best not to look at each other.

'I guess this is goodbye, Alex,' she murmured sadly. '"All good things must come to an end", and all that bullshit.'

Despite the recriminations of the last few hours, my heart was desperately looking for a reason to justify its existence, and suddenly, out of nowhere, it came up with this crazy idea. 'Listen, Martina, this doesn't have to be the end. Why can't we still remain friends?'

'Are you serious?' she asked. 'You are going back to your girl in Australia, and I have to move on with my life. And I definitely don't have time for penpals.'

'Just because I have a girlfriend doesn't mean that we can't keep in contact with each other. I will likely return to Europe next year. We can meet up anywhere you like, far away from Samos.'

'You really want to be my friend?'

'Aren't we friends already?'

'I am not sure what you mean to me,' she said. 'Tonight, I wanted to screw you, mother you, and kill you all in the space of five minutes. You bring out far too many raw emotions in me, Alex. And after what Marco did to me tonight, the last thing I need is to have another man hurt me, even if he is just a friend.'

'I would never hurt you in a million years.'

Really, Alex? You might want to think that one through.

'To use your own words, how do you know that? You don't do hypotheticals, remember?'

'Touché. Trust me when I say that I wouldn't.'

'You really want to be my friend?' she repeated as if the whole concept made no sense to her.

'How many times do you want me to answer? Of course I do. If it now ended like this, I would always worry about you.'

She cleverly identified the one weakness in my argument. 'Is this the real reason you want to keep in contact with me? To satisfy your guilt over what happened tonight?'

'How about this for a reason?' I retorted. 'I actually care about you.'

'I care about you as well.'

'Then, why are we even debating this?'

Martina twisted her head in deep contemplation before landing back on my face. 'Okay, there is a post office box I use in Vienna, and I clear my mail maybe five, six times a year. Come down to the ferry terminal tomorrow morning at eight-thirty, and I will provide you with the details.'

'Thank you,' I replied. However, nothing about this night was straightforward. She suddenly swivelled her hand upwards towards the sky as if she was about to touch the moon. 'Not so fast, mister. I will give you my address on one condition. You have to tell me your big secret. If we are to be the best of friends, I need to see the real person, not the one that is currently hiding behind a wall of lies.'

'That's blackmail,' I growled.

'No, it's just the way it is. No secret, no address. Your choice—take it or leave it. Now, I suggest that you go home and sleep on it.'

'You're incorrigible.'

'And you wouldn't have it any other way.'

Somehow, Martina found the energy to fall on top of me, and we squeezed out one last hug. 'You know, we are possibly the world's two most fucked-up people. Have you ever considered that?'

'No, but I will take anything from you at this late stage of the evening.'

'Promise me that you will come to the terminal, regardless of your decision,' she implored, a tinge of concern staining her beautiful face. 'Don't say that you want to be my friend and then not turn up to say goodbye. That would devastate me.'

'I will be there on time, right on eight-thirty. Trust me.'

'I do trust you, Alex. That's why I am so scared.'

She released herself from my arms and skipped towards the hotel courtyard before twirling around on her heels one last time. 'Did you really put heat cream on your haemorrhoids?' she asked, with a glimmer of a smile.

'Yeah, I did.'

Her ruby lips sparkled against the silhouette of a coal-black sky. 'You're such an idiot.'

She blew me a kiss, and I watched her disappear behind a concrete wall.

I would never see her again.

Marlena

Samos
May 1995

The antique clock in the hallway struck two-thirty just as I crept back to my room. I was tired, miserable, emotionally drained, and desperately needed a frozen steak to relieve the pain in my throbbing cheek. As I searched for my room key, I heard some noises emerging from the hallway and turned to find my least favourite Greek teenager grinning at me from behind a flowerpot. He was wearing shorts, a loose-fitting singlet, and carrying a faded, orange basketball.

'Hello, mister,' he said, bouncing the ball against the floor in an effort to impress me.

'Hi there,' I replied rudely. The last thing I needed at that moment was a prolonged conversation with this geezer.

'Will we see you at breakfast, sir?' he asked through a row of gleaming white teeth. 'We were extremely disappointed to miss you yesterday!'

Okay, I may have been tired, miserable, and emotionally drained, but after everything I had gone through, I was definitely not going to let that comment pass without a reply.

'What do you mean, I missed breakfast?' I glowered at him. 'When I came to the dining room in the morning, it was completely empty! I was the only person there!'

'That's a shame, mister,' he replied, totally ignoring my point. 'Because you see, we have the best breakfast in all of Samos. The best!'

All I could do at this point was scratch my head in bewilderment and wonder whether I had been living in an alternate universe for the last twenty-four hours. But as I stared curiously into his blank face, I concocted this rather absurd plan—one that would have drastic ramifications for the rest of my life.

'Listen, kid, can you please do me a favour in the morning? Can you knock on my door at eight o'clock and make sure that I'm awake?'

He beamed excitedly. 'Yes, mister! I can wash your socks, shine your shoes, cut your hair!'

'No!' I waved my hands at him. 'All I want you to do is knock on my door at eight o'clock. Got it?' I pulled out my wallet and passed him some spare change just to square everything away.

'Yes, mister, I got it,' he cried as he greedily stacked his newfound wealth into one of his socks. 'I will knock on your door at nine o'clock.'

'No, not nine o'clock,' I replied impatiently. 'I want you to wake me up at eight o'clock.'

Just to confirm my instructions in a more practical way, I held up five fingers on my left hand and three fingers on my right hand. When he repeated the signal back to me, I rewarded him with a thumbs-up sign. Not unexpectedly, given how keen he was to please me, he also shifted his thumb upwards in front of his tiny nose, and then we celebrated with a customary high five.

Back in my room, I produced my small travel clock, manoeuvred the alarm hand exactly onto eight o'clock, and then pressed down on the activation button, just like I had done every other night so far during my holiday. Between my natural body alarm, the travel clock, and the kid, I would safely wake up on time, have a shower, and then meander down to the ferry terminal. I wasn't sure what I would say to Martina when I got there, but I would work all that out along the way. All I cared about was getting that damn address from her. *Is that too much to ask? I mean, what could go wrong?*

*

'Mister, mister! Wake up! It's nine o'clock!' The kid's frantic banging on my door pulled me out of some wretched dream.

Nine o'clock! What the fuck?

I scratched away the cobwebs from my eyes and inspected my cheap alarm clock. What? It was only twenty-five minutes past five! For a fleeting moment, I felt a sense of exhilaration rush through my body as if I had somehow survived the executioner's axe by sheer luck. But the sunlight streaming through my curtains and the constant knocking on the door urged me to recheck my watch. *Oh my God! It really is nine o'clock! The battery in my clock must have died while I was asleep! In fact, now that I think about it some more, I haven't changed it since visiting Liverpool!*

I rolled out of bed, flopped on a fresh T-shirt and my jeans, and then opened the door. Remarkably, the Greek kid was still romping around in his basketball gear, as if he never went to bed.

'What's going on?' I screamed at him. 'I said eight o'clock, not nine o'clock!'

The kid shook his head at me in defiance. 'No, sir—you said nine o'clock. Remember?' He placed eight fingers in front of my nose and then one of his thumbs. 'You see? Eight fingers and one thumb! Nine o'clock!'

Oh my God! Oh my God! Oh my God! Can you believe the extent of this stupidity—especially mine?

'That's not what I meant, you idiot!' I cried. Overwhelmed with panic, I desperately shoved on my runners, stuck my wallet in my pocket, and long-jumped out the door.

'Where are you going, mister?' the kid bawled at me as I pushed him out of the way. 'You must have breakfast first! We have the best breakfast in Samos, mister! The best!'

My first stop was the citrus trees where, barely twenty-four hours before, Martina had been waiting for me. Maybe if I wished hard enough, she would reappear from behind the thickets, teasing me with that wondrous smile as she explained that she had missed her ferry on purpose just to see the look on my face. But the sound of a horn bellowing in the distance bludgeoned me into reality, and I finally realised that the promise I made to Martina last night was all but sinking beneath the deep blue sea.

I arrived at the terminal ten minutes later, out of breath and out of my mind. As I watched the ferry to Chios slowly fade away into a murky horizon, everything around me stood still. Within the withering remnants of my sanity, I found a way to change myself into a werewolf, pulling at my hair as if it was on fire, shrieking and howling aimlessly into the crisp morning air. Without even thinking how I must have looked, I began to sprint up and down the main pontoon with every last drop of energy I had, begging for someone to lend me a boat or a yacht or even a life raft, so I could chase the ferry down and find Martina.

But as I frantically scoured these ancient docks, all I could find at my disposal was the occasional dilapidated fishing trawler floating lazily in the breeze. I doubted whether any of these rust-buckets could even remotely catch up to a turbo-charged ferry with a twenty-minute head start. Unsurprisingly, the bemused faces from a row of moustachioed Greek fishermen, swallowing down their early morning coffees, only reinforced this pathetic observation.

Undeterred, I then came up with my next brilliant plan. This one involved jumping headfirst into the water and swimming madly through a rough tidal surge until I reached the ferry. I was sure that I could do it! *I could do anything if I put my mind to it*!

Of course, only someone who had completely lost his marbles could have come up with such a ridiculous scheme. But here I was, slipping off my shoes, socks, and jeans in front of a crowd of curious onlookers who didn't know whether to laugh or call the local police.

'Alex, what are you doing?' a woman's desperate voice raged across the platform. I turned to see Marlena striding towards me, her long, sandy hair blowing wildly across her face.

She offered the group of locals mulling around me an apologetic frown and convinced them in fluent Greek that it was all a misunderstanding: that we were actually hypersensitive lovers who recently had a very bad fight. She then slid up to my chest and ordered me to get my 'bloody jeans back on, right now'. Despite her embarrassed indignation, Marlena's presence seemed to calm everyone down, especially me, and I quickly reconstituted my clothes just as the crowd began to disperse.

'What the hell were you thinking?' Marlena asked, pointing at the sea. 'Are you totally insane?'

'I missed the ferry, Marlena,' I replied. 'I missed saying goodbye to Martina.'

'Yes, I realise that, maestro. Now, let's get out of here before we are both arrested.' She took my hand and calmly escorted me down a hidden pathway until we arrived at a small, run-down café. For some reason, its faded walls smelt like dog shit, and I desperately felt like retching. Marlena didn't even bother to ask me what I wanted, and she quietly ordered two black coffees.

'What happened to you this morning?' she sneered, her hands thumping the table in front of me. I explained to her about the battery and the clock and the dopey Greek kid, and she rolled her eyes in disbelief. 'You are absolutely clueless, aren't you?'

'I didn't do it deliberately, Marlena,' I replied angrily. I tried to find a sliver of sympathy inside her scornful blue eyes, but there was nothing there. 'It was just one screw-up after another, and I feel bloody terrible about it.'

'I am not here to crucify you, Alex,' she promised me. 'But Martina was terribly upset when you failed to show up.'

My heart sank deep into my bowels. 'On a scale out of ten, how bad was it?'

'I'd say an eleven. She was totally inconsolable. For some reason, she really believed in you, Alex.'

She really believed in you, Alex.

Marlena's last comment cut me deeply, and I said nothing more to her until I finally regained some semblance of composure. 'You really have a poor opinion of me, don't you?' I asked Marlena, just as the waiter delivered our coffees.

'Actually, you are wrong,' Marlena replied. 'I liked you from the very start, and I especially loved the way you treated Martina the other night. But I warned you about getting too involved with her. Instead, you thought you knew it all and ignored my advice. As a result, there are damaged people strewn across the Greek Islands because of your arrogance.'

'You don't understand,' I protested firmly. 'Marco was using her in ways that I can't bear to describe.'

'I know. Martina told me this morning. Not everything, mind you: she seems to have mostly burdened you with that responsibility.' She rolled her head in disbelief at the mere thought of it and then dropped a couple of sugars into her coffee. 'It was commendable that you stood up for her as you did, but in the end, all she wanted you to do was listen to her story. She did not ask you to fight her battles.'

'If not me, then who?'

'Lots of people, but not someone who has his own personal issues to resolve.'

Not for the first time, I was offended by Marlena's brutal disregard for my feelings. 'Are you referring to me?' I asked, childishly pointing to my chest.

'There isn't anyone else here in this dump other than the two of us.'

I glared at her. 'What makes you think I have personal issues?'

'Well, for a start, you're the first person I've met who decided to strip off all their clothes at a public ferry terminal in a futile attempt to swim after a ferry.'

'Oh, that.'

'Yes, that.'

I tried to hide my growing frustration with her. 'Look, I broke a promise to someone I care about very much and temporarily lost the plot. Give me a frigging break.'

Unfortunately, Marlena was not the type of person inclined to give me a frigging break. 'She also told me how you cried last night after Lottie and I left,' she snorted. 'And that you have a secret you were supposed to reveal to her this morning.'

'Gee, thanks Martina,' I replied, grim-faced. 'Did she also broadcast these facts on the local radio station before she left?' If the floor was to have opened up right now, I would have gladly fallen right into it.

'Listen to me, Alex. I am thirty-three years old, and I have been through some tough times. My close friends and family often criticise me for not taking life too seriously, but they didn't have the luxury of seeing their fiancé commit suicide in front of them like I did when I was just twenty-one.'

'I'm sorry to hear that,' I replied with genuine remorse. 'That must have been awful for you.'

'Yes, awful,' she said sadly. 'It's particularly hard when you know that someone you love needs help desperately, but you don't have the life skills to deal with the situation by yourself.' She finished her coffee before pushing the cup away to the side.

'I did try, of course. I put an arm around him every day, promising that things would get better, even though I had no way of knowing whether they would or not. I was simply this young, immature girl just out of my teenage years, obsessed with designer clothes and make-up, trying to help someone with a serious mental illness. But in the end, I failed him.'

'His death was not your fault, Marlena,' I reassured her.

'Of course it was my fault,' she replied. 'My love was supposed to have cured him, but what he needed was professional treatment. In the end, I didn't have the skills to help him overcome his condition, and my feeble efforts only served to damage him even further.'

'So if I am reading you correctly, what you are saying is that I am a clueless busy-body, and I should butt out of other people's lives, especially Martina's.'

'Pretty much,' Marlena said bluntly. 'I am sure you mean well, Alex. But this makes you even more dangerous, in my opinion. People naturally warm to you, and they trust you. But it would be best if you got your own life sorted out first before walking the Earth, offering free advice to the poor and oppressed. Otherwise, you will cause greater damage to those who believe that you can help them, like Martina.'

'There is nothing wrong with me wanting to be her friend, Marlena.'

'For what purpose?' she snapped. 'So that you can string her along for the next few months while thousands of miles away in Australia you are enjoying the fruits of another woman? Or is it because you want to have Martina as a fallback option in case your new relationship falters?'

'That's very unfair,' I said. 'I never even touched Martina, other than to give her a hug when she needed one.'

'Bullshit. She said you kissed her at Ephesus.'

'I did that to comfort her, nothing more.'

'Even if that were true, you must have thought about her in a sexual way,' she pressed me further.

'Of course I did. But nothing happened last night after you left because I made sure that it didn't.'

'So if you saw her again? How long do you think you could hold out?' Before I could answer her, Marlena rubbed her chin. 'Men and women aren't meant to be friends, Alex. Oh, we can pretend to be on a peripheral level, I guess. But sooner or later, the never-ending curse of sexual attraction will always raise its murky head.'

'I don't agree with you,' I replied boldly. 'I have many female friends.'

'Goody for you,' Marlena said sarcastically. 'But Martina never saw you as a friend, did she? To her, you were a knight in shining armour, someone who tried to understand her, someone who could take away her pain. Then you forgot to change the battery in your alarm clock and overslept.'

'That's very harsh,' I grunted. I nodded to the waiter, and he refilled my cup with more scalding coffee.

'You must think that I am a total bitch,' said Marlena. 'But I am just telling you how it is. Martina may have seen the brave knight within you, but all I see is an Australian version of Don Quixote. You are exceptionally well-intentioned, I am sure, but you were playing with fire with a complex, traumatised woman who must now find her own way back into the world. So let it go, Alex. Please.'

My tasteless coffee froze inside my throat. 'Are you saying that I am supposed to forget about her and everything that she told me yesterday?'

I could tell by the intensity of her sighing that the tables had turned, and Marlena was fast losing patience with *me*. 'What is the alternative? Are you thinking about catching a ferry to Chios tomorrow morning and trying to find her?'

'Maybe.'

'Oh, you are a silly fool,' she groaned. 'We both know that there would be no going back if you did—that you would immediately fall under her spell and never leave until she finishes with you. Is that what you want? Because I am not sure that your current girlfriend and family back in Australia would be so understanding.'

Even though I would never admit it to her, Marlena was right. If I followed Martina to Chios, I wouldn't be able to resist her charms for more than a few days. What man in their right mind could?

'All I want to do is explain to her what happened this morning.'

'Does it really matter anymore?' asked Marlena.

'Of course it does. I made such a big thing last night about the need for us to remain friends. I just can't leave Greece with this disaster hanging over my head.'

'She thought you were too scared to reveal your secret to her,' Marlena admitted. 'I think her exact words were, "he is such a self-obsessed coward".'

'And that is supposed to make me feel better?' I replied with a scowl. *Jesus, I wonder if the world could get any shittier than it was right now.*

'Why don't you write to her and explain what happened?' Marlena suggested. 'Did she leave you a forwarding address?'

'No,' I replied glumly. 'That was going to be our trade-off this morning—my secret for her post office box address in Vienna.'

'What about posting a letter to the hospital in Chios?'

'That won't do, either,' I said. 'She is working for a private doctor, not for the hospital. Besides, she wouldn't tell me her real surname. She didn't even tell Marco. Perhaps she was too scared that the Serbian Army would find her—I don't know. But given the efforts she has gone to hide her identity, getting a letter to her is virtually impossible.'

Marlena stuffed a mint into her mouth before touching my hand. 'I am going to regret this, but please give me your contact details in Australia. You see, I gave Martina my phone number this morning in case she needs to talk to me when I get back to Italy. Whether she decides to or not, I have no way of knowing. But if she does call me, I will explain to her what happened today and pass on your number. It's up to her whether she contacts you or not, and I'm not going to get involved in that decision. Okay?'

I quickly produced my last crumpled business card from my wallet and placed it on the table in front of her. 'This has everything you need,' I explained. 'Thank you, Marlena. I appreciate this very much.'

Her generosity, however, came with a catch. 'Everything that I said to you before still stands, Alex. Think very carefully about what you will say to her if she does call. Nothing will be gained by giving her false hope. Explain what happened this morning if you must, then let it go. That is the only proper thing for you to do.'

'All I want is the opportunity to apologise to her, that's all.'

'I'm not sure whether I should believe you or not, but I always have faith that common sense will somehow prevail in people, no matter how stupid they are.'

It was a quarter past ten, and I had to be out of my room in forty-five minutes' time. I paid for the coffees, and Marlena offered to walk back to the hotel with me.

'Just to make sure that you actually leave Samos today,' she said rather acidly.

As we strolled down the main promenade that led back to my hotel, it suddenly occurred to me that I had not yet asked Marlena about her and Franco.

'We decided this morning to have a break from each other,' she calmly announced. If she was upset by this outcome, she was able to hide it remarkably well.

'That sucks,' I said. 'I'm so sorry. Where is he now?'

'Both he and Marco left for Turkey this morning. I am sure that they will have a great time together.' Her last words were spat out with a predictably scathing undertone.

'What about you? Are you okay?'

'I will be fine. I never liked Marco; he had such a destructive influence on our relationship. Franco always changed into a different person whenever he entered our lives. It is best that we deal with this issue now rather than wait until things get more serious between us. We will see what happens when we both get back to Milan. I have had so many breakups in my life that one more isn't going to define me.'

'I feel so responsible for what happened.'

'You were just the torch that lit the fuse,' she reassured me. 'I was the one who picked the shovel up and slammed it right into Marco's stupid face. If it didn't happen last night, it would have happened soon enough. Besides, it was Franco who betrayed me, not you.'

'I have to say, though, you really gave it to Marco.' I smiled mischievously. 'I mean, it was rather impressive.'

'You weren't so bad yourself. Did you really call him and Franco a pair of piss-weak wankers?'

I blushed but nodded my head. 'I regret that like everything else I did last night. I can be such a hothead at times.' We walked a little more before I raised the other thorny issue. 'What about the others? Are they okay?'

Marlena glided a hand through her wavy hair. 'All three couples have now officially broken up, if that's what you mean. Tom and Karl—what complete idiots. What were they thinking?'

'I thought that was fairly obvious,' I offered. 'You said yourself: it's hard for a man to resist Martina.'

'Yet somehow you did,' Marlena replied. Her new grimace was quite brutal.

'Yeah, but I am the Australian Don Quixote, remember?'

Despite herself, Marlena managed to laugh. 'Listen,' she said, 'both Tom and Karl were stomping around like wounded bulls this morning. Make sure that you keep a low profile in the town before you leave. I don't want to find out later tonight that the police are peeling you off the side of the road somewhere.'

'I will be fine, but thanks for the warning. And what about you? When are you going to leave Samos?'

'I am not sure yet. I am waiting for Julia and Kitty to come back from the hospital this morning. A lot will depend on when Julia is able to travel again. I can't just leave them both here, especially after everything that's happened. They are my friends, after all.'

We finally reached my hotel before we turned to face each other one last time. 'Maybe we will see each other again.'

'Oh God, I hope not!' Marlena said with a frown. 'You are far too much trouble for a quiet Italian girl like me!' Nevertheless, she surprised me with a long, affectionate hug. 'You take care of yourself, Alex. And remember what I said to you before.'

'I promise.' But just like my promise to Martina the previous night, it would be one of many I made over the next few years that I ended up breaking with mindless regularity.

'Thank you for being Martina's friend. *Buono Fortuna*.'

'*Buono fortuna*,' Marlena replied.

'And maybe if you are ever in Australia—'

But before I was able to finish the sentence, Marlena glared at me in abject terror, ruthlessly dropped my hand and then scurried away as fast as her tiny legs could carry her.

Lottie

Samos–Aegean Sea–Athens
May 1995

I was trapped inside a torn shower curtain, the cold, stinging water tumbling over my aching limbs. Suddenly, the tiny bathroom began to shudder violently.

My God, an earthquake! Just my bloody luck! I did my best to remain calm. *Think, Alex, think.* Lucky for me, the bathroom was usually the safest place to hide during a natural disaster. Reacting quickly, I turned off the water and then curled myself into a frenzied ball across the tile floor.

Time stood eerily still. All I could hear was the sound of my heavy breathing. A feeling of dread nibbled at my fingers. There was something wrong, and I couldn't work out what. I carefully bent my neck upwards towards the light to see what was happening. To my amazement, my towel, brush, razor, toiletry bag were all sitting calmly on the bench next to the washbasin. *What the hell is going on?* It was then that I realised the bleeding obvious. The room wasn't shaking—I was.

I tried to push myself up from the floor in my haste to escape, but my legs suddenly collapsed beneath me, just like they had at Syntagma Square and the party. At the same time, an intense spasm of pain tore through my left shoulder blade and into the middle of my chest. Damn it! Was this a heart attack?

'No, Alex,' a distant voice whispered in my ear. 'This has happened to you once before. Remember? When you were a twelve-year-old boy? That rainy day when you came home from school and found your father beating your mother.'

I desperately dragged myself upwards onto all fours and crawled my way out of the shower cubicle. A fresh white towel stared at me from a wooden rack. For some reason, its lonely presence represented my last kernel of hope.

I have to get there, I told myself. *Whatever else happens, I have to get there.*

Step by step. Inch by inch. Each new gasp of air was nothing short of a miracle. After several torturous minutes, sliding myself across a splintered floor, I finally made it. I reached out with trembling hands and wrapped the towel around my twisted body. Its soft fibres burned my skin. *Okay, let's make the bed my next target.* But the shaking had become so intense, so merciless, that I couldn't even find a way to lift myself onto my knees.

Despite my growing anxiety, I tried to remember what our family doctor, Doctor Skerman, had said to me all those years ago. 'It's all about your breathing, son.' *Of course! I was able to calm myself that day through my breathing. Surely if I could do it then, there is no reason I can't do it now.* With one last effort, I opened my mouth as wide as I could and sucked down a series of long, deep breaths. *One, two, three, relax; one, two, three, breathe.*

'Mister, mister, it's time for you to leave!' screamed the teenage kid from the hallway. 'It's almost eleven o'clock!' He started to bang loudly on the door for special effect, to make sure that I had heard him. After all, he didn't want any more misunderstandings after that morning's fiasco.

'I'm not ready,' I yelled back at him. 'Come back at a quarter past eleven!'

A temporary silence.

'Will do, mister! I come back at eleven-thirty—just like you said!'

'Yes, you do that.'

Perhaps I should have asked the kid to seek urgent medical assistance. Call me petty, if you like, but despite my current predicament, I still hadn't got past the whole eight o'clock/nine o'clock thing. If that silly little bugger couldn't do something simple like waking me up on time, what hope was there that he could find a doctor before I died? No, if I were about to shuffle off this mortal coil, the satisfaction I would get in the afterlife from seeing the kid and his mother discovering my lifeless body would somehow make this all seem worthwhile.

But I didn't end up dying, did I? In fact, straight after that dopey kid wandered off into the unknown, the shaking gradually receded until every muscle in my body eased back into place. After several more repetitions of controlled breathing, I felt confident enough to lift myself off the floor. Apart from a slight bout of dizziness and some gentle numbness in my fingers and toes, I seemed to have survived the entire ordeal without any serious damage.

I silently peered out my window into the distant ocean, naked and afraid, wondering what the hell had just happened to me. If I was honest, a part of me didn't really want to find out. As my father used to say, some questions were best left unanswered. Perhaps I would contemplate these issues further that night when I was rolling about the Aegean Sea, drunk as a skunk, without a care in the world. But for the time being, all I wanted to do was leave this absurd hotel room in one piece and make doubly sure that I was sitting on that ferry at three o'clock when it departed for Piraeus.

Time was fast running out, so I jumped into some fresh clothes and carelessly stuffed everything I owned into my little travel bag. Minutes later, I was sprinting down the hotel's recently waxed corridors towards freedom. With one final effort, I dived straight through the front door onto the wooden patio, where mother, son, and cat all happily waved to me as I flew past their noses.

'Please come back soon, mister,' I heard the boy shout behind me. 'Next time, we will make you a special breakfast. It will be the best breakfast ever seen in Samos, mister. The best!'

I had several hours to kill before I was due to meet Lottie. But what was I going to do until then? I wanted to avoid the passenger terminal after the drama that morning, and I had no intention of returning to the café, especially with Karl and Tom on the prowl. In my opinion, there was only one place on the island where I could safely keep a low profile.

With my plan in place, I raided the local grocery store, bought a cheese and salami baguette, and scoffed it down in seconds. Double-checking that Karl and Tom weren't waiting for me behind some hidden corner, I quietly followed the path to the old pontoon where Martina and I had spent our final hours together. At first, everything felt so tragically empty without her. But the intoxicating memory of her beautiful smile soon became a most welcome companion. I wasted away the next two hours in peaceful solitude: sipping at a bottle of water, seeking wisdom from the early afternoon sunshine, and wondering how I would ever recover from the last few days.

Just before it was time to leave, I took one last glance into the lonely rock pools below me. Deep within their afternoon shadow, I saw the reflection of a man who, over the past few days, had lost his way. It was of little comfort to me that I had first courted, then narrowly averted, disaster. To ensure that this never happened again, I had to stop looking backwards and begin to embrace the future. Yes. It was time to return to my world, my reality, for there was nothing in the Greek Islands for me other than sadness and regret.

When I arrived at the terminal, I secured a table outside the tiny passenger lounge and waited impatiently for Lottie to join me. I passed the time by counting the number of seagulls gathering on the pier. When I finally reached one hundred, I decided that she wasn't coming anytime soon. *What a surprise! Let's face it, Lottie has been playing me for a sucker since Ephesus.* I laughed silently at my reckless naïvety before finally deciding to board the ferry.

I found a quiet corner seat on the business deck and thrust the complimentary pillow behind my head. Given the traumatic events of the last twenty-four hours, it was no surprise that I drifted off into a fitful slumber almost immediately.

'Typical,' Lottie said as she ruffled my hair. 'Always falling asleep at the wrong time.'

The familiar smell of her perfume caused my body to snap upright.

'What the hell are you doing here, Lottie?' I asked impertinently.

'Do you greet every girl you know with such enthusiasm?' she replied with a frown.

'Only the ones that stand me up.' Despite my petulance, I noticed she was holding a large, blood-red suitcase.

'I received an alert on my pager this morning,' Lottie explained. 'My board of directors want to discuss a financial report tomorrow afternoon. I have been ordered back to Athens.'

'That's a shame,' I observed dryly. 'And your parents?'

'They will make their way to Istanbul tomorrow morning. I will join them on Saturday.'

'That's even a bigger shame.'

'You now have me all to yourself.'

With no adults around to supervise us anymore, I could only wonder whether my brittle self-control would survive the night.

Once the ferry made open water, Lottie and I agreed to have that long-overdue cup of tea. We barely had time to sit down before she asked me for an update on Martina. Ashen-faced, I explained everything that had happened since we last saw each other in Martina's hotel room. When I finally finished my sordid little tale, Lottie offered me a sympathetic smile.

'What are we going to do with you, Alex?' she asked.

'You can start by calling me the world's biggest loser,' I replied sadly. 'That's certainly how I feel.'

'You do seem to have an incredible ability to get yourself into complex situations.'

'That's an understatement,' I muttered, desperate for more of her sympathy.

'Even so, if I had been you, I would have also punched Marco after what he said about Martina. Disgusting little pig. In fact, he was incredibly lucky that I didn't stick a fork right into his nose.'

Despite my bleak mood, I began to chuckle. 'After last night, I don't think he and Dieter will hit on any Dutch girls too soon.'

'And I'm the quiet one in the family,' replied Lottie, with a grin. 'You should meet my older sister, Jana. She's a real tomcat.' She poured some more tea from her pot and laughed at herself. 'Look,' she continued, 'I really liked Martina, but she reminded me of an elastic band, stretched out between two bedposts, waiting to snap at any moment. Unfortunately, it finally happened last night, expedited by the grubbiest man in the universe. You weren't to blame for what happened.'

'Marlena wasn't so forgiving.'

Lottie laughed again. 'Honey, perhaps Marlena has her own reasons for wanting you out of the picture.'

'How so?'

'She has feelings for Martina. Don't you get it?'

I screwed up my face. 'What? Are you trying to say that Marlena is gay? No chance! What about Franco?'

Lottie seemed bemused by my unworldliness. 'She is bisexual, Alex. She likes both men and women. Do you understand?'

Obviously, I didn't. 'Are you sure?'

'Oh, quite sure,' she said. 'What do you think Martina and I were both talking about last night while you were drinking with Marlena and Franco?'

'She actually told you this?'

'Yes, of course. Marco let the cat out of the bag some weeks ago. I will leave it to your imagination, but he was encouraging Martina to explore certain opportunities, the sick little bastard. Martina made it perfectly clear to him that she wasn't into that sort of thing.'

'Wow,' I shook my head in astonishment. 'I must be living a sheltered life. But just because she is bisexual doesn't mean that she has feelings for Martina.'

'Think about it, Alex. Remember how upset she was last night in Martina's hotel room? She even said that she loved her!'

'I noticed that too, but girls say things like that all the time, don't they? It doesn't necessarily mean that they are about to jump into bed with each other.'

Lottie flicked her used teabag at me in disgust. 'You really do need to get out of Australia more often, Alex. Must I explain everything to you?'

'If you could, please.'

'Where do we start?' She gave it some thought before continuing. 'Over a long period of time, Marlena develops feelings for Martina. With me?'

'With you.'

'You then ride into town with those swarthy Richard Hunte looks. What girl can resist them, especially someone as confused and vulnerable as Martina? In a moment of weakness, she reveals to you that she was gang-raped three years ago. After much soul-searching, she then agrees to keep in touch with you because deep down, she really likes you, and after all, she has just told you her biggest secret—'

'You are going to have to do better than this,' I interrupted her.

'When you fail to turn up this morning,' Lottie defiantly raised her eyebrows, 'Marlena comforts her and explains that all men, including you and Franco, are total bastards and not to be trusted. She, on the other hand, will always be there for her. So let me give you my phone number, and please call me whenever you want because I care about you. And then, when Marlena finds you this morning, she uses all of her feminine wiles to convince you that any further contact with Martina is detrimental to her wellbeing.'

'What are you trying to say?' I challenged her. 'That she has no intention of passing my details to Martina?'

'Argh!' Lottie pretended to scream. 'You really don't understand women, do you?'

'I refuse to say anything on the grounds that it might incriminate me.'

'Yes, I think there is a strong chance that she won't pass on your details. She was leading you on; making you think that she would help you so you wouldn't get too suspicious about her true motives. If you still want to find Martina, I suggest that you have a backup plan. Do you know anyone in Greece who can help you?'

Do I know anyone in Greece who can help me?

My thoughts wandered back to the party in Athens on Saturday night and my meeting with Reginald Crump. *What did he say to me? 'Everyone needs some help during their lives.' Was this how the whole 'Reginald Crump Affair' was supposed to end?*

'There was a man I met in Athens called Reginald Crump,' I said. I proceeded to tell Lottie the whole story, hoping that she would somehow suspend reality for a few minutes and believe me.

Her initial expression didn't inspire a lot of confidence. 'I'm finding it hard to accept that this Reginald Clump knew that you were going to Samos when you only made the decision that very morning. And that thing about the old woman, that's downright weird.'

'That's Crump, by the way.'

'What?'

'His name is Reginald Crump, not Clump.'

'Whatever,' she said irritably. 'The whole thing sounds like something out of *The X-Files*.'

'I was thinking more *Twilight Zone*, but yes, I see your point.'

'I don't know,' Lottie pondered. 'Personally, I would stay well clear of this man. But if you think he can help you find Martina, then you must follow your conscience.' Lottie reached over to her handbag, pulled out a pen and a small notebook, and then pushed both items across the table towards me.

'Here, write down your Australian phone number. I have some contacts in my line of work who regularly visit Chios. They seem to know everyone important on the island. I will pass on your details to them and see if they are willing to do some detective work for you.'

'Thank you, Lottie,' I said after I finished writing down my contact details. 'I'm not sure if I can live with myself if I don't try to find her.'

'You're a romantic fool.'

After Lottie and I finished our teas, we strolled upstairs to the special outdoor viewing deck reserved only for business-class passengers. We found a couple of empty seats on the port side of the ferry and peered back across the water towards the blurry outline of Samos Island.

'Any regrets?' Lottie asked.

'A few,' I reflected sadly. 'I mean, Samos and Ephesus are both amazing places, but I will forever remember my time there for all the wrong reasons.'

'It doesn't have to be that way,' said Lottie, the golden tips of her hair gliding between snippets of sunshine. 'You can control how you feel.'

'Before yesterday, I definitely thought I could. Alex Gerrick, the man in total control, the man who never cried. But ever since Martina told me her story, something inside of me has changed.'

'Perhaps nothing has changed at all,' remarked Lottie softly. 'Perhaps Martina's story has opened old wounds that have never properly healed.'

True to form, whenever someone made a comment that I didn't like, even though it was probably true, my stomach began to percolate, and I found myself withdrawing inside an imaginary cocoon. Needless to say, Lottie was perceptive enough to realise that I had gone quiet for a reason.

'My last boyfriend, Markus, served in the Yugoslavian War,' she suddenly began. 'He was an infantry officer in the Dutch army, on attachment with the United Nations.'

'That would have been tough,' I replied.

'He saw some terrible things in Bosnia during his nine months on deployment, most of which he refused to discuss even with me.'

'It's never easy to talk about these things, Lottie.'

'True, and I never forced him, either. But one day in September last year, he and I were having a casual walk in the middle of Amsterdam. It was a beautiful autumn day, and we were so happy. He had been back in the Netherlands for almost six months, and everything seemed perfectly fine with him. He was laughing and joking with me like he always did. Then out of nowhere, this little kid walking on the footpath in front of us escaped his mother's grip and ran onto the street, right in front of an oncoming delivery van.'

'Oh, God. Did it hit him?'

'No, luckily, the driver was able to stop in time. But something inside of Markus just snapped. I have never seen such unadulterated rage in another human being. One minute he was the kind, funny, caring man I had known since high school, and then he was this monster that I had never seen before. Without saying a word to me, he pulled the driver out of the vehicle by his hair, threw him onto the ground and started kicking him all over his body like a football.'

Lottie's hands began to quiver, so I asked her if she wanted a glass of water. 'No, I'm fine,' she reassured me. 'So, I begged him to stop—I thought he was going to kill the poor man, I really did. When Markus didn't respond to me, I tried to grab him around the chest, but he turned around and slapped me hard across the face, knocking me to the ground. I was so stunned that the man I wanted to marry had just hit me; I couldn't speak for the next two hours. Luckily, a policeman was walking behind us at the time and was able to pull Markus away from the man before he could do any further damage to him.'

'Was he arrested?'

'Yes,' Lottie nodded. 'The driver eventually dropped the charges when he found out that Markus was in the military, but the army wasn't so lenient. He was ordered to face a court-martial. Before the trial, he was examined by several doctors, including a psychiatrist. They discovered that during the war in Bosnia, Markus had given some chocolate to a group of young boys while on a patrol in Sarajevo. He turned his back on them for a moment and then heard a shot. When he looked behind him, one of the boys was lying dead on the footpath, with a bullet to his head. For some reason, a sniper indiscriminately targeted this kid and just shot him cold. Apparently, Markus was inconsolable for days afterwards and blamed himself for the boy's death.'

'So when Markus saw that kid run onto the road, it triggered memories of what happened to him in Bosnia?'

'That's right. Reliving such horrible events or having flashbacks are common occurrences in people who suffer from post-traumatic stress disorder.'

Through my army reserve service, I was very much aware of the impacts of excessive trauma. 'Was he diagnosed with PTSD?'

'Yes, after much internal debate between different medical experts. The army doesn't always understand these things. Men who show any semblance of emotion must be weak and not fit for military service. But the charges against him were dropped, and from what I understand, he is still recovering in a facility in Rotterdam.' She dropped her head as if retelling this part of the story was one step too far. 'We broke up soon after he hit me, you see.'

I put my arm around Lottie and gave her shoulder a gentle squeeze.

'I know what you must be thinking,' she whispered. 'Why is yet another woman opening up to you?'

'It must be my doleful eyes.' I smiled sadly. 'However, I guess you want me to draw some parallels between Markus and my own situation with Martina.'

'I'm no expert on these things, Alex, do you understand?' Lottie continued. 'But just like Markus and the boy that day in Amsterdam, Martina's story has triggered something inside your head. Your fight with Marco, breaking down in tears inside Martina's hotel room, your behaviour at the ferry terminal, and shaking uncontrollably in the bathroom. These are most likely delayed reactions to some form of trauma in your past.'

I pretended to consider her views before then rejecting them out of hand just as quickly. 'PTSD mainly impacts soldiers who have experienced bad things in war, like Markus, or policemen and women who deal with car accidents and murders. It doesn't affect ordinary people like me.'

'As I said, I am not an expert, honey. But just like you encouraged Martina to seek professional advice about her issues, I am now suggesting that you do the same.'

'That's great,' I replied with a contrived frown. 'I came to Samos to see the sights and absorb its history, but instead, I get psychoanalysed by three different women, all of whom have me riding off into the sunset with men in white coats. Martina believes that my past will one day destroy me, Marlena thinks I'm not stable enough to help other people, and you have me walking around like a time bomb with PTSD.'

Lottie's casual smile was devoid of sympathy. 'Perhaps we can see what others have missed because you have become adept at hiding the truth. That's the beauty of meeting new people, Alex: we see you for who you are, stripped of the shield you have built to protect yourself from the rest of the world.'

'I am not sure if that makes me feel any better,' I said. 'You make me sound like the star attraction at some psychiatric conference in Switzerland.'

Lottie gently touched my forearm. 'Maybe it's because I really like you. If I didn't care, I doubt whether I would have bothered to say anything at all.'

This was how the conversation about my mental health ended, and I was grateful that it did. My head was cluttered with so many different emotions that all I wanted to do was hit the rewind button on my life and return to how things were before I ever came to Greece. I was certain that Lottie realised this as well, so she allowed us to sit quietly together while we watched the early strands of twilight descend into the dark-blue ocean.

The outside temperature quickly plummeted as nighttime approached, and we wrapped ourselves tightly against each other's bodies to keep warm. I wasn't going to pretend otherwise; I was enjoying every minute of this unintended intimacy, and it was evident that Lottie was as well. Without warning, she slowly bent her lips into my face and then kissed me firmly on the lips. I was at first stunned by the brazenness of her attack, but to my eternal shame, the soft, sensual feel of her skin on my cheek only made me want more.

'That was for the other night—before I knew you had a girlfriend,' she explained once our faces separated.

'And now that you know that I do have a girlfriend?' I asked hopefully.

'Nothing more can happen, can it?' she said with a mournful smile.

'No, it can't,' I replied, unable to hide the disappointment even from myself.

We spent the rest of the evening talking about our lives, our hopes, and our dreams, all in the company of several bottles of red wine. Unlike our first ferry conversation a few nights before, there was no-one to distract us, no secrets left to confuse us and no rules by which to judge us.

Just after midnight, we finally succumbed to exhaustion, and so we belatedly made our way back to the business-class deck. We shuffled endlessly around with our gear in a futile effort to make ourselves more comfortable before we decided that snuggling next to each other with a pillow lodged between our heads was the only practical way to get a good night's rest.

We mucked around for a while, exchanging dirty jokes before finally surrendering to the darkness. Just before dawn, I woke up to see the pillow and Lottie's head wedged tightly into my lap. I took the liberty of gently stroking her soft blonde hair, and she smiled at the deftness of my touch through half-closed eyes. 'Go back to sleep,' she warned, 'or I may have to do something that we will both regret later.'

We arrived in Piraeus just after eight o'clock, and Lottie offered to drive me back to Athens in her hire car. As soon as we left the port terminal, we realised that we would soon have to say goodbye to each other, even though that wasn't what either of us wanted. We flirted around the topic aimlessly for what seemed like a lifetime before I finally obtained the courage to raise the dead cat in the boot.

'So what happens now?'

'I will drop you off near Syntagma Square, and then I will go home to get dressed for my meeting.' Lottie's tone was annoyingly flat, devoid of any emotion.

'No, that's not what I meant,' I replied. 'I meant what now happens to our friendship?'

We came to a sudden halt at a set of traffic lights, and Lottie took the opportunity to twirl her fingers through her hair. 'You are not going to insist that we keep in contact with each other, are you? Look what trouble that has already caused you with Martina.'

'This is different.'

'How so? Last time I checked, you still live in Australia, and you still have a girlfriend. Do you honestly expect me to sit by the phone every night for God knows how long, hoping that your situation changes? Show me some respect, Alex.' When a green light appeared, she slammed her foot on the accelerator.

'So it's just meant to end like this?' I muttered sulkily.

'Yes, it is, Alex. Our friendship was always meant to be a shooting star. Last night we stared into its flames together and fleetingly saw something magical. But now, a new day has arrived, along with the reality of our situations. I still need to recover from Markus, and you need to go back to Australia and make your new relationship with Rachel work.'

'And the kiss last night? What was that all about?'

Lottie somehow managed to keep her eyes on the road. 'I wanted to feel the magic just once, Alex.'

'That is a selfish thing to do if you always intended to cast me aside,' I replied angrily.

'Of course it was selfish!' She laughed at my naïvety. 'But now, the next time I meet a man that I like, I will be able to remember what it feels like.'

'And what do I say to Rachel?' I tried to reason with her. 'I am barely out of her sight for three weeks, and I find myself emotionally entangled with a mysterious Bosnian girl and hopelessly smitten with a beautiful Dutch girl.'

'Why do you have to say anything to Rachel at all? You didn't sleep with me or Martina. You are not the first person ever to have their head temporarily turned while on a holiday! Goodness me, it happens to some of my girlfriends every weekend! This was just four days in the rest of your life—a drop in the ocean if you think about it. In a week, when you are with her in London, none of this will matter anymore.'

'I don't know. Surely there has to be a reason for all of this?'

'Of course there is a reason,' said Lottie. 'It's all part of your growth as a man. Learn from this experience, explain to Martina what happened yesterday, if you do end up finding her, then forget about both of us. All you need to focus on is your mental wellbeing and making Rachel happy.'

We reluctantly agreed to drop the topic, even though there were still so many things left unresolved between us. When we eventually arrived in the city centre, Lottie manoeuvred her car into a five-minute parking bay close to Syntagma Square. With clockwork precision, we both leapt out of our seats simultaneously and met each other halfway on the footpath. I held Lottie firmly around her slender waist while she nudged her face deep into the crevice of my neck. Warm tears began to roll down my chest.

'Despite what I said before, this does suck big-time,' she sniffed. 'I really do like you, Alex, and I wish we had more time to explore our friendship.' Lottie's tender voice filled me with a humble sadness that would gnaw at my heart for many years to come.

'I will never forget you, Lottie,' I whispered into her ear. 'I really won't.'

'Neither will I, Alex,' she replied, trying ridiculously hard to compose herself. 'However, I am going to give it a damn good try.' We exchanged another ferocious hug before she somehow found the courage to dive back into her car. When our eyes connected through the passenger side window for the last time, I swore that I could detect a hint of regret on her face. But before either of us could seize the moment, she kicked over the ignition, and her car slowly faded away into the smothering Athens traffic.

I waved blindly into the wind before trudging sadly towards the Adelphi Hotel in one final gesture of regret. When I arrived at the hotel reception, Spiro and Selene glared suspiciously at me through ice-cold frowns. Gone were the enthusiastic ramblings about relatives in Melbourne, offers of freshly cooked baklava, and access to the best room in the hotel. Instead, Spiro growled something about the daily rate increasing since the weekend, and Selene carelessly threw me the key to a small apartment on the second floor.

Could it be that arsehole Marco had warned them in advance that their favourite Australian tourist was really an ungrateful prick who deserved no more treats? Possibly. I wouldn't have put anything past that idiot. Nevertheless, I quietly collected my backpack from the storeroom and soon found myself rolling inside a miniature bathtub.

After I made myself a pot of Earl Grey tea, I reached across to the phone and tapped in the numbers of the Company. To my relief, someone finally answered my call, even if it was a woman speaking Greek and not Reginald Crump.

'Hi, do you speak English?'

'Of course,' the woman replied in a thick Slavic accent. 'My name is Edna Krajicek. How can I help you?'

'I would like to speak with Reginald Crump, please.' Just saying his name made me squirm in my chair, and I wondered whether this was a good idea.

'Who did you say you want to speak to again?' asked Edna, in a naturally haughty tone.

'Reginald Crump.'

'I'm sorry, but there is nobody here with that name.'

'That's impossible. I met him at the Hotel Hellas just the other day. He gave me this number.'

'Are you sure you have the correct name? Because you see, my colleague Oliver Browne normally works at the Hellas.'

'No,' I replied angrily. 'He was sick that day. I was met at the hotel by someone called Reginald Crump.'

'Oliver was sick?' Edna laughed insanely. 'He has never had a sick day in his life!'

'Are you sure?'

'Of course I'm sure.' I could hear her deep, frustrated breathing bounce down the line. 'Now, if you don't mind, I'm very busy.'

Fuck you, Edna! I wasn't going to sit in this stinking hotel room and take her lies one second longer! The entire country had been conspiring against me from day one, and I simply wouldn't put up with it anymore.

'You are a lying bitch!' I yelled at her in a strange falsetto voice that I barely recognised. Every cell inside my body was screaming at the world in exasperation.

'And you are a rude, disgusting man!' *Slam!*

Once Edna hung up on me, I twirled the phone line tightly around my neck before yanking it clear out of the wall socket. Stunned by the magnitude of my own ferocity, I dropped my eyes to the floor and started to search desperately for any last fragments of sanity.

'*Well, well,*' Jemima cried from the top of my backpack. '*You have finally lost it, haven't you? Just like I always said you would.*'

I stumbled across the floor and roughly grabbed Jemima by the beak. 'Shut the fuck up!' I screamed at her until my lungs wanted to burst. Without even attempting to rationalise my actions, I tore Jemima's flimsy head right off her delicate neck until I was completely covered by pounds and pounds of white, inner stuffing.

'*What the hell is wrong with me?*' I screamed into a nearby mirror. '*What is going on?*'

I wiped away the sticky residue clinging to my shirt, picked up my wallet and room key, and stomped towards the Hotel Hellas, ranting and raving at scores of confused pedestrians in my rage. Just as I expected, Dumbo was standing at the front counter, chewing dreamily on a pencil. When he saw me, the blood pumped into his downtrodden face, and he reeled back in terror towards a photocopier.

'Do you remember me?' I asked in mad desperation. My head was about to explode all over the lobby.

'How could I possibly forget?' Dumbo responded with a tortured smile.

'Do you also remember the complaint that I made?'

Dumbo slowly raised his hand at me. 'Of course I do. Oliver Browne had accidentally been given your contact details before you checked into the hotel. I thought we cleared this all up on the night?'

'No!' I cried out in despair. 'Not Oliver Browne. He was sick that day; you told me so yourself. I was met by someone called Reginald Crump!' I reached into my pocket and pulled out the business card that Reginald Crump gave me on that very first night we met. Without even checking its fine print, I slammed the card down on the counter in front of Dumbo's bloodshot eyes.

'See? He gave me his business card!'

Dumbo rubbed the card several times with his scaly fingers and then stared at me with genuine concern. 'But sir, this is Oliver Browne's business card!'

I rudely snatched the card from Dumbo's hand and pressed it hard against my eyes. Sure enough, Oliver Browne's name was printed boldly in refined gold letters.

No, no, no! This is bullshit! What about the café at Syntagma Square? What about the party? He isn't a figment of my imagination; for the love of God, he exists!

But does he, Alex? Think about it some more! How quickly did he disappear from the lobby on that very first night? Why didn't anyone react to the argument at the café? How easily did you fall over yourself when you tried to stop him from leaving the party?

No! You are wrong. Do you hear me? He is real! This is fucking crazy!

I dropped the business card onto the waxed floor. With the lights from the lobby chandelier shining above me, I furiously stamped the edges of the card into the ground with the corner of my shoe, cursing and screaming out every profanity I had ever known at Dumbo and his insidious cohorts. Several tortured seconds later, my old friend, the concierge, pushed me towards the revolving door and then hurled me headfirst into the forgotten world outside. Stranded on a lonely footpath, a beggar in a black coat brushed my arm, a Volvo blared its horn at some pedestrians, a young woman in a tank top lit up a cigarette, and all I could see everywhere around me was yellow, yellow, and even more yellow.

Post Script

London
Four days later

I was lying on my hotel bed in London, waiting for Rachel to arrive after almost four weeks apart. Even now, with only minutes remaining before we would see each other again, I still didn't know what to say to her about my time in Greece. Over the last few days, as I lingered somewhere in that lonely space that existed between sanity and madness, I had exhausted every option in my mind.

How many occasions had I analysed the sequence of events to make sense of it all? That very first night with Reginald Crump, my chance meeting with Marco, the party from hell, the old woman dying on the street, my time with Lottie and Martina, Martina's secret, fighting with Marco and his friends, rejecting Martina's advances on her couch, sleeping in on the day Martina left for Chios, my meltdown at the ferry terminal, kissing Lottie on the ferry and then discovering that Reginald Crump might be … well, let's not go there.

If I wrote a novel around these events, people would have laughed at such an outlandish plot. How could I explain this all rationally to my new girlfriend when it was apparent that I couldn't even explain it rationally to myself?

I wasn't scared of telling Rachel the truth about my time with Lottie and Martina. Sure, I could sometimes act like a selfish bastard, but I prided myself on the fact that I was usually honest with the women in my life. I could see Lottie's point that I didn't sleep with anyone—so why create unnecessary drama for myself? But for three straight days, I acted like a kid in a candy store whenever she or Martina was around me.

If Rachel and I were to have a future, then it had to be a relationship built on trust. It might be painful in the short term, and yes, there was also a good chance that she could break up with me, but that was the risk when you took liberties with your integrity as I had done.

But if I told Rachel the truth about the two girls, I was also compelled to reveal everything else that happened to me as well. There was no way of getting around it. Every piece of the Greek puzzle was intrinsically linked with another.

Did I want Rachel to know about my two-way conversations with a fluffy toy? That the character who followed me all around Athens may or may not have been real? Or that I tried to jump into the ocean to swim after a ferry? And that ever since I was five years old, I was sometimes visited by an evil clown dressed in yellow who could change his appearance whenever he wanted?

Either way, I was screwed. If we stayed together, Rachel would rightly insist that I obtain professional help, which put the onus on me to inform my workplace and the army reserve about my condition. But if we didn't stay together, there was always a chance that she might accidentally reveal something to one of our mutual friends in Canberra, and the entire city would then know that Alex Gerrick was nutty as a fruitcake.

Was this really what I wanted from my life? After everything that I had worked so hard to achieve over the last few years, just as my career had begun to prosper, did I now want it all destroyed as people viewed me as an oddity?

You know how these things worked, especially in a dog-eat-dog city like Canberra. Every abnormality, every point of difference, was open slather to ridicule and abuse. Imagine what it would be like for me as a public servant trying to get ahead in such a competitive world with this burden hanging over me? How could I possibly retain the respect of my work colleagues and ever get promoted again if people knew that I suffered from a mental disorder?

And what about the Spiders? How would they react? Rest assured, they would abandon me without even a second thought. No, I was not going to limit my opportunities in life just because of a few crazy days in Greece.

Lottie was right: I needed to forget about the past week. I wasn't sure what was wrong with me, but perhaps the stress of my recent marriage breakdown and all the issues with my father before he died had finally taken their toll. Or maybe Martina's story had stirred something terrible inside my psyche that I couldn't explain.

Things had been good before I arrived in Greece: I was a man in control who understood where he was going in life and how he would get there. What I had experienced in Athens and Samos was nothing more than a temporary ailment, a diabolical melting pot of miscalculations that would somehow disappear once I saw Rachel again.

If anyone had the resilience and fortitude to put this all behind him, then surely, I did. *Lick'em tomorrow, Alex! Of course!* Once I realised that this was my only option, there was no way I could ever turn back.

I suddenly heard the door creak open, and Rachel fell excitedly into the room, her tiny hands barely clasping her oversized suitcase. I staggered up from the bed, smashed my arms around her petite body, and then lifted her triumphantly above my shoulders into the air.

'I am never going to let you go ever again,' I finally whispered softly into her ear before we shared our first kiss in weeks.

To be fair, for the next three and a half years, at least, I was true to my word.

*

Canberra
Five Weeks Later

I was at work on a Friday afternoon, microwaving some leftover spaghetti bolognaise in the lunchroom while discussing last night's episode of *Absolutely Fabulous* with Jenny Shaw, when Linda Falk suddenly tapped me on the shoulder.

'Alex, there is a t-telephone call for you on the t-telephone,' she stammered in her usual dreary monotone. She was a lovely girl, Linda, but clearly not the sharpest tool in the shed.

'Oh my God!' I yelled out in pretend fear. 'Really? A telephone call. On the telephone? Whatever should I do?' Jenny giggled, and my spaghetti made a loud *plopping* noise inside the microwave.

'It's an overseas call, too,' Linda announced, completely ignoring my awful sarcasm. 'She says her name is Martina and that she met you in Greece.' She gave Jenny a wicked grin, and Jenny, who, according to some mutual friends, believed that she was next in line should Rachel and I ever break up, warily lifted her brow at me.

My knees began to buckle. *Oh my God, Martina! Someone found her! Was it Marlena? Was it one of Lottie's friends? Does it even matter who?*

A small part of me desperately wanted to hear her voice again, to know that she was doing well and that she had forgiven me for what had happened that morning in Samos. But no, I made a pact in my London hotel room four weeks ago to put all of this behind me. So far, everything had worked out perfectly.

My relationship with Rachel was booming; I was off to Sydney for the next six months on a temporary promotion, and most importantly, I was back to being normal, happy-go-lucky Alex, without any side effects from my time in Greece. I couldn't afford to jeopardise any of this now, primarily to satisfy some latent guilt I felt for a woman I had only known for a few days. Martina had to move on with her life, just like I had done since returning to Australia.

'Listen, Linda—I wonder if you could do me a huge favour?' My tone was pathetically sweet. 'I met this girl on my holiday, but I don't want to talk to her.'

'Oh, you have been bad, haven't you, Alex?' Linda tortured me some more. 'Very bad! And now you want me to cover up for you by telling her that you have left for the afternoon.'

Okay, maybe Linda was a lot smarter than I initially thought. 'Yes. No. Well, yes,' I sank further into the mire while Jenny bludgeoned me with her evil eye. 'If you could do that for me, Linda, I will owe you big-time!'

'Do you think I could take Monday morning off on flexitime?' she asked, with a series of excited nods. 'That would be cool!'

'Of course you can,' I replied, even though I wasn't sure whether I had the authority to give Linda Monday morning off on flexitime.

'Super-duper! And by the way, your lunch is burning!'

Several minutes later, as I was foraging through my plate for edible lumps of burnt bolognaise sauce, Linda returned with a super smug smile stamped on her ashen face.

'She wasn't happy with you, Alex,' she lectured me. 'I think she knew you were deliberately avoiding her. But she will leave a message on your phone later today.' I thanked Linda for her trouble and then quietly finished my lunch.

The following day, I arrived early to tidy up my desk before leaving for Sydney with Rachel. While packing my belongings into a small cardboard box, I became transfixed at the red light flashing on my phone, indicating that someone had called during the middle of the night and left a message for me on voicemail. It could only have been one person.

'Let's just get this over and done with,' I sighed. I picked up the phone, tapped in my security code, and waited for that raw, husky voice to shout down the line.

'Alex, why didn't you come to the phone before? I don't understand. You went to all that trouble to find me, and now you ignore my call? Something bad has happened, and I need to talk to you. I will be in Vienna for the next few days, and you can reach me on the following number. Please get a pen!'

Before I allowed Martina to finish, I gently pressed the escape button and arrived back at the main menu. I listened quietly to all the options until the hollow computerised voice reminded me that I could delete my messages at any time by simply pressing the number five button on the telephone pad. I pictured Martina's sad eyes one final time, then slammed down on the number five button with all my strength, permanently deleting every message I had stored on the tape.

I wasn't to know it then, of course, but with this one simple action, I would condemn myself forever into the fires of Hell.

Reflections

Canberra
7 March 2016

'Martina!'

Bubbles of perspiration fell like snowflakes across my T-shirt. In my desperation, I found a way to blink my eyelids several times until Martina's apparition slowly evaporated into tiny embers of sunlight. Finally convinced that she was gone, I turned to face my wife, who was asleep next to me in bed, and our pet beagle, George, snuggled closely beside her.

I wanted so much to find the courage to wake her up and tell her about everything. To explain to her about Ringo Bingo, Martina, and the turmoil that raged like a fire inside my turbulent mind—to release this unforgiving burden that had overwhelmed me for so long. But with so much at stake, I couldn't bring myself to share my fears with her or anyone else who cared about me.

I quietly slipped out of bed and glanced at our clock. *Five forty-five. There is no way I can go back to sleep, not after that.* The only sensible thing I could do was get dressed, go to work, and wait for this looming disaster, whatever it was, to reveal itself to me. I somehow fell into our ensuite and closed the door behind me. For several minutes, I stood in front of the bathroom mirror and pondered my immediate fate.

You are afraid, aren't you? Afraid of her. Afraid of what the day will now bring.

I turned on the tap and splashed cold water across my face. However, it did nothing to alleviate the feeling of dread burning inside my chest. A warning sign, I concluded, of the oncoming storm that was about to engulf my life. But then, I was never good at listening to the warnings, was I?

I gently pushed my thumb over the jagged lines of my forehead. I was a different man in 1995 to the one now growing old with his endless list of regrets: young, bold, confident, and yes, maybe a smart-arse as well. But in a way, you could understand the reasons for my cockiness: I was on the brink of something special, waiting impatiently for all the pieces to fall my way.

Then came Samos.

For some reason, this forgotten island, deep within the bowels of the Aegean Sea, had discovered the combination to my Pandora's Box and then unleashed a legion of demons onto an unsuspecting world. If my plan to contain their wrath was to return to Australia with Rachel in tow as if nothing had happened, then I deserved all the misfortune that would eventually come my way.

Sure, that first month back in Canberra appeared to validate my strategy. Everything fell neatly into place, and my world once again exploded with possibilities. Yet, the nightmares began a week after I erased Martina's number from my work phone.

At first, I assumed these unwelcome intrusions were merely an aberration, a natural consequence of my callous disregard for Martina and her pitiful cries for help. Perhaps if I could ignore them for just a little longer, they would gradually fade away like most of my unwanted memories.

Alas, only a fool chose to ignore the inevitable because, over the next four years, their intensity grew more potent by the night until I could no longer separate fact from fiction. When I finally surrendered to their fury in Bateman's Bay, everything in my life crumbled around me until I somehow found the strength to fight back.

But for every action, there was a consequence. For me, the man who finally emerged into the light that cold winter's morning was different from the one who had innocently blundered his way across Greece several years before.

Didn't Brother Rojo say something about this? That a man must assume many guises before he could escape the Season of Clouds? From memory, it was on that very first day we met in his hut in Manila, as we drank that lemongrass tea that he loved so much.

I even remembered his exact words: 'The man who survived Bateman's Bay was no more capable of escaping the Season of Clouds than the innocent man who disembarked the ferry that day in Samos.'

Yes, it was all flooding back to me: the rickety bamboo chairs, the heavy smoke, the foul aroma of incense. And how Brother Rojo was surprisingly impressed with my 'Lost Week', even though, ultimately, I fell at the final hurdle.

'It simply was not your time,' he said to me in that polluted voice as he wrung his arthritic hands over his motley-looking gas stove. 'Only you can explain how you missed this chance at redemption.'

How indeed. How did one explain the irrational mysteries of the heart to a man as pure as Brother Rojo? Because the answer to his question did not belong to me, but with two remarkable young women, who, to compensate for their own frailties, would search the depths of my heart and find something inside the emptiness that was worth saving.

And when the time finally came for me to choose, Martina's grieving hand would seek its revenge, and everything I had achieved in this incredible week would be lost forever inside the Season of Clouds.

Part Two

The Lost Week

Eleanor

London
October 1999

I have a theory that life is nothing more than a demented jigsaw puzzle that controls your destiny from the moment you are born. As a result, you spend every second, every minute, every hour, every day, every month, every year collecting every shitty little piece you can find, in the vain hope that once you complete your task, it will somehow open the doorway to eternal wisdom.

But then, just when you are about to twist in that very last piece, just when you are about to discover the answers to all of your pathetic little questions, a total stranger enters the room, picks up the puzzle you have worked so hard to complete and then dumps the whole damn lot on top of you just for the hell of it. Okay, it's not much of a theory, I know. But at least it's mine, and I'm still its most faithful disciple.

Indeed, whenever life gets me down, I will often share these insights with strangers to see their reactions. Most of the time, they will shake their heads in disbelief and suggest that mine is a foolish explanation for how the world really works. Instead, they like to argue, we all inevitably shape our lives through our very own words, deeds, and decisions.

Their hypothesis goes something like this. We take a man—let's call him Jim—and offer him two different paths he can take in his life. The first path provides Jim with the usual touch points that shape our future: birth, school, sweetheart, job, marriage, mortgage, kids, holidays, retirement, grandkids, death.

Jim tops his last year of high school, studies to become a lawyer, marries Loretta in the dewy meadow where they first meet, opens his own successful legal business among the white picket houses of suburban Sydney, has yearly holidays at Terrigal, produces three lovely daughters who all marry men just like their dad, takes his wife on their first overseas trip when he retires at sixty-five, dotes on his six grandchildren and lives to be 78.2 years old, when he dies happy and contented with his family beside him.

Jim's second path offers precisely the same touchpoints, but the choices he makes are quite different. Instead of attending law school, Jim becomes a policeman. He doesn't marry Loretta because she doesn't understand him or the job anymore, and besides, Constable Rose is much better in bed and doesn't nag him about a future.

Children? You're kidding. Given Jim's daily exposure to the degenerate street kids of inner Sydney and their obsession with drugs, alcohol, and sex, he wants nothing to do with them.

Then, one hot December night, while patrolling somewhere near Rooty Hill, Jim responds to a burglar alarm at a local bottle shop, and some scared little punk with a two-hundred-dollar-a-day drug habit puts a bullet straight between his eyes. Not only does Jim die alone in agony on a bloodied driveway in the middle of nowhere, but Constable Rose doesn't even care enough to attend his funeral.

In the end, it's all about cause and effect. Depending on which path Jim takes, his ultimate decision will determine his fate. One path has him living a fulfilling life with his family, while the other path has him lying prematurely in a box.

All sounds relatively straightforward. Of course it does. You can convince anyone that something makes sense if you try hard enough. But trust me, everything I have just said is a total delusion: cranked-up nonsense peddled by an army of do-gooders who want you to believe that some divine force is responsible for shaping our lives. In fact, should you ever accept this theory, you are naïvely supporting the notion that the decisions ordinary people like Jim, you, and I make actually matter and that we ultimately have the power to influence the world around us.

However, not even the most gullible of optimists would seriously believe these outlandish lies because most of us are too preoccupied with the minutiae of everyday life to consider the consequences of our actions, or indeed, furnish a perfect process in our minds for how we make the correct life-dictating decisions.

There is no greater purpose to our lives, no greater entity that empowers us to make the right choices. All we have is a deeply complex world, mesmerising us with its subversive bag of tricks. Furthermore, should you decide to fight this irresistible force along the way, you will more often than not end up getting screwed. Just like I have been screwed, time and time again.

'You are quite the pessimist, aren't you, darling?' said Eleanor in her throaty Austrian accent as she casually flicked a loose strand of hair from her eyes. We were lying next to each other on a pair of mangled deck chairs in St James Park, London, as the warm, late-morning autumn sunshine began to creep suspiciously through a blanket of thick clouds. Her long ballerina legs, covered by those faded, tattered jeans she loved to wear, dangled mischievously over the side of her chair in the vain hope that they would somehow intertwine with mine.

I considered her comment with a twitch of my nose and thought about how to respond. She was right, of course. Almost overnight, I had become the world's most enduring pessimist, for my entire existence thrived upon a basic assumption that no matter what I did, I would always find a way to screw it up.

Even now, with this beautiful, sophisticated young woman nestled beside me, I found it almost impossible to enjoy myself, for every minute that I spent with her, the more I worried that something would go wrong. And the more I worried that something would go wrong, the more likely it would.

Perhaps I should just cut my losses before this goes any further before people end up getting hurt again. So why don't you spill the beans about everything in your past: Samos, Lottie, Martina, Rachel, the nightmares—the whole box and dice? Let her decide right now whether she wants to waste her time with someone as messed up as me.

But just when I unearthed the courage to say something to her, I became overwhelmed by a litany of excuses. *Aren't you just being a tad selfish, Alex? The two of you have only just met, and there is still plenty of time for Eleanor to work things out for herself. After all, why spoil her journey of discovery?*

Satisfied with the purity of my logic, I leaned across Eleanor's chair and kissed her softly on her blood-red lips. 'Just my way of keeping you interested.'

'Of course it is,' she said. I watched with amusement as she focused on a tiny squirrel dancing happily along a nearby footpath. I loved how she bounced around from one issue to another and didn't get too stuck on things. If my life had been different, I could have quickly fallen for her.

It might have sounded implausible to those who witnessed our naked passion for themselves, but Eleanor and I had only just met forty-eight hours before. If you must know, the events that brought us together made quite a story. How we then dived headfirst into a full-on, bells-and-whistles, up-all-night, let's-go-for-it love affair was even more riveting.

Most of my friends in Australia were under the impression that the purpose of my holiday to the United Kingdom was to support our national Rugby Union team—the Wallabies—in the opening rounds of the 1999 Rugby World Cup. For the most part, that was the truth. But, as life often dictated, behind every fact existed a much bigger lie, or at least, a more deceitful way of explaining that truth.

Such was the tragedy of my current predicament, for my holiday had masked an especially shameful episode in my life. Five months previously, the culmination of everything that had begun in Samos triggered a bout of depression so severe that I attempted suicide inside a squalid little motel room in Bateman's Bay, on the south coast of New South Wales.

For the record, I came close to succeeding. If I try hard enough, I can still see the events of that lonely night unravel in my mind.

I see the bottle of prescribed sleeping tablets sitting on top of the bathroom sink. I see myself pour a glass of water and place ten pills in my hand. I see myself writing a note that explains why I have decided to take my own life. I see myself putting one of the pills to my lips. I see myself rolling the pill around in my mouth for several seconds. I see myself reaching out for the other pills.

An unholy darkness drifts across my room, and I temporarily lose myself within its ghostly embrace. When the light returns several seconds later, I see myself walking into the bathroom and flushing the pills down the toilet. I see myself overwhelmed with such uncontrollable anger that I collapse in exhaustion onto the floor. Finally, I see myself sinking into a troubled sleep on the very spot where I fall, my clothes soaked in sweat.

While I lay unconscious on the damp, cold ground, the ocean waves that smashed violently against the rocks outside my motel room guarded me jealously throughout the night. I woke up to the warm embrace of a new morning and watched through sizzling red eyes as fragments of sunlight waltzed happily through the half-drawn curtains of my room with military precision. I had somehow survived the night, and I was incredibly grateful.

The new day carried with it a simple message. I had been given another chance, and it was probably not one that I really deserved. Later that morning, as I strolled wearily along Batehaven Beach to clear my mind, I cursed my stupidity and vowed to make some immediate changes to my life. I could never allow something like this to happen again. As such, I needed to find a circuit breaker, a distraction that would resurrect my fallen spirit over the difficult months ahead.

As usual, whenever I needed some moral guidance, Jack had the answer. 'Mate, you have become the shell of the man that we all love,' he said with that cheeky smile as we sipped at our coffees in our favourite café in Manuka, Canberra. 'You need to have some fun again, be the old Alex, and take life less seriously.'

After a two-hour discussion, we finally agreed that partying in the United Kingdom for two months during the World Cup was the perfect tonic I needed to turn my life around. And so far, everything had gone exactly to plan.

I spent my first few days in London, getting over the usual jet lag and catching up with my sister, Anne, who was in England visiting her daughter, Vanessa. After visiting Buckingham Palace with Anne, I hopped on a National Express bus and began my long-awaited trek to Belfast, where I planned to meet up with Bill, my oldest friend.

We went back a long way, Bill and I—twenty-five years, to be precise—to another time when we were two skinny kids kicking a football together in a secluded, lonely park, lost within the dusty backstreets of Gladstone. But no matter where life took us, Bill always retained a telepathic ability to read my emotions. Whether he fully appreciated the extent of my pain as I walked off the ferry to greet him, I couldn't say, but he was never one to flounder in my self-pity either.

When I stored my luggage away in the boot of his car, he slapped me on the back, assured me that we were about to experience some great craic, and then dragged me off to his favourite Belfast pub. Yes, he knew what I needed: an old friend, a few laughs, good music, and many pints of amber fluid. After a few rowdy hours with Bill and the local Belfast populace, the blurry crucifix that I had been carrying on my shoulders for months gradually disappeared.

Then came the rugby. At first, I didn't care whether the Wallabies had a successful World Cup or not. The rugby was nothing more than a convenient excuse that explained my absence from Australia and created a platform through which I could have some fun again.

Australia was one of the favourites for the tournament, and they started off like the champions that they would ultimately be. Their first three games were all played on the Irish mainland, and one by one, Romania, the USA, and even Ireland fell to their collective might.

Bill accompanied me to Australia's opening game with Romania in Belfast. We both killed ourselves laughing when a female streaker danced onto the field during the second half of the game and was duly rewarded for her efforts with a blanket and a warm cup of tea by a local security guard. On the way back to Bill's house after the game, I decided that night had been a terrific omen for the rest of my holiday and promptly became infected with World Cup fever.

Now that I was formally behind the Wallabies, their progress through the tournament and the opportunity to celebrate their successes became my new obsession. If the World Cup had attracted my full attention, then damn it, the rest of Ireland was coming along with me for the ride.

From Belfast to Limerick to Dublin to Galway, I made new friends everywhere. I partied with such careless abandon that I fell in love with a different Irish woman every night, as well as many, many more Irish bartenders. When I visited some swanky Dublin hotel one cold Friday night and won a karaoke competition singing an unrehearsed mix of my favourite U2 songs, Ireland belonged to me!

But it didn't take long for the inevitable cracks to appear. Perhaps I was too old to party like a carefree adolescent, for it soon became apparent that if I didn't leave this wonderful country soon, I would die from that horrible Irish affliction: stout poisoning.

Indeed, on one incredibly bleak night in Galway, where I visited with all the best intentions of taking a short break from my excessive partying, I was about to enter the last hours of my life. I was sweating profusely; my stomach lining had dissolved entirely, and I looked as green as a clump of pure Irish clover.

As I prepared to die with as little dignity as possible, Norman, the morosely gruff owner of the hotel that I was staying in that night, reassured me that the symptoms I had were quite familiar with Galway's adult population most days of the week. He brazenly told me to grow some balls and then poured me another pint of Guinness for my trouble. I was genuinely amazed by how quickly I recovered.

Given that Australia had qualified for a quarter-final showdown with Wales in Cardiff on Saturday week, new worlds beckoned, and I couldn't justify my stay in Galway any longer. No-one understood this better than Norman, and he did everything possible to ensure that I stayed true to my cause. Indeed, he ruthlessly insisted that my time to leave had finally arrived.

'Aye, lad, the Wallabies need you, not Galway,' he reminded me during happy hour the following afternoon.

'But—' I tried to protest.

'No more excuses, lad.' His face seemed to catch fire whenever he spoke to me. 'You need to escape the temptations of this fine city and help your compatriots face their destiny. If you don't, I fear you will drink my bar completely dry. I have virtually run out of fookin' beer already, and for the life of me, I can't cope with your fookin' boring stories about fookin' Australia any fookin' longer! So please leave, I beg you! If you don't do this for your team, then at least fookin' do it for me!'

I didn't want to see a proud man like Norman cry, so I cheered him up with my bawdy collection of English jokes and promised him that I would depart Galway by first daylight. When he realised I was serious, he cracked a relieved smile and bought me a beer on the house, just for being such a good sport.

'I will miss you, lad,' he finally admitted to me after he refilled my empty glass one last time.

'Really?' I replied hopefully.

'Nah, not really. I'm just fookin' with your head.'

So with Norman's heartfelt blessing, I said goodbye to my lovely friend Kym, who had been travelling with me for the past few days, and began the arduous journey by ferry, bus, and train that would lead me back to London.

Although I hadn't washed or changed my clothes in over twenty-four hours, my priority upon disembarking at Victoria Street station was finding a travel agency. My new plan involved spending the next week bunkered down in hibernation before revisiting the World

Cup madness all over again in Cardiff. Indeed, as I explained to an overweight, balding travel agent while he sprayed air freshener around his desk, what I needed was guaranteed sunshine, a quiet place to read my book, and somewhere that didn't sell Irish stout.

He circled his computer terminal, tapped his feet once or twice on a plastic doormat, and then pointed excitedly to a loose bunch of travel brochures on his desk. 'What about Barcelona? Everything you need right now is there at your fingertips,' he cried out with all the conviction of a used car salesman. The 'five "S"s' he called it: soccer, sun, siestas, sangria, and senoritas. He even promised to book a Barcelona FC game for me on the house!

It didn't take long before I agreed to his indecent proposal. *Of course—Barcelona! Why hadn't I thought of that? Barcelona was indeed the perfect place to dry out for a few days, take in the local culture, eat some great food, and veg out next to a swimming pool. Well done, my chubby, hairless little friend, you have nailed it!* Although this change of plan would put a substantial hole in my limited budget, Barcelona would undoubtedly be the highlight of my holiday so far.

With my travel plans finalised, I needed to find somewhere to kip for the next two nights before my scheduled flight to Spain. Whenever I visited London, I usually stayed in the Bloomsbury precinct. Twenty minutes later, I jumped off the tube at Russell Square station and shuffled with my luggage towards one of my favourite hotels, the Royal National.

With the details of my trip to Barcelona fresh in my mind, I was overwhelmed with excitement for what the next few days offered me. There was no better feeling in the world than being on holiday in a large city like London, where no-one knew your name, and you had the ultimate freedom of your own company.

'Gerrick, you ugly bastard!' my old primary school friend Dick Reilly suddenly yelled from a car window as he weaved past the nearest set of traffic lights. *Er, didn't I last see Dick Reilly in Gladstone in Grade 6, twenty-five years ago? Or was that Grade 7?*

Unperturbed by Dick Reilly's uninvited appearance, I inevitably became distracted by a local bookshop and then wasted more time ordering a takeaway coffee. Only when I walked back along the footpath to throw away my empty Styrofoam cup into a bin did I notice a freshly painted three-star property staring at me from across the road. The Royal National suddenly felt miles away and I decided that it would be fun to try a different hotel.

Okay, the room I soon purchased was disturbingly small, the bathroom smelt of seaweed, and there was a weird-looking brown stain running down my shower curtain. But it was mainly spotless, the double bed was large and firm, a spacious dining room served breakfast, and most importantly, it was very cheap! Look, I wasn't expecting the Taj Mahal. All I needed was somewhere to flop, a laundromat to wash my filthy clothes, and a local barber to get a much-needed haircut. And if I had enough time, I would also take the opportunity to visit the British Museum, which was barely a ten-minute walk down the road.

Everything ran like clockwork on that first night. I discovered an outlandishly decorated Indian restaurant in Southampton Row, where I treated myself to a mouth-tingling beef vindaloo curry, which helped to clean out my clogged sinuses. I then dived into an animated discussion with the head chef on whether Sachin Tendulkar was a better batsman than Brian Lara. After I finished dessert, he gave me a complimentary glass of wine because I knew so much about cricket, and I left him a healthy tip in return.

Following dinner, I strolled dreamily along Oxford street for a lazy hour, bought some much-needed toiletries from a Boots pharmacy, and returned to my hotel around ten-thirty. I picked up a spare copy of the *London Times* from the lobby, bumped into a raucous group of young Spanish tourists out for a night on the town, and then fell asleep during a re-run of *Minder* on television.

I woke up feeling refreshed for the first time in weeks and ready to take on the world. I quickly showered and dressed, ran a razor over my pale face, and hurried downstairs to the dining room. It was seven-thirty, and I was confident that this would be the quietest time of the morning to have breakfast as most guests would either still be asleep or just getting ready for the day ahead. But alas, as always, an assumption of mine was misplaced.

Far from being a quiet sanctuary, the dining room was a conveyor belt of loud, disorganised chatter. An eclectic collection of businesspeople, holidaymakers, and excited school children were all crammed in shoulder to shoulder as they contemplated their upcoming day over bacon, eggs, and baked beans.

Bugger! It will have to be takeaway, then. At least I will be better prepared for tomorrow morning.

A small, plump Pakistani waiter named Jamal with a wide smile and even wider girth shuffled his way over to me to state the obvious: 'We are pretty much full at the moment, sir—pretty much full.'

I quickly explained to him that I was happy to go elsewhere for breakfast.

'No, no,' he demanded. 'I will find a seat for you, sir. Just you wait and see!'

He skipped away excitedly before I could lift a hand in protest and soon returned with a satisfied grin on his cherubic face.

'I found somewhere for you, sir. Yes, indeed. Just over there with the young lady, and she is happy for you to sit with her.'

Jamal's skinny index finger pointed to a table barely several feet away, and we both focused on an empty chair wedged next to a young woman with shoulder-length black hair. I watched closely as she delicately stole tiny sips of coffee from a gleaming white mug before burying her head into a glossy magazine.

Even from where I was standing, I could tell that the woman was beautiful. She was probably in her late twenties, with crystal blue eyes that could sink a cruise liner and a deep brown tan that seemed to glow in the shadow of the room's drab interior. She had the look of someone who knew that she was good-looking but didn't care what mere mortals like me thought about her. True to form, I was immediately smitten.

My leering was interrupted by a burst of laughter blaring from the table directly behind her. Over recent months, I had become annoyingly short-sighted, and the new glasses that I rarely wore—due to my vanity—were packed somewhere at the bottom of my suitcase. So, while I could see the woman's table, what lay beyond her was a complete mystery.

It took some high-level squinting before I finally made out that this crude racket belonged to those four Spanish punks who I had briefly met last night in the hotel lobby. Having finished their coffees, it presented them with the perfect opportunity to compare their sordid little notes about the woman's physical attributes as loudly as they could.

They seemed rather determined to use the word '*senos*' in their sentences, and whenever they did, it made them laugh even louder. Yeah, I did know a word or two of Spanish: *senos* meant 'breasts'. *Idiots.* Their tawdry behaviour only reinforced the unfavourable first impression they created with me last night.

Unfortunately, one of them suddenly caught my eye and furiously waved his hand at me to say hello. When I refused to return the compliment, he sneakily whispered something to his friends behind his hands, and they all collectively laughed in my direction.

I should have said something about their appalling behaviour, but if I did, this would have made me quite the hypocrite. After all, I was secretly delighted with the situation that was unfolding before me. I had been awake a little over an hour, and I was suddenly about to meet a beautiful woman over breakfast. Wasn't this the single man's dream while on holiday? I was sure those Spanish guys realised this and were equally convinced that I stood no chance with her. *So, go ahead and laugh—I dare you to. Because I am standing here, and you are all sitting over there.*

Despite the growing butterflies in my stomach, I felt strangely confident as I strode towards the woman's table. But halfway across the room, I suddenly froze dead in my tracks and stared hopelessly at the cracked ceiling for further guidance. Only then did I realise that my knees were shaking in abject terror at the thought of talking to a stranger. The sad reality was that ever since Bateman's Bay, I had completely lost my mojo with the opposite sex—if, indeed, I ever had one.

But that was the risk you took when you specialised in destroying relationships, especially your own. Consequently, I avoided one-on-one meetings with single women whenever I could. Those halcyon days of charming Lottie on the ferry or serenading Martina on the beach were nothing more than the faded illusions of some other man. So rather than embarrassing myself further in front of the Spanish Inquisition, I decided that the time had come for me to leave.

What I failed to appreciate, though, was that Jamal had been designated my guardian angel for the day, and he had written an entirely different script for me. Before I could disappear into the abyss, he dropped some cutlery into my hand, picked up the empty chair next to the woman, and then calmly lifted it over to the other side of the table so that it was directly facing her. Delighted with the precision of his work, Jamal snatched at my forearm and then catapulted me headfirst towards her. 'Go on, sir,' he urged. 'I'm sure she won't bite.'

'That's easy for you to say,' I snarled back at him before crash-landing right next to the empty chair. Although the sound of my clumsiness vibrated across the room to everyone else's amusement, the woman, who I can now reveal to be Eleanor, barely found the time to lift her head from her magazine.

I nervously swallowed several bubbles of smoky air and invented a new way of sitting down without falling over my feet.

Okay, so what do I do now? Well, how about an attempt at meaningful conversation?

'Thanks for letting me sit at your table,' I offered tentatively.

Eleanor barely flinched at the sound of my voice. 'Whatever,' she quietly grumbled into her coffee.

Hey, look at me! What a stud! A few more spectacular pick-up lines like that one, and I will soon be swinging with the best of them.

Not wishing to court further rejection, I shuffled around uncomfortably in my seat to relieve the growing tension in my backside. With nothing else to offer, I decided to hide my growing embarrassment by trying to guess Eleanor's accent. I eventually settled on either German or Scandinavian but then realised I would never have a proper conversation with her to determine whether I was right. Happy to concede defeat at last, I buried my head into the breakfast menu and dreamt about the different ways I would kill Jamal.

'Excuse me. As much as it is none of my business, I think your menu is upside down. You will find that if you turn it the other way around, this will help you make a much better choice. It certainly worked for me.'

It took several rounds of abject humiliation before I realised that Eleanor was talking to me. I slowly absorbed every word she had just said, allowed them to swirl around my brain some more, and then nervously peeked back at my menu. *No! Tell me I haven't! Please! Oh God, she is right! You moron!*

I tried to avoid the inevitable as long as possible, but I couldn't stare at my skinny knees forever. When I finally found the courage to raise my eyes to her, Eleanor was waiting for me with a reluctant smile. Okay, it was more like a contrived smirk, which said something along the lines of: 'I think you are a loser, but a nice one, nevertheless.' Her newfound conviviality convinced me to rock my head back at her in fake surprise, just to see where it would take me. Of course, she had no choice other than to laugh at my clumsy attempt at self-deprecation.

I slowly turned the menu around and placed it on the table. 'Thank you, but I'm not that hungry,' I replied sheepishly, even though, in truth, I possibly *could* have eaten a sheep if someone had served it to me.

'No, you are having the hot breakfast,' she demanded. Her accent may have been coarse, but her words were perfectly constructed as if English was her natural language. To ensure that I had understood her point, she slammed her mug down on the table and snapped her fingers at Jamal.

'I am?'

'Yes, you are. You see, I partied late into the night, and I desperately need another coffee. And I don't intend to sit here by myself while there is a chance that one of those morons at the next table will come over here and hit on me.'

'You can speak Spanish then?'

'Yes, Einstein, I can speak Spanish. So, if you can indulge me for just a little longer, you are ordering the hot breakfast.'

Now, here is a tip for all the single guys out there: if a strange, beautiful woman ever asks you to order the hot breakfast, that's what you do. I did, and it was the catalyst for the most unforgettable week of my life. Indeed, should you be fortunate enough to find yourself in such a situation, I can only hope that your cause, like mine, is greatly enhanced by the likes of an overly persistent waiter and a group of sleazy tourists.

Despite her glorious mystique and self-contained persona, Eleanor was surprisingly quick to reveal details about herself. For a moment, I wondered whether she had just graduated from a speed-dating course. Through various snippets of disjointed chatter, I quickly discovered that she was twenty-seven years old and had grown up in the beautiful Austrian city of Salzburg.

Sometimes coincidences are wonderfully enigmatic, especially when you are chatting up a gorgeous young woman. I explained to Eleanor with an excited smile that I had visited Salzburg two years before in 1997, which made her beam with pride. The birthplace of Mozart was indeed one of the most majestic cities in Europe, I told her, richly adorned by a myriad of baroque and medieval architecture that left one breathless. When Eleanor then asked me whether I had visited Salzburg Cathedral, where she had gone to mass every week as a child, I was able to easily wax lyrical about its exquisite beauty for several heartfelt minutes.

However, there was one thing about Salzburg that still disturbed me after all this time. It involved the city's association with *The Sound of Music.* I recalled my very first night in town when that sinister group of tour guides accosted me in the main square of the city and unsuccessfully tried to push Maria Von Trapp's epic story into my wallet at every opportunity. And how, after I bravely resisted their evil advances, they then attacked me with an entrée of meaningless trinkets and T-shirts to further demean the experience.

Don't get me wrong: *The Sound of Music* is a beautiful movie, but after you have watched the same film 999 times across three consecutive nights, fully dressed in lederhosen, like the overly parochial owner of my B&B in Salzburg insisted I do, it suddenly loses its charm. Indeed, when I finally escaped my confinement by digging a tunnel beneath the television room, I promised myself that I would never watch *The Sound of Music* again as long as I lived.

No, the bottom line for me was that *The Sound of Music* was a deal-breaker. After all, one should always be loyal to their values. If Eleanor admitted that she loved the movie, I was out of there.

'Of course,' Eleanor continued, 'Salzburg is also home to that wonderful movie, *The Sound of Music*. Have you ever watched it?'

'Are you kidding me?' I yelled out so everyone in the dining room could hear me. 'Several times, if you must know! It is my favourite movie of all time, and those songs are just something else. I can hardly wait to see it again!'

(I should add here that this is another lesson for the superficial single man. If you need to choose between a beautiful woman or your values, then feel free to betray those values whenever you want.)

Impressed that I was a fellow admirer of Rodgers and Hammerstein, Eleanor proceeded to reveal even more about herself. While my brain worked overtime to keep up with her rapid-fire delivery, she painted a vivid picture of an impressive young woman who had the world at her feet.

Her occupation? Eleanor was a high school teacher with degrees in history and languages who worked at an exclusive all-girls school in Paris. She was at the wrong end of a six-week holiday of Scandinavia and the British Isles with Danielle, her French best friend and co-worker. Danielle was currently visiting Oxford on a personal matter, and the two of them would reunite in London next week before they began a bus tour of Scotland.

Eleanor spoke four languages fluently: English, Spanish, French, and, of course, German. Just like me, she was an avid lover of history who had spent much of her time in England trampling through many of its fabulous museums.

Her interests? She loved to ski and snowboard, which explained her deep snow-tan, and enjoyed amateur theatre and ballet, which explained her quirky self-confidence. Her favourite band was Radiohead, and her favourite author was Stephen King. She possessed a curious addiction to B-grade horror movies and low-budget chick flicks for someone so educated. Her ultimate dream was to one day work in America.

Her status? She was single (yippee!) and revelled in being the dedicated party girl. She became engaged to her high school sweetheart at twenty-three but then broke up with him weeks before their wedding after discovering that he had cheated on her with a close friend. *Ouch.* Apart from the occasional dalliance, Eleanor was determined to remain her own woman.

I would agree that this was an incredible amount of information to glean from one breakfast conversation. But that's what made our time together that morning so special. There were no uncomfortable pauses or misplaced thoughts that so often embarrassed single people when they met for the first time. We had become curiously relaxed in each other's company, and I wanted to spend even more time with her.

With that thought on my mind, Jamal suddenly appeared out of nowhere and pointed to his wrist. 'Hello there. We close soon, so you need to finish up. Yes, please!'

I glanced at my watch to make sure that Jamal wasn't bullshitting us. But as usual, he was right on the money. It was nine-thirty! I couldn't believe that Eleanor and I had been talking for nearly two hours! We had become so engrossed in our conversation that we didn't even notice when those Spanish misfits left the dining room.

With Jamal's warning lingering over us, Eleanor and I waited for the other person to make the first move. Yes, what we had here was a good old-fashioned stalemate. Neither Eleanor nor I wanted to get scorned and humiliated—there was the bigger picture to think about. But given my newly acquired shyness around women, the ball was definitely in Eleanor's court. Thankfully, she had more grit than I did and didn't let either of us down.

'I am going to the British Museum this morning. Would you like to join me?'

Would I like to join you? I wanted to wake up the rest of London by screaming out 'Yes!' as loudly as I could, but instead, I did my best to look calm and collected. 'Sure, I would love to,' I replied in a cool, baritone voice.

'Brilliant! Meet you in the lobby in an hour.' It was as simple as that.

After Eleanor left the dining room, I offered Jamal an excited salute and then galloped up to my room with the speed of a lovesick gazelle. There was much work to be done! For it was imperative that I arrived at the lobby well before Eleanor did. You see, I still couldn't believe that she wanted to spend the morning with me, and I didn't want to give her any excuse to change her mind. Motivated by my fragility, I re-showered, squirted on some extra aftershave, blended in a smidgin of hair gel here and there, and finally reached into my suitcase for that unworn navy-blue shirt I had bought for half-price in Dublin.

Hey, don't overdo things, Alex. That might scare her away. So I kept on the same pair of dark-blue jeans and black runners I had worn at breakfast and took one last look at myself in the mirror. *Damn it!* As usual, I found so many things to hate about myself. And why didn't I get that damn haircut? But I quickly realised that I was looking for excuses to have a miserable time.

So, just this once, stop it, shit-for-brains. Drop the whole 'woe is me' crap and go out and enjoy yourself for a change. I mean, apart from my pride, self-confidence, and sanity, what did I have to lose?

The Movie

London
October 1999

By the time I reached the lobby, my lungs were pleading for air, but I was delighted that I had been able to beat the clock and Eleanor so easily. That was until I found her propped up against the reception desk, scrunching her hair into a ponytail. The smile that she offered me alternated between cunning and sweet as if she knew of my plan well in advance and was always destined to outsmart me.

'I wasn't expecting you so soon,' she said playfully.

'I never like to keep a lady waiting,' I replied. I graciously waited for Eleanor to stop her stifled giggling before I pointed towards the front door. 'Shall we?'

We were greeted by a sumptuous London autumn morning, and the beautiful daffodils on display in Russell Square only sweetened the air around us. If I needed any other reason, the allure of such a gorgeous day only reinforced why Bloomsbury had become so special to me.

I explained to Eleanor that I found myself transported back in time to Victorian England whenever I walked along these lonely, narrow streets. I spent idle days and cool, lazy evenings engaging with writers, artists, courtesans, and scientists about everything and nothing within this fantasy world. Lunch with EM Forster. Tea with Virginia Wolfe. Dinner with HG Wells. It was a place where I had the freedom to create my destiny for the universe. Eleanor listened politely before laughing at my curious imagination.

The British Museum was open for business, greeting visitors from all over the world. Mothers shooed in bored young children. School teachers barked out orders to their restless minions to line up in an orderly fashion. Overweight tour guides tried to explain to equally overweight tourists that admission was perfectly free. But the only thing that mattered to Eleanor and me was the undeniable attraction that was growing between us.

While Eleanor and I had ignited our mutual attraction at breakfast, it was our love of history that consolidated our spiritual connection. Every moment that we spent together in the museum created another step in our magical journey—one that ferried us through the halls of time itself and bound us to a force that we could never explain. Within this prism, we saw everything as it was, as it is, and as it should be.

We saw Greek philosophers create new worlds out of words, ideas, and the desires of others. We saw Roman consuls fire their chariots across stoned pathways, looking for new lands to conquer. We saw pharaohs build pyramids through the sweat and toil of faceless men who craved their freedom. Everywhere we went, we saw light, we saw darkness, we saw good, we saw evil, we saw faith, we saw despair. We rejoiced in the sanctity of these emotions and understood how they would shape our futures. For Eleanor and me, nothing was more important.

That was until I got exceptionally randy in the Egyptology exhibition and thought of ways of whisking her back to my hotel room for a quickie. You see, while Eleanor was thoroughly inspecting an Egyptian artefact, I was thoroughly inspecting her. The more I succumbed to her intoxicating charms, the more I became this gormless, blithering, imbecile with one thing on my mind. So much for the sanctity of history and our spiritual connection.

Yes, part of me felt like a total sleazebag, no different at all to those Spanish sleazebags at breakfast. One, perhaps, could even mount an argument that I was a higher level of creep because of my feigned outrage at their behaviour. But, given my track record in Greece with Martina and Lottie, it didn't surprise me that it had taken me barely half a day to become hopelessly smitten with a beautiful girl like Eleanor.

'Having a good look, Alex?' Eleanor muttered coldly, her hands folded firmly against her chest.

Oh God, not again!

Just like Martina in that stupid little jeep four years ago, a woman had caught me ogling her. Well, if it was any consolation, at least this time it was intentional. Although Martina's ire was immediately evident and her retribution excruciatingly swift, it was difficult to ascertain from Eleanor's stony silence whether I was in trouble or not. So I slithered behind the Egyptian mummies to my left for protection and decided to go on the attack.

'It's impossible not to look at you. You are so beautiful.'

Those spineless mummies were quick to betray me. Rather than supporting me during my time of adversity, they screamed out in terror and skulked into the afternoon shadows to escape the oncoming bloodshed.

But, to our surprise, Eleanor's lips undertook a complete U-turn and curled into a cheeky grin. 'I will let you in on a little secret, shall I?' she said while readjusting her ponytail. 'I was watching you before while you were studying the Rosetta Stone. Has anyone told you that you look like Richard Hunte?'

'Well, now that you've mentioned it—'

'So,' she interrupted me, 'I have decided, based solely on this criterion, that you are allowed to escort me around London for the rest of the day.'

'And I thought that you were impressed with my knowledge of Ancient Rome.'

'Are you kidding?' she said, laughing. 'I know more about Rome than you do! My sole focus is *LA Hero*, Rodeo Drive, and some outrageous cocktails.'

'*LA Hero* is so overrated,' I replied, pretending to be serious. 'And in my humble opinion, you are so much better-looking than any of his female co-stars.'

Eleanor allowed my latest compliment to wash right over her, but I could see the innate smugness in her eyes. She then pressed me further. 'Which of his films would you recommend?'

'*A Gentleman and a Patriot,* of course.'

'Yes, that was indeed a very romantic film,' Eleanor said with a seductive twitch of her nose. 'But now the big question: are you really a gentleman or are you just pretending to be one so you can get into my pants?'

Come on, Alex! Your big moment has arrived! She has left it open for you to make the next move! It's time to reply with something clever and flirtatious!

But despite my willingness to progress this erotic game of cat and mouse, my capacity for the witty retort sadly abandoned me. As much as I tried, nothing intelligible was able to escape my wretched lips. I was so overwrought with stage fright all I could do was bobble my mouth up and down in front of Eleanor.

Just when all seemed lost, I suddenly remembered that I had exclusive access to the greatest Casanova the world has ever known—my friend, Bill. He could charm the skin off a snake, the wings off a fly, the hind legs off a donkey, the habit off a n—Well, you get my point. I could hear him yelling at me from across the Irish sea.

'Tell her that you are definitely not a gentleman and that she should come back to your hotel to find out why!'

Of course! That's perfect! Why didn't I think of that?

Alas, even though I appreciated Bill's contribution very much, I quickly decided against offering her such an unruly invitation. On another day, I would have called it cold feet, and I'm sure that this was what Bill would have called it too. I could see his incredulous red face bursting down at me from above. '*What the hell are you doing, son?'* he implored. '*Are you crazy? Probably, Bill, but this is solely my decision.* Damn me with faint praise, but on this occasion, I did the right thing.

'Lucky for you, I am both a patriot and a gentleman. So you're safe for the time being.'

'Just as I suspected,' Eleanor teased me. 'But your punishment for being such a frightful bore is to buy me lunch.'

We ordered some toasted sandwiches at the museum café and then found a table next to a middle-aged couple arguing about a half-eaten apple.

'Yeah, marriage is real fun,' she quipped, and I laughed at her cattiness.

Now that our museum date had finished, I tried to work out in my head what my next move should be. I did some computations, multiplied a couple of fractions, subtracted Y from X, and then settled on a plan to take Eleanor for a gentle stroll to Buckingham Palace. But just when I was about to make this suggestion, she released an almighty yawn which managed to dismantle my fragile ego completely.

'You look tired,' I offered sadly. 'Have you had enough? Do you want to go back to the hotel?'

She glared at me as if I had just won the London Idiot of the Year Award. 'Aren't you enjoying my company, Richard Hunte?' Her icy cold stare gave the impression that I had mortally offended her.

'I'm just worried about you, that's all.' It sounded positively trite and positively stupid, and she positively agreed with me.

'Here's the deal,' she lectured me. 'How about you let me worry about how I feel, and you can worry about how we are to spend the rest of the afternoon.'

I accepted her fierce rebuke with a plastic smile and then offered up another brilliant idea. 'How about we see a movie?'

Happily, this suggestion received a much better reaction, and her face immediately brightened. 'Good thinking. See? You have now added value to my day.'

We decided to walk down to Leicester Square, where several movie theatres were waiting for us. The first one offered us a choice between two films: *The Last Wedding*, which just happened to star Richard Hunte, or *The Blair Witch Project*. I was inclined to see a chick flick that starred, well, me! How could Eleanor possibly say no?

'No,' she said rather emphatically. 'I'm not watching a movie about weddings.' She suddenly shook her tiny hand at me. 'And between you and me—as an actor, I think Richard Hunte stinks!'

She spat out that last bit like she wanted to hurt my feelings, and I couldn't figure out why. Then it all made perfect sense—*The Last Wedding*. Remember? She was recently engaged.

But wait! Eleanor also loved horror films, did she not? So what about *Blair Witch*? 'No, Danielle and I only saw it a few weeks ago.'

I was just about to acknowledge that this whole movie idea had 'A-grade disaster' written all over it when Eleanor suddenly belted me excitedly on the arm. 'Look, Alex.' She pointed to a massive black and white poster in the foyer. 'They are playing classic movies here this week, and *The Sound of Music* is about to start in fifteen minutes! What a coincidence!'

Noooooooooooooooooooooooooooooooooooooooooooooooooooooooo!

A cold, dark panic erupted from the bottom of my stomach, but there was nowhere for me to run. *Please, God, there has to be a way out of here!* My eyes darted hopefully across the floor for an emergency exit, anything, but all I could see were people lining up for candy and drinks.

I can't do it! I won't do it! Not even for her!

But Mini-Alex, the irritating voice that lived inside my head and occasionally told me what to do, suddenly intervened. *'Pull yourself together, Alex,'* he ordered. *'When did the word* can't *enter your vocabulary? This isn't about the movie. This is about spending time with a beautiful Austrian woman in a dark, cosy theatre. Now, get your shit together and buy those tickets!'*

God bless Mini-Alex! Usually, he was an utter moron, but that day he actually made a positive contribution for once, and I suddenly became inflicted with a half-witted desire to make this all work. Yes, I could even sit through 'My Favourite Things', I reassured myself.

But just when I was able to find a crumb of positivity out of this unfolding madness, a horrendous thought circulated inside my head. *How would I respond if Eleanor, God forbid, suddenly asked me to sing along with her during the movie? No, don't even think about it, Alex! The implications are way too awful to contemplate. Besides, I could always fake a heart attack if things became desperate.* Satisfied that I had all angles covered, I managed to buy two tickets and some popcorn without incident, and pretty soon, we were snuggled together in the middle of the theatre.

But who was I trying to kid? Admittedly, things started to come apart at the seams as early as the coming attractions, but once the theatre manager drew the curtains, the lights began to dim, and Maria came bouncing over the hill singing the title song; I wanted to slam my head into a meat-grinder. And when those horrid nuns started to belt out 'How to solve a problem like Maria', I suddenly remembered that my mother's birthday had arrived three months earlier this year and that I had to ring her immediately.

But alas, my prevarication was always destined to bite me on the arse. As I was about to leap out of my chair towards freedom, Eleanor suddenly collapsed on top of me, sinking her weary head across my forearm. Within seconds, dainty snippets of air began to leak out of her mouth while I was left to counter the pins and needles driving their way along the contours of my neck.

What a disaster! Not only had she fallen asleep, but I was insanely trapped beneath her, forced to endure the never-ending horror of seeing the same movie for the 1,000th time all by myself! What's more, any chance of making out with her in the dark had slowly evaporated into the snow-capped Austrian Alps.

But despite my outrageously childish behaviour, I somehow managed to steer myself through the next two hours of misery with something resembling good humour. Incredibly, I soon found myself humming to 'Do-Re-Mi' and even shed a few tears when Baron Von Trapp sang 'Edelweiss'. Eleanor woke up just in time for the Von Trapp family to begin their escape from Austria. Her face exuded sugar and spice, and we both knew that I wouldn't get angry with her.

'I'm so sorry,' she said with a laugh. 'I normally don't fall asleep on top of strange men like that.'

She brushed away popcorn crumbs from her blouse, and we quietly stepped into the late-afternoon twilight only to be greeted by a savage burst of stinging rain.

It was the perfect time to take the initiative. Or at least I thought it was. 'Can I buy you dinner?' I offered her.

Eleanor's bloodshot eyes were telling. 'You know what, I might take a raincheck if you don't mind. I really ought to have an early night. I'm so sorry about the movie, Alex.'

Her words struck me with the force of an intercontinental ballistic missile. *What a fool I was to believe that a woman like this would be interested in me for more than a few hours.*

'Okay, then,' I grumbled. 'Let's go back to the hotel.' I didn't want Eleanor to see the worms of disappointment crawling across my face, so I stormed off in front of her like a spoilt child, desperate to lose myself within the oncoming crowd.

But before my legs could gain any traction, Eleanor grasped my hand and yanked me towards an open kerb in the street. With a ballerina's touch, she swivelled her hips into my body and then kissed me on the cheek.

'There, you idiot. Are all Australian men thick like you? I am not trying to brush you off. I'm exhausted and need a good night's sleep so I will be better behaved tomorrow when you show me the rest of London.'

Her words immediately sent me spiralling into an enormous crater of euphoria. *She likes me! There I go, silly me again! Worrying about nothing! Thinking of the worst!* The thought that I would see her again the next day overwhelmed me with pure happiness.

Yes, tomorrow! When I'm in Barcelona.

What?

Uh-oh …

'You look worried, Alex. Is something wrong? Do you have other plans tomorrow?'

I avoided answering her at first because my brain had suddenly become entangled in a high-stakes game of mental tennis.

Barcelona. Eleanor. Barcelona. Eleanor. Barcelona. Eleanor.

While the longest rally in mental tennis history continued to unravel, Eleanor stood impatiently in the rain, waiting for my response.

'How could you even think about not going to Barcelona?' Mini-Alex angrily snarled. *'Remember all the things that we wanted to see? Las Ramblas? La Segrada Família? The Picasso Museum? And what about Barcelona Football Club? This might be the only opportunity you will ever get to see them play a live game. Are you that desperate that you would give this all up for a woman you have barely known for a day?'*

'I thought we might visit Windsor Castle tomorrow if you would like that?'

'Sounds great,' said Eleanor. Her striking blue eyes dazzled brightly against the grey sheets of rain that tumbled all around her. 'Lucky for you, though.'

'How so?'

'If you delayed your response any longer, I was going to beat you over the head with my handbag.'

And I knew her well enough by that stage to believe every word she said.

Mary Queen of Scots

London
Saturday, October 1999

Once we had returned our deckchairs to the attendants inside St James Park, Eleanor and I thought it would be fun to visit Westminster Abbey. I suggested that we walk back down Pall Mall and make a right turn at Trafalgar Square, but Eleanor insisted that we follow what she contended to be the more scenic route through the park. I had learnt enough about Eleanor over the last forty-eight hours to realise that it was pointless to defy her wishes once she had decided on something, so I casually nodded my head in agreement.

When I finished dusting away the leaves and twigs that somehow found their way into my jeans, Eleanor snatched at my hand and clenched it tightly against her upper thigh. We managed to stay connected like this until we reached the relative safety of Downing Street, after which I used the bellowing crick in my neck as an excuse to release myself from her grip.

Dear God, Eleanor! Do you realise what you have just done? Surely, she must have been familiar with the universal checklist for new relationships and understood that she had just defied all protocol by jumping several steps. I mean, the implied holding of hands in public. That was like, number six. Man, we hadn't even argued yet about leaving the toilet seat up! If I remembered correctly, that was a locked-in, sure-fire, number ten!

No, the implied holding of hands had set a dangerous precedent, one that I was reluctant to oblige at this stage of proceedings. This could only mean one thing—Eleanor thought we were a legitimate couple. After only two days, might I add! Understandably, my body tensed at the mere thought. You see, this whole 'couple' thing rarely worked for me.

My mind wandered back to the previous morning and how quickly we fell down the love well together. Of course, I cancelled my trip to Barcelona and lost one thousand Australian dollars in the process. The chubby, balding travel agent was not impressed with me at all, even when I explained to him over the phone that my poor sick grandmother had recently died in Glasgow from bacterial pneumonia.

Look, I wasn't motivated by money. I was a generous person who didn't care about personal wealth as long as I could travel, buy my history books, and watch sport on the most prominent TV I could afford. House. Car. Expensive clothes. I did not need any of these things. But yeah, I bitched and moaned like crazy when I realised that I had lost a large amount of cash for no other reason than to satisfy my lurid desires.

But when Eleanor joined me for breakfast, every negative thought I had about the situation disappeared into the bottom of my porridge bowl. She was wearing a short tartan skirt with black pantyhose and shiny leather boots, while her overly tight red woollen jumper left nothing to the imagination. A light pasting of make-up dazzled her skin while her hair, released from the burden of the previous day's ponytail, fell enticingly over the contours of her chest.

'*Okay, I take back what I said yesterday,*' admitted Mini-Alex. '*You made the right choice, bud.*'

'No shit, Sherlock,' I whispered back at him.

She greeted me with a sensual kiss that narrowly missed my lips. From the corner of my eye, I could see Jamal smiling at me, proud as Punch that he was responsible for all the chaos spinning inside my head. *Righto Jamal, you have had your moment in the sun. Now piss off.*

'So, how do I look?' Eleanor asked with a smug smile.

'Do you have a job interview this morning?' I replied, trying hard to be funny.

Her frown was downright scary. 'Are you always this complimentary to a girl who has made a huge effort to look nice for you?'

'Can I get back to you on that one?'

'Alex!'

'Okay, how about this? There aren't enough adjectives in the English language to describe how incredible you look'.

'Perhaps you should invent some just to please me,' she demanded.

'Perhaps I will.'

After we finished our coffees, we ran down to Russell Square station as fast as possible to avoid the early morning rush on the tube. After a couple of line changes, we safely boarded the waiting train to Windsor. We negotiated the next few stops with some idle chitchat about football and the weather. Everything was friendly and relaxed between us, and I genuinely looked forward to a fun day. But when the train gently pulled up at Earl's Court station, Eleanor suddenly tugged at my arm.

'Do you have your heart set on Windsor Castle, Alex?'

'I'm not married to the idea; put it that way.'

'Good.'

'So, what would you like to do instead?'

She warily placed her hand on my thigh. 'What I really would like to do is get a proper hotel room and spend the day with you.'

I took my time to respond to her request, as it required careful consideration. One point two seconds later, I replied: 'Yeah, why not?'

We both giggled as we sprinted up the station escalators and hailed down a taxi. We drove back to Bloomsbury and chose a four-star property just around the corner from our other hotel. Eleanor worked her acting magic and somehow convinced the hotel's bemused reception staff that two people with no luggage urgently required a room at nine-thirty in the morning. Her performance was worthy of an Academy Award if, indeed, they gave out awards for impromptu performances like hers. We eventually made it to the lift, and then our hotel room, where …

Nothing more to see here, I'm afraid. All I can divulge is that our time together felt special for both of us. My desire to be with a woman again was incredibly potent after my year of turmoil, and I could tell by the softness of her touch that Eleanor felt the same way. Whatever personal demons had bedevilled us in the past, there was a sense of relief that we could forget about them, even if it was for a few short hours.

We didn't join the rest of humanity until dinner, when we reluctantly made our way downstairs to the hotel restaurant. She ordered pasta, and I grabbed a steak. After some needless chatter, we shared a bottle of merlot and then smiled curiously at each other.

'Any regrets?' she suddenly asked me.

I was not ready for such a question. 'Of course not. You?'

'Not at all. However, I am a little surprised at myself. I have old-fashioned, Catholic views about sex, and I rarely do one-night stands.'

'Is this a one-night stand?' I asked inquisitively.

She pretended not to hear me. 'Oh well,' she said to herself before slurping down more wine. Eleanor looked remarkably guilty for someone who insisted that she had no regrets. I found this a little odd initially, especially given how she appeared at breakfast dressed like the Mata Hari. But things often changed with two people after they shagged for the first time. The quirky, confident Eleanor that I met the previous morning had become a reflective, fragile version of the same person. It was almost as if our time together had stripped an invisible veneer from her heart.

After we ordered dessert, she started to discuss her life, and I was strangely intrigued by the intricacy of her sadness. She talked mainly about her ex-fiancée, Otto—her childhood sweetheart since primary school—their plans, dreams, all the places they wanted to visit. How it all went up in smoke because of some blonde floozy Otto admitted he didn't even like. His betrayal had placed an emotional line in the sand for Eleanor that she could never cross.

'I just don't think I am capable of a long-term relationship again,' she admitted. 'I was so hurt by what Otto did to me. I find it extremely hard to trust men anymore.'

If you must know, I had nothing appropriate to say to her—no soothing words or cheeky witticism that would make her feel better. A year ago, I had also betrayed the woman I had planned to marry. You see, I was in no position to take the moral high ground by criticising Otto or even attempting to explain his motivation for hurting her. Indeed, I was sure that Eleanor would think poorly of me if she only knew how I had treated Rachel.

Rather than being an active participant in my demise, I sat back quietly in my chair and carefully listened to her desperate ramblings, hoping to God that this was all she wanted me to do. As luck would have it, my patience seemed to have been the perfect antidote for her sombre tale. By the time our desserts arrived, she had completely lost her train of thought. Once we started an unintentional food fight with our strawberries, she was back to being her old self.

After dinner, we strolled down to Trafalgar Square. The evening was cool and crisp, and we remained lost in our thoughts until we arrived at Nelson's Column. Despite the hundreds of other tourists who had also decided to assemble at this iconic London meeting place, Eleanor and I somehow found ourselves a lonely set of steps, far away from the gathering crowd. I heroically drew her into my body to protect her from the growing cold, and she displayed her gratitude with a dazzling smile. We sat together like this as we marvelled at a shooting star that whisked across the moonlit sky.

'Thank you for listening to me at dinner,' she said, suddenly breaking the silence. There was no need for her to thank me, and I told her so.

'Sometimes a girl just wants a guy to listen to her,' she explained. 'No questions or solutions. Just listen without any interruptions. And you did that. I like that about you.' I wanted to congratulate myself, but this wasn't the time or place to tempt fate.

'Have you given any thought about what happens tomorrow?' she asked me in a half-whisper, tiny strands of her hair bundling into my face.

'Not really,' I replied. 'Have you?'

'Just as I thought.' Eleanor laughed. 'Do you always leave it for the woman to make the first move?'

'Pretty much.' I smiled. 'I come from a long line of procrastinators.'

'I leave for Scotland with Danielle next Friday, and your game in Wales is the following day. I want to stay with you until then, if that's okay with you, of course.'

'How many nights is that?' I tried to count them in my head.

'I make that eight, including tonight.' There was a cold snap to her voice. 'I don't want to cramp your style if that's what you are worried about.'

I gently stroked her fairy floss hair. 'I reckon I can do that easily.'

Of course I could. There was never any doubt. I had become intoxicated by Eleanor's intelligence and beauty, and I wanted so much more of her. But I was also a realist, battle-hardened by my unfortunate experiences in Greece four years before. If I had learnt anything from that debacle, it was that these overseas dalliances had a limited lifespan. No, I didn't intend to get caught in the same Venus flytrap as I did with Martina and Lottie. As long as I remembered this was nothing more than a guilt-free holiday fling before I returned to my unhinged existence in Australia, then no-one, including me, would need to get hurt.

But that was then, and this was now, and we found ourselves plodding through the steel gates of Westminster Abbey, excited at the prospect of exploring this wonderful building together. Eleanor and I both shared an unswerving love of English history. She completed her honours thesis on Henry the Eighth and the 'great question' of his divorce from Catherine of Aragon. Although my degree focused on military history, I retained a unique passion for English kings and queens.

While Eleanor and I had visited the Abbey many times before, it was the first time we had undertaken such an excursion with another historian. To begin with, we had so much fun. We started our tour by marvelling at the lavish shrine of Saint Edward the Confessor, and I listened carefully as Eleanor regaled a well-known fable about how he once gave his gold ring to a struggling beggar because he had no money.

Eleanor was a natural storyteller, with that sing-song voice and her perfectly crafted facial expressions. Indeed, a group of Dutch tourists veered towards us and began to bombard Eleanor with questions about Edward. I did what I could to explain that Eleanor wasn't a tour guide, but when I failed to make any progress, she intervened herself and sent them on their way with a mere wiggle of her nose.

We inspected some more gravestones, after which Eleanor recited a riveting lecture about her namesake, Eleanor of Aquitaine, mother of two kings and wife to one of the most influential monarchs in English history, Henry the Second. When I playfully told her that the only Queen Eleanor I cared about was her, she smacked me on the bottom and ordered me to behave myself.

But it wasn't all one-way. I soon took the opportunity to impress her with my knowledge of Edward the Third and his great-grandson, Henry the Fifth, my two favourite English kings. I regaled to her past battles of the Hundred Years' War, the code of chivalry they both maintained, loves won and lost, and how the bravery of a few key men influenced an entire generation.

Eleanor listened carefully before making a vow to read more about the legendary Black Prince, Edward the Third's famous warrior son. When I teased her that finally, I knew more about something than she did, she promised to rectify this indiscretion as soon as she could. We were having such a fabulous time that it only occurred to me when we entered the crypt containing the grave of Mary, Queen of Scots, that we were once again holding hands.

One of the great ironies in history was that, in death, arguably England's greatest monarch, Elizabeth the First, was forced to spend eternity only feet apart from her biggest rival: the tempestuous first cousin she never met. It was Elizabeth, of course, who, after being manipulated by her court, signed Mary's death warrant in 1587 on a trumped-up charge of treason. I casually mentioned this fact to Eleanor to help kickstart our analysis of this critical set of events.

'Oh my God!' Eleanor suddenly roared at me. 'Don't tell me that you are a Mary apologist.'

At first, I thought she was talking to someone else.

'What do you mean?' I replied, stunned by the tone of her voice.

'Mary deserved everything she got! That's what I mean!' She childishly hurled my hand away from her body in defiance. Her actions were so outwardly aggressive and out-of-character that at any moment, I half-expected to be arrested by a platoon of Beefeaters and whisked away to the Tower of London.

I never imagined that I would find myself arguing with a woman next to the coffin of a dead Scottish queen. But one should always be ready to embrace new adventures. Although I first wanted to believe that Eleanor was playing some weird joke on me, the jagged lines on her face suddenly made me realise we had hit a potential snag in our embryonic relationship.

You see, Mary Queen of Scots was my favourite female historical figure, and she came second to no other woman. Not only had I read every book ever written about her life, but I also considered myself to be a self-professed expert on her reign as the Catholic Queen of Scotland during the Reformation. Mary demanded my total loyalty, and I didn't concede to some second-rate Austrian high school teacher who thought she knew better!

'How can you say that?' I growled at her. 'All Mary ever wanted was Elizabeth's affection, but she never lifted a finger to help her out of spite. Far too preoccupied with the fact that Mary was better-looking than her.'

Eleanor's sultry blue eyes threatened to burst into hot red flames. 'What a typical male comment!' she roared. 'Mary was nothing more than a useless bimbo who craved Elizabeth's crown. And look who she married? That idiot the Earl of Darnley, who she then helped murder, followed by that horrible despot Bothwell.'

'Bothwell raped her and forced Mary to marry him. Besides, there is no solid proof that Mary was in any way involved in Darnley's murder. Just loose speculation by revisionists. She was poorly treated by everyone, even centuries after her death.'

'And you call yourself a historian?' Eleanor cried out. 'All she ever did was play the perpetual victim who went running to the first man she thought could save her from her stupidity!'

Okay, blow the whistle—half-time people! Eleanor has just crossed a huge line! How dare she talk about my Mary like that? And right in front of her coffin, too. Well, she wasn't going to get away with it.

I angrily lurched over her. 'Do you want to know something?'

'What?'

'*The Sound of Music* sucks.'

'What did you say?'

'You heard me,' I snarled back at her. 'And what the hell is an edelweiss anyway?'

Make no mistake; I had just entered uncharted territory. Unashamedly, I had come up with some lame excuses in the past for ending relationships with women. But this was a whole new ball game, even if you took the time to consider my chequered history on these matters.

First, there was that girl in Brisbane I once dated who had regular conversations with her handbag.

'Say hello to Alex, Miss Handbag. He is buying us dinner tonight!'

I was too embarrassed to admit it to my friends at the time, but I decided to end that one in the middle of the dessert. Miss Handbag? I might have also skipped out on paying the bill just to get the hell out of there.

Then there was Jill. A perplexing individual, if you must know. On our first and only date, I took her to see *Out of Africa*, which was fair enough, I guess, until she began to sob uncontrollably at the movie's *opening* credits. I was so outraged by this nonsensical behaviour that I told her I was going to the bathroom and never returned.

Finally, we had that American girl I met in Canberra's most notorious nightclub, the Private Bin—the one that looked like a famous 1940's film star. That in itself was enough to give me hope for a meaningful relationship. Unfortunately, she had the annoying habit of whistling every time she finished a sentence. It was unbearable: like having a bottlenose dolphin for a girlfriend. Ironically, she saved her loudest whistle for the end of our relationship when I announced over dinner that we had to break up because I was gay. Man, she almost blew my eardrums out.

As my critics would no doubt concur, I ventured into unparalleled levels of stupidity at each step along the way. But this was something different. I mean, dumping a woman over

English medieval history. Undoubtedly, this would be the pinnacle of my career so far. So I happily rubbed my hands in anticipation and prepared myself for the inevitable.

However, two elderly couples who entered the crypt mainly at their peril rudely interrupted Eleanor's impending execution. When they found Eleanor and me standing eyeball to eyeball with each other, they waved their hands apologetically at us and then quietly slinked back outside. We stared at them, stared at each other, and then burst out laughing. With diplomatic relations between us temporarily restored, I put my plan to dump Eleanor on hold.

'I'm so sorry,' she said once we left the crypt. 'I hate all this stuff about Mary and Elizabeth. The whole story has become sanitised to satisfy the demands of popular culture, and it's not history anymore.'

'I was somewhat surprised by your reaction,' I replied. 'You are a Roman Catholic, just like me. Mary was the beacon for our religion during that time.'

'I don't like women who manipulate men with their good looks and self-indulgent stories—such a weak way out for any woman. Elizabeth got hurt once and never put herself in that position again. I respect her for that.'

We walked around in silence for a little longer before we landed in the Abbey cafeteria, and I bought us some coffees as a final peace offering. When we found some seats, Eleanor twirled a sugar sachet between her long, pale fingers.

'So, tell me, Alex. Transport yourself back to the sixteenth century after Mary's sentence was announced. Would you have tried to rescue her?'

Jesus, why can't she leave this alone? 'Of course I would. But that's easy for me to speculate four hundred years later in the relative luxury of modern London. It's pure conjecture—a nothing question, and I don't do hypotheticals.'

Just ask Martina.

Eleanor laughed. 'You can find out so much from a person through a hypothetical question. Therefore, I am not surprised by your answer.' She flicked the sachet across the table with her index finger, and it skimmed off my wrist.

'Admit it, Alex—you like saving vulnerable women, don't you? All they have to do is bat their little eyelids, and you will come running out with your sword and armour to rescue them. How cute.'

'That's very unfair,' I tried to protest. 'How can you make that sort of judgement about me after only three days?'

'Oh, don't get so defensive.' She giggled at my discomfort. 'We both know it's perfectly true. I came to this conclusion on the first day we met when you lectured me about Cleopatra at the British Museum. Remember? How horrible it was that the men of Rome used her as a pawn. '

'Well, she was treated appallingly by some men,' I replied angrily.

'She brought everything on herself, just like Mary Queen of Scots did. When she landed on her backside, screaming out for help, men like you came running out of the woodwork, desperate to reinforce her bad behaviour.'

'You are wrong. She was a delicate rose.'

'Man, you can be such a dick,' she scolded me.

Eleanor soon got bored with assassinating my character, and we slowly made our way back to the hotel. Earlier that morning, I had bought tickets to see *The Phantom of the Opera,* and we wanted to give ourselves plenty of time to get ready before the show. But somewhere near Churchill's Cabinet War Rooms, she suddenly pulled me onto an empty park bench. A homeless guy swigging a bottle of rum next to a nearby bin looked on curiously.

'I shouldn't have spoken to you like that in the café.'

I kissed Eleanor on the cheek to prove that I had forgiven her. 'Don't be silly. You're not the first person to tell me that I am a sucker for a crying woman.' I thought about Marlena and decided that she and Eleanor were both cut from the same cloth.

'Alex, so you know, I don't need to be saved. I'm not a vulnerable woman looking for a man to rescue me. I must say this to you right now before we go any further.'

Despite the one hundred and one comebacks floating through my mind, I somehow managed to keep a straight face. 'I have no intention of trying to save you, Eleanor. I can't even look after myself. So, please, you have nothing to worry about.'

Eleanor nodded happily. 'Good. All I want is us to have fun, okay? I don't want this to get too crazy.'

'Sure—not too crazy.'

As we lumped our way towards Trafalgar Square, I felt the urge to scream. She must be kidding me, surely. *Was it not Eleanor who poured her heart out to me last night about her sad life? Was it not Eleanor who made us hold hands this morning like husband and wife out for our daily walk? Was it not Eleanor who just used my love of Mary Queen of Scots as an excuse to rip into my personality? If anyone had been getting too crazy about things, it was Eleanor, not me.*

When we arrived at Trafalgar Square, Eleanor marched off to buy us some cold drinks while I picked out a spare patch of concrete next to one of the famous lions at Nelson's column. I looked upwards to the statue of the Admiral himself and stared into his stern, marble eyes.

'What do you think about my situation, sir?' I asked in a low whisper so that the swarms of school children buzzing around my ankles couldn't hear me.

'You are asking the wrong person,' he replied glumly. *'Haven't you heard? I have several issues to sort out myself. Lady Hamilton, my wife and that mad man, Napoleon, if you may.'*

'Good luck with all that,' I muttered back at him. 'And, by the way, a fat lot of help you were, too.'

A pigeon flew dangerously close to my nose while Eleanor returned with our drinks. She handed me a can of lemonade, then opened her bottle of orange juice.

'I will let you in on a little secret about women,' she finally announced.

'Oh, please,' I groaned, altogether too loudly. 'Haven't you confused me enough already for one day?'

'Shut up, Alex,' said Eleanor.

'Yes, shut up, Alex,' ordered Lord Nelson.

'Alright, go ahead. Tell me your big secret about women.'

She began once she was satisfied that both Lord Nelson and I were genuinely listening to her. 'While I was going through everything with Otto, there was this lovely guy I met through my sister called Gunther. We quickly became good friends, and he was a great sounding-board once I decided to break off my engagement. He was very kind-hearted and especially gracious with his time. He insisted that we meet at a local café every week to talk through my issues, and I never missed any of those appointments. Twice I became distraught with things and needed a friend to talk to, and on both occasions, Gunther dropped everything he was doing to come and see me.'

'Sounds like a sweet guy,' I mumbled, completely disinterested.

'He is—I mean, he was. After a while, I gradually got back on my feet and started to go out again with my friends. All I wanted to do was relax on a Friday night, have a few drinks, dance the night away, and not overthink stuff. You see, I was ready to move on. But Gunther? He didn't quite understand that. He started to get upset when I missed our weekly coffees and would often ring my mother to see if I was okay. Soon I felt so paralysed by his intrusion into my life that I angrily called him at work one day and told him never to contact me again. We haven't spoken since.'

'That's some story,' I admitted after finishing my drink.

'Do you see my point?'

'Gunther was an axe-murderer?'

'No, you moron.' She considered me with a rueful glare. 'Have you ever heard the term: a knight in shining armour?'

'You mean like Don Quixote, Marlena?'

'Did you just call me Marlena?'

'No—'

'I think you just called me Marlena.'

'You misheard me. It must have been the pigeons.'

'What I was going to say,' she sighed, 'is that women don't like knights in shining armour. Oh, our mothers like to tell us as little girls that a handsome prince is waiting to save us from the evil witch. For a while, we believe in all the hype. But in reality, princes and knights only serve as a convenient stopgap until we get our lives back on track. For a while there, I thought Gunther was my prince. But when I was ready to have some fun again, he became nothing more than a pain in the neck.'

She picked up my hand and held it tightly. 'These knights? Well, they become a burden, don't you see? As Gunther indeed was. They remind us of why we were so sad in the first place when all we want to do is move on and forget about the past. So we end up treating these guys like dirt, just like I did with Gunther. Remember that, my Australian knight in shining armour. I don't want to see you get hurt one day by some unscrupulous princess.'

I tried to imagine what Gunther looked like in the flesh, and for some reason, I came up with some scrawny guy in a scrunched-up velvet suit and a gold stud in his ear. He either genuinely cared for Eleanor or figured that the best way to see her naked was to become the understanding friend who was always hanging around until they went to bed by default. Indeed, I had played this same role many, many times, to universal condemnation.

'Any more deranged stalkers I should know about?' I grinned.

'You're patronising me, you bastard,' Eleanor growled.

'I wouldn't dream of it.'

She glanced at her empty orange juice bottle. 'I could smash you over the head with this, but I don't know where you put the tickets for tonight.'

I puffed out my chest in victory. 'Well, perhaps I will let you in on a little secret about men. We can be totally unscrupulous.'

We soon arrived back at our old hotel and took our time to dress up for our big night out. If I did say so myself, I looked especially spiffy in my sports jacket and dark corduroy slacks, while Eleanor appeared in this stunning black, off-the-shoulder exposition that almost knocked over half of London. *Where the hell does she hide all these clothes?*

We caught a taxi down to Leicester Square, where we swallowed a couple of schnitzels at a steak restaurant. After we shared an apple strudel, the two of us walked arm in arm down Haymarket Street to Her Majesty's Theatre. On our way, we stumbled upon a local flower girl, and I bought Eleanor a single red rose. She blushed when I gave it to her, and I blushed when she rewarded me with a kiss. The night was ours to claim, and nothing else in the universe mattered.

Once inside the theatre, a skinny kid dressed in a Phantom mask gave us two complimentary glasses of champagne, and we stood quietly in the corner of the waiting room, sipping our drinks while the rest of the audience slowly arrived. A bell rang to warn everyone that the show would soon commence, so we guzzled down our champagne and quickly settled into our prime seats, five rows back from the front of the stage. Once the overture began, we smiled at each other excitedly and then made out for the 357th time that day.

Not everyone enjoyed the sound of young lovers going for it in a packed theatre, especially the woman with the hooked nose and the canary yellow dress sitting in front of us. She immediately took toffee-nosed umbrage at our slurping before twisting her head around towards us in silent protest. Our faces briefly connected for several creepy seconds before I decided to piss her off even more by kissing Eleanor again for the 358th time that day.

The Phantom of the Opera had a special place in my heart. Indeed, Andrew Lloyd Webber's masterpiece was a compelling tale of obsession, unrequited love, betrayal, and sacrifice set to some of the most haunting music ever written. Although we had both seen *The Phantom* before, he did everything in his power to mesmerise us once again.

Given how perfect the night had been so far, it was difficult to explain what happened next. Perhaps the only explanation that made any sense was that someone had silently crept up from behind and smacked me over the head with a dirty great big fly swat. Because just as the Phantom commenced his signature song—'The Music of the Night'—my entire body began to spin wildly, and everything inside the theatre collapsed into a melting pot of pure yellow.

'Is this happening?' I screamed at the darkness.

'Yes indeedy, Mr Squeezy,' the woman in the yellow dress laughed through her black, cigarette-stained teeth. I could hear the bones in her neck begin to creak and splutter as her head spun 180 degrees on its axis to greet my terrified eyes. 'The cat got your tongue?' she shrieked happily. 'Not so much of a smart-arse now, are you?'

'Go away! Leave me alone!'

As I stared helplessly in terror at her yellow, lizard-like eyes, a putrid mist boomed from her nostrils, driving a floating wedge underneath my body. It wrapped itself around my legs, pressed me upwards into the air, and then sling-shot me across a dark, barren corridor. When I dared open my eyes several minutes later, I found myself alone inside a rat-infested dungeon, a tribe of sliding metal chains creeping along my arms and legs like tiny hordes of deranged caterpillars. I heard something click over my head, and then the chains simultaneously interlocked with each other across my entire body.

'Help me!' I cried out into the unknown. However, all I could hear were the strains of music creeping through the dungeon's hollow walls. They gradually became louder and more precise, buzzing up and down and around my head.

'This old man, he played three / He played knick-knack on my knee / With a knick-knack paddywhack, give a dog a bone / Poor old Martina never came home.'

No, it can't be!

I pulled furiously at my chains over and over again until blood poured from my scratched fingers and my aching lungs dissolved into bowls of putrid dust. If only I could sell my soul to the devil right now, maybe I could find my way back to Eleanor. But not even the devil could stop the terrifying reality that finally awaited me, for you see, the battle for my atonement had finally begun.

'Alex! Wake up!'

I cranked my head around in semicircles, looking for some proof of life, only to find Eleanor staring at me, her frightened eyes trapped inside the theatre's eerie shadows, anguished tears pouring down her stricken face.

'Are you okay?' she sobbed, her hand running along the back of my shoulders.

'I had a bad dream,' I tried to convince her. Eleanor's tears soaked my shirt. 'Why are you crying?'

'I thought I had lost you. God help me, I thought I had lost you.' The very same girl who didn't need saving was now shaking in fear.

What were my obligations here? *Do I leave Eleanor alone because of what she said this afternoon? Or do I comfort her because I am the irrepressible Australian Don Quixote? Fuck it, I don't know anymore.* Thankfully, I swallowed my pride and wrapped my arms tightly around her body.

'Everything will be fine,' I stroked her hair. 'Just like I promised you in Samos.'

'Samos? What are you talking about?'

Samos? Did I really say that?

'N-n-nothing,' I stuttered. I turned my eyes frontwards and watched while my nemesis, the woman in the yellow dress, crumpled in her chair. Her demonic face remained transfixed on the chandelier prop hanging above us.

I tapped Eleanor on the shoulder. 'That woman in front of us in the yellow dress. Do you see her?'

'Of course I do,' she whispered. 'Why would you ask me such a stupid question?'

'That's good,' I said. My eyes flickered from Eleanor's confused face to my shaking hands.

We somehow made it through the rest of the show unscathed, the warmth of our bodies the only protection from a subterranean world that neither of us fully understood. Afterwards, we went for a late-night coffee at Piccadilly Square, where our strange ordeal was deliberately absent from our stifled conversation. In fact, for the remaining time Eleanor and I spent together, we never once spoke about these events again. It was as if we had both decided that the secrets of this bewildering night should be locked away in a secure vault for eternity, never released for the sake of our collective sanity.

Despite seeing *Phantom* several more times in my life, I always stayed true to the non-verbal pact I made with Eleanor in London. Never once during those performances did I think about the strange events of that night.

But sometimes, when the rest of the world was asleep, I would reach for my iPod and press play on 'The Music of the Night', in the vain hope that its enduring secret would somehow be revealed. Occasionally, as the song's haunting words meandered through the valleys of my heart, I was sure I could hear Eleanor's pitiful crying in the distance, her desperate voice calling out to me, begging me to find her.

Brighton

Sunday
October 1999

The following morning, I suggested to Eleanor that we take a break from London. 'Let's spend some time beside the seaside, just like that old English ditty says.' After last night's strange events at the theatre, the salty air and quiet ambience were the possible tonics we both needed.

But there was an ulterior motive as well, for Eleanor had become needlessly fixated on our relationship. Too much analysis caused sexual paralysis. All that nonsense about knights in shining armour, Mary Queen of Scots, and vulnerable women was wrecking my evil plans for a no-strings-attached fling. Eleanor needed a peaceful setting where she could clear her head and reconnect with her womanly desires. Once she did that, we could then go back to having fun again. So, I proposed this wonderful, quaint little village in Kent called Deal. We could go for long walks on the beach, eat freshly cooked fish and chips, and generally chill out.

'What do you say, Eleanor?'

She thought it was a fabulous idea. But there was a catch. *What a surprise.* She didn't want to go to Deal because she and Danielle had visited Deal only three weeks before. They stayed at some horrid little hotel next to a swamp and got into this whole thing about their bill with a prickly owner who reminded them of Basil Fawlty.

No, she wanted to go to Brighton instead and visit the Royal Pavilion and Brighton Pier.

'Can you take me, Alex? Please? Please?' She pleaded with me with those deep, voluptuous eyes because she knew that no man could resist them. It might surprise you, but I was indeed a man—well, a sort of one, I guess—and I agreed to her proposal immediately.

However, there was one small problem: Brighton was the last place I wanted to visit with Eleanor, for Brighton was where Rachel and I first became a couple. Wouldn't I be tainting those special memories by spending time there with another woman barely four years later? Of course I would be. But in my haste to manipulate Eleanor, everything had backfired on top of my miserable head, and it was too late to do anything about it.

After breakfast, I convinced Eleanor that we should take one day bag between us and leave our oversized luggage inside my London room, which I had just secured for another two nights. We quickly agreed that this would be the plan, and everything looked promising at first.

That was until I realised what a woman had to take with her for one night in Brighton. Mobile phone, charger, camera, portable CD player, headphones, shampoo, conditioner, purse, a ladies' razor, a bra, panties, pantyhose, toothbrush and paste, a spare pair of bobby socks, perfume, a brush, a white top, tissues, a *Lonely Planet* guide, sunscreen, body lotions, a mini-hairdryer, contraception, and the latest edition of *Time* magazine were all thrown into my bag without a second thought. I pathetically stood in front of her and looked at my razor and toothbrush with genuine concern, and then quietly found a small space in the bag to place them. She initially giggled at my dilemma but then raised her ire when I tried to fit my novel inside the bag as well.

'Hey—you carry that, mister,' she retorted.

We made it to Victoria coach station just in time to hop on a departing bus. As we settled into our seats, Eleanor casually turned to face me. 'I never asked you this morning—have you ever been to Brighton before?'

I had no reason to lie to her. 'Yes. I went there in 1995 with my girlfriend at the time, Rachel.'

'I see,' she replied, her eyes suddenly betraying a stark coldness. I waited for Eleanor to ask me a follow-up question, but she decided to pass up on the opportunity for some reason. That suited me just fine. So I opened my novel, Tom Clancy's latest tome, and allowed Eleanor to immerse herself in her *Time* magazine. Thirty minutes later, Eleanor suddenly placed her magazine on her lap and poked me in the arm.

'You're exceptionally quiet this morning,' she said.

I looked surprised. 'Am I?'

'Yes, you are. You are not your usual talkative self.'

'What would you like to talk about?' I didn't mean for that comment to come out in such a sarcastic way.

'We haven't discussed your personal life. The focus has purely been on mine.'

Oh, I get it now. That was why Eleanor was so cold to me before. I told her that I had visited Brighton with Rachel. Wrong move, Alex. No woman in your present life wants to hear about a woman from your past life. You have to keep these things compartmentalised. Once you let the genie out of the bottle, you leave yourself open to all sorts of irrational scrutiny.

'Okay, what do you want to know?'

'That Rachel girl. What's her story?'

Bingo! I nailed it in one! My priority was to keep my response as low-key and uninformative as possible. Otherwise, I could subject myself to a mindless interrogation that lasted for hours.

'There's not much to say,' I replied, shrugging my shoulders. 'I was married for four years. That didn't work out, so we broke up. I then went out with Rachel for four years. That didn't work out either, so we also broke up. Then I started to see another girl called Toni, and we went out for nine months. That didn't work out either, and guess what? We broke up too. So here I am in England with you. There you go. Now you know everything about my personal life.'

Eleanor silently stared at the seat in front of her. Before I could add to my perjury, she twisted around and pulled out her portable CD player and headphones from the magazine pocket. Once she quietly checked whether the identity of the CD she was about to play suited her belligerent mood, she swatted the headphones over her ears and pressed the play button. It was the most elegantly designed 'fuck you' I had ever received from a woman in my life.

I knew that I had misbehaved with my unfounded, immature theories about the opposite sex. I wasn't particularly proud of myself, but there was a reason why we men sometimes acted the way we did. Call it self-protection, but I had been through the wringer over recent months that the last thing I wanted to do was give Eleanor an excuse to judge me. The whole point of my holiday was to enjoy myself, not to engage in futile examinations about my private life.

But if I had one redeeming quality, I was a very forgiving person who couldn't stay angry with someone for too long. After several minutes of brooding silence, I swivelled around, gently removed Eleanor's headphones, and apologised to her. She turned off her CD player and tried hard not to smile.

'You are a strange man.'

'I never lied about that, did I?'

'Why can't you just tell me what happened with Rachel?'

'It's all a bit messy, that's why,' I revealed. 'Rachel is a terrific girl. The sweetest, most caring person you could ever meet. For a long time, I wanted to marry her. But those seeds of doubt I had about remarriage that I kept hidden away from everyone suddenly grew into this gigantic monster that I could no longer control. In the end, I wasn't able to commit to the relationship.'

Why don't you tell her the whole truth? Those awful dreams about Martina, night after night. How they slowly twisted your mind. How they almost led to your suicide.

'But instead of doing the right thing, I took the coward's way out, told her that I didn't want to do a long-distance relationship anymore, and began to pursue another woman.'

'Toni?' Eleanor interrupted.

'Yeah. I met Toni on a work trip to Sydney. She is a flight attendant. Hindsight is a wonderful thing, but given her busy schedule, it was never going to work. Even so, I behaved appallingly during our short time together—like a jealous, spoilt brat. Man, I was such a shit person; I can hardly believe it. She was smart enough to get out while she still could.'

'I'm sorry,' said Eleanor. 'So you ended up losing both of them?'

'I guess you could say that. Look, I'm not angry at Toni at all; she's a fantastic girl who deserves someone better than me. But I'm still racked with guilt over how I treated Rachel.'

'Oh, Alex, she will get over it,' said Eleanor. 'Probably has already, and I'm sure she is more resilient than you give her credit for.' I must admit that I found her comment somewhat confusing, given her own vulnerability to Otto's treachery.

'Maybe you're right.' I nodded. 'But the whole reason for this trip was to forget about the last twelve months and have some fun.'

'And that's when I conveniently came along. Or have there been others on this redemption trip of yours?

'No, just you,' I promised her.

'Why didn't you just tell me this before?'

'Well, there are obvious similarities between what I did to Rachel and what Otto did to you.'

'And you thought I would judge you?'

'Possibly, yes.'

She slapped me on the wrist. 'You can't assume these things with people, Alex.' She sneezed twice, and I passed her a tissue.

'Everyone has their own story to tell. I can't judge your life, just like you can't judge mine. But you showed more remorse in the last two minutes than Otto ever did in his entire life. That's something I can work with, I think.' She nudged her lips close to mine.

'It's all in the past, Alex. There are just the two of us now. No Otto, no Rachel, no Toni. Just you and me. So, let's enjoy Brighton while we can.'

Our bus arrived in the Brighton CBD just after twelve-thirty, and we soon found the B & B I booked before we left London. The owner who greeted us at reception was a pleasant lady in her late fifties, with a squirrelled nose and light grey streaks in her hair. She didn't attempt to hide her sly smile when she examined our passports.

'The room has a huge double bed,' she giggled. 'And you can come down to breakfast whenever you want, as long it is before ten o'clock.' Eleanor laughed playfully in response and asked her to knock on our door if we didn't get up in time.

After we enjoyed a quick pot of tea, Eleanor and I spent the next two hours exploring the decadent Royal Pavilion, the notorious oriental holiday palace built for King George the Fourth when he was but a mere prince. I was a disinterested spectator, for the most part, having visited this unique building with Rachel, but Eleanor predictably found the Pavilion's luscious apartments absorbing. She took her time inspecting every item on display and expected me to mirror her enthusiasm whenever she wanted to start a conversation.

After she had finally seen enough, we obligingly inspected the gift shop for any interesting trinkets before retreating into a tiny laneway known as the Pavilion Buildings. We targeted a nearby café and then settled outside with our toasted sandwiches and cold drinks. Eleanor smiled sweetly at me when I had to leave for the bathroom and ordered me to hurry back. Her beautiful complexion glimmered in the afternoon sunshine, and I couldn't wait to be with her again.

Several minutes later, I returned to find an empty chair and a huge black raven pecking at Eleanor's half-finished sandwich. I tossed my head towards the gift shop, but I couldn't see her anywhere inside. A dreadful suspicion suddenly overcame me. *Did she have second thoughts about us following our conversation on the bus? Surely not.*

But hang on a minute, is that her? I slowly walked towards the laneway entrance and heard her distinctive laughter chime above the noise of a car backfiring. Yes, I could see her now, caught in the middle of that small crowd of tourists. She was talking to a man in his late twenties with short-cropped blonde hair and a deep cowboy tan. It didn't worry me at first that he looked like a model from the cover of a *Men's Health* magazine. But then …

Okay, what's going on here? I watched in utter disbelief as Eleanor's hands brushed provocatively across the man's chest until they landed on his massive biceps. If that wasn't bad enough, he brazenly managed to squeeze himself right into her plunging breasts, and she didn't seem to mind at all. In fact, from where I was standing, I'd say she was encouraging him.

For some reason, my mind wandered back to when I was a little boy in Year 1. As I had previously mentioned, I had a secret crush on Bettie Scott, Doctor Scott's precocious niece and the prettiest girl in my class. One day after school, she asked me to walk home with her, and I decided, in my confused little world, that her invitation meant she was also secretly in love with me. Of course, I was utterly mistaken: she was just a normal seven-year-old kid who wanted to make friends with one of her classmates.

The following day, when the school bell rang for home time, I ran out of the classroom as quickly as I dared and glued myself to the very same spot where Bettie and I had met. Ten seconds later, as I waited for her to find me, I looked over my right shoulder and watched in horror as she casually wandered off into the distance, arm in arm with my arch-nemesis, Robert Saunders.

If people wanted to derive some morbid pleasure from this tale, then yes, my fragile self-confidence splattered like roadkill afterwards, and I wanted to run away from home forever … well, until at least dinner time. However, the betrayal I then felt watching my new girlfriend debase herself like this in front of me far outweighed the lost memories of my first broken heart.

Suddenly, the toxic forces bubbling inside my head took leave of their senses. *It would be best if you made this tantrum a special one*, they urged me. *So do your goddam duty to our cause.* Emboldened by their burning rage, I threw the tourist brochure I was carrying onto the ground and marched angrily towards Eleanor and her new love interest.

Eleanor failed to acknowledge my presence until I brushed up against her shoulder, my lips rattling against the bottom of her chin. As she turned to face me, I quickly adopted the attack position and blasted out a succession of swearwords at both her and Mr Knucklehead for ten hate-filled seconds. Satisfied with my work, I took one last look at their bemused faces before I propelled myself into the adjoining street.

Once that was all over, I had no idea where I should go next. *I didn't plan this very well, did I?* Let's face it, my options were pretty limited. Our room was definitely out of bounds, and I had no idea when the buses left for London. A passing seagull kindly pointed me in the direction of the distant sea. Failing any other ideas, I decided that Brighton's rocky beach was about as good as it was going to get. So with the afternoon sea breeze snaking through my hair, I dragged my knuckles along Steine Street and waited impatiently for the traffic lights to change. I was just about to make a detour through the Steine Gardens when I felt a woman's hand on my shoulder.

'Alex, what are you doing?' Eleanor screamed at me, that persistent snow tan dripping off her face. 'Why did you swear at me like that?'

'As if you don't know,' I snarled.

'What?' she snarled back at me. 'Do you mean the guy back there?'

'Who else? I go to the bathroom for a few minutes, come out to find you missing, and then see you feeling up a total stranger.'

'You're talking about Hans?'

'If that's his name.'

'You fucking idiot!' she roared. It was the first time I had heard Eleanor swear in either German or English, and I had to admit: it scared the hell out of me. 'Hans is a family friend, and I have known him since I was five years old. He is the guy I told you about the other day who now lives in England, working for an advertising firm.'

Oh yeah—I remember now. 'Him,' I replied morosely. My throat began to sting, and I wished I was back in London.

'Yes, him. He has been working here in Brighton for several months, and I called him from the bus station this morning when you were booking our room to see if he was free this afternoon. I wanted him to meet you.'

I desperately longed to tell her that I was an absolute fool, that I would never put her through something like that again. But all I could do was stoop my head towards the gutter, a victim of my irrational behaviour.

'And by the way,' she shouted, 'Hans is gay. Totally fucking gay. Danielle and I often joke about trying to turn him, but never in a million years. Even you have got a better chance of screwing him than I do.'

'Do you have to be so crude about it?' I pretended to be outraged. However, Eleanor was in no mood for my deceitfulness.

'Don't patronise me, you bastard. How dare you make out that I am some tramp that would screw the first guy she sees? How dare you!' The last *how dare you* was released with such venom that it almost knocked over a nearby telephone pole.

'I never implied that at all,' I lied. By this time, several people were walking towards us, and I could see that they had become fully attuned to our argument.

'You were implying exactly that, Alex.' Hot, boiling lava flowed from her eyes. 'I'm going back to our room now, and I may not be there when you return.'

Eleanor offered me one final glare before she hurried down the nearest footpath, her arms ricocheting off her hips. There was a part of me that wanted to chase her down and hold her tightly in my arms until she forgave me, but all I could do was stand paralysed next to the traffic lights, blowing imaginary bubbles into the air. A young English girl with plaited blonde hair suddenly tapped me on the shoulder and politely asked if I was okay.

'I think my new girlfriend has just dumped me,' I replied bluntly.

'Go after her,' she scolded me. 'That's what she wants.'

I shook my head sadly. 'No point. It's all over, red rover. But thanks, anyway.'

I flicked my hair for dramatic effect, in case God was filming this debacle for some later interview when I was dead, and then lost myself in one of Brighton's famous old laneways. *What do I do now?* Nothing immediately came to mind, so I took the only option that a man had left for him in such circumstances—I went to the pub.

I targeted a gloomy little bar next to a Chinese grocery store and ordered a pint of brown ale from a muscular barman, who, in return, offered me a curiously morbid smile. I was pretty sure that I wasn't the first loser he had served today, and that, at least, provided me with some solace. Even so, I spent the next miserable hour dissecting my rotten behaviour, hoping that the pain I had caused Eleanor would miraculously disappear.

If I was truthful, before that afternoon's fight, Eleanor had meant nothing more to me than a beautiful overseas fling; a convenient stopgap in my life that was helping to restore my shattered self-confidence after a forgettable twelve months. My sole motivation for leaving London that day was the need to put our affair back into its proper context after the previous day's bizarre events. But as I wondered whether I would ever see Eleanor again, I realised something important that had been lost on me from the moment we met at breakfast the other day: I really liked her.

Come on! Admit it, Alex. It was so much stronger than that. There, I said it. Even though she lived in Austria, and I lived in Australia, it didn't change how I felt about her. Besides, this was about being honourable to a woman who had enriched my life as few others had done before her. There was no way I could let it end like this—not without apologising first.

The barman sized up my empty glass and offered me a refill on the house. I allowed him the chance to exercise those massive forearms before I pulled myself up from my chair and politely declined.

'It's like this, squire,' I told him. 'I need to take care of some unfinished business. But, by all means, have one ready to go just in case things don't go to plan.'

I was soon sprinting along Marine Parade towards our B & B as if my life depended on it. In so many ways, it did. I had lost Martina because of my stupidity, and there was no way on God's earth that I was going to lose Eleanor in the same way.

When I finally arrived at our B & B, I found the owner still sitting behind her desk with a cup of tea, busily at work on her books. For some reason, she reminded me of Edina's mother from *Absolutely Fabulous,* and I wanted to laugh along with her as she made another caustic remark to Patsy. But when she heard my footsteps, she carefully placed her cup on the polished desk. The deliberately constructed scornful look she gave me made me fear the worst. Eleanor had left Brighton and gone back to London.

'No, she is still here,' Edina's mother reassured me. 'But she is terribly upset, and you need to give her the biggest hug you can.' I tried to say something in response, but all I could do was whistle some bizarre mating call through my nose.

'Go on, son,' she demanded. 'Get in there and apologise for whatever it is you have done. Because if you don't do it soon, you won't have to worry about your girlfriend. I will kick you fair up the backside myself!' Something in her granite eyes told me that I should take her threat very seriously.

I stumbled upstairs and prised open the door to our room. I found Eleanor sitting cross-legged in the middle of our bed, her eyes staring blankly at the ceiling, my duffle bag crammed closely beside her. The smudgy stains on her cheeks and her ruffled hair were monuments to her recent crying. When I saw her on that bed, her face contorted in anguish, I couldn't bear the thought of upsetting her any further.

But at this critical moment, just when I was poised to walk out of her life forever, Eleanor pleaded with me to sit next to her on the bed. When I did, she lifted herself onto her knees and reached for my hand. Once she had me firmly trapped within her arms, she pulled my body across the orange quilt, and we kissed each other violently until there was nothing left in our lungs to expel.

'I'm so sorry, Eleanor,' I whispered once our lips separated. 'What I did before was unforgivable. I—'

'Please stop, Alex,' said Eleanor. She looked a completely different person to the one that had screamed at me in town barely an hour before. 'Some men would not have come back after the way I treated you. But you did, and that says everything I need to know about you.'

I wasn't going to let her forgive me so easily. 'No, Eleanor. Don't let me get away with it. Just this once, I need a woman to tell me that I was wrong.'

'What more do you want me to say, Alex? That you acted like a jerk? Yes, you did. But if we are honest with each other, so did I.'

'What do you mean?'

'I goaded you on purpose yesterday about Mary Queen of Scots. The whole thing was so trivial, and I knew it. And I should have told you this morning that I had invited Hans to meet with us, but I deliberately chose not to. Why? Because I wanted to play a game with you; to see how you would react. I have been testing your boundaries from day one to prove that I am in total control of this situation. In many ways, I have been a total bitch to you.'

Her frank admission stunned me at first, but I quickly realised I had no right to be upset with her: not after my disgraceful performance that afternoon. Instead, I reflected that our dubious behaviour was perhaps the natural consequence of two damaged people using the pain that we both carried to define the strange chemistry that existed between us. If our relationship was to work, we both had to find other ways to manage our insecurities.

'It has been an amazing four days,' I began slowly. 'We don't know each other all that well, yet we have expended more emotional energy than most couples do in a lifetime. And the thing is, we may never see each other again after Friday.'

'I am sure this explains my poor behaviour,' Eleanor agreed. 'It is all because I feel something for you, and I don't know how to respond. I wasn't looking for a man on this holiday, and that's why I am so scared about Friday. Is this all going to be for nothing, just when I allow myself to like someone again? You tell me.'

'I don't know the answer to that,' I replied truthfully. 'But I do know that I have never met a woman quite like you.'

I pointed to a 1999 puppy calendar hanging next to a small, wooden bookshelf.

'Look—today is Sunday. Why don't we leave things the way they are until Thursday night? We can talk about the next steps then. In the meantime, let's start again with a clean slate. No more tears, no more arguments, no more deep and meaningful conversations.'

'I will try,' she said with a smile. The sincerity in her eyes convinced me that she was serious about keeping her promise.

Later that evening, Eleanor and I strolled down to Brighton Pier, arriving just before sunset. A magic panorama of swirling lights and thumping music welcomed us to the night. Before long, we lost ourselves among the exuberant Sunday night partygoers who battled each other for the best rides and the best games.

Over the next hour or so, we gulped down hot caramel crêpes, guzzled a Heineken or two at some lousy bar, and then tried our luck on a whiz-bang pinball machine. After that, we wandered into sideshow alley, where Eleanor challenged me to a duel on the dodgem cars. Of course, there was no way that I could refuse her request, even if every other driver around us was under the age of ten. I also understood that whatever happened, I had to allow her to smash into me whenever she wanted.

After the dodgem cars, Eleanor guided me towards a mobile football stand. 'You said you played soccer, didn't you? Come on, go ahead and win me something!'

Yes, I played soccer when I was younger, and I was rather good, too—well, for a short time at least. All I had to do was kick three balls through three holes at a distance of around ten feet. *Easy!* One by one, I successfully slotted each kick with consummate ease and then offered myself a triumphant fist pump. Even the skinny little kid operating the booth seemed impressed.

Eleanor was impressed as well. She jumped on top of me as if I had just scored the winning goal for Liverpool in the FA Cup final at Wembley and then carefully considered all the prizes on display. Eleanor finally picked out a white fluffy teddy bear sitting on the top shelf. When the booth operator handed it over to her, she hugged it like a little girl and proudly held it aloft in front of us. Yes, the whole thing seemed so silly, but it made Eleanor gloriously happy.

'Only the most beautiful girl in Brighton deserves such a present,' I whispered to her as we strolled back along the pier towards the exit sign.

'I love it,' she replied gleefully before giving Teddy another hug. We made our way over to an empty bench, and she leaned her head on my shoulder.

'Thank you, Alex. Tonight has been simply wonderful. I love being with you.'

'I really don't know why,' I said. 'You could choose any man in the world.'

Eleanor slapped my thigh. 'You're wrong. I want no-one else but you. Why do you find that so difficult to believe?'

Why do *I find that so difficult to believe?*

Should I take up her challenge? But where to begin? My childhood? My marriage? My attempted suicide? Martina? Oh God, Martina …

I kissed Eleanor softly on the cheek instead. 'Hey, we agreed to do no more D and Ms, remember? Let's drop it and talk about something else.'

'You started it, silly man.' She laughed softly. 'You are now going to listen while I explain why I like you so much.'

'Eleanor, please,' I started to protest.

She pushed Teddy right into my face. 'We both think you are intelligent, extremely funny, and incredibly kind. Furthermore, every time I stare into your eyes, I discover something new about the world. What girl would not want to take that journey with you?'

'One who doesn't want to end up getting hurt,' I replied truthfully.

'Perhaps,' she agreed. 'There is always that risk with men like you. But do you want to know what I like about you the most? Do you want to know the real reason why I don't want to run away from you just quite yet?'

She politely waited for me to answer, but we both knew that I had run out of ideas a long time ago.

'You never give up on other people,' she finally announced. 'Even after everything I said to you in the street this afternoon, you never gave up on me. Just like you never give up on Mary. Or Cleopatra. Or even Rachel. That is such a wonderful quality for a man to have, and you have it in abundance, my love.'

Eleanor cupped my chin into her palm and breathed softly into my face.

'However, there is one person who you have indeed abandoned. He is someone who wants the world to love him but has prematurely decided that it never will. So he continues to ignore all the good things in life that might make him happy. That person, of course, is you.'

I wanted to tell her that she was wrong—that I had also abandoned Martina, too—but instead, I tried to hide the cold tears swelling in my eyes. No woman had ever made me feel as vulnerable as Eleanor did then, and I was genuinely frightened by its implications.

'Look,' Eleanor began, 'I want to show you something.'

She reached into her purse and pulled out a small plastic bag. Inside were three coins, and she carefully pulled one out to show me.

'My father was a computer programmer,' she explained. 'He is retired now, of course. Dad used to travel all over Europe for his firm but spent most of his time here in England.

My sister and I missed him terribly when he travelled, especially when we were in primary school. Every time we saw the taxi come to pick him up for the airport, we would cry and beg him not to leave. He would give us this look of total despair when he hugged us goodbye, and then he would try to ignore us from the taxi as we were waving to him.'

For a moment, Eleanor stared wistfully at the black ocean and smiled.

'Lena and I would mark off the days until his return on a blackboard we kept in our playroom. When it was the night of his return, we would both sit on my bed and stare out the window until we saw the lights of the taxi beam into our room. Mum would knock on our door, and we would come screaming down the stairs and into Dad's arms.'

I used her quiet pause as an opportunity to fold my hand into hers. I could see the intense love Eleanor had for her family, and it touched my heart.

'One day, Dad came back from England and called Lena and me into the lounge room. He said that he did not want us to be sad anymore when he went away to work. Dad produced six British pound coins and gave three each to both of us. After we had hidden them in our bedrooms, he told us that they were special coins and that we weren't to tell anyone else about them. He then fed us this ridiculous story about how the Queen of England gave him the coins and that they had magical powers.'

'Whenever we felt sad or lonely, all we had to do was pull out one of the coins, put it in our pocket, and it would immediately make us feel better. We fell for it like the two gullible little girls we were. But oh my God, it worked, and it still does. I swear there is something in it. I don't know what it is, but throughout my life, these coins have helped me overcome so many bad experiences, even with Otto.'

There was a stony silence between us, but she took my hand and placed the coin into my palm. 'Here, you gave me a present, and now I am giving you one, too. I hope that this coin can help you when you are sad as it has always helped me.'

I stroked her hand gently in appreciation before dropping the coin back into the plastic bag. She tried to protest, but I placed my finger on her lips.

'Please listen, Eleanor. This coin can only work for you, for it's full of your father's love. In the hands of a stranger like me, it will mean nothing. It is something you should give to your grandchildren one day—not some guy you have just met on holiday.'

Eleanor resigned herself to the fact that maybe this once, I was right.

'I want you to have it, but I see your point.' Eleanor casually watched two young girls while they bickered with their mother, and I wondered if she was thinking of her sister Lena. 'I do think it would have worked on you; I really do. If anyone can connect with its innocence, you can. Now I have to buy you another present instead.'

I gleefully pointed to my stomach. 'How about you buy me dinner at that Italian restaurant we saw before, and we call it even?'

She grinned mischievously before nodding her head. 'That sounds like a fair deal.' We sauntered towards the centre of town, the evening sea breeze blowing wildly in our faces.

'What do we do now?' Eleanor asked after a waiter at the Italian restaurant informed us that he had no spare tables.

I treated her question far more philosophically than I should have done. 'We find another place to have dinner and then get the hell back to London tomorrow.' I kissed her on the forehead and temporarily lost myself in the fireworks swirling above the pier. 'Because if you want to know the truth, two trips to Brighton in my life are more than enough.'

Danielle

Brighton–London
October 1999

The telephone ringing brought my dream about eating a bucket of chocolate ice cream inside a Russian gulag to an abrupt end. My brain tried to work out where I was before I focused on a strand of newborn light that twisted its way through our Venetian blinds. Half-awake, I turned to see Eleanor sitting stark naked on the corner of the bed, her beautiful black hair flung wildly over her shoulders, her mobile phone drawn to her lips. She suddenly reminded me of a modern-day version of Lady Godiva.

I quickly realised that Eleanor was talking to her best friend, Danielle, and because the dialogue was in animated French, I assumed that the topic of discussion was me. I was initially curious about Eleanor's excited chatter, but I figured there were some things you just had to leave alone. As a result, I turned onto my stomach, burped out some cold morning air, and tried to reconnect with that endless bucket of ice cream.

'Alex!' Eleanor playfully tugged at my elbow. 'Danielle had to return to London earlier than expected, poor darling. She wants to know if we would like to join her in Stratford-Up-on-Avon tomorrow. She has bought some tickets for a Shakespeare play.' She brushed away a loose strand of hair from my lips. 'Please say yes. It will be such fun.'

Given my general dishevelled state, I could have agreed to almost anything she had asked, so I muttered something like 'sure thing' in response and then fell back into my pillow. Eleanor blew me a solitary kiss and picked up her phone.

'Alex said that would be great,' she exaggerated. *But you know what? I don't care that she did. Now, let me get back to sleep.*

But before I could get too comfortable, Eleanor thumped me on the back, and it bloody well hurt.

'Time to get up, sleepyhead. We have a busy morning in front of us.'

I groaned and grumbled and grizzled but somehow stumbled to the shower. Apart from a change of underwear, I had brought no other fresh clothes with me, and I cursed the fact that

I had been so compliant with the duffle bag. Eleanor, meanwhile, looked unconcerned as she dazzled herself with an array of creams, lotions, and oils. She then smiled at me in a way that said: 'Hurry up, sunshine, or I will go to breakfast without you.'

We made it downstairs by eight-thirty, where Edina's mother was busily serving breakfast to her guests, while her weather-beaten husband sauntered morosely from table to table as if he was barely awake. He somehow managed to take our order without falling over, and soon we were both swallowing down egg and bacon rolls and endless pots of coffee while talking through the day's plan.

We decided to catch the train back to London with Hans, who had to be in the city that night for a work event. The three of us would then meet Danielle for lunch at an Italian restaurant near Trafalgar Square at one-thirty. We would all stay in London overnight, and then Eleanor, Danielle, and I would take the first bus to Stratford-Upon-Avon the next morning.

I ran a hand across my head and decided that my overdue haircut was the main priority when we arrived in London. After the obligatory 'it's nice as it is' comment, Eleanor agreed to drop my duffle bag and her new teddy bear back at our London hotel room to save time. Once everything was sorted out, we gathered our things, paid our bill, and caught a taxi to Brighton railway station.

After the previous day's debacle, I was thoroughly nervous about meeting Hans, but his initial smile was genuine and compassionate, and I immediately felt relaxed in his company. He happily pulled out three tickets from his coat and gave one each to Eleanor and me.

'I thought I would save some time,' he explained. When I reached into my pocket to reimburse him, he held his hands up and grinned. 'Please—my treat.' His natural kindness made me feel even worse.

We boarded a half-empty carriage at the rear end of the train. Eleanor and I sat next to each other, facing the front, while Hans sat opposite with Teddy snuggled next to him, content to ride backwards for the one-hour journey to London. Once we departed, the topic of conversation quickly turned to football, where I discovered that Hans was also a mad Liverpool fan. Eleanor, who unfortunately was an Arsenal supporter, rolled her eyes in quiet indignation as Hans and I proceeded to regale stories about our love for the greatest football club in the world.

'I should have known better than to put you two together,' Eleanor grunted before throwing herself back into her magazine. Hans winked at me mischievously, for he wasn't going to let her get away with being such a crybaby.

'Oh, come on, Lennie Bennie—stop sulking,' he teased as he pulled at her wrist.

I broke out in laughter. 'Lennie Bennie?' I repeated. 'Lennie Bennie? Is that your nickname?'

'What if it is?' she stared at me menacingly.

'Nothing. I mean, it suits your personality, and if you must know, you even look like a Lennie Bennie.'

Eleanor swore at me in German. In response, the old woman sitting in the aisle seat behind us growled loudly in exasperation so that we could all hear her displeasure. Convinced that we were anarchic fringe-dwellers from the Weimar Republic, she pushed herself towards the nearest window so she didn't have to become infected by our rampant foolishness. Of course, this only made us snigger at her expense.

After we left the next station, Eleanor gently put her arm around me. 'Hey, we need to tell you something about Danielle before you meet her.'

Hans released another cheeky grin.

'What?' I asked her. 'Does she have two heads or something?'

'If only that were the case—things would be much simpler,' Eleanor replied. She looked at Hans for encouragement. 'Do you want to tell him?'

Hans shook his head. 'No. She is your friend, and this should come from you.'

I started to grow impatient. 'Come on; I can deal with it, I'm sure. Just tell me.'

'Well, it's like this,' Eleanor began. 'Danielle? How shall one put it? She is beautiful.'

I looked at her curiously. 'That's it? That's the big issue? She is beautiful?'

'Yep, pretty much,' said Hans, with his trademark chuckle.

I leaned over and kissed Eleanor on the cheek. 'I am sure that she is no match for you, gorgeous.'

Eleanor looked like she was about to break wind. 'How sweet. But also, how terribly naïve. You see, there is beautiful, then there is insanely beautiful. And Danielle is insanely beautiful.'

'Insanely,' repeated Hans.

'You know,' I pleaded irritably, 'I don't understand the fuss. There are plenty of beautiful women in the world.'

'That's what most men think at first,' Hans interrupted. 'Then they meet her. It's around this point that they start to lose all control of their bodily functions.'

Eleanor patted Hans on the arm. 'Except for you, darling,' she said. 'You are always cool and collected around her.'

'That's because I am gay, you idiot.' He laughed loudly, and I could hear the old woman stir in her seat.

Eleanor gave him a playful 'fuck you' stare and tried to explain further.

'You must understand, Danielle is a very sensitive girl. Everyone focuses on her beauty and nothing else, and she is utterly sick and tired of it.'

'Does she have a boyfriend?' I asked inquisitively.

Eleanor and Hans shared a quiet smile. 'That's not a feasible option, I'm afraid,' said Eleanor.

'Why not? If she's as beautiful as you say she is, surely that counts for something.'

Eleanor released one of the brooding expressions that made her look like an ice queen from a fairytale. 'It is not that simple. Every man she meets eventually becomes completely intimidated by her looks. Can you imagine how frustrating that must be? Please try not to make a big thing about it when you meet her.'

'Okay, Eleanor,' I promised her. 'I'll try not to make a big thing about it when I meet her.'

We arrived at Victoria Station just after eleven. Eleanor and Hans immediately caught a tube back to Bloomsbury while I wandered off searching for a barber. I spent some time walking around the Victoria Station shopping complex with my head up my backside before I chanced upon a hairdressing salon that didn't look especially busy. A bouncy young thing with orange and purple locks and an acute Cornish accent offered me a seat and quickly attacked my hair with her scissors. After fifteen minutes of snipping and snapping, she completed a pretty decent job and was ecstatic when I thanked her with a twenty-pound note.

On my way to the tube station, I passed a men's store and got the urge to buy some new clothes. I felt ridiculously shabby next to the classy, elegant Eleanor, especially when she seemed to be able to access a never-ending supply of designer clothes at a whim. Compared to Hans, who resembled a refined Roman statue, I looked like a hapless vagrant auditioning for some fashion contest exclusive to homeless people.

Besides, shouldn't I try to look my best for Eleanor's best friend? Indeed, it was essential to making a positive first impression. So out came my credit card, and in came an expensive woollen polo top and a pair of brown-coloured slacks.

After I changed into my new clothes at the hotel, I walked down to Trafalgar Square in a remarkably buoyant mood. That was until I became lost in the Strand, mainly because I had refused to wear my glasses yet again. Luckily, several fellow pedestrians came to my aid and kindly escorted me to the restaurant. A blonde-haired waitress whose face resembled a rockmelon welcomed me at the front counter.

'Oh, you're with her,' she spat out with venom when I mentioned the name of the booking. 'I know which table you mean. It's the one situated in that little alcove towards the back of the restaurant. Come on—I will take you there now.'

As I passed by a row of tables along the way, my ears began to connect with tiny fragments of aggravated conversation.

'For God's sake, Bob. Can you stop looking at her?'

'Mummy, why are you fighting with Daddy over that girl?'

'What does she have that I don't?'

'If you don't stop staring at her, John, I swear, I will cut your tackle off right here and now.'

What on earth is going on? The waitress suddenly stopped and pointed to a table in front of me.

'There they are,' she snorted loudly. 'Have fun with Helen of Troy.'

My eyes briefly followed her as she stomped away to meet another guest. 'Have fun with Charlie Manson and the rest of the family,' I shouted at her.

'Alex, you're late!' The blurry outlines of Eleanor and Hans were waving at me from across the wooden floor.

'Sorry, but I had some trouble finding the restaurant,' I replied.

As I walked towards their table, the features of a third person gradually came into focus. *That must be Danielle. Now, remember. Take it all in your stride and act natural. And whatever you do, stay calm and don't make a big deal about her looks.*

Sweet holy mother of Jesus!

She was simply the most stunning woman I had ever seen. Indeed, her allure was so outrageous, so potent it was almost impossible to make any sense of it, let alone describe it. The only explanation I could find was that after being commissioned by the archangel Gabriel, Van Gogh painted a portrait of the most desirable woman on Earth. When he completed the task, God was so pleased with his work that he immediately brought the painting to life.

How else could one explain her heavenly perfection? Every dimension of her face was elegantly structured. Her lips were full and sensual, and her petite nose jealously guarded them with perfect symmetry. If you managed to get past her face, you would notice that her never-ending brown hair tumbled carelessly down the length of her back. Yet, it was her emerald-green eyes that completely mesmerised you. Every cell inside your body wanted to explode with delirium when they fixed on you.

I somehow managed to shuffle blindly towards the table, my legs wobbling on a sixpence. When Danielle stood up to greet me, I couldn't help but notice that the audacious perfection of her face also extended to her model-slim body.

'Hi, I am Danielle,' she said in the sexiest French accent ever created.

I tried to remember my name, but once I gazed into those eyes, all I could come up with was an unintelligible grunt beginning with the letter 'A'.

'Your name is Alex,' Eleanor reminded me.

'That's right,' I muttered in reply, taking Danielle's hand. 'It's Alex.'

'That's enough, sweetheart,' Eleanor continued. 'You can let go of Danielle's hand now.'

'Sorry, Ellen.'

'My name is Eleanor.'

'Yeah, right. Eleanor.'

I did my best to sit down on a chair, but I became so obsessed with Danielle's face that I completely missed my target by several feet. Embarrassingly, I found myself sprawled on the ground, my legs flapping in the air, a white napkin floating on top of my nose. Hans laughed hysterically before leaning across to help me up.

'You see?' I heard the man at a nearby table explain to his wife. 'It's not just me.'

Danielle remained remarkably demure throughout this entire episode but somehow managed to smile at me when I finally crawled back onto my chair.

'Can you please excuse me while I go to the bathroom, Alex?' she asked very politely.

'Sure,' I replied, trying to cover my overtly red face covertly.

My eyes followed her for the entire journey to the bathroom until she disappeared behind a huge pot plant. *Damn my myopia! Why didn't I bring my glasses?*

'Are you going to remember to kiss one of us hello?' asked Hans.

'Let him work out what planet he is on first,' said Eleanor. Hans couldn't stop himself from laughing yet again.

'Of course; how could I forget?' I turned towards Hans with puckered lips and was just about to plant one on his cheek when he reeled backwards in terror.

'Not me, Romeo,' he retorted, pointing to Eleanor. 'Her!'

'Oh, sorry.' I somehow found a way to lean across the table and then gave Eleanor a peck on the cheek.

'We told you, but you wouldn't believe us,' she gloated. 'You thought you knew it all, didn't you?' Her grin was so evil that I feared I only had several miserable seconds to live. 'And I assume that the new clothes and haircut are for her?'

'Don't be silly,' I pretended. 'I did it all for you.'

'Liar.'

Hans decided to come to my rescue. 'He does look cute with that new haircut. I can see why you think he looks like Richard Hunte.'

'He looks like a complete fool,' Eleanor said, fuming.

Despite my rather pathetic performance, Danielle and I quickly became friends. When she returned to our table, she immediately put me at ease by poking fun at my clumsiness before we casually fell into a private conversation about Paris. Having visited the City of Lights several times myself, I possessed a unique understanding of its charm and history, enabling me to connect easily with Danielle's everyday life. Whenever I acknowledged something that she cared about, Danielle politely touched my hand as if each contact would enhance our newly discovered bond even further.

After we finished our chat, Hans regaled us with some stories about his life growing up with Eleanor. He proved to be an amusing man, and he soon had us rolling around in hysterical fits of laughter when he explained to us the April Fool's joke he once played on Eleanor when she was twelve years old. I laughed so much that I almost choked on my ravioli, much to the pleasure of Miss Rockmelon Face.

Hans finally announced that he had to leave for his work event, and we organised to meet up with him later that night for a drink. It was incredible how much I had enjoyed his company, and I missed him instantly. Meanwhile, the girls said that they wanted to visit the National Gallery. I could have done with an afternoon nap, but we all knew that my obligation was to remain at their side no matter what. Although art was not really my thing, I enthusiastically pretended to be a new age fan, and we soon made our way outside into the warm afternoon sunshine.

During our short walk to the National Gallery, I quickly concluded that Danielle was a softer, more emotional person than Eleanor. There was an innocence and unworldliness about her personality that did not match the turbulence of her beauty. She had no pretensions about herself, just a desire to be a thoughtful and kind person whenever she could. Her natural instinct was to defy the curse she had inherited and adhere to the fundamental values of decency and honesty. However, her ongoing tragedy was that the world was unable to comprehend her ravishing beauty. She couldn't understand why no-one seemed interested in her as a person but only as an object of sexual desire.

When we passed a filthy middle-aged man sitting on the footpath caressing a sad-looking Jack Russell terrier, that became abundantly clear. The placard placed in front of the man indicated a Gulf War veteran fallen on hard times. Eleanor at first pretended that she didn't see him and ignored his pleas for charity. But once Danielle noticed the dog, her heart melted immediately. She reached into her purse, gave the man ten pounds, and then scratched the dog under his chin.

'Please also buy him food,' she begged the man. 'He is starving.'

He smiled back at her with vulgar, black teeth. 'Whatever you say, sexy girl. But only if you kiss me.'

I could tell by Danielle's venomous stare that she was deeply offended by his comment. Once again, she had tried to help someone in need, but their only response was to focus on her beauty. Eleanor, meanwhile, rushed over to Danielle, her arms thrashing madly about in the air.

'What did you expect, darling?' she admonished her right in front of me. 'You want to be Florence Nightingale all the time but can't seem to accept that the rest of the world doesn't see you that way.'

I was at first taken aback by Eleanor's insensitive comments to her best friend. The cold stare that I gave her hopefully reinforced my displeasure. Despite my outrage, I decided to leave it alone for the time being. It was not my place to comment on their friendship, and all I could do was sit back and observe their interactions. But it was obvious that their close relationship was an overly complex one, fraught with potential dangers for both women.

Eleanor had a deep affection for her younger friend and felt the need to protect her from all the bad people who might conspire to do her harm. She didn't want her innocent and naïve friend to become a victim of a shallow, heartless world. Eleanor had seen it, had experienced it, and had been traumatised by it, and no-one would ever do that to her beautiful companion.

On the other hand, Danielle looked up to her worldly, intelligent, and flamboyant friend like a big sister and wished she could be confident and strong like her. When Eleanor was not around, she struggled to understand who she was and how she should progress her life. Given that Eleanor was about to leave Paris and return to Salzburg, I wondered how Danielle would survive without her close confidante beside her.

Just after five o'clock, we finished our art-watching and walked back to Trafalgar Square. As we approached a water fountain, Eleanor suddenly announced how we were all going to spend the rest of the evening. First, we would participate in a Jack the Ripper walking tour in Whitechapel, and afterwards, we would dance the night away in the West End. She eyed a sign for an internet café next to a Boots pharmacy and quickly rushed to make an online booking. Meanwhile, Danielle and I decided to grab a coffee at a corner café while waiting for her.

I wondered whether things might become awkward between the two of us without Eleanor, but I again underplayed our obvious connection. After ordering our coffees, she grinned at me and said: 'So, then—Jack the Ripper.' We both laughed at the same time.

'Well, if you weren't going to say anything, I certainly wasn't,' I said.

'Eleanor doesn't like to be disappointed,' Danielle replied.

'Oh yes, I have experienced that already.' A sudden pause in our conversation allowed me to ask Danielle what was really on my mind.

'I hope that I haven't intruded upon your holiday. I know that this was supposed to be your farewell tour before Eleanor returns to Austria.'

Danielle released a slight frown, but not enough of one for me to worry.

'I won't lie. I was a little surprised when Eleanor explained the situation to me this morning. But I like to think it was destiny. A couple of weeks ago, I became fixated on this Swiss guy I met at our youth hostel in Copenhagen, and I drove poor Eleanor insane. So it's all cool, Alex. She and I are even.'

She placed her hands on the table in front of her. 'Look, stop worrying about what I think. I like you, and I'm happy to have you tag along with us for a while. Providing, of course, you don't fall off too many more chairs.'

I felt my face flush red but laughed, nevertheless. 'I am so sorry. I embarrassed myself at lunch.'

'No, you didn't; I thought you were quite adorable.' I temporarily lost myself in those amazing eyes and only snapped back into reality when the waiter delivered our coffees.

'How long have you known each other?' I asked her while I waited for my cappuccino to cool down.

Danielle unbuttoned her denim jacket. 'Almost three years now. We both started our jobs on the very same day and mainly taught the same group of girls. It was only natural that we would become good friends.'

'She told me she would never have made it through that first year in Paris without you.'

Danielle nodded her head. 'Yes, the poor darling was grief-stricken. That whole business with her ex-fiancée was awful, and she missed her family terribly at first. But she got through it all. Eleanor is one tough girl.'

'Do you think she is ready for another relationship?' I wasn't sure why I had chosen to ask Danielle such an impossible question in a run-down coffee shop near Trafalgar Square. Thankfully, she was happy to respond.

'Yes, I do. I don't have to tell you that Eleanor is very popular with the boys back in Paris. She has gone out on so many dates, I have lost count - nothing serious, though. The hurt caused by Otto still consumes her emotions, don't you see? But it is time she—please help me with the expression—get back with the horse?'

I tried very hard not to laugh. 'Close. It's "get back *on* the horse".'

'Oh,' she replied sweetly. 'Yes. Get back on the horse.' She paused and locked that phrase into her memory bank. 'It does not surprise me that she wants to be with you.'

'Really?'

'Of course. Eleanor loves tall, interesting men with dark hair and brown eyes. And they have to be brave enough to challenge her. You seem to be all those things from what I can see. Even Hans thinks you are a good match, and he is very protective of her.'

'I am not sure if I'm all that interesting, but thank you, nevertheless.' Danielle's compliment made me smile because I knew she was incapable of lying.

'What about you? What do you think of her?'

'She is amazing, but I don't want to hurt her either.'

Danielle dropped her chin on top of her hands and attacked me with an inquisitive frown. 'Are you intending to hurt her? Because I wouldn't be happy if you were.'

'Of course not,' I reassured her. 'But everything has happened so quickly. We are from different countries, different backgrounds. Then there is the whole issue about what happens after Friday.'

'That won't be easy,' Danielle admitted. 'However, I'm sure you will both work it out. You have to let things take their natural course.'

'I guess so. Because between you and me, I think I'm falling for her.' *Oh God, did I really say that? Will Danielle now say something to Eleanor?*

'Don't worry,' Danielle smiled warmly as if she had just read my mind. 'I won't say anything. That is something you should tell her, not me. But please do me one favour.'

'Anything.'

'Not before Jack the Ripper!'

We both laughed just as Eleanor entered the café. She was incredibly excited. 'I was able to get us some tickets!' she declared. 'But we have to leave for Aldgate East station right now.'

Danielle and I desperately finished our coffees before joining Eleanor in a mad sprint to Charing Cross tube station. Despite a minor delay at Embankment, we eventually found our tour group with plenty of time to spare.

I did a similar Jack the Ripper tour with Rachel in 1995, so this was all second nature for me. The tour guide, a short, stocky man who could have passed for a Beefeater at the Tower of London if he ever wanted another job, claimed to be the foremost expert of Ripper lore in London. While Danielle seemed impressed by his pedigree, I quietly told her that my tour guide in 1995 made the same claim.

The tour commenced at six-thirty, and we faithfully followed the guide as he manoeuvred us through a series of winding streets. After such a crazy few hours, I used the walk as an opportunity to clear my head. So many interesting things happened: breakfast in Brighton, a train ride with Hans, coffee with the most beautiful woman in the world. And we were about to solve the Jack the Ripper case all by ourselves. I foolishly wondered if my friends back in Canberra would ever believe any of this nonsense.

Danielle and Eleanor had left me in their wake, and for the first time, I was able to observe them together from afar. What a pair they made, too! Eleanor—intelligent, feisty, sensual, complex. Danielle—breathtaking, kind, naïve, and, yes, vulnerable. A divine connection between two incredible women, weaved together by a mystical spell from a long-forgotten world. Suddenly, I felt like an intruder who had hijacked a storyline that didn't belong to him. Where I fitted within its pages left me breathless in anticipation.

Katie

London
Monday Night, October 1999

The Jack the Ripper tour took two hours to complete. Eleanor had the time of her life, while Danielle and I tried to reassure her that we were having a ball as well. We did the usual Whitechapel sites, speculated on some theories on who the Ripper might have been, and then ended up at the 8 Bells Hotel where his final victim, Mary Kelly, was last seen.

We passed on the guide's invitation to stay behind for a drink and then hailed a taxi that transported us back to the West End. After a quick supper, we entered some fancy nouveau bar that Danielle discovered the last time she was in London. Surprisingly, the streets were full of willing people for a Monday night, and the bar began to fill up quickly. The clientele included a selection of professional people looking for that one last drink after a shitty day at work and carefree tourists like us who didn't have any reason to get up too early in the morning. Everyone seemed to be in a good mood, and we graciously commended Danielle for her choice of venue.

Hans soon joined us, and he couldn't hide the fact that he was drunk. Despite his slipping and sliding, his mind was still sharp as ever, and he effortlessly resumed where he left off at lunchtime with his boundless repertoire of Eleanor stories. Within seconds, he had us screaming out in laughter once again, and I could already tell that this was going to be a fun night.

I always knew it was time to party hard when I swapped from beer to my favourite alcoholic pursuit: double Baileys on ice. This momentous event had arrived, so I strode confidently towards the bar, a twenty-pound note gripped between my eager fingers.

As I waited for the bartender to serve me, I noticed a group of five young men standing next to a cluttered table full of empty beer bottles, bantering playfully with each other. I heard enough of their accents to tell that they were Liverpudlians. If I had been sober, I would never have dared to disturb them, but because this was happy Baileys Alex and they were from the city I loved, well, I needed new people to hug!

I continued to listen carefully for several more minutes while they passionately debated the merits of Michael Owen, the brilliant young centre forward who played for Liverpool Football Club. *Excellent! They all seem to be Liverpool fans and not supporters of the other Merseyside club, the archenemy, Everton.* With my Baileys in hand, I shamelessly embedded myself into their discussion. At first, they considered my slightly effeminate drink and uninvited intervention with suspicion. Still, when I told them that I had been supporting Liverpool for over twenty years, their faces suddenly wrinkled with approval. Pretty soon, they were all slapping me on the back as if I was an old friend they had just met again after years of unexplained absence.

I quickly discovered that they were visiting London ahead of a friend's wedding on Saturday. They were out enjoying a few quiet beers after a long day travelling on the bus from Liverpool. They naturally quizzed me about Australia and how I became a Liverpool fan, and we all laughed in response to a scathing comment that one of them made about *Neighbours*.

The obvious leader of the group was a friendly, handsome guy who also happened to be the spitting image of an old friend of mine from university called Will Johnson. We immediately developed a rapport, and he asked me several questions about Sydney because his sister lived there, and he was planning to visit her in the new year. We talked about Bondi Beach, the Opera House, Kings Cross, and venomous snakes, and I then bought them all another round of drinks. I promised Will I would catch up with him later in the night and then slowly made my way back to Hans and the girls.

'Where have you been, stranger?' asked Eleanor.

'Just socialising,' I said. I looked at Hans and pointed across the floor to my new friends. 'They are all Liverpool supporters!'

Hans checked them out from afar. 'Any of them like boys, do you think?'

Eleanor slapped his arm. 'Hans!'

He offered his best friend a withering stare. 'Alex knows I'm gay, and he isn't offended by my comment. Girl, what's your problem?'

I was just about to take a raincheck from their constant bickering when Danielle tugged at my sleeve.

'That tall guy that you were just speaking to? He is unbelievably cute.'

'You mean Will Johnson?' I asked.

'Is his name Will?'

I wanted to explain; honestly, I did. However, I was sure that this would only confuse Danielle even more.

'No, not really. But he is a great guy. Would you like to meet him?'

Danielle suddenly reminded me of a beautiful Persian cat that had recently drunk a saucer of sour milk. 'Oh, I'm just being silly, Alex,' she whispered sweetly.

'Danielle, you are a single, beautiful young woman. There is nothing silly about wanting to meet a man that you find attractive.'

'You think I should?' she asked me in that incredible French accent.

I wanted to hug this beautiful, fragile creature for the rest of the evening. 'Of course I do. Look, why don't you stay here, and I will see if my friend wants to meet you.'

She mumbled in mild panic. 'Alex … but, oh, okay.'

I walked back over to the boys and dragged Will aside.

'Mate, do you see the girls I am sitting with?' I turned towards our table, and he followed my line of sight.

'See them? We have been admiring them all night. You are one lucky man, Alex.'

'Well, you see, it's like this. The brunette and I are a couple, but the other girl is single. Very single. And she thinks you're totally cute in every way.'

Will raised his eyes at me with suspicion. 'Are you messing with my head? She thinks I'm cute?'

'That's right. Danielle thinks you're cute.'

'She said that?'

'Yes! God forbid I ever lie to a fellow Red. Come over and say hello.'

Will wanted to consult with his mates first. 'Go on, soft lad,' they all predictably teased him when he did. 'Do it!'

He took a deep breath and slowly followed me across the dance floor towards our table. Danielle had switched on her man antenna to high altitude, and she dived into her bag for some extra lipstick in anticipation of our arrival. Ah, the sweet mysteries of sexual attraction! Will and I made it halfway across the floor when he suddenly stopped and pulled me back towards him.

'I'm having second thoughts.'

'Are you bloody crazy?' I laughed at him. 'She is this amazing, gorgeous woman, and she has picked you out from everyone else here.'

'I'm not in her league,' Will murmured.

'Dude, of course you are in her league. You are the most handsome guy in the bar. If I were a girl, even I would go for you.'

'If you were a girl, you'd go for me?' Will asked with a worried frown.

Okay—unnecessarily confusing, Alex. 'Look,' I replied in a much deeper voice, 'she wants to meet you! Surely that counts for something?'

Will went through the motions of reconsidering his decision, but he had made up his mind. 'Sorry, mate. I appreciate what you are trying to do, but I would just make a fool of myself.'

I wanted to knock some sense into him, but he was a grown man after all. 'No worries, mate. In the end, it's your call.'

We exchanged a high five, and I moped back to our table empty-handed.

Danielle looked despondent. 'Let me guess,' she asked gloomily, 'he has roostered out at the last minute?'

I almost swallowed my chin in an effort not to laugh. 'Yes, he has, er, chickened out,' I replied in the most serious tone I could muster. 'That's all on him and nothing to do with you.'

'It's always on them,' she said sadly.

'I'm so sorry.'

She touched my face, and the scent of her perfume propelled me onto the ceiling. 'You have nothing to be sorry about,' she said. 'You tried to help me, and I appreciate that very much. As a reward, I am now going to buy you another drink.'

As Danielle strode to the bar, I noticed that a group of women had squeezed in behind our table during my absence. There were six of them in total, all in their early to mid-thirties, and it seemed they were there to celebrate the birthday of one of their friends.

The identity of the birthday girl soon became apparent. She was an attractive woman, with long sandy hair and a cute little dimple on her chin. She was clinging to a bunch of roses with one hand while the other struggled to hold a glass of champagne. The celebrations were altogether strangely muted, and she seemed somewhat depressed. Her friends were courageously doing what they could to lift her spirits.

Danielle eventually returned with my drink, and she and Eleanor then started to berate Hans about his faltering relationship with his parents. Mum and Dad still wouldn't accept his sexuality, it seemed, and as a result, he hadn't spoken to them in over a year. At first, I tried to take an interest, but the unfolding conversation between the birthday girl and her friends was far more riveting. Their accents were loud and strained, and I decided that all of them could have walked straight off *EastEnders.*

The birthday girl's name was Katie, and I was confident that this was her first night out in a very long time. She started to cry as she explained to her friends how hard it had been without her husband. It wasn't clear whether she was single because her husband had died or whether they had broken up, but whatever the reason, I heard 'three years' mentioned several times.

There were kids involved too—a boy called Jamie and a girl named Ellie—and she struggled to give them the life they deserved. It was also bloody hard to meet someone when you were entirely devoted to your children. Next came the part that shredded my stomach into tiny, worthless pieces. Wiping away her tears, Katie revealed to her friends the full extent of her loneliness and why she couldn't understand how this had happened after so many years of happiness.

Katie's story completely absorbed me, and as hard as I might, I couldn't take my eyes off her or her worried friends. Perhaps I was tired and more than a little tipsy. But I soon found myself choking back the tears from my throat and wishing to God that I had minded my own business. All this talk about loneliness had ripped open my unhealed wounds, and it was impossible to forget that not so long ago, I had been asking myself the very same questions as Katie.

In particular, I remembered how desperately alone I felt during that horrible night in Bateman's Bay. That overwhelming fear of abandonment and a terrifying realisation that you had no-one in your life who cared about you. When we were young, we never truly appreciated the destructive curse of loneliness. No matter what the circumstances, there was always another possibility waiting for us just around the corner. But life also had a way of screwing you over when you least expected it, and before you knew it, you were propelled into an empty, callous world that you never knew existed. For some of us, there was no going back.

I looked out towards the dance floor and wondered how many people then bopping it up to the raucous music were as equally alone and desperate as Katie was that night. Just like I was in Bateman's Bay. How many had come to this bar in the forlorn hope they would meet that one, special person? Over half, I believed.

You see, I worked out an awfully long time ago that loneliness didn't discriminate. It chose everyone and rejected no-one. It didn't matter whether you were a garbage collector or the heir to a billion-dollar fortune. It took whoever it could, whenever it could, and it didn't care who it offended.

I considered our very own table. We were four bright, intelligent young people with the world at our feet, yet each of us carried a personal burden.

Hans was lonely because his parents could not accept his sexuality.

Eleanor was lonely because she could not forgive Otto's betrayal.

Danielle was lonely because people were scared of her beauty.

And me? Why was I so lonely? Well, if I had only known the answer to that, I wouldn't be a single thirty-six-year-old man sitting in a bar at one o'clock in the morning in London, bemoaning my life, would I?

'Typical,' Mini-Alex snorted angrily. *'Always taking the easy way out and waiting for everyone else to take the lead. Rather than feeling sorry for yourself, why don't you do something constructive for once?'*

Well, screw you, mate. Maybe I will.

The music grew louder with each new song, and the dance floor soon became a coliseum of sweaty, twisting bodies. I suddenly came up with an outrageous idea, so I hustled back to the bar to find my Liverpool friends. Will felt obliged to shake my hand and tried several times to apologise for his previous bout of cowardice. I could tell that his mates had been badgering him mercilessly over Danielle.

'No worries, mate,' I replied with a sympathetic smile. 'However, I was wondering whether you guys could do me a small favour?'

'Name it,' said Will.

'There is a group of women next to our table. One of them is called Katie and today is her birthday. She is having a miserable time, and I think it would be great if one of you guys asked her for a dance.'

They all stared at Rodger, a handsome-looking specimen with an overly spiky haircut. He seemed a decent lad.

Will explained. 'It's Rodger's birthday tomorrow, and it makes perfect sense for him to ask the birthday girl for a dance, don't you think?'

Happily, Rodger was all for it. 'I can't have a lady having a shite time on her birthday, can I? It's bad enough that I have to spend mine tomorrow with you bell ends.'

We all laughed together at Rodger's expense before he declared that he needed to visit the heads before he did anything else. Convinced that my cunning plan would work, I sneaked back to our table, where the girls and Hans were still deeply immersed in the same conversation. *Good—no-one has missed me, so no irritating questions to answer.*

I quietly sipped on my drink and then twisted my head back towards Katie's table in anticipation of Rodger's arrival. Only then did I realise that one of her friends—a voluptuous woman with curly red hair—had been watching me all this time. When our eyes eventually met, she offered me an inquisitive scowl which asked: 'What the hell are you up to, sunshine?'

Thankfully, Rodger swaggered over to Katie's table, armed with nothing more than a baby-faced smile and a bucket load of balls. He introduced himself to everyone in his finest Scouse accent and then targeted Katie's sullen eyes.

'Excuse me, miss, but I understand that today is your birthday?'

'So what if it is?' she snapped back at him.

'It's my birthday tomorrow, and I would consider it an honour if you could join me for a dance!'

Katie seemed initially bemused by Rodger's audacious request, but her friends conspired to intervene on her behalf. 'Go on, Katie, do it!' they all screeched out at her, shaking their fingers towards the disco lights. Rodger used their approval as the excuse he needed to slide out his hand, and remarkably, Katie grasped it firmly without so much as a by-your-leave. He whispered something in her ear and then expertly whisked her off to the dance floor.

Meanwhile, Katie's stickybeak friend suddenly walked across to where I was standing and screamed out at the top of her voice. 'You did that, didn't you? Yes, I saw you listening to us before and then you went over to those guys to talk to them.'

'I'm sorry,' I gulped nervously. 'I just wanted your friend to have a good night out on her birthday.'

'Sorry? Are you fookin' serious? You are a fookin' legend, son! If you weren't with your bird over there, I'd jump you myself!'

Her wild shouting attracted not only her friends but Eleanor, Danielle, and Hans as well.

'What on earth is going on?' Eleanor asked angrily, visibly annoyed by the woman's uncouth language.

Katie's friend gathered everyone around her, and I stood quietly while she explained what I had just done. Her companions barked out some cockney rhyming slang that I didn't understand and joyfully lifted their glasses at me in appreciation. *Wow, this could all go to my head if I am not careful.*

'Playing the knight in shining armour again?' said Eleanor, smirking.

'Just this once,' I promised her.

'You can't help yourself, can you? Even so, that has to be one of the sweetest things I have ever seen. I would not dare think to do something like that.'

'You're wrong. You see, I did this *because* of you.'

'How so?'

'From the moment we met, I wanted to make you proud of me.'

Eleanor insisted that we kiss in honour of such a beautiful line.

'Oh, give it a rest, you two!' Hans begged when we failed to come up for air.

After we completely ignored him, he offered to drive us back to our hotel for free.

'Love Shack' by the B-52s blared across the room. Eleanor ruthlessly dropped my hand and pulled Hans towards her. 'Our song, Lennie Bennie,' Hans shouted back at her. 'Shall we dance?' Eleanor pirouetted on her heels and then bulldozed Hans out onto the dance floor.

I quietly returned to our main table, where Danielle was chatting to one of Katie's crazy-arsed friends. I really wanted to make it up to her in some small way after the whole debacle with Will, but apart from flaying myself alive with a cat-o'-nine-tails, I was totally devoid of any ideas. But when Katie's friend suddenly went to the ladies, I used it as an excuse to drag Danielle aside.

'Are you okay?' I asked hopefully.

She greeted me with another heavenly smile. 'I'm fine. However, I still can't believe that you found a man for Katie, but you couldn't find one for me!"

'I've let you down,' I admitted sadly.

Danielle touched my forearm, and I did my best not to tingle all over. 'Oh, don't look so serious,' she said, laughing. 'I am just teasing you. I am used to this by now.'

A new song whistled across the dance floor: 'Say a Little Prayer' by Diana King.

'Did you see *My Best Friend's Wedding* with Julia Roberts?' I asked Danielle.

'Yes, I did. 'Say a Little Prayer' was the hit song from the movie.'

'Do you remember the film's ending? Julia and her gay friend share a dance together, not knowing what their future friendship might hold for them.' Danielle was struggling to keep up with my train of thought. 'Yes. Why do you ask?'

'Well, I am not sure what the future holds for us, either, but it would be remiss of us not to have at least one dance together.'

Danielle threw her long hair around her beautiful long neck and laughed. 'Yes, you are right. Perhaps we should.'

Now, although I might have looked vaguely like Richard Hunte, John Travolta I definitely wasn't. My dancing usually involved lurching aimlessly on the same spot, hammering my two left feet into the ground, and waving my hands around in windmill-like motions. However, when I was half-drunk, these little details didn't seem to matter.

Before I knew what was happening, Danielle and I were grinding our hips together on the dance floor, barrels of sweat dripping off our clothes. At first, I found it challenging to keep up with her as she effortlessly glided about the dance floor. But after taking my hand, she guided me down a narrow opening between a group of teenagers until she found enough room to pull me towards her. Once she had me snapped firmly against her body, she clasped her hands together into a pretend microphone and thrust them under my mouth.

'This was your idea, Alex,' she cried. 'If you are going to be my best friend, you need to sing along with me and mean every word of it!'

We waited for Diana King to finish off the next verse before our time in the sun arrived, and we hollered out the chorus as belligerently as we could to the rest of the world. I wasn't sure if it resembled singing, but Danielle and I could hardly have cared. 'I want this song to last forever!' she sang, her sweaty fingers stroking my cheek.

Yes, forever! Occasionally in life, your emotions, thoughts, and desires become perfectly aligned with the universe, and you develop incredible insights about other people. For whatever reason, dancing with Danielle inside this murky bar somewhere in the corner of London's West End allowed me to experience this sensation for the very first time.

I first considered Danielle as she delicately swung her hips in front of me. Her angelic perfection eroded the fallacy that life only rewarded terrible people. The pureness of her beauty and compassion was proof of the goodness that existed within us all.

I then watched while Hans hugged his beloved Lennie Bennie, and I rejoiced in the passion of their friendship. Two beautiful people joined together by childhood innocence and their love for one another, defeating every challenge put in front of them. It reminded me of my friendships and how lucky I was to have so many good people in my life.

Finally, I laughed at Rodger and Katie as they shared their first tentative kiss on the dance floor. Katie's wonderful smile demonstrated that indeed, if you gave life a chance, maybe something good would come your way. All you needed was someone to help guide you through the darkness. *Perhaps I got it wrong before. The world might be full of lonely people, but there was a way out as long as we believed in each other.*

Following a few more '80s classics, we entered the domain of the inevitable late-night love songs, and so Danielle decided that Eleanor and I should have some private time together. Herb Alpert's take of Burt Bacharach's 'This Guy's in Love with You' started to play, so she gently pushed her best friend to where I was standing with Hans. We dramatically fell into each other's arms like Bogie and Bacall and then celebrated our new song with a horribly slow waltz.

Eleanor gradually nestled her head next to mine and whispered: 'This is one of the happiest days I have had in a long time. Thank you for making it so special.'

'I haven't done all that much, Eleanor.' *Honestly, I don't think that I have.*

'You have been amazing! The way you have indulged my every whim and have welcomed my friends.'

'I hope they like me,' I replied.

'Like you? One has found a friend for life, and the other would hit on you if only you were that way inclined!' She laughed softly, then dropped her head back on my shoulder.

'Lucky for you then that I am not that way inclined,' I smiled back at her.

'Yes, lucky for me.' She lifted her head, and I allowed her sad, beautiful eyes to express themselves. 'Alex, I don't want Friday ever to arrive.'

I held her a fraction tighter. 'Please, not now. Let's enjoy this song and forget about everything else for the next few minutes.'

'You win.' Eleanor sighed before sliding back into my arms.

After more tear-jerking drivel, the DJ announced that this would be his last set for the evening, and he was open for final requests. Eleanor and Hans mysteriously shuffled over to him, and I could see them all nod in agreement. They were plotting some devious plan, and I was pretty sure that it involved me. Sure enough, the DJ pointed his bony finger in my direction and announced: 'This next song is for Richard Hunte.'

'Da Ya Think I'm Sexy?' by Rod Stewart began to scream out from the speakers and, just like that night on the ferry to Samos with Marco and Lottie, I wanted to wither away into a dark corner and die. Eleanor skipped over to me with a delightfully cheeky smile that made her face light up in the darkness. 'Come on, Richard, don't be shy.' At some point between our flailing arms, I promised her that my eventual revenge would be swift and brutal.

By the time this song ended and the next one, 'King of Wishful Thinking', started, most of the crowd were on the dance floor, slightly drunk and primed for action. Many of us had entered the bar burdened with negative thoughts, but over the last few hours, they had disappeared down a vast black hole we had created out of our hope for a better life. As I looked around the dance floor, everyone was having a wonderful time.

Rodger and Katie were still grinding their hips to the beat of the music while finding countless opportunities to kiss in between choruses. Will finally found the courage to ask Danielle for a dance, and she flushed with real happiness for the first time that evening. The Liverpool lads had, amazingly, dropped their beers and had coaxed a posse of young girls to dance with them. Katie's friends were either dancing with each other or pummelling into any unsuspecting male that took their fancy. Hans, in the meantime, was twirling around some gorgeous young girl who had yet to work out that he was gay.

This one big, happy family had achieved so much in the last hour, but we had one last song to navigate before the night sadly ended. And what a song it was! Yes, it had to be 'Walking on Sunshine' by Katrina and the Waves, and we immediately shouted our approval.

Hans and his new lady friend decided to start a conga line, and one by one, we all became consumed by it. I somehow misplaced Eleanor in the melee that followed and took hold of a woman I had never seen before around her tiny waist. She turned around, inspected me with a dubious frown, and said, 'You look nothing like Richard Hunte at all!' I reluctantly agreed with her, and we bumbled around the floor, chained together in this rather bizarre huddle.

Much to our disappointment, the song finally came to an end, and we all gave the DJ an almighty roar of approval before tumbling back to our tables. Hans made sure he caught up with me before we reached the girls and then pulled me towards him.

'There is one last thing we both need to do before we leave,' he announced. I thought about what Eleanor said about Hans before and wondered if he was about to kiss me.

Hans offered me the filthiest of looks. 'This is not a proposition, you idiot. I am talking about all of us singing the song. Do you know? The song!'

Ahhh—I now know what he means. Every Liverpool FC fan would no doubt know as well. It was time for the anthem! Hans somehow managed to prise Rodger away from Katie, and Will collected the rest of the boys and a few other hangers-on who wanted to join us.

When we all finally squeezed into the same patch of floor, we stood united, arm in arm, and began to belt out a thunderous rendition of 'You'll Never Walk Alone', the song made famous by Liverpool fans across the world. Sure, there were some in the room who booed and hissed just to big-note themselves, but our undying passion soon drowned out any lasting scraps of discontent from these Neanderthals. After we finished, we all jumped on top of each other and offloaded a series of hugs to anyone we could find. It was a fantastic way to finish off a fantastic evening.

While Hans and the girls began to search for a cab outside, I decided to take that one last, necessary trip to the bathroom. When I re-emerged several minutes later, I found Katie standing by herself in the doorway, her eager hand busily working in that last touch of make-up for Rodger's benefit. The crestfallen, emotionally crippled woman on display earlier in the evening was an Energizer bunny, bubbling with excitement for what the rest of the night might bring. When she found me studying her, she snapped shut her make-up kit and stumbled her way towards me.

'You're not going anywhere, mister,' she scolded me. 'The girls told me what you did tonight. I mean, getting Rodger and I together like that. I am not sure why you did it, but whatever your reasons, I want to say thank you—from the bottom of my heart.'

'You don't have to thank me, Katie,' I explained. 'In fact, you were the one who did *me* a favour.'

I could immediately tell from Katie's blank facial expression that she was confused by my comment.

'Look, I am way too bloody drunk for a deep and meaningful,' said Katie. 'But you deserve a reward.' She pushed herself into my chest and traced the contours of my face with her puppy dog eyes before planting a gentle kiss on my lips. 'That's for helping out a girl in need'.

I said nothing more because there was nothing more she would want me to say.

Across the universe, a thousand dying stars suddenly called out my name, and Katie watched in stunned silence as I followed a trail of forgotten tears into the cold autumn night.

The Picnic

Stratford-Upon-Avon
Tuesday/Wednesday, October 1999

We arrived at Stratford-Upon-Avon just before midday. After getting directions from a cranky older woman walking a crankier Irish setter, we eventually found our hotel: a beautifully converted nineteenth-century mansion surrounded by a fortress of aging beech trees. We successfully secured two rooms next to each other in the most secluded part of the hotel and then slowly strolled back into town. We spent the rest of the afternoon recovering from our substantial hangovers, lamenting how much we missed Hans and visiting some of the local tourist attractions, including the house where William Shakespeare was born.

Just before seven-thirty, we arrived at the Royal Shakespeare Theatre, where we had tickets for a production of *Hamlet.* Danielle had indeed done wonderfully well: our seats were located right in the middle of the front row, with the best view in the house. Before I could inspect my ticket, Eleanor insisted that it was standard European custom for me to sit between both girls while watching the show. Honestly, I had never heard of such poppycock in my life, but I nodded my head in agreement to keep her happy.

I was one of those irritating nerds who loved Shakespeare and *Hamlet* was a personal favourite. Pretty soon, I became deeply engrossed with the trials and tribulations of the Mad King of Denmark. So much so, for a short time at least, I was oblivious to the simmering presence of both women sitting beside me. But when Eleanor popped her head on my shoulder, I was reminded once again of her brooding sensuality. And when Danielle began to rub the bottom of my back, it sent me spiralling into an interplanetary orbit around Mars. Afterwards, as we barrelled our way into a taxi, Danielle winked at me slyly when Eleanor wasn't looking to confirm that I hadn't imagined things inside the theatre.

The persistent sound of a dripping tap woke me up just after four-thirty. I was lying at the edge of our king-sized bed, tiny streams of sweat nibbling at my neck. It took several seconds before I realised that Eleanor's bronze arms were welded tightly around my torso. She groaned softly as I gently removed her limbs from my body and rolled my legs over the side of the bed. Ignoring her protests just this once, I tiptoed to the cupboard, where I discovered a rose-coloured blanket. Careful not to activate the creaking floorboards, I shuffled back to the bed and carefully placed the blanket over Eleanor's shivering body. I blew her an imaginary kiss, put on some clothes, and quietly made my way outside towards the public garden at the front of the hotel.

An icy wind poked at my face. I found a bench next to a broken water fountain and stared forlornly into a mysterious green fog that snaked its way along the street in front of me. In the distance, a dog howled at an iridescent half-moon. If I didn't know any better, I had walked straight into a scene from *The Hound of the Baskervilles.*

My thoughts gradually turned to the events of last night. Did Danielle really rub my back? Did Eleanor see her do it? Bloody hell—nothing was ever easy with me, was it?

Yet, I couldn't deny it any longer. Ever since we danced together the other night in London, I had felt an eerie kinship with Danielle—weird stuff that you only read about in some trashy novel and never believed happened to real people, let alone you.

There was something else, as well. On the bus ride to Stratford, while Eleanor was sleeping, there was a moment when Danielle and I shared a quiet, intimate smile. The way she blushed and dropped her eyes afterwards left me both struggling for breath and answers.

There is something there, God dammit. There is something there.

'Hey, what are you doing out here in the cold?'

I turned around to see Eleanor staring at me with half-opened eyes.

'I couldn't sleep,' I muttered.

'Me neither.' She sat down next to me and manoeuvred her head against the top half of my chest. 'There, that's better,' she said.

'Yes, so much better,' I replied.

Together with my growing guilt, we sat like this in the darkness until the unmistakable melodies of a new morning forced us to seek permanent refuge inside the hotel.

*

It was fast approaching eleven o'clock, and the three of us were walking through town in search of a car rental company. The girls had decided over breakfast to hire a car for the next few days. They wanted to visit Warwick Castle that afternoon and the next day we planned to drive to Birmingham to do some last-minute shopping. If we had time on the way home, we might also visit the farm where Shakespeare's mother, Mary Arden, had spent her childhood.

That Friday morning, Eleanor and Danielle would drive to the nearby city of Coventry to catch the first of a series of buses to Edinburgh.

None of us had any real idea about cars, so we chose the first rental shown to us: a white 1994 sedan. Eleanor was the only member of our little group who had an international driver's license, so she was especially keen to showcase her lack of driving skills. She soon took us on a terrifying expedition through the backstreets of Stratford-Upon-Avon, culminating in her failed attempt to sideswipe a harmless old man trying to negotiate a pedestrian crossing.

Despite her lazy attempt at manslaughter, Eleanor continued to ignore our screaming and cursing until she finally managed a controlled semi-burnout several feet away from the local police station. 'I need to get my hair and nails done,' she finally announced before backing into the first empty car space she could find.

It didn't take us long to find a beauty salon, and Eleanor booked an immediate appointment. She explained that she also wanted to do some souvenir shopping for her mum and that we would only get in her way.

'Why don't we all meet back here in two hours?' she suggested.

Before I could work out what that meant for me, Danielle excitedly jumped in front of my face. 'How about we have a picnic beside the river?' she suggested.

'Sure.' I gulped loudly. 'That's a great idea.'

We walked back to our hotel, gathered some vital essentials like a blanket and a hat for Danielle, and then raided a nearby convenience store. We purchased cheese and smoked ham, French bread from the store's bakery, apples and peaches, and a couple of bottles of mineral water. Danielle and I eventually chose a secluded patch of grass underneath a handsome birch tree overlooking the Avon River. After we staked out our blanket, Danielle prepared our ham and cheese baguettes while I found a tap to wash our fruit.

Once we finished lunch, we sat quietly together on the blanket and admired a team of dragonflies that treated us to a specially choreographed acrobatic display. Danielle's long brown hair soon became brutally tangled inside a growling breeze, so she dived into her handbag for a brush and started to drag it across her head with firm, savage strokes. After several minutes of failure, she cursed to herself in French and then waved the brush in my face.

'Do you mind?' she asked.

'I beg your pardon?'

'Could you please brush my hair? I always find it easier if somebody else does it for me. Normally Lennie Bennie would volunteer, but since she is not here …'

She closely examined my terminally pale face and poked out her tongue. 'You have brushed a girl's hair before, haven't you?'

'Me? Of course I have,' I tried to kid us both. Look, maybe I did it for one of my ex-girlfriends: who could remember? But this was a whole new ball game. The person in front of me was an insanely beautiful French woman who also happened to be my new girlfriend's best friend and who, only twelve hours before, had been rubbing my back during a Shakespeare play.

'Good,' she said, dropping the brush next to me. 'Please be gentle with me.'

Please be gentle with me? Oh my God! Can you believe this?

I picked up the brush with nervous little fingers, collected a fistful of Danielle's soft hair, and started to push through with long, firm strokes, all the while trying ridiculously hard not to touch her body. After several minutes of undignified pulling and tugging, Danielle suddenly closed her eyes and emitted a moan so intense that it almost sliced the birch tree in half. *Bloody hell: this is nuts. Is this for real, or is she getting off on this?* I had wasted so much of my adult life trying to understand women, I never once thought about brushing their hair!

This stuff was beyond the limits of my feeble brain, so I looked upwards to the sky for inspiration. *Someone, please tell me what to do; I am swimming in shark-infested waters here.* Thankfully, Mini-Alex came to my rescue for the second time in a week and calmly suggested that I keep going until she lost interest. So I brushed and brushed like a madman until Danielle finally opened her eyes, smiled at me with a smack of her full lips, and then lifted her hand for me to stop. Despite my extraordinary efforts, I had barely untangled anything—apart from several knots in my chest—but she seemed relatively pleased, nonetheless.

She carefully patted down her jacket, tossed her brush back into her bag, and considered me with her green, seditious eyes. Something was coming, something big. I could feel it in my bones.

Oh God, Alex, your brushing was divine. I think I am falling in love with you.

'Are you happy, Alex?'

Okay, slightly disappointed.

'The last twelve months have been pretty tough,' I said. 'But things are slowly improving. Meeting you and Eleanor has been a bonus.'

There was a hard edge to Danielle's gentle nod.

Oh, I saw that. A grimace of self-doubt?

'And what about you, Danielle? Are *you* happy?'

She deliberately stretched her incredible legs right past my nose and then gazed out towards the river. 'I used to be, but I am not so sure anymore.'

'I find that hard to believe,' I replied honestly. 'You have so much going for you, and this should be the happiest time of your life.'

'Thank you. You're lovely. But unfortunately, your kind words don't make me feel any better.'

'I wish they did.'

'I am sure this feeling will eventually pass,' she added. 'Lately, I feel so directionless. So, so …'

'Lonely?'

She swatted away a pesky fly from her face. 'Yes, loneliness is one way to describe how I feel. But it is so much more than that. I have become—this will sound strange, I'm sure—a talking zombie. I look and sound like a living, breathing creature, but when you scratch the surface, there is nothing inside except an emptiness that I can't explain.'

You don't have to explain anything, Danielle. I know exactly what you mean.

'I have experienced that emptiness too,' I reassured her. 'Many times. You will eventually find your way out. We all do.'

Liar, liar, pants on fire.

'I wish I could believe you,' she said. 'You have now seen firsthand how men react to me. How am I supposed to live my life like this?'

She waited for me to say something profound, but I was temporarily baffled by my impotence. Honestly, I didn't know what to say to her.

'I've had to put up with this for years,' she continued. 'I am so sick of it. And you know what? Looks aren't even all that important to me. I would happily go out with Quasimodo as long as he treated me for who I was and not how I looked in a short dress.'

Well, you do look unbelievably hot in a short dress, Danielle. But putting aside my lurid fantasies, for the time being, I suddenly had one of those light-bulb moments that usually ended in disaster.

'Do you want to know what I think?'

'Of course I do.'

'The only person who is obsessed with your beauty is you.'

'What do you mean by that?' Her cute little nose trembled at the edges, and I reckoned that I had about twenty seconds to make my point before she fired me from her team.

'If you spend all your time thinking about how you look, it's only natural that everyone else will too.'

'Well, I can't change how I look, can I?' she replied irritably.

'Of course not. But you can flip things around. Turn everything on its head.'

'What do you mean?'

You now have less than ten seconds, buddy.

'Start focusing more on your other qualities. You are funny, intelligent, and compassionate. If you give priority to those things that make you uniquely special, it will change the way you see yourself and the way that other people see you.'

I wished it were that simple, and I wasn't even sure I was making any sense. But what did Danielle have to lose—apart from years and years of further humiliation and regret?

'I wouldn't know where to begin,' she said sadly.

I started to draw crop circles in the dirt with my finger just for the fun of it. 'Okay, let's imagine that you are about to enter a crowded room. What's the first thing on your mind?'

'Everyone is looking at me!'

I thumped my fist into the ground, almost breaking three fingers in the process. 'Exactly! And the tension that you now feel will dictate the way that you look at other people. As a result, they will wrongly assume that you are arrogant, aloof, and unattainable.'

'Just like Will,' said Danielle.

Who? Oh, yes. Him. 'Just like Will.' *Now, where the hell was I?*

'But if you enter that room with a different mindset: determined to show the world what a thoughtful, caring, and interesting person you are, everything about you will change. The way you look, the way you talk, the way you interact with people, everything. When they see how relaxed and friendly you are, they will naturally feel more comfortable around you.'

Danielle mulled over my brilliant proposal some more and then offered me a smile of approval.

'You think they will?'

'Of course I do!' *Okay, I have no idea whether they will or won't, but work with me here.*

'Why don't you give it a try next time you go out? Pick someone in the crowd when you arrive and start talking to them. Once you take the initiative with people, they will flock to you. Trust me.'

Danielle's next smile was ridiculously perfect. 'You know, you are right. I'm always so self-conscious when I go out by myself. More often than not, I sit there by myself like a loser and hope someone will come over to me. It sounds positively insane, but I am going to give it a try. Thank you so much.'

'That's what I do—I solve problems,' I replied triumphantly. *How about that, Marlena?*

Deeply impressed by the scale of my incompetence, I slid back down onto the blanket for a well-deserved rest. But somewhere along the way, Danielle caught my arm.

'Hey, not so fast, Alex. You solved my problem—now it's my turn to solve yours.'

'I have a problem?'

'I'm not sure yet,' she giggled. 'But I want to find out. So, come on, Alex. Tell me your life story.'

I released a tiny groan. 'I wouldn't even know where to start.'

'Well, how about we start at the beginning? Where did you grow up?'

'Where did I grow up?'

'Yes, you know.' She looked at me with a bemused frown. 'Your childhood.'

My childhood? That is the last place I want to start! I never talked to anyone about my childhood. I thought back to Martina and that whole *Strangers on a Ferry* fiasco and wondered whether I was in danger of taking yet another fall.

'It was pretty horrible,' I exclaimed. 'I almost died four times before I was ten years old.'

'Four times?' Danielle asked incredulously. 'No! How?'

'Well, I almost drowned when I was five.'

'Really?'

'Yes. We were at a public swimming pool in a place called Mudgee. It was a scorching day, and so I decided to cool down by jumping into the deep end of the adult pool.'

'But you could swim?'

'Um, no.' I picked up a small rock and hurled it into the Avon River. We watched together as it disappeared into the dark waters. 'I sank to the bottom just like that rock did, but my father jumped into the pool and saved me in the nick of time.'

'Wow. I bet you were always grateful to your father.'

'Oh yes, always grateful,' I said. I could still remember that incident like it was yesterday. How peaceful the world seemed at the bottom of that pool, with Ring—

Well, let's not mention him now.

'And the other three times?'

Do I have to?

'I had two major operations to rectify an exceedingly rare form of hernia. If they had perforated, as one almost did, I would have most likely died.'

'Poor darling,' said Danielle.

'Oh, and I was playing in my front yard one day when someone shot me.'

Danielle's mouth dropped to the ground like a character in a Tom and Jerry cartoon. 'Someone shot you?!'

'Yes. Lucky for me, though, whoever shot me wasn't particularly good.'

When Danielle's beautiful white teeth started to rattle around her mouth in horror, I rolled up the shirt sleeve on my left arm and revealed to her the small scar that still existed above my elbow. She stared at me in amazement for several seconds.

'Is shooting children customary in your country?' she eventually asked, altogether way too seriously.

'Only during school holidays.' Danielle didn't get the joke, but she was never going to. 'It was just one of those things that occasionally happened in a small country town during the sixties.'

'Did they catch the person who did it?'

'No. The police lost interest very quickly. I have some theories, of course, but I will probably never know for sure.'

Unless, of course, the Spiders knew something that I didn't.

Danielle stroked my arm. 'What about you? How did it impact your life?'

'Well, it can be a perfect pick-up line if used wisely. Sometimes I rock up to a beautiful woman and ask her if she wants to see my gunshot wound. They find my scar irresistible; you see.'

'You're teasing me,' she said, unimpressed.

'Ah, you caught me out,' I replied.

'It was a serious question,' she scolded me.

'I'm sorry.' I stroked Danielle's hand as a peace offering. 'It did affect me as a teenager, I guess. I became obsessed with locking the doors to our house whenever I was by myself, staying away from people I didn't know, that sort of thing. Eventually, you move on.'

Maybe.

'It's just unbelievable,' Danielle whistled. 'I have never met a person with such a story.'

And I haven't even told you what happened when I was eight years old.

'Yep, it's a doozy, alright.'

'Eleanor also told me that you are obsessed with saving vulnerable women.'

That comment came out of nowhere, and my face wrinkled with surprise. 'Did she, now?' I replied coldly. 'How much more has Eleanor told you about me?'

'Please don't get angry with her, Alex,' Danielle pleaded. 'That's just Eleanor; she likes to dissect people before she invites them into her life. I am just amazed how much she trusts you already.'

'That's something, I guess.'

'May I ask why? I mean, why do you feel it necessary to save vulnerable women?'

'I don't know. Maybe because I am the youngest child in our family.'

'How so?'

I told her about my life as a young boy, living alone with my mother and father after my siblings had left home. I told her about the fighting, the hitting, and the screaming. I told her how I came home one day to see my father beating my mother. I told her how I always hid under my bed whenever they started to argue. I told her how my father threatened to kick me out of the house if he ever caught me talking to my brother. I told her how I had built an imaginary world around me to escape this insane battlefield.

Danielle's eyes flickered in the wind. 'You had an awful childhood—just awful. I am so sorry I made you talk about it. Please forgive me.'

Danielle reached for a lock of her long, beautiful hair. It was her way of saying that she understood. 'It all makes sense, Alex,' she said. 'You know, this desire to save women? I did several psychology subjects at university, and I once completed a paper on this very topic. People often carry their childhood experiences into adulthood. You were impacted by seeing your mother abused. When you were a child, you were powerless to do anything about it. But now, as an adult, you are trying to save your mum by helping other women. I am sure that most therapists would agree with me.'

Therapists? The last therapist I saw knew jack shit. She was a typical Freud apologist who thought that all my problems extended to my penis. 'I'm not so sure. All I know is that the last time I tried to help a woman, it exploded in my face.'

Do you really want to go here, Alex? Strangers on a Ferry, *mate. Remember,* Strangers on a Ferry.

'Do you want to talk about it, Alex?'

My head was full of conflicting emotions, but I had come too far to deny Danielle a proper explanation. So I revealed everything to her: from the moment I met Marco at the Adelphi, right up to the night I nearly committed suicide in Bateman's Bay.

The entire confession took about fifteen minutes. 'I don't know what to say,' Danielle whispered as we both slumped onto the blanket together in total exhaustion. A small pocket of wind ripped across the collar of her blouse. 'Have you told Eleanor any of this?'

'No. I was going to raise it with Eleanor in London the other day, but I thought better of it.' I paused for a second or two. 'Do you think I should?'

'I don't know,' she replied honestly. 'Maybe I wouldn't just yet. She is still dealing with her own issues. But if you are going to have a future together, you will have to say something to her sooner or later.'

'Yes, of course. Thank you.'

Danielle inspected me closely. 'Those nightmares, Alex. You poor darling. They sound positively awful.'

'Trust me, they were.'

'When did they stop?'

'Probably a couple of months ago. Even so, I still lay awake every night in bed praying that they never return.'

'Did they always involve Martina's gang rape?' Danielle pressed further.

I swallowed hard. 'Mostly, yes. Sometimes other women in my life would make a special guest appearance, but mainly Martina.'

I could tell that Danielle wasn't going to stop asking me questions until I told her everything.

'They usually start the same way,' I began. 'I'm walking through a dark forest at night with Martina by my side when she suddenly disappears into the moonlight. How or why, I have no idea. Put it down to the reckless absurdity of dreams. I call out her name over and over again, as loud as I can until I completely lose my mind. Then somewhere beyond the horizon, I suddenly hear a woman scream. It is a foul, animalistic scream, too, and I know straight away that it's Martina. I cautiously follow its trail until—' My voice started to crack.

'You don't have to continue, Alex,' said Danielle.

Of course I do. I gulped down some water and peered out towards the river. 'There is a house. How I hate seeing that fucking house. I know that Martina is trapped inside, and something terrible is happening to her. I pick up a lump of wood and make my way towards a window. I then look past the olive curtains and—'

'Oh God, Alex ...'

'The room is full of men. Maybe, fifty, one hundred, who knows? All screaming and yelling and laughing. Martina is stripped naked, held over a table, crying hysterically. A man is behind her, howling in ecstasy. Sometimes the man is a stranger to me; sometimes it's Marco, her ex-boyfriend, and other times it's'—I swallowed some more water—'... well, it's me'.

'I see,' said Danielle softly. She paused to catch her breath, then leaned towards me. 'It's just your subconscious playing tricks on you, Alex. You can see that, can't you? It's taking advantage of the guilt that you feel about abandoning her.'

'But you don't understand,' I replied, stony-faced. I pushed Danielle's hand away, and she looked mortally offended as a result. 'There is something about the expression on my face that concerns me.'

'What?'

'I'm smiling.'

Danielle shuffled uncomfortably to the other side of the blanket. Maybe I had gone too far this time: perhaps she was petrified of being alone with such a monster. But to my surprise, she swept herself on top of me until our lips were almost touching. The smell of her French perfume caused my heart to flutter.

'Oh, stop it, Alex,' she lectured me. 'Just because you have a dream doesn't mean to say that it is a true reflection of who you are. You are a good person; anyone can see that.'

'I hope so,' I tried to convince both of us. 'But I keep thinking back to my last night in Samos when Martina asked me whether I could ever hurt someone during a war. Ever since then, I have questioned every fibre of my existence.'

'You are over-analysing things, Alex.'

'Perhaps. But when you have the same nightmare over and over again for four years, it makes you somewhat disconsolate.'

Danielle ferociously bit into a bright red apple. 'Did you ever discuss any of this with your girlfriend—sorry, what was her name? Rachel?'

'No. I decided that it would only complicate our fledgling relationship if I did.'

'What about a professional counsellor?'

I remembered how I once asked Martina this very same question. 'Yeah, I saw someone who claimed to be a professional counsellor. Well, she had a degree stuck up on her wall, so I assumed that it was legitimate.'

Yes, Janet M Culpepper, FCCLP. At your service, Mr Gerrick, you pathetic pile of white male trash.

'After three consultations, it all came down to my misogynistic tendencies. I wanted to control Martina; I wanted to control every woman I ever met. She even claimed that I secretly wanted to control her. When all else failed, she then suggested that I start chronicling my nightmares on paper to help me desensitise things in my mind. But all it did was make things worse.'

Danielle dropped the ravaged apple core onto the ground. 'I can understand your frustration, Alex. But nothing you have said diminishes you in my eyes.'

'Really?'

'Really.'

'I'm not sure why but thank you.'

'You need to believe in yourself more.'

'That's easier said than done.'

'Then you should try to find her.'

'Try to find who?'

'Martina, of course.'

'That's impossible.' I shook my head sadly. 'Martina is dead.'

Danielle reeled back in horror. 'Dead? Oh, dear God! When?'

'Not long after I deleted her phone message.'

'When did you find out?'

I tried to recall the exact moment when I first realised that she was gone. It was during that work function at the Sydney Opera House, that's right. The nightmares began not long afterwards. 'I just know, that's all.'

'What do you mean? Do you know for certain, or do you think she is dead?'

'I never received any official confirmation, if that's what you mean. But I was drip-fed certain bits of information over several months.' *Courtesy of the Spiders.* 'I'm pretty certain she committed suicide not long after that phone call.'

Danielle threw her hands up in exasperation. 'Oh, you are a silly, silly man. You blame yourself for her death, but you are not even one hundred percent sure that she is dead. That is one of the craziest things I have ever heard. And easily the saddest.'

Okay, we needed to end this charade. 'Danielle—'

'Listen to me!' she cried. 'You can't live the rest of your life like this, for it will drive you insane.'

'I reached that point some time ago, Danielle.'

'Is it any wonder?' she snapped back at me. 'You want so much to believe that you have failed your mum and Martina, when in fact, the only person you have failed is yourself. You need to sort this out before the next vulnerable woman comes along and confuses the situation even more.'

Like you, perhaps, Danielle? I sucked in some air. 'Don't worry, Eleanor has already lectured me on the pitfalls of being a knight in shining armour.'

'Yes, I know—she told me all about it.'

'Naturally.'

'She wanted my reassurance that she did the right thing.'

'And did she do the right thing?'

'Yes, she did. We both know that some women can be unforgiving when a man disappoints them. You are never going to meet the lofty expectations of every woman you try to help.'

'Not so long ago, I had a similar conversation with another woman,' thinking back to Marlena in Samos. 'As a result, I turned my back on Martina, and look what happened? It seems that I can't win either way.'

'Perhaps that's a sign that you should put yourself first.'

'Yes, perhaps. But long as *you* are never angry at me, then everything will be sweet.'

She did her best to think about my statement carefully. 'I could never turn on you, Alex. You have such a gentle heart. But unfortunately, there are people out there who will take advantage of those qualities and try to manipulate them for their own benefit. I would hate to see you get hurt again.'

We soon ran out of things to say about this topic, so I thanked her for listening to me.

'You must think I have a screw loose and that Eleanor is in mortal danger.'

She offered me a puzzled frown. 'There's a screw loose? Where? On what?'

I couldn't stop myself from laughing. 'No, it's an Australian expression, and it means that I am mentally deranged.'

Danielle took her time to analyse my response. 'Ah, I see,' she finally relented. 'Screw loose. Yes, I understand now.' She laughed again at the irony. 'I don't think you are mentally deranged, Alex. A little naïve, perhaps. And traumatised by your past experiences.'

'You are not going to tell Eleanor what we have spoken about today?'

'Absolutely not!' she protested. 'As I said before, what you decide to tell her is your business. Ours was entirely a private conversation, Alex. You have my word.'

'Thanks. I appreciate that very much.'

We quickly tidied up our mess, threw out our leftovers to some wandering geese, and rolled up our blanket. Satisfied that we had left nothing of value behind, we began our return journey into town.

We walked for several minutes before Danielle suddenly tugged at my shirt.

'Thank you for the picnic. I had a wonderful time, and I especially appreciate the thoughtful advice you gave me.'

'I enjoyed it, too. And thanks for listening to my story as well—it felt good to get some things off my chest finally.'

She moved closer towards me. 'Would you mind if I kissed you?' she asked almost too sweetly.

'Of course not.'

She gently caressed my neck with both of her hands and then pressed down hard on my lips. Just like with Lottie, all those years ago, on the ferry to Piraeus, I fell backwards in delirious bemusement, fuelled by a desire that I didn't understand.

She wiped away a smear of her pink lipstick from my nose. 'I hope I didn't embarrass you.'

'Of course you did!' I said. 'But apart from Eleanor, who the hell cares?'

'Please don't tell her I did that,' she begged me.

'Once again, our little secret.'

'Do you think you would have asked me out if you had met me before Eleanor?'

I would have usually baulked at such a leading question, but after that kiss, she could have asked me to give her the world, and I would have done it for her. 'I think you know the answer to that, Danielle. You are an amazing woman, and I love being with you.'

'Thank you,' she whispered.

You are not getting off that easily.

'And if I had asked you out, would you have accepted?'

Danielle's eyes squinted at the fierce sunlight. 'You know that I can't answer that question, Alex, for that would betray my friendship with Eleanor.'

'Sure,' I replied, slightly disappointed at her response but not wanting to push her any further. But given what was about to happen, I should have seen right through her façade. Because if you scrutinised it some more, if you broke down everything she had just said over the last few minutes, none of it made any sense. But as usual, I happily blundered my way through life, totally oblivious to the machinations of others.

We soon found Eleanor at the edge of the park, waving madly at us while holding a plastic shopping bag tightly to her chest.

'Have fun, you two?' she asked with a quirky smile.

'Sure did,' I replied. 'Danielle makes one hell of a baguette.'

'I see.'

She quietly turned to Danielle. 'So, did you get him to brush your hair?'

What the fuck? Her words rebounded off my forehead. I turned to condemn Danielle's guilty face, but she had conveniently dropped her head to the ground by this stage.

'Yes,' she mumbled.

'Did he then make a move on you?'

'No. Alex was the perfect gentleman—completely loyal to you.'

Steam began to pour out of my otherwise stuffy nose. 'What the hell is going on, Eleanor?'

'I just want to make sure that I can trust you,' she said.

'By tempting me with your best friend?'

'Don't take it so personally, Alex,' she said with an irritable calmness. 'You know how much Otto's unfaithfulness hurt me. If I'm going to commit myself to you long-term, I need to know how you will act with other women when I am not around.'

I raised my eyes angrily at Danielle. 'And you were party to this?'

Eleanor answered for her. 'After she rubbed your back last night during the play, we both became genuinely concerned. Alarm bells went off, don't you see? Then we came up with the idea of a picnic today to test, your, how should I put it? Self-control.'

I wanted to throw up, make no mistake about it. 'You mean the whole thing was a set-up right from the start?' I hissed at them.

Before Eleanor or Danielle could reply, I bashed a hand against my chest. 'I never said anything last night because I didn't want to cause a rift between the two of you.' Okay, not one hundred percent accurate, but it didn't stop me from pointing an accusing finger at

Danielle. 'That rubbish you said to me just before. How I had to be careful about people manipulating me? All that time you were manipulating me yourself?'

'Alex, I—' Danielle began.

'I have nothing more to say to you,' I roared at her as I childishly threw our blanket into a nearby clump of bushes.

Eleanor was razor-quick to admonish me. 'Come now, Alex; don't be so melodramatic.' She licked her lips several times as if she had been waiting eagerly for this next part and then grasped Danielle by the hand. 'Now sweetie pie, did he let you kiss him?'

You have to be fucking kidding me! Danielle's normally rosy cheeks seemed to have miraculously turned a fierce white while I stared down at her with red-hot eyes.

If I were right, Danielle's following sentence would be the ultimate nail in my coffin. Go straight to Hell—do not pass 'Go', do not collect two hundred dollars. In some ways, I felt almost relieved that everything was about to disintegrate in such dramatic circumstances. After all, it was always going to end on Friday, regardless of this tawdry episode. Who was I trying to kid?

Danielle's beautiful long hair tossed silently in the wind. I could tell that she was on the verge of tears. *Even if you start crying, Honey Bunny, there is no chance I am rushing to your aid.*

'No, of course he didn't!' she blurted out. 'I tried to kiss him, but he pulled away immediately. He is one hundred percent loyal to you, as I always knew he would be.'

Well, I wasn't quite prepared for that! *What the hell are you playing at, Danielle?* Eleanor raised her eyebrows at both of us. She had the look of someone who had seen her evil master plan easily defeated. That might explain why she suddenly perpetrated the most inappropriate long-distance kiss in the history of male–female relationships. 'There! You did yourself proud, Alex! I officially declare the experiment over! Come on! Time to go to Warwick Castle!'

My feet were submerged in concrete by this stage, the hairs on my arms bristling with anger. 'If you somehow think that this makes us all friends again, then you are both mistaken.'

'Oh, don't be so silly, Alex,' Eleanor lectured me, her face sweltering with concern for the very first time. 'It was just a silly game.'

'A silly game!' I yelled out these words so loudly that the rest of Stratford-Upon-Avon came to an indignant halt. 'If that is what you both think, then the pair of you can rightly piss off out of my life!'

Of course, my reaction was way over the top, especially when considering my dubious motives during the picnic. But to be deceived so callously, so shamelessly, by two women who I had welcomed into my heart was simply the last straw. All I wanted to do was to get away from them, to get away from every woman I had ever known. With my head caught in the gathering rain clouds, I turned my back on both Eleanor and Danielle and pounded furiously along a narrow pathway that led into the middle of town. Somewhere behind me, I could hear a series of heated voices trapped inside a howling wind.

'Never make me do something like that ever again!' someone shouted. Thousands of desperate footsteps rattled along the path behind me, begging me to stop. Even for a hopeless, shallow man like me, it didn't take long to realise that the footsteps belonged to Danielle.

The Proposition

Stratford-upon-Avon
Wednesday-Friday
October 1999

For the next twenty minutes, Danielle chased me down an endless maze of side streets until I finally yielded to her relentless pleading and agreed to return with her to our car. During this short journey, my demeanour towards her was far from gentlemanly, which was somewhat unbecoming when she had just lied to her best friend to save my sorry arse.

But if being a gentleman involved an open invitation for people to tip a bucket of shit right over your head whenever they felt like it, then I no longer wanted to belong to that club. To further illustrate my feelings on the topic, when we found Eleanor sitting wistfully on the car bonnet, admiring a cotton toy she bought for her mother, I released an especially obnoxious grunt in her direction before jumping into the back seat.

The mood inside the car during our ride to Warwick Castle was hardly convivial. Danielle wasn't talking to Eleanor, and I wasn't talking to either woman. Mind you, this didn't necessarily stop Eleanor from talking to both of us in the vain hope that we would somehow forgive her.

But Eleanor's incessant chatter soon drew to a premature end when she failed to slow down at a T-junction and almost sideswiped a lorry for her trouble. It was about then that Danielle pulled her neck back from its socket and screamed at her best friend in English: 'Just fucking well shut up, for once, and drive!' Of course, the by-product of this incident was that Eleanor was now refusing to talk to Danielle.

It was an absurd way for three mature and intelligent adults to behave, but at this point, I couldn't see any of us backing down—especially me. After all the support I had given Danielle over the last few days, this was the way she went about showing her appreciation—by agreeing to participate in Eleanor's offensive little scheme.

Then, of course, there was Eleanor! The Austrian Ice Princess from Hell. What a piece of work she had turned out to be! She dared to tell me in Brighton that she was setting relationship traps from day one, begged me to forgive her, and then did it all over again for fun barely three days later!

But if I was so enraged by their malice, why did I feel so bloody guilty when I saw the flurried look of anguish stretched across Danielle's face? Perhaps it was because I desperately wanted to believe that Danielle was interested in me. Indeed, for a few hours that morning, I wanted to believe it more than anything else in the world. Our shared glances on the bus, the rubbing of my back, the brushing of her hair— these were all pointers that proved beyond reasonable doubt that something special was developing between us.

Of course, I had lapped it up like the self-obsessed fool I was, especially right after that kiss. Notches on the belt, no less. Two beautiful, classy European women in one week—best of friends, too! My mates back in Australia would be so impressed. 'Alex is back in the game,' they would gleefully shout when they had learnt of my exploits. Yes, Eleanor indeed had every reason to be wary of my intentions.

Feeling suitably admonished, somewhere near the outskirts of Warwick, my anger towards both women began to wane considerably. My only concern now was to sort out this ridiculous mess before everyone's stupidity, including mine, permanently fractured their friendship. Thankfully, we made it to Warwick Castle with little fanfare, and after several painstaking attempts, Eleanor finally managed to squeeze our car in between two minibuses. Whether it was the stress of driving or the fact that she was not used to so many people being upset with her at the same time, Eleanor dropped her head onto the steering wheel and began to bawl her eyes out. Seconds later, Danielle also collapsed in a blubbering heap right on top of her. Soon a bizarre competition commenced to see who could out-wail the other.

No, I didn't join in the festivities. Instead, I clumsily leaned forward and stuck my head between their delicate bodies as far as I could go. 'Please stop crying,' I said calmly. 'I'm not angry anymore. Can't you both see that this has been a horrible misunderstanding?'

If I thought this was going to calm the situation, then I was grossly mistaken. Eleanor immediately looked up at Danielle's blotchy red face and snivelled out: 'He's not angry with us anymore,' which caused both women to howl even louder.

Okay, I needed a different approach before I drowned.

'Come on, guys, how about we all go outside and give each other a hug?'

Surprisingly, my call to arms worked. We all managed to jump out of the car at precisely the same time and smashed into each other from thirty-five different angles. Arms, hands, necks, torsos, and hair were all attacked simultaneously with savage enthusiasm. I wasn't sure who was supposed to hug who and how, but at one point, I could feel Danielle's hands subtly running up and down my back, which was quite ironic in hindsight, given that this was how the whole mess began in the first place.

Our reconciliation finally came to an end, and we quietly gathered around in a semicircle. Eleanor's crystal blue eyes were full of regret. 'I am so sorry, Alex,' she said. 'That was a horrible thing to do after you have been so wonderful to me over the last few days.' She then turned to face her best friend. 'And Danielle, I should not have involved you in my scheming. I took advantage of our friendship, and that was very wrong of me.'

Danielle transformed herself into a beautiful hummingbird and flew straight into Eleanor's chest. She gave her best friend a ferociously tight hug before forcing me to connect with her beautiful face. 'I want you to know how much I like you, Alex. You gave me such good advice today. I let you down badly, and I am deeply sorry.'

'You have nothing to be sorry about,' I replied. 'Both you and Eleanor have enriched my life over the last week in ways I cannot describe.'

Maybe I should have chosen my words less elegantly because both women tackled me headfirst into a nearby ditch and then started to bawl all over again. Thankfully, after a few more minutes of ritualistic hollering, I was able to restore calm. We silently walked towards the castle entrance when suddenly Eleanor stopped dead in her tracks and stared angrily at Danielle.

'Back in the car, you told me to "fucking shut up"!'

For one horrible moment, I feared that Eleanor's unwelcome intervention would be the touchpaper for yet another huge fight. But instead, we all looked at each other with confused glances before bursting out into mutual laughter.

It took an hour or so, but things gradually returned to normal. I made sure that I gave Eleanor special attention, and we hardly left each other's side for the rest of the afternoon. She loved that I made such a renewed effort to shower her with affection, and she beamed whenever I touched her. For the first time since the British Museum, it felt like she was genuinely smitten with me.

As we explored the castle further, Danielle mostly wandered off by herself. She realised that her role, for the time being, was to leave the two of us alone as much as possible. She pretended to smile when we talked to her, but it was done with a curt flick of her hair and wrinkling of her nose.

The day's events had upset her very much, and I thought about our conversation during the picnic. I couldn't help but feel that my intrusion into their holiday had only added to her unhappiness and made things more uncertain for her. I would have loved nothing more than to take Danielle aside and discuss it with her, but we had an unspoken understanding that this couldn't happen. I needed to focus solely on Eleanor and no-one else. Besides, my selfish behaviour had damaged Danielle enough for one day.

When we arrived back at our hotel, Danielle suddenly announced she was going for a walk. She looked incredibly deflated, and so I left her alone with Eleanor for a few minutes and sulkily trampled back to our room by myself. I wondered how much of her sadness was down to me, and I wished I could start the day all over again. But Eleanor soon returned and reassured me that Danielle would be fine.

'She just needs a little time to herself,' Eleanor promised. 'Nothing to worry about.'

Sure enough, an hour later, Eleanor received a call from Danielle on her mobile phone, begging us to join her at a local pub. A trivia competition was about to begin, and she had registered us as a team.

When we entered the pub some fifteen minutes later, we noticed that Danielle was in the middle of a large circle of people, laughing wildly at some handsome hulk who had a Canadian maple leaf tattooed on the back of his sweatshirt. When she saw us standing next to the jukebox, she released a loud squeal and jumped over fifteen tables to greet us. Without explaining, she pushed us into her new group of friends and excitedly introduced us to them. It was the happiest I had seen her since we met.

I usually didn't enjoy trivia nights, but we had a fabulous night. Of course, we were always going to win, which made Eleanor extremely happy. It was a team effort, too. But even though I was the only person in the room who knew that Don Bradman's test batting average was 99.94, Danielle and I made it clear that we owed our victory to Eleanor's unmatched brilliance. She naturally beamed with pride when we showered her with never-ending praise, and, as a reward, she bought us a bottle of champers for helping her win.

Our team prize for this magnificent victory was an enormously large food hamper, complete with twenty cans of baked beans and a gigantic leg of ham. Because there was no way we could take it with us, we gave it to a local family, which made us incredibly popular with everyone inside the pub.

As the night wore on, everything that had happened earlier slowly became a distant memory. Danielle seemed to have taken my advice and had discarded her fears and inhibitions. Every time I turned my head, a new group of people surrounded her, all of whom seemed besotted by her beauty and contagious personality. Just as I predicted during the picnic, she loved her newfound popularity. Her emerald eyes dazzled in happiness, and her infectious laughter radiated pure joy. She looked like a woman completely reborn.

When we crossed paths later in the night on my way to the bathroom, she ran over to me and kissed me on the cheek. 'You were right,' she whispered into my ear and then rushed off to meet her new Canadian boy.

With Danielle entirely preoccupied, Eleanor and I spent the rest of the night sitting quietly next to a log fire that crackled to the beat of the bar's funky music. There was a tenderness and honesty to our relationship that brought us closer together after such a difficult day. Although we still felt guilty, we also knew that there was little time left for us to comprehend our feelings for each other.

Over several hours, we ran our eyes over the rest of the world, shared one too many secrets, and then finally concluded that we were nuts for each other. When we sealed this with a beautifully constructed kiss, Eleanor nestled her head blindly into my jumper, and I softly caressed the lifelines on her palm. Then strangely, my memory of what happened for the next several hours disappeared into the fire's ferocious, red flames.

*

The first thing I remembered the next day was Eleanor and I feeding the ducks along the Avon River during our early morning walk. We shared several kisses, bought some takeaway coffees, and then Eleanor dragged me towards a park bench where she hit me with a proposition.

'I want you to come back to Salzburg with me, Alex.'

Today was always a decision day for our relationship, but I wasn't expecting this.

'What, now?'

Eleanor gave me a dirty look. 'No, you fool. I have to go to Scotland first, and you have to go to your game. But I mean afterwards, in two weeks.'

A thousand questions entered my head. *Where would I live?* was the most obvious one.

'With me, of course!' said Eleanor. 'When I return home, Dad and Mum are going to spend several months fixing up a little villa they have bought on the Costa De Sol in Spain. I have agreed to look after the family house for them while I sort out the next stage of my life. If you want to be a part of the next stage of my life, we can live together for a few months in Salzburg and see what happens.'

It was apparent that Eleanor had thought this all through at least a hundred times over. I, on the other hand—

She sensed my trepidation. 'Look,' she continued, 'I don't want an answer now. It's a huge decision to make, and I appreciate that you need some time to think it through. Why don't you mull over things during the day, and then we can talk some more when we return from Birmingham this afternoon?'

That was how the last day of my Lost Week began. You might think that with such a big decision hanging over my head, I had a positively miserable time for the rest of that day, trying to figure out what I was going to do. But nothing could have been further from the truth. After all these years, our trip to Birmingham and Mary Arden's farm remained my favourite memory of that week.

I take out the three photos I have kept from that incredible day. The first photo shows both girls laughing hysterically in front of the department store in Birmingham, minutes after Eleanor had accidentally set off the building's security alarm. The next one was of Danielle pretending to strangle Eleanor at the food court after she deliberately spilled sushi over her best friend's new sweater. But the third photo was my personal favourite: both girls inspecting their shoes after they'd stepped in a pile of horse manure at Mary Arden's farm. Didn't Eleanor look cute in that red beanie of hers? And Danielle must have been the only woman I ever knew who still looked gorgeous when immersed knee-deep in shit.

Yes, each photo perfectly illustrated the prevailing mood of that day: one of happiness, laughter, and enduring friendship. Then slowly, everything began to unravel once we entered our hotel room later that afternoon.

'So, what is your answer?' Eleanor demanded before I even had time to take off my jacket.

The truth was that I had been having such a wonderful time, I hadn't considered Eleanor's proposition until then. Thinking quickly on my feet, I came up with a lame excuse that I had to use the bathroom first and then took whatever time I had left to collect together my thoughts.

By the time I returned a few minutes later, Eleanor was sitting on the edge of our sofa, her long fingers tapping impatiently on a small coffee table. I suddenly realised how much this all meant to her.

'Look …' I began. I coughed several times to make sure that my voice didn't betray the seriousness of the situation.

'Have you ever seen the movie *Brigadoon*? The musical where two American tourists travelling through Scotland stumble upon a village from another century?

'Sure,' replied Eleanor. Her grim face only enhanced my ongoing apprehension.

'Well, just like Van Johnson's character in that movie, I have fallen for the film's beautiful heroine, and I want to be part of her idyllic world. I think that we can make the world sing together if we want to.'

'That's something, I guess.'

I blurted out one random thought after another. 'But I also have responsibilities in Australia. I have an important project for work that I have to finish. My mother is coming to Canberra for Christmas. I have debts to pay. I'm going to be the best man at a friend's wedding. Blah, blah, blah.'

'Do you want to come back to Austria with me or not?' she asked after I finished my long-winded diatribe. Her tone was worryingly impatient.

'What I am proposing'—I cleared my throat once again—'is that I meet you halfway. After the rugby is over, I will return to Australia, settle my affairs as quickly as possible, and apply for some long-service leave. I will meet you in Salzburg in late February or early March.'

If Eleanor was disappointed, she didn't show it. Instead, she scrunched her nose and then reached across for her handbag, submerging her hand inside for several seconds before pulling out a notebook and pen. After scribbling something on the first spare page she could find, she ripped it out from its binding and plonked it safely into my lap.

'Here, this is my Hotmail address,' she said. 'Don't lose it because I never give it out twice. Not even to you.' There was no discernible change in the tone of her voice, so I couldn't decide whether she was pissed with me or not, just like that very first day at the British Museum when I told her how beautiful she looked in front of the Egyptian mummies.

I safely secured her email address inside my wallet and wondered whether it was time to offer her some cheap trinket of affection to test out the waters. But as always, Eleanor was one step ahead of me.

'Don't look so scared—I am not going to eat you.'

'That's a relief because I'm not all that tasty. String-bean soup if you must know.' She desperately wanted to laugh but finally decided against it.

'I hope I haven't disappointed you with my decision,' I continued.

'I half-expected something like this, so I'm not really surprised.'

'I'm sorry.'

She raised her hands in protest. 'You don't need to apologise, for at least we have agreed on a way forward. I much prefer your solution than the alternative, which was ending it on a cold Thursday night in Stratford-Upon-Avon.'

'I will come to Salzburg, I promise.' Even though I had said those words as passionately as possible, I wasn't sure if I believed them, and I suspected neither did Eleanor.

'Sure, you will,' she half-whispered. 'But there is one thing about the movie *Brigadoon* that you forgot to mention.'

'What's that?'

Her eyes were cold and ruthless. 'The town was cursed, remember? It only appeared for one day every one hundred years.'

'So?'

'So you have a short window to follow me into my world before that door closes forever. If you don't come to Salzburg by early March, it's over. Okay?'

'Okay.'

We soon found Danielle in the hotel lobby, and the three of us wandered off to have an early dinner. Eleanor and I wanted to spend our last night alone while Danielle had a hot date with the Canadian guy. Dinner turned out to be a miserable affair, with each of us knowing that this extraordinary time was about to come to an end.

Just after dessert, which none of us enjoyed, Eleanor peeled off to the bathroom while Danielle sipped quietly on her glass of red wine.

'Did Eleanor tell you?' I asked her.

'Yes.'

'What do you think?'

'Sounds like a plan,' she replied unconvincingly.

When Eleanor returned, Danielle offered to pay the bill, and we all tramped outside into the arms of a chilly, autumn evening.

Eleanor pointed to a nearby pharmacy. 'I need to get a few things, so I will let you two say goodbye in peace.'

When Eleanor entered the store, Danielle used it as a cue to push her arms around my back and kiss me on the cheek. 'I wish we had more time,' she said sadly.

'Me, too.' I could feel the usual pangs of regret gather inside my throat.

She managed to pull herself away from me and delved into her coat pocket.

'Here,' she said as she passed me an envelope. 'Please read this when you have some time, preferably when Eleanor isn't with you.'

I folded the envelope neatly and slipped it into my jacket. I wanted to say something profound that did justice to the occasion, but Danielle pressed a finger against my lips. 'Sometimes the best friendships are those that last but a short time,' she said, smiling.

We hugged each other again, and I felt the same implacable feeling of loss that I did when I said goodbye to Lottie in Athens four years ago.

Once we squeezed out every last drop of regret, Danielle straightened her back to feel the wind against her face, those incredible green eyes flashing down at me. 'That question you asked me yesterday?' she whispered. 'The answer is a definite "yes".'

Before I had a chance to contemplate her response, the most beautiful girl in the world leapt into a nearby taxi and disappeared down a lonely side street.

Eleanor soon re-emerged, and we walked silently back to our hotel room, where we then made love. Afterwards, we cradled each other in our arms until we both fell asleep to the sound of trees crackling against the windowpane. Our spluttering heater jolted me from my slumber just before midnight, and I panicked when I realised that Eleanor's soft body was no longer beside me.

I carefully searched into the darkness, where I now found her standing naked at the end of the bed, sinking her nose into a clump of tissues. I pounced upwards and gathered her in my arms.

'What's wrong, Eleanor?' I tried to comfort her. 'Why are you crying?'

'We will never see each other again,' she insisted.

I kissed her on the forehead. 'Of course we will.'

'I am not going to Scotland. I want to go to Cardiff with you.'

'Don't be ridiculous,' I replied sternly. 'What would Danielle think?'

'Danielle, Danielle, Danielle,' she roared. 'It's always about Danielle with you, isn't it?'

'Don't be ridiculous,' I found myself repeating. 'Danielle is your best friend, and you can't let her down. You'll always regret it.'

Finally accepting defeat on the whole Danielle angle, Eleanor changed tack. 'You don't want me to come to Cardiff because I will get in your way. Admit it!'

'Eleanor, please calm down. You're not thinking rationally.'

She collapsed onto the floor, her crying bordering on hysterical, but after some careful negotiation, she allowed me to help her up to the side of the bed, where we stayed locked together in silence for the next ten minutes. For some reason, that Cutting Crew song 'I Just Died in Your Arms Tonight' rolled around inside my head, and I started whispering the chorus into Eleanor's ear.

Despite the gravity of the situation, she suddenly erupted into laughter. 'Is that the best you can do?' she asked.

'Off the top of my head, yes.'

'Sometimes, I wonder how I would describe you to my family and friends.'

'How about the word "harmless"?' I offered. 'That description has worked well for me in the past with other women.'

I reassured her once again that everything would be fine. Of course, she still didn't believe a single word I said, but at this late stage, she had no choice other than to give me the benefit of the doubt.

'I promise you one thing,' I whispered, reaching out for her hand. 'When we see each other again, I'll allow you to give me one of your father's coins.'

Eleanor's smile was disturbingly muted. 'You have a deal. But a word of warning—you know better than to dishonour their power. Don't tempt fate by not keeping your word.' We sealed our new covenant with another kiss and then sneaked back beneath the sheets, emotionally drained. I couldn't remember how quickly we fell back to sleep, but it seemed like barely five minutes had passed before I opened my eyes again and heard Eleanor rustling inside the bathroom.

I glanced at my watch and discovered that it was almost six in the morning. The time had come for Eleanor and Danielle to leave. I swung my legs over the side of the bed and switched on a light. Eleanor soon appeared, wearing the pink woollen top she bought in Birmingham and those favourite jeans of hers. She looked just as stunning as she did on that very first day I met her over breakfast, and I cursed myself for letting such a woman slip through my fingers so easily.

Eleanor quietly packed her toiletry bag into her suitcase, fiddled around with the zipper and then reluctantly switched off the bathroom light.

'This is it,' she said to me with a shrug of her shoulders.

I crashed into her arms, and we passionately kissed for what would be the final time in our lives. All I wanted to do was consume every last taste of her so that I could savour it in my dreams forever.

'I had the best time,' she finally whispered when we both dropped our hands. Her tone belied an icy calmness that had been absent just a few hours before.

'Me, too,' I replied, holding back my tears.

'Until we meet again, my love.'

'Until we meet again, gorgeous girl.'

She pulled herself towards the door, opened it, and then stopped midstream. 'You're wrong, you know,' she said.

'About what?'

'Your theory on life. Remember? The other day in St James Park? We do have the power to shape our lives. That is, of course, if we want to try. You see, I think you are looking for excuses.'

'Eleanor…'

'Please don't make me a forgotten piece in your jigsaw puzzle, Alex.'

I turned away from her, not sure how I should respond in the extraordinarily little time we had left.

'You are the most incredible woman I have ever met,' I finally told her.

But she never heard me.

For the sound of the door closing behind her was always going to beat us.

Epilogue

Somewhere on a train between Birmingham and Cardiff
Friday
October 1999

Dear Alex,

Thank you for agreeing to read this letter in private. Given what happened the other day, I am not sure if Eleanor would have understood why I felt the need to write to her new boyfriend, and she can be susceptible to such things.

I just wanted to say what a privilege it was to meet you. I don't make friends that easily, but I felt a natural affinity with you when we met at that restaurant in London. My only regret is that there was never enough time for us to explore our friendship further. I could have learnt so much more from you, and I am sure you would have also greatly benefited from my insights about women!

Just before she died a few years ago, my grandmother, a wise old lady, revealed a massive family secret that she had hidden for decades. Even though she was married to Grandpa for nearly fifty years, I was surprised to learn that the most significant influence on her life was not him, but rather an American soldier she had met by chance at the end of the Second World War. While their affair was very brief—a flickering speck in the wind, she liked to call it—Grandma believed that the American had unlocked the chains to her heart, allowing her to discover the emotions that raged inside of her. She was adamant that, if not for him, she would never have pursued the life she did with Grandpa. Her dying wish was that I would meet such a person who would change the way I viewed the world one day. She was right, of course. Everyone does get to meet such a person at least once in their lifetime. In my case, I was exceptionally fortunate to meet you. I don't have the words in English to explain how grateful I am for our conversation the other day. Your faith in me during our short time together is something that I will always cherish. Thank you so much.

I am sorry that I betrayed you. In my desperation to please Eleanor, I temporarily forgot about the things that make me who I am. Please don't blame yourself. You see, I used every one of my feminine wiles to entrap you, and to my utter shame, I enjoyed every minute of it for a while there. But trust me when I say that I will never do something like that ever again.

I wish you every happiness in your life, Alex. I hope things work out with Eleanor. Despite her many eccentricities (!), she is a beautiful human being, and she will be good for you. I understand why you are going back to Australia—if I am not mistaken, you need to sort out your head about Martina and all the other terrible things that have happened to you this year before you can commit to a new relationship. I just hope you told Eleanor everything before you left—she is a naturally impatient girl, and she won't stay still forever. Please trust me on this.

I am not sure if we will ever see each other again. Alas, life is so short, so rushed, so full of choices. But no matter where it takes me, I will never forget the last few days.

Fais attention mon ami,

D.

Canberra, Australia
Australia Day 2000

Email from Eleanor to Alex

Dear Alex,

Happy New Year. I am sorry that I have taken so long to respond to you, but I needed to be clear in my mind about everything before I sent you this email. Regardless, I am just going to come out and say it now: I have met someone else, and I have decided to pursue a relationship with him.

Sometimes in life, we have to seize the opportunity when it arrives. That time for us was in October. I could understand why you needed to go back to Australia for a few weeks to sort out your affairs, but I could never accept the reasons why you wanted to delay your visit until this year. It was clear that you couldn't commit to a long-term relationship: that you were hiding something from me. As a result, my feelings for you began to waver almost immediately. I then went to a Christmas party in Salzburg with some friends, and you can guess the rest.

Please don't be angry with me, Alex. We both know that you will be relieved by my decision. I could have easily fallen in love with you if things had been different, and I will always have fond memories of our time together in England, despite all the little dramas we encountered along the way. I wish you the best and hope that you eventually meet a lovely Australian girl that will make you happy.

As Shakespeare once wrote, parting is such sweet sorrow, but I really do hope that we will see each other again. After all, I have kept a coin for you as promised.

Love,
Eleanor

Canberra, Australia
28 January 2000

Email Alex to Eleanor

Dear Eleanor,

There is no need to apologise: when you failed to contact me on New Year's Day, I knew the jig was up. You are right: I am somewhat relieved by your decision. I have just been sitting around at home, waiting for you to formally dump me, as I always knew you would. Thankfully, now that you have, I can get on with my life.

Yes, there was something holding me back and, in hindsight, I should have told you this before we said our goodbyes. But thanks to you, I tricked myself into believing that just for once in my life, fate would intervene and make everything work out. What a fool I was to believe that my theory about life may have been wrong.

Likewise, I wish you all the best for the future.

Alex.

P.S. Save the coin for someone else. Unless we bump into each other by accident in a coffee shop somewhere in Europe in twenty years' time, it's unlikely that we will see each other again.

Recriminations

Canberra
7 March 2016

I shuffled into our shower cubicle and pulled the tattered white shower curtain tightly across my body. Once I finished fumbling around with the taps, I crumpled to my knees and allowed the warm water to cascade over my face.

Surrounded by terror and confusion, I scoured my conscience for any lasting memories of Eleanor and our time together. But instead, all I could see was Danielle's beautiful face bearing down at me from the edge of a fallen star, her ghostly smile my final connection with the infidelities of my past.

Not that I should have been surprised, for only Danielle had been able to see beyond the anguish of my self-deceit. While Eleanor knew how to penetrate the barriers to my world, it had been on her terms and when her expectations of me outmatched her desires. She had viewed my Lost Week for what it was: a lost opportunity for redemption, the failure to commence a new life with a woman who had fought her own battles inside the Season of Clouds and had won.

But after I received her email, I slowly realised I had misjudged the entire situation completely. Eleanor had not won any battles at all: instead, her ongoing fragility, demonstrated so many times during our brief association, had left her swaying precariously on the edge of a precipice. Her search for stability, for a calming presence in her life, dwarfed even my preoccupation with Samos.

Yes, Eleanor's belief that she didn't need saving was merely a trap, her way of hiding the unpalatable truth from herself. For when I failed to accept the terms of her proposition—when I didn't follow her to Salzburg as she insisted—she surrendered herself to the loneliness and despair that had stained her life since Otto and embraced the passion of the very next man she met.

No-one understood this better than Danielle. She had warned me in her letter: she had implored me not to procrastinate; she tried to make me appreciate that Eleanor's needs were far more important than resolving the guilt I still felt for Martina. But when you've been trapped inside the Clouds as long as I had, such subtleties passed you by like raindrops from a gathering storm. Rather than celebrating the vast strides I had made during my Lost Week, I rebelled against its insincerity and then threw myself into the waiting arms of the Philippines. As such, my life would never be the same again.

PART THREE

THE CRY OF THE LYREBIRD

The Quiet Australian

Manila
July 2000

The first thing you noticed about Manila was the smell. It stuck to you like aging confetti: a disturbing cocktail, if you could imagine, of scorched gas delicately intertwined with the sweetest, most exotic spices ever known. Once you inhaled that first rancid scent, it either purged every last drop of humanity you had left inside of you or sucked you down a vortex of your most forbidden desires. Over the next fifteen months, I would alternate between both realities.

'You will get used to it,' Terry from the Australian Embassy reassured me. *I bet you say that to everyone*. He picked up my heavy red suitcase and carelessly tossed it into the back of his station wagon with one hand. 'All part of daily life here in Manila.'

I quietly slid into the front passenger seat and wondered whether it wasn't too late to hijack a Qantas plane back to Australia. *Most probably,* I decided. We soon bumped along an empty road full of rain-beaten potholes and dirt patches before leaving the lights of Ninoy Aquino Airport behind us.

'Is it always this humid?' I enquired as the sweat dripped down my cotton shirt.

'Pretty much, mate,' he replied. He carefully twisted a few knobs on his air-conditioner dashboard just for my benefit. Satisfied that he had done everything he could to end my whinging, his chiselled features bore down at my lonely face. 'Everything will seem strange at first, but after a few weeks, you will be fine.'

'Sure,' I replied with a whiff of sarcasm. 'After a few weeks, I'll be fine.' We spent the next part of our journey making obligatory small talk: where we were from, what football teams we supported, that sort of thing.

But when we squeezed onto EDSA, the main freeway that encircled Metro Manila, my incredulous eyes became transfixed on a bloodcurdling traffic jam that defied all common sense: cars zoomed left and right, in and out, up, and down; sirens and horns blared out with the intensity of a deranged orchestra; people screamed at each other in strange dialects through half-opened windows.

'That's the other annoying thing about this place,' Terry roared out in frustration while belligerently staring down a traditional Filipino jeepney trying to cut in front of us. 'The traffic here sends you bloody crazy!'

We eventually arrived at the Shangri-La Hotel in Makati, the main business and government district of Manila. A young valet, somehow dressed in a suit and tie despite the savage humidity, opened my door, and Terry gestured towards him.

'Get yourself a good night's sleep, and I'll pick you up in the morning at eight-thirty.'

'Got it.'

'You'll be staying here for the next two nights before we move you to your new apartment on Friday.'

'Thanks, Terry.' I offered him my hand. 'Not sure if I could have negotiated this madhouse by myself.'

'Any time.' He suddenly gave me one of those looks that my father gave me before my Grade 12 formal. 'Don't go out night-clubbing tonight, will you?' he grinned. 'Plenty of time for that later.'

'No chance,' I reassured him. 'I'm bloody exhausted.'

That part was true. I had been awake since four o'clock that morning, Australian time, and the seven-and-a-half-hour flight to Manila had strained both my patience and the tiny little muscles tearing down my lower back.

The valet carried my luggage to reception, and it took me several minutes to check in. Once I was inside my room, I searched for the obligatory can of drink from the minibar, thought about ordering a late-night snack from room service, then decided to slide into one of those pornographic bathrobes usually found in expensive Asian hotels.

I was soon rolling down the blanket on my bed, eyes drooping, hands caressing those freshly washed sheets. Minutes later, I was tossing and turning on the rock-hard mattress, drowning in sweat, and staring aimlessly through my bedroom window at the bright neon lights of Makati.

'Fuck it.' I eventually admitted defeat. I picked out a fresh T-shirt from my suitcase, snapped back into my Levi jeans, and hustled downstairs to the hotel bar. I ordered a nightcap, inherited a free bowl of peanuts, and looked for somewhere quiet to sit.

'You can sit with me, mister,' offered an attractive Filipina with big hair, big breasts, and even bigger teeth. Perversely, I wondered whether she was the big bad wolf from *Little Red Riding Hood,* sent there to gobble me up.

'Watch out for those Filipino women,' Percy, the Philippines expert, had begged me during his in-country briefing before I left Australia. 'A single white man like you will have a target on his back from the moment you step outside the airport.'

'I can look after myself, Percy,' I reassured him at the time, wondering if he had me mixed up with someone else. But as I became increasingly mesmerised by the woman's colossal overbite, I wished Percy was there to protect me.

I did my best to convince the woman that I was waiting for a friend. She knew that I was lying, of course, but still seemed perversely satisfied with my explanation.

'I come and see you another time, okay, big boy?' she implored.

'Yes, you come and see me another time,' I promised.

I gratefully found an empty chair in the corner of the room. Carlos Santana's 'Smooth' swept across the room, making a small group of young girls squeal excitedly in my direction. I raised my drink at them to be friendly and then quietly contemplated the events which led me to this hotel bar in Manila.

After I returned to Australia in late October 1999, the excitement generated by my Lost Week and Australia's World Cup win quickly waned. Before I could even attempt to make sense of everything I had just experienced, I soon found myself once again trapped within the endless Canberra treadmill of work, fast food, alcohol, sleep, and even more work. Yes, I was back to being what I had always been: another monkey playing the public service organ grinder, pushing out crap daily that went nowhere. The only thing that sustained me was the prospect of seeing Eleanor again in the new year.

But of course, this was nothing more than a pitiful illusion. I was never going to Salzburg, no matter how much I missed Eleanor. When she sent me a muted Christmas message and then didn't respond to my new year's greeting, I merely sat back and prepared myself for the worst.

Surprisingly, her email on Australia Day didn't upset me at all. Just like she predicted, I felt curiously relieved by her decision. In one fell swoop, it eradicated every fear I had accumulated over the previous few months about entering into a new relationship. With ruthless efficiency, I cut my losses and went looking for other distractions to amuse me.

Unfortunately, they failed to materialise as quickly as I would have liked, and pretty soon, my life began to drift at a snail's pace. Every new day mirrored the previous one. Despite my lingering feelings for Eleanor, I became attracted to this wonderfully precocious woman at work who, naturally, had a boyfriend and who was, naturally, unattainable. When an acquaintance of her boyfriend warned me to back off, I became even more attracted to her. Undeterred, a few weeks later, I bumped into my former girlfriend Toni at Canberra Airport and decided, based on one distant smile, that maybe we could get back together again. But the sight of her kissing her new boyfriend at the security gate ended that speculation as well.

Both incidents reinforced a reality that I was unprepared to face—I was fast approaching middle age, and my personal life was a mess. You see, there comes the point in your late thirties when you realise that the rest of the world is leaving you behind. The girls you chat up are less receptive; the jokes you make don't get laughed at the same way; the young punk with the pointed beetle-crusher shoes soon starts cutting in on you on the dance floor. Before you know it, your implied Saturday night date involves your single friends.

Then, one by one, my friends began to disappear as well. Clemmons and his new girlfriend, Kayla, went to Melbourne. Charles and Brett left for Sydney. Josh deployed to Bougainville, and Jack was off to Salt Lake City for the Winter Olympics.

'I'm going to miss you, mate,' I admitted to Jack one night after he allowed me to beat him at a game of pool.

'Don't be stupid,' he said with that audacious action hero smile. He racked the balls together for one last game, which he was always going to win easily.

'It's true,' I replied, somewhat hurt by his indifference.

'Your problem, Alex, is that you are always trying to find happiness through other people.' He then smashed two balls into adjacent pockets straight from the break. 'Perhaps it's time you found happiness within yourself.'

He was right, of course: I was always looking for someone to cure me of my pain, that special person who could unlock the chains to my heart, as Danielle had put it in her letter to me. But as luck would have it, there was no-one in this damn city who I could entrust with the key. So after weeks of more self-reflection, I decided that I wanted to leave Canberra as well.

Of course, that was never going to impress the Spiders. 'Out of the question,' Funnel Web Spider snarled a few days later. 'We put you where you are for a reason, and that's where you are staying until we tell you otherwise.'

Man, I was starting to hate those Spiders. For the next two weeks, I bumbled around work in a foul mood, formulating all sorts of devious plans for how I could escape their hold over me when my friend Matt Smith suddenly dropped a piece of paper on my desk.

'Here,' he tapped his finger on my chair. 'This has you written all over it.' Despite myself, I glanced down at the internal work memo.

'Applications are sought from Executive Level One officers to attend masters' programs in Singapore and the Philippines,' it screamed out at me. 'Must have an undergraduate degree in strategic studies.'

'You're an EL1,' Matt reminded me.

'I also have an arts degree majoring in strategic studies,' I replied.

'What do you think?' I asked Funnel Web Spider the next day.

'Sounds interesting. I will make some calls on your behalf.'

'No, you won't,' I begged him. 'I want to do this my way, for once.'

'If you must,' Funnel Web Spider said begrudgingly. 'But really, cheating and deception are the only ways to guarantee success in the public service. Haven't we taught you anything?'

Later that night, I started to work on my application. I was halfway through the usual nonsense about how wonderful I was and what an asset I would be when God and a bottle of red wine helped me make a decision that would ultimately shape the rest of my life. You see, God felt that I should solely focus my energies on the program being offered by the Philippines Defense College.

'After all,' he said with a holy frown, 'Manila is a dangerous place, and you're delightfully dispensable. 'While God made a fascinating point, I explained to him that I didn't know much about the Philippines, apart from that stuff about Douglas MacArthur during World War II and the People's Revolution in 1986, which ousted a much-hated dictator, Ferdinand Marcos. To rectify the situation, I marched into the work library the following day, buried my head into countless articles and books, and then God and I cobbled together the most brilliant soliloquy about the Philippines ever written. Several days later, a lovely young woman with a reassuring smile parked herself at my desk, explained that mine was the most brilliant soliloquy about the Philippines she had ever read, and enthusiastically congratulated me on my selection.

'And should I screw up,' I said to her with a grin, 'we can both blame it on God.'

Over the next few months, I undertook several briefings, had a hundred needles stuck in my arse, and before you knew it, I was on that plane to Manila.

As my first night in Manila extended into the early hours of the morning, I sank some more beers, trialled some Filipino rum, and got into a verbal argument with some Poms about football. Three hours later, I staggered back to my room, either half-tanked or jet-lagged, wondering how I was going to survive the next few days.

'Just take your time,' said Captain Roderick, my new boss, the very next morning. He was a handsome senior navy captain with a prickly beard and seashell eyes, which suited me fine because I had always got along with handsome senior navy captains with prickly beards and seashell eyes. 'You can achieve great things here if you try,' he promised.

'Providing, of course, you don't get yourself killed first,' noted Marty Booth, his deputy. His black sense of humour immediately lifted my prickly mood, and I was relieved at last to find a kindred spirit inside the embassy.

After lunch, we jumped into Captain Roderick's car and drove out to Camp Aguinaldo, the principal military base in Manila. Along with the Defense College, it also accommodated the headquarters of the Armed Forces of the Philippines and a variety of other critical military units. It would become the centre of my world for the next twelve months.

The college consisted of a crumbling two-storey building, hidden next to a deserted car park and a dusty parade ground. At first glance, it looked as if it could use a coat or two of paint and a generous surge of electricity.

'This is the most prestigious academic institution in the Philippines,' Professor Moreno, the college's kind-hearted principal, boasted while pouring me a glass of chilled water. I did my best to nod attentively just as a majestic golden cockroach brushed the side of my shoe.

We talked some more about the course, and then she escorted me to the primary classroom. The rest of the course members—a broad collection of high-flying Filipino military officers, public servants, and civilians—were already inside, eager to greet the new Australian student. As such, thirty pairs of eyes considered me with morbid fascination while I nonchalantly swiped at the geyser of sweat erupting on my chin.

Will someone please turn on the fucking air conditioning?

As I acknowledged their bewildered faces, the absurd reality emerged that I was the only foreign student on the course. Like it or not, this would mean that I would always be the centre of attention, the exquisite anomaly for everyone to critique. How I wished they had informed me of this before I left Australia.

The following day, Terry and Marty escorted me to my new home in San Lorenzo Village, an upmarket locale built for the pleasure of diplomats and their families in Makati, close to both the embassy and Glorietta Mall.

'You're kidding me, right?' I muttered several hours later once I completed a full tour of the apartment. 'This is obscene.' I pointed to the spiralling staircase that led to the second floor. 'Do you seriously expect me to walk up those stairs every night? I need a bloody lift to go to bed.'

'It's a tad opulent,' admitted Marty. 'But it works for me.'

'A tad opulent? It has six frigging bedrooms! What am I supposed to do with six frigging bedrooms?'

'I don't know, grumble bum. Use your imagination.'

Fely, my new maid, Gip the Gardner, and Hector, my driver, giggled from the kitchen corner. Unaccustomed to this lavish lifestyle, I assumed they were all extras from *Upstairs/Downstairs*.

Despite all the friendly warnings about the country I had received from embassy officials and colleagues back in Australia, the Philippines and I were a perfect match right from the start. Sure, there were lots of intangibles that I had to deal with along the way: the country's bizarre gun culture, how no-one turned up to meetings on time, why it took four sales assistants to process one department store purchase, and why I was being confused with some

South American crooner called Fernando. But I knew that if I wanted to succeed on the course, I had to accept my new environment with good humour and not be distracted by its many cultural anomalies. Adaptability: that was the key to success.

It didn't take me long to discern that the Philippines was a country caught in a widening rift between two extreme cultures, which served only to exacerbate its many inequities. On the one hand, the touch, the smell, and the feel of its cluttered and dirty streets were uniquely Asian and Roman Catholic. However, how many Filipinos saw the world beyond their poverty-ridden existence mirrored the worst aspects of western consumerism.

To be a Filipino sometimes meant a life connected to a false American dream of fame, fortune, and looking your best. Even a young Filipina from the dirtiest, run-down hut on the street had to have their hair perfectly curled, their dress bearing the latest designer logo, and their face made up like a supermodel. Unfortunately, unlike its big sister America, which had ruled the Philippines for the first half of the twentieth century, the Philippines lacked the institutions, governance, and community endeavour needed to turn these untapped dreams into a reality.

Instead, it was a developing nation unsure of its place in the world, beset by nepotism, corruption, violence, and economic dislocation, where the ordinary Filipino citizens—who I would learn to love more than life itself—suffered terrible injustices every day. Even after my first week inside the country, I was angry to see how poorly the ruling elite treated their people.

To complicate matters, the Philippines was the victim of several insurgencies raging out of control across the country. On the main island of Luzon, a group of communist rebels calling themselves the National People's Army roamed the northern highways, kidnapping or shooting the odd government official and demanding an end to the status quo. Meanwhile, no-one could ever adequately explain to me what the status quo involved. While the NPA painted themselves as the good guys, their plans seemed to spin around in circles, like everything else in this country.

However, the biggest threat to Filipino national security was undoubtedly the various Islamic insurgencies prospering in the southern island of Mindanao. Although the Philippines was predominantly a Roman Catholic country due to Spanish colonisation in the sixteenth century, a small but significant Islamic minority—the Moros—made Mindanao their home. But centuries of neglect, poverty, and suffering at the hands of the Christian majority had caused many Moros to pursue sedition as the only means for survival.

Various separatist Islamic groups had formed over the decades, engaged in a brutal armed insurgency in Mindanao and its neighbouring islands. Worryingly, a common goal of independence connected some of these groups to wider extremist Islamic movements in Indonesia and Malaysia. Like the Abu Sayyaf, other groups were simply brigands out to make a quick buck through kidnapping and blackmail. By the time I arrived in the country, the situation had descended into chaos, and no-one in Manila seemed to have any idea how to curtail it.

That's where I would come in. Over the next twelve months, the plight of Mindanao's Muslim population would become my obsession. While I hated the violence associated with their struggles, I had learnt enough from my father to know that the looking glass always worked both ways. Behind every insurgency was a root cause that was often conveniently ignored by those in power. Furthermore, I had long held that behind most of the world's conflicts, poverty, economic neglect, and a fight for resources were the leading causes.

The situation in Mindanao was no different. It was a beautiful island, blessed with golden beaches and bountiful resources. As I walked among its people in the months to come, I became more convinced that accelerating the local levers of prosperity would improve their lives. If you gave people a job, a house, new clothing and hope for a better future, they would less likely want to join an extremist organisation.

To facilitate a better way of life for its Moro citizens, the government had a responsibility to encourage foreign investment, build better infrastructure, and clamp down on dissent in a proactive way. Perhaps only a dangerous outsider from another country like me could propose such a hair-brained scheme. Regardless, I was determined to incorporate these solutions into my thesis that all students had to submit by the end of the course. Not only did I owe it to the Philippines to get things right, but I owed it to every Australian taxpayer whose taxes were funding my fifteen-month sabbatical.

However, obtaining the evidence I needed to prove my thesis was not going to be easy, for when the darkness arrived, I had to turn myself into a false prophet, the Quiet Australian, who lived silently between the shadows and pulled strings with the audacity of a puppet master. I had to watch, wait, and learn. I had to train my mind to understand what motivated a terrorist, to experience their fears and desires. I had to engage with the prostitutes, the pimps, the dope addicts, the crooked policemen, the single mums with their thirty dirty children and, when that was all over, like a chameleon, slip back into the light to resume a quieter life.

As the months slowly passed by, the living remnants of my servitude to this inglorious quest would become startlingly obvious. They included the empty bottles of rum in my garden, the endless stream of women's undergarments strewn across my bedroom floor, the filthy smell of decadence on my shirt. Every day in the Philippines presented a new challenge, a new absurdity. In a country full of madmen, I figured one more addition was not going to make a hell of a difference.

Sally

Manila
July 2000

Before leaving Australia, my close friend and mentor, Chris Taylor, gave me some critical advice. 'The one thing I learnt during my career in the air force is that life rarely gives you these opportunities,' he said to me one day over a beer. 'Make your good fortune count, and don't look back.' In the weeks before my departure, Chris would often ask me to repeat these exact words over and over again to make sure that I had understood him: 'See everything. Regret nothing.'

He was right, I decided later that afternoon as I began to unpack one of my infernal boxes. It would have been so easy to spend my weekends lost inside my obscenely salubrious apartment instead of experiencing the local Filipino culture.

'Resist that temptation,' Chris warned me when I rang him after dinner. 'Be active, don't get lazy, and explore as much of the country as you can.'

With our telephone conversation still on my mind, I woke up on my first Saturday morning in Manila in an excited mood and with an overwhelming desire to follow Chris's instructions to a tee. After Fely spoiled me with something that I assumed were corn fritters, I strolled down to the Shangri-La Hotel, where I ordered a taxi to take me to Intramuros, an ancient walled city located in the heart of Metro Manila.

At first, I tried hard to make Chris proud of me. But after two hours of bouncing through a slew of crumbling Spanish landmarks, the names of which I could barely pronounce, the oppressive heat, the persistent sweat, and some overly obese flies finally got the better of me. Pretty soon, I was wandering cluelessly around the Ermita district, not knowing where I was or what the hell I was supposed to be doing.

Luckily for me, I soon discovered a lonely white taxi parked in the middle of a cluttered alleyway. When I dangled my legs across the front passenger seat, the driver dismissed me with a lazy frown, indicating that he was well inclined to remain where he was for the rest of the afternoon.

However, as I would often find out during my stay in the Philippines, the lure of the five-hundred-peso note did wonders in improving a local's motivation. An hour later, after negotiating some more baffling traffic jams, I hurried through the main security entrance to Glorietta Shopping Mall, relieved to be back in the relative safety of Makati.

I frittered away the early afternoon exploring Glorietta's endless maze of specialty shops and bookstores before deciding to take in a movie—a new Hollywood offering called *Autumn in New York*. Even though it starred two of my favourite actors, Winona Ryder and Richard Gere, the film wouldn't win too many Oscars. But what the next two hours did provide was a unique insight into how Filipino people liked to enjoy their cinematic experience.

The first thing I noticed was that the whole concept of observing silence during a movie was an extremely outdated one. That wasn't to say we didn't get off to a promising start: the audience curiously welcomed the coming attractions with almost religious deference. Not a peep from anyone, you might say.

But as soon as the main feature commenced, trillions of mobile phones suddenly appeared from out of the darkness. Within seconds, the entire theatre had erupted into a whirlwind of beeping and whirring, as text messages were sent and received with mindless regularity. If you were fortunate—like I indeed was—you might also get to sit next to Dolly, who got a phone call from Daisy, and pretty soon you had in your possession every intimate detail of last night's shenanigans.

Halfway through the movie, a large group of people sitting to my left—virtually half the audience—decided to lurch forward for no apparent reason and left the theatre in an orderly, single file. As I alluded to before, the movie wasn't exactly my cup of tea. But these were two of my all-time Hollywood heroes. Why couldn't they have shown just a little respect and watched the whole thing through to its logical conclusion?

Just as I finished eating my popcorn, a flood of people swarmed through the doors and dived into the empty seats around me. It took several minutes before I realised what was going on. The people who recently left the theatre, well, if I wasn't mistaken, did so because they began to watch the movie halfway through the previous session.

What about the guys who had just turned up? When the final credits rolled, and the rest of us were throwing our used tickets in the bin, I was confident that they would still be there, clinging onto their seats in anticipation, waiting for the next session to begin so that they could watch how the first half of the movie went down.

As much as I tried to understand why anyone would want to watch the last part of a movie first and the first part of a movie last, it just wasn't doing it for me. So when Winona's character died from her incurable disease, I decided to ponder these issues over a beer. For the next twenty minutes, I staggered around the crowded streets of central Makati, desperately looking for somewhere to buy a drink before I accidentally found a flashy-looking nightclub.

Once inside, I happily negotiated a highchair at the main bar, ordered an ice-cold Filipino beer, and then asked Jo-Jo, the bartender, the obvious question.

'Why am I the only person here?'

'What do you mean?'

'The place is empty.'

'You're obviously new in town.' Jo-Jo giggled. 'Things don't liven up in Makati until about nine o'clock at night.'

That was a bloody shame, given that it was only ten past five. While I was still desperate to please Chris, I wasn't sitting there by myself like a loser for the next four hours. I was about to bring my first Saturday in Manila to a premature conclusion when the redoubtable Jo-Jo encouraged me to persevere. 'Get some dinner and then come back later this evening, sir. You won't regret it! The women that come here at night are unbelievable!'

Admittedly, this additional piece of information sparked my curiosity. I left Jo-Jo a few extra pesos because I was such a nice guy and then navigated my way back to San Lorenzo Village. I treated myself to a soothing cold shower, slapped on some duty-free cologne, and thirty minutes later, I was tucking into an Aussie T-bone steak at a cosy little restaurant situated inside Glorietta Mall.

Everything was good with the world until my stomach threatened to explode several hundred feet into the air. Ever since Greece, my intestinal issues had become an ever-present curse, especially when I ventured overseas. However, this felt markedly different from the ailment that had inflicted me following the party in Athens: something akin to an erupting volcano stuck deep inside my intestines. To avoid any potential embarrassment—like shitting all over the restaurant's brand-new carpet—I quickly cancelled dessert, paid my bill, squeezed in my bottom cheeks as tightly as I could and shuffled safely back home.

Afterwards, as I stared out into the smoggy night sky from my bedroom window, I realised that the time had come to call it quits. But when I pulled out a clean pair of pyjamas from the top drawer, a mysterious hybrid apparition combining both Chris and Jo-Jo's disappointed faces stared at me from the back of the mirror. 'Come on, Alex,' it demanded. 'Don't be such a wuss. Go out and have some fun!'

Right, that was it: I would never allow some half-baked hallucination to call me a wuss. So I splashed some cold water across my face, flicked on more aftershave, and headed back to Glorietta.

As I turned down yet another filthy side street, I passed an all-night pharmacy and remembered that I didn't have any of those implements that single men sometimes needed to use in an emergency. Yes: I had run clean out of condoms. Of course, I wasn't expecting anything to happen, but it was always prudent to be well-prepared.

For a woman, buying contraception is seemingly a mundane affair. But for a man, there is something about buying condoms that makes you feel like you have made the FBI's Ten Most Wanted list. You begin by tiptoeing carefully into the pharmacy, hoping that you won't bump into anyone you know. More often than not, you are wearing sunglasses for that extra bit of disguise, even though this is the third time you have visited the pharmacy in a week.

For the next ten minutes, you pathetically wander around from aisle to aisle, your face caked with sweat, convinced that they have deliberately relocated your favourite brand to trick you and hoping you will fall upon them by chance before the young female sales assistant catches you out.

When you ultimately fail—when she finds you skulking behind the shaving stand, pretending to look at razors, and asks with that knowing smile whether she can help you—you are obliged to come out with the most absurd excuses ever invented justifying why you have to leave.

That was all jumbling around in my head as I lined up in what soon became a ridiculously slow queue. To my horror, when I finally arrived at the front counter, I realised that they didn't stock actual boxes of condoms. Instead, they were all neatly laid out individually in endless rows of trays in front of me, akin to jellybeans in a candy bar.

'Good evening, sir!' offered a sweet-looking girl behind the cash register. She couldn't have been more than eighteen or nineteen. 'How can I help you?'

"I would like to buy some condhdhdhdhdhd,' I mumbled in a low whisper.

'Sorry, but I didn't quite hear you. Could you please repeat that?'

'I would like to buy some condoms, please.'

'Oh, you want condoms?' she screamed out, partly to herself, partly to the other fifty people in the line behind me. 'How many would you like?'

'Er, ten?'

'Ten!' Her face exploded with disbelief as if the mere thought of me having sex ten more times in my life was utterly incomprehensible to her. 'Are you sure you need that many?'

'They are not for me actually—they are for a friend,' I reassured her.

'If you insist.' She produced a thin plastic bag and then pointed to the trays in front of her. 'Would you like the ones with the pink wrappers or the blue wrappers?'

By then, I had shrunk from six foot four to about two foot five. 'I'm not sure,' was all I could say.

‘Buy the pink ones,’ the Filipino woman directly behind me suggested. ‘They are usually pretty good.’

‘Okay, the pink ones then.’

The sales assistant held out the plastic bag in front of her with one hand and then slowly dipped her other hand into the pink tray, pulling out a single condom. ‘One!’ she announced to the world. She casually dropped the condom into the bag and then repeated the process all over again. ‘Two!’ she bellowed out even more loudly.

I could already hear the impatient murmuring emanating from the back of the line. ‘What’s going on?’ asked a Filipino man who had just entered the store with his wife and two children.

‘Some Australian guy up there is buying out all the pink condoms,’ a young girl explained.

‘Three!’

‘You missed one there.’ The woman directly behind me pointed to a lone condom stuck to the side of the plastic bag.

‘Oh yes!’ the sales assistant cried out gleefully. ‘You are right. Four!’

By the time she reached five, I had shrunk to the size of a dormouse. There was no feasible way I was going to make it to ten without gurgling down the nearest drainpipe. ‘How about we just go with five?’ I finally conceded.

The girl’s fake smile belied her disappointment, but she happily took my money anyway. ‘Have a good evening, sir!’ she proudly said once she handed over the plastic bag. ‘Come back soon!’

My humiliation complete, I left the pharmacy with something resembling a tail stuck firmly between my skinny legs. Ten minutes later, with my new condoms hidden safely in my back pocket, I was back giving Jo-Jo a high five while he produced another Filipino beer and an ‘I told you so’ smile.

‘You were right,’ I conceded, darting my eyes across the dance floor. ‘This place has gone completely off.’

Indeed, what a difference a few hours made. After chairing the lonely hearts club meeting, I was herded into a boisterous crowd of excited young couples, their mingling sweat falling in cadence to the thumping dance music blaring across the room. Unperturbed, I dragged my beer over to the only spare stool I could find, parked myself down, and began chatting with several German backpackers at an adjoining table.

Once I finally convinced them that Australia wasn’t full of serial killers knocking off their compatriots, I forced my way back to the bar for a much-needed refill. While waiting for the guy in front of me to complete his order, something caught my attention through the mass of bodies encircling me. There were three young women in the adjacent drinks line smiling right at me.

The two standing closest to the bar were Filipino, and they were both stunning. Even so, their skirts were way too short, their make-up was way too thick, and they both looked way too young. Without any further discussion, I turned my decadent musings onto the third woman, who moved closer towards me.

She was much older than her friends—late twenties, if I had to guess—but even considering the flickering strands of disco light sweeping across her face, I struggled at first to work out her nationality. She was tall enough, perhaps five foot seven, or at a stretch, five-eight in heels, which accentuated her slim waistline and tree twig legs. Her hair was fashioned into a shiny dark bob that barely skimmed the bottom of the neck, while her charcoal eyes radiated a childish mischievousness more akin to a boisterous teenager. 'Hi there, stranger,' she said in a distinctly southern American accent.

American? Well, knock me over with a feather. I didn't see that coming.

I returned the favour. 'Hi there.' She pushed me aside and then rolled her head around to face her friends, both of whom were giggling madly. It didn't take me long to work out that I was the source of their amusement.

'What's so funny?' I asked Miss America with a snap to my voice. 'Why are your friends laughing at me?'

'I am only guessing here, of course,' she said. 'But it might have something to do with the packet of condoms sticking out of your jeans.'

Of course it did.

I nervously pulled my hand over the contours of my bottom and then squashed the plastic bag deep into my pocket as far as it would go.

'Thanks. I thought I had lost them.'

'Expecting a big night, are we?'

I tried lying to her. 'They're not mine. If you must know, I bought them for a friend.'

'If you insist,' she said with a laugh. Without warning, she reached across with her long fingernails, scratched out the condoms from my pocket and then dropped them into her small handbag. 'Maybe I should look after them—for your friend. You know, while we have a dance.' Wow! *This was quite the development. After all, it wasn't every day that my stupidity paid off so handsomely.*

We danced together for maybe twenty minutes. She didn't seem to mind my two left feet or the usual windmill motions I made with my hands. And I was positively flippant when she accidentally kicked me in the balls.

She let slip that she had a boyfriend somewhere in between Madonna's 'Papa Don't Preach' and the B52s' 'Rock Lobster'. I wasn't sure why she was telling me this and, to be honest, I didn't care. But whatever her reasons, it didn't seem to diminish her growing interest in me. When we returned to the bar, I bought her another drink, and then she whispered something deliciously naughty to her friends.

'What's your name?' I finally asked after she had sipped at her vodka and orange drink.

'Sally Wojistchow …'

'Wow, that's a difficult—'

'—bilkowski—'

'—name to pronounce.'

'—rockow.'

'And what do you do for a living?' she asked inquisitively as if the answer to this question would be the deal-breaker in our embryonic relationship.

'I'm a famous Australian warrior monk.'

'Well'—she began to chuckle—'you don't look like a warrior.' She dived into her handbag and swung the packet of condoms deep into my face. 'Given these, I doubt that you're much of a monk either.'

'They're for a friend,' I insisted once again.

We shouted at each other some more over the music, shared a few more dances, and sank a few more screwdrivers before Sally announced that she and her friends had to attend some high-rolling party in Quezon City. Before I could decide my next move, she placed her business card into my palm and suggested that we catch up for a drink next weekend.

'What about those, ahem, you know?' I pointed to her handbag.

'I am holding them for ransom until you call me.'

'What if my friend needs them?'

'He won't,' she assured me.

*

The following Saturday afternoon, I arrived at the Hobbit House, a bar in central Manila owned and operated by a family of little people, wondering how things would play out.

I found Sally sitting quietly at a table, reading a copy of the Manila Times. She released a tiny squeal of delight in my direction and then kicked out at the spare seat in front of her.

'Well, if it isn't the warrior monk.'

'Well, if it isn't Sally with the ridiculously long surname'.

We ordered some drinks and soon lost ourselves in animated conversation. Who was I kidding? It was Sally who did most of the talking. Pretty soon, I realised that she was one of those gym-freaking, party-loving, fast-talking, wise-cracking, neo-feminists who called everyone 'darling' and loathed any food that may have had parents.

'Really, darling?' she implored when I ordered some chicken wings for a snack. 'Think of what they did to those poor chickens before they killed them.'

While her views about battery cages were quite compelling, I found her family background even more fascinating. Despite that Slavic sounding surname, her grandfather on her father's side had been an immigrant from Glasgow who settled in Louisiana after the Second World War. He fell in love with a Creole woman, and they had one child, Sally's father. He grew up on the outskirts of New Orleans and joined the navy as soon as he finished high school.

'Had a woman in every port,' Sally proudly boasted with a grin, which somehow contradicted her feminist predilections. Eventually, he would meet Sally's mum, a Filipina working as a secretary at the US naval station at Subic Bay. They got married after a whirlwind romance and then returned to New Orleans when her father retired from the navy. Sally was the oldest of three girls: 'Dad's penance,' she called it. She was the first person in her family to have completed a university degree and was a highly regarded corporate financial expert specialising in business development.

'What made you come to the Philippines?' I asked. I examined the intriguing texture of her face and tried to determine which part was Creole, Filipina, and Scottish.

'Career, mainly,' she explained. 'My company in the States suggested it would benefit my career if I worked in one of our Asian offices for a year or two. Manila was the obvious choice since I speak Tagalog and understand the local culture.'

We talked some more about my course, the downsides of living in Manila, and the usual trivialities when a boy first meets a girl. To be fair on Sally, I wasn't sure where this was all heading. She was way, way over the top for me. Altogether too wacky and too much in my face. I needed to be around someone a lot calmer who could counter my many eccentricities. There was also the whole boyfriend thing, too, a topic which she deliberately continued to avoid. Therefore, I wasn't too disappointed when she had to leave for another appointment.

But just when I thought it was all going to end in a damp squib, she offered to take me on a day excursion to the island of Corregidor in Manila Bay next weekend. A part of me wanted to decline her invitation, but the other decided to give her one more chance. We gave each other a friendly hug goodbye and resolved to see each other again next Saturday.

The week at college went far too quickly, and I rarely had time to think about Sally or our impending adventure until Friday night, when she texted me to confirm the timings for the next day. I woke up around five-thirty, covered in a voluminous sweat and trying incredibly hard not to vomit. Those ongoing stomach issues were driving me insane. Looking for the ideal excuse to pull out of our trip, I was seconds away from texting Sally with an apology before I tossed my mobile phone onto a separate pillow. *Damn it! Let's just get it over and done with, pal. But you're ending this today.*

I was in a particularly gloomy, non-social mood when she picked me up on that sultry Saturday morning. But by the time we arrived at the Port of Manila passenger terminal forty minutes later, I found myself infected by Sally's persistent exuberance. It was like every doubt I had invented about her had been erased, one by one, by some benevolent computer virus. Before I could do anything to counteract this audacious attack, I was laughing at her jokes, blushing at her inappropriate comments, and swimming inside her petulant eyes.

They say that time flies when you're having fun. That's an apt description of how I spent the next several hours. Corregidor was a treasure trove of fading artefacts and interesting information for a military history buff like me. It was Corregidor where Douglas MacArthur had based his headquarters during the Japanese invasion of the Philippines, following the surprise attack on Pearl Harbour. It was also from these same rocky shores that McArthur had controversially left his men and embarked on a long, arduous journey to Australia by boat and plane.

We spent the morning exploring the haunting Malinta tunnel, taking in a delicious seafood lunch at the former officers' club, and then wandered through a procession of weather-beaten war ruins, hidden delicately inside the island's sprawling vegetation. Everything around us seemed a world away from the chaos and poverty of Metro Manila.

'Corregidor makes you forget about the city, doesn't it?' Sally suddenly remarked.

'It sure does,' I replied.

'I could easily spend the night here with you.' At first, I wondered whether this was another one of her deliberately suggestive comments aimed at getting a reaction. But I could sense something different from how she looked at me, so I gratefully took the bait.

'Me too—if you didn't have a boyfriend.' I paused for several seconds while considering the specks of sunlight on her face. 'Or is this whole boyfriend thing just made up to string me along for your amusement?'

'Oh no, he is real, alright.' She picked up several small pebbles and hurled them down a nearby gully just for my benefit. 'But I am getting that sorted out real soon.'

'I see.'

'If I do, how would you feel about that?'

'I would feel pretty darn good, I reckon.'

'Great,' she whispered into my ear. 'Because I am worth the wait.'

'I bet you are.'

When Sally made a detour to the bathroom, Mini-Alex suddenly returned after six months on sabbatical. I wasn't necessarily pleased to see him.

'What are you doing, Alex? Haven't you been down this path before? Not even a year ago. Need I remind you of that fiasco with Eleanor?'

Butt out, shit-for-brains. What I do with Sally is my decision, not yours.

'Mark my words; you will only get hurt again.'

No, this was different, I explained to him. There was something about the last eight hours that invoked a beautiful lullaby from my future. An inexplicable feeling that a critical piece of my life's jigsaw puzzle was standing right next to me. All I had to do was grab it with both hands, snap it into place, and everything about my life would finally make sense.

Experience everything. Regret nothing. Remember?

So screw you, Mini-Alex; I am going for it with everything I've got.

After all, Sally and I have the next twelve months to make this all work.

What could go wrong?

Anguish

Manila
August 2000

'I have to quit my job and go back to New Orleans,' Sally explained on the phone the following Monday night. 'My father has inoperable bowel cancer, and I leave Manila on Saturday afternoon.'

Don't say a word, Mini-Alex. Not one bloody thing.

'I'm so sorry, Alex,' she continued. She was crying.

'You have nothing to be sorry about,' I replied, trying to hide my total devastation. 'Besides, we're not even—'

'Yeah, I know. We're not even going out.'

We talked some more; I stupidly reassured her that her dad would be okay, and she promised to give me a call later in the week. When she eventually said good night, I glared at my phone, considered the options available to me, and then hurled it across the room towards the nearest wall, smashing it into a million pieces.

I moped around college for the next few days, convinced that I was doomed to be alone for the rest of my life. Whenever I heard the sound of a newly arrived text message, I dived for my replacement mobile phone and expected to see Sally's name light up my screen in stars, telling me that her dad had somehow made a miraculous recovery. But with each passing disappointment, all I could do was curse my growing selfishness. By Friday lunchtime, I finally accepted that I would never hear from Sally again.

I spent the rest of the afternoon sipping iced tea, reading Christopher Koch's magnificent book about war-torn Cambodia, *Highway to a War*, and staring at the recently painted white ceilings. Inevitably, I soon drifted off to sleep on my extra-soft upstairs lounge.

Just before sunset, I was jarred awake by the unmistakable sound of semiautomatic rifle fire. For one absurd moment, I thought that I was re-enacting a scene from my book inside an impossible dream. But when I saw tracer flares streaking upwards past my window, I realised that this was bloody well happening.

My army training automatically took control, and I instinctively bellyflopped off the bed and landed facedown on the polished floor. Once I caught my breath, I quickly stretched my body out as far as it could go and then rapidly executed a series of fire and movement drills that carried me safely towards the windowpane. Once the firing had stopped, I ducked my head upwards and peered outside into the emerging moonlight.

I couldn't believe what I was seeing. Four kids, probably no more than fifteen or sixteen, were standing in front of my apartment block, admiring their M16 rifle. In hindsight, they were nice boys, especially the one wearing the balaclava.

I quickly prised open the window, caught hold of the security screen, and pulled myself up. 'Oi!' I screamed out angrily through the metal grill, 'what the hell do you think you are doing?'

Of course, there was always a chance that one of them would blow my head right off. But that was a risk I was willing to take. After all, I was used to being shot.

'Sorry, sir!' the tallest of the boys yelled at me. 'It's my birthday present! We were just testing it out!'

'Let me explain to you one of the basic rules of gunfire. Those metal things that you put inside the magazine. You know, the bullets?'

'Yes, sir.'

'Well, I am not sure if you are aware or not, but clinical tests have confirmed that once they penetrate the human body, they usually kill you.'

'Yes, sir.' Another pause. 'But sir, we were shooting them straight in the air!'

'Where do you think the bullets go after you shoot them straight in the air?'

The four boys stared at each other with confused faces. Okay, I really couldn't vouch for the boy wearing the balaclava, but you get what I mean.

'Straight down?' the ringleader offered.

'Hole in one, dude,' I replied facetiously. 'Hole in one! Now, don't get offended by what I am about to say next, but can you please get the fuck off my property and fire your rifle elsewhere? Like on a firing range, for instance?'

'Yes, sir,' they all waved back at me. 'Sorry, sir!'

I stood next to the window for several more minutes just to make sure they had all buggered off before I shuffled back to the couch. Not for the first time since arriving in Manila, I wanted to scream at the insanity unfolding around me.

Unperturbed, I picked up my book, read a few more pages, and then decided to check my mobile phone. That's when I realised I had missed several calls from Sally.

Damn it! They were from an hour ago! Hoping that I could still catch her, I pressed down on the recall button and sweated on several dial tones.

'Hi,' Sally thankfully answered.

'Hi.'

'I didn't think you would call me back.'

'Why not?'

'I just didn't.'

'Well, I have.'

'Can I come over?'

She really shouldn't, but I had to see her again. 'Of course you can.'

She arrived ten minutes later by taxi. Streaks of blurred mascara lined her pretty face, ominous signs that she had been crying.

'Are you okay?' I asked, inviting her to sit on my downstairs sofa.

'I just broke up with Nathan, my boyfriend.'

'Ah,' I replied knowingly.

'He didn't take it well.'

'Men rarely do.'

She asked for something to drink. I returned from the kitchen with a bottle of sparkling mineral water and two huge glasses, after which she poured herself a drink and then pretended to toast me.

'This is a mess,' she finally admitted.

'Breakups usually are. It will pass.'

'I am not talking about Nathan. I am talking about you and me.'

'Oh, I see.'

'I desperately wanted us to get together.'

'I did too. But it wasn't meant to be.'

'No, it wasn't.'

Sally ordered me to sit down next to her, and I pathetically obeyed without a murmur of protest. It was obvious where this was heading. She gently took my hand and pinned it against her chest. 'I don't want to be alone tonight, Alex.'

I thought back to Martina and my very last night on Samos. Didn't she say those exact words to me in her hotel room?

'Are you sure?'

Her scowl was rightly vicious. 'Am I sure? What, do you want a written invitation or something?'

'No. But when it's over, please don't ask me about my secrets.'

'Secrets? What secrets? What are you talking about?'

You know damn well what I am talking about, Martina.

'Just thinking out loud.' I nudged my face towards her, and we kissed. Her lips tasted like wild honey.

'Take me to bed,' she insisted.

Such an erstwhile proposal required an equally gallant response. So, channelling Rhett Butler from *Gone with the Wind*, I gathered Scarlett in my trembling arms and heroically carried her up the seventeen hundred steps that led to my bedroom. Alas, when we finally arrived some three years later, my back completely locked up, and I found myself prancing around my bed as if my soles were on fire.

'What should I do?' asked Sally.

'Um, bathroom? Hot water bottle?'

Eventually, we both became settled beneath the sheets when Sally suddenly revealed a vital bit of information.

'I forgot to take the pill today.'

'That should be fine.'

'And yesterday, as well. Maybe the day before, too.'

'I see. What about my—'

'I threw them away.'

'Really?'

'Really.'

'Okay.' I pressed pause. 'May I ask why?'

'They were for your friend, remember?'

Stupidly, we decided to carry on regardless. When we finished, Sally leaned up against a bedpost and pulled the sheet around her.

'Any chance you could emigrate to the States?'

'What would I do there?'

'Make me laugh every day.'

'You would get bored very quickly.'

'I doubt it.'

She dropped her head back onto my chest, and I caressed her soft hair.

'This is insane,' she began. 'First guy I fall for in a long while, and now I have to leave. I just don't get it.'

'There's nothing really to get,' I replied bleakly. 'You see, I have a theory that life is nothing more than one huge jigsaw puzzle that determines your life from the day you are born.'

Ten minutes later. 'That has to be the dumbest theory on life I have ever heard,' said Sally.

I scratched my head. Perhaps it was time I developed a new theory on life. This one wasn't going down too well with the chicks at all.

'Anyway, what's the story with Nathan?'

Sally coughed. 'He was supposed to be a casual fling while I got myself settled into a new city, but somehow it turned into a full-on relationship.'

'You must have felt something for him.'

'Not really. As a friend, maybe. Nothing else.'

'I see.' I hadn't meant to sound condescending, but even so, Sally belligerently poked me in the ribs.

'Don't be so judgemental. Haven't you ever felt confused about a woman before?' I went completely silent. 'Alex?'

'Sorry, but I need some more time to consider your question.'

She giggled and then slapped my wrist. 'You're quite the conundrum, aren't you?'

'Let's not go there.'

'What was that nonsense before about your secrets?'

'Let's definitely not go there.'

'You can't deny a woman who you have just screwed.'

'No? Watch me.'

She tugged at my arm. 'Come on, tell me.'

Strangers on a Ferry number 3.

Okay, why not? What the hell did it matter anymore, anyway?

So, I told her everything. Just like Lottie and Danielle before her—well, almost everything.

'That's quite a story,' she whistled.

'I told you.'

'And that Reginald Clump guy? All true?'

'Crump. His name was Reginald Crump. And yes, it's all true.'

'And the clown? Ringo Bingo?'

'Yes.'

'Do you see him, like, now?'

'Of course not.'

She quietly licked her lips.

'Your life is almost as crazy as mine.'

'I doubt it.'

'You don't believe that I lead a crazy life?'

'From where I'm sitting, no.'

'Well, try this one,' she said. 'My grandmother is steeped in all the ancient rituals of the Creole culture. So much so, she held a seance with her friends to decide who I should take to my high school prom. Can you believe that? A seance?'

'A tad perplexing now that you ask.'

'Do you know who they chose for me?'

'Let me guess. Damian from *The Omen*?'

'No. Jackson—my first cousin.'

'Wow. I assume Jackson wasn't your first choice?'

'Are you insane? He was like … like …'

'Like?'

'Damian from *The Omen*.'

'Not good.'

'No, not good at all.' She coughed some more. 'Have you any idea what it's like to be a cheerleader and then turn up to your prom, the biggest night in your short life, with your fat, pimply cousin?'

'No, I don't. I have never been a cheerleader before.'

She ignored me. 'It was so embarrassing. Then the little bastard audaciously made a move on me afterwards in the car. I kicked him so hard in the balls he couldn't walk for days.'

'I'm sorry,' I said, double-checking my groin for good luck. 'I get so focused on myself sometimes that I forget other people have bad things happen to them as well.'

'You ain't half a magnet for shit, are you?' she said in that sexually charged Southern accent. It was as if she belonged on the set of Dallas.

'You got that right, honey.' My JR Ewing needed a lot more work, but Sally didn't seem to mind.

'So now that's settled, what was the secret you didn't want to tell Martina?'

I ducked my head under the sheet in horror. *You witch! You have been playing me all this time. I bet a bucketload of bourbon that you don't even have a troglodyte cousin called Jackson at all.*

'What makes you think I would tell you?' I replied after coming up for air.

Sally pounced on top of me and straddled my chest with her knees. Her once-delicate brown eyes turned into a vicious shade of purple, and her long fingernails began to scrape at my skin.

'Because if you don't, I am going to screw it out of you, word for word.' To prove her point, she started to rub her body up and down my legs while I tried hard not to swallow my tongue.

'You have never submitted yourself to a woman before, have you?' she boasted, her wet lips gnashing at my neck. 'Go on! Admit it!'

'I'm sorry to disappoint you.'

Okay, this was not the dirty talk she had been expecting, so she thumped the side of my thigh with her fist in protest. 'What is that supposed to mean, smart-arse?'

'I'm simply pointing out that the girl who sexually abused me when I was a boy had a thirty-year head start on you, that's all.'

As conversation-stoppers go, that one was pretty special. It was also fair to say that for the next five minutes, you could hardly hear a pin drop anywhere in the room. Indeed, Sally used the uninvited silence as an opportunity to carefully disconnect herself from my body, her breasts swaying gently across my face. When she pulled a T-shirt over her head, I concluded that sex was no longer high on her agenda.

'I put my foot in it, didn't I?' she whispered as she nudged her face closer to mine.

'Nah, both feet, I reckon. Size eights as well.'

'I am a seven; I'll have you know.'

'I will remember that.' I laughed before I leaned across to kiss her.

'Please forgive me,' she begged. She sounded genuinely remorseful.

I tickled her on the chin. 'There's nothing to forgive. I was always going to tell someone sooner or later. I'm only glad that it was you.'

'Really?'

'Really.' This was the absolute truth. Because after all these years of silently managing my pain, I had finally met someone who needed to understand more than I did.

'Do you want to talk about it some more?'

'I guess so.'

She rustled my hair with her long fingers to make sure. 'When did it happen?'

'On the day of my first holy communion.'

'Are you joking?'

'I wish I were, kiddo.' It was somewhat ironic in a way. It was easily the proudest day of my short life: when I partook of God's holy host for the very first time in front of my mother and sister Rosemary. After all those wasted months at Sunday school, learning those silly little prayers off by heart until I could say them backwards in my sleep, I was on my way to becoming a man! Well, that's what the old nuns led us to believe, anyway.

Then barely an hour later, my childhood innocence was stolen forever, without God even entering into the conversation.

'After we finished at the church, this kind old lady who helped us prepare for our holy communion convinced our parents to allow the kids to come back to her house for a party,'

I explained to Sally. 'There was cake and balloons and fairy floss. Some older teenagers were hanging around as well; they were probably around thirteen or fourteen, but I never found out what they were doing there. Anyway, we started to play hide and seek—Jenny Ferguson was "it", if I recall—when a tall, red-haired girl I had never seen before convinced me to hide inside an old tool shed with her. It was a good hiding place as any, and she seemed genuinely nice, so that's what I did.'

'Dear God.'

'Next thing I know, she was lying on a ball of hay, stark naked from the waist down. She then made me do things to her. As you can imagine, I had no idea what was going on. I was so innocent, just a shy eight-year-old kid who barely spoke to girls at all.'

Sally began to sob. I wanted to comfort her, to tell her that I was fine, but all I could feel was the ice squeezing inside my veins.

'Did you tell anyone?' she finally asked.

'Of course not. The girl told me that everything was my fault, that boys my age shouldn't do these things to teenage girls like her. If I said anything to anyone, I would get into lots of trouble and never see my family again. What can I tell you? I was scared shitless. So I ran out of the shed, hid behind a pile of chopped wood, and kept my mouth shut forever and a day.'

'It's not too late, you know.'

I screwed up my nose. 'For what purpose? It's been nearly thirty years, and I have no proof to back up my story—hell, I can't even remember her name.'

'Are you still angry about it?'

I shrugged my shoulders. 'What's the point of being angry? I can't change the past. Nor do I bear her any ill will, either. She was just a kid herself—albeit a slightly messed up one—but a kid, nevertheless, experimenting with her unspoken desires. I only wish she had selected someone else for her sordid experiment rather than me.'

Sally began to rub my scalp, and I liked it very much. *Maybe we should drop the entire subject entirely and make love again.*

'In the States,' she continued, 'if a fourteen-year-old boy had been found guilty of sexually assaulting an eight-year-old girl, he would go to jail.'

'This was Australia, honey,' I replied mournfully. 'Most men I know would see what happened to me as a badge of honour, not sexual abuse.'

Sally released an exasperated grunt and then twisted her body around until our faces were almost touching.

'Don't you see the irony?' she asked.

'Not really.'

'Your friend, Martina? When she told you about her rape, you insisted that she do something about it and get help. But you have done absolutely nothing to help yourself.'

'Her situation was different,' I replied.

'Who says?'

'I do.'

'You happen to be wrong.'

'Well, the Spiders agree with me.'

'The Spiders? Who are the Spiders?'

'Never mind.'

Before she could utter another word, I managed to lose myself in her warm, naked flesh. We then made love for a second time. When it was over, we threw on whatever clothes we could find and then tumbled downstairs for a well-deserved coffee. As the percolator rumbled away, Sally jumped onto the kitchen table and wriggled her toes in my direction.

'Has it affected you?'

My lips tightened. 'Has what affected me?'

'What happened that day. Has it ruined your life?'

I considered her question briefly. 'Well, I don't care too much for redheads, if that's what you mean.' I thought about it some more. 'Although I do have this thing for Nicole Kidman.'

'Be serious for once.'

'I am serious.'

'No, you're not. You're deliberately deflecting my question.'

'Why would I do that?'

'To avoid the truth.'

I clasped my hands together in frustration.

'Look, I try not to think about that day anymore.'

'Bullshit.'

'I beg your pardon?'

'You know, "bullshit". Codswallop. Baloney.'

I switched off the percolator and did my best to look offended. 'Why are you doing this?'

'Because I care about you.'

I released a bewildered sigh. Why was it that every woman I met wanted to psychoanalyse me? 'Okay, maybe those events have screwed with my emotions. Exactly how, I don't know.'

'But I think you do,' Sally pressed further.

'And what makes you such an expert on these things?'

'Growing up as a girl of mixed race in Louisiana, for a start.'

I wasn't going to win this one; that much was clear. 'Okay, tell me your theory.'

Sally pouted her breasts as if she was about to address a worldwide conference on the subject. 'It's quite simple: you don't trust women.'

'I don't?'

'No, you don't,' she reinforced. 'Oh, you desperately want them to like you, Alex. It's your obsession, I think. But once you get their attention, you can only go so far before you find a reason to pull back. The thought of being hurt and betrayed by a female again, like you were all those years ago, scares you to death. Am I right?'

I blinked at her red-coloured toenails. 'If you think so.'

'You know I'm right!' she said.

'But that means I wouldn't have trusted you, either,' I muttered through gritted teeth.

'No, I'm different.'

'You seem very sure of yourself.'

'Tell me that I'm wrong.'

I said nothing at first, probably because I had nothing more to say. Deep down, I knew that there was an element of truth to Sally's theory. But now that she was leaving for good, her words were utterly useless—nothing more than autumn leaves floating in a deserted park.

'So,' I commenced, 'only you could have saved me?'

'Pretty much,' Sally replied.

'That's something, I guess.'

I reached across and pulled her towards me. The scent of her perfume smothered my face.

'You know what I find amazing?' she asked as she caressed my cheek. 'Despite everything, you still can't turn your back on a woman who needs your help.'

'That has more to do with my psychosis.' I tried to laugh.

Sally dismissed me with a wave of her hand. 'No, it has more to do with the person you are.'

'I'm not so sure that Martina would have agreed with you.'

'Maybe not.' She took a deep breath. 'But men and women sometimes see the same issue differently, Alex. That's why you always need to consider both sides.'

We finally stopped this nonsense, made our way to the TV room, and watched some chick flick together until the wee hours of the morning. We laughed, we cuddled, we kissed. Inevitably, we fell asleep on top of each other on the couch like an old married couple.

Just before dawn, Fely's scrawny little cat woke us up with his infernal meowing. We both showered and dressed, and I escorted Sally back to the taxi rank at the Shangri-La. We agreed to meet for lunch at the hotel restaurant, and I would then arrange for Hector to take us to the airport afterwards.

For the rest of the morning, I tried very hard to keep it together. Sally had been right. This whole thing was insane. After all this time, I had finally found a woman who knew who I was and where I had been, and she would soon depart for another world. Furthermore, there was nothing I could do about it, not one little thing. I had rarely felt so powerless in my life, and my heart wanted to shatter into a million pieces.

After lunch, we arrived at the airport just before three o'clock. Hector and I carried Sally's two large suitcases to the United Airlines check-in counter, and the clerk quickly provided her with a boarding pass. I asked Hector to return to the car before Sally and I found a quiet space in the departure hall.

We hugged each other and, for a brief moment when I closed my eyes, the life that I would never have with her flashed past me. Picnics beside the lake. A wedding in a rose garden. That honeymoon in Paris. Two beautiful daughters in striking pink dresses.

'What are you thinking about?' she asked me.

'The life we could have had together.'

'It would have been good.'

I pathetically began to cry. 'I am not sure if I can do this anymore. First, there was Martina, then Lottie, then Danielle, and then Eleanor. Every farewell broke my heart just a little more. But you are about to smash it into a different solar system.'

She rested an index finger against my cheek, allowing my tears to fall calmly across her palm. 'To think all of this started because you bought some condoms.'

'They were for a friend,' I muttered.

She found a way to laugh. 'Defiant to the end.'

'Only with you.'

'Alex, I think I am in lo—'

I stood before her in self-condemnation, weak-kneed and defeated, my legs sinking inside a pool of smouldering tar. 'No, please, Sally.'

'But, Alex, it's how I feel.' She lifted her tiny hand towards me.

'It hurts enough as it is.'

I gently pushed her arm away until it was resting against her thigh.

'Alex, please don't.'

'I have to, Sally.'

Not for the first time in my life, I took the cowardly option and ran away.

Delilah

New York
October 2000

'I can't be certain until the tests come back, Mr Gerrick,' said the embassy doctor, 'but I think a stubborn parasite has made your stomach its new home.'

'Would that explain the constant bloating, shitting, and farting?' I asked with a quizzical frown.

'Pretty much.'

'Wow. A parasite. Cool.'

He put his clipboard down and wondered if I was taking the mickey out of him. 'Have you eaten anything different over the last few weeks? I mean, stuff that you normally wouldn't eat in Australia?'

Well, there was that class initiation where I was encouraged to eat wild buffalo. Then there was the barbecued viper I ate for a dare during a night out in Quezon City and, of course, all the *balut* I had been gulping down like sugar candy.

'Nothing that readily comes to mind.'

I could tell he didn't believe me. 'Even so, your stomach is a right mess. You need to take extra care in a country like the Philippines.'

'I will do better,' I responded glumly.

'You will if you know what's best for you. Didn't you say before that you have a mid-term break coming up later in the month?'

I nodded my head.

'Then if I were you, I would go back to Australia for a few days and eat some proper food. Lots of fruit and fresh vegetables for a start, for they will help clean out your gut.' He then pointed to my emaciated chest. 'You never know, you might even put on some weight as well.'

Maybe the doctor had a point. As much as I had tried to fit in, I could tell that my body and Manila were having relationship difficulties. The smell, smog, poverty, and the barbecued viper—they were all conspiring to wear me down in different ways. Returning to Australia for a few days wasn't such a bad idea at all, as long as it didn't involve Canberra.

Later that night, I sat down at the local internet café and whisked through some Australian travel sites. I thought about booking three nights at Hamilton Island on the Great Barrier Reef before I decided to check my Hotmail account instead. Lucky for me, that I did because sitting in bold letters underneath the usual rows of porn spam was an email titled *Hi* from Sally.

Two months had passed since that dreadful afternoon at Manila Airport. After Sally landed in the States, she had texted me to see whether I was okay. That was Sally to a tee—always caring about other people. Following some more desperate exchanges, we agreed not to contact each other for a while. But here she was, emailing me out of the blue. Despite all of my regrets about that day, my heart was overwhelmed with joy.

Her first three paragraphs were full of news from New Orleans. Her father's condition had stabilised, she had found a new job, she recently kicked Jackson in the balls again, and her grandma was still holding seances about her love life. Good. Everything seemed back to normal.

Then came the opening sentence of the fourth paragraph: *Anyway, don't be alarmed, but I have missed my period.*

Don't be alarmed?

Okay, if there was one thing that was guaranteed to cause me alarm was when a woman I had recently slept with admitted that she had just missed her period. So I wrote back immediately and calmly explained to her my long-held views on the topic. I waited anxiously for several days before she finally emailed me a reply and convinced me that I had nothing to worry about.

> *Dear Alex,*
> *You have nothing to worry about!*
> *It came back this morning.*
> *It must have been the stress. So relax.*

I celebrated this news by getting drunk at dinner with some friends from the embassy. But during dessert, my paranoia and I decided to undertake a more thorough analysis of her email. Something didn't sit right, we both decided. Was Sally lying? Okay, maybe not *lying* so much, but stretching the truth just a little so as not to worry me?

Why would she do that? Well, I, … look, I don't know! I want to reassure myself that she is not pregnant if that's not too much to ask.

After dinner, I managed to crawl on all fours back to the internet café. It was time to send Sally another email.

Hi Sally
Thank you for letting me know. I wasn't worried, simply curious.
Anyway, exciting news.
Remember how I have a mid-term break?
I have decided to go to New York for a few days to visit an old friend who has been very unwell.
If you want, I can come down to New Orleans later in the week to see you.
That's if you have the time.
Alex

My half-hour internet slot was just about to expire when a return email from Sally suddenly appeared in my inbox.

Hi Alex
Wow, that's sensational news!
I am so happy!
Let me know the details!
You can stay with me!
My family will be so delighted to meet you.
(Okay, maybe not Jackson.)
P.S. And don't bullshit me; you were worried like crazy!

A week later, on a plane somewhere over the Pacific Ocean, I thought about Sally's last email one more time and then realised I was a complete idiot. I mean, if Sally were pregnant, wouldn't she want to avoid me at all costs? Of course she would, because it would have been impossible for her to keep something like that a secret from me. Therefore, assuming that Sally was at least half as deceitful as I was, if she were pregnant, unquestionably, she would have come up with some bullshit excuse for why it wasn't a good time for me to visit.

But that's not what Sally did at all, was it? Her reaction was completely heartfelt. Not only was she overjoyed by the news that I was coming to New Orleans, but she also planned to introduce me to her family as well.

As I skulked through immigration at JFK Airport several hours later, I decided that maybe visiting New York instead of the Great Barrier Reef wasn't so bad after all. Sure, I had just wasted three thousand dollars on an airline ticket that was certain to cause me more misery. But New York was still my favourite city in the world, and I adored America and its people. *So why not take advantage of my lunacy and enjoy myself for a few days?*

When I obtained my first glimpse of that incredible Manhattan skyline from the sanctuary of my taxi, I felt so excited that I even belted out a few crumpled verses of 'New York, New York' to a bemused driver. *Hey, Mister Sinatra—this is my town, and don't you forget it!*

Later that afternoon, I checked myself into a delightful boutique hotel on the east side of town near Bloomingdales. For the next few days, I did my best to forget about Sally. I made sure that I enjoyed everything that the Big Apple had to offer, like early morning strolls through Central Park, daily excursions to the Guggenheim, and free ferry rides across to Staten Island.

Of course, now that I was in New York, I was at the mercy of fast-food heaven, exposed to an alarming array of decadent temptations aimed at increasing my cholesterol and sugar levels. But despite raiding fifty burger joints within my first forty-eight hours, I finally made a poorly-lit diner on Third Avenue my new home for the week, given that it served the banana split from heaven and a Mexican pizza that would rock your socks off.

I woke up on Wednesday morning pain-free for the first time in weeks but with a realisation that Sally was expecting me in New Orleans the following afternoon. After I scoffed down a huge breakfast of pancakes and grilled bacon, I bumbled along Seventh and Broadway in search of a travel agency before I allowed myself to become distracted by a popular music store.

Once inside, I hung around the video section for a while. When I got bored with that, I moved to the CD section and hung around there for even longer. When I started to inspect the store's Red Hot Chilli Peppers collection, I somehow became entangled in deep conversation with a middle-aged American couple and their adult daughter about Australia.

While we innocently chatted away, I was slowly drawn back to that night with Lottie and her parents on the ferry to Samos. You see, just like Lottie, this girl was drop-dead gorgeous, with long, never-ending hair and even longer, never-ending legs. Every time she smiled at my coarse Australian accent; my face began to melt just a little bit more.

After we finished discussing U2's latest album, she shook my hand to say goodbye, and I joyfully flew over to the counter with a clutch of CDs in my hand.

I was greeted at the cash register by some gawky guy wearing rusted-on jeans and a red bandana. He was gaping at the side of my head while threatening to swallow the extra-large headphones that seemed to be permanently attached to his neck.

'Man, are you someone famous?'

'Not the last time I checked. Why?'

'Then how do you know her, man?'

'What do you mean?"

'The girl you were just talking to, man?'

'I have never met her before. We just started chatting.'

'Wow, man! Do you know who she is, man?'

'No,' I replied honestly.

'It's her, man.'

'Who?'

'That girl, man. From that TV show, man.'

'You're going to have to be a little bit more specific here, I'm afraid. Man.'

I suddenly became distracted by high-pitched shrieking from behind me. We turned to see a group of teenagers, slithering like demented ants all over the girl and her parents as they tried to weave past them for the safety of the footpath.

'Man,' the guy behind the counter moaned.

I shuffled towards Times Square, none the wiser to the identity of the television star that I had just been talking to and still none the wiser about what I was going to do about Sally. That meant one thing: I was in danger of wasting the rest of this beautiful autumn afternoon tormenting myself with this whole 'will I—won't I' routine.

I still had feelings for Sally – that was obvious. I thought about her every day. Seeing her again would be amazing. But what was the point of going to New Orleans if it meant taking yet another sucker punch? Did I want to put myself through another heartbreaking farewell?

After several hours of fruitless indecision, I finally got the balls to make that long walk down to the New York library on Fifth Avenue and its free internet service.

Dear Sally,

I'm sorry to do this to you at such an extremely late stage.

But I am unable to travel to New Orleans as planned.

My friend is still very unwell, and I cannot leave him alone.

I hope you understand and can find it within yourself to forgive me.

Regards, Alex.

I hesitated briefly before pressing the 'send' button and then allowed the parasite inside my stomach to devour what was left of my conscience.

Thoroughly miserable, I staggered back to my hotel room, hoping that my new CDs would provide me with the solace I needed to get me through the rest of the day. But after listening to the brilliant but introspective Smiths for the next half an hour, I felt so emotionally drained I had to get out of my room. So I snatched my leather jacket from the coffee table and went searching for a bar.

I eventually found an Irish pub on Seventh Avenue and secured myself a table in the darkest corner of the room after purchasing a pint of beer and a packet of crisps. It appeared to be one of those places where everyone did their best to look thoroughly miserable, just to add to its ongoing mystique. As such, I half-expected to see Billy Joel enter the bar at any moment to belt out a few verses of 'Piano Man'.

I polished off a couple more beers, nodded my compliments to two hippies from Greenwich Village sitting at the table next to me, and then whizzed off to the men's room. I returned minutes later only to find some chubby guy wearing a bow tie sitting proudly at my table, eating all the crisps and swirling his finger around the top of his beer glass.

'What the hell?' I asked incredulously. 'I was sitting there first.'

'Not when I arrived, you weren't,' he sneered.

'I was using the toilet.'

'How do I know that you are telling the truth?'

I pointed to my leather jacket, strung up untidily over the back of my chair.

'What do you call that? A ham-fucking-sandwich?'

He wanted so much to stand his ground but soon realised that the existence of the jacket meant that he had lost all moral authority on the matter. Sure enough, he reluctantly pushed himself up from the chair and began to waddle his way across to the other side of the room.

As he passed by the next table, one of the spaced-out hippies pointed his finger accusingly at the man's fat stomach. 'Hahaha, he showed you who's boss, motherfucker!'

Meanwhile, his drinking companion lifted his glass at me in cheesy admiration. 'Stay cool, motherfucker!'

I waved back to him. 'Will do, bro.'

'That motherfucker didn't know who he was motherfucking dealing with, did he?'

'He sure didn't, bro. The motherfucker.'

Twenty minutes later, my two new admirers decided to leave. The first one bounded over towards me with rapid-fire steps and smacked out a high five. 'You are one crazy motherfucker, man. But I like your motherfucking style.'

His friend soon replaced him, and he farewelled me by sticking five fingers into my face. 'I like what you're doing, motherfucker.'

'What I am doing?' I asked with a puzzled frown. 'I'm not doing anything!'

'Then just keep doing it, motherfucker!'

Convinced that I had just imagined this entire sequence of events, I decided it might be safer if I occupied a seat at the main bar instead. After ordering a bottle of beer, I started talking to a middle-aged guy in a dark-blue suit who worked for a nearby accounting firm.

'Where you from, boy?' he asked with genuine interest.

'Australia.'

'Australia?' he roared out so everyone could hear him. 'My wife and I, we try to drive up there once a year.'

The bartender thankfully beat me to it. 'What the hell are you talking about, Mitch?'

'You know? Australia? The country to our north?'

'That's Canada,' he informed him.

'Goddammit, I always get those two countries mixed up.'

He soon mumbled something about needing to cook dinner and then kindly bought me another beer. Once he left, I read the food menu from front to back and then back to front, rearranged some business cards in my wallet, and made idle chitchat with some old guy sporting a ponytail. But before I could buy him a drink, an avalanche of oversexed twenty-somethings rudely crushed up against the back of our stools and railroaded us into their conversation about the upcoming baseball World Series.

Lost inside this frantic world, I soon found myself talking to a pretty young African-American woman. She had long, platted hair, a cute button nose, and withering black eyes. The bright red dress that tightly hugged her ample breasts told me that she enjoyed being the centre of attention, while her infectious smile said to me that she didn't take shit from anyone.

'What's your name?' I finally got the courage to ask.

'Delilah.'

Look, I wasn't proud about what I did next, right? I was only trying to be funny. Really. Because I shamelessly broke out into that incredibly famous Tom Jones song whose lyrics I can't repeat for copyright reasons.

'Jeez, I've never heard that one before,' she growled when I finished the song. 'Would it be possible for you to hit on me with a cornier line?'

'Anything is possible, I guess.' I sank back into my beer, suitably chastened. Surprisingly, she didn't tell me to F off but instead carried on with our conversation as if nothing had happened. We discussed movies, music, prawn toast, and breast implants before she offered to take me dancing. Soon we were making out in the back of a taxi and then jumping all over each other at some dance bar on 54th Street.

About two o'clock in the morning, she challenged me to a tequila slammer duel.

One, two, three, slam!

'You don't know who you are dealing with here, Delilah.'

One, two, three, slam!

'Yes, I do.'

One, two, three, slam!

'No, you don't.'

One, two, three, slam!

Blank.

I woke up with a family of tree frogs croaking inside my mouth. The constant tapping of a ceiling fan buzzed over my face. I gingerly glanced towards the other side of the pillow, where I found Delilah smiling at me.

'Hi there,' I offered.

'Hi there,' she replied.

An air-raid siren suddenly went off in my head. 'I am guessing that you won the tequila slammer duel?' I groaned.

'Hands down.'

I lifted the flimsy cotton sheet. To my surprise, I was wearing nothing apart from an orange T-shirt that I had never seen before.

'Um, could you please explain to me and the readers how I got here?'

'Sure. You hit the wall after four slammers, and I then invited you to stay here for the night.'

'And where is "here", exactly?'

'Central Park West. West 75th Street, to be precise.'

'I see.' I stared at Delilah and noticed that she was also naked. 'Er, did we?'

'Yes, we did.'

'Was I …?'

'You were fine.'

'Good. I normally am when I can't remember what I am doing.'

She laughed and then touched my face. Luckily it didn't burst. 'What's up? You look totally confused if you don't mind me saying.'

'Nothing,' I replied, wondering if I needed to be sick. 'It's just that I've never—'

'Had sex with a black woman before?'

'—woken up next to a total stranger in New York before.'

'Well, we are not total strangers, are we? After all, we did—'

I held up my hand, and even that turned out to be a struggle. 'Yeah, I get your point. But I am sure that you're a busy person, so I'll now get out of your hair.'

She looked offended. 'Why do you have to leave? Are you catching a plane today or something?'

'No, but I assume you have to go to work?'

'I'm a theatre nurse, and I have the next few days off.'

Oh no! Get out of here! Not another nurse! 'I see.'

'Why don't you grab some more sleep while I make breakfast?'

Given how nauseous I felt, it was an invitation I could hardly refuse. So I drifted off into a quick-fire nap full of glorious psychedelic mumbo jumbo before Delilah shook me awake. 'Time to get up, soldier. Breakfast is about to be served!'

I stretched myself precariously across a bedpost while I slid on my jeans and black boots and then walked out into a bright, breezy apartment full of plastic furniture, wooden coffee tables, and scattered magazines. Delilah was waiting for me on the balcony, pouring hot coffee into three huge mugs from a flask. A tall blond-haired man in his mid-thirties, with narrow blue eyes and a bottomless dimple, was peering out over the railing. When I took my first tentative steps outside, he thumped out his muscular arm towards me. 'Hi, I am Dwayne —Delilah's roommate.'

'Alex,' I replied, shaking his hand.

'Here, have some of this,' Dwayne insisted as he pushed out a plate of sliced mango in my direction. The nonchalant way he treated my presence suggested that I was not the first stranger he had encountered under these circumstances.

Delilah watched me closely as I chewed on my lone piece of fruit.

'Don't worry, Alex. Dwayne is used to me bringing stray puppies home, aren't you, sweetheart?'

'Makes my life all the more interesting,' he replied, smiling. The three of us caressed our coffee mugs and took a moment to appreciate a sunlit view of Central Park.

'This is some place you have here,' I said to both of them. 'Such an amazing view.'

'I never get sick of it,' admitted Dwayne. We talked some more while I tucked into the best French toast I had ever tasted. Slowly but surely, my dreadful hangover started to disappear, and I relaxed some more. After I greedily wiped away muffin crumbs from my mouth, Dwayne announced that he was off to work, leaving Delilah to rest her bare legs over my lap.

'So what do you have planned for today?' she asked, with a twinkle in her eye.

I dropped my fork next to my plate. 'Well, you see, I was supposed to go—'

'Yeah, I know,' Delilah interrupted. 'You were supposed to go to New Orleans to see some gal you think you are in love with. Then you chickened out at the last moment because you couldn't bear facing her again.'

'I told you this last night?'

'Several times. It's old news, baby.' For some reason, I decided to massage her foot, and she giggled. 'You're pretty much a lost soul, aren't you?'

'That's the understatement of the year.'

'How would you like a proper tour of New York, then?' she offered. 'The one that tourists rarely get to see.'

'Are you sure? I mean, I don't want to impose.'

'You're not imposing at all; it'll be fun, I think.'

I chose the following words carefully. 'But you *barely* know me. How do you know that I'm not some deranged serial killer?'

'How do you know that I'm not?'

'True.'

'Besides, you look harmless enough.'

We agreed to meet at the top of the Empire State Building at midday.

'Just like in that scene from *When Harry Met Sally*,' I said.

'That's *Sleepless in Seattle*, you idiot,' Delilah replied.

After my third cup of coffee, I stumbled back to my hotel, had a well-needed shower, and disposed of my alcohol-laden clothes. After drinking several gallons of water, I checked myself out in the mirror and decided I looked vaguely human again.

I might have been an infantry officer, but my navigation skills were bloody useless without a compass. As a result, it took me over an hour to walk from my hotel to the Empire State Building. After I went to the bathroom several times, bought a ticket, and lined up in a queue, I realised that I was running late. So when my lift eventually reached the main observation deck on the 102nd floor, I rushed through the growing crowd in a mild panic until I found Delilah tapping her hand softly against one of those rusty telescopes. She looked gorgeous in those light-blue jeans and a white, frilly top.

Delilah pointed to her watch. 'You're late,' she growled.

'I'm sorry,' I replied. 'But I lost all track of time. Blame it on my hangover.'

'I thought you had stood me up.'

'Why would I do that?'

'Others have in the past.'

'That was their loss then, wasn't it?'

She smiled. 'You know, for someone completely clueless, you do have a way of making a woman feel special.'

'I once read about it on the back of a chip packet.'

She wrapped my hands around her waist, and we both gazed out towards the Statue of Liberty. Like everyone else on the observation deck, we witnessed the most impossibly clear blue sky that God had ever created. Yes, I believed that I could see the living edges of the world itself, just like the travel brochures promised.

'What are you thinking about, Alex?' asked Delilah.

'That this building somehow connects Manhattan with heaven.'

For some reason, she found that funny. 'Apart from your absurd philosophical observations.'

'Just how much I love this city, I guess.'

'Do you wish you were here with your girl from New Orleans?'

Her question knocked me over. 'Why would you ask that?'

'Just curious, that's all.'

Is it possible that she's jealous after an alcohol-fuelled one-night stand? Surely not. 'At any given moment in time, everyone belongs somewhere. And at this very moment, here on top of the Empire State Building, you belong with me.'

'Hey, that's quite beautiful,' she joked. 'I didn't realise you Australians were such romantics.'

'We do our best.'

In reality, though, my head was spinning out of control. I came to America for all the wrong reasons, fell victim to my cowardice, and found myself on top of the Empire State Building with someone that I only met last night in a bar. Meanwhile, the woman who I loved was barely a two-hour flight away in another city.

Was this where my life was heading? To be constantly moving from one miscalculation to the next. I didn't know anymore; I really didn't. And you know what? Maybe I didn't want to know anymore, either. That probably explained why I then drove Delilah into my arms and initiated the most extended kiss in literary history.

After such a virtuoso performance, Delilah had no option but to keep her promise to show me another side of New York. So when we bid farewell to the Empire State, she lulled me down several delicate little alleyways before we reached Greenwich Village, where we lost ourselves for the rest of the afternoon.

During this time, we discovered an ancient Gaelic harp in a dusty little antique store, watched a juggler negotiate several basketballs at once while smoking a cigar, heard a rap artist belt out a tribute to Tupac Shakur, saw a skateboard rider spin recklessly in the air in defiance of all gravity, had coffee and fudge cake in some hidden underground café, pestered an older man selling hot chestnuts, and rummaged through one of the best second-hand bookstores on the planet.

Close to seven o'clock, Delilah hailed down a yellow cab, and she begged the waiter at her favourite restaurant in Little Italy to give us her very own special seats. Over dessert, we discovered that we both shared a love of jazz music, and she then quickly dialled a number on her mobile phone. 'You want jazz? Well, you're going to get some jazz, baby!'

After I paid the bill, we caught another taxi and landed at Poughkeepsie Blues in Harlem, one of the most famous jazz clubs in New York City. Yes, this was Angel of Harlem territory, and Delilah was seemingly one of her more famous acolytes. From the moment we entered the main bar area, everyone we met knelt in her presence.

The most beautiful thing about all this was that every person who showered her with that tight hug or that warm kiss made no judgement whatsoever about who I was and what I was doing with their friend. Instead, they lifted their shoulders with a pleasant smile and assumed that I must be one pretty cool guy to be with their Delilah.

One by one, they told me their life stories.

Dan was a radiologist from the Bronx who wanted to become a writer.

Janelle was a beautician from Harlem who was looking after her sick mother.

Garth was a waiter from New Jersey who was putting his sister through law school.

Gloria was a secretary from Connecticut who wanted to have six children.

Mama Cass was … well, Mama Cass.

With the next set of music about to start, we invaded a table close to the stage, polished off several bottles of expensive red wine, and watched in awe as Mama Cass belted out the most insanely beautiful version of 'Dream a Little Dream of Me' ever attempted. Somewhere up in heaven, the real Mama Cass would have been proud as Punch.

'Are you having a good time?' Delilah asked me later in the night. Pools of sweat were pouring down her face, and she sounded amusingly drunk.

'The best,' I replied. 'And you?'

'Fabulous, babe.'

I picked up a napkin from a nearby table and carefully dabbed away the droplets of perspiration gathering on her chest.

'Thank you,' she said. 'You're adorable.'

'I try and do my best.' I ran my hand softly over the back of her neck. There was something about a woman's neck that defied Darwin's theory of evolution. Only a divine being with an imagination could have created something so wildly perfect. 'You have a beautiful suprasternal. Has anyone ever told you that before?'

'Not really,' she replied. She took the time to offer me a resigned smile. 'Lucky for you, though, I have watched *The English Patient* several times.'

'Damn it,' I said. 'I thought that I was the only person on the planet who can quote the entire movie.'

'Not a chance. It's my favourite film ever. Besides, I can always remember my basic physiology even when I'm drunk.'

'Nothing's worse than a very pissed nurse.'

'I am not that drunk to whip your ass.'

'Undoubtedly.'

'Can I ask you a question?' she rudely changed the subject.

'Sure.'

'That kiss at the Empire State Building?'

'What about it?'

'Was that for real?'

Was that for real?

It was way too late in the evening to unpack this one, so I decided to cut straight to the chase. 'You are going to have to help me, Delilah. What's the correct answer you are expecting here?'

'There isn't one, babe,' she said. 'As long as you remember that this ends when you leave on the weekend. No emotional baggage, okay?'

'What is it with you, nurses? Always so goddamn rational about everything.'

'I'm serious.'

'So am I,' I replied. 'You see, I only want you for your suprasternal.'

Thankfully, I could see the relief on her face. I wasn't out to trick Delilah in any way, for my only motivation was to forget about Sally for the rest of my holiday. Once Delilah understood that, she jerked her head forward, slammed her lips onto mine, and for the second time that day, we created literary history.

Windows on the World

New York
October 2000

I woke up once again in Delilah's double bed. My hair smelt of barbecued eel, and someone had stapled my tongue to the side of my cheek. But other than that, I felt pretty darn good. So I threw on some clothes, sucked on a Junior Mint hiding inside one of my trouser pockets, and wandered into the living room.

Dwayne and Delilah were sitting next to each other, laughing at a re-run of *Seinfeld* on TV. It was one of my favourite episodes, too: the one where George changed his religion to Latvian Orthodox to impress his new girlfriend. When Dwayne heard me knock over one of the kitchen chairs, he released a pretend groan. 'Oh no, not you again.'

'You're stuck with me, I'm afraid.'

'Man, Delilah must like you. Usually, by the second day, I'm scraping them off the kitchen floor.'

Delilah smacked him hard on the shoulder. 'Don't listen to him, Alex. He is just jealous.'

'You wish, girlfriend,' he smirked.

I turned towards Delilah. 'I want to say thanks for last night. I had the best time ever. I don't know how I can ever—'

'Oh, don't get soppy with me, Alex,' she demanded. She stared at Dwayne with her big, pleading eyes. 'Dwayne, tell Alex not to get soppy with me.'

'Don't get soppy with her, Alex,' Dwayne ordered while munching on a piece of toast.

'Can I get soppy with you instead?'

'No. Fuck off.'

'Now, Alex,' said Delilah, throwing the TV guide at me. 'Have a shower and get dressed. We are having brunch at Windows on the World at the World Trade Center.'

'Don't we have to book, like, three weeks in advance?' I asked curiously. 'My good friend Clemmons and I tried to have lunch there when we were in New York last year, but they just laughed at us.'

'This one has connections everywhere in the city,' Dwayne moaned. 'I just don't ask questions anymore.'

'It's amazing when you're a theatre nurse how many influential people need you to help them pee after their operation,' explained Delilah. 'You end up developing some close bonds.'

'I can imagine.' It only occurred to me then how much Delilah reminded me of Martina.

Dwayne jumped up from his seat, disappeared into his room, and quickly returned with a dark-blue sports jacket. 'Here, take this.' He tossed the jacket over to me. 'It should fit you nicely. You'll need to wear a jacket to be allowed entry into the restaurant.'

'Thanks, mate. Rest assured; I'll look after it.'

'Of course you will. Otherwise, you're buying me a new one, and I'll settle for nothing less than the most expensive suit from the latest Italian catalogue.'

We arrived by taxi at the North Tower of the World Trade Center just after ten-thirty. The foyer was a conveyor belt of trendy, beautiful people rushing around with the world at their fingertips. But of course, when you worked at the Twin Towers in New York City, who said that you couldn't go that little bit higher and aim for the universe instead?

We snared one of the two express elevators that led to the Windows on the World, and Delilah pushed the button for the 107th. A friendly African-American security guard carrying a copy of *USA Today* joined us just as the door began to close.

'What's happening in the world today?' asked Delilah, pointing at the paper. She had her hair rolled up into a bun which made her look astonishingly sophisticated.

'Mostly about the World Series,' he laughed. 'Those Yankees will do them in four, I reckon.'

'Nah,' dismissed Delilah. 'The Mets are going to whip their arse, baby.'

They both looked to me for the deciding vote. 'Hey,' I threw my arms up in protest, 'I'm Australian! Leave me out of this one!'

The security guard chuckled before tapping his finger against another headline. 'The bombing of that American warship in Yemen is still making news, as well.'

'The USS *Cole*?' I asked. Last week, two Islamic suicide bombers in Yemen had blown a hole in the side of a visiting American guided-missile destroyer, killing seventeen crew members and injuring many more.

'Yeah, the USS *Cole*.'

'It's a bit worrying,' I agreed. 'The bad guys are getting more daring by the day.'

'You don't have to convince me of that,' said the security guard. 'I was working right here in ninety-three when those sons of bitches tried to blow up this very same building. I will never forget that day as long as I live.'

'Well, here's hoping you never have to go through anything like that again.'

We finally reached the 107th floor. The security guard stepped aside as the lift door opened and extended his hand out to me. 'Here's hoping that you're right, sir.'

A gangly waiter with mutton sideburns escorted us to our table. What an incredible place! Everything in the restaurant, from the napkins to the cutlery and then the glassware, were of the highest quality, while the view we had of New York Harbour on such a beautiful morning defied mortal description. It was almost as if I was watching the city from another dimension.

'Something else, isn't it, babe?' Delilah asked me. I wasn't into those silly romantic nicknames, but I liked how she called me *babe*. It somehow made this whole thing seem more surreal than what it was.

A tiny Hispanic waiter, with parted greasy black hair and a failed moustache, skittered quickly towards Delilah. 'Miss Delilah!' he roared. 'So happy to see you again! It's been over a month!'

'Hello, Raul,' she smiled generously. 'How's my favourite waiter?'

'Always better for seeing you.' His skinny hands gestured nervously in my direction, his face beaming red. 'You must be an exceptional person to be friends with Delilah!'

'This could all go to my head,' I replied.

We ordered some food and coffees and then silently stared out the window once again. I mean, it was the *Windows on the World,* after all. What else were we supposed to do?

'I was working in the hospital that day,' said Delilah.

'Which day?'

'When those terrorists bombed the World Trade Center.'

'Oh, that.'

'I had only been in the job for several months following my graduation. A hell of a way to start my career as a nurse. Some of the things I saw that day were simply horrific.'

I slumped back into my seat. We had been having so much fun together, yet I realised I knew nothing about Delilah as a person. Who was she? Where was she going? What were her hopes and dreams?

'I'm sorry. You guys never get it easy.'

'I like being a nurse, don't get me wrong,' she explained. 'But over time, we learn to detach ourselves from reality.'

'You are not the first nurse who has said that to me.'

She raised her eyebrow. 'Really? Have you known other nurses?'

'Not many—just one.' Damn it; I had broached the one topic I wanted to avoid. I had no choice other than to tell Delilah about Martina.

'Poor girl,' Delilah said ten minutes later, just as Raul returned with our food and drinks. 'What you did to her was so uncool.'

'Gee, thanks,' I replied sarcastically. I just assumed she would show me the same level of sympathy for my story as Danielle and Sally had done. So I told her that.

'Well, if you think I will indulge your selfish behaviour, you're wrong.'

'How about just a little?'

'No,' she snapped. 'You should have called her that day; she needed your help.'

For a moment, I had a genuine fear that this would be the end of our association. The nurses' union sticking together, and all that. But instead, she flipped out her hand and tapped the table in front of me. 'Don't beat yourself up too much. We all make mistakes. But I hope you learnt something.'

'Just to have less faith in myself.'

It's probably right after this remark that I first noticed the people at the next table whispering to each other. Closest to me sat a prim young woman with a pink ribbon tied vertically into her ridiculously long blonde hair. Next to her was the apparent boyfriend, fiancé, or husband, a mountain of a young man who looked as if he had just walked straight off a marine recruiting poster. Across from them, we had Ma and Pa Redneck direct from Hicksville. Without even knowing anything about them, I could tell that this was their first visit to New York City.

The longer they sipped at their expensive mineral water, the more obvious it was that we were the topic of conversation.

I meant Delilah and me.

You know, a white man with a black woman.

Of course, Delilah was no wilting flower. One could also argue that her decision to lean across and kiss me on the lips served only to escalate their appalling behaviour even further. But seriously, what were her options?

'Disgusting,' said Miss Prim. 'They should be locked up,' said Ma. 'Where I come from, he would get a stern talking to, and she would get a damn fine whipping,' said Pa.

Perhaps it was because we had just been discussing Martina's rape, and I wasn't especially thrilled at the prospect of another act of physical violence against a woman. Or maybe it was because I desperately felt the need to lash out at someone after all these years of built-up frustration. Whatever my reasons, Pa's comment unleashed an eruption of anger inside me that I had not experienced since my fight with Marco.

'Excuse me.' I targeted his balding head, my fists shaking hard against my hips. 'You do realise that the American Civil War is over, and that Lincoln freed the slaves?'

Pa looked at me in total shock. Was this insolent creature actually talking to him? He tried to spit something out, but his tongue became stuck to his fork. As a result, it was up to Miss Prim to jump to his defence.

'What would you know about it?' she said, picking up on my strange, foreign accent.

I directed my ire at her stupid pink ribbon. 'A lot more than you do, it seems. But then, I figure that they don't teach history in Bum Fuck, Idaho.'

'Alex, enough,' chided Delilah. She looked as if she was about to cry.

'Yes, why don't you listen to your little nigger girlfriend?' Miss Prim sneered at me. Being seated next to Meathead gave her the confidence to say whatever she wanted. After all, this was how they did things back on the cotton plantation.

'Better to have an *African-American* for a friend than a worthless, spruced up, little pom-pom queen like you.' *Okay, slightly provocative.*

'Darren!' she suddenly screamed out, her purple face threatening to explode all over the beautiful satin tablecloth. 'Did you hear what he just said to me?'

Darren, or Meathead, whatever your preference, angrily threw his napkin onto the ground and rocketed up behind his chair—all six foot five inches of him. I figured by then that I had approximately five seconds left to live. But hey, it was mostly fun while it lasted.

Mostly.

But sometimes, you really can't judge a book by its cover because Meathead wasn't targeting his wrath at me at all, but rather at Miss Prim and her parents. 'Get up. We're leaving,' he shouted at them.

'What?' Miss Prim exclaimed as if her whole world had just come plummeting down on top of her racist head.

'You heard me. Get your parents and meet me outside. We are leaving.'

That seemed to have the desired result. I mean, if Meathead had told me to jump off Niagara Falls, I wouldn't have given it a second thought. So after the obligatory hugs and tears between mother, father, and daughter, and instant speculation on whether the wedding was still going ahead or not, they thankfully disappeared from my life.

Darren slowly walked over to Delilah, who, by this stage, couldn't stop shaking, and slumped in front of her. 'Ma'am, I deeply apologise for my fiancée's terrible behaviour,' he began politely. 'I hope that in time you can forgive her and her parents for their ignorance.'

'Thank you,' Delilah replied, choking back her tears.

But when Darren turned his granite jaw to face me, not so cheery. 'And as for you: you're lucky that I didn't tear you a second arsehole.'

'More's the pity,' is all I could say. 'I really could have done with an extra one.'

An hour later, we were slowly walking through Battery Park. Delilah had spent a good portion of that time crying. A group of scantily clad joggers appeared from behind a row of cars, and I immediately grasped her hand in defiance. I wanted them, Delilah, and the rest of the world to know that what had happened in the restaurant was fucking disgraceful. What's more, I was incredibly proud to be holding this woman's hand in public.

We eventually found a park bench, and after I shooed away a pesky squirrel, I convinced Delilah to sit down. Her eyes momentarily mingled with the sunlight bouncing off the ocean surface before she kissed my cheek.

'Thanks for standing up for me before,' she whispered. 'That was very noble of you.'

I tightly squeezed her hand. 'God, I am the least noble person you will ever meet, and I was just trying to do the right thing for once.' I searched for the appropriate words before adding: 'I can't believe that it's the twenty-first century, and there are still people who think and talk like that.'

'What you saw today happens to me and some of my friends regularly,' she sighed. 'It's not easy being black in this country.'

'I'm so sorry.' We shared another deep hug. It felt incredibly intimate, and for a moment, I didn't want to let go of her.

'By the way, Mr History,' she said as she flattened down my collar. 'Idaho fought on the Union side during the Civil War.'

'I was hoping you wouldn't pick up on that.'

'And a pom-pom queen?' She giggled as we pulled away from each other. 'Really? Was that the best that you could do?

'I folded under pressure,' I said with a muted smile. 'But you're right; I've got to learn to hold my temper better in those situations.'

'Does that worry you?'

'Sometimes,' I admitted. 'I often wonder how I will respond if I ever find myself in real trouble one day. You know if my career, or even my life, was somehow in jeopardy.'

She fumbled around with the top button of her blouse and then watched a seagull as it screeched proudly above us. 'Can I tell you a story?'

'Of course you can.'

'My father was a very gentle man,' she began. 'I don't recall him ever raising his voice at my younger brother or me when we were kids. It was always Mom that smacked us if we did something naughty.'

'Where did you grow up?' I asked, embarrassed that I had not bothered to find this out sooner.

'Savannah. In Georgia?'

'I visited Savannah in 1997. Fascinating place. *Midnight in the Garden of Good and Evil* and all that.'

'Fascinating for visitors, boring for those of us who lived there, which leads to the next part of *my* story. You see, I desperately wanted to live in New York; it had been my dream ever since I was a little girl. When I entered my final year of high school, I decided that becoming a nurse would be my meal ticket out of Georgia.'

'Did your folks support you?' I asked, thinking back to how Sally had been the first person in her family to obtain a university education.

'Definitely,' replied Delilah. 'Nothing made my parents happier. But money was the issue. Dad was a bus driver, and Mom was a kindergarten teacher. They made enough money to give us a nice house and a comfortable lifestyle but contributing to a four-year college degree was entirely different. So Dad took a second job on weekends, working at a nearby airport.' She took a deep breath, and I wondered whether she was about to cry again. 'You have to understand my father,' she said. 'He would always stand in the background when there was a disagreement in the family, rarely saying a thing, and sometimes that annoyed the hell out of me. I would often watch my mother walk all over him. But rather than biting back, he would try to appease her. Over time, I began to lose some respect for him, even when he worked his arse off just for me.'

'We don't always get to understand our parents,' I said. 'I went through the same thing, trust me.'

Oh yes, I did.

'Sure—such a normal occurrence for many kids,' she agreed. 'But then, one Sunday afternoon, I returned from seeing a movie with my boyfriend when I noticed a police car in our driveway. At first, I thought someone had died, so I rushed inside in a blind panic. But instead, when I entered the living room, Dad and Mom were being interviewed by two uniform policemen.'

'Were they involved in an accident?'

'Not quite. Dad never told us, but he was working at the airport with a couple of local rednecks who had been teasing him mercilessly for weeks. You know, the normal racist stuff, which I don't have to repeat. He had turned a blind eye for most of it, as was his due, but today something had changed.'

'What exactly?'

'They asked him during a smoke break why he was working a second job, and when he explained that it was to help his teenage daughter go to college, they opined that a hot bit of black scruff like me would better serve society by making a living on my back. One of them even offered to come home with him that afternoon to give me some tips.'

'That's crazy talk,' is all I could say. 'What did your dad do?'

'Oh, he put them both into hospital; one with a fractured cheekbone and the other with two broken ribs. They failed to realise, and what I had forgotten too, was that dad had been an infantry platoon sergeant during the Vietnam War. And a pretty tough one as well, I later found out.'

'Did the police charge your father?'

'No. Those rednecks never made a formal complaint, either. The airport handled everything quietly behind doors, and they then found him another job. But later that night, with a newfound respect for my father, I politely asked him why he did what he did.'

It seemed like she wanted to keep me in suspense for as long as possible. 'So, what did your father say?'

She dry-gargled her throat in an attempt to replicate his broad accent. 'Sometimes you have to stop pretending and show people the real person.'

I allowed Delilah's shoulder to connect with mine, and we quickly kissed. 'It sounds like he knew what he was talking about,' I said when we finished.

'You still don't get it, do you, Alex? I mean, why I've told you this story?'

'You might have to explain further,' I replied. 'You see, I'm not very bright.'

I could tell that she was getting exasperated with me. 'That question you asked before? About how you would respond if the world ever turned against you?'

'Yes.'

'When that day comes, stop pretending to be a man without a soul and show them the real you, Alex. Just like Dad did all those years ago. Just like you did today at the Windows on the World. Because if you do, you will never have to fear anything in your life again.'

The rest of the afternoon passed by very quickly. After paying homage to the Statue of Liberty, Delilah and I joined Dwayne for dinner at his favourite restaurant near the United Nations building. At his insistence, we then accompanied him to a housewarming party on the Upper East Side, which ended up being fifty people cramped up inside a small apartment. Nevertheless, unlike that forgettable event in Athens five years ago, I enjoyed the evening immensely. I met some more fascinating New Yorkers, deliberately spilled wine over Dwayne's jacket, and then tried to set Delilah up with a handsome young doctor who had just arrived in town.

Early next morning, the three of us took the subway out to Coney Island, where we goofed around on a ride or two before Delilah took the exciting call that she had just scored three tickets to the opening game of the World Series that night. We immediately dropped our tokens for the Spook-A-Rama onto the ground and then scrambled back to Manhattan.

Although I was not a huge baseball fan, I appreciated the basic plot due to my love of cricket. There was also something about the screaming, partisan crowd inside Yankee Stadium that stirred my endorphins into a fever pitch. Pretty soon, I was screaming along with the best of them. Sitting next to two crazed Mets fans didn't hurt either, especially when the game went to an exciting twelfth inning. But unfortunately for the dynamic duo, with the bases loaded, Jose Vizcaino drove his fourth hit of the game to win it for the Yankees, 4–3. We finished the night drowning our sorrows at some cosy little wine bar in Harlem.

My arduous journey back to the Philippines on Sunday morning began with a ten-thirty flight to LA. Delilah kindly offered to drive me to the airport. I checked out of my hotel, which I had barely used for the last four days, picked up Dwayne's dry-cleaned jacket, and walked back to their apartment.

When it came time to leave, the indomitable Dwayne hugged me. 'Stay safe, dude, and try not to be a miserable shit all your life,' he offered with something resembling a grin.

'I will try,' I promised. 'But being a miserable shit is what I do best.'

We jumped into Delilah's Audi A6 Sedan and burrowed our way through the early morning traffic. She had to yell in my direction a few times, but she finally convinced me that the trip would only take forty-five minutes. So I sat back in my seat, tried to relax, and listened as she then talked about her work.

But as we drove through Queens, it suddenly dawned on me that this was the calmest I had ever been before saying goodbye to a woman. There were no regrets like with Lottie, no recriminations like with Martina, no sadness like with Danielle, no confusion like with Eleanor, no emptiness like with Sally. Just a sense of fulfilment and a realisation that something that had been good was reaching its natural conclusion. Surely, there had to be a reason. So I tapped Delilah on the knee and asked her why.

'It's because you have never met a more brilliant, sensational, sexier woman in your life than me. That's why.'

'No, seriously,' I replied, twisting the side of my mouth.

'How about I toss you out at the next set of traffic lights?' she snorted.

'You know what I mean, Delilah.'

She glanced into her rear-view mirror. 'I have a theory on life.'

Oh God, not you too.

'You see, I believe that everyone is born with a broken heart.'

'That would explain a lot,' I noted sarcastically.

'Don't be an arsehole.'

'Okay,' I replied, deciding to play along with her for the moment. 'Why is everyone born with a broken heart?'

'Because life is all about putting it back together again.'

'Just like Humpty Dumpty?'

'If that makes it easier for you to understand, yes.'

'Interesting,' I pondered. 'You see, I have a similar theory, but mine involves a jigsaw puzzle.'

She didn't seem surprised. 'Regardless,' she continued, 'when we become adults, we start to connect all the broken pieces, one by one, through the people we meet, the lessons we learn, until one day, your heart is finally mended.'

'And what happens then?'

'Well, after that, there is nothing more for you to do. You are ready to take the next step. Meet a girl, get married, and have a family. That sort of thing.'

I attempted to humour her. 'Indulge me here for one moment. Are you suggesting that I now possess a mended heart despite everything I have gone through lately?'

'Hey,' she calmly said. 'You're not as dumb as you look!'

'And Sally wasn't the one?'

'Of course she wasn't. Don't you get it? She was just another broken piece, floating out there in the ether. Every woman up to this point in your life has been just that and nothing more. Your ex-wife, your previous girlfriends, Lottie, Martina, that French chick, the Austrian girl, and even Sally, they were all tests. Sure, you fell in love with some of them, maybe all of them. Who knows? But in the end, they were merely stepping stones in your emotional development. I will admit that it's taken you longer than most to figure this out, but that's because you are an idiot.'

I flushed red with irritation. 'Am I getting this abuse for free?' I muttered. 'Or do you want my credit card details as well?'

'Consider it a personal favour.'

'And what about you?' I pressed her further. 'Does this mean you are my perfect match?'

'Oh God, no,' she replied. Her laugh was somewhat insulting for a woman who had shared my bed for the last several nights. 'All I did was ensure that the last broken piece is now rigidly attached to the rest of your heart.'

'What do you mean?'

'In simple terms, you needed someone to help you get over Sally. For some reason, someone decided that this responsibility should fall on my shoulders.'

'When did you come to this conclusion?'

'Pretty much during the tequila slammers.'

Like everything else in my life, none of this made any sense. But as I would soon find out, nothing made sense when you were indebted to the Clouds.

'You know,' I began with a laugh, 'I thought my theory was crazy, but yours belongs in another stratosphere.'

'Laugh if you will,' she replied after we stopped at a red light somewhere in Little Jamaica. 'But even they agree with me.'

'Who do?'

'The Spiders.'

'You know about the Spiders?'

'Of course I do. Who do you think I am?'

'I only wish I knew.'

When we entered JFK, Delilah quickly found a parking space in departures, and we embarked on all the usual formalities people went through when they said goodbye to each other. I told her that I had the time of my life and that she was a wonderful human being. To her credit, Delilah didn't laugh in my face, as I half-expected she would. Instead, she said all these lovely things in return that I wanted to hear about myself, and then she gave me a massive kiss on the lips. Whether she was being sincere or not, I had no idea, but it was an indulgence that I allowed myself for the time being.

'Look after yourself, crazy guy,' she said with a smile as I collected my carry-on bag from the car floor.

'You too. Maybe next time I'm in New York, I will look you up.'

Delilah waved her finger at me. 'The next time you are in New York, you will be with your new wife, and I'm sure she won't appreciate meeting someone you had a fling with several years before.'

'You think so?'

'I know so.'

I moved across to open the door, but Delilah braced sideways and caught my forearm. 'There is something you can do for me, Alex.'

'Of course. Anything.'

'Please write to Sally and end it, once and for all. While you are at it, tell her that you love her as well, for she needs to hear that from you at least once.'

I promised her that I would give it proper consideration. 'Of course I will.'

'You better.'

I jumped outside, threw everything I owned onto the footpath, and quickly sidled back to the car.

'One final thing.' I stared at Delilah through the half-open window. 'What about you? You never said whether you have a mended heart.'

She imparted one of those frowns that people seemed to throw when they never wanted to see you again.

'I tossed away my broken pieces a long time ago,' she said. To my surprise, a single tear balanced itself on the tip of her nose, and only then did I understand the true extent of her loneliness.

'Delilah—'

But before I had the opportunity to rectify the hurt I had just caused, she released the handbrake, sucked in her cheeks, and made a dash for the late-morning rain.

Minutes later, I checked myself in at the American Airlines counter and then searched for the nearest Admiralty Club. Once inside, I poured myself an OJ and found a spare computer terminal. I locked in the daily internet password, then scrolled down to the Hotmail icon.

As I predicted, the email I had avoided since Wednesday afternoon was waiting for me in bold letters.

Dear Alex,

You silly man. There is no need to apologise, even though we both know that there is no sick friend in New York, and you have been lying your socks off.

Funnily enough, being such a silly fibber is one of the reasons why I fell in love with you. But we both know that the time has come to say a proper goodbye. I deluded myself into thinking that seeing you again would make everything right, that somehow, we would both find a way to live happily ever after. But fairytales don't exist, despite what they say, and I must now accept that reality.

Please promise me one thing. Don't let all this stuff between you and me set you back in any way. Finish your course, go back to Australia, and become the person you always wanted to be. And Martina? She is not the issue, Alex. But other things are. And you need to come to terms with that one day very soon.

At a time like this, I recall the words of my favourite poet, Henry Wordsworth, who wrote: 'Great is the art of beginning, but greater is the art of ending.' I think this perfectly sums up how I now feel. I must end this today, and it's the most courageous thing I have ever done.

Goodbye Alex.

Ever since Samos, I pretended that I had a heart made of stone. Even though it was all an illusion, I deliberately carried this lie with me everywhere I went purely for occasions such as this. That was why I was so surprised at how quickly I engaged the reply button.

Dear Sally,

I am sorry that I lied to you. The reasons for doing so are far too complex to explain in one email. But none of them detracts from how I feel about you and what you have meant to me in the short time we have known each other. You are an incredible woman, and I know that you will have a wonderful life,

Regards,
Alex.

My flight began to board. I stared back at the computer screen, knowing that if I submitted to my cowardice, I could never go back. With Armageddon getting closer by the second, I finally relented to Delilah's prophetic voice stirring inside my head and drafted some further words.

P.S. I love you, Sally.

But even then, as the announcer called my name over the intercom to urgently leave for the departure gate, I still dithered. So I tried to re-imagine the desperation inside Sally's pleading eyes that day at Manila Airport, reassured myself that there was no other way, and finally told her what she deserved to hear.

After all, when you considered how many times I had already lied to her, it was the least that I could do.

The Comedy Club

Manila
December 2000

It was early December, and Ramon, a laconic former army officer with a mysterious past, had just warned me that my life was in danger. Over the last few months, he had become one of my closest friends on the course, along with Taffie, a bubbly solicitor with an iconic grin; William, the charismatic head of a retail chain; and Therese, a charming and intelligent journalist. We were an exceptionally tight group that looked out for one another, and that was what Ramon was doing now.

'There are a lot of bad people out there who are desperate to take advantage of the current situation,' he said, as we sipped our lemon iced teas at the Robo Range, a cosy little restaurant situated inside Camp Aguinaldo. 'A foreigner like you, attending Manila's most prestigious national security course, is a prime target for kidnapping or'—he kept me in suspense for several more seconds—'something far worse.'

'Such as?'

'You know.'

'You don't mean?'

'Yes.'

'A vasectomy?'

'This is no joking matter, my friend,' he said earnestly. 'These are dark times.'

On that score, I did agree with Ramon. These were indeed dark times for the Philippines. Since early October, the political situation in the country had turned into a complete shit show. I started to seriously question whether I would be allowed to complete the course.

The crisis began when the president, former movie action hero Joseph Estrada—or Erap to his followers—was accused by his best friend of profiteering from an illegal numbers game called *jueteng*. These explosive allegations precipitated a burgeoning political scandal that culminated with Estrada's impeachment several weeks ago. His trial had just commenced, but each day brought with it a new whiff of scandal. As a result, his many enemies were beginning to circle him, including his former vice president, Gloria Macapagal-Arroyo.

As an impartial observer to the crisis, I could see how much the unfolding situation impacted my coursemates, many of whom had survived their own harrowing stories from the 1986 EDSA revolution.

None more so than Ramon.

'Look,' I reassured him with my usual mindless bravado, 'I appreciate your concern; I really do. But I can take care of myself. If the embassy thought I was in any danger, they would have told me by now.'

Ramon responded with one of his notoriously sceptical scowls. 'Don't get offended, Alex, but your embassy knows shit.' He pronounced the word 'shit' like 'sheet', but regardless, it had the same startling effect. 'No-one knows what will happen, not even those plotting the next coup.' He reached into the red and white sports bag he had been mysteriously carrying all day and dropped something onto the table, right next to my iced tea.

'Do you know what this is?' he asked quietly.

I picked up the handgun and inspected it closely. 'If I'm not mistaken, it's a Glock 17 nine-millimetre semiautomatic pistol.'

'I assume you know how to use it?'

'I get the basic plot. You point it at someone you don't like, squeeze the trigger, and then call an ambulance.'

'Good. It's all yours.'

I swallowed hard. My Filipino friends had tried to sell me the concept of owning a gun once before, when Hector drove some of us to an obscure restaurant in Pasig for lunch and then parked the passenger side of the Land Cruiser straight underneath a broken water pipe. After we all got drenched with filthy, disease-laden sewage, my friends felt that Hector was an imbecile. They reassured me that he would become a better driver if I brandished a pistol at him every morning before we left my apartment. However, I calmly tried to explain to my Filipino friends that in Australia, attempted murder was illegal.

'How about this?' one of them had then offered. 'There are some men that I know who can take him to an undisclosed quarry outside of Manila for a few days and beat him to a pulp until he agrees to lift his performance.'

'How about this?' I quickly replied. 'You're frigging insane!'

With that incident in mind, I politely raised my open palms towards Ramon. 'I can't accept your gift, mate. If the embassy knew I had a gun, they would send me home on the first Qantas flight out of Manila.'

'Please take it, my friend,' Ramon begged. 'Better to go home in controversy than go home in a coffin.'

'Well, since you put it that way.' Without further discussion, I kindly accepted his disturbing gift to honour our friendship, emptied the magazine of its contents as soon as I arrived home, and then hid it safely away beneath a pile of spare blankets inside an unused cupboard.

I respected Ramon well enough to recognise that he wasn't someone to exaggerate such things. He had seen his fair share of military coups—Jesus, he probably helped plan a few himself. So I wasn't that foolish to ignore his warning. Instead, I briefed Marty about our conversation—well, up to the part about the Glock—started to look over my shoulder and viewed every stranger with suspicion. As soon as I did, the weird stuff started to happen. First, Fely began to complain about strangers milling around the apartment while I was at college. Then, the following Wednesday, I received a series of disturbing phone calls during the middle of the night from some dusky-voiced woman, asking if I was alone. If that wasn't scary enough, then came the Saturday afternoon when I bumped into Frank at Glorietta Mall. Well, at least, I thought it was Frank.

'Hey, Frank!' I yelled out to the guy squatting in front of the camera shop. When he heard my voice, he deliberately tilted his head upwards towards the ceiling. For a moment, he reminded me of a magpie in search of a lost melody. His pale grey eyes, squat nose, and receding hairline were almost exactly how I remembered them when we both attended the Capricornia Institute of Advanced Education together in Rockhampton some twenty years before.

'Frank, it's me—Alex Gerrick,' I happily stretched out my hand. But to my surprise, he continued to sit on his arse, his fingers nervously grasping at the tips of his trouser pockets.

'Sorry, but you've got the wrong person,' he said somewhat testily. 'My name isn't Frank; it's Jeremy.'

'Jeremy?' I began to laugh. 'Your name is Frank Madsen, and you went to school in Bundaberg. We both played soccer together, remember? You follow Leeds United.'

'Soccer? I hate fucking soccer,' he insisted. 'You've got the wrong guy, okay?'

'No, I don't.'

'Yes, you do.'

'So you never attended Capricornia?'

'Never.'

'Never lived in Rockhampton?'

'Never.'

'You sure?'

'Perfectly. I have never been to Rockhampton, never attended Capricornia, and never played soccer with you.'

I sucked in my cheeks and stepped away from him. 'My apologies. You look exactly like an old friend—'

'Goodbye,' he rudely cut me off.

Usually, a case of mistaken identity wouldn't have bothered me. But this was the Philippines, and as such, everything bothered me. For when I diverted my eyes from Jeremy's scolding face to the reflection in the camera store window, I realised that my initial observation back at the bookstore some fifteen minutes previously had been correct: I was being followed.

People would rightly argue that I was hopeless at relationships and equally clueless about the practicalities of everyday life. But when it came to this cloak and dagger stuff, I was without peer. Put it down to my inborn Croatian paranoia or my fascination with spy novels. But ever since Athens, my mind had always been on high alert for the inexplicable, the tiny little things that seemed out of place, even in such a bewildering, rampageous city like Manila, where *everything* seemed out of place.

At the bookstore, I had quickly deduced that there were three of them. One was a scrawny-looking Filipino with a black Led Zeppelin T-shirt hanging around the travel section, pretending to flick through a book about America. Ten feet to his left was a more diminutive fellow, with closely cropped hair and a double chin. He nervously thumbed his way through a Robert Ludlum novel, trying hard to avoid any eye contact with his friend. Several feet behind me was their leader, an athletic type with a shoehorn for a nose and thighs the size of concrete pillars. If he thought that I hadn't spotted him yet, then he had one hell of a shock when I walked up to him and casually asked how his day was going.

As I paid for my book at the counter, I swept my eyes across the store exit and noticed that the three men had joined forces and were waiting for me to make my next move. I felt a sense of relief: whether their purpose was to kidnap me, rob me, or tell me dirty jokes, they weren't very professional. Only complete amateurs would congregate like this in full view of their intended victim. They all seemed somewhat nervous, agitated, and just a little scared.

I had read enough about spy tradecraft to know how to lose a tail, and it was all about upsetting your pursuer's thought processes and not doing what they expected you to do. So, rather than recklessly stomp out the main door, I backtracked in between some aisles, lost myself within a train of school kids, and then sneaked out through a side entrance. *Yes, round one to me!*

If followed, one of the first things you should do is to change your appearance as quickly as possible. Luckily for me, I had just bought a new T-shirt from a department store. In front of a pack of bewildered shoppers, I quickly swapped shirts and then flicked on my glasses for double effect. To be on the safe side, I also ruffled my hair around so that it looked less coiffed than usual and then ventured carefully towards the camera store, glancing sideways whenever I could.

But somewhere along the way, either by design or sheer luck, the three of them had found me, and I reconsidered my options. Another basic rule of tradecraft was to use the environment to your advantage. The mall was full of people; security guards manned every entrance, and I was also standing next to another Australian. The perfect scenario for what I was about to do next.

Without a moment to spare, I deliberately spilled the contents of my plastic carry bag onto the ground, leaned downwards, and grabbed Jeremy around the armpit.

'Hey, what the fuck do you think you're doing, you maniac?' he shouted at me.

'Listen, Jeremy, Frank or, whatever the fuck your name is,' I whispered angrily, pointing to the three Filipinos. 'Those guys over there are following me for some reason, and you're going to help me scare them away.'

Jeremy's pallid complexion teetered on the brink of white-sheet territory, but to his credit, he lifted himself without any help.

'What do you want me to do?' he asked nervously.

'Just stay with me and don't say a word.'

I puffed out my chest to look more brutal than I was.

'Are you ready?'

Jeremy said nothing but nodded his head.

'Okay, let's do it.' He waited for me to roll my fists into two concrete balls, then with our imaginary Colt 45s by our sides, we bustled along the shiny floor with all the swagger of Wyatt Earp and Doc Holliday on their way to the OK Corral.

'Hey, you three!' I screamed out loudly so everyone in our immediate vicinity, including a couple of burly security guards, could hear me. 'What's going on? Why are you following me?'

If I intended to confuse their scrambled little brains, then my hollering seemed to do the trick. When Jeremy and I came to an audacious halt right in front of their faces, you could see how panic-stricken they had become. I'm talking about legs shaking, knees knocking, fingers twitching, that sort of thing.

It was only a matter of time before one of them cracked under pressure. Surprisingly, that honour went to Mister Shoehorn Nose. When he realised that the security guards were striding towards us, batons in hand, he cried out to his mates in Tagalog to make a run for it.

Before any of us had time to react, they arranged themselves into a deranged three-by-one-hundred relay team and then sprinted towards the nearest set of escalators.

'Don't come back here ever again, or we will kick your butts!' Jeremy triumphantly whooped. 'You don't fuck around with a couple of Queenslanders!'

I initially intended to discuss the incident with the local security guards but then got distracted by Jeremy's last sentence.

'I want to make sure that I correctly heard what you just said,' I interrupted him. 'Did you just say, "You don't fuck around with a couple of Queenslanders"?'

'Yes. What if I did?'

'So, you are from Queensland, then?'

'Of course.'

'But you have never been to Rockhampton?'

'Never,' he insisted.

'You're certain?'

'How many more times do I have to tell you?'

Although I would never see those three Filipino miscreants again, the incident rattled me more than I cared to admit. It was an issue I raised rather solemnly with Jack a week or so later when he stopped over to visit me in Manila on his way back to Australia from Singapore.

'Mate,' he began in his customary laidback drawl, 'if someone dropped an atomic bomb on Manila and only one guy walked out of the ashes completely unharmed, I'd bet my life savings that it would be you.'

I studied his rugged jawline and inquisitive hazel eyes with amusement. If that description had applied to anyone, it was Jack, not me. 'Coming from you, Jack, that's a compliment.'

'You are the proverbial cat with nine lives,' he said, as he completed another beer. 'Trust me; you will be the last one standing after the rest of us have gone, waiting to turn the lights on for the next generation.'

'I am not so sure about that.'

'You're wrong.' He slapped his hand hard against my knee. 'Besides, you can't die yet—not until I get my revenge.'

'You mean for the airport thing?'

'Yeah, I mean for the airport thing.'

The more Jack and I talked that afternoon; I realised that he was there on a mission. Some of the guys back in Australia were worried about me. In recent weeks, the emails had become less regular, the humorous anecdotes had all but stopped, and I appeared to have gone, well, slightly native.

Over dinner, I reassured Jack that nothing could have been further from the truth. I explained to him I was still recovering from my stomach illness, that the course workload had become more strenuous, and I was writing a top-class thesis. He left for the airport the following day, partially satisfied with his work, but with a brotherly proviso, I should call him whenever I needed to chat. But of course, it was impossible to fool Jack. After all, he was the only person I ever knew who could navigate a pathway through the maze of my self-deceit and still come out the other side with his love for me intact. His suspicions had been correct: I was deliberately shunning my friends and family. For want of a better description, I had indeed gone native.

Perhaps it was the natural by-product of my indulgent trip to America. Despite my fascination with Delilah's theory, I returned from New York with a broken heart and a restlessness that infested every molecule of my body. I couldn't see myself finishing the course under these circumstances, and I wondered whether the best outcome for everyone was to quit right then and head home.

There was no clear catalyst for what happened next, but almost overnight, my perspective about life started to change slowly. I suddenly began to shun the local diplomatic community, I put more effort into my Filipino friendships, I wined and dined the occasional Filipina, and I welcomed every new person I met with heartfelt enthusiasm. *From now on*, I decided, *I'll try to see the Philippines through the eyes of the very same people that I had once shamelessly pitied.*

When I did, everything about the country that had initially perplexed me—the poverty, the chaos, the passion, the beauty, the tragedy—became a refuge for my affectations and an opportunity to cleanse the insincerities of my past. I knew that the only way I could maintain the sanctity of my utopia was to temporarily expunge every prejudice, every bias that lived within the confines of my privileged Australian existence.

Of course, I needed to hide my infidelities from those who cared about me the most. So I returned to Australia for the holiday season, determined to allay any residual fears about my state of mind.

I celebrated Christmas with my family. I went to the Boxing Day test match with Clemmons. I invited my army friends Jeff and Craig to accompany me back to the Philippines for New Year's Eve. On the outside, I portrayed the comfortable, plastic version of Alex Gerrick that everyone wanted to see, with a reassuring smile and a quick-fire joke. But beneath all the flim-flam, the only thing on my mind was how quickly I could return to Manila.

When college finally resumed in the first week of January, I was initially overwhelmed by a sense of gratitude. Through any reasonable calculation, I shouldn't have been allowed to return to the Philippines, given the escalating political tensions.

While I was absent in Australia, a spate of bombings had rocked Manila, including one across the road from the Dusit Hotel, not far away from where I lived in San Lorenzo Village. In total, twenty-two people were killed, including two police officers. If that wasn't reason enough to review my ongoing attendance on the course, then I didn't know what was. It was as if those in Canberra had forgotten that I existed.

Sure, Ramon's dire warning and that whole thing with the Three Stooges had alerted me to the inherent dangers of my situation. But what was the alternative? Return to Canberra to a life that no longer interested me? No thanks—I'd take my chances fending off communist insurgents, Islamic terrorists, or right-wing coup plotters. Besides, it wasn't as if I had to contend with the danger by myself. I had my Filipino friends; I had my colleagues from the embassy, and I had a Glock 17 nine-millimetre semiautomatic pistol in my linen cupboard. Furthermore, my old army reserve buddy, Harry Wright, had arrived in Manila to stay with me for several weeks.

The night before Harry landed, I attended a local comedy club in Quezon City with a girl named Liki, who I had recently met at a private function. She was pretty enough, although probably a bit too young for me—which in itself wasn't a surprise given that most of the single Filipino women in Manila were a bit too young for me. However, there really wasn't much to it; I had no interest in pursuing a night of passion, nor was I interested in anything long-term. It was nothing more than a case of being polite to a girl who had asked me out.

When we arrived at the club, Liki jumped out of the Land Cruiser first and immediately swung her fulsome hips to get my attention.

'What is it?' I tried to smile.

'I forgot to mention that we are also meeting a friend of mine tonight. I hope you don't mind.' *As if I have a choice in the matter.*

'Of course not.'

'She is bringing her boyfriend with her. He is Australian, too.'

'Really?' I replied with a modicum of interest.

'You may know him.'

'I doubt it.'

Liki and I shuffled around the club entrance for several minutes before I heard several screams behind us.

'Liki!'

'Sandi!'

I watched in stunned amazement as a petite Filipina and Jeremy made their way towards us, their hands locked together in something resembling a death pact. Jeremy had a haircut since we last met, and he looked dignified in his faded blue jeans, brown cowboy boots, and white Capricornia Institute of Advanced Education sweatshirt.

'Alex!' he stuck out his hand out jovially. 'Good to see you again!'

'Jeremy,' I replied warily.

'Why did you call him Jeremy?' Sandi screwed up her face. 'His name is Frank.'

'Of course it is. How could I have forgotten?'

'You two know each other?' asked Liki.

'Yes,' Frank replied with a twinkle in his beady eyes. 'We played soccer together in Rockhampton many years ago, didn't we Alex?'

'We sure did.'

'I suppose you want an explanation, Alex,' he whispered to me while Sandi and Liki collected our tickets from the front office.

'About what?' I grumbled.

'Why I pretended at Glorietta that I didn't know you.'

'Now that you mention it, no, I fucking don't.'

After a few drinks, we settled into our seats and made salacious small talk before the first act arrived on stage. The announcer proudly introduced us to two young female twins called Ying and Yang, the joke being that we were never actually sure which one was Ying and which one was Yang. They bleated out a couple of off-key tunes, made some colourful observations about President Estrada, and then left us with some weird gymnastic act that served only to thrill the many male perverts inside the room. I clapped politely because everyone else did.

Next up, we had Tina the Terrific, direct from some obscure island in the Visayas. If I had the freedom to choose any word that described Tina's act, then it definitely wouldn't have been *terrific*. She began by mumbling her way through some dreary monologue about how difficult it was to tell octopuses apart until the whole production inevitably ended with the punchline: because they are all 'i-tentacle.'

By this stage, I contemplated gnawing off one of my arms just for the fun of it but then got sucked into Tina's following spiel about Goldilocks and the three bears. When no-one laughed at that one either, she dropped her head politely at the audience, suggested that she wasn't feeling very well, and announced the arrival of the night's main attraction, Raul Gonzolo the Third.

Now Raul was one of those gay comedy acts that obtained his laughs by not admitting that he was gay but by making outlandish, ambiguous comments in an effeminate voice that only suggested that he was gay. But even under this dubious premise, he was still a vast improvement from the previous two acts. Raul sang a few bawdy songs, poked fun at several audience members, and then regaled a riveting story about an astronaut's daughter. When he finally ran out of daughter jokes, he slowly walked up to the edge of the stage and calmly pointed his finger right at my head.

'Oh my God, it's Alex Gerrick from the Australian Embassy! Let's make him welcome everyone!'

A stage light spewed out a toxic blue beam right into my eyes. I wasn't sure what I found more disturbing: the crowd applauding my presence or the fact that I had never met Raul Gonzolo the Third before in my life.

'Look at you,' Frank said with a sarcastic wink.

'Yeah, look at me,' I replied tersely.

Raul raised his microphone to his mouth as if he was about to scoff down a banana. 'It's been so long since we've been together; I have forgotten how handsome you are!'

Everyone in the room was laughing at my expense except, of course, Liki, Sandi, and possibly Frank. Without even a murmur, they each folded their arms against their chests and stared down at me accusingly. I might have been imagining things at this point, but Liki gave the impression that she was about to burst into tears.

'I'm not gay,' I tried to convince her. Not that it would have mattered if I were.

'You don't have to hide your sexuality from us,' Frank said. 'You're among friends here.'

'Fuck off, Jeremy.'

Raul forgot about me for the next five minutes and plodded on with more high-octane jokes about the president and the current political situation. I was thoroughly impressed by how many people found an impending revolution so humorous. He ended his act with some naughty gym-room innuendo and then announced that there would be a fifteen-minute intermission before the next act.

As people began to file out of the auditorium, I wandered over to where Raul Gonzolo the Third was disconnecting his microphone. He reminded me of a young Sal Mineo.

'Excuse me, Raul?'

He pointed his bone-white teeth right at my nose. 'Ah, Mr Gerrick! So good to see you again.' He seemed remarkably cocksure of himself.

'Well, that's just it, Raul,' I replied as politely as I could. 'I don't recall ever meeting you before tonight.'

'Just like your friend Frank couldn't remember meeting you?'

'How do you know about that?'

'Word gets around.'

Ah, I get it now. The whole thing was a stitch-up. When we were having drinks before the show, Frank bumped into this guy, and they concocted this entire thing between them.

'Okay, you got me. You and Frank set me up. Well played.'

He seemed offended. 'Mr Gerrick, I am shocked that you would even suggest such a thing! We met in Athens. Don't you remember?'

'No, I don't,' I insisted. 'I never met any Filipino people during my visit to Athens.'

'Friends come in many forms, Mr Gerrick.' He pressed his hands into his stomach as if he had just removed them from an oven top. 'Truth be known, we met several times.'

This guy was a piece of work, I decided. *It was all part of his act, don't you see? He couldn't let go, even when caught out. Because you have to keep them wondering. You have to keep them talking to their friends about your act. More people through the door the next time you appeared at the comedy club. More cash in your hand after your next gig. But I wasn't going to fall for it.*

Instead, I did my best to itemise the people I had met in Athens to prove a point to myself. There was Marco, of course, and his three girlfriends: Sophia, Marcella, and Dominica. Then there were the various hotel staff members like Spiro, Selene, Dumbo, and Dumbo's boss. Everyone from the night of the party: the guy in the demountable, the cockney security guard dressed up as a Greek soldier, that slimeball Scott Farmer, the couple from Texas, the swimsuit model, Cassandra, Tammy, and Reginald …

'Oh my God.' Thousands of tiny membranes inside my brain began to detonate one at a time. *No, it can't be! It's not possible!*

'What do you mean we met several times?' I screamed back at him.

'You see?' Raul replied knowingly. 'You do remember, after all.'

'No, this is insane.' I shuffled back towards the creeping darkness, but Raul stood calmly in front of me.

'Get out of my way,' I ordered him. Several production staff wandered over towards us to investigate the developing commotion.

'Don't be scared, Mr Gerrick.'

Don't be scared? Are you fucking kidding me? A gay Filipino comedian was claiming to be the same person who had appeared to me as an English travel clerk in Athens six years ago, and now he was telling me not to be scared? No, I wasn't scared; I was fucking petrified.

'Please, Mr Gerrick.' He drew closer towards me, just like the wolf once did with Little Red Riding Hood. But not even the brothers Grimm could have made this shit up.

'I'm warning you. Don't screw with me, Crump.'

'Why, I'm here to help you, Mr Gerrick,' said Reginald Crump. 'I'm not here, as you put it, to screw with you.'

'I don't need or want your help.'

'We could all use some help in our lives, Mr Gerrick. Just like the baby crying out for his mother's milk or the blind man crossing the road or the suicidal Bosnian nurse.'

'What did you say?'

'Please be careful, Mr Gerrick. These are difficult times.'

For a paltry second, I swore to God that Reginald Crump's terrifying charcoal eyes exploded from their sockets and their remnants splashed hard against my face. I could almost taste the particles of slime pouring into the corners of my mouth. High above me, a swarm of yellow balloons drifted slowly towards a solitary window.

Yes indeedy, Mister Sneezy!

'Mister Gerrick, are you okay?' asked Raul Gonzolo the Third.

'I have to go home!' I cried out.

Yes indeedy, Mister Sleazy!

I weaved through a group of half-pissed teenagers, who waved a bottle of local rum at me in disgust and then scampered towards the front exit.

'Here,' said Frank, trying to catch my arm as I rolled past him. 'I've bought you a beer.'

'Shove it up your arse, Frank.'

Yes indeedy, Mister Greedy!

'Alex!' Liki cried out. 'Where are you going?'

'I'll call you later' was the only reassurance I could provide her.

Yes indeedy, Mister Wheezy!

The sultry night air temporarily calmed my nerves. After tying up a loose shoelace, I followed the foul stench of rotten sewage through a row of parked cars before my Land Cruiser miraculously appeared in the next allotment. I did my best to collapse dramatically into the front seat, where I found Hector lying half-asleep against the steering wheel. When he realised it was me, he jolted his head upwards and automatically engaged the ignition.

'Get me out of here, Hector,' I ordered.

'Are you okay, sir?'

'I will be fine. Just get me home.'

Despite all those times I had inappropriately made fun of him, Hector performed miracles that night. He discovered every shortcut, beat every red light, and missed every traffic jam. Fifteen minutes later, we were pulling into San Lorenzo Village.

'Thank you, Hector.' I dropped a thousand-peso note into his hand to show my appreciation. 'You did very well.'

He offered me a dull smile as if he had been waiting for this compliment for several months. 'You worry, sir?'

He didn't need to explain any further. I knew what he meant. 'Yes, I worry, Hector.'

'Let's check the apartment, sir.'

We opened the side security door, and, not for the first time, I tripped over Fely's filthy cat, which pounced at me from beneath the shadows. 'I am going to kill that fucking thing if it's the last thing I do,' I announced simply for Hector's benefit.

We slowly moved from room to room, turning on every light, looking under every bed, watching every movement. Satisfied that we had finally secured the house, I thanked Hector for his troubles and encouraged him to go home. He tried to convince me that he should stay the night, but I calmly told him it wasn't necessary. I didn't want an innocent man caught up in my insanity.

After Hector left, I wandered upstairs and pulled out Ramon's Glock from the cupboard. I carefully reloaded the magazine, then sneaked back into my bedroom and locked the door behind me.

'Come and get me, you arsehole,' I screamed out into the darkest corners of the universe.

Once I made the invitation, I dropped the Glock onto my spare pillow, pulled a blanket over my legs and waited for Ringo Bingo the Clown to arrive.

The Coup

Manila
Friday 19 January 2001

Ringo Bingo kept me guessing for several more days. But that was just the way he liked to do business. From the beginning, it was always about the mind games with him, always about making me doubt my sanity when I had more important priorities to consider. He could argue as much as he liked, but Ringo Bingo never had my best interests at heart when he made that deal with me all those years ago. So when I woke up that morning to the sound of his evil laughter, I wasn't surprised at all to find the decaying corpse of the woman I once loved lying next to me in bed.

Granted, Ringo Bingo had thirty years to develop a new disguise, so his next effort was always going to be a real humdinger. Ever since Samos, I had given him endless material with which to work his devious magic. *But honestly, Ringo Bingo, did you have to include those maggots tearing away at her cheeks? Or the vile, yellow pus dribbling out of her mouth?* You see, I had to twist my body into all sorts of impossible angles to escape the rivers of blood pouring over my legs.

Her blood. Sally's blood.

I rolled off the side of the bed and hit my head on the wooden floor. As I leaned on my elbows, I stared at a tiny moth pulling itself over one of my new slippers, and I wondered whether this was also part of Ringo Bingo's grandiose production.

Hahahaha! Gotcha! Just like the good old days! Remember the good old days, Alex? Proudly brought to you by Ringo Bingo the Clown and his band of merry perverts!

I grabbed hold of the wooden bed frame and somehow pulled my body upwards.

Gosh, she was a pretty one, Alex. But that's your dilemma, isn't it? All the pretty ones in your life end up dead!

My hands frantically crackled through my bedside drawer, pushing aside pancake stacks of neatly folded underpants. When I felt the tingle of the Glock's cold steel barrel scrape against my fingers, waves of adrenaline seeped into every curvature of my spine. *Today is the day that I get rid of this fucker forever!*

I snapped my hands around the gun's stock, slammed in the magazine, pulled back the slide, and then released a cartridge into the chamber. Fully loaded and ready to rock, I twirled around to face my mortal enemy one last time. But instead of Sally's rotting carcass, all I could see was a single, crumpled sheet hanging pathetically over the bottom edge of my mattress. *No, don't fall for it again. This was another one of his tricks.* With my heart pulsating, I carefully scanned the length of the bed, looking for further evidence of his trickery.

Hang on! What's that? It was the book that I had been reading last night before I fell asleep, still lying face down next to my spare pillow, exactly where I had left it. Right next to the book was the T-shirt I pulled off my chest at two-thirty in the morning, scrunched helplessly into a tiny ball.

'Jesus Christ,' I whispered as my heart began to thump inside my head. I stared down at the barrel of the Glock, and for one crazy, ill-conceived moment, I wondered whether this was the only proper way to release myself from all this madness.

'Mister Alex!' cried out Fely from behind my locked bedroom door. 'Breakfast is ready!'

I dropped the gun onto the floor and ran my hands over my unshaven face in despair. While Fely continued to bang away at the door, I slowly counted to ten in French to ensure that I had re-entered reality.

Un, deux, trois, quatre, cinq, six, sept, huit—

'Thanks, Fely. I'll be right down.'*—neuf, dix.*

I bent over to pick up the Glock, unloaded the magazine, and ejected the round from the chamber. With a minimum of fuss, I laid the T-shirt out on my bed, placed all the spare parts and other remnants from the morning's wreckage on top of it, and then tied everything up into a neatly compressed bundle. Come hell or high water, this gun wouldn't see another day inside my house.

Minutes later, I was sitting at the kitchen table, my trembling hands squeezing out some honey onto a burnt piece of toast. Harry had his nose firmly locked behind the *Manila Times* and seemed impervious to my dishevelled state. It gave me a precious few seconds to calm the fuck down.

'How did you sleep, mate?' he asked, finally dropping the paper onto the table. There was something about Harry's relaxed demeanour, curly blonde hair, and judicious blue eyes that inspired confidence, and I was suddenly pleased that he was with me.

'Fine,' I replied. Of course, I was lying through my teeth. But what was I supposed to have said? That I had almost emptied seventeen rounds from a Glock into the deranged apparition of my ex-lover? Instead, I sucked on my piece of toast and pointed to the paper. 'What's the latest?'

'Looks bad. I think today might be the day.'

I blinked at the headlines:

More crowds at the EDSA shrine last night.

Film stars and musicians join the protests.

Military tipped to defect to Macapagal-Arroyo.

The Philippines is on the brink of civil war.

'Media trash talk,' I replied flippantly.

'You don't believe that, not even for a second.'

No, of course, I didn't. Any hope of resolving the current impasse disappeared on Tuesday afternoon during President Estrada's impeachment trial after senators gathered to vote on opening a single envelope.

But this was no ordinary envelope, for many speculated that its contents would finally prove that Erap had acted corruptly over the *jueteng* scandal. So, as the nation looked on nervously, the smoking gun in this whole controversy was about to be revealed.

However, there was only one problem. Erap's supporters held a majority in the senate. To their credit—or discredit, depending on where you stood on the matter—they all voted against opening the envelope, ensuring the motion's defeat by the irritatingly small margin of eleven votes to ten. Once the result was declared, nine opposition senators and the eleven prosecutors presiding over the trial walked out of the senate in protest.

The following day, the prosecutors announced their resignation. Senator Tessie Aquino-Oreta, one of Erap's closest supporters, celebrated this news on the senate floor by dancing an outrageous jig of delight for the benefit of the television cameras. That only incensed the anti-Erap crowd, which began to gather at the shrine of the Virgin Mary on EDSA Avenue in Quezon City, the symbol of people power during the peaceful ousting of President Marcos.

That night, Cardinal Jaime Sin, the Archbishop of Manila and the most influential person in the city, encouraged his flock to join the protest. Now that the Catholic Church had declared its hand, the nation was again at the mercy of God's curious will.

'Do you think the military will withdraw their support today?' asked Harry. He topped my mug with coffee and waited for a response.

'After what we saw on Wednesday, I'd say there's a good chance.'

Two days ago, Harry and I had gone to the Robo Range for lunch, where we chanced upon a group of retired Filipino generals huddled in the corner of the room engaged in animated discussion. Our entry into their private domain caused them to bolt upright in their chairs: it reminded me of one of those old western movies where the bad guy entered the saloon, and the piano player stopped playing in anticipation of a gunfight. Of course, we weren't privy to the details of their conversation, but given the unstable political environment, it was apparent what they were doing.

'Mmm,' Harry pondered. 'What about you? Are you still attending lessons today?' Depending on my answer, it could have enormous implications for his entire visit. Harry was conducting research for his employer and had scheduled several meetings for later in the morning. The plan was for Hector to drop me off at Camp Aguinaldo and then chaperone Harry for the rest of the day.

What I couldn't tell Harry was many years ago, I had made a Faustian bargain with a vile, imaginary clown, and whenever he reappeared in my life, everything around me turned to custard. Perhaps it was best that Harry and Hector kept their distance from me.

'No, let's stick to the plan,' I whistled into my coffee. 'Besides, I have my French class this afternoon, and I am not missing that even for a military coup.'

Thirty minutes later, we clambered into the Land Cruiser, where Hector greeted us with his usual relaxed grin. If he was worried about how the day might unfold, he didn't show it. Instead, Hector frantically groped at his tattered white T-shirt while listening carefully to my instructions. When I finished talking, he repeated everything back to Harry, who then jumped into the front passenger seat.

'I will drop Alex off at Camp Aguinaldo. I will take Harry wherever he needs to go. I will pick Alex up from the college at four o'clock.'

We soon choked our way through the usual early morning pollution. As we approached the last set of traffic lights before entering EDSA avenue, the alert tone on my mobile phone screamed out from my trouser pocket, causing both Harry and Hector to jump out of their seats.

'Liki,' I explained to Harry after I read her message. 'The whole country is about to fall apart, and she wants to know whether we are still going out for dinner tonight!'

'You can't leave the girl in suspense,' Harry said with a chuckle. I got the impression he found my extracurricular activities highly amusing.

'No, I can't,' I agreed. 'It seems that she doesn't want to be alone this weekend.'

Hector tried to get my attention by coughing wildly at me.

'What is it, Hector?'

'Miss Liki, she no live alone.'

'How do you know that?'

'Her friend's driver told me. She has *bebe*.'

'What?' I asked, dropping my phone onto my lap.

Harry burst out laughing.

'She has *bebe*,' Hector repeated.

'How many *bebe* does she have?' I demanded to know.

'She has two *bebe*!'

What do you know? I have been out with Liki twice, and she never mentioned anything to me about having two bebe.

We chugged along in silence for a few more miles before the statue of the Virgin Mary appeared from out of the rising smog. As I often did, I greeted her with the sign of the cross in a pathetic attempt to look religious to my colleagues.

Harry, meanwhile, seemed transfixed by the tens of thousands of people who had maintained their vigil all night. 'They're not going anywhere, are they?'

'Filipinos take their democracy very seriously,' I replied, as I lost myself within the endless sea of protest signs. 'Maybe I should, too.'

'Don't even think about it,' warned Harry via the rear-view mirror. 'Attending the protest is the last thing the embassy would want you to do. You have to be impartial and not take any sides. That's if you don't want to be sent home early.'

'Spoilsport,' I replied gloomily. I allowed some quiet time to pass between us before I changed the topic. 'Once we get inside Camp Aguinaldo, I'll lend you my security pass. Don't worry, I'll stay at the college all day. If anything goes wrong, call me on my phone. Otherwise, I'll see you at sixteen hundred.'

'Right on the dot,' said Harry calmly.

When we pulled up at the college car park, Harry shook my hand. 'Promise me you won't do anything stupid,' he said with a wry smile.

'Hey, it's me you're talking to.'

'That's what I'm worried about.'

I found my Filipino colleagues scattered around in small groups inside the library, gossiping about overnight developments. There was a touch of gallows humour to their conversations as if the time had finally arrived for them to accept the inevitable. In fact, rather than lamenting the situation, most seemed more concerned about my welfare and how their clueless Australian friend was going to survive the following few days without their help.

'You still have my gun?' asked Ramon as we entered our primary classroom.

'Almost used it this morning,' I replied.

Lessons began right on time: well, as close to right on time as you could get in the Philippines. But I could tell within minutes that no-one was interested in the latest economic statistics from Mindanao, not even the lecturer. Text messages were flying around rapidly as we all sat glued to our mobile phones, waiting for the latest updates. Then, just after ten o'clock, Mathilda, our class president, shouted out from her front seat: 'The military has defected!'

Right on cue, Professor Moreno entered the room, her gentle face belying the seriousness of her announcement. 'Good morning, class,' she began with a nervous cough. She exuded strength and calmness. 'I have just been advised that the military and police have officially declared their support for Vice President Arroyo. Things are escalating within Camp Aguinaldo even as we speak.' Now that it was all official, I could feel the tension seep into the room.

'Your safety is my main concern,' Professor Moreno continued. 'So I have decided to cancel this morning's lectures. Would you please go home to your families? We will contact you once we have more information. God bless you all.'

While most of the students began assembling outside the main building, my priority was to get back to the embassy as quickly as possible. I was, of course, apprehensive about Harry and Hector and wished I had arranged a mobile phone for them. All I could think about was both men wandering around the outskirts of Manila together, oblivious to the fact that the revolution had well and truly started.

I was not entirely sure, but there was a chance I had a copy of Harry's itinerary in an email he had sent to me on my work account. If I could find out where he would be at lunchtime, perhaps I could get a message to him.

'I will take you to Makati,' kindly offered Ramon. We wished our colleagues the best of luck and then jumped into his jet-black Land Rover. As we slowly weaved our way back along EDSA, I was surprised that he looked scared.

'You must be careful now, Alex,' he warned me. 'Don't trust anyone.'

'I trust you, Ramon.'

'Then you are a fool.'

By the time we reached the Makati city centre, a large demonstration had poured down Legazpi Avenue towards the Australian Embassy. It was difficult to determine from my car window whether these demonstrators were supporting Estrada or Arroyo.

'My best advice is that you keep a low profile for the rest of the day. All it takes is one idiot with a rifle who thinks you're an anomaly …' Ramon didn't finish the sentence, but then, he didn't really have to.

'I will,' I promised. Ramon dropped me off at the side of a kerb and gave me a savage hug. 'Stay safe, my friend.'

'You too, mate.' I connected with his shrunken eyes. 'By the way, you still haven't told me which side you support in all this.'

'Whichever side wins, of course.' He managed to smile and then roared off through a red light.

Minutes later, I jumped onto the only spare computer I could find and frantically began to search my emails. *Bugger it.* I couldn't find anything from Harry which outlined his plans for the day. I then bumped into Marty, and he reassured me that everything would be fine. 'The best thing you can do is return to San Lorenzo and wait for him there.'

I pretended to agree with him, picked up my latest payslip, and made myself a cup of instant coffee in the breakout room. For the next thirty minutes, I weighed up the options available and then conveniently remembered that I had a French class scheduled for that afternoon. That was the lame excuse I needed to make the fateful decision to return to Camp Aguinaldo.

Later that night, Harry would ask me the obvious question: why did I return to Camp Aguinaldo with the country on the cusp of a revolution? I agreed with him that I had made a controversial choice. But I felt a personal responsibility to meet him and Hector at our preordained meeting place. You didn't leave your mates behind to face the music by themselves. Besides, didn't Professor Moreno cancel the morning lessons? She never mentioned anything about those scheduled for the afternoon. Mine was a specious argument, of course, but if my Catholic upbringing taught me one thing, it was always to respect the rules. If that meant I was required to be at French lessons, then that's where I would be unless somebody in authority told me otherwise.

I found a taxi and asked the driver to take me to Camp Aguinaldo. By the time we bypassed our first set of traffic lights, I was already regretting my decision. The overly tight seatbelt began to bite hard into my stomach and thighs while the traffic along EDSA resembled a medieval time-warp. A journey that would have usually taken thirty minutes soon became an epic fight for survival where we were competing with every other lunatic in the city.

We soon became wedged between two monstrous semi-trailers, so I randomly checked my mobile phone for messages to pass the time. To my horror, I realised that the battery had almost drawn down its power, and pretty soon, it would be completely flat. In my haste to leave the embassy, I had forgotten to recharge it. My only option was to switch the phone off and save whatever juice I had left for an emergency.

It took us a mind-boggling one and a half hours to reach Camp Aguinaldo. By that time, I was so punch-drunk with claustrophobia, all I could think about was getting out of this damn car before I blew several gaskets inside my head. Dispensing with the usual courtesies, I yelled at the driver several times in confused Tagalog before he stopped in the middle of the road some two hundred feet away from the main security gate. After we finally agreed on a fee, I paid him in cash, collected my bag from the back seat, and then stumbled back towards the base.

Most normal people would have recognised the danger signs immediately. First, one could point to the hordes of workers scurrying out the main gate, their terrified faces covered in sweat. Or the countless arguments that had broken out among those lining up for a jeepney across the street. Yes, any idiot with half a brain could tell that the country was descending into lawlessness apart from this one absurd Australian who was far more concerned about missing his French lesson.

The security guards at the main gate didn't seem to be all that interested in me either as I gently tiptoed past them. Maybe they remembered my face from the morning or, most likely, they were too preoccupied with their futures to worry that much about some harmless-looking white guy carrying a schoolbag. So I wandered down the road without a care in the world, oblivious to the swarms of squabbling Filipinos heading in the opposite direction.

I first noticed them when I arrived at the next T-junction. There were six of them in total, mulling around a lone patch of grass to my right, all with M16 rifles slung ominously over their backs, looking incredibly badass. What especially pricked my interest about the group was that none of them was wearing military uniforms. Instead, they all seemed to have made a deliberate effort to look like civilians. I decided that they must have been either special forces, members of the Philippines National Police, or some form of a local militia. Who could tell? But whatever their station in life, I didn't necessarily have a good feeling about them, so I immediately spun a diagonal left to remove myself from their line of sight.

'Excuse me, sir! Please stop!'

Shit.

I came to a halt and wheeled around to face a muscular Filipino in his mid-thirties. Although I towered over his much smaller frame, a hard edge to his dark, grimy eyes suggested he was not someone to be taken lightly. 'My apologies, sir,' he said, almost too politely. 'Do you have a pass that allows you entry into the camp?'

'I am a student at the Defense College,' I explained. 'My driver is picking me up this afternoon, and he has my security pass with him.'

'I see.' He didn't look convinced, not by any stretch of the imagination. 'Do you have any other form of identification?'

'Yes, I have my embassy pass.' I plunged my hands into my pockets, and nothing. I looked inside my bag, and not there either. I patted myself down all over again in mild panic. Nope. *Damn it; I must have left my pass at the embassy.* I suddenly thought about Martina and how she forgot to bring her license with her on the day she was raped.

'Sorry, but I don't seem to have my embassy pass with me.'

My explanation was never going to wash with this guy. 'Please come with me, sir.'

'Look, I am a student at the Defense College!' I repeated.

'I am sure you are. But for the moment, you must come with me.'

I had no choice other than to obey his order and follow him. When we finally reached his companions, he pointed to a mound of dirt sitting in the middle of an open field and ordered me to sit down.

'Please ring the Defense College. They will tell you who I am.'

'I know what I have to do,' he replied rather testily. 'In the meantime, please sit down and be quiet.'

Despite the burning frustration building up inside of me, I decided not to test his patience for the moment. The ground was still damp from overnight rain, so I eased myself into a half squat position and then placed my bag underneath me. Once I was secure on the ground, one of the men casually walked over to me as if he was about to take my lunch order and then dangled a half-filled bottle of water in my face. I was in no mood to be grateful, so I carelessly dismissed him with an arrogant wave of my hand. He returned the favour by muttering something indiscernible in Tagalog—which his friends mostly found rip-roaringly funny—before pouring out the water in front of me. Not the best way to start forced confinement.

While my captors continued to share whispers inside the semicircle they had created for themselves, I tried to figure a way out of that mess without getting myself shot. The urgency of my situation became magnified when the leader pointed his rifle at my head and growled out those dreaded letters 'C-I-A' to his mates.

Estrada and his cronies had often insisted that the CIA was colluding with the opposition forces to destabilise the country. I understood the implications of this accusation better than anyone. Blaming America and the CIA was the standard public relations response for failing regimes when faced with a potential coup.

In summary, it didn't matter which side these guys supported. It was their erroneous conclusion that I was there to do something provocative that worried me the most. I was the guy who spent his childhood wanting to be James Bond. Now I was faced with the grim irony that I was alone and trapped in a foreign country, face to face with a bunch of baddies carrying loaded M16 rifles. But wasn't this the lifestyle I had always desired?

For the next hour, I sat aimlessly underneath a blazing afternoon sun, rubbing the mobile phone in my bag for comfort, looking for any opportunity to call the embassy. I was sure that Marty would be able to help me if only I could talk to him. Meanwhile, the group leader refused to contact anyone in authority as he had promised. Instead, he continued to walk up and down along a concrete pavement with his hands in his pockets as if I didn't even exist. But this was a deliberate strategy. You see, he was waiting for all the civilians to leave the base first before dealing with his captured CIA operative. That could involve handing me over to the authorities or putting a bullet in my head when no-one looked. In the Philippines, anything was possible.

I should have been scared shitless, but I didn't have the energy. What an idiot I was for not going home to my apartment when I had the chance. Even so, I was in no mood for self-reflection, and these guys were going to pay for my stupidity if it was the last thing I did. And in many ways, it almost was.

When the leader turned to complete his fiftieth lap of the pavement, I jumped to my feet and then lunged my way towards the group. As I heard my feet thudding loudly against the soft grass, I thought back to my conversation with Delilah in October and those words of wisdom from her father: *Sometimes in life, you have to stop pretending and show people the real person.*

Yes, the time had finally arrived to show the world exactly who I was: the talented, frustrated diplomat who could handle any volatile situation with tact, integrity, and decency. I was sure that by the end of the day, Delilah would have every reason to be immensely proud of me.

'Hey, fuckhead,' I shouted at the leader. 'What the fuck is going on? You said that you would contact the college and you haven't. You're a bloody liar!'

Unfortunately, on this occasion, my tact, integrity, and decency only went so far. The leader, stunned by the audacity of my verbal attack, puffed out something suitably cantankerous through his trembling lips before farting loudly. There was a stifled giggle or two from his mates—and perhaps even from me—but this didn't stop them from immediately squirrelling around him in defiance, their rifles pointing at my head.

'Please sit down, sir!' the leader barked. 'I won't ask you a second time.'

'You can all go fuck yourselves!' With my latest insult rattling around their dumbfounded faces, I quickly stampeded my way back towards the T-junction. Man, I couldn't even begin to describe how good I felt.

'Sir!' the leader screamed at me again. 'Stop! I order you to stop!'

Yeah, right. As if a thinly veiled threat from this scrapper would make any difference to me at this stage.

Click, click, click, click, click!

Okay, that might.

It was the unmistakable sound that rifles made when they were engaged from action to instant and primed, ready to fire.

'Choose your next move wisely, sir.'

It's amazing what goes through your head when you have seconds to live. Most people would spend these precious moments thinking about their families or loved ones and wishing they could see them one last time. Many more would take the opportunity to say one final prayer, just in case God was hovering up there, somewhere.

As for me? Well, at first, I was mainly preoccupied with the thought that being murdered in broad daylight in a strange country was a thoroughly appropriate way for my crazy, screwed-up life to end. Then to my astonishment, I realised that death would most likely mean that I would never get to see Liverpool Football Club win another English league title.

'Okay, take it easy,' I shouted at the leader. 'I'm turning around, okay?' The thought of missing out on another Liverpool title was too much for me to bear.

I silently walked back to the group, one hand grasping my bag, the other raised high in the air in defeat. Best to look compliant, I decided.

'My apologies,' said the leader as he ripped the bag away from my hand. 'I hope we did not frighten you?'

'I might have to sleep on that one and get back to you.'

The other men seemed to find my comment exceptionally funny and decided to ease springs for the moment. *There's no way we will waste a precious bullet on this joker,* they seemed to be thinking. Meanwhile, the leader continued to lecture me as if I was a runaway teenager.

'I told you that I would sort this out. Why didn't you listen to me?'

'You've done nothing but sit on your backside for the last hour,' I angrily replied. 'I just want to leave here before the situation deteriorates any further.'

'You should have thought about that before you entered a military base without any form of identification. If you were in my position, what would you do?'

I didn't answer him at first. Instead, I thought back to something that had happened to me a couple of years before. When I worked for the Department of Workplace Relations in 1998, I developed a negotiation skills training course for public service managers. Included in the manual that all attendees received at the start of the course was a list of different tactics that people could adopt during an industrial negotiation.

One tactic listed involved 'making false demands' to your opponent—in other words, trying to lead them astray by basically lying. You say something like: 'If you don't accept the one-dollar-a-week pay rise that I am offering you, I am going to sack everyone here and hire contractors instead.' Of course, in reality, you have no intention of sacking your staff at all. It's all a ruse to get the poor sucker on the other side of the table so scared by the threat that they cave in immediately.

However, when delivering the course, I never once suggested people should use such a nefarious ploy against their staff. As a former union industrial officer, I only informed my audience what to expect during most high-level negotiations. Rather, I encouraged them to apply the appropriate ethical standards when choosing their tactics. I mainly advocated the use of 'principled negotiation' during industrial disputes, where both parties focused on the key issues rather than personalities and positions.

Yet despite my good intentions and the popularity of the course, it didn't stop the union movement and the federal Labor opposition from seizing the manual and turning its contents into a ridiculous political issue.

The government encourages public service managers to lie to their staff! blared the newspaper headlines! You see, certain saintly people from the left tried to use this manual to demonstrate how the conservative government wanted bosses to crush workers everywhere! Never mind that no-one in the government knew that the course even existed or that many of its participants were actually union members! These were precisely the points I made to the local secretary of the public sector union at the time after I tended my resignation as a member over its handling of the affair.

In the end, the controversy washed over quickly. Still, as I faced the leader and his band of trigger-happy brigands in the middle of a revolution, I wondered whether it was time to reveal the true evil underbelly of the manual's desperate author. So I whisked it out from one of the many unused memory banks inside my brain and offered the leader a gruesome smile.

'The longer you hold me here, the worse it gets for you.'

'How so?' For the first time that afternoon, he looked vaguely worried.

'I am a close friend of General Rocho, the head of the armed forces.'

That was total rubbish, of course—I didn't know General Rocho from a bar of soap. But remember what happens when you make false demands in a negotiation? You get them frightened, and you get them thinking, and you get them questioning their own ludicrous position.

The group's leader corrected me. 'The former head of the armed forces.'

'Regardless,' I snapped back. 'He is still an especially important man in your country, and he won't be impressed when he discovers that you have harmed me.'

'How do I know you are telling the truth?'

'How do you know that I'm not?'

Incredibly, my total disregard for the facts seemed to have had an immediate impact. The leader began to nervously fidget with the strap on his rifle before shooting a conciliatory glance towards his colleagues. Their eyes all seemed to connect in one perfect Kumbaya moment.

'We never had any intention of harming you,' he said nervously. 'We just wanted to know who you are—for your protection.'

'Of course. Pointing six fully loaded rifles at my head was perfectly understandable in the circumstances.' I paused to see whether he appreciated my sarcasm before adding: 'To answer your question from before: if I were in your position, I would have done the same.'

That was what he wanted to hear. He calmly reached for my bag and tossed it against my chest.

'I suggest that you leave soon before things around here get much worse.'

'Thank you,' I replied, my heart thumping with euphoria. I had successfully dodged a bullet—literally—and was determined to get the fuck out of there at the speed of sound.

I wasn't prepared to allow him to change his mind. Before he even had time to say anything else, I charged headfirst down the road that led to the college, not looking behind me even once. To my enormous relief, I arrived at the college ten minutes later and found a small group of students and staff whooping it up around a barbecue.

'Hey!' Taffie cried out. 'What are you doing back here, mate?'

'Er … French lessons?'

'French lessons? Are you insane?'

I pointed to the crowd gathering around him. 'More's the question, what the hell are you guys doing here?'

'What does it look like we are doing? We are having a party.'

He flipped open a can of beer and passed it over to me. 'Here, I am sure you can use a drink.'

I sure could, and I swallowed the whole damn thing down in record time. After I tossed the empty can into a nearby bin, I described my ordeal to Taffie.

If I was expecting sympathy, he didn't indulge me. Instead, he shrugged his massive shoulders and smiled. 'What did you expect, mate? We are in the middle of a fucking coup!'

Thankfully, this latest round of insanity ended prematurely when a security guard told us to move on and go home. Taffie mysteriously disappeared into the afternoon shadows before I could say goodbye, and those left behind to fend for themselves included several of the college's research assistants and two classmates, Wilma and Howie. Professor Moreno employed some young female university graduates to assist her with running the college. They were all intelligent, lovely young women, and I was close to many of them. My favourite was a feisty twenty-something called Jade, who boasted a wide pair of bubbly eyes and a permanently cheeky grin. When she came over to say goodbye, I could see the worms of fear wriggle through her delicate cheekbones.

'Please be careful, Alex,' she said after giving me an extra tight hug. 'I don't know how this is all going to end.'

'We will see each other on Monday,' I promised her, and for a moment, I didn't want to leave her behind. However, I soon dawdled back down towards the car park, where Wilma and Howie were in deep conversation. Neither of them lived in Manila, so they stayed at the college's student hostel during the week. But they were also forced to leave Camp Aguinaldo with the rest of us, and they had nowhere to go for the night.

'You are both staying with me,' I insisted to their enormous relief. With this settled, we quickly gathered our things and decided what to do next. We eventually agreed that our best option was to walk out to EDSA and somehow find a taxi that would take us to Makati. It was almost three-thirty, tensions were rising, and there was no way I could see Hector and Harry being allowed back onto the base. When Harry saw the situation's futility, I was confident that he would return to San Lorenzo Village and wait for me to come home.

While this was indeed a sensible plan, it didn't take us long to realise that our escape might be more difficult than first envisaged. There were three main entrances to the base, and in my desire to avoid another confrontation, I suggested we make our way to the western entrance first. Once we were safely outside, we could detour along an adjoining road that led straight back to EDSA.

But as soon as we approached the gate, drowning in our afternoon sweat, a group of soldiers immediately waved us away. 'Go back to the main entrance,' a tough-looking sergeant informed us. 'You're not safe here.'

Unfortunately, after such a long, arduous walk, this change of plan didn't do much for our fading morale. Everywhere we looked, we saw soldiers barking out orders from behind their rifles or army lorries screeching up and down the road with extra fierce intent. If it wasn't apparent before then, things were starting to get profoundly serious. The thought of being caught in the middle of a random firefight was very much on our minds.

With no other option available to us, we reluctantly turned around and started to plough our way back towards the front gate through a row of flimsily constructed wooden huts. In the distance, automatic rifle fire snapped through the air, reminding me once again that during the 1986 revolution, the main fighting between the opposing factions occurred on the base.

We soon reached a clump of lonely trees standing next to another car park, and Wilma requested that we stop for a rest. With the sound of rifle fire still ringing in my ears, my immediate reaction was to keep going. But the oppressive heat and humidity had left all of us exhausted, so I pointed to a patch of shade, and we gratefully took a few moments to refresh ourselves away from the scorching sunlight.

While my friends chattered away in Tagalog, I reached into my carry bag and finally pulled out my mobile phone. For some reason, I had deliberately ignored its presence from the moment the group leader released me. Rather than drinking beer with Taffie, I would have better spent my time if I had asked him for a phone charger. But there was nothing I could do now, so I pressed a few buttons and waited to see if Harry or Marty had left a message for me on my voicemail. Once I fully activated the phone, an alert tone immediately roared from my screen.

Hi Alex. I hope U R well. I have booked Santiano's tonight for 7.30. C U then! Liki!

After everything I had endured, it was completely understandable that I wasted several precious seconds of the phone's remaining battery life by staring at the screen in utter bewilderment. At what point in my journey did I become the main character in a Filipino production of *Alex in Wonderland*? Was it just me, or was everyone in this city completely bonkers?

Recognising that I didn't have much time left, I tapped away at the keyboard.

Hi. A bit preoccupied actually, trying not 2 get killed. Suggest U turn UR TV on. U mite notice that the country is turning 2 shit. Alex.

Send.

I thought about calling the embassy before deciding that I really couldn't resist a follow-up text message to Liki. After all, I might never get an opportunity like this again.

P.S. Why didn't you tell me that you have two bebe?

Send.

Man, that felt good. But more often or not, there was always a price to pay for being a total prick. My penance on this occasion soon became apparent when I made that overdue call to the embassy only for my phone to go flat before the switchboard operator could even mutter hello. Disgruntled once again by my stupidity, I tossed this useless artefact back into my bag and called out for Wilma and Howie to join me.

We trudged unmolested through the simmering afternoon heat for another fifteen minutes before we finally dropped exhausted in front of the security gate. An eerie silence greeted our arrival, and I quickly deduced from the security guard's deadpan face that we were the last civilians to leave the base.

Regardless of this dubious honour, I was just relieved to have made it to EDSA alive, so I gazed thankfully into the heavens and promised God that I would be a much better church attendee from this point onwards. My belief in religion temporarily restored, I jumped onto the road in front of a slow-moving taxi and thrust streams of peso notes in front of the driver's confused face.

'Here!' I yelled at him. 'Three thousand pesos. It's all yours if you take us to San Lorenzo Village right now.'

One should never underestimate the power of entrepreneurism during a revolution because the driver immediately pushed out his pearly false teeth until they almost fell onto his lap and then invited us all to jump inside. Before long, he was spinning his wheels in and out of every tiny crack in the road he could find.

I became temporarily lost within an ocean of car horns, burnt rubber, and falsetto screaming. But nothing could ameliorate the feeling of elation when we eventually sped down San Lorenzo Drive and found Harry and Hector sitting calmly on the bonnet of the Land Rover, parked right in front of my apartment.

We gave ourselves plenty of time to enjoy a three-way man-hug. I had never been happier to see two people in my life. After we staggered inside and guzzled some cold drinks, Harry explained what had happened to him and Hector. They discovered that things were escalating in Manila before lunch and had quickly decided to cancel their afternoon meetings. They tried several times unsuccessfully to enter Camp Aguinaldo only to be turned away on each occasion by angry security guards. Harry then desperately tried to call me on my cell phone, not knowing, of course, that it had been out of action for much of the day. As I predicted, his army reserve officer training had come to the fore, and he decided to return to that one guaranteed rendezvous point that he knew was safe—my apartment.

I soon encouraged Hector to return home to his wife, and the four of us then crumpled wearily in front of CNN. Watching a coup unfold in real-time made us very hungry indeed, so I ordered some pizza, rocked out a few beers, and soon we were having a mini party in our dining room. Harry took a wonderful photo of me lying on a couch, a can of beer in my hand, humbly satisfied that I would get to see Liverpool play another game on the weekend.

Later that night, when everyone else was tucked away safely in bed, I thought about how close I came to being killed. I wasn't sure how I felt about that yet, but I did know that my nine lives were fast running out. I thought about Martina and how, like her, I had been exposed to a life-threatening situation—alone, afraid, and hell-bent on survival. While I bluffed my way out of a thorny confrontation, unharmed and unrepentant, Martina had been less fortunate. Sometimes in life, there was a fine line between hope and despair.

Marlena once said that Martina lived on the edge of a rainbow. That exactly described how I felt about my crazy existence. Even my jigsaw puzzle was struggling to keep up with me. There would come a time soon—I was sure of it—when I would inevitably fall off the edge. When I did, my only hope was that someone would be there to catch me before I joined Martina in the abyss. But for now, all I could do was marvel at my genius for reckless adversity and rejoice in the fact that I had beaten Ringo Bingo at his own game.

As for the Philippines, well, just like in 1986 when people power ignited hope for everyone in the world living under tyranny, the strength and will of its resilient citizens prevailed once again. The following afternoon, Gloria Arroyo defied Estrada's call for an election and took the oath of office in the crowd's presence at the EDSA Shrine. Thirty minutes later, President Estrada announced he would relinquish the presidency and then planned for his escape. He officially resigned from office later that afternoon.

I could never really decide whether this was a win for the people or a calculated, illegal grab for power by Arroyo and her supporters. What I did know, however, was that on 20 January 2001, the course of Filipino history changed, and I somehow made a ludicrous contribution to that story. Not bad for a skinny kid from Gladstone who once dreamt about saving the world.

At the height of tensions that afternoon, Harry and I watched closely on television as a large group of protesters began to march towards the historic Mendiola Bridge, determined to force Estrada to resign. A shiny black Land Rover crawled at the head of this ramshackle crusade, its familiar grey headlights glimmering in the afternoon sunshine. When a muscular arm jolted its way out of the window and purposefully directed a group of people on the side of the road to fall back behind the vehicle, I immediately realised that Arroyo had won the day. Yes, Ramon had finally picked the winning side, and for the Philippines, there was no going back.

Two Little Girls

Mindanao
May 2001

By the time I completed a tour of the village, filthy black grime had smothered my shirt, and the brutal midday sun was frying out my brain. A murder of crows squawked voraciously over my head, eagerly waiting for my demise, so I reached into my backpack and took leave of my last bottle of water to make a point.

After taking a drink, I slumped next to a splintered telephone pole. The foul aroma of animal faeces and rotting fruit swamped the air around me. A grey, skinny dog with its bitch against the world emerged from behind a palm tree, huffing and puffing angrily at my growing shadow. He casually sniffed at the foreign odour of my aftershave before I ended his demonic wailing with a loud clap of my hands.

'Go shit somewhere else, Fido,' I muttered as it dived back into the foliage.

Satisfied with my work, I slowly walked back towards our car, dreaming of the refreshing swim and cold iced tea waiting for me in my Davao hotel. But as much as I tried, the prospect of civilisation couldn't mask the despair I felt after my brief walk through the broken streets of this dying community.

Four months had passed since my epic adventures during the EDSA II Revolution, but it felt like a lifetime ago. While Manila remained a hotbed of political intrigue, I had focused my energies on finishing that damn thesis before the next national crisis threatened to terminate my overseas posting.

Even last week's seminal events, when a group of Estrada supporters attempted an unsuccessful countercoup against the Arroyo government, failed to excite my treacherous curiosity. During the height of the tensions in Manila, I had ignored all those missed calls from friends and lovers and locked myself away within the dungeons of my apartment until it was safe to go outside. Maybe, at last, I had learnt something about personal commitment.

This was my third trip to Mindanao since January and the last opportunity to validate my field findings before submitting my paper in early June. So far during my stay, I interviewed a former Islamic freedom fighter in a McDonald's restaurant, chatted with a lovely old nun who served me fairy cake and tea, and lectured a prominent local businessman about my plan to achieve prosperity in his village.

But I needed more. To give my paper that cutting edge, that one special thing that would make it stand out from the others, I had to experience Mindanao's economic dislocation for myself. So, that morning, I paid a local Davao driver three thousand pesos to take me on a high-speed masterclass through the middle of tiger country.

Of course, I was taking one hell of a gamble. Mindanao had become a clearing house for every ambitious Islamic terrorist and power-hungry warlord in Southeast Asia. I was sure they would have loved nothing better than to get their greedy hands on a smarmy, white Australian like me. I would be worth ten thousand dollars on the kidnap/blackmail market at least. *Yes, imagine that! Me!*

Fortunately, I had floated through my two previous trips unscathed. After surviving an excursion to the island of Basilan, the birthplace of the Abu Sayyaf—where my army escort got lost on his way to the local army base—I then wandered carelessly by myself through the streets of Zamboanga, one of the most dangerous cities in the Philippines, and was hailed an all-conquering hero by the good folk of Pagadian.

I was a great believer that familiarity did, indeed, breed contempt. Although my presence in this forbidden world may have initially generated mild curiosity amongst the locals, it was merely a temporary aberration, a whimsical extravagance that briefly enriched their desolate lives before it, too, became another unwanted memory. Each new day, as more people passed me on these silent, murky streets, their heads bowed in ignorance, I somehow felt safer there than I ever did in Manila.

That was the third village my driver and I had visited that day, but I wondered whether anyone else in the Philippines was aware that this morbid graveyard of humanity even existed for, if they had, they would surely understand why Islamic extremism in Mindanao was on the rise. I mean, what hope did these people have for a better life? No health, no education, no capacity for personal advancement. My father had often said that if you removed hope from people, you removed their sense of worth. Generally speaking, people who felt worthless usually had no loyalty to the government.

Although it was marked on my map as a village, in truth, it was merely a collection of rusted-on shanties and dilapidated wooden boxes. Inside lay swarms of miserable wretches, all of whom were victims of the burning heat and suffocating red dust that swelled up like mini-tornados from the ground. The village may have survived for centuries, but finally, its luck was running out.

Perhaps I never really understood poverty until this very moment. Oh, I had seen examples of similar devastation throughout Metro Manila, but I was far too busy having a good time with my new friends to let it consume me. But this was different; these hapless surroundings reflected a cruel subjugation by a government that didn't care anymore. Those I had spoken to in Manila before leaving on this trip considered these travesties merely a consequence of God's will. Yet if Manila's God had decided this for his people, he was a heartless false idol and no friend of mine.

A group of dirty young children crawled out from the bottom of a clump of corrugated iron and considered me with suspicious eyes. As I watched them closely, a little boy with a mop of curly hair found the courage to tug at my shirt.

'Hello, mister,' he said, exposing his missing front teeth. 'You American? GI Joe?' The other children—two boys and a cute little girl—laughed at his audacity and then ran towards me, their tight bodies ramming into each other as they tried to wrap themselves around my legs.

I squatted to my knees and rewarded them with an approving smile. Whatever the state of my mood, I could never turn my back on a Filipino child, and I wondered ruefully when these poor little devils had last received a proper meal.

'No, I am Australian,' I replied. 'Do you know where Australia is?' *Of course they don't, you idiot.*

I reached into my backpack once again and quickly found the object of my search. The sight of my chocolate bar immediately created a chorus of delighted squeals, and I calmly broke off four equal portions. Without recourse to the civility they had never known, they greedily snatched the pieces out of my hand and devoured them within seconds.

As I admired their tragic innocence, I retreated to the memories of my own childhood, trapped as they were inside a lost corner of the universe. My posting was supposed to have healed the twin wounds of broken love and a devastating past. And for a short time, I thought it was working. But ever since the coup, caught inside a culture I never really understood, I found myself fighting a moral crusade that struck at the very heart of my existence.

I wanted to be a better person. But in my pursuit of the perfect solution, I had abandoned every principle from which I had previously sought comfort. Faith, compassion, honesty—they were all useless baubles to me. Instead of denouncing the corrupt and greedy Manila society in my paper, I released myself from this burden and ignored the truth. In doing so, I had become equally culpable for the desperation that prevailed throughout the country.

In my shame, I had become a hollow man, a pathetic man, unsure of my purpose and what I was trying to prove thousands of miles away from Australia. At least within the lavish, suburban sanctuary of Canberra, I had stood for something: career, money, self-indulgence; there was indeed a method to my madness. But there in that godforsaken place, in front of those four beautiful children, I had become nothing. They may have led impoverished lives, but they were better human beings than I would ever be.

I suddenly felt a bony hand scrape my shoulder. I swivelled around to find an old lady glaring at me, her wrinkled, brown face scarred with tears. For a moment, I assumed that she was the grandmother to one of these children. So, I picked up the chocolate wrapping from the ground and waved it in front of her eyes. 'I gave them some chocolate, that's all. Don't be afraid.'

The old lady's grip on my shoulder tightened. 'Please? You a good man? You a good man?'

Despite my self-loathing, I pushed my face towards her. 'Yes, I am a good man,' I hopelessly lied.

She began to cry. 'Please help me. My granddaughter is very sick.'

I didn't want to give her false hope, so I shook my head wildly. 'I am not a doctor.' I comically tried to mimic a stethoscope to emphasise the point further, but she didn't understand. 'You need a doctor,' I repeated.

The old woman squeezed my shoulder even tighter and, with an incredible strength that belied her wizened frame, she dragged me closer towards her. 'No, you a good man. You help us, please.'

I looked at the four children for inspiration, their innocent giggling urging me forward.

'Okay, I will help you.' The old lady bowed her head several times before leading me down a maze of putrid streets. She eventually invited me inside a rusted tin shed cramped in between two wilting palm trees. I walked into a single room smothered by a ferocious, stifling heat and the smell of rotting fish. She pointed to a simple wooden bed with one of her skeletal fingers, and I observed a middle-aged woman frantically wiping the forehead of a little girl. Two little boys were by their mother's side, holding hands and sobbing while their sister lay prostrate on the bed.

The mother turned to face me, her red eyes filled with a relentless fear. She muttered something to me in her local dialect, but when I raised my hands to indicate that I didn't understand, she reverted to broken English: 'She is boiling.'

I politely pushed aside the two boys and bent over to discover an elfish little figure stretched out on the bed. She couldn't be more than five years old. Her long black hair hung limply around the bottom of her neck and her cute little nose glittered in the sunlight. Next to her sat an old, raggedy doll, which stared at me accusingly with pitch-black eyes.

'Hello, princess,' I whispered, brushing away a lock of tangled hair dangling from her forehead. 'You're such a pretty girl.' I held her tiny little hand and rubbed my fingers along her wrist until I found a pulse. To my horror, her heart was beating violently.

I thought about all those travel warnings I had received from Marty before I first visited Mindanao in late January. This whole village was likely to be Malaria Central, and there was nothing to suggest that the family had taken the necessary precautions to protect themselves from this debilitating disease. Whether my diagnosis was right or wrong, it was evident that she needed urgent medical assistance. But did I risk taking her to a hospital in Davao, or should I try and find a local doctor?

The little girl released yet another painful moan. Despite my rising anxiety, the girl's mother stared at me in hopeful anticipation, as if I might magically click my fingers and suddenly perform some outrageous miracle that would cure her daughter.

'We have to take her to Davao,' I informed her. 'She needs a doctor.'

While the mother sought guidance from the grandmother, I was fast losing my patience. 'She needs a doctor urgently,' I repeated.

Both women huddled away into a corner as if my presence was no longer necessary. They began to scream at each other in those high-pitched, sing-song shrieks that sometimes grated my mind in this country. Meanwhile, my driver, who had been following me around like some misguided disciple, mercifully entered the house. I quietly took him aside and asked him to explain to the two women in their dialect that I wanted to take the little girl to a hospital in Davao. He squinted his eyes, then interrupted them with a snarling cough. After more senseless chatter, he frowned at me.

'I am afraid they won't allow you to do that.'

I growled out the usual Alex Gerrick swear words under my breath before inspecting the girl once again. Tiny droplets of phlegm trickled down from the side of the girl's mouth, and her raggedy doll begged me to do something quickly. It dawned on me that the girl was slowly dying, and there wasn't a damn thing I could do about it.

'For God's sake, this is serious!' I shouted at the room. The other two children shuddered at the brutality of my outburst and rushed over to hug their ailing mother, bawling their scared little eyes out. Suddenly I had become the school bully trapped inside a pyramid of his cowardice.

'Her husband is a fisherman, and he is away for the next three nights,' my driver explained. 'He will be angry if they let you take her without his permission.'

What sort of insane joke was this? Her daughter was dying, and all she was worried about was what her husband would think if we left without him?

I gazed at the grandmother in desperation, figuring that she was my only hope. Was I not the good man who had promised to help her granddaughter? Maybe I could somehow reach inside that patch of common sense that encouraged her to approach me in the first place.

'Please understand,' I begged her. 'She will not last one more day. She needs urgent medical attention, and I have to take her to the hospital in Davao. We cannot wait any longer.'

The old lady's frightened eyes offered a patch of sympathy, but before she was allowed to talk, her daughter shouted: 'We must wait!'

Given my track record, this was the perfect time to lose the plot. Just like I did at Camp Aguinaldo, I found myself swearing and shrieking inside a bubble of my vanity. But it achieved absolutely nothing. You see, the negotiation manual I had written several years ago offered no advice about what you should do when faced with an irrational mother protecting her child.

Unfortunately, the only thing that my tantrum succeeded in doing was hardening the mother's resolve. She ordered me to leave the house, the anger caught within her scaly hands rising in tandem with the frightened groans of her sick daughter. I was no longer her saviour but a man who had lost his right to be heard.

But I had one last card to play. Before I left, I instructed the driver to tell her that I would find a doctor. That seemed to calm things down a little, and the mother thankfully stopped her incessant wailing. Hoping that I had secured some common ground, at last, I leaned over the little girl and stroked her hair one last time. Red-hot tears burned my cheeks.

'I will be back soon, sweetheart, I promise.' She didn't understand a word I was saying to her, but I liked to think that her eyes blinked in gratitude. Through my tears, I noticed a tattered copy of the Holy Koran sitting on the kitchen table. Maybe this was the only hope we had. *Please Allah, God, whoever—don't let her die.*

I picked up the damp, ragged cloth next to the girl's pillow and poured some more water over it. I handed it over to the girl's mother and explained slowly: 'Keep her cool, do you understand?' However, the mother snatched the cloth from my hand as if I had contaminated it irreparably with my blasphemy.

I waved to my driver, and we stumbled together into the churning sun. His endless sneering made me wish I had brought Hector with me on this trip. 'We need to find medical assistance quickly, or that little girl will die. Do you know if there is a doctor or a hospital in this area?'

He scratched his chin. 'We see a policeman, for he will know what to do.'

I didn't want to waste precious time looking for a police officer, but what choice did I have? I was a stranger in these parts. There were no Yellow Pages or ambulances or emergency lines to assist me. I was operating in the middle of nowhere, where no rules of normalcy applied. So we drove through a grid of lonely streets before we thankfully arrived at a wooden hut, with the letters *PNP* signposted across a letterbox.

The policeman on duty was a kind but bellicose man who listened to our tale with the occasional twitch of his pink cracked lips. When I finished speaking, he belched loudly and then folded a fleshy arm over his enormous pot belly.

'You have to understand the local culture,' he explained in rapid English. 'An infidel like you can't walk into a Muslim house and demand to take a child away from their parents. Do you understand? That's not going to get you anywhere.'

'You can all sue me later,' I replied. 'We need to find someone who can help that little girl.'

'There is a doctor who lives in the adjoining village, but we may not find him in time. So I agree with you that the best option is to take her to Davao. I will see if I can coax the mother into releasing her into my custody.'

As we jumped into our respective vehicles, I was, at last, hopeful that we had a chance —a small one, but an opportunity, nevertheless. *Please hang on, sweetheart. For the love of God, please hang on.* But when we returned to the hut several minutes later, all I could hear were the echoes of the dead calling out my name.

It was almost impossible to describe how I felt. Every living organ inside of me disintegrated at the same time. Although I could not hear myself speak, I could feel my mouth cry out the word 'No!' repeatedly until it blocked out every sound that the universe had ever made. Then the hollow man without a soul, who somehow thought he could save a little girl on his own, fell to his knees and howled at the sun.

The earth stood still for several minutes before I dared raise my head. Several interested onlookers, crowding around the hut, sneered at my pathetic form. Meanwhile, the policeman crept silently towards me and kindly helped me to my feet.

'She is dead, I'm afraid,' he informed me. I nodded my understanding and then wept some more. When I eventually found a way to compose myself, I wiped away the rampant red dust from my jeans and waited for the policeman to tell me what to do next.

'Do you want to see her?' he asked.

'No,' I replied. 'I should return to Davao.'

'It wasn't your fault,' he lied. 'You did your best, and sadly, you would never have got that little girl to Davao in time. From what I understand, she had been sick for several days, but they were waiting for the father to return. He is a fisherman.'

'So was Peter,' I mumbled back at him.

'I beg your pardon?'

'It doesn't matter.' I thanked the policeman for his help and then asked him one last favour. 'Please tell the grandmother I am sorry that I couldn't keep my promise to her.'

'Don't do this to yourself,' he implored. 'There is no way you could have saved her.'

'Of course not,' I replied. 'How does a man who cannot save himself save the precious life of a little girl?'

Somewhere in Italy, I could see Marlena clapping her hands in delight. 'Finally, you get it, Alex!' she hollered triumphantly. 'Finally, you get it!'

As I slowly began to walk along the main road, a pair of young fruit sellers suddenly appeared behind a ditch and tried to block my path. Even though they must have known that I wasn't interested, they nevertheless pushed their daily produce of half-rotten melons and bananas right into my face. 'Hey, Joe, buy our fruit!' they demanded. I did my best to ignore them with an angry crack of my arm, but it only encouraged them to persevere.

Their constant hissing and cajoling only made me angrier. A little girl from their miserable community, the daughter of people they had probably known all their lives, had just died, and their main priority was to take my money? Was this all there was? Did the life of one innocent little girl mean nothing in this place other than a bunch of half-ripe bananas?

I didn't want to answer that question anymore. Instead, I roughly targeted the youngest of the two men—a tall, stinking skeleton with a lace of seashells strung around his scrawny neck—and wrestled a watermelon from his hands. Laughing at the terror pouring out from his treacherous eyes, I raised the melon high above my head with all my strength and then slammed it into the dirty ground beneath me, splitting it into a thousand atoms.

'You are all *fucking savages!'* I shouted at them. 'Do you hear me? *Fucking savages!'* I reached into my pocket and threw several one-hundred-peso notes into the air. 'Here! Money is the only thing that matters in this fucked-up place. Take it *all!'*

Ignoring the barbarity of my meltdown, the men began to claw savagely at the paper notes as they slowly floated above their heads, laughing and whistling at their good fortune. Inside this bizarre paradox of human existence, I wondered whether I was any better than them.

My driver jingled his keys in front of me, his arrogant face locked in a silent grin. At this point, I seriously thought about smashing a fist into his dirty, rotten teeth, but I decided that there had been enough tears for one day. 'Take me back to Davao,' I barked at him.

The afternoon sun licked fiercely at my face. As I followed him down the road, I could see another little girl crying near a broken tree stump, her dirty hair rustling to the sound of a sweltering breeze. If I didn't know any better, I would swear I was watching a videotape of the little girl who had just died. *What sick joke was this?*

I ran towards her, skipping past a feral cat that screamed out at me in a fury. When the little girl stood to greet me, I pushed my hand against her chin, half-expecting it to melt straight through her like one of Ringo Bingo's evil apparitions. But when I only felt flesh and bone, I realised that I was staring at the little girl I had given chocolate to earlier that afternoon.

'What's wrong, darling?' I asked softly, her tears spilling over my sunburnt wrist.

'I can't find my brothers,' she cried.

'Don't worry,' I reply. 'I know where your brothers are. I will take you to them now.' I took hold of her filthy little hand, and we slowly walked together until we reached my car. Her brothers were exactly where I last saw them, throwing tiny pebbles at a shattered soft drink bottle. The little girl immediately dropped my hand in delight and tumbled headfirst into their dirty little bodies.

After a flurry of needless hugs and kisses, the boys hopefully turned their eyes towards my backpack, in the vain chance that I still had more chocolate to give them. But to their disappointment, I merely dropped to my haunches in exhaustion and pointed at their delicate little sister.

'Promise me that you will never abandon her again.' The boys carefully studied my parched lips, their bony fingers twitching in shame.

'Okay, Joe,' the oldest brother promised.

'Good. Now, please take your sister home.'

Perhaps their pitiful, innocent little minds understood why my heart was full of pain. But more likely, my usefulness to their cause had come to an abrupt end, and they became distracted by that damn feral cat instead. Within seconds, they scampered down the road in hot pursuit of their new target without even saying goodbye.

As I remained frozen to the ground, the little girl suddenly darted away from the rest of the group and sprinted back towards me as if she sensed the world was finally welcoming her to another life. When she reached me, she took careful aim, nuzzled her neck into my sweaty face, and hugged me tightly. With that one lonely gesture, she giggled, gathered up her filthy skirt, and ran out of my life forever.

Brother Rojo

Manila
May 2001

Later that evening, as I lay wasted on my bed, staring mournfully at the half-crescent moon, I suddenly realised that my tragic visit to the village hadn't been an accident. Like everything else in my life, the little girl's death had been preordained inside my secret jigsaw puzzle. Given that every piece had finally been twisted in together, it painted a horrifying picture of my demise.

What I hadn't expected, though, what I hadn't understood until I boarded the flight to Manila the next day, was that some of us were allowed to complete a second puzzle. While I was asleep, the Spiders had hit the reset button on my life to ensure that I fulfilled my obligations to their insidious cause. And to prove my allegiance, as soon as I entered my San Lorenzo apartment, I calmly flushed my old puzzle down the toilet bowl and went searching for a new product that would help guide the rest of my life.

But where do you start when you are close to forty and everything you thought you knew about yourself was an absolute lie? Sure, I had picked up some valuable tips along the way from people like Sally and Delilah on how I might be able to live a more fulfilling life. But I needed more; I needed someone to guide me through the darkness before it finally consumed me forever.

But finding such a person wouldn't be easy. I had already exhausted far too many relationships in my shameless pursuit of salvation. Furthermore, when you considered my endless stream of personal disasters, I doubted whether anyone would have the patience or nous to take on such a challenging task.

However, as with so many other things in my story, I had misjudged the good intentions of others. For when I finally threw in the towel and accepted that the world was no longer my saviour, Brother Rojo emerged from beneath a pale, red sky and somehow found *me*.

He first came to my attention back in January when I was part of a delegation of ten Defense College students touring Western Mindanao on a fact-finding mission. We had spent much of our time skirting the coastline of the Zamboanga peninsula in a navy patrol boat, occasionally bludgeoning our way into selected townships to discuss the Islamic insurgency with the local population.

On the day we visited Pagadian, the second-largest city in the province, we attended a sumptuous lunch sponsored by the local mayor. I spent the first half-hour accosted by an awful woman from some foreign consulate, who smelt like blue-vein cheese and who sincerely believed all poor people should be permanently locked up in ghettos. Thankfully, a local priest offered me a glass of punch and a coffee-stained smile, so I used his intervention as the perfect excuse to leave her stranded next to a mosquito net.

Inevitably, our conversation turned to my thesis, and I asked the priest whether he had any unique insights on how Christians and Muslims could work more effectively together. To his credit, he provided me with some valuable anecdotes before adding: 'However, the real expert on this topic is a man called Brother Rojo.'

'Brother Rojo?' I replied. 'Does he live in Padagian?'

'No, he doesn't,' said the priest, laughing raucously at my ignorance. 'Brother Rojo is a citizen of the world; he doesn't call any particular place his home.'

'Why is that?'

'Many reasons, but mainly because he is a man still searching for answers.'

'Sounds like my sort of guy.'

'Please don't be fooled by his never-ending quest for knowledge,' the priest continued with a slight frown. 'He is the wisest man I have ever known. However, his wisdom has also become his curse.'

'Where can I find him?'

'The last I heard, he was recuperating in Baguio after a recent illness, but he never stays in the one place for too long. Let me make some enquiries, and I will get back to you.'

We politely exchanged phone numbers and left it that. Months went by with no contact when, out of the blue, I received a text message from the priest on the day that I left for my most recent trip to Mindanao.

Brother Rojo is living in Manila. He is happy to meet with U. His number is …

I took a punt and called Brother Rojo from the airport before I boarded my flight. After several unanswered rings, his phone went to the message bank, so I left him my contact details and waited for him to return my call. He never did, so I decided not to pursue him any further.

By the time I returned to Manila, I had forgotten entirely about Brother Rojo until I noticed another missed call on my mobile phone. When I dialled back the number, a high-pitched voice answered, inviting me to attend a morning tea with him at his house the next morning.

'Thank you, Brother Rojo,' I replied, having not yet decided whether I would turn up or not. You see, my main focus was not on him or my thesis, but solely on my upcoming date that night with Charisma, a rather attractive Filipina flight attendant that I met a month or so ago inside the main bar at the Shangri-La Hotel. At the time, I was hiding under a table from Liki, who I had dumped just minutes before.

'You are quite funny for an utter slimeball,' Charisma may have said to me later in the evening, perhaps after I bought her the third bottle of expensive champagne. 'But are you wealthy?'

'You bet I am,' I lied. 'Just ask my bartender back in Australia.'

She didn't laugh; she didn't call me a dickhead; she didn't do anything. She just sat there on a stool, glaring at me with those huge chocolate eyes, wondering whether it wasn't too late to latch onto some other single guy in the bar. But, to her credit, she decided to persevere with me for a little longer. So we consulted our little black books and finally agreed that this evening would be the perfect opportunity for our next dalliance.

But, as I was to find out, sharing your first date with a girl's close friends is a sure-fire recipe for disaster. A connection between me, Charisma, and six of her flight attendant buddies was never going to work. Besides, she was far too distracted with that handsome French pilot—who had conveniently, miraculously, fortuitously bumped into our group at nine-thirty—to pay too much attention to me. Suitably chastened, I did the gentlemanly thing by sneaking off to another bar and getting drunk with a couple of English guys who I vaguely knew through the embassy.

I woke up that morning with another booming headache, my male pride ruthlessly dented and my mobile phone vibrating out of control, courtesy of the indomitable Brother Rojo. I secretly hoped that he was going to cancel the meeting. But instead, his primary purpose was to harass me with a series of precise questions aimed at my preference for tea or coffee and the type of biscuits I liked. *Damn it! I can't put it off now; I have to go.*

Despite the malevolence of my hangover, I somehow staggered out of bed and crawled to the shower. After I snapped on a pair of jeans and a Filipino barong, I managed to fall downstairs without injuring myself before calling out for Hector. Concerned for my safety, Fely handed me a boiling black coffee and reminded me that I had given Hector the week off. I used our conversation as an excuse to throw some more water over my face and then walked down to Makati on my two wobbly legs to find a taxi.

Fifteen minutes later, I was staring at an old wooden shack that supposedly functioned as a presbytery. An old nun in a fading grey habit greeted me at the front gate and advised that Brother Rojo lived at the back of the main building. I jumped through a couple of broken fences, tiptoed past a rabid dog, and then strode straight into a rickety old hut, barely floating on a set of wooden pillars.

I knocked several times on something resembling a screen door, only to be greeted by the hugest rat I had ever seen. After exchanging business cards and briefly chatting about the weather, a squat little figure emerged into the sunlight. Even without my glasses, he immediately reminded me of Mister Toad from *The Wind in the Willows.*

Indeed, he couldn't have been more than five feet tall, with huge, goblin eyes and a tumbling, flat nose.

'Good to meet you, Mister Gerrick,' Brother Rojo said warmly. 'Please come inside.'

The first thing I noticed when I entered the main living room was a pungent aroma—as if a flock of seagulls had just crapped out countless balls of marijuana onto the splintered floor.

'Do you like my incense?' he suddenly asked, with a hopeful smile.

'It's very unusual,' I replied as politely as I could. I didn't want to tell Brother Rojo so early in our relationship that the smell made me want to throw up.

He pointed to a bamboo chair, and after I sat down, he shuffled over to a white stove. 'Are you sure that lemongrass tea is fine?'

'Yes, thank you.'

Brother Rojo pottered around in silence before dropping two steaming white cups and a plate of assorted biscuits onto a coffee table separating our two chairs.

He inspected my bulging head and politely asked, 'Are you feeling okay, Mister Gerrick?'

I tried to hide my embarrassment as best as I could. 'I'm sorry, but I had a very late night. I must look terrible.'

'How a person may or may not look doesn't concern me,' he said with a crooked smile. 'I am only interested in what prevails inside a man's heart.'

'Then I am likely to disappoint you even more.'

'Let me be the judge of that, Mister Gerrick.'

'Please, call me Alex.'

We saluted each other with our cups of tea before Brother Rojo bounced into his chair.

'If I'm honest, you're not what I expected,' he said.

'How so?'

'I thought you would be much younger.'

'I'm actually twenty-five,' I told him. 'But all my partying has finally caught up with me.'

He laughed again. 'No, I meant to say that you sounded younger on the phone. That's a compliment, I should think.'

'Thanks, I'll take it,' I said. 'Rest assured; I don't bite.'

'Of course not; you look harmless enough.'

'That much I can guarantee.'

I didn't reveal too much of my background at first. Just where I was from, what I was doing in the Philippines, that sort of stuff. I didn't want to scare him senseless so soon into our meeting. Besides, his story was far more interesting than mine.

'I was born in Manila during the war,' he commenced. 'My mother was the daughter of wealthy landowners, and her parents were able to flush most of their money out of the country just before the Japanese invaded.'

He proceeded to tell me how his family suffered the most extreme brutalities during the city's two-and-a-half-year occupation. His grandfather was shot for being a spy on Christmas Day 1942, and both his grandmother and mother were savagely gang-raped in their backyard by a squad of Japanese soldiers. At some point during this attack, his mother, who was sixteen, must have fallen pregnant.

'Unfortunately, Alex,' he said wistfully, 'my mother didn't celebrate my birth. I hope you understand.'

'Only too well,' I replied calmly. 'A friend of mine was brutally raped during the recent war in the former Yugoslavia, which devastated her.'

And me.

'Yes,' he replied. 'No woman should have to experience such terrible things. My mother didn't handle this outrage very well and wanted nothing more to do with me after my birth. It was my grandmother who cared for me until the war was over. To hide the family embarrassment, they shipped me over to America on the first boat they could find to live with my grandfather's brother.'

'I'm so sorry. That's a heartbreaking story.'

He seemed impressed by my unnatural empathy. 'Thank you, Alex. But it was probably for the best. My mother eventually killed herself not long after I left the Philippines, you see. So I consider myself lucky that I didn't have to witness that terrible event. Besides,' he added with a reflective smile, 'my uncle, as I called him, and his wife both treated me like their own son. It doesn't shame my mother to say that I still consider them to be my real parents.'

He went on to explain how he inherited much of his family's wealth after his mother died. That paid for a university degree in economics and law in a prestigious American university and then a round-the-world trip that lasted almost three years.

'I must have travelled to nearly every country on Earth,' he joked.

'Even Australia?'

'Even Australia,' he said, with a hastily composed Australian accent. '*How ya going, cobber? Dry as a dead dingo's dick!*'

We laughed some more, and I decided that I liked him very much.

'So what made you transition from international jetsetter to a man of the cloth?' I asked inquisitively.

'A good question,' he said. 'One morning—in Mexico, I think it was—I had a vision from God and realised that no woman would ever find my unusual form attractive.'

'That's very unfair on yourself,' I tried to lie.

'Unfair, perhaps, but an uncontroversial assessment, nevertheless. As you Australians would say, I'm no oil painting. If we are both being truthful, I look like Mister Toad from *The Wind in the Willows*, don't you think?'

I said nothing at first as we both struggled to deal with my obvious embarrassment. 'You said yourself that looks mean nothing,' I eventually replied.

'Of course they don't!' he exclaimed. 'Besides, I knew since university that my calling involved a higher plane which extended beyond the temptations of the flesh. So, I eventually joined a monastery in Italy and took my vows with the Marist order a few years later.'

'And your inheritance?' I asked boldly.

'I have given most of it away to the church, although I have enough to keep me comfortable in my final years.'

I stared at his tattered sandals and sweat-stained *barong* and decided that he was lying for my benefit.

Half an hour had passed, and I began to wonder how I should divert his conversation to my topic of interest without appearing rude and ungracious. But I need not have worried. After pouring himself another cup of tea, he began to regurgitate a detailed account of his twenty years working as a counsellor and peace coordinator in Mindanao.

Accompanied by the occasional rasping cough, he recounted a spellbinding tale of military conflict, religious intolerance, bureaucratic bumbling, and lost opportunities. Whenever he spoke about something that made him especially angry, his mouse-like ears would bend underneath the tips of his sagging jowls, and he would hiss out his words with a fierce intensity. When he finished speaking, I felt pretty deflated.

'After listening to your story, I'm no longer certain that my thesis makes any sense,' I muttered gloomily.

'Nonsense,' he scolded me. 'Your theory is a very sound one. I agree with you that poverty and economic dislocation are the main reasons why some Muslim men are turning to crime and terrorism. But simply throwing money at the problem won't fix things, not by a long shot. You also have to win their souls, Alex. That's the tricky part.'

His imperfect smile temporarily made me feel better about myself. He sure had a way about him. 'You tried, though?'

'Yes, I did.' He took a few mouthfuls of tea before dropping his arms into his lap. 'Have you ever put your trust in someone, thinking that they were doing the right thing by you, only to find out that they weren't?'

I quietly nodded. 'Yes, I have. When I first moved to Canberra in 1985, I met an older man who convinced me that he could help me with my career. For the next two years, he led me on a wild goose chase before I eventually found out that he was a complete fraud and playing with me for his amusement.'

'Why do you think it took you so long to work this out?'

I could see the man's dark, swarthy features as clear as day as if he were sitting in a chair next to us. 'I was young and gullible, I guess.'

'Nothing more?'

I gently sucked on my lip. 'Okay, I wanted to believe him; I was so desperate to succeed that I couldn't see beyond his deceit.' *Maybe that's why I joined the Spiders.*

'Exactly, my friend.' Brother Rojo clapped his hands. 'Sometimes we invest so much time and effort believing in that one special person, and then, without warning, they pour burning oil over you.'

'Did that happen to you?'

'Many times, Alex. On one occasion, I remember negotiating a deal with a local Muslim leader to deliver a telephone service in his village. I thought we had become good friends and that we trusted each other implicitly. I finally secured the necessary funding to construct some telephone poles. All these important people came from Davao to witness the agreement.'

'What happened then?'

'Oh, we built the poles alright. But barely a week after we erected them, I returned to the village only to find that someone had cut them all down. You see, my friend had convinced some of the more radical people around him that the poles symbolised the Christian crucifix and were, therefore, an affront to Islam. It turned out that the whole thing had been a deceitful pantomime on his part to demonstrate the wastefulness of the Manila government.'

'You must have felt betrayed.'

'Yes, you are right. I did feel betrayed. But I learnt a valuable lesson as well. Good men finally succeed if they persevere and have faith in God. You see, I refused to turn my back on the people who lived in the village, and I persevered and did what I could to improve their living conditions, despite constant interference from my former friend.'

I found myself smiling at him. 'I suppose this is your way of telling me that I should persevere with my thesis and see it to its conclusion.'

'Ah, you are a man blessed with far more wisdom than the normal twenty-five-year-old.' We both laughed at his joke, and he offered me another biscuit. 'Because of this, I will now reward your wisdom with my assistance. Drop me a copy of your draft later today by email, and I will examine it during the week. I promise that I will make some sturdy observations wherever I can.'

'Thank you.' We stared at each other like two people who had nothing more to discuss.

'Can I ask you one question?' Brother Rojo finally asked.

'Sure.'

'Why did you pick this topic?'

I thought the answer was obvious. 'To get a good mark for my paper, of course.'

'But there are a thousand topics you could have chosen. The Philippines is a country beset with many problems, so why did you choose this one in particular?'

I gave him the standard response that I had parroted to people for much of the past year. 'I want to make a difference in people's lives.'

'Yes, but why?'

'I'll be forty soon,' I muttered bleakly. 'All my life, I have battled mediocrity. Perhaps this is my last chance to do something special.'

'What if you are wrong?' He challenged me further. 'What if your tutors dislike your paper? What do you do after that?'

'I don't know,' I replied honestly. 'I haven't thought that far ahead. I guess I go back to being the no-hoper that I have always been.'

His gnome-like face shrank inside a ray of brilliant sunlight. 'You're not a no-hoper, Alex—anyone with half a brain can see that. I have spent many years separating the clever ones from those who bask in stupidity.' He lifted a finger and pointed it at my heart. 'In fact, you're quite an extraordinary young man, but you refuse to realise it.'

Although I felt chuffed at his compliment, I still found it impossible to believe him. 'Well, whatever is supposed to happen, it better happen soon because my patience is fast running out.'

He rose from his chair, shuffled back into the kitchen, and refilled our cups with tea. When he returned to his seat, his face exuded an intensity that overwhelmed his fragile body.

'Many, many years ago,' he began, 'I became aware of a holy man who lived in Nepal. People travelled from all over Asia to meet him.'

'Was this before you entered the church?'

'Yes,' said Brother Rojo. 'I had reached a decision point, but I needed that final piece of guidance before I signed on the dotted line. So you can understand my desire to meet such a man and learn from his wisdom. Letters were sent, representations were made, and eventually, I was invited to stay with the great man for a few days before winter set in.'

'What was he like?' I asked politely.

'He was the wisest man I ever met. Unfortunately, he was also old and frail when I visited him. Our time together was brief. But every night after dinner, he would graciously take the time to see me. Our conversations were uniquely fascinating.'

'What did you talk about?'

'Oh, many things. The moon, the sun, and the sky. The issues facing our different worlds. But he always brought everything back to his favourite topic: how the earth and humankind connected with one other.' I could tell that he wanted to cry and that my presence was the only thing stopping him. 'One night, when I was feeling especially pessimistic about my future, he explained to me about the four seasons and how they shape a person's life.'

'You mean autumn, winter, spring, summer—that sort of stuff?'

'No, Alex. These are different seasons, spheres of magic from the dawn of time that you and I know little about and perhaps will never fully comprehend.'

'Right.'

He smiled at my sarcasm. 'Please hear me out.'

'I'm sorry.'

'The first season is called the Season of Thunder. This season defines the events which led to your birth. How you mother and father first met, how they brought you up as a child, and the values they taught you.'

'Interesting,' I said. *The last thing I wanted was to have my childhood explained to me by a fable.*

'The second season,' he continued, 'is called the Season of Fire and usually begins when you become a teenager. It draws upon those unexplained flames of passion that burn inside your soul and turn you into the person you eventually become.'

Yet again.

'Then there is the Season of Wisdom, which draws its power from the sun and the stars. This season represents a state of permanent grace that we all aspire to reach. Self-actualisation if you have read Maslow's *Hierarchy of Needs*. It ultimately means that you have passed all of life's tests and are ready to bind your soul with the light.'

'And this is where one finds true happiness? Inside this Season of Wisdom?'

'Yes, that's correct.'

Well, as life theories went, this one was certainly unique - so much more avant-garde than talking about jigsaw puzzles.

'But you have missed a season, haven't you?' I tightened my eyebrows. 'You said there were four, but you have only mentioned three.'

'Ah, behind that facetious smile, you have been listening.' He spun his hands across the table and rubbed me affectionately on the knee. 'The fourth season is called the Season of Clouds.'

'The Season of Clouds?' As soon as I repeated those words, tiny lumps of fear began to fester inside my throat. 'What happens inside this season?' I asked, even though I didn't want to know.

'Imagine that it's a dark stormy day,' began Brother Rojo, 'and you are seeking shelter from the rain. You desperately want to see the sun, to feel its warmth on your body, and to offer you the wisdom of a better life. But everywhere you turn, a different storm cloud consumes the sun's rays, denying you of its mercy. You walk from town to town, year upon year, looking for that break in the cloud, hoping to find sustenance from the light before your time expires. As a result, you can never settle in that one place where the sun always shines.'

'But the clouds eventually lift, don't they?' I replied indignantly. 'I mean, we all get to see the sun at some point.'

Brother Rojo's placed his empty cup onto the table. There was an obscure tenderness to his movements as if God had created his entire world solely for my benefit. 'Not always, my son. Most people are fortunate to find a way through the clouds, and once they do, they can connect with the sun and lead happy and productive lives.'

'And the others?'

'Well, for some, that cycle takes a little longer.'

'How much longer?'

'It depends.'

'On what?'

'On many things, my friend. You see, for some people, the Clouds are all they have.'

'Meaning?'

'Meaning, they have no choice but to spend the rest of their lives in darkness.'

I wanted to take the cowardly way out, to avoid Brother Rojo's accusing eyes altogether, but all I could do was glare at his tattered sandals.

'You have to face the truth, Alex.' He gently clasped my hand.

'And what is the truth?'

As if you don't already know.

'You have been trapped inside the Season of Clouds for most of your life.'

The Villa

The Philippines
May 2001

We spent the next two hours talking. With honesty I never knew I possessed, I told Brother Rojo everything about my life. During this conversation, he explained to me how a man must wear many guises before he could leave the Season of Clouds and where he praised my efforts during the Lost Week. By the time he finished dissecting the universe for my benefit, everything I knew about myself was lying in a pool of regret beside me.

'I am sorry if I have spoken out of turn,' he said while rocking gently in his chair. 'Once I start talking about the four seasons, I get somewhat carried away.'

Out of courtesy, I firmly shook his hand. 'I'm grateful for your advice. If anything, you have opened my eyes to my foolishness.'

'Sometimes we have to face the things that we don't want to hear about ourselves before we can move forward with our lives. You shouldn't be afraid of that.'

'I'm afraid of everything.' I replied. 'But at least you have put my own miserable theories about life into perspective.'

Brother Rojo frowned. 'Ever since Adam and Eve, we have invented stories to help explain our true purpose in the world. It doesn't mean to say that they are perfect in their construction. For instance, do you believe everything contained in the Old Testament?'

'Of course not.'

'But you will agree with me that certain lessons in the Bible are still relevant today?'

'Yes. We have built an entire civilisation, an entire way of life, around the Bible.'

'Exactly. Every story, every parable, every theory has something we can use. It's up to us to decide what is helpful and what is not. For example, your friend Delilah was probably right. Your heart may well be ready to find true love. And perhaps there is a second jigsaw puzzle for you to complete if that's what you wish to believe. But your pursuit of these things will always fail unless you establish the true cause of your unhappiness.'

'I have already looked several times,' I mumbled. 'But nothing I found made any sense. I don't know who I am anymore.'

Brother Rojo's face glowed in the afternoon sunlight, and it made him appear even more pious if that was at all humanly possible. 'The Clouds are not our friends, Alex. They don't want us to escape the control they might have over our lives. They feed on our doubts and insecurities and thrive on our confusion. They take us to places where we don't want to go. For they know that they can only survive through the accumulation of our fears.'

'Then I should beg for their mercy,' I replied sadly. 'Because fear is the only thing I have left.'

'It doesn't have to be that way, my son.'

'You said yourself that I have become their prisoner.'

'There is a way out, Alex. There always has been, but for some reason, you refuse to see it. We need to find that reason.'

Brother Rojo shuffled his hands across the coffee table and reached for his mobile phone. He politely tapped away at his keyboard before a noisy text message rattled across the room in response.

'My cousin Denny owns a magnificent villa just outside of Baguio,' he explained. 'It's built next to a winding valley, surrounded by a series of majestic mountains. I think it's one of the most peaceful places on Earth, and a man can easily dispose of his afflictions within its cool, early morning mists. Whenever Denny is away on business, I often use the villa to escape the madness of Manila.'

'Does he have a family?' I asked with a smidgin of disinterest.

'He lost his beloved wife to cancer eighteen months ago, but fortunately, he has a beautiful daughter named Dulcie to share his life. She lives in a separate part of the villa and mainly keeps to herself. But to her credit, she wanders across every day to make my meals and share some quiet words with a lonely old man.'

'And you're telling me this because?'

'It just so happens that Denny is travelling to Malaysia next week, and he has asked me to keep Dulcie company for a few days. However, I think you should go in my place, for I can't think of a better place for a man like you to undertake some quiet reflection.'

I furiously waved my hands at him. 'I cannot possibly impose on your family. In any case, I have to remain in Manila to work on my thesis.' I surely had the perfect excuse, but Brother Rojo was having none of it.

'Nonsense,' he replied firmly. 'You will work so much better at the villa without all the petty distractions of a big city. And you will also be doing me a huge favour. I'm sure that you are aware that I've been very unwell recently. Things are now better, but these trips to Baguio sometimes wear me out.'

'But what about your cousin? How would he feel about a strange man he has never met spending the entire week alone with his young daughter?'

'My cousin is a gracious man who would be forever indebted to you. Besides,'—he dropped his voice—'you are in your late thirties; Dulcie is nineteen if I remember correctly. Such an age difference surely represents nothing more than a fatherly disposition, does it not?'

'I guess so.'

'One more thing, if you can indulge a fading old Marist brother. I don't want you to be alarmed, but I am duty-bound to warn you. There is something mysterious about the villa I can't explain. Maybe I won't go as far as saying it's haunted—that's way too risqué for a devoted Roman Catholic like me. But something unusual lives inside the villa's lonely walls, which only emerges at night.'

'Rats?'

'What?'

'Does the villa have rats?'

He grunted when he realised that I was taking the piss. But what he didn't appreciate was that he was talking to the king when it came to the supernatural.

'Okay, tell me more,' I reassured him with an apologetic smile.

He picked up a dirty photo album from the coffee table and flipped it open. 'This is a photo of me a few days after my heart operation. As you can see, there must have been a tube stuck inside every hole of my body.'

'I'm sorry. That doesn't look good at all.'

'Following the operation, my doctor advised me that I only had a few weeks to live—there was considerable damage to my ventricle, you see. So, upon hearing this news, Denny insisted that I should stay at the villa until such time death came to collect me. Time stood still for the next few weeks, as it always does for the condemned man.'

'But then one night, something incredible happened. I was drifting in that lonely space that sometimes exists between two alternating dreams when I felt something unnatural tug at the side of my sheet and pull me towards a bright, shining light. I naturally thought I was dying, and, to be honest, nothing made me happier. It was the most wondrous feeling.

'Then, all of a sudden, I rapidly changed direction, entering a brand-new dimension that I never knew existed. As I floated slowly towards the most beautiful rainbow I had ever seen, a presence, perhaps, or some form of entity touched my face, reassuring me that my time had not yet come. I woke up startled but feeling better than I had for a very long time. So here I am now before you, months later, not cured, as I said, but a living by-product of that miracle.'

'You think that there is a miracle waiting for me at the villa?' I asked.

'If you keep your faith, perhaps there will be.'

'I'm not sure that my faith is as strong as yours, Brother Rojo. But if there is an entity living in the villa, I guarantee you that it will find me.'

'Then we have a deal?'

'We have a deal.'

'Good, because I have just texted Cousin Denny telling him that you are arriving on Sunday.'

Three days later, I appeared at the bus station in Makati just after breakfast, Brother Rojo's ticket wedged tightly between my fingers. I wasn't sure why I thought that a six-hour bus trip to Baguio would be anything other than a complete shit fight. But as soon as we began to board, it became apparent that I had entered a war zone, involving a vast array of humans, animals, and vegetables, all trying to cram into one filthy, dilapidated bus.

Whether these dubious characters had actually purchased tickets or not, I was not willing to say, but there was absolutely no limit to the stampeding bodies that tried to squeeze their way through the front passenger door. Caught in the middle of this insidious melee, surrounded by scores of people screaming out at me in Tagalog, I desperately engaged in a fight for survival.

Waves of people slamming into my buttocks suddenly sent me sprawling down the corridor headfirst before I accidentally landed into one of the last available seats; predictably, right next to the toilet that no-one remotely sensible was ever going to use. Somehow, I wriggled up to the glass window, closed my eyes, and hoped to God that no-one wanted to sit next to the angry-looking white guy.

But I could only be so lucky. Within a nano-second, a mother and her teenage daughter crammed into that empty space, complete with several plastic bags full of bananas, and God knew what else. Before I knew it, I became violently wedged up against the glass window, covered from head to toe in banana peels and busting to pee like you would not imagine.

Thankfully, this unique Filipino water torture came to a premature end three hours later at a service station somewhere in the middle of Luzon. It was there where I broke Carl Lewis's world record for the one-hundred-metre dash after I beat every other sucker to the men's toilet. When I returned, a policeman ordered most of the original passengers from the bus, including the girl and her mother. I didn't know why, and in my selfishness, I didn't care. All that mattered was that I could complete the rest of the journey in relative comfort.

Somewhere outside Baguio's city limits, my phone snarled out a new text message. It was surprisingly from Dulcie, Cousin Denny's daughter, and she informed me that her father's driver had taken ill and would pick me up from the bus stop instead. 'Sure thing,' I replied before returning to Pink Floyd's *The Wall* on my CD player.

When we finally disembarked in Baguio, there was no young Filipino woman to greet me amongst the crowd of growing well-wishers, so I wandered across the courtyard to what looked like a bakery to order some food. I ordered a ham and cheese sandwich and began to melt in the late-afternoon sun.

After a few more minutes of loafing around, I became distracted by the noisy chimes of a car horn. I followed its trajectory to a white station wagon parked in a lonely bay across the street. A beautiful, young Filipina stood impatiently in front of the bonnet, her thin arms dangling next to her light-blue jeans.

'Are you Alex?' she demanded.

'Possibly, but I might have to check my bus ticket first.'

She didn't react to my attempt at humour at all. Instead, her cantankerous, doe-like eyes generated the undeniable impression that the very sight of me pretty much revolted her. Her undeserved antipathy followed me all the way to the front passenger seat.

'You drive very well for a nineteen-year-old,' I soon blurted out after Dulcie executed a tricky U-turn. I had to say; it was one of the dumbest, most condescending conversation-starters I had ever used on a woman.

'Who said that I was nineteen?' she growled behind the steering wheel.

'Your cousin Rojo,' I replied tentatively.

'He wouldn't know if his head was on fire,' she sneered. 'I have just turned twenty-three.'

'Oh, I see.'

I did my best to make small talk, but since Dulcie's responses were limited mainly to monosyllabic grunts, I decided to quit while I was ahead. When we finally reached the villa ten minutes later, she pulled into a muddy driveway and then haphazardly leaned her elbow against the car horn.

'Thanks for the fascinating conversation,' I said above the deafening roar. Dulcie offered me a very constrained 'fuck you' smile and then pointed to the main security gate, which slowly began to open.

'Are you sure your name isn't Martina?' I asked her.

'Very sure. Why?'

'Just curious.'

'Don't get out yet,' she then warned me as she hit the accelerator pedal.

'Wouldn't dream of it. I'm having too much fun.'

Once we were safely inside, I took my first look at the villa. I must admit it wasn't what I had imagined. For some reason, I had my heart set on some colonial, kick-arse Spanish mansion, concreted next to a botanical garden. But whoever dreamt up this monstrosity must have been tormented by copious gallons of alcohol. It was like someone had stacked five versions of my apartment block next to each other on wooden stilts and then built an additional two stories on top of them just because they could.

Its light-blue walls were ridiculously out of place, while the ivory-stained verandah did its best to gobble up everything around it, including a large cluster of trees, the spiralling vines that crept along its uppermost roof, and even the sullen valley that meandered its way around the side porch.

'Ah, Mr Gerrick,' a tall, slim Filipino man cried out as he appeared from the front door. 'Welcome to our humble abode.'

Cousin Denny was a rather handsome man in his late forties, with a thick shock of black hair—which I was sure he dyed—and sunken eyes that threatened to combust at any moment. As I accepted his welcoming smile, I tried to understand how he and Mister Toad could be related.

'My cousin speaks very highly of you,' Denny said after we shook hands.

'Unfortunately, he was very drunk when we met,' I replied. 'He has me mixed up with someone else.'

Denny laughed. 'If only that were true! The occasional glass of sherry is his only vice.'

'Right you are.' I was about to grab my belongings from the car when Dulcie silently appeared next to her father, carrying both my laptop and suitcase in her tiny, delicate hands. She greeted her dad with a simple kiss, and I witnessed the immense pride on his face.

'I trust my daughter has looked after you so far?' asks Denny.

Dulcie raised her eyebrows at me in disdain, and I happily smirked at her discomfort. However, we both knew that I was about to engage in a series of outrageous lies for her benefit. 'Yes, she kept me entertained throughout our journey,' I replied with an abundance of faked enthusiasm. 'She is a charming young lady.'

'Excellent!' Denny shouted before clapping his hands. 'Now, let me show you around the villa.'

'I will take these to your room, shall I?' Dulcie growled as she brushed past my shoulder. Even so, I was sure that I could see a satisfied smile in between her general fits of snarling.

Over the next hour and a half, Denny provided me with a riveting history of the villa. Of course, I lost interest after about ten minutes, but I did what I could to pretend otherwise. I laughed happily at the occasional anecdote, released that expected gasp of wonderment at an exquisite piece of Spanish pottery, and dazzled him with a flume of targeted questions whenever the situation required a pick-me-up.

What I did learn through Denny's excited ramblings was that a rich American army officer had built the villa in the early 1900s, just after the United States claimed the Philippines as a colony. It exchanged hands several times over the next several decades before Denny's grandfather purchased it at a bargain price before the Second World War.

Although never substantiated, rumours abounded that General McArthur once stayed there for a weekend with his young family. On a more sinister note, the local Japanese commander had used the villa as a place of recreation for his senior officers during the occupation. I got the impression from Denny's pallid facial expressions that some disturbing things may have happened during that time.

Upon inspecting a piece of medieval armour, Denny realised that I could barely stand up, so he graciously brought the tour to a premature halt. He guided me to my room and suggested that I freshen up before dinner.

'We shall see you at seven o'clock in the main dining room,' he announced before I fell into one of those afternoon naps that we all cherish.

I woke up just before seven, ran a travel brush over my hair, and threw on a clean shirt. When I entered the dining room, Denny greeted me with a slap on the back and invited me to sit down at the main table.

Dulcie soon emerged from the kitchen, her hands clasping at a huge metal pot. Whatever concoction was bubbling inside, it smelt bloody delicious, and I deliberately made this point out loud just for her benefit.

'Ah, pork adobo,' Denny enthused. 'My favourite.'

Dulcie offered her dad an approving smile but wholly ignored my compliment. *Never mind—at least I tried.*

Despite her latest rebuff, dinner was mainly a pleasant affair. Denny was a man blessed with a thousand stories, and he kept me entertained while I continued to scoff down several large helpings of delicious pork.

'Trust me, Alex,' he demanded. 'There is lost Japanese treasure in these hills, and one day I am going to find it.'

'What do the locals think about that?' I asked.

'They think that I have spent too much time in this villa,' he replied with a smile.

'And have you?'

'I am an architect, Alex. Two things inspire me: solitude and self-indulgence. Fortunately, the villa provides me with both.'

His confession seemed to be the perfect opportunity to raise the dead vampire in the coffin.

'The villa is haunted, according to your cousin Rojo,' I mentioned matter-of-factly.

'Nonsense,' Dulcie spat at me. She had said very little all evening, and so her sudden intervention almost knocked me off my chair.

Denny wiped his mouth with a napkin and then gazed ruefully at her. 'We shouldn't discount things that we don't understand, my child.'

'There is nothing to understand, Father,' Dulcie replied glumly. 'With due respect to our beloved Rojo, he is just another sad person clinging onto a bunch of useless fairytales. There is nothing to look forward to after death, only emptiness.'

Denny swirled his glass of Chardonnay in my direction, and I wondered whether my presence was the only thing stopping him from chastising his daughter more harshly. 'Rojo has devoted his life to helping people, Dulcie. Whatever you may think about his faith, please remember the sacrifices he has made to assist others less fortunate than us.'

'Yes, Father,' she replied, clearly regretting her outburst. 'However, I'm not feeling all that well. May I please be excused?'

Before Denny could respond, she quietly stood up and respectfully gave him a peck on his cheek. 'I will see you in the morning before you leave.' She swivelled around to consider me, decided that I was the cause of her sudden predicament, and said nothing more before leaving the room.

'You must excuse my daughter,' said Denny. 'She hasn't been the same since her mother died.'

'I'm sorry,' I replied genuinely. 'Were Dulcie and her mum close?'

'Surprisingly, no.' He slumped in his chair. 'The two of them were always fighting, and I constantly found myself in the middle, trying to adjudicate a solution. My wife, Grace, was a very traditional woman, you see, who had extreme views about how a young Filipina of Dulcie's standing should behave. Unfortunately, Dulcie inherited my independent spirit and would rebel against her every whim. They did not reconcile their differences before breast cancer took my Grace.'

I swallowed more of the sour wine, and it burned my throat. 'I'm no expert, but she must still be feeling guilty about her mother. It will take time, I'm sure.' *Bloody hell. Who am I trying to kid?*

'You are right,' Denny said sadly. 'Her guilt now defines her life. She has assumed the persona and responsibilities of her mother, like it is a penance that she must endure. She won't even allow me to hire a maid or a cook to help her out. This is a girl, by the way, who last year graduated with a master's degree in economics. I'm scared that she is wasting her life.'

'Has Rojo spoken to her? I mean, he is a man of infinite wisdom.'

'Indeed, he is,' Denny agreed. 'Dulcie adored him when she was a young girl. However, Grace never warmed to Rojo. His odd appearance and the manner of his birth didn't quite fit the high standards she had set out for our family. Now that she has gone, Dulcie has decided to take over the mantle of family protector. You heard what she said tonight about him.'

'I don't think I should be here,' I said, suddenly making it all about me again. 'Despite what I said before, Dulcie and I haven't exactly got along.' Of course, Denny already knew that. 'To be honest with you, she barely says a word to me most days, let alone to a stranger like you.' He paused to catch his breath. 'Don't worry—you won't see that much of her, except when she is making your meals. Please remember you are my honoured guest and free to use my house in any way you see fit.'

'Thank you, Denny. I appreciate that.'

'Besides, having someone different around may be good for her.'

After a glass or three of sherry, Denny did what all good Filipino hosts did and introduced me to his vast collection of semiautomatic rifles.

'Dulcie has many potential suitors in Baguio,' he explained. 'Most of them are completely unsuitable, of course. Don't be afraid to use one of these beauties should any of them visit the villa during my absence.' Given that I was unlikely ever to have a daughter, Denny's instructions excited me to the core, even if it did potentially mean twenty years in jail.

The sound of a car humming drearily in the driveway woke me up just after dawn, and I assumed this was Denny's driver picking him up for the airport. With no hope of further sleep, I launched myself off the mattress, put on some tracksuit pants, and crept into the kitchen to make myself a coffee. As I waited for the kettle to boil, I heard several loud noises behind the pantry door. Convinced that it was either a rat or Dulcie plotting to murder me, I picked up my mug and sneaked back to my room like the coward I was.

After I finished my coffee, I reached into my suitcase and produced a small envelope. I ripped open the top corner, cursed myself for having spilt a droplet of coffee over my clean shirt, and then pulled out a single white sheet of paper.

Dear Alex,

Escaping the Clouds won't be an easy task. But you are a man of considerable gifts, and I'm confident that you will eventually succeed.

Over the next few days, I want you to consider three questions:

1) How would you like people to describe you when you reach fifty?

2) How many of those qualities do you currently possess?

3) What changes do you have to make to your life to achieve your target?

I honestly believe that your quest to unravel your life's riddle will become easier once you answer these questions honestly. Remember, Alex—God's will shines only on those who succumb to the truth.

Should you need to talk to me at any stage, I am but a phone call away.

God bless you, my son, and good luck.

R

I chewed on my pencil and then scribbled a few lines at the bottom of the letter.

Question 1:
-A successful leader widely admired for his integrity and intelligence.
-A man who treats everyone with care and compassion, especially women.
-Someone who is happy with himself and his relationships.

Question 2:
-Bugger all!

I mulled over question three for what seemed like an eternity, decided that I needed a break, and then fired up my laptop. For the next two days, I largely forgot about Brother Rojo's letter and did very little other than work on my thesis and go for quiet, lonely walks in the afternoon along the cluttered edges of the valley. I might not have discovered the meaning of life as Brother Rojo had anticipated, but I felt at peace with myself for the first time in months.

Fortunately, I didn't see much of Dulcie, except at dinner time. On both nights, she had left her latest meal for me on the dining room table, muttered out a few instructions, and then disappeared for the rest of the evening. I could almost taste the hostility in the food that she had prepared for me. It was going to be an excruciatingly long week.

On Tuesday night, I fell asleep on top of my bed while attempting to read *Lord of the Rings* for the 857th time. I woke up around two-thirty to find the blurry outline of a middle-aged Caucasian woman sitting on a chair next to the dressing table, humming some long-forgotten melody to herself. The woman was wearing a white ball gown that barely clutched the contours of her tiny body, and she had pinned her snow-coloured hair into a beehive.

'Hi there,' I remarked casually once the urge to shit myself passed.

'Hello,' she replied sweetly.

'Can I help you with anything?'

'No, thank you. I'm happy where I am.'

'I see. In that case, do you mind if I go back to sleep? I'm exhausted.'

'Of course not.'

I paused briefly. 'You're not going to turn into a horrible yellow clown, are you?'

'Don't be silly.'

'Okay. Well, good night then.'

'Good night. Sweet dreams, now.'

A scale-feathered malkoha perched insolently on my windowsill woke me up with its infernal singing just after sunrise. I rubbed both eyes with my hands, thought about the lady in my room last night, and vowed to stop drinking that foul Filipino wine with my dinner.

Once I finished breakfast, I decided to explore more of the villa. After losing myself inside several broken closets, I soon entered a large, breezy room full of dusty bookshelves. *There must be at least two thousand books here.* Upon closer inspection, as I moved from shelf to shelf, I realised that each book had been perfectly catalogued, first by genre and then by the author's name. Someone had dedicated months of their precious time to designing this wonderful room.

Curious at what I might find, I breezed past a substantial crime fiction collection before falling upon a cluster of history books about the local Baguio region. I casually browsed at a couple of promising titles before settling on a slim, tattered hardcover called *Baguio During the War.* I released the book from its imprisonment with gentle precision, blew away a few cobwebs and sat down at a polished, wooden reading table in the middle of the room. I was enjoying the peace and quiet when …

'What are you doing here?' a voice shrieked at me from behind. I shunted my chair around to find Dulcie standing at the doorway, her arms folded menacingly against her breasts, her eyes spitting out streams of poison in my direction.

'Um—I'm reading a book.'

'You have no right to be here. This library belonged to my mother.'

'I'm sorry, but—'

Before I could finish my sentence, Dulcie suddenly took a step backwards towards the door in horror and then released a bloodcurdling scream that almost blew my eardrums out.

'What is it?' I cried.

'Over there!' She pointed at a lone patch of cream wallpaper in the far corner of the room. 'A spider!'

Yeah, it was a spider, alright, and a huge mother at that. Even if I had placed both my hands out in front of me, side to side, its body span would still have been more prominent. And on top of that, it was a hairy little blighter as well—obviously, some sort of local tarantula that looked far nastier than its actual bite.

'It's okay,' I reassured her. 'I'll capture it and take it outside.'

'Are you crazy?' she shrieked, her head threatening to spin into a nearby lampshade. 'Kill it! Kill it!'

No-one understood the potential consequences of what I did next better than me. There was an unwritten rule, you see, one which only became apparent to me well after I committed my life to the Spiders. Never kill an underling because someday, one of their brothers or sisters would most likely seek their revenge.

But what was I supposed to do? Ignore the hysterics of a fragile young woman or hope that that the Spiders never discover my discretion?

Oh, sweet Jesus. Here I go again—saving a vulnerable woman from herself.

I reluctantly slipped off one of my shoes and silently crept across the floor. The spider immediately sensed the danger and courageously tried to stare me down with its million and one eyes. 'This just isn't cricket, old man,' it pleaded with me in a posh English accent before I whacked it over the head as hard as I could. When it dropped helplessly to the floor, pretending, as they always did, to be dead, I took further aim and smashed its puny exoskeleton a few more times just for good measure.

'There.' I smiled triumphantly at Dulcie. 'Dead as the proverbial dodo.'

Now, throughout my story, I have often demonstrated my inability to understand the female brain. But what happened next totally stupefied even me. Before I had time to put my shoe back on my foot, Dulcie suddenly scampered across the fading carpet and wrapped herself around my chest. 'I am petrified of spiders,' she cried as her tears poured down the back of my T-shirt.

We walked back to the dining room, and I made us both a cup of tea. Dulcie sat quietly at the table, her shivering hands barely able to grip her cup, her treasure chest eyes never leaving me. 'It's not the first time I have seen that spider,' she finally admitted. 'I know this sounds ridiculous, but I am certain it has been following me for weeks.'

I thought back to my situation in Brisbane during that thunderstorm and the beautiful money spider hiding in the kitchen cupboard. It almost wanted to seduce me. Come to think of it, it probably did. 'It's not ridiculous at all, Dulcie. The same thing happened to me many years ago, and it simply means that they are interested in you.'

'What are you talking about?' she replied. 'Who is interested in me?'

'The Spiders.'

'The Spiders? I don't understand.'

'No-one ever does.'

'Try me.'

How could I explain the enormity of this tale to someone as vulnerable and naïve as Dulcie? 'Have you ever stared into a mirror and caught a reflection of something that you can't explain?'

'Those are the Spiders?'

'No. I'm curious if these things happen to people other than me.'

'No, I haven't,' she said impatiently. 'Why is this important?'

'It isn't. Anyway, the Spiders I am referring to are not arachnids, although they do seem to wield a special power over our eight-legged friends.'

'So, they are human?'

'Of course they are.'

'What do they want?'

'That's a good question.' I rubbed my chin and searched for the right words. 'We assume that our political leaders control our destiny. But power is a much more linear concept. Behind every government exists an elite cabal of people who exercise ultimate authority over the rest of us. Subliminally they tell us what to do, what to think, and how to act.

'Who are they, exactly?'

'The bureaucracy, big business, the media, the security services. The usual lot. Well, the Spiders act as their proxies. They work silently behind the shadows, pulling the strings, negotiating the deals, doing their dirty work.'

'For what purpose?'

'I haven't figured that part out yet.'

'Do they want to rule the world?'

'Nah, they're not clever enough for that. The Spiders are obsessed with enriching their own lives, you see. I wouldn't call them evil, necessarily; the word "overbearing" comes to mind. They don't care about you as a person, but generally speaking, they allow you to lead your own life within certain boundaries. Occasionally, they will ask you to do them special favours.' I tried to look serious. 'Make no mistake, when the Spiders ask you to jump, you jump quickly, efficiently and without asking too many questions. It's all about crossing the t's and dotting the i's with them.'

'So, if you don't like them, why did you join them?'

'Seemed like a good idea at the time.'

'And what are they doing in the Philippines?

'From what I can tell, every country has its own cadre of Spiders. That's my theory, anyway.'

'But what do they want from me?' I could see the lines of panic stretch across her lovely face.

'To recruit you, of course. Just like me.'

'But why?' she asked, her tone descending into disbelief. 'I'm nothing special.'

'Neither am I, Dulcie. But importantly, they think we are, and they only approach a small number of people. Their strategy is to make us feel important and valuable so that we keep wanting more.'

We spent the rest of the afternoon talking. I told Dulcie everything I knew about the Spiders, and she remarkably took it all in her stride. Despite her arachnophobia, she was one calm individual. Afterwards, she cooked me a fantastic spaghetti sauce for dinner, and we finished the evening with several glasses of red wine on the balcony. Somewhere along the way, we became friends.

When I returned to my room just before midnight, I gave the *Lord of the Rings* one last chance before the small television sitting on top of the dressing table suddenly turned itself on without warning. I reached over to grab the remote sitting at the end of my bed, clicked the 'off' button several times, and then resumed reading. Twenty seconds later, the TV switched itself back on again. I swore out loud a few more times, engaged the off button once more, and waited for something to happen. Sure enough, barely a minute later, CNN magically returned to the screen.

'Listen,' I barked out into the night. 'I've had a shitty day, and I need some rest. Can you please go away and annoy someone else!' Petulantly, the TV immediately morphed into black nothingness, and I soon fell asleep.

The following morning, Dulcie and I packed some goodies in a basket and hiked into the mountains. Despite my previous history with women and picnics, I had no sexual interest in Dulcie, and my sole ambition was to be her friend—a platonic father figure who could help her navigate the stormy waters that lay ahead.

We picked out a gorgeous stretch of grass near a small waterfall, and Dulcie handed out the salmon and cucumber sandwiches that she made for us after breakfast. Pretty soon, she began talking about her life.

'I feel so unsettled,' she admitted while playing with a bread crust. 'Ever since Mum died, all I want to do is lock myself away in the villa.'

'Were the two of you close?' I asked softly. Of course, I already knew the answer to this question, but I wanted to hear it from her.

'On one level, we weren't,' Dulcie replied. 'But deep down, she understood me better than anyone I know. I loved her very much, despite our heated arguments. How I wish I told her that before she died.'

'We all have our regrets,' the King of Regrets told her. 'I'm sure your mother knew how much you loved her and would have wanted you to get on with your life.'

'You're right.' She hung her head sadly. 'In a way, I have been using her death as an excuse to remain here in Baguio with Dad. But all it does is hide the fact that I have lost confidence in myself.'

I smiled at her just as a large bumblebee whizzed past her nose.

'What so funny?' she asked pointedly.

'I find it hard to believe that you lack self-confidence.'

'Well, I do.'

'Come on, Dulcie. You are beautiful, intelligent, and charming company when you're not ripping heads off people. You have the world at your feet.'

She picked up a loose twig and playfully threw it at my chin. 'You dirty old man,' she said, laughing. 'I bet you say that to all the girls.' In an attempt to prove her point, she pulled her dress a little bit further up her bare thigh to see what my reaction would be.

But I didn't take the bait. 'You got me all wrong,' I replied with a fatherly frown. 'I just want to help you and other young women like you.' Even though some people would refuse to believe my explanation fifteen years later, that was indeed all I ever intended.

Over the next two-and-a-half days, Dulcie and I became inseparable. She helped me with my thesis, we went for long walks together before sunset, and we talked incessantly about the meaning of life. Slowly, I began to learn that there was nothing more beautiful for a man than to mentor a young woman on the brink of her destiny. All those *My Fair Lady* fantasies I had collected suddenly made sense. I was indeed living the life of Professor Higgins, and Dulcie was my new Eliza Doolittle.

Least of all, I no longer cared what Marlena thought about my meddling. I was proud that I could connect so easily with a young woman and provide her with the benefit of my life experience, the lessons I had learnt through my various tortured relationships. As long as I set firm boundaries between us, where was the harm?

On the following Saturday afternoon, Denny received the shock of his life when Dulcie and I greeted him at the main security gate. As soon as he leapt out onto the wet grass, Dulcie surged forward towards him and planted a smothering kiss on his pudgy cheek. 'I missed you so much, Daddy,' she declared.

'What the heck is going on?' he whispered to me when Dulcie was out of earshot. 'She hasn't called me Daddy since she was five years old!'

'She has been reborn,' I announced.

'So it seems.' He put his arm around my shoulders. 'How in God's name did you manage that?'

'I'm not sure, but it's nothing short of a miracle.'

'Blasphemy is not usually welcome in my house. But on this occasion, I will make a rare exception.'

'That's a wise choice.'

'Anything else I should know?'

'Yeah, your villa is bloody well haunted.'

That night, the three of us had dinner at a wonderful Malaysian restaurant in Baguio. We had a simply marvellous time eating, drinking, and laughing, with a bit of karaoke and dancing thrown in for good measure. When we returned to the villa just after eleven-thirty, there was little doubt that the bonds created between the three of us would last a lifetime.

*

I was lying alone in my bed, her delicate hands gently caressing my face.

'Alex,' she whispered, 'your time has come.'

'Am I going to die?'

'Please come with me' is the only thing she was allowed to say.

I took her hand, and she led me outside into the raging twilight.

We walked for an eternity, her golden hair shining like a beacon against a pure night sky.

'Where are we?' I soon asked. 'This is not the Philippines.'

'Hush now, Alex. You will soon find out.'

We traversed a little further before I realised that I had been there before. Everywhere I looked, some ancient relic from my past facetiously greeted me.

A café.

A stone footpath.

The roar of the sea.

The chill of the wind.

'Do you know where you are now, Alex?' the woman demanded. Her voice sounded like a million sirens luring me to my demise.

'Yes, I'm in Samos,' I replied bitterly. 'This is where Martina and I spent our last night together.'

The woman said nothing but merely stared at me with her soulless eyes.

'Why have you taken me here?'

'Why don't you ask her?'

Several feet away, I saw the outline of a young woman standing at the edge of a familiar rocky cliff. She was holding her arms out towards the ocean, crying out for the waves to catch her soul, the howling midnight wind pulling at the locks of her long flowing hair.

'Martina!' I cried out in desperation. 'Please don't jump. I'm so sorry that I betrayed you.'

I turned to the apparition beside me and begged her to intervene. 'Please stop her. I can't live with the guilt anymore.'

'But I'm not Martina!' the woman at the edge of the cliff cried.

I swivelled my head back towards the water's edge to find Dulcie scowling at me.

'What are you doing, Alex? she demanded to know. 'Why are you here?'

'I'm here to help you,' I promised her.

'But I don't need or want your help.'

'We could all use some help in our lives.'

She twisted her body once more to face the lonely horizon, to a place where the Spiders often called home.

'Go with him,' they now ordered her. 'He is one of us, and he will tell you what to do.'

Now that everything made sense to her, she hesitantly stepped backwards from the edge and rushed into my arms.

'Thank you for caring,' she whispered.

'That's all I can ever give you.'

We held hands, and I then asked the woman if I could leave.

'Of course.' She smiled at me. 'But only if you promise never to return.'

*

I jolted upright against my bedframe and switched on the reading lamp. I pinched my arm several times to convince myself that I was in the same room, in the same villa, on the outskirts of Baguio, before reaching for my phone.

'It's me!' I shouted.

'Alex, what is it?' Brother Rojo cleared his throat. 'It's three o'clock in the morning. Is something wrong?'

'I did it, Brother Rojo,' I declared. 'I've solved the riddle of the Clouds.'

And for the next fifteen years, I tragically believed that I had.

Aftermath

Manila, 2001

'It's Martina,' I explained to Brother Rojo a week later in Starbucks. 'She is the reason why I can't escape the Season of Clouds.'

Brother Rojo twiddled around with his thumb, his eyes never leaving me. I could tell that he had his doubts. 'Are you confident in your assessment, Alex? Because she is the most obvious answer and sometimes the most obvious answer is not always the most obvious answer.'

What the hell does that even mean?

'What about the villa?' I replied.

'What about it?'

'There's something mysterious within its walls that unshackles your mind—you said it yourself. During my stay, every question I asked about my life, every fear I tried to unpack led me straight back to Martina. How else am I supposed to rationalise all this?'

He poured me another cup of lemongrass tea. 'You know what I love the most about your country?' he asked, changing the subject. He pointed a skinny finger to the sky. 'The birds! Gosh, Australia has some of the most beautiful birds in the world.'

'Sure …' For a moment, I wondered whether he had been sniffing too much of the local office glue.

'My particular favourite is the lyrebird,' he enthused. 'Are you familiar with that species?'

'Of course. It's probably Australia's best known native bird.'

'A magnificent creature, wouldn't you say? And they are intelligent, as well.'

'If you say so.'

'From what I understand,' he said, ignoring my indifference, 'they have a unique ability to mimic other sounds they hear.'

'They have a very distinct call,' I admitted.

'How would you describe it?'

Shit, I don't know. I thought back to when I was a teenager, visiting my sister Anne on the Gold Coast during the Christmas school holidays. Her family house was situated very close to a well-known bird sanctuary containing a large contingent of lyrebirds. Sometimes when I had trouble falling asleep, fearing that Ringo Bingo was close by, I would find comfort in their nightly chorus.

'When it's dark, and you have no context about what might be happening outside, a lyrebird's cry almost sounds like a woman calling for help.' When I finished my sentence, I realised I had walked right into Brother Rojo's trap.

'Funny you should say that, Alex.' He beamed. 'Because I think the cry of the lyrebird sounds like a fire alarm. Perhaps it's because I have always been scared about dying in a house fire.'

Yes, Brother Rojo had hoodwinked me again, and we both knew it. 'So, you are saying that my interpretation about lyrebirds represents some fundamental flaw in my character.'

'No, Alex.' He shook his hand at me. 'I am merely making the point that we often see things through the same lens. I fear being burnt alive; you think every woman who walks past you needs saving. However, we must not use these afflictions as an excuse to absolve ourselves from the truth.'

Tiny drops of morning rain skimmed across the pavement. 'Life was good before I visited Greece,' I began. 'My career was blossoming, I had just met a girl I truly admired, and I felt good about myself. Then I met Martina. For the last six years, I have carried her guilt around my neck like an iron collar, and it has gradually choked away every last drop of happiness from my soul. But when I left the villa on Sunday, I felt optimistic for the first time in years. I honestly believe that life has given me a second chance. If I don't take this opportunity now, I'm not sure that I will ever get another one.'

'I hear you, Alex.'

'Then you understand why I must forget about Martina.'

Brother Rojo tried to reassure me. 'Yes, I do.' He paused for a moment as he considered the thickening rain. 'If you believe that you have found the answer, who am I to disagree? That is a matter entirely for you.'

'But you are not convinced?'

'Of course not,' he said. 'Those of us who follow the light for a living have a divine right to be wary. We have the disadvantage of witnessing so much sadness in the world. That's why I know that the Clouds will never let you go without a fight. At least give a dithering old fool his parting wish and think things through carefully a second time.'

'For you, I will,' I promised him, even though, as he paid our bill, we both knew that I was lying. For he realised, like I did, that this was my final chance to remove the shameless guilt that had stained my heart for years, to become the man I should have been, had I not agreed to visit Samos with Marco.

Indeed, many years later, long after I had returned to Australia, I triumphantly reminded Brother Rojo of our coffee in Makati and that I had been right all along. By then, I had trained my conscience to erase every last one of Martina's sad memories, together with everyone else who had flirted inside our world: Marlena, Lottie, Eleanor, Danielle, and my God, even Sally. Although I could sense a tinge of sarcasm in his emailed response, he eventually accepted—like I did—that when you finally farewelled the Season of Clouds, the collateral damage was unavoidable.

Muzak

7 March 2016

I finished blow-drying my hair just in time for the alarm clock to detonate outside. George twisted his head and wondered whether my sudden appearance in a suit meant breakfast for him. I reached out to stroke one of his floppy ears, and he licked my hand as a reward.

My wife stirred from underneath the sheets and demanded to know why I was up so early. I told her that I had to get to work to finish a report and would call her later. She wearily fell back into her pillow and wished me a good day. I briefly gazed at her and George and wondered if I would see either of them again.

It took two buses and thirty minutes to travel from my home to where I worked in the city. By the time I waved down that first bus, I was paralysed with fear and couldn't even get my travel card out of my wallet. When the driver greeted me with a welcoming smile, I pretended not to see him.

I dawdled down the aisle and curiously sat next to a skinny teenage schoolgirl, who was bellowing into her iPhone as if there were no other people on the bus. Before we could even make it to the end of the street, her insane wailing stabbed at my throat, and I wanted to scream out at her to stop.

I closed my eyes and slowly counted backwards from one hundred until we arrived at the next terminal several minutes later. I muttered something uncomplimentary to the girl as I stepped off the bus and then jumped behind a queue of people waiting for the next connection into the city. My heart was bouncing furiously inside my chest, but my focus turned sharply to the crisp terminal muzak that blared all around me.

'This old man, he played seven / he played knick-knack up in heaven / with a knick-knack, paddywhack, give a dog a bit / Poor old Alex is in the shit.'

Why won't it stop?

Why can't it leave me alone?

What does it want from me?

I somehow managed to board my next bus and found an empty seat just behind the driver. A young woman with pink hair and a large tattoo of a rose on her forearm gazed at me inquisitively from across the aisle. When our eyes met, she smiled apologetically and then pretended to bury her head into a book. I briefly considered her strange innocence, as if she was a mirage from an old movie I had never seen before, and then dropped my head into my chest.

Come on, Alex, compose yourself; you still have some time left. Maybe there is a clue from the Philippines that can now help you. Some obscure lesson you learnt that could defeat the toxic forces lining up against you.

In desperation, I searched the corridors of time for something—anything—that would guide me through this pervading nightmare. But all I found was an empty void that led to nowhere, for there were no defined boundaries that shaped my life anymore. Instead, it had become a confusing tale of success and failure, love and hate, triumph, and tragedy. Only Brother Rojo might have been able to help me, but he was long gone, taken by lung cancer last year. Was it any coincidence that my descent into madness started not long after his death?

I recalled the last email he sent me before he died. 'Promise me that you will never give up. That you will continue to find true happiness, no matter where it takes you.'

You see, he had always known that I had been wrong. Every letter or email he had sent to me after our chat at Starbucks that day in Makati contained lingering evidence of his doubt. But in the end, he refused to interfere anymore. Even during his final weeks, he knew that this day would arrive and when it did, I would have to face it alone, without his hand guiding me.

Yes, you were right, old friend. I can see that now. For I finally understood what became of a man when he tried to deceive the Season of Clouds. And now that I did, I screamed at myself for having ignored the truth for so long.

PART FOUR

RISE AND FALL

The Big Lie

Canberra, 2001

When I think about the trajectory my life would inevitably take over the next fifteen years, the warning signs were evident almost from the moment I returned to Australia from Manila in early September 2001. If I had been a more discerning person, if I had accepted my fate, I would have carefully reflected upon my time in the Philippines and realised I was missing some vital clues. But I was like the fisherman lost at sea in his leaky boat, frantically trying to plug the holes while wave after wave, lashed against its fragile stern.

Yes, that was me, for I didn't have time for such trivialities. I only cared about progressing a career that had been interrupted because of my emotional frailties. My sole motivation was to prove to those who had previously doubted me that I was back in the game. So I rowed out to sea every morning, oblivious to the fact that my boat was slowly falling apart, and I had no idea how to repair it.

My last three months in Manila were mostly uneventful. Despite all the distractions, I finally confronted a panel of three distinguished Filipino academics on a hot, misty Wednesday afternoon in early June. But it didn't take long to realise that these fine gentlemen were justifiably confused by my thesis. To be fair, so was I.

As I had often done in my life, I managed to overcomplicate the simple parts and over-simplify the complex parts. What was left was a self-indulgent checklist of demands that fell short of proper intellectual rigour. How it could make a difference to the citizens of Mindanao none of us were sure. But thankfully, in the end, I had done enough to secure a pass. So they smiled kindly, poured some iced tea into helping me relax, and then offered me their congratulations. The only sensible thing I could do was smile back at them and say nothing.

After that came a study tour to Russia, weeks of partying and drinking and making inane promises that I was never going to keep, and then finally, a congratulatory trip to the presidential palace where I received my master's degree from the president herself, Gloria Macapagal-Arroyo. Then came even more partying, even more drinking, and even more inane promises that I was never going to keep.

Leaving the Philippines was never going to be easy. Saying goodbye to Marty, Terry, Fely, and Hector was hard enough. But nothing could prepare me for the enduring feeling of loss I experienced when I left the Defense College for the last time. Despite all the promises of reunions in the future, I knew that regardless of the abiding love I felt for the country and its people, I could never return to these tormented shores. The Spiders had set my new jigsaw puzzle in stone, and I was on the way to becoming a new man, leaving the old one to fade away with his dreams and regrets in the backstreets of Mindanao. Such were the laws of physics, time, and jigsaw puzzles, that a new person could never meet his previous, soulless incarnation under any circumstances.

When I landed in Sydney on a balmy spring morning, I realised that Australia had also changed during my absence. Over many years, the issues of immigration and refugees had rankled the country's working class. *They were jumping the queue*, they roared. They were *taking our jobs!* They were *bumming off our taxes! They were threatening our wives and daughters!*

As often was the case, such a cocktail of lies and half-truths soon masqueraded as fact, spurred on by several radio shock jocks who professed to represent the views of ordinary people. A spate of boat arrivals in the first half of the year, carrying asylum seekers from the Middle East, served only to inflame the national debate further.

In late August, a Norwegian ocean freighter, the MV *Tampa,* had rescued hundreds of Afghani refugees from their sinking vessel in the middle of the Indian Ocean. As the United Nations Law of the Sea decreed, the ship's captain immediately sought permission to enter into Australian waters so that the Afghanis could claim asylum.

Sensing that the national mood was behind him, and with one eye on the forthcoming federal election, Prime Minister John Howard decided to disregard international convention and refuse the *Tampa* entry into Australia. At the same time, Howard rushed through legislation confirming Australian sovereignty over its borders. The same headline blared everywhere inside Sydney airport: *We determine who will enter and reside in Australia*.

'Fucking Lebos,' offered my taxi driver as he drove me to my hotel. 'We showed them bludgers who's boss. Too many darkies already in this country, ripping it off if you ask me.'

I thought about Delilah and the hillbillies at the Windows on the World. I thought about the little girl in the village and her desperate cries for help. I thought about all of the poverty, the destitution, the lost helplessness that I witnessed every day for fourteen months. I thought about punching the taxi driver square between his beady, racist eyes. The only thing that stopped me was the metal grill locked between us.

'You crazy fucker,' he roared at me after I paid his fare. 'You're one of them bastards, aren't you? A lousy Arab dickhead.'

When I landed in Canberra the following day, I regretted my decision to return almost immediately. I had come home voluntarily, mainly because I owed my allegiance to the Australian taxpayer. Of course, I didn't want to attract *their* displeasure, either. In doing so, I had rejected several job offers, including one with a major investment company in Hong Kong that would have paid hundreds of thousands a year.

But as I drove past Australia's Parliament House on my way to Matt Smith's apartment, where I would stay until I found myself somewhere to live, I was overcome by a sense of betrayal. Over the last year, I had risked my life promoting what I thought was Australia's values to our South-East Asian neighbours to strengthen our strategic relationships with a part of the world naturally suspicious of our motives.

But what did I get in return? A realisation that everything I told my Filipino colleagues about Australia had been bare-faced lies. All thanks to the politicians sitting inside that grotesque building, spreading their ill-conceived judgements about the suffering of others solely for political gain. For the first and only time in my life, I was thoroughly ashamed to be an Australian.

Several days later, I sent an email to the Hong Kong company, reaffirming my interest in the position. *Fuck the Spiders! Fuck Australia!* I was going to look after myself for once. Hours later, their recruitment manager rang me and requested my availability for a telephone hook-up the next day: Wednesday, 12 September 2001.

That night I celebrated with a home-cooked Indian dinner before going to bed early, excited by what might unfold the following day. A half an hour later, I woke up in the darkness to see Matt hovering over my face. 'Mate, you may want to see this,' he said sternly. I stumbled out into the lounge room, just in time to see the second plane crash into the South Tower of the World Trade Center.

My initial thoughts turned to Delilah, the African-American security guard, Raul, and the wonderful Windows on the World staff. *My God! Remember what I had said to the security guard that day?* Over the next few weeks, I would scour the plethora of victim lists, hoping never to find Delilah's name among them. Eventually, I reassured myself that she did not visit either building on that horrible day, although I suspected that the security guard and Raul weren't so lucky.

In the wee hours of the morning, as more reports started to flood in about an attack at the Pentagon, I immediately understood the implications for the world. I had studied, lived, and breathed Islamic terrorism and insurgency for the previous twelve months, and I knew immediately that this was the work of Osama Bin Laden. I also understood that the world was about to change and that this meant I was no longer going to Hong Kong. My responsibility was here in Canberra, helping to protect my fellow Australians. I had to put aside my personal disappointments and outrage over *Tampa* and contribute in whatever way I could.

For the first few weeks after the attacks, I waited for someone to enlist my services. The United States had already announced that it would provide extra military assistance in battling the Islamic insurgency in the Philippines, and who could better provide their expertise on this issue than me? But for some reason, the calls never came. No matter how hard I tried or how much I used other people to advocate my cause, I could not find a suitable position inside the public service that utilised my recent experiences and skills.

Just before Christmas, exasperated beyond belief, I finally accepted that I was pushing shit uphill. So I put aside my dreams and took the position of director of national logistics within the Department of Defence. I would be responsible for developing strategic partnerships with infrastructure providers like Qantas and Australia's port facilities to support our military operations. It was important work, and I quickly grew into the role. Over the next few years, my team and I would contribute to the logistics planning for operations in Afghanistan, Iraq, and the Solomon Islands.

Just before Easter 2002, the nightmares returned. At first, there was no obvious trigger for these attacks. Things had been working out; I had settled in my new bachelor pad and was focused solely on doing a good job. My mind was preoccupied with work, so I had rarely given much thought to the events of my past.

But gradually, I descended into old habits. Sometimes the nightmares would involve the little girl; sometimes, they would involve the strange events in Baguio, sometimes they would involve being held at gunpoint in Manila, occasionally they would involve Martina. More often than not, I would wake up as I had during my darkest days with Rachel, dripping in sweat, shaking with fear, paralysed by grief.

In June 2002, I delivered a talk about my time in the Philippines. During the obligatory question-and-answer segment, I casually mentioned to the audience that I sometimes experienced nightmares due to my posting. Maybe it was a cry for help, or maybe I was trying to impress the lovely female army psychologist smiling at me from the front row. Afterwards, when everyone was leaving the auditorium, she wandered over to the lectern and matter-of-factly informed me that I was suffering from PTSD in a perky, friendly voice.

'That's rubbish,' I replied sternly. 'I'm perfectly fine.' But she obviously knew that I wasn't, so we never spoke to each other again. Unsurprisingly, that was the last time I ever mentioned my nightmares to anyone.

Of course, I should have seen a doctor. But this would have meant accepting that something was wrong with me, and there was no way I was ever going to do that. Even though I must have known that I was suffering from a severe mental illness, it didn't fit the script I had written for myself. Besides, I had to keep my focus on the bigger picture. Everything bad in my life emanated from my guilt over Martina as it seemingly made one last attempt to infect my psyche.

But I was equally determined that she wouldn't prevail. I had left the Season of Clouds for good, and there was no turning back. Only when I was free from Martina's curse could I ever be normal again. So that's how the biggest lie of my life started to grow.

While I pushed myself down this lonely road, I soon turned my attention to my personal life. If I wanted to become a different person, to have a successful career, and meet someone special, I had to make some changes. One Saturday afternoon, I made a list of things I no longer liked about myself and decided to eradicate them one by one. Out went the meaningless one-night stands, the binge-drinking sessions, and all my stupid reasons for remaining single. Instead, I made new female friends, changed my diet, exercised more, and tried to be a better son and brother. I began to wear my glasses, dropped my obsession with other people's looks, and explored new hobbies that tested my intellect. I did everything I knew to become a normal person, to put the madness behind me once and for all.

They say that you often meet your life partner when you least expect it. Remarriage was the furthest thing on my mind: heck, I hadn't been out on a date since I returned from Manila. Then one rainy afternoon, towards the end of 2002, a work colleague introduced me to a young woman called Miriam with a funny, French-sounding surname, who wanted to join my team. From the moment our eyes met, I knew that I would marry her. Everything about her looks, sense of humour, intelligence, and values seemed destined to cure my inherent loneliness. Without even realising it, she had politely drawn a curtain across every other woman who had graced my past. Delilah had indeed been right—the circle of my heart was now complete, and, at last, I had found my perfect match.

We were married three years later, bizarrely, some might say, on my birthday. My best man Clemmons joked at the reception that this was the only way I would be able to remember our anniversary. Later that evening, we all sang *'You'll Never Walk Alone'* on the dance floor and then regaled tall stories from my past. Before leaving for the night, Jack reassured me that just because I was now married didn't necessarily mean that he had forgotten about the 'airport thing'. His revenge was coming, and when it did, it would be swift and brutal! I laughed at his persistence and then told him how much I loved him.

Miriam and I spent our honeymoon in our two favourite countries: Croatia and Scotland. It would be the first of many trips together that would continue to define our relationship. A year later, we visited New York together, just as Delilah had predicted. On a glistening autumn morning after weaving our way through Central Park West, Miriam and I suddenly found ourselves walking past the Dakota Hotel, where the former Beatle, John Lennon, had been shot and killed in 1980.

'Is there something wrong?' Miriam asked me as I dreamily turned my eyes upwards towards the apartment building where I had once spent three incredible days with Delilah and Dwayne. Inside a prism of golden sunlight, I swore I could see Dwayne staring down at me from his balcony, arrogantly chewing on a slice of mango.

'Nothing,' I replied quickly, having smiled at my lost memories. 'I thought I saw someone I knew, but my eyes were playing tricks on me.' With a final twinge of regret, another chapter in my life had now closed.

Given that I had sorted out my private life, the focus now returned to my career. 'It's time you fulfilled your potential,' Funnel Web Spider texted me one day. For once, he was right. It was evident that as a man in his mid-forties, I had a noticeably short window of opportunity to make it to the Senior Executive Service. I needed to plan every move to perfection, and there was no room for failure.

Without stopping for breath, I ticked off win after win, swapped jobs, got some more wins, and then at the beginning of 2007, found myself working as the chief of staff to the head of Defence personnel. Over the next twelve months, I served two outstanding army generals with distinction, winning their trust and admiration in the process. I was rewarded for my efforts the following year, securing a place on the prestigious strategic studies course at the Australian Defence College. During those twelve months, I completed another master's degree, represented the Department of Defence in China, Japan, the USA, Papua New Guinea, and New Zealand, and published one of my academic papers. Everything boded well for the next stage of my career. Little did I realise that for the first time in my life, I would become the beneficiary of fate's beguiling hand.

Mister Fixit's Mister Fixit

Canberra, 2009–2011

The Labor government's Minister for Defence had become embroiled in a political controversy and submitted his resignation to the Prime Minister, Kevin Rudd, in early June 2009. As a result of the subsequent ministerial reshuffle, the former high-profile union official and the government's rising star, Tony Drake, was promoted to the dual roles of Assistant Minister for Climate Change and Minister for Defence Personnel.

The Ashes in England had now commenced on television, so I had barely paid any attention to these developments. A few days later, the head of Defence Personnel contacted me at home. Would I be interested in working for the new minister on secondment for three months to help establish his new office?

Would I ever! Tony was the only politician in the country that I truly admired. He had risen to public prominence during the infamous Waterfront Dispute in 1997, impressing both friend and foe alike with his integrity and diligence. His leadership in rallying voters against the previous government's hard-line industrial relations policy was something I admired as well.

Regrettably, I no longer considered myself a partisan Labor man: the issues surrounding that damn negotiation manual had soured any allegiance I once had for the party and the trade union movement. But I also knew that experience as a ministerial adviser would open a succession of doors for me. So I dry-cleaned my best suit, got myself a haircut, and prepared for my upcoming interview.

It was love at first sight. I fell in love with Tony's rapid intelligence, quirky sense of humour, and natural compassion for people from the moment I shook his hand. He was not overly demonstrative or ambitious like other politicians. If you saw him walking up the main street and didn't know who he was, you would barely give him a second glance. He was one of those extraordinary guys who looked ordinary, a man blessed with many gifts and an overwhelming desire to help people in any way he could. Luckily for me, he hired me on the spot.

Most people assume being a ministerial adviser is exciting and glamorous, that power lies at the touch of your fingertips. It certainly felt that way at first. Just walking along parliament's shiny corridors of power on my first day was enough to unleash an unparalleled sense of accomplishment I had never felt before. I had finally made it; I convinced myself! But it didn't take long before I realised that this was yet another false illusion. For the most part, an adviser's world proved to be a bleak, lonely existence, punctuated by periods of extreme stress and personal turmoil.

When parliament was sitting, you were often held hostage in the darkest corner of a permanently cold office with little personal contact other than your chief of staff and the department officials constantly ringing your Blackberry. It was usually much worse during the winter months. You arrived in darkness at six-thirty in the morning and then left in darkness at nine o'clock that night. Sometimes you could spend the whole day without seeing the sun.

There was rarely time for a proper lunch. Even seeking a leave of absence to go to the bathroom could have drastic consequences for your day. If you were lucky enough, you could sneak out at morning tea to get a coffee, if prepared to risk the long queues at the legendary Aussies Café.

You worked ridiculously long hours, sometimes seventy-five hours a week, including weekends. As a result, you rarely saw your friends and family, and when you did, your Blackberry never left your side. You dedicated your entire life to keeping your minister out of the shit, twenty-four hours a day, seven days a week. Some of the younger ministerial staff took solace in this bizarre lifestyle through raucous bouts of drinking and partying. I, on the other hand, took every opportunity to catch up on my sleep.

In years to come, several unsavoury revelations would emerge about the work culture in Parliament House, including horrific details of alleged rape and sexual harassment. Although these disclosures didn't surprise me—I had witnessed and been at the receiving end of some appalling behaviours myself—there was no distinction in my eyes between heroes and villains. Men, women, Labor, Liberal—we were all ultimately responsible for institutionalising a poor workplace culture. Parliament was a place that attracted the power-hungry elite, where testosterone and bravado ruled every conversation and decision. Weaklings were eaten alive and spat out with endless regularity. At the same time, the strong believed their victories entitled them to act in any devious way they saw fit. You rarely had friends when you worked in politics, only political colleagues. As a result, loneliness was rife, and you always had to prevent your mind from wandering down some forbidden pathways.

My first three months passed quickly. I spent most of this time familiarising Tony with Defence's personnel policies and processes and learning to become a good adviser. I must have done something right because he asked me if I would like to become a permanent member of his staff during a trip to Singleton army base. 'Sure, that would be great,' I replied, without giving it too much thought.

I was hardly the greatest admirer of the government, but I wasn't going to abandon Tony now. He was the best boss I had ever worked for, and I wanted to learn so much more from him. So I was granted leave without pay from Defence, diligently beavered away for several more months, and even found myself regaining respect for the broader labour movement.

Everything changed in February 2010. As part of the Rudd Government's stimulus package to pump prime the economy following the Global Financial Crisis, Cabinet approved a program to provide Australians with cheap, effective home insulation. However, in an attempt to implement the program quickly, its design and scope had been poorly conceived.

Hundreds of unskilled workers suddenly flooded an unregulated industry, their shoddy work practices barely passing a basic understanding of what was required. As a result, houses began to burn down daily due to faulty installations. Tragically, four young men with little training behind them died horrible deaths while installing insulation. The entire program had turned into an absolute farce.

With an election looming, the PM realised that the public would punish the perception of incompetence. As a result, the government turned to the one man who could get it out of the mire—Tony Drake. He was the government's Mister Fixit, after all. On a bleak Sunday afternoon in February 2010, Tony called all of his advisers together and told us the bad news: cleaning up this mess was going to be a massive task, and he would need to drop some of his Defence responsibilities. I went home that night, thoroughly depressed, realising that my time in Tony's office was coming to an end.

The following day, Tony, accompanied by his Chief of Staff, Allan Beaton, called me into his office. I had my brief case by my side, ready to leave at a moment's notice. Tony looked at me quizzically from behind his black, horn-rimmed glasses. For a crazy moment, I thought I was staring at Clark Kent.

'What do you think about this home insulation stuff, Alex?' he asked me in a stern voice.

'It's an absolute shit fight,' I replied.

'One hundred percent.' He smiled. 'So, how would you like to help me fix it up?'

I felt the air blow out of my stomach. *Really?* 'I don't know anything about pink batts.'

'Well, you better bloody hurry up and learn,' was all he said before dismissing me with a wave off his index finger.

'Why me?' I asked Allan a few minutes later.

'Because he trusts you and knows that you won't leave a stone unturned until it's all over. Now get to work!'

Get to work I did. Over the next forty-eight hours, I read everything I could find on home insulation until my eyes popped out of my head. By the beginning of the following week, I had become a self-professed expert on the topic.

It took me a while to realise it, but the pivotal moment of my career had now arrived. Yes, this was the big crisis I had dreamt about as a kid, and now I had the opportunity to save the world. Okay, it wasn't necessarily chasing Carlos the Jackal across Europe or finding Nazi treasure in the Amazon, but thousands of Australians with faulty insulation installed in their rooftops were now depending on Tony and his team. I, for one, wasn't going to let them down.

For the next several months, I worked myself to near exhaustion: scrutinising and selling our new safety programs, cajoling departmental officials, reassuring insulation installers, organising safety inspections, and helping Tony keep the political wolves at bay. If I wasn't shouting down the line at some unfortunate public servant, I was pleading with a failed installer not to commit suicide. I was at the top of my form: confident, meticulous, compassionate, and brave. Word soon got around the floors of Parliament House that I was a fixer and a doer: 'Mister Fixit's Mister Fixit', as one female member of parliament would call me. Nothing made me prouder.

I was so busy that I barely had time to witness the political storm brewing around me. After weeks of speculation, Prime Minister Kevin Rudd finally met his Waterloo on 24 June 2010. A majority of Labor MPs, spooked by sliding polls, ruthlessly shifted their support to his deputy, Julia Gillard. Weeks later, as the new Prime Minister, Julia called a federal election to legitimise her position. Despite my misgivings about his style, I had a lot of sympathy for Rudd, and I wondered how the Australian public would react to a PM being knee-capped in his first term.

The answer became abundantly clear on election night when the votes pointed to a hung parliament. For the next seventeen days, Gillard and Tony Abbott vied for the support of a handful of independent members who would hold the balance of power for the next three years. Incredibly, two former National Party members, Rob Oakeshott and Tony Windsor, decided to throw their support behind Julia, and we were back in business, baby, albeit as a minority government.

During the election campaign, I spent most of my time working alongside Tony, advising him on policy issues. Tony expected that he would most likely become Minister for Defence if Gillard won the election. So we talked about the things we would do, the challenges we would face, and how we would change Defence for the better. I went to bed every night afterwards, praying for a Labor win, hoping that my dreams would now come true. However, to my utter dismay, Julia announced after she formed the government that Tony would become the new Minister for Climate Change.

Of course, I kept my current job—there was still much to do in remediating the home insulation fiasco. But deep down, I was bitterly disappointed. You see, I readily accepted that the climate was changing due to carbon emissions, but it wasn't something necessarily keeping me up at night. Terrorism, poverty, indigenous health, domestic violence, and the possibility that China might bomb the shit out of us one day were things keeping me up at night, but not climate change. That was just the way my brain worked. Consequently, I viewed Tony's new role as nothing more than a lost opportunity for both of us, and it left me slightly bitter as the new parliament commenced.

Over the next few months, my mental health issues slowly returned. The constant pressure and stresses of the home insulation program, as well as working in a maniacal minority government where you never knew if you still had a job by the end of the day, began to take its toll. Every morning, the first thing I did was listen to the radio to find out whether there had been any house fires overnight. If there hadn't been, I would stumble into my shower, barely relieved. If there had been a fire, I would immediately snap out my Blackberry and order the department to investigate whether the damaged house had insulation installed under our bullshit program.

I constantly lived in fear of someone dying from a house fire, rarely sleeping at night as I pondered the implications of such a ghastly scenario. To make matters worse, I was deteriorating physically. Along with rising blood pressure, I would often wake up in the morning with severe, stabbing pain in my kidneys and head-splitting migraines. It was a terrible way to live.

Just before Easter 2011, my mother died at the age of ninety-one. We had never been close: as she often reminded me, I was a mistake, a quirk of circumstance which, at forty-three years old, came too late in her life. Although she had provided for me as any mother would do without fuss or bother, I could tell there was always a tinge of resentment behind every cut lunch and pressed school shirt. There were other things she could have been doing as a woman in her fifties rather than looking after a teenage boy.

As an older man, I regretted how I had treated her: the sarcastic comments over nothing, the frustration with her forgetfulness, the arguments about her neighbours. I tried to reconcile the situation by accompanying her on a holiday to England in 1996, but all it did was test my patience with her even further and made me realise that we belonged to different planets.

Nevertheless, I broke down in tears when I heard the news. Mum's life had been a tragic exercise in futility: one where she spent the best years of her life with a complex and unfaithful man who mostly put his interests first before hers. In another life, perhaps her star could have shone brightly if luck brought with it other choices than my father. But alas, her jigsaw puzzle had been preordained, just like the rest of us.

Mum died days before Tony was due to deliver a keynote address on home insulation. The government had successfully completed the safety inspection programs designed to mitigate the crisis, and Australia could now rest easy. Despite the importance of this event, Allan, being the thoughtful man he was, insisted that I should be with my family in Brisbane at such a distressing time. But no, that simply wasn't going to happen. I had worked so hard to get to this point, and I didn't attend to go AWOL at the time of my greatest triumph.

Later that week, I stood proudly next to the stage while Tony delivered the best speech of his ministerial career. Afterwards, as I made myself a cup of instant coffee in the office kitchen, he silently surged towards me with an intended bear hug. 'Thank you for everything,' he said, tears swelling in his eyes. 'The government is greatly indebted to you.' I was crying too, of course, but for markedly different reasons. Without anyone telling me, I knew that my time with Tony had come to an end.

Sure enough, barely a fortnight after my mother's funeral, he called me back into his office. The government's Cabinet Secretary needed a new chief of staff, he explained. It was a very prestigious job, and everyone thought that it would make perfect sense if I assumed the role. I had earned it, after all.

I could see the benefits. The Cabinet Secretary was a person I admired, and it also meant that I would be able to observe firsthand how real power worked. Indeed, I found it all quite exciting in the beginning. I would get to sit inside the Cabinet Room, watching the government's key ministers determine Australia's immediate future and then help record the outcomes for prosperity. I was living in a bubble that few people ever experienced, and it made me feel so damn important. And even though I did my best to keep an even keel, it eventually all went to my head. I soon found myself flitting around the halls of Parliament House like King Shit, thoroughly untouchable and impervious to my own machinations. There was only one way this would end, but even I didn't think it would happen so spectacularly.

One afternoon in mid-June, as I busily perused a chapter of the government's one-million-page climate change package, I received an email from Jack.

> *Mate, we haven't seen you for ages. My brothers are having a beer with me tonight. Why don't you come along?*

Jack was right—I hadn't seen him since late January. It was the job, you see. I looked at the eight separate piles of rubbish I was reading and decided there had to be more to life than assessing the 'ins and outs' of a carbon pricing mechanism. But just as I was about to reply in the affirmative, I knew my hands were tied. I owed it to my boss to get my final comments to the Prime Minister's office that night. There was no way I would get out of there until at least ten o'clock.

> *Sorry, mate, I would love to, but not today. I'm doing my bit for Queen and Country and the Spotted Owl, so let's try to catch up next month.*

A week later, Jack was dead, killed in the prime of his life, only forty-eight years old. He left behind a beautiful partner, three gorgeous children, and another child on the way who would never get to meet their dad. As Matt, Josh, and I sat huddled together at Jack's funeral, I felt paralysed with pain. All I could think about was Jack's last email to me and how I had rejected his invitation. Even when one of our mutual friends, Rob, recalled the 'airport thing' during his eulogy, I could barely raise a smile. My entire world had temporarily lost all meaning, and the shadow of Jack's death would never leave me.

For the next two weeks, I was overwrought with grief. It was a constant empty feeling that gnawed at my heart every day. I couldn't think straight; I couldn't make decisions; I no longer cared about others. All I wanted was to see Jack again. Pretty soon, my fragile state of mind began to impact my work. I yelled at staff; I missed important deadlines; I made shit up to protect myself. On the day the government finally released its climate change package, I raised my voice at anyone stupid enough to cross my path. It was a disaster; I was a disaster.

That afternoon, I went home and told Miriam, who I had barely spoken to for over a week, that I was quitting. I had enough of Labor, enough of a minority government, and enough of waiting for the hole in the ozone layer to zap me out of existence. So, I went back to work the next day, told some people that I was about to quit, unintentionally offended someone I cared about very much, had some more arguments, and then desperately tried to recant everything I had just said. Later in the week, I made another attempt to backtrack my decision to resign, got into some more arguments, and finally decided that I had let down my boss and hurt too many people. I had run out of tickets, and it was time to go. I took some extended leave, returned for a few days to clean out my office, then quietly slid away into anonymity.

Someone once told me that you never get to choose the way you leave politics. She was right, of course. In the space of three months, I went from the exalted prince, lauded for his efforts with home insulation, to the irrational pauper who trod on his dick. But it was precisely the way God always intended me to leave. Because in politics, only the insane man is able to appreciate the limits of his usefulness.

Descent Into Madness

Canberra, 2012

It is an intriguing proposition. You can spend your entire life chasing a dream, and when you finally achieve it, you feel no emotion at all. Nothing. Such was my reaction when told of my promotion to a senior executive position with the Agency in mid-2012.

I initially put my trepidation down to a morbid sense of relief. After all, it had taken me almost twenty-seven years to get there. 'Five years too late,' Funnel Web Spider had grumbled when I told him the good news. But something was not right, and I could feel it in my bones. It would take several more years before this constant dread would eventually lead me down an inevitable path towards oblivion.

The Agency was a relatively large organisation responsible for providing medical support services, infrastructure, and supplies to regional Australia. It had a staff of around two thousand people, ninety of whom would work directly for me, with offices scattered across the capital cities. My new role involved managing the Agency's parliamentary support, media, and governance operations.

Deep into my first day, I vowed to staff that my door would always be open to anyone who needed my help, regardless of who they were. Early in my career—if you discount the dubious motives of the Spiders—I never had anyone who cared about my personal development and wellbeing. Given my success with people like Dulcie, I was determined to be a mentor to anyone who needed a kind word or some advice, regardless of who they were or what position they held.

Initially, it seemed to work. The majority of my new team quickly grew into the Alex Gerrick Project. They liked how I joked about myself, how I would rarely get angry with them, how I stood up for them if something went wrong, how I made decisions quickly, how I praised them for even the smallest of victories.

'What's your new branch head like?' I heard someone ask one of my staff members through the flimsy walls of the coffee room.

'Amazing!' she enthused. 'Alex is the best leader I have seen here in over twenty years!'

I went home that night feeling one hundred feet tall. Of course, all of us are prone to slight bouts of exaggeration, as this staff member was, but I knew I had hit the mark. I may have had tickets on myself, but I felt different from the other senior leaders in the Agency. Sure, they were, by and large, a talented group of people. But while they may have known more about budgets, policies, and flow charts than I ever would, to my knowledge, none of them possessed the same operatic scale of my life experiences. For so many of my staff, that was crucial to how they saw me as a leader.

Every interaction I had with them brought the scars accumulated from my time in Samos, the Philippines, and Parliament House. As a result, I had a rare ability to connect with people at all levels: to delve into their hearts, understand their hopes and dreams, unlock their hidden potential and make them believe in themselves. They saw in me the flawed person I happened to be, with the same frailties, same emotions, and doubts that they experienced every day of their lives.

As a result, they grew to trust and admire me. Over the next few years, the leadership ratings I obtained during the annual staff surveys consistently hovered at twenty points above the departmental and public service averages, something that no-one could ever take away from me.

But every leader is imperfect, and every leadership style is susceptible to criticism. The problem with my leadership style was that it was unsustainable. Sooner or later, someone would get disappointed when I didn't live up to my values and their expectations.

'Gerrick is so full of shit,' I heard a guy say to his colleague over the urinal while I was messing about in one of the cubicles. 'He talks the talk, but when it comes to the crunch, he toes the management line like everyone else.'

Oh well, back to the drawing board. But the occasional straggler from my cause was the least of my problems, for it soon became apparent that a small group of people inside the organisation didn't particularly like me or the way I approached my job. I didn't find this especially unusual: for some, working in the public service often meant white-anting the person next to you to obtain an advantage. The higher you went, the worse it got. But there was something uniquely sinister to this campaign that I hadn't experienced before, not even in Parliament House.

It began with a rumour that suggested I only wanted to hire women in my branch. That then morphed into 'He only wants to hire *young* women.' That then morphed into 'He only wants to hire *pretty, young* women.' That then morphed into 'He is having an affair with one of his female directors.'

I was frigging appalled when I found out. Frigging appalled. What made the situation so untenable in my eyes was that certain people in the organisation had known about the rumour for weeks, but no-one had the fortitude to tell me.

Of course, it was all a lie, all of it. For a start, around sixty percent of the Agency's employees were women, so if you did the maths and extrapolated it further, there was always a chance that this trend would be replicated in my team as well. Sure—I enjoyed having young staff work for me, male or female, and neither did I deny that my branch contained several attractive young women.

But for God's sake, I was fifty-three years old and had been faithful to my wife from the first day we met. What's more, I had supervised women of all ages for the last fifteen years, and I never looked at any of them sexually. While I may have retained a fatherly disposition for some of my younger female employees, that was all it ever was, all it ever would be. As for the alleged affair: well, all Miriam and I could do was laugh at its recklessness. Neither of us enjoyed spreading rumours about other people, and we couldn't understand why anyone would want to do this to us.

The Agency eventually slapped some wrists, but apart from one honourable person, I never received any apologies. Frustrated, I decided to pull up my socks, tried to forgive people as I had always done, and continued onwards. But the long-term impacts of this incident were incalculable, for this was exactly when my descent into madness truly began.

Slowly, the paranoia that had laid dormant inside my head ever since I was a child started to consume me. I now viewed everyone outside my team with suspicion. I tripled-checked every email, replayed every conversation. Little things that usually wouldn't bother me suddenly became magnified. *What did that comment mean? Was that other rumour true? Did she that behind my back?* I would go home every night in a foul mood, snapping at Miriam over the most trivial of matters.

Pretty soon, my paranoia even extended to her. *Why was Miriam spending so much time at the gym? Who was that guy at the shop who smiled at her? Are they having an affair?* I would sit alone until three o'clock in the morning, stewing over these absurdities, while the holes in the boat beneath me grew wider and wider.

Throughout this period of growing anxiety and paranoia, I somehow maintained a high level of work performance. As a reward, my superiors gave me a new job, responsible for leading the reform of the organisation's service delivery arm. But I wasn't in the best frame of mind to take on such an important task. For you see, overnight, I had become the living, breathing zombie that Danielle had talked about in Stratford-Upon-Avon, full of self-doubt and confusion.

Luckily, I had some wonderful senior colleagues who supported me during this time. There was Angela, whose unswerving friendship knew no bounds; Meg, a former policewoman, whose joyful laughter lifted my spirits every morning; Rizzie, whose motherly affections inspired me to become a more patient person; Lois, another former policewoman who swamped me with her heart of gold; and a family friend, Karen, who regularly took it upon herself to check on me. On top of that, I inherited a fantastic new team, full of bright, enthusiastic youngsters and hardworking, experienced professionals, and a supportive new boss, Steve, who gave me the freedom to express myself as a leader.

For that first half of 2015, we worked damn hard, achieved many wins, and had lots of fun together. There were weekly cakes, trips to the zoo, and birthday presents for everyone. Sometimes, I spent more time mentoring staff than actually doing work, but I didn't mind. I was trying my best to look after everyone, to keep the façade going.

But that constant buzzing in my head, those tiny spasms of impending doom, would not go away. Soon the noises became louder and louder like a power drill burrowing into my brain. I would wake up in bed at four every morning, barely an hour after I had fallen asleep, believing that a coven of horrid witches had surrounded me. They would scream and shriek at me with their shrill voices, warning me of the evil to come, until I slid further under the sheets in fear.

'Who were you talking to then?' Miriam asked me one night while I stared in horror at my mother and father standing at the end of our bed.

'No-one,' I promised her. 'Just a bad dream.'

'You need to see someone, Alex,' Angela begged me the next day. 'There's a guy I know.'

I took the card Angela gave me, promised her that I would make an appointment, and then had a conversation with myself over the matter later that night, which lasted for two hours.

At this point, I thought an overseas holiday might cure my ills, but all it did was hasten the process. At Narita Airport in Japan, I had a massive meltdown after discovering that I had left my phone charger at the hotel. My public hollering, howling, and cursing almost caused an international incident. Then, a fortnight later in Paris, I caught the worst stomach bug in modern history. When Miriam joined me in Hong Kong a few days later, she found me crying in agony on the hotel room floor.

Things rapidly deteriorated when I returned to Australia. *Splash! Splash!* The water was pouring inside the boat. *Someone, please help me! I'm drowning! But no—not today, son.* So I roused on my support staff for failing to control the noise blaring outside of my office, threw a hissy fit at Steve on Melbourne Cup Day, and cruelly upset my favourite staff member for no reason at all.

I spent Christmas Day secluded in a hotel room on the Gold Coast while I watched thousands of spiders crawl across the ceiling.

'Be warned,' a gigantic huntsman screamed at me. 'You killed our brother in Baguio. We will have our revenge, mark my words.'

In mid-February, a car sideswiped me while I was crossing a road near our local shops. The driver was staring at his mobile phone and didn't see me until the last second. Or perhaps I was so lost in the clouds that I never saw him coming. I wasn't injured—not even a scratch—but it triggered something inside my head that I couldn't even remotely explain to other people. Over the next hour, every close encounter in my life suddenly came tumbling down on top of me until I almost choked in their collective horror.

Stupidly, I rejected Miriam's calls to go to a doctor and turned up to work the next day in an exceptionally foul mood. I snapped at several staff members for no reason at all and then spent the remainder of the afternoon pathetically trying to offer them an apology. But it was too late: the boat had now sunk to the bottom, and all I could do was tread water until someone volunteered to rescue me. I was alone and afraid, doing crazy things I had never done before, incapable of making rational decisions, and unsure where to run.

'Your time is short, Mr Jerrick with a J,' Dumbo gloated on Sunday night. While he giggled and laughed outrageously, a pod of yellow balloons slowly floated above the TV. 'They are coming for you,' he cackled. 'Just you wait and see.'

There was nothing I could do but scream at the walls until an intense pain ripped at my chest. I turned on my iPhone in my panic and saw the millions of work emails that would dictate the rest of my week.

'How do you expect me to do all this?' I cried out at them. 'Can't you see that I am going mad?'

The clock suddenly struck twelve, and Monday, 7 March 2016, finally arrived. While I wiped away my exhausted tears, somewhere in another dimension, Ringo Bingo the Clown laughed and considered his next move.

The Spiders

Canberra, 7 March 2016

'Excuse me, sir, but we have arrived in the city,' a voice gasped into my ear.

I slowly opened my eyes and gazed wearily at the girl with the pink tattoo on her arm. She was standing tightly against my seat as a swarm of passengers began to squeeze past her.

'You fell asleep,' the girl explained. 'We sat next to each other last week, if you remember. I know that this is your stop.'

No, I didn't remember, actually, but I nodded at her as a gesture of goodwill, nevertheless. 'Thank you so much,' I replied coldly. 'I don't know what came over me.'

When did I fall asleep? Wasn't I just in Manila? How in God's name did I get back to Canberra so quickly?

'Mondays can be a real bummer, don't you think?' she asked with a grin. 'Anyway, I hope you have a good day.'

A good day? I suddenly wanted to tell her about Ringo Bingo and Martina and the Spiders and everything else wrong with the world, but I pushed myself up from my seat instead. 'I appreciate your help,' I offered as we reached the exit door together.

'My pleasure, Alex,' she whispered into my ear. 'We can all use some help in our lives.'

I rolled backwards with such ferocity that I fell right into the bus driver's unsuspecting lap. He released a loud 'What the fuck?' and I managed to escape his Popeye forearms by flinging myself forward into the direction of the girl's midriff. But before I could secure her arm, she leapt out onto the pavement and skipped harmlessly away towards another bus.

'Hey!' I screamed at her, my trembling hands trying desperately to cling onto a safety rail. 'Come back!' I kept up this insane hollering for several more minutes until her new bus disappeared beyond the next set of traffic lights.

Realising that the remaining passengers on the bus had become fixated on my insanity, I lifted my briefcase and limped towards Café Essen, where I usually got my early morning coffee.

The kind Vietnamese waitress who doted on me every day brought out an extra hot café latte with her usual smile, and I gripped it firmly in my hands. For some reason, its smothering heat gave me a slight sense of comfort.

My iPhone suddenly whirled out a new text message, and my eyes widened. Only they usually texted me so early in the morning.

Sure enough.

We need to see you now, ordered Funnel Web Spider.

Just as I suspected, it was all about the Spiders. If there were one small consolation, it would surely be over very quickly.

Why? I texted back. As if he was ever going to tell me over the phone.

You will find out soon enough. Just get here. Pronto. The usual place.

The usual place was an abandoned office on the top floor of a building in Marcus Clarke Street, and it provided the perfect environment to host a cluster of spiders.

It didn't take long to find my way there—ten minutes at the most. Several drops of rain parted my hair just as I was about to enter the building. *Yes, they love the rain, don't they?*

I fell into the first lift I could find, ignoring a giant man wearing suspenders and a wrinkly old lady wrapped in a dark velvet skirt. They both considered me with soulful frowns as if they already knew the true nature of my crimes and the awful fate that awaited me.

When I reached the abandoned office, I punched in the security code and quietly walked inside. They were waiting for me in a semicircle, just as I had expected. From left to right: Black Widow Spider, Golden Orb Spider, Daddy Long Legs Spider, Funnel Web Spider, Mouse Spider, Huntsman Spider, and Dickhead Spider. In front of them was a single, lonely chair.

'Sit down,' Funnel Web Spider ordered. I deliberately dropped my briefcase in front of him from a great height, causing the other spiders to huff and puff in protest.

'Has anyone anything to say before we start?' Funnel Web Spider asked his companions.

'Yes,' Dickhead Spider said. 'We must remember that Australia is a glorious nation—'

'Not now, Dickhead,' moaned Funnel Web Spider. Black Widow Spider was now laughing so much I wondered whether her head was about to fall right off.

'It just occurred to me,' I said, smiling. 'I have known all of you for nearly thirty years, but none of you has grown older. Why is that?'

The spiders now looked at each other curtly with their eight sets of eyes.

'Never you mind,' Black Widow Spider shrieked. Her sickly grey teeth had an extra sharp edge to them, and I knew I had to be wary. But then, I never really liked Black Widow Spider. Altogether way too highly strung.

'Enough of this,' shouted Funnel Web Spider. 'We have brought you here for a reason, Alex.'

'I've figured that part out already.'

'We once had high hopes for you,' he said. 'But you never quite matched our expectations.'

'How so?'

'Well, look at you now. A branch head still working in a meaningless organisation like the Agency.'

'I'm next in line for a promotion,' I replied confidently.

'Perhaps,' Funnel Web Spider said. 'But even if you are, what help can you seriously provide us? We wanted you to stay in the national security domain, to play an important role in the grand scheme.'

I shuffled in my seat. 'Maybe I never wanted to be a part of the grand scheme. Did you ever consider that?'

More growling and hissing.

'If not the grand scheme, then what?' Golden Orb Spider demanded to know.

'To live a normal life. To sleep easily at night. Things that people like you will never understand.' Surprisingly, those words came out so much easier than I had ever dared imagine.

'Then you're a fool,' said Daddy Long Legs Spider. 'You can't have a normal life when you serve the Spiders.' The rest of them mumbled out their agreement, and I now realised they were setting me up to take an almighty fall.

'What's this all about?' I finally asked. 'Everything you have ordered me to do over the years, I have done to your satisfaction. Despite what you may think of me or my motives, I have never let any of you down. Not once.' The eerie silence that now prevailed proved that I was right.

'Yes, that much is true,' Funnel Web Spider conceded. 'You have always succeeded in your tasks. But times have changed since you joined us. The world is a different place. There are new rules to abide by; new agendas that have emerged that even we can't ignore any longer.'

'What does this have to do with me?'

I was never going to like their answer.

'We have examined your past, and we no longer believe that you have the moral fortitude to serve our cause.'

'What do you mean by that?' I demanded angrily. 'Moral fortitude? You guys dare to talk to me about moral fortitude?'

'That's enough,' snapped Funnel Web Spider. 'This isn't a decision we take lightly. But the facts are the facts: we have in our possession a report that found you have consistently gaslit women throughout your life. We cannot sit back and let that continue without investigating these claims further.'

Gaslit women? What the hell does he mean by that?

'This is crazy,' I roared back at him. 'If what you are suggesting is that I have done something inappropriate to a woman, then that's an outright lie.'

'Yes,' snarled Black Widow Spider. 'We have heard you say that before. But didn't you once tell a married woman who worked for you in Sydney that you wanted to explore your friendship with her further?'

I could not believe what I was hearing. *Are they seriously raising this old chestnut again?*

'I explained that to you before,' I heard myself screaming. 'I swear to God that I didn't mean that comment sexually: it was a term that women had often used on me and which I often used on other people. If I wanted to hit on her, surely I would have said something less ambiguous.'

All seven spiders now withdrew into their seats. It was clear that they wouldn't countenance my explanation, no matter what I said.

'Excuse after excuse,' Black Widow Spider began. 'Just like when people accused you of stacking your branch with pretty young women.'

'But that was all bullshit, don't you remember? I was the victim in that situation.'

'You're always the victim, it seems,' Huntsman Spider interrupted spitefully. I knew that he hated me with a passion ever since that day in Baguio. 'But we received some interesting information from our brothers and sisters in the Philippines, which further condemns you.'

A bound plastic folder was thrown at me with utter contempt, almost hitting me in the face. 'Read it,' he ordered.

I tucked the folder neatly into my lap. 'I don't need to read it, for Dulcie can vouch for everything I did in the Philippines.'

'Oh, can she now?' asked Huntsman Spider, an evil grin pasted onto his hairy face. 'You may wish to think again. You see, Dulcie agrees with us that your behaviour in the Philippines requires further scrutiny.'

'What?' Dulcie had been working for the Spiders for several years now from her new base in Singapore. But during that time, we had remained very close friends.

'Is this some sort of a joke?' I asked hopefully. 'Dulcie supports this bullshit?'

'No, this isn't a joke,' Funnel Web Spider warned.

'But she's my friend. We spoke only last Friday.'

Mouse Spider, who always had a soft spot for me, was quietly sympathetic. 'I'm sorry, Alex. I know how close the two of you are.'

My hands began to shake loosely against my chest, and I carelessly dropped the folder onto the floor. *What the hell? Was this the same Dulcie who I had mentored in Baguio? Who accompanied me to Russia a couple of weeks later? Shit, this never happened to Henry Higgins. Or did it, and I just never saw it coming?*

'I'm not accepting this bullshit,' I doubled down on the Spiders. 'I have done nothing wrong.'

'Don't tell it to us,' said Funnel Web Spider. 'Tell it to the special investigator.'

'What do you mean?' I replied nervously. 'What special investigator?'

'We have written to the public service formally to express our concerns about your behaviour in the Philippines. An independent person will examine these claims. If you are found guilty of an indiscretion that contravenes your employment contract, you will either be sacked or demoted. And you won't be much use to us if you are sacked or demoted, will you?'

I kicked out the chair away in disgust and picked up my briefcase. If only I could travel back in time to that rainy day in Brisbane and shoot the whole damn lot of them before they were able to infect me with their neurotoxic poison.

'Don't bother going to work this morning either,' said Black Widow Spider. 'You are suspended on full pay until further notice.'

I barely had time to absorb this latest insult when the air inside my lungs exploded. 'Why are you doing this to me?' I squealed pathetically. 'Where's your goddam loyalty?'

'Loyalty only goes so far, Alex,' replied Funnel Web Spider. 'Now get the fuck out of here.'

I tumbled blindly to the door, defeated and humiliated, before I twisted my head back towards their table. 'Screw you!' I shouted at them. 'Screw all of you.'

'Typical,' said Daddy Long Legs Spider.

'Very sad,' said Mouse Spider.

'Arsehole,' said Huntsman Spider.

'Pervert,' said Black Widow Spider.

'Loser,' said Golden Orb Spider.

'He had so much potential,' said Funnel Web Spider.

'We must remember that Australia is a glorious nation—' began Dickhead Spider.

When I reached the foyer, I ran towards the nearest bathroom. A large group of office workers, caressing their morning coffees, parted like the Red Sea to avoid my stench.

'Bing, Bang,' Ringo Bingo cried out as he opened the toilet door for me. For the first time in forty-five years, he had reverted to being a clown, and it was so good to see him again.

'Leave me alone,' I screamed at him, locking the cubicle door behind me.

'You know what to do,' he guffawed through his extra set of yellow teeth. He somehow squeezed his ugly head through the gap beneath the toilet door. 'Yes indeedy, Mister Greedy. I'm sure you know what to do.'

Yes, I know what to do. Trapped inside that horrid little cubicle, with my sanity breaking into pieces, I finally realised that Ringo Bingo's meddling in my life had reached its natural conclusion. Because all of his planning, all of his vile yellow scheming, was about bringing me there to that very moment in time. And to his enormous credit, he kept the promise he made to me so many years ago and ensured that, at last, I had the means to release myself from his ongoing treachery.

Meg

Canberra
7 March 2016

By the time the rain stopped, I would be dead.

They say that you can tell someone is serious about committing suicide when they can explain how they are going to do it in fine detail. For me, I knew how mine was about to go down to the finest detail. I would first put George inside the house, lock the door behind me, and then wander out into the backyard, holding a spanking new razor blade that I had just purchased from the local supermarket.

The outdoor BBQ area was the best place to execute my plan, I decided. It was hidden beneath a rickety old tin roof and a clump of sprawling eucalyptus trees, so none of the neighbours would be able to see my demise. The concrete pavement meant that it would be relatively easy for Miriam to wash away the blood afterwards. After all, the last thing I wanted to do was to ruin the house. She would be angry enough with me, you know, me being dead and all, so there was no need to make it worse for her. *There, I had thought of everything. Even when faced with my suicide, I was thinking of other people. What a guy!* Yes, this would be the most perfectly planned suicide ever attempted. So, I watched the tiny droplets of rain pound silently against the windowsill and waited for the perfect moment to arrive.

I only found out later, but right at that time, Rizzy, Karen, Angela, Lois, and Meg were having their own conversation. From what Karen later told the special investigator, it went something like this:

Rizzy: 'Guys, I'm really worried about Alex.'

Karen: 'I'll call his wife.'

Angela: 'I'll call his lawyer.'

Lois: 'I'll call the head of corporate.'

Meg: 'I'll call Alex.'

*

Ring, ring.

Damn it! It's Meg. Why is she calling me now? I couldn't remember this being in the plan. Why can't they leave me alone?

'Alex, where are you?'

'I'm at home.'

'We're genuinely concerned about you. Is it true that you have been suspended?'

'You shouldn't listen to rumours, Meg.'

'Alex, what's going on?'

'I—' Jesus, I couldn't get any words out.

'Alex, please talk to me.'

I coughed and spluttered until my voice returned. 'Meg, if you must know, I am about to top myself. Nothing for you to worry about.' Yes, it sounded a tad flippant, especially given that I was talking to an ex-policewoman.

'Alex,' Meg said sternly. 'You are not doing anything of the sort.'

'But, Meg.' I began to cry.

'Listen to me. Make yourself a cup of tea and wait for me to arrive. I will be there in fifteen minutes. In the meantime, I'm calling the police.'

'You don't have to call the police,' I begged her. 'I will wait for you.'

Exactly fifteen minutes later, I heard several frantic knocks on the door.

'Thank God,' Meg sighed once she saw me. 'Get your coat—I'm taking you to Canberra Hospital.'

'I don't want to go.'

'Too bad. That's where we are going. I won't repeat myself. Get your things; we're going to the hospital.' Meg was no longer the staff member who made me laugh every morning with her zany sense of humour. She was one serious ex-copper who was used to saving lives and was not going to take no for an answer. At that precarious moment in my life, God had selected the perfect person to help me survive.

The following two hours descended into a blur, but I did remember getting shuffled from General Admission to suicide watch, a thousand eyes poking inside my head. During the transfer, I lost my work phone, house keys, and Medicare card. Nothing inside my brain computed with the stark reality of my situation, so I responded to the doctor with simple, one-syllable answers. Only when Miriam barged through the nearest door, crying hysterically, did my brain begin to function again. And when she held me tightly against her body, I promised her that no matter what happened in the future, I would never put her through such an ordeal again. Despite my abysmal track record over the years, this was one promise I was determined to keep.

Fight Back

Canberra, March 2016

The man who raised me from the dead was a tiny Indian psychologist called Roy. I had been referred to him by my GP after he prescribed me the usual drugs to counter my depression and hallucinations. Of course, I didn't want to go—my views about therapists hadn't changed since that Culpepper specimen back in 1999. But my doctor was not taking no for an answer. 'You have suffered a major breakdown,' he warned. 'If you want to get better, we have to reconstruct your mind.'

'I wouldn't put it quite that way,' Roy said with a laugh at our first consultation. 'What we need to do is plot a way forward for you, that's all.'

Sure, easy as pie.

'But the first thing you have to do for me is to accept that you have a problem.'

He could have dropped an iron ladle on top of my head. After everything that had happened since Samos, including two attempts at suicide, it still didn't fully register with me that I was seriously unwell. At different stages of my life, I knew that things weren't right, but I had always found an excuse to follow a different path. Besides, if I was dead-set crazy, how did I finish officer training, five academic degrees, and sort out the home insulation fiasco?

'Because you can still function as an ordinary citizen yet hide your debilitating illnesses from the rest of society,' he replied sternly. 'And from what I can see already, you are quite the chameleon.'

He was right, of course. Gradually over time, I became the world's most accomplished actor. While pretending that nothing was wrong with me, I strode to work every morning, that same confident, sassy leader loved by his staff. But at two o'clock in the morning, I was hiding beneath my blanket, fantasising about ugly witches dancing at my bedside.

When I finally accepted, in that consultation room, that I had a problem, a considerable weight lifted from my shoulders. At last, I could see things with clarity.

'Good,' said Roy when I told him. 'Now we can make progress.' The first thing we discussed was that my career and reputation stood to be permanently ruined.

'It's such a shame that you have let your career define you.'

'Well, I have worked bloody hard to get where I am.'

'Yes, but to what purpose? How much has your health, marriage, and friendships suffered by all those endless hours in the office?'

I thought about Jack. *Okay, you got me there.*

'You are assuming that your friends and family will disown you, Alex. But you are wrong. Look how quickly your friend Meg responded to you on that awful day. Think about the steadfast love of your wife. These are not the actions of people who will readily abandon you. Those who love you will always be at your side, and the rest of them can go to hell.'

For the first time in over a week, I actually laughed. 'But I don't want to lose my job either,' I muttered. 'Not after everything I have gone through.'

'But what if you did?' Roy snapped at me. 'Would that be such a tragedy? Might it not open another door for an intelligent man like you?'

I really didn't know the answer to that question, so I said nothing. I simply sat in that chair, with that same hangdog expression I had used all day, waiting for him to create some magic from another world that would make me feel better. Lo and behold, he actually did.

'This is what I want you to do, Alex. Consider it your homework. I want you to create a narrative about yourself. Who is Alex Gerrick? What are his values? What does he like to do? Then come and see me the day after tomorrow.'

I thought it all too silly at first, and I wasn't in the right frame of mind for another person's silliness. But nevertheless, I went home and penned some thoughts straight away to get him off my back. Two days later, I returned, waving a single sheet of paper in front of him.

'Okay,' he ordered triumphantly. 'Read it out to me!'

I puffed out my chest. 'Alex Gerrick is a kind, compassionate man, who works hard, never shirks his duty, and tries to help people whenever he can. He loves his wife, family, and friends. He is passionate about Liverpool Football Club and world history.' Pretty low-key, even by my standards. But that's all I could come up with at short notice.

'Excellent.' Roy clapped loudly. 'Very nice words, Alex.'

'If you say so.'

'I do. And you want to know why?' He didn't let me answer. 'It's because nothing you have just said connects specifically to your current job at the Agency. Rather, they reflect a set of values that could be used anywhere.'

'I see.'

'This is what I want you to do. You will now learn this little ditty of yours off by heart until you can recite it backwards. Then whenever your depression and anxiety get the better of you, especially about your job, I want you to repeat those words over and over again until you feel better.'

I didn't know what to make of his request, but what option did I have? So, I nodded my head and then caught a taxi home, agreeably nonplussed by the whole episode.

Later that afternoon, as I walked down to the local shops, I was suddenly swamped by waves and waves of panic. The reality of my situation had become mind-numbingly stark. *I was going to lose my job, wasn't I? Oh, God! What would I do next? Where would I go? Would I ever work again? What about the mortgage?*

The rain clouds that came bearing down from the west threatened to burst all over my groggy head. But in one last act of desperation, I began to recite those silly words I had learnt:

Alex Gerrick is a kind, compassionate man, who works hard, never shirks his duty, and tries to help people whenever he can. He loves his wife, family, and friends. He is passionate about Liverpool Football Club and world history.

And you know what? It worked! It bloody well worked! After five minutes, I was struck with a feeling of calmness I had rarely experienced in years. As if by a miracle, everything was brought back to its proper perspective.

Perhaps it wouldn't be so bad leaving the public service after all. I'm sure there was a role for me in the not-for-profit sector. Or maybe I could do some army reserve work? How good would it be to work for the military again?

As soon as I got home, I texted Roy immediately.

Roy, it worked! I was feeling really depressed before, so I followed your advice, and it worked!

Several seconds later: *Of course it worked! Why would you think otherwise?*

I had reached the turning point in my battle against PTSD and mental illness. A line in the sand had finally been drawn after all these years, and I would never cross it again. Most importantly, I had found someone I could trust, someone who understood the intricate nature of my condition without pre-judging my motives as Culpepper had done. For me, the critical point in my recovery was finding the right person who knew exactly how to help me.

Over the next twelve months, Roy would recommend several techniques to help me take the next step towards a normal life. For instance, he showed me how to reduce my predilection for catastrophising by regulating my breathing patterns. Through cognitive therapy, Roy helped me dissociate the Philippines from the trauma-related episodes which had dogged me since 2001. He encouraged me to focus on hobbies like digital 3D art that reduced my stress and helped desensitise my adverse reactions to the violent memories of Martina's story.

Over time, with Roy's help, I developed a toolbox that I could use whenever my condition threatened to overpower me. Every problem I raised with him, he always offered me a solution. Well, all except for one. But even then, he put me on the right track.

You see, I desperately needed to understand what happened; how someone who had always tried to do the right thing by people suddenly found himself in such a precarious situation. I had my theories, but the trick was finding someone I could trust to help validate them. Roy had some views, of course, but he was less focused on the past and more concerned about how I would manage the future. Nevertheless, he encouraged me to do my own research, seek the views of friends and family and then go back to him when I was ready.

But it wasn't going to be easy, for I had spent the majority of my adult life deliberately hiding my mental issues from everyone who knew me, including Miriam and my closest friends. The only two people who really understood the true nature of my cognitive decline were Jack and Brother Rojo, and both of them were dead.

As I sat in my lounge room chair, trying to think of a way forward, something Lottie had said to me over twenty years ago suddenly leapt into my head. We had been talking about my mental health on the ferry ride back to Piraeus, just after she shared her story about Markus, when she said, 'That's the beauty of meeting new people, Alex—we see you how you really are, stripped of the shield you have built to protect yourself from the rest of the world.'

I allowed her words to sink in for a while before I realised that I had discovered a key—a very unique key. Lottie, Marlena, Eleanor, Danielle, Sally, and Delilah had all met me at a time in my life when I was at my most vulnerable, with my shield well and truly down. Was there a clue hidden inside our brief associations that could help me better understand my current predicament?

Trying to remember every conversation I had with all six women wasn't going to be easy. It had been twenty-one years since my visit to Samos, seventeen years since my Lost Week, and fifteen years since I farewelled Delilah and emailed Sally in New York. Time often destroyed past memories ruthlessly, while there was absolutely no thought about contacting them. No, they all had their own husbands, children, and friends to worry about, and I had no right to force myself back into their lives after all these years.

But I had another idea instead that was crazy enough to work. I bought myself a new notebook and one of those multicoloured pens with the sliding notches and began to write down every little detail, every little snippet of conversation that I could remember from those relationships. After two days, I had produced over fifty pages of disorganised, priceless chatter, written in a different colour for each girl.

Once satisfied that I had everything I needed, I started to carefully sift through each page, looking for anything worthwhile that could help me unravel my past. It was a comment made by Danielle, written in bright red ink on page five, that first caught my attention. During our picnic at Stratford-Upon-Avon, she suggested that people usually carried their bad childhood experiences into adulthood. Of course, most of what she said during the picnic had been lost inside that tense car ride to Warwick Castle. But suddenly, her words made perfect sense.

I never forgot what happened to me as a kid: the near-death experiences, the sexual assault, and exposure to domestic violence. They were part of who I was. But I had merely viewed them as isolated incidents: obscure pieces of that jigsaw puzzle that slotted into place separately after each episode. Never once did I consider how these incidents may have collectively impacted my older self. Oh, Culpepper tried, but she was too fixated on my sexual peccadilloes to make any real progress. So, I researched everything on childhood trauma that I could find and tried to work it out for myself.

Incredibly, every journal or article I read simply reinforced Danielle's previous comment: people who experienced early childhood trauma were highly likely to develop mental health issues as an adult. Trauma, I further read, was accumulative—it could lie dormant for years and years until some fateful trigger unleashed the next stage of its fury.

As I continued to read case study after case study, my mind temporarily wandered back to my childhood. I remember how I felt after being shot that day: lying in that hospital, wrapped in bandages, frightened, alone, and thinking I would die. I recall how I felt at Mudgee pool, knowing that I might never be able to retake another breath of air; my father's fists thumping on my brittle little chest as waves of water spooled out of my lungs. Or how disgusted and confused I felt when I was forced to lick an older girl's vagina in a woodshed. I was eight years old, for God's sake.

When I became a teenager, I repressed these memories inside the fantasy world I had created for myself. I mean, why focus on those bad things when I could be having fun, masquerading as James Bond? But once my fantasy world crumbled into dust like everything else from my youth, the real truth about those years became grotesquely stark.

Like why I hid in the toilets during maths class throughout Grade 5, how I broke down in front of my classmates in Grade 6, and why I hardly spoke to any girls until Grade 9. Or why I hid in the bushes for the entirety of the Grade 10 formal and why I then repeated Grade 11. They were all indicators that the emptiness I felt for most of my young life wasn't exaggerated. I really did dance between the raindrops, and it was the loneliest feeling in the world.

In my late twenties, I somehow found the determination to turn back the tide. That was my one great strength; the ability to counterattack before I became totally overwhelmed with fear. *Lick'em tomorrow, Alex*. But as the experts revealed, it only needed one spark to burn the whole fortress down. That spark, of course, was Martina.

I turned my computer off and went for a long walk. *There was a reason why Brother Rojo always doubted my Martina theory,* I thought. He knew that I wasn't truthful to myself, that I was only focused on everything that had happened after Samos. But fifteen years of living the big lie had finally opened my mind to his wisdom. Despite all the hubris and self-congratulation after my visit to the villa, I never actually solved the riddle of the Clouds at all.

As I stretched my legs across a splintered park bench, waiting for the afternoon breeze to soothe my blushes, everything in my life finally made sense. It wasn't Martina that prevented me from enjoying a happy life: it was the severity of my mental illness caused by a potpourri of senseless childhood traumas. The events of Samos, being held at gunpoint in Manila, the little girl in Mindanao, Jack's death, the rumours inside the Agency—these were nothing more than triggers that reopened my pre-existing wounds.

I rushed back home and re-examined my notebook. Yes, my friends all tried to warn me, didn't they? Marlena in the coffee shop, Lottie on the ferry to Piraeus, and Sally in her final email.

But why? Why had I become so obsessed with Martina? Why did I allow this tragically fragile woman from Bosnia, who I had only known for a few days, to dominate my life as she did? Once again, Danielle had the answer. At Stratford, she insisted that my desire to save vulnerable women was driven in part by the guilt I felt for not protecting my mother when I was young. So I stormed back to the internet to see what other information I could find on the topic.

After several hours, I eventually found an article by a leading psychiatrist that confirmed Danielle's theory. Men who suffered sexual abuse as children or witnessed violence against their mother or other females often became overly protective of women as adults. Conversely, other men used these adverse childhood experiences to justify their own violence against women later in their lives.

My thoughts returned to that final night in Samos, when Martina asked me that confronting question of whether I could ever hurt a woman. She was testing me, trying to work out if I really was one of the good guys. Despite her apparent carefree persona, Martina was actually very vulnerable and afraid. She needed someone in her life who understood what she had experienced, who would always protect her without destroying her fierce independence.

By forcing me to reappraise my own life that night, by demanding that I tell her my biggest secret, I was unwittingly undertaking a job interview for that role. Later, when I convinced her that we needed to remain friends, she clung to that hope as if her life depended on it. Until, of course, I refused to make that phone call.

When I finally realised the extent of that betrayal and how it must have impacted Martina, I became obsessed with my own guilt; a consequence made easier by my increasingly fragile state of mind. Despite all of my pathetic attempts to erase her memories, I took that guilt with me everywhere I went in my life, including to the workplace. Every woman I mentored, every woman I rescued, became a byword for Martina. It didn't matter if they were old or young, fat or thin, big or small. I was determined to never let a woman down again, even if it meant inflicting my wisdom upon them when they didn't need or ask for it. Only when there were no other women to help could Martina finally rest in peace.

But there was something else that I had neglected as well. I recalled how Sally had remonstrated with me in the kitchen all those years ago in Manila. *'You don't trust women, Alex.'* Absolutely I didn't, Sally. Ever since that girl pinned me between her legs when I was eight years old, I became inherently petrified of women and the power they wielded over me. Helping women like Martina, Danielle, Dulcie, and the young women at the Agency and receiving their praise was the only antidote I had to prevent myself from being hurt all over again. But unfortunately, my pursuit of this antidote ultimately turned into an obsession.

At times, I became so fixated with doing the right thing in my relationships with women, even as a mentor, that I became overbearing and intrusive. I realised that my compulsive and obsessive behaviour had contributed to destroying at least two close female friendships.

'*Women don't respond well to knights in shining armour, Alex,*' Eleanor once told me in London. After her story about Gunther, she had warned me about divulging too much about myself, of overplaying my hand with women. Danielle had done the same, even suggesting that some women took advantage of men like me. And then there was Marlena, who had been sceptical about my mentoring ability right from the word go.

These issues continued to swirl inside my head for several more days until I read something else Sally had said to me on that final night in Manila. '*Men and women sometimes see the same issue differently, Alex. That's why you always need to consider both sides.*'

My thoughts immediately returned to the married woman in Sydney. I had been so dismissive of her after she had taken umbrage at my comment about exploring our friendship further. After all, how many women had repeated the very same line to me over the years? Lottie? Danielle? Others? How often had I said it to other people—men and women—without offence being taken?

In the end, I viewed her complaint as merely another case of a woman screwing me over: just like the girl who sexually assaulted me, or the girl who bullied me in my first job, or the older woman who sexually harassed me when I first joined the public service or the woman who tried to mask her affair with another man by falsely telling her husband that I had hit on her. Yes, why was I even giving her bullshit any credence?

But what if my comment had indeed genuinely offended her? *Men and women sometimes see the same issue differently, Alex. That's why you always need to consider both sides.*

Thanks to Sally's belated wisdom, I realised that I shouldn't have dismissed the woman's concerns so willingly. She had a right to be heard and a right to have her concerns taken seriously. Furthermore, it blackened my heart to think that my well-intentioned mentoring and support made her feel uncomfortable about my motives. So, I decided to write down my recent interactions with staff members until I filled ten more pages in my notebook.

After scrutinising this additional information, I accepted that on one or two occasions, I may have unintentionally crossed the professional boundaries between mentor and protege, where I had inserted myself into a person's life in such a way that most likely made them feel uneasy, where my desperation for attention and acceptance bordered on fixation. Without me even realising it, I had inadvertently become the monster I always vowed to defeat.

Furthermore, in my haste to exorcise Martina, I had betrayed the sacredness of her despair and that of every other woman who had been subjected to sexual assault and harassment. Ever since the Philippines, I had turned a blind eye to the evil that existed within their lives for the pitiful sake of my convalescence.

Most women I knew bore the burden of my deceit, for they lived in fear every day of their lives. My only solution to this travesty was to put a patronising hand around their shoulders, tell them how terrible the world was and reassure them that things would get better.

Well, things weren't getting better. Indeed, things wouldn't get any better until all women were able to walk the streets at night without getting attacked or go to work without some twit staring down at their legs. With this on my mind, I went to bed that night, thoroughly ashamed of my self-deceit.

But rather than catastrophising over my potential fate, I woke up the following day with a renewed sense of purpose. After such a comprehensive self-analysis of my life, I finally had the unequivocal answer to that question Martina had asked me during our last night in Samos. I knew with one hundred percent certainty that I could never intentionally hurt a woman, no matter who they were.

I reminded myself of that old Latin maxim: *Actus non facit reum nisi mens sit rea*—the act is not evil unless the intention is evil. While I accepted responsibility for my actions and behaviour, there was a massive difference between those unintended failures of judgement and the accusation that I had deliberately 'gaslit' women. I had done nothing of the sort, and I refused to allow such a spurious allegation to define the rest of my life. *So, what was I going to do about it?*

Eleanor had suggested to me in Brighton that I had given up on myself. For far too long, I had failed to heed that advice, to the detriment of everyone in my life who loved me. Instead, I had nonchalantly accepted the curse of my jigsaw puzzle without fear or favour—that everything in my life had been preordained and there was no way to turn back from the path it had selected for me. But as I was about to fall off a rainbow, I realised that I owed it to Miriam and my family, friends, staff, and those extraordinary women from my past, to make a final stand against this perfidy. The time had come for me to fight back.

End of the Line

Canberra,
April 2016

In mid-April, I finally met with the independent investigator. My friend Karen accompanied me for moral support. Before I even had time to put my feet under the table, the investigator began to hound me with a thousand questions about my time in the Philippines. So, I sat there calmly and answered each question truthfully.

I explained how I once prevented a group of men from raping a young girl in the backstreets of Makati.

I explained how I gave money to selected Filipino women to help them advance their education.

I explained how I provided financial assistance to an eighteen-year-old Filipina to enable her to escape a life of prostitution.

I explained how I tried to save the little girl in Mindanao.

I explained how I helped people like Dulcie to enhance their careers.

I explained that while I wasn't a saint and certainly had my issues, I had always tried to treat women with respect and kindness.

Throughout that harrowing three-hour interview, I did everything I could to prove my innocence. When I finished, I made sure that I left that damn room with my head held high. Whether the investigator believed me or not, I wasn't sure, but I had kept my promise to Delilah and showed her and everyone else involved the man that I truly was.

Several weeks later, Mouse Spider rang me with the news. The investigator had completed her deliberations and found that I had not contravened the public service's code of conduct. It was finally over. I was not going to lose my job.

Although I was initially relieved by the outcome, I had no reason to celebrate. For the last three months, I had been dragged through the pits of hell, and all that remained was a rump of the man I used to be. My physical and mental wellbeing had been permanently compromised, while the stress experienced by my wife, staff, and friends was immeasurable.

I was especially sickened by the way the Spiders had used Dulcie in this process. Despite everything, I was genuinely remorseful for what she had gone through herself during that time and equally concerned for her wellbeing. She was a good person, and my life had been enriched by our association. It was simply heartbreaking that I had lost a valued colleague and a friend, someone who I cared for deeply, for no bloody reason.

My initial anger at the Spiders soon turned into incandescent rage when I realised that the stain on my reputation would remain with me for the rest of my life despite the outcome. That whole thing about mud sticking was true. In the cutthroat world of the Senior Executive Service, a question mark against your name could be used for devastating effect. No matter how hard I tried to release the shackles, the complaint would continue to loom menacingly in the background as I tried to resume my career.

The first challenge I faced following the verdict was my eventual return to work. I was determined to face the music, even though I was still suffering the debilitating side effects from my breakdown. Yes, it would be hard at first, but I just had to grit my teeth and see it through.

My first day back was especially traumatic. I lost count of how many times my anxiety caused me to vomit in the backstreets of Canberra as I meandered towards our building. My biggest fear was the unknown. I didn't know what people had been told about my situation or how they would initially react to my presence. I was going back into the trenches completely blindfolded, and it scared the living bejesus out of me.

Thankfully, most of my staff were delighted to see me again. People like Meg, Angela, Lois, Karen, and Rizzie were simply grateful that I was still alive after that crazy day back in March. But when confronted with the cold, quizzical looks offered to me by some other people in the lifts—actual or imagined—I wanted to hide in the darkest corner of my office and never come out.

During my absence, Steve, my boss, had accepted a promotion to another department. A new team had arrived to reform the Agency, and I quickly realised that my professional status had abruptly changed. Overnight, I had gone from being someone at the top of the pile to being relegated towards the bottom. I could see it in the way people spoke to me, how they 'forgot' to invite me to meetings, and how quickly they disregarded my previous work.

The Agency head was a kind, fair, and intelligent man who had always valued my contribution. While he remained at the helm, I knew that I would be treated fairly for the time being. I also had several other friends at the senior levels, including the Head of Corporate, who understood what I had gone through and supported me.

But some of my critics saw this as an opportunity to sink the knife into my back once they realised I was vulnerable. Soon the insults began to fly thick and fast and always behind my back.

Gerrick is useless.

Gerrick can't make decisions.

Gerrick no longer has a future in the Agency.

Gerrick doesn't know what he's doing.

Gerrick doesn't support agency reform.

What? Come again? Gerrick doesn't support agency reform? What the hell had I been doing for the past eighteen months? If you were going to take a crack at someone, at least get your facts straight.

Then came that staff meeting several weeks later. As hundreds of people poured inside the main auditorium one afternoon, one of my colleagues looked at me square in the eye and suggested that I had to smile more. To be fair, I'm confident they never meant to say it in such a cruel way, but at the time, rarely had I felt so belittled in my life. Two months earlier, I had been sitting inside the suicide watch ward at Canberra Hospital with my wife crying on my shoulder, but now I was being told to smile more in public.

I found these personal attacks particularly unedifying for someone who had spent his professional life regularly achieving results and receiving praise for his efforts. Sure, I was nowhere near at the top of my game following the investigation, but where was the fucking compassion? I had suffered a severe mental breakdown and was lucky to still be alive. Did some people genuinely expect me to return to work and carry on where I left off as if nothing had happened?

But if the attacks against my work performance cut deeply, nothing prepared me for the plethora of false rumours and gutter innuendo sweeping the Agency's water coolers. I knew the identities of those who were behind the rumours, but at times, some of the things being said about me were so ludicrous, so insane, I wondered whether they had hired a scriptwriter.

The final insult occurred one Friday afternoon as I was about to go home for the weekend. I was standing inside a lift with two women, minding my own business, thinking about what I would make for dinner. One of the women was a known problem child who, three years before, had sought my advice on a workplace issue because she was told by her friends that I was a good guy. I had gone out of my way to help her, and she seemed grateful at the time. But now, as the lift reached the ground floor and I was the first person to walk out, I could hear the woman behind me loudly say to her companion, 'Scumbag!'

Later that night, I called Miriam into our lounge room and bawled my eyes out in front of her. It was not fair. Was that how you treated someone in the workplace who was suffering from PTSD and depression? After everything I endured during my life, was that the future that now awaited me—to be viewed forever as a pariah, just because the Spiders had made unproven allegations against me?

For the rest of the weekend, Miriam and I discussed our options. By Sunday night, we had formulated a plan for me to resign in several months. We both agreed that I shouldn't remain in the Agency one minute longer than I had to.

But just when I thought all hope was lost, things at work started to slowly improve. The catalyst for change was undoubtedly my new boss, who began to realise my worth as a person and as a senior leader. With her support and compassion, I gradually regained my self-confidence and started to kick some goals again.

Then there was my incredible team, which had continued to stick by me, despite the uncertainty over my future. Even as my confidence returned, my supporters never stopped believing in me and kept pushing me upwards. That was especially true of the young female staff members, who wouldn't entertain anyone saying a bad word about me despite all the vile rumours. As one of them cheekily put it: 'You might be a sleaze, Alex, but you're our sleaze, and we love you.' Their unwavering support and sense of humour meant so much to me, and I vowed to treasure their memories until the day I died.

By the end of 2016, the worst year of my life, I had managed to turn things completely around. I had regained people's trust again, and, importantly, my team was finally rewarded for their hard work. But they say that success breeds many orphans, and as we rolled into 2017, all those orphans seemed to find a new home with me. With that came a hugely increased workload, which at times became almost impossible to manage.

In a typical public service agency, a branch head like me would have four, at the most, five directors and their sections working for them. But by the middle of the year, I had somehow accumulated a grand total of thirteen directors, almost three times more than any other branch head in the Agency. The situation became so absurd that several colleagues simply refused to believe me when I told them about the size of my team.

On a sunny autumn day in May 2017, I walked into Roy's office for another consultation. Before I could make it past his front counter, he came storming out of his office, waving his arms at my head. 'No, no, no,' he said with a half-smile. 'I don't need to see you anymore.'

'But, Roy—' I tried to implore.

'I have taught you everything I can, Alex. It's time for you to move on and lead a more productive life. Now go for it!'

As I jumped into a waiting cab, I swore that I could see his crumpled little nose inspect me morosely through a glass window. Nothing I could possibly say would ever adequately demonstrate my gratitude for what he had done for me. He had indeed reconstructed my brain, just as my doc said he would. But as the taxi zipped around the next street corner, I prayed to God with all my heart that I would never have to see him again.

By the beginning of 2018, I finally accepted that my public service career was all but over. Despite my hard work, achievements, and sacrifice over the previous twelve months, it was evident that the promotion I felt I deserved was out of reach. Oh, the occasional compliment would be thrown my way just to whet my appetite, but I knew where I stood. The organisation was going in a different direction, and I wasn't part of its long-term plans. Fair enough; I had no problems with that.

That realisation would have devastated me two years ago, but in January 2018, I couldn't have cared less. Sadly, I no longer felt any loyalty or connection to the Agency. Instead, I was like the person who realises they have nothing in common with their partner anymore after several years of a loveless marriage. I was physically and mentally exhausted by the sleepless nights, the ridiculous workload, the constant sixty-hour weeks, and the internal politics that rarely made sense.

No, I was finished with the Agency and the public sector. They had served me well, and I was grateful for the opportunities they had provided me, but I wanted to work for an organisation where my contribution was genuinely valued; that allowed me the freedom to pursue my own legacy. There was another world out there waiting for me—if I could only find the courage to take the next step.

In late January 2018, I attended a Foo Fighters concert in Sydney. Seeing them play live again somehow mitigated the loss I felt over the recent suicide of the Linkin Park frontman, Chester Bennington. My love of both bands had played an important role in my recovery, and the loss of such a brilliant talent so young left me speechless. But that night, it was all about Dave Grohl and the boys, and as always, they didn't let me down. For two hours, I rocked along through all their best songs until they played my favourite title, 'These Days', from their brilliant album, *Wasting Light*.

A quarter of the way through the song, I suddenly became overcome by a weird sensation. I struggled at first to work out what was bothering me before a Chris Shiflett guitar riff made everything seem so obvious. Remarkably, I hadn't thought about work all day. Yes, for the first time in over twenty years, I had gone through an entire day not thinking about work. It was at that very moment that I decided I would leave the public service for good.

But before I could make the announcement, there was one thing that I had to do, and I wasn't looking forward to it.

'Hello, Alex,' Funnel Web Spider grumbled when he answered my call. It was the first time I had spoken to him since that awful day in 2016. Up until then, my only contact with the Spiders had been through Mouse Spider. 'What do you want?'

'I'm letting you know that I am leaving the public service.'

'Impossible,' he roared. 'Only I can sanction such a move, for those are the rules.'

'Fuck your rules. They don't apply to me anymore.'

'That isn't how it works. You know that as well as I do.'

'Any allegiance I had to your cause evaporated when you sold me down the river in 2016. All bets are off, and so I am leaving for good.'

'No-one ever leaves the Spiders without our permission. We can destroy you.'

I laughed at him down the receiver. 'I don't think so. There are things I know about you, things that I have done for you, that would destroy the whole rotten applecart in minutes. We both know that. So I've made a list and sent it to a lawyer who will release it to the media if anything ever happens to my family or me.'

'You wouldn't.'

'Try me.'

We both knew he had one last card left to play, and so he played it without remorse. 'You're forgetting that we know. Don't you remember? The identity of the man who shot you when you were a kid?'

'What of it?'

'He may be in his late seventies, but he can still hurt you. If you leave us before he dies, we cannot stop him from coming after you again.'

'Let him come,' I replied sternly. 'And you can join him if you like. Because if you do, I promise that I will send both of you to hell together.'

Click.

The following Monday morning, I handed in my notice to retire from the public service. Some eyebrows were raised, noses were put out of joint, and my team was generally saddened by my decision. However, one of them came up to me after my announcement and explained why she was happy that I was leaving.

'You were going to die in this job, Alex.' Rightly or wrongly, I felt the same way.

Over the next few weeks, many speeches were given, many farewell afternoon teas were eaten. The Agency head was incredibly kind to me, ensuring that my final days in the public service were appropriately celebrated. Despite all the dramas of the last two years, I was privileged to have worked at the Agency and genuinely happy we were departing on relatively good terms.

On the night before my last day at work, I finally sifted through the many farewell cards and emails I had received over the previous few days. As I read one after the other, I couldn't help becoming overwhelmed with emotion.

Alex, you are the most inspirational man I have ever met.

Alex, you were the best leader the Agency has had, or ever will have.

Thank you for being the best branch head and mentor I could have asked for. You taught me so much about being a leader.

Alex, you are a most inspirational leader; you will be greatly missed by all of us.

Thank you for always taking the time, Alex. I am grateful for all of your support and wisdom over the years. It meant so much to me.

Alex, it will never be the same here without you. In my own dark times, I needed a father figure who could make me see the light. And you were that person.

Alex, thank you for all of your support and encouragement over the years. You remain the best boss I ever had.

Alex, thank you for being a great boss, an inspirational leader and having the strategic vision that always flowed to your people. Above all, thank you for being a kind and generous friend—you will be greatly missed.

Alex, you taught me so much and had faith in my ability, which I had lost completely. I will never forget you and what you did for me.

All of those comments, and many more like them, had been written by women. It made me think of a line I once wrote for a play when I was a university student: *The ordinary man will always find the greatest of ironies in the smallest of things*. While my complex relationships with women almost destroyed my career, it was the women I had mentored and led who gave it true meaning. It might never remove that permanent stain, but I was hopeful that one day each of them would take whatever they had learnt from me and use it to do something incredible with their lives. For any leader, such a wish is the best farewell gift you can ever receive from your staff.

The following day started out like nearly every other one in my thirty-five-year career. I put on a suit and tie, scratched George under the chin, and kissed Miriam goodbye. On the bus, I listened to 'These Days', 'Boulevard of Broken Dreams' by Green Day, 'The End' by Linkin Park, and 'Wish You Were Here' by Pink Floyd. They all seemed appropriate songs for such a momentous day. I took my usual coffee at Café Essen and spent the first couple of hours doing a final clean out of my office.

Just before midday, I realised the time had come. One by one, I slowly visited each part of my massive team and said my farewells in the best way I could. There were tears, there was laughter, and there were plenty of photos. None of us really believed that this day had come, but now that it had, we were doing our best to make it memorable.

My next stop was the senior executive wing, where I thanked the Agency head for everything he had done for me. His support during the most challenging period of my career was something that I would always cherish. Sometimes good people do indeed get to the top.

The last person I visited that day was my boss. She had opened her mind to my worth at a time when so many others had abandoned me. Without her support, I would have left the Agency long before now. We hugged each other tightly, and I told her how much I would miss her.

I was met at the lift by my lovely EA, Kathy. Over the last two years, she had been my rock, always looking after me with that contagious smile, even during my darkest days.

'Oh my God, this is it,' she said, tears rolling down her cheeks. 'It just won't be the same without you.'

'Of course it won't,' I smiled.

We jumped into the lift together, and I pressed the button for the ground floor. Each of the thirty-five seconds that it took to reach our destination represented a year-by-year celebration of a career mostly well done. I had started out all those years ago as a dishevelled drunk, lucky not to be sacked for my poor behaviour and work performance. I was leaving as an SES officer on my terms, having achieved many things that I was proud of, with my dignity and integrity intact. I couldn't ask for much more than that.

When we reached the ground floor, I handed Kathy my security card, followed by a final embrace.

'Do you know what I still can't get over?' I asked her.

'What?'

'Two years ago, I fought like hell to save my job. Now, I can't wait to get out of here!'

We both laughed, and I slowly made my way towards the revolving exit door. Just as I was about to walk outside, a hand tugged at my shoulder to reveal the woman who had made that awful comment about me that Friday afternoon in 2016.

'Alex, I just wanted to say goodbye,' she crawled. 'This place is going to be so much poorer for your absence.'

I looked at her with the derision I kept for special occasions like this. 'Yep. Not bad for a scumbag, huh?'

I watched as her face turned violently red, stole one final glance at the busy foyer, and then turned my back on her and the public service for good.

Excerpt from *The Search for Martina*

Kiama, New South Wales
June 2046

October!

Greta woke up just before lunchtime, Alex's manuscript splayed out on the floor beside her. Damn it! She had slept for far too long. She had to see Alex, and there was no time to lose. Despite the nagging twinge of pain in her back, courtesy of a troubled, twisted sleep, Greta dragged herself out of bed and sneaked in a hot shower. She picked out the first set of clothes she could find in her suitcase—a tight pair of jeans and a golden silk top—whisked on some mascara and quickly swallowed a cup of instant coffee to make sure she was fully awake.

Thirty minutes later, she was back in her car, trying to remember the name of the street that she needed to turn into.

October!

Greta hoped she wouldn't be late. She knew within her heart that Alex didn't have much time left. Weeks, days, hours, maybe. Who could tell? There was so much more she needed to know. So much more she needed to understand.

October!

She couldn't believe that her mother and Danielle had both lied to her. Of course, she understood the reasons, but she was a grown woman, and there was no excuse for sending her on a wild goose chase halfway around the world when the absolute truth lay closer to home.

October!

Everything had changed now. Greta's book was no longer the main priority, and all that mattered to her was finishing Alex's story before it was too late.

When she arrived at the front counter, thankfully, it was Mary who greeted her and not the head nurse.

'I need to see Alex,' Greta begged.

Mary was instantly shocked by Greta's appearance. The day before, she had been the epitome of Aryan beauty and elegance; now, she looked like she had just been run over by a truck.

'I can't do that, Mrs Schumacher,' Mary replied sternly. 'You have to call us twenty-four hours in advance to make an appointment. Those are the rules. We explained that to you yesterday. If my boss found out that I allowed you inside, she would sack me on the spot.'

'Oh, screw her,' Greta scowled. 'Who cares about her stupid rules? We may not have much time, and I must see Alex now.'

Mary's pinkish cheeks almost collapsed into a smile, but she quickly regathered her composure.

'I'm sorry, Mrs Schumacher. There is nothing I can do.'

Usually, Greta wouldn't have time for niceties, but a change of approach was required; such was her desperation. 'Please, Mary.' She grovelled softly for special effect. 'I know how much he means to you. Trust me when I say that I have to speak with him again before he dies. There is no time to lose. What I have to say might give him the final peace of mind that he deserves. I'm sure you want to see that, just as much as I do.'

Mary sighed a million times before she finally lifted her eyes towards the reception clock. 'Okay. The old bulldog isn't back for another hour. You have twenty minutes.'

'God bless you, Mary.'

She found him in the exact same spot as the previous afternoon. But this time, when she kneeled in front of him, he immediately acknowledged her presence.

'Ah, Eleanor Kuhn's daughter. I am surprised to see you back here so soon.'

'I read your book last night.'

'All of it?'

'All of it.'

'What did you think?'

'It was amazing.'

Alex didn't react at all, as if he had expected this praise from her.

'And now that you have read my book, do you still want to tell me your story?'

'No, I don't.'

That wasn't a surprise either. 'Did you also figure out why I couldn't write that final chapter?'

'I think so,' Greta replied. 'After everything you went through, you never actually found a way out, did you? You remained a prisoner inside the Season of Clouds.'

'Not entirely true,' Alex replied wistfully. 'When I left the Agency, the sunlight eventually found me. For a while, at least, I bore witness to its beauty. It allowed me to see life through various emotions that were never on offer to me in the past: peace, security, contentment, tranquillity, love, and dare I say it, hope.'

'What happened?'

'The world succumbed to COVID-19; that's what happened. After that devastating first year, all I saw around me was death, misery, and sadness. There was no way I could continue to grow inside the sun, to find the true happiness I had always sought at such a desperate time. So, I returned to the only world I had ever known before the doors were permanently sealed behind me.'

'I'm so sorry,' was all Greta could say.

'You shouldn't be because, for all his wisdom, Brother Rojo forgot to tell me one thing. There was only ever the Season of Clouds for me.'

Yes, I can see that now, admitted Greta to herself.

'And the book?'

'I wanted the last chapter to be a celebration of my life. To put the previous five hundred pages into perspective. How I beat PTSD, what you could learn from my experiences, you know what I mean. But nothing had really changed, don't you see? I was now back inside the Season of Clouds, where I belonged. There were no victories to gloat about, no lessons to impart, no magic wands to wave. There was only me, the same man I had always been. So I tossed my manuscript in the cupboard and decided that writing a book about my parents was far more interesting.'

October!

Don't mess this up now, Greta. Make him understand.

'But there is another way to write the final chapter,' Greta said firmly. 'Make it end in 2019; before anyone had ever heard of COVID.'

'What do you mean?' Alex asked as he bent his ear closer towards her. She could tell that she had finally succeeded in impressing him.

'I once read an old interview that you gave where you said that life is all about how you deal with that one specific moment in your timeline. Do you remember?'

'I do. How is that relevant now?'

'Don't you get it? At that point in your timeline, just before Covid, you had triumphed. You had won your battle against PTSD and depression and were living a happy, fulfilling life, helping other people. Look at all the incredible work you did with FearLess, the organisation you led after leaving the public service. You were an inspiration to so many people suffering from PTSD and mental illness. The lessons that underpinned your journey are just as important now as they were back in 2019. A new generation needs to hear your story, Alex.'

He momentarily whipped his head towards the sun before callously throwing his woollen shawl onto the ground.

'An interesting concept,' he finally admitted. 'Everything after 2019 never happened, is that right?'

'Yes, that's right.'

'Brilliant,' he said, chuckling some more. 'But there is one tiny flaw in your plan. How do you expect a decrepit old man like me to give this his full attention? Such a task could take me several weeks, and I do not have the luxury of time, unlike you.'

'I will write it for you, that's how.'

October!

'Really?'

'Really.' Their eyes glittered together. 'Oh, I do want something in return, though.'

'Naturally.' He laughed at her.

'I want to know more about the man who shot you.' She offered him a sly smile. 'For my next book.'

He thought it through for several seconds before replying. 'You really are Eleanor's daughter, aren't you?' he said. 'Okay. I don't see what harm it can do now. You have a deal.'

She took his bony hand and shook it gently.

'But this might take a few days,' Greta said awkwardly. 'We need to get started immediately, if you know what I mean.'

Alex laughed again. 'If it makes you feel any better, I have no intention of croaking it just yet, so I think I can manage a few more days just for you.'

Some things had to be resolved first. Later that afternoon, Greta, Miriam, and the head sister managed to thrash out an agreement on how all of this would work. And while Mary never got the sack, she reckoned afterwards that she had only survived by the skin of her teeth.

Over the next four days, Greta and Alex would meet beneath his favourite weeping willow, just after the other residents had finished their lunches. They were curious, at first, about the goings-on between their notoriously silent companion and this beautiful, mysterious woman with the strange accent. But once the novelty wore off during the middle of day two, they all grumbled together into their Thai chicken salads and allowed the couple's incessant chatter to drift aimlessly towards the nearby ocean.

Greta and Alex quickly developed a routine. He would spend their first hour pouring out his random thoughts with bullet-like precision while Greta sat steadfastly next to him, furiously dictating copious notes into her iPad. Occasionally, she would interrupt him to ask a question or clarify a point, but things were always resolved amicably after Mary brought them out a pot of tea. Throughout that special time, Alex remained entirely lucid, cooperative, and even, well, happy.

'I'm going to miss you,' he said sadly on the last day after Greta had passed him a Tim Tam biscuit. 'You have given me a reason to get up every morning.'

'Oh, you're not getting rid of me that easily,' she said. 'I will type up the first draft over the weekend and come back on Monday to get your final approval.'

'Damn. I guess I'll have to hang around for a few more days, then.'

'You know you want to,' she replied, laughing. She reached for her handbag and shuffled inside with her fingers. 'Oh dear, I almost forgot. In all this drama, I haven't given you Mum's present yet.'

Alex pushed his hands in front of her in protest. 'No, Greta, please. I think I know what you're about to give me, and if I'm correct, today is not the right time. Give it to me next week when you say goodbye. It will help soften your absence further.'

'You have a deal,' she said, nodding. They tapped their teacups together for a job well done and then gazed out into the distant shore.

'There is one question I wanted to ask you,' Greta suddenly said. 'The manuscript you gave me the other day. A yellow Post-It note was attached with a message in your handwriting; do you recall it?'

'Yes,' Alex replied softly. 'It says: *Please give this to her when I die.*'

'Who did you mean?' pressed Greta further. 'Was it Miriam?'

Alex placed his teacup on the table and scratched his chin. 'It was so many years ago, Greta. I can't be sure if you must know. Maybe it was Miriam, but then, maybe it was a close female friend who I thought deserved an explanation of my behaviour.'

'I see.'

'Or maybe it was the daughter I never knew I had.'

October!

Please, not now.

'Greta, may I ask you a question?'

Say nothing, Greta. Please say nothing.

'Of course.'

'Are you my daughter?'

A lonely gust of wind smothered her blank face. 'Why would you ask me that?' she cried out, confused at her own tempestuousness. At the same time, her eyes began to tighten around her growing tears.

'You let slip yesterday that you were nineteen years old when you and your mother saw me that day in Potsdam. You don't have to be a mathematical genius to work out that you were born in 2000: a year after your mother and I had our affair.'

October!

'I—' She wanted to say something, anything that might distract him from this madness. But she was far too preoccupied trying to stop the waterfall plunging down her jawline. *Damn you, Mum, why did you have to leave it all to me?*

'The thing is,' Alex continued, 'if you were my daughter, nothing would make me happier.'

By now, Greta was lost within another world. Everything she had hidden from herself had been revealed. The pain, the anger, the self-recriminations. *Why hadn't I seen this before now?*

'Greta, please don't ...'

Alex never completed his sentence, for there was a howl. There was a whimper. There was the sound of a body crashing over a wheelchair.

'Mary, please help me!' Greta screamed. Everyone was looking at them, and everyone wanted to know how the whole thing was going to end. Everyone, that was, except for Greta.

'He'll be okay,' Mary promised her after they helped carry him back to his room. 'This has happened to him before, and he just needs some rest. I'll call you when he's better.'

After three days, Mary still hadn't called her. Then on Monday, just as Greta finished her breakfast, she received a text message from Miriam. Alex had died the previous night during a thunderstorm. Mary found him lying peacefully on his bed in the morning, a sheet of paper crumpled in his hand, a final smile etched onto his lonely face. High above him, a mangled spider web hung delicately from the ceiling. He was eighty-four.

His funeral was held a week later. It wasn't a sumptuous affair by any means, but that would have suited Alex fine. Clemmons paid tribute to their time together in the army reserve. Harry regaled that crazy day when he and Alex had stopped a revolution. Matt reassured everyone that Jack would now get his revenge for the airport thing. And then everyone cried when they played 'You'll Never Walk Alone'.

Later that afternoon, Alex's close friends Luke, Mary, Karen, and Greta escorted Miriam to a lonely hilltop overlooking Kiama beach. 'This is what he always wanted,' Miriam said as she held the urn out in front of her. 'The freedom to go anywhere in the world.' She pushed back her shoulders, and with one final surge, released his ashes into the air. Tiny pockets of wind joyfully scattered them high across the heavens. Once satisfied, Miriam finally turned to the others, smiling. 'At last, Alex is now at peace.'

In the weeks and months that followed, controversy continued to rage inside the literary community about Alex's death. One rumour centred around the piece of paper found in his hand on the day he died; another involved the identity of a strange woman dressed in black who attended the funeral. The usual maze of twisted conspiracy theories swirled on social media, night after night, driving the sane world crazy until Greta decided to do something about it. Two weeks after *Season of Clouds* was finally published, Greta went on the ABC's *The 7.30 Report* to end the nonsense once and for all.

Interviewer: Can you confirm that the piece of paper found in Alex's hand contained a will that gave you most of his estate?
Greta: Don't be ridiculous. Why would he do that?
Interviewer: The Twitter rumours suggest that you are his daughter.
Greta: Then I suggest that your viewers don't always listen to Twitter rumours.
Interviewer: So, what was written on that piece of paper?
Greta: It was a poem given to him by a friend from the Philippines many years ago.
Interviewer: And the woman in black? Many people believe it was Martina, the woman who Alex met in Samos. Can you confirm that?
Greta: No, it wasn't Martina.
Interviewer: But you do know who it was?
Greta: Of course I do, but you will need to buy my book later in the year to find out. (Both laugh.)
Interviewer: Getting back to Martina, why didn't you tell Alex the truth before he died? Didn't he have a right to know?'
Greta: (A slight pause). Alex's guilt about Martina was the driving force for everything good he did in his life. Who was I to tell him during his final days that the one thing that gave his life meaning had actually been a lie? No-one had that right, not even me.
Interviewer: Do you think he suspected something?
Greta: What you have to understand was that Martina and Alex shared the same soul.

When he thought she had died, he inherited her pain willingly. In the end, whether he knew or not, Alex would have always carried that pain for her. He had no choice, don't you see?

Interviewer: Yes, I see ... And then there is all this conjecture now about who shot Alex when he was a boy. Do you have any further information about that?

Greta: Not much (she lies again). But then, I suggest that you wait for my book. You never know what might be revealed.

Interviewer: (Laughs) Okay, everyone—cut! (She turns to Greta). Thank you, that was great.

Greta: Thanks for having me.

Interviewer: By the way, I finished reading A Season of Clouds *last night. If you don't mind me saying so, I still can't work out if Alex was a hero or actually a villain.*

Greta: He had the same problem.

(Greta stands up and quietly leaves the studio.)

Kandos

Kandos, New South Wales
September 2019
(As dictated to Greta Schumacher)

I knew I had to go back to Kandos one more time if I was to ever finish my book. But that wasn't the reason why I had returned. Ever since I found that old school photo in our garage just before Easter, the spirits of my childhood, lost within the rugged mountains that surrounded this long-forgotten town, had been crying out to me every night, calling me home to face one final reckoning. So, with the FearLess conference over, Miriam dropped me off at the Kandos Rural Hotel last night, realising that whatever demons I had to face, I had to face them alone.

I woke up that morning just in time for breakfast. The woman who served me was convinced that she had seen me before. 'Have you been on the telly or something, love?' she asked with a glint in her eye.'

'Unlikely, not me,' I reassured her. 'You've mistaken me for someone else.'

'That's a shame,' she sighed. 'We don't get too many famous people visiting Kandos anymore.'

I examined the freckles on her dimpled cheeks and tried to smile. She was yet another victim of this once-thriving industrial community. What did they use to call Kandos?

'"The town that built Sydney",' she reminded me. 'The cement from our factory helped build institutions like the Sydney Harbour Bridge and the foundations of Central Railway Station. Not bad, huh?'

No, not bad at all. Furthermore, during the 1960s and 1970s, Kandos had extended a welcoming hand to migrants from all over the world, people like my father and brother, who brought various specialised skills with them. It was a culturally diverse, one company town that looked after its people and dreamt of opportunities that the future might bring.

'We couldn't compete, you see,' she continued. 'Not with the rest of the world being as it is. So, after nearly one hundred years of blood, sweat, and toil, the cement factory finally had to close its doors for good.'

'I know,' I replied. 'It's a bloody shame.'

'Yes, that's exactly right! It's a bloody shame!'

'Samantha, for goodness' sake,' moaned Bill, the hotel manager. 'Our guest doesn't need a history lesson at nine o'clock in the morning.'

'Actually, I probably do,' I said, grinning. 'Fifty years away from Kandos is an exceptionally long time.'

I collected my small overnight bag and shoved a twenty-dollar note in Samantha's hand. 'Thanks for the conversation. I really enjoyed it.'

She squeezed the note around her fingers to make sure it was real. 'Anytime, sweetie!'

I was just about to exit the front door when she squealed out in excitement.

'Now I know where I have seen you! Yes, you look like that actor!'

Here we go again.

'You know, Eric Bana!'

*

My first stop was Kandos primary school. I couldn't really decide whether it had changed or not since the last time I saw it. True, there were more buildings to observe, more facilities to admire, and I didn't even remotely remember that clump of trees ever being there. But as I peered into the same playground I once graced, watching a group of kids screaming over a plastic football, I realised that I was looking at a video compilation of my own childhood. That was me out there, competing with the rest of them, with my gangly legs, pageboy haircut, and grazed elbows—just another innocent child, waiting for the world to catch up with him.

That same little boy wandered over to where I was standing, his big brown eyes glaring at me in confusion.

'What are you doing here?' he finally asked me.

'Just checking to see how you are.'

He looked curiously at my short, cropped hair. 'Do I really go that grey?'

'Getting old sucks,' I replied grimly.

He chuckled to himself while I waited for him to ask me that million-dollar question.

'So, what do I end up doing with my life? A doctor? A lawyer? An astronaut?'

My answer would surely disappoint him.

'None of those things,' I replied. 'A public servant.'

He let the concept sink in. 'A public servant? Really? How? I mean—why?'

'Things don't always go to plan,' I explained. 'Sometimes you have to adapt and take the first opportunity that comes your way.'

'Wow, I never saw that coming. I mean, I like the idea of becoming a diplomat, but other than that, I don't even know what a public servant really does.'

'You'll find out one day, trust me.'

He scratched his chin. 'Do I have fun?'

'Sometimes it will be rewarding—other times it will have its frustrations. Along the way, you'll travel to places you never dared imagine. You'll meet prime ministers, presidents, and even a princess. You'll work with some terrific people. Eventually, you'll become a leader that many people will admire.'

'And will there be many girls?'

I laughed at my own innocence. 'Sometimes when you want them, sometimes when you don't. But one day, you'll end up marrying a wonderful woman who will love you forever.'

'Cool, because you see, I have this crush on Bettie Scott.'

'I know you do—you're talking to *me*, remember?'

He laughed as if it all made sense to him now.

'And what will be the biggest regret in my career?'

What a question for a little boy to ask; and with such little time to reply.

'Perhaps you become so invested in your dreams that you miss out on other things that are more important.'

How right I am.

'But do I eventually find my true calling?' he asked pointedly. As I admired his pale, blank face, it suddenly occurred to me that at this point in his timeline, he had already been shot and nearly drowned in Mudgee.

'Yes, you do. You will become the head of FearLess, an influential charity that supports people suffering from post-traumatic stress.'

He offered me an insanely wide smile as if he already knew what post-traumatic stress meant, and I noticed for the first time that his front tooth was missing. 'I like the name FearLess,' he finally said. 'It makes me not want to be scared. I have nightmares, you see. About a clown dressed in yellow.'

'Yes, I know. He will disappear one day, I promise.'

He squatted down to re-tie his shoelace and almost hit his head on the fence separating us. *Typical Gerrick clumsiness.* 'And how do you help those people? You know, the ones that have that post—whatever—thing.'

I tried not to laugh at myself. 'I explain how I repressed my own trauma for many years until it was almost too late, how it was the biggest mistake of my life. Then I get them to understand why it is so important to admit that they have a problem and then do something about it.'

'And does it always help?' he asked hopefully.

'That's one secret I'll let you find out for yourself.'

The school bell rang, and he gave me a forlorn grin. 'Gotta go. You know how it is.'

'I sure do.' Even so, I tried to prolong things just a little longer. 'You're in Grade 1, right? Who's your teacher again?'

'Mrs Gilbert.'

'Ah—she was nice.'

'Yes, she is.' He was about to skip away from me when he swivelled on his left leg and stared back into the sun. 'One more thing—who is the wisest person I will meet in my life?'

I ran my hand carefully through my hair. That was a toughie. There were so many people I could have mentioned: those six girls, Miriam, Tony, Charles, Clemmons, Luke, Harry, Matt, and of course, Brother Rojo. But in the end, there was only one person who deserved that title. 'His name was Jack.'

'Jack? I like that name. Was he your friend?'

'Oh yes, one of the best.'

'What made him such a good friend?'

'He was brave, funny, compassionate, and of course, very wise. Rest assured; he will always be there for you.'

'I see.'

'One day,' I began with a smile, 'he will visit you in the Philippines, and for a joke, you will use your contacts to have him arrested at the airport for suspected drug trafficking.'

My younger self could barely understand the implications but still laughed anyway. 'Was Jack angry with you?'

'When he realised that I had set him up, he couldn't stop laughing. That was him all over. But he still vowed to get his revenge on me.'

'And did he?'

I looked up at the heavens and smiled. 'One day, he will. And I can't wait.'

My younger self and I laughed at each other in a way that suggested we both still had so much more to learn about ourselves.

'Is that it?'

'Oh, and watch out for Robert Saunders. He's trying to undercut you with Bettie.'

He unleashed a cheeky wink solely for my benefit before disappearing into a tornado of his classmates.

I left the school behind me and took a left turn into Rodgers Street. Minutes later, I was standing in front of our old home, the house we moved to after all the dramas in Pomenay Street. As I crept closer to the driveway, a golden labrador angrily screamed at me from behind a steel railed gate, not realising, of course, that I had once ruled that very same patch of grass he was protecting.

Just like at the school, time had not expunged my memories of the house. The gum tree that I used to climb every day was still standing proudly in the front yard. The letterbox where I waited for imaginary letters from imaginary friends was located exactly where I remembered it. That old brick chimney was still proudly protecting the rest of the street.

I walked back towards the centre of the road when I saw my father's battered brown EH Holden splutter up the driveway. There he was, still handsome and virile in his late fifties. He was carrying that same faded orange soccer ball that he bought for me on my seventh birthday. 'Come and have a kick, Alex,' he called out at me. 'We haven't done that for ages.'

I nervously followed him into the backyard, and we took up our usual positions: he was perched on the driveway, right next to the drainpipe, while I was standing in front of the chook pen. A freshly cut lawn lay between us while the labrador had seemingly vanished into thin air. We began to exchange a series of well-timed passes, Dad favouring that powerful left foot he always liked to boast about, while I focused on my trusty right instep as much as I could.

'You're still very good,' he observed while trapping a delicate chip with his chest. 'You may not have been the most naturally gifted player around, but you had an iron will on the field. You never gave up.'

'No,' I replied wistfully. 'I never gave up.'

He flicked the ball up with his right foot and then bent a low pass with his left, stroking it just that little harder. I trapped the ball with my sole before flicking it up with the back of my heel, juggling it several times with both feet and then hitting a return pass.

'I wanted to play professional football,' I reflected ruefully, 'But I never became the player I wanted to be. I don't know why.'

'Quite often, it's nothing more than bad luck,' my father replied. 'I also had my dreams, but the war completely destroyed them. It's a terrible feeling, knowing that you can never go back. I tried my best, as did your mother, but we made mistakes. Awful mistakes. But life is never one straight line, don't you see?'

For the very first time, we were separated only by our honesty. 'I agree,' I replied. 'It's never one straight line.' We kicked the ball some more before he announced that he had to go to bed. 'Night shift,' he said grimly. 'You know how much I always hated the night shift.'

'Always.'

We gave each other a final hug. 'From now on, I promise that I will try harder to understand you and Mum.'

'Maybe you can write a book about us one day.'

'Yes, maybe I will.'

He tucked the ball under his arm, and I faced him one last time. 'Thank you for always watching me play soccer when I was a kid, Dad. That meant so much to me.'

'And to me as well, my son.' As I slumped against the gum tree to catch my breath, the tears I never shed for my father when he died suddenly came back to haunt me.

I soon began walking down Angus Street towards my brother's old house. All the ancient icons of the Kandos I once knew were gone. The old co-op where my mum did her shopping. The furniture store where Dad bought that toy army jeep that I cherished. The old picture theatre where I was forced to watch *Sound of Music* for the very first time. All gone—missing relics of a bygone age. But as I got closer and closer to Pomenay Street, I realised that I must not be fooled by the past. The old Kandos was never my friend, and I had to guard myself against the malevolent forces that might be still out there, waiting for me.

I eventually found our old house. I was confused at first because the picket fence that once guarded my bedroom from the Daleks and Cybermen had been stripped away. But there was no mistaking that long, narrow driveway, the shrivelled front steps, and the peculiar angle of the front yard.

The hot midday sun began to beat against my pale neck. I looked back across the street, where the girl with the droopy eye and the harelip once lived. I marvelled at the close proximity of the nearest mountain to this bizarre allotment of houses. It would have been so easy for him to shoot me from behind that enormous rock near the gum tree, calmly observe the situation, and then scamper up the mountain without anyone seeing him. Yes, so easy.

And what could stop him from doing it again?

'Can I help you?' The voice startled me. I turned around to face a woman in her fifties, with dark, auburn hair and glistening black eyes. Her mildly suspicious looks were somewhat contradicted by the gorgeous lemon beagle she was walking, who immediately began to sniff my bag for potential goodies.

'My apologies, but do you live here?' I asked casually. There was something about the woman's calm assuredness that made me think we had met before.

'My friend lives here,' she explained with a smile. 'She is visiting her family in Sydney, so I am picking up her mail, that sort of thing.'

Her beagle demanded my full attention, so he jumped at me excitedly, his tiny paws clambering at my thighs.

'Henry,' she shouted at him. 'Stop being so rude!' She looked at me apologetically. 'I'm so sorry; he's normally not that forward.' I bent down to scratch his tummy, and he immediately rolled onto his back, wanting more.

'He likes you,' she said happily, finally convinced that no person who was so comfortable with dogs could be a serious criminal.

'I have my own beagle back in Canberra. His name is George; they are a wonderful breed.'

The woman's pleasant smile indicated that everything made sense to her. 'Oh, you're that writer fellow that Samantha told me about this morning—the one who gave her a twenty-dollar tip.'

'Word sure gets around,' I laughed.

'Well, this is Kandos. There is not much that happens here without other people finding out straight away.' She held out her hand. 'My name is Bettie Scott.'

No fucking way! This is absolutely crazy!

My heart skipped a dozen beats, but I tried not to flinch. In my panic, I even forgot to tell Bettie my name.

'Wasn't there a Doctor Scott who worked here many years ago?' I finally asked after composing myself.

'Yes, he was my uncle. He practised here for decades until he died in 1989.'

'Oh, I'm sorry.'

'Don't be. Uncle Frank was a good man, but a lot of water has passed under the bridge since then.'

'It sure has.'

'So why do you find this house so interesting?' she asked me, deliberately changing the subject.

Mini-Alex suddenly made another unwanted return, and he told me to run away as fast as I could. *'Nothing good will come from this,'* he cried. But this was Bettie Scott. The first girl who I ever 'loved'; the first girl who broke my heart. There was no way on God's earth I was leaving just yet.

So, I told her everything. How I was once visited by a yellow clown in this very house when I was five, how I was shot in the arm a few days later, how this very same clown, and his counterpart, Reginald Crump, kept screwing with my life at every juncture. When I finally looked at my watch, I was amazed that I had garbled all of it out in less than five minutes.

'Wow, that's an incredible story,' said Bettie. Her spectacular eyes had not changed one bit since her childhood. 'And what do you hope to gain from this visit today?'

'I'm not sure. Some form of closure, I guess. Something to make me understand what happened here all those years ago.'

'I see,' she said softly. 'But perhaps you are looking for answers in the wrong place?'

'What do you mean?' I asked, scratching Henry on the belly again.

'You obviously believe that your apparitions were caused by something evil inside this house. But there is probably a simpler explanation.'

'Such as?'

'It's funny that you mentioned my uncle before. Poor guy. He had some harebrained ideas. Some people didn't think he was much of a doctor, but he took an avid interest in the power of the mind. He believed that some people were more gifted than others, that they could externalise their feelings to such an extent that they could even manifest into real-life events. He also believed that in times of great stress, these emotions became so conflicted, they sometimes appeared to people as duelling entities, like they were fighting each other for the possession of the same soul.'

'Your uncle was indeed a smart man,' I replied, thinking about the day my testicles turned into mini-grapefruits. 'But are you saying that Ringo Bingo the Clown and Reginald Crump were the dual manifestations of my own conscience, one good, one evil?'

'It's possible, isn't it? Look into it. Do your research. You're obviously a very bright man. The world is always a bigger place than what we know it to be.'

'And if that doesn't work?

'Then you have to seriously think about the other possibility.'

'Which is?'

'You're bat-shit crazy.'

We both laughed, and I then outrageously asked her out for coffee. There was so much more I wanted to find out about her; so many years to cherish. But alas, she blew me off again as she did that day with Robert Saunders almost fifty years ago.

'I'm so sorry. Normally I would have said yes, but I need to get this fellow back home and then bake a cake for afternoon tea. You're welcome to come along if you like.'

'I have to get back to Mudgee. But thanks, anyway.'

Her final smile took me all the way back to kindergarten before all the shit in my life truly began, and it filled my heart with rare happiness.

'It just occurred to me,' she said, stroking the back of her hair. 'We're about the same age. Did we ever go to school together?'

'No,' I replied, 'I think I would have remembered you.'

'Oh, that's a shame. You remind me of a little boy I once knew, that's all. His name was Alex if I remember correctly. He was a funny boy in a way, always following me around like a lovesick puppy. He never dared to tell me what was on his mind. But he had such a beautiful heart, and I desperately wanted him to be my friend. When he never came back after second grade, I bawled my eyes out for a week.'

'Wherever he is'—I gently took her hand—'I'm sure he still remembers you. How in the world could he possibly not?'

We reluctantly said our goodbyes, and I watched with sadness as Bettie and Henry scurried along the footpath until they melted in the welcoming sunlight.

There was one last place I needed to visit before I left Kandos, and it didn't take me long to find it. After all, I had been there so many times in my nightmares that I could walk through its dreary halls almost blindfolded. Unsurprisingly, I found it in a state of ill-repair, as if it had been deliberately neglected just for my benefit. The front screen door was ripped at its hinges, several windows were smashed, and the old barbecue area was nothing more than a pile of bricks. The only thing that had remained the same after all this time was that fucking woodshed, standing stoically in the middle of a patch of overgrown grass.

'Are you a prospective buyer?' an elderly woman with fierce red hair and a crinkled chin asked me. She sidled up next to me with a familiarity that suggested we had known each other all our lives. In another time, she would have been a most striking woman.

'Excuse me?' I replied.

'Are you interested in buying this house?'

'No. I am just visiting, that's all.'

'Good for you. Because this is a house full of bad memories.'

Yes, I can attest to that. 'Do you live here?'

She cackled with all the charm of a cartoon witch. 'No, I live in Orange, and I'm selling this house for a friend who is extremely ill.

'I see.'

'So, what brings you to Kandos?'

'Something bad happened to me in this house an exceptionally long time ago.'

She seemed to squirm at all the possibilities. 'Too many bad things have happened here, so that's not a surprise.'

'Such as?'

I could see that something had been playing on her mind for years and that she was desperate to cleanse her soul. And there I was, her knight in shining armour, ready to deliver her salvation.

'I once did something to a little boy in that shed that I've regretted all my life. I was just a teenage girl, you see, overwhelmed by my uncontrolled pubescent desires. But what I did was wrong. Very wrong. A day has not gone by where I haven't begged for his forgiveness.'

I silently took her hand and did my best to comfort her. '*Forgiveness* is such an overused word,' I told her. 'For people like you and me, it's what we do at certain points in our timeline that counts. If we make a mistake, all we can do is learn from it and do better next time.'

'But do you think he would actually forgive me?' she repeated. Her voice sounded desperate, belligerent, as if I were her last chance at atonement.

'I'd say he is far too busy forgiving himself for all of the mistakes he has made in his own life to worry about other people. But I also think he would want you to be happy and not feel guilty anymore. It was so many years ago, after all, and life is way too short. You are obviously a good person who once did something wrong, and that is the only way he will ever judge you.'

She smiled at me for the first time. In her confused, contorted face, all I could see was a loving and devoted wife, mother, and friend who had mainly led a noble life. *How could I ever sanction any retribution against someone like her? No, sometimes in life, you have to accept that what's done is done and simply move on.* Yes, it was finally time to erase this shadow from my life for good.

After leaving her behind, I wandered back into the main street and bought myself a meat pie and a soft drink from the local bakery. The stifling afternoon heat whistled past my face, so I discovered a bench beneath a shady tree at the local park and began to eat my lunch.

'May I sit down?' asked a handsome-looking woman, perhaps in her early sixties. Her brand-new hat masked a strikingly familiar face.

'Do I know you?' I asked.

She inspected me with the same sarcastic blue eyes that once preyed on my soul in Samos. 'Really, Alex—still completely clueless, I see.'

'Marlena,' I cried out. 'What the hell are you doing here?'

'I always said that I wanted to see Australia, didn't I? And I'm having such a ball visiting the local wineries.'

'This is crazy,' I replied. 'After all these years.'

'Yes, it has been a while. But I have been keeping an eye on you.'

'Why am I not surprised?'

She laughed wickedly before wiping her face with a tissue. 'You disappoint me, Alex. I'm not here to criticise you at all.'

'Then why *are* you here?'

'To tell you that you're on the right track. To encourage you to keep going. That sort of thing.'

'That must be hard for you.'

'Oh, don't be so melodramatic,' she berated me. 'I know what you went through in 2016. But you survived, and that's something you can be proud of.'

'Proud?' I looked at her with disgust. 'How many people did I hurt because I failed to do something positive about my mental health? My first wife, Rachel, Toni, the married woman from Sydney, Dulcie.' A deep breath. 'Martina.' Another deep breath. 'I don't feel proud about that at all.'

'Yes, you have hurt people, without question. And you rightfully need to reflect upon your behaviour. But look at all the good things you did. How you stood up to Marco that night, how you made sure that Katie had a birthday to remember, how you helped Danielle with her self-confidence, how you supported Delilah at the Windows on the World, how you tried your damnedest to save that little girl in the Philippines, all the young women that you successfully mentored at the Agency. These are not things to be sneezed at, my dear.'

'Then why do I still feel so guilty?'

'Because we are all frail human beings who live by the seat of our emotions,' said Marlena. 'There are good people who do bad things and bad people who do good things. Sometimes we go through life unable to distinguish between the two. In the end, I guess that God tallies everything up and then has a heart-to-heart discussion with you when you die. In the meantime, like you just said to the woman with the red hair, all we can do is admit our mistakes and learn from them.'

'And what do you think was my biggest mistake?' I asked her curiously.

Marlena guffawed loudly. 'You are a sucker for punishment, aren't you?'

'I'm serious.'

She took off her silly hat and unfurled her curly black hair. 'I said this to you before, an awfully long time ago. You are an eighteenth-century knight living in the twenty-first century. While you rode your beautiful white stallion, acting all chivalrous to anyone in a short skirt, the world passed you by. Women no longer wanted to be objectified, to be told that we were beautiful or that they needed male protection. We really just wanted to live the lives that men do—without having to look behind our backs all the time. All you were doing through your naïvety was serving us up on a dinner plate to the bad guys.'

'What can I do differently?'

'For a start, you can use your current position in FearLess to agitate for change.'

My smile was both reckless and solemn. 'I'm a man in his fifties, once accused of gaslighting women, living in the middle of the #Metoo movement. As soon as I put my head above the parapet, there will be thousands out there ready to blow it right off.'

'You're also a military historian,' Marlena replied. 'You know that to win a battle, sometimes you have to be courageous and take risks. Sure, some people will denigrate you. But so many others will follow you. You're a natural leader, Alex, and always will be. So go out and strut your stuff. Develop programs, spread the word, fight like hell for your wives, sisters, and daughters. Make men understand that the only people who can stop men from abusing and hurting women are other men. That is your only role now. If you truly wish to honour Martina, get your arse moving.'

'I'll try.' I somehow managed to laugh at her shrillness.

'Good!' said Marlena as she stood up and reconstituted her hat. 'Here ends the lesson. Now, the wineries at Mudgee await me.' She bent over and pecked me on the cheek. 'You're a good man, Alex. I've always said that. A little misguided, perhaps, but your heart is in the right place. I wish you well.'

'Hey, wait a minute,' I called after her as she sidestepped a newly planted flowerbed. 'What about Martina? What really happened to her?'

'Spoilers, Alex,' she yelled back at me. 'It's not my station to tell you that. That's a path that only you can take, and I hope one day it leads you to everlasting peace.'

She took a few more steps before I goaded her one last time. 'Hey, I heard that you became a high-flying lawyer. How on earth did you manage that?'

Marlena's laughter sprinkled the air, and I gathered her reply just as she magically faded from view. 'I got rid of all the men in my life, that's how!'

I had some time to kill before Miriam picked me up at four o'clock. I walked down Angus Street again and turned right into Darbee Road. In years gone by, this was the main artery that led to the cement works. One day, when I was barely four years old, I was determined to see where Dad worked at the big factory, and so I sneaked out my bedroom window while no-one was watching. For hours I walked up and down this lonely road, bewildered and confused, searching for a way out before my brother Charlie finally found me sleeping next to a tree.

In many ways, my life mirrored this very same journey. For so long, I had remained bewildered and confused by my mental illness, trapped in a remote corner of the forest, waiting for someone to find me. But just when I thought everything was lost, a light came shining through the darkness and showed me the way home. Only then did I recognise how lucky I was, for not many people like me were so fortunate to get a second chance.

I recently listened to a podcast from a woman with PTSD who said that she wouldn't have changed anything about her life, that her trauma had opened up her mind. What a load of bullshit! I would have given my last cent to have avoided this curse. Imagine—to be able to wake up every morning knowing that the sun will shine on you all day.

So many things could have been avoided; so many people need not have been hurt. But I refused to use my mental illness as an excuse. I wasn't a victim, and I took personal responsibility for everything that had befallen me. Apart from Martina, nor did I want people to forgive me for what I had done to them. All I could do was offer them an explanation, continue to reflect upon my actions, and dissect the errors I made. By doing so, I knew that I could encourage other men like me to consider their own behaviour and help them become better people.

At the FearLess conference two weeks ago, a lady walked up to me and called me a hero for having the courage to tell my story. I wasn't a hero at all, I explained to her. I was just an ordinary man who, at the time of his greatest crisis, realised that to survive, he had to discover who he really was. I told her that other people suffering from PTSD and mental illness had far more compelling stories to tell than mine. They included our veterans, their families, our first responders, women who experienced domestic abuse and sexual violence, and refugees and their children who had been locked away for years and years.

The woman then told me that her son, an army corporal who had served five tours of the Middle East, still suffered stigma associated with his PTSD condition. His wife had left him, he was forced to leave the job he loved, and he had lost many of his friends. Only the support of his family prevented him from taking his own life. I thought about my own situation at the Agency and the stigma and hurt I carried with me for nearly two years after the events of March 2016. Nothing can adequately describe the pain one feels when they aren't believed or feel abandoned by those who should know better. That's why the woman and I both agreed that the only way we could defeat this scourge was through a national, coordinated campaign where everyone's story was taken seriously. As I later said to another conference delegate, it's a dream well worth fighting for.

As I approached the end of my journey, I thought back to the many people who had helped me along the way. Danielle was right; we all get to meet at least one person in our lives who can unlock the chains to our hearts. Fortunately for me, during my thirties, God entrusted my heart to six incredible young women, all of whom witnessed the depths of my despair and tried to show me a different way. Their collective wisdom, together with Miriam's unconditional love, and the support of my family, work colleagues, and friends, helped save my life and led me down the path towards redemption.

Of course, I still have my bad days. I still have my nagging doubts. I still desperately long for Martina's forgiveness. Indeed, I always will. But I now have the one thing that I never had before: hope.

For me, the Season of Clouds was finally over, and the Season of Wisdom had begun.

And as I left this mysterious, ancient forest for the last time, I was sure that I could hear Brother Rojo's voice calling out to me from beyond the mountains.

Laughing at me.

Telling me that I was right.

The Gift

Potsdam, October 2019
Three weeks later

I have an hour to kill before the bus returns to Berlin. The rain that has been flitting around the edges of our tour to Potsdam now lashes fiercely against my face. Fearful that I will get absolutely drenched, I hive off into a charming little café in Potsdam's beautiful old market square and order a coffee and a piece of strudel.

I've had a wonderful day so far, visiting several historical sites that have fascinated my intellect for years, including Sanssouci Palace and the infamous Glienicke Bridge of Spies. It has been the perfect way to end my week-long stay in Berlin. Over the last few days, I have worked strenuously on my manuscript, hoping that the historical ambience of my favourite city in Europe would inspire me. So far, I haven't been disappointed. My creative juices have been overflowing, I'm happy to report. Last night I began writing the final chapters of *A Season of Clouds.* Hopefully, by the time I return to Australia, my manuscript will be completed.

My attention turns to my iPhone, where I have receive an alert on my Liverpool FC app about some injury news ahead of our crunch game with Manchester United later that afternoon. I didn't want to jinx things too much, but I am confident that only a worldwide plague can stop us from winning the title this season for the first time in thirty years. *I mean, a worldwide plague, how stupid was that?*

'Randolph, can you please behave?' For some reason, these inane words whisk across the narrow floor of the café and land right in my coffee. I immediately swivel my head upwards with intrigue, certain that their unique cadence has unplugged some unknown memory from my past. My eyes warily follow their suspected path towards a table at the front of the room. Luckily, there is a clear line of sight between us, so there can be no mistake about the origin of that comment.

There are three of them sitting at the table, all, I assume, belonging to the same family. The boy, who I conclude must be Randolph, is a handsome young teenager with typical blonde curly hair and an imperious-looking nose. The girl sitting next to him is slightly older but no less impressive. Her long black hair dangles against the table, and her pretty face stares ominously at her iPhone. She looks thoroughly bored, as if she needs to be somewhere else, and is utterly disinterested in the ongoing tensions between mother and son.

'Randolph, do you want me to call your father?' He blows out some hot air in defiance, and I wonder what his mother will do next. It's only now, when she lifts her iPhone to her lips, that I finally get to see her face.

No, it can't be. Surely to God, this has to be a mirage caused by my overly active imagination. But the more I try to deny my memory banks, the starker the realisation becomes. Sure, the hair has been cut short, but there is no mistaking the clarity of her blue eyes and the precision of her exquisitely crafted mouth.

Don't look, please don't look. But of course, she does. In that one moment of absurd synchronicity, our eyes are drawn to each other like magnets, and the confusion they now display defies any recollection that we were once lovers. So I drop my head back into my iPhone and hope to God that she and her children decide to leave the café soon.

Fifteen, twenty minutes go by. Out of the corner of my eye, I see some movement at the station. Her son and daughter lazily put on their jackets while she now stumbles directly towards me. *Oh my God! What am I going to say to her after all these years? What could possibly be gained by our separate lives intersecting once again?*

She is seconds away from me before another patron pushes past my table. Unavoidably, she gets caught in a slipstream of her own making, as other patrons stampede towards my table. As a result, her shoulder gently rubs against my back. But no, this was not some prelude to an unwelcome conversation. It was an accident, pure and simple. Because she now asks for the bill, and after the squeak of a cash register, a flurry of thank yous in German quickly follows. She finds a way to bypass my table without getting close as last time, and I finally sink back into my chair.

Just to be sure, I wait impatiently for another five minutes before I stand up to pay my bill. The guy at the cash register now asks me in broken English whether everything was to my satisfaction.

'All good, thank you.' I glance at the bill and leave him a twenty-Euro note for his trouble. 'Keep the change,' I tell him politely.

'Thank you, sir,' he replies. I am just about to turn and leave when he puts up his hand. 'By the way, the lady who left before asked me to give you this.' My stomach churns as he passes me a crumpled piece of paper, and I open it up carefully:

Alex, thank you for finally keeping your promise. Now I can keep mine. E.

‘Did the woman give you anything else?’ I calmly ask the cashier.

‘Yes, she did.’ I open my palm, and he places a small, cold object across my fingers. I immediately drop my eyes and stare at a single British one-pound coin.

I place the coin in my wallet, slowly wipe the tears from my cheeks, and walk out into the waiting rain.

THE END

Acknowledgements

Writing *A Season of Clouds.* was the most difficult thing I have done in my life. From its inception in early 2018 until the completion of my initial manuscript some three years later, the book became an emotional commitment that at times stretched the boundaries of my intellect and spirit. Thankfully, I was able to lean on the support of so many people who helped me reach the finish line in one piece.

Special thanks go to my close friend Amber Vardos who convinced me to write the book as a fictional memoir after I struggled to make initial headway. Amber and my good friends John Clements, Renee Wilson, Luke Fraser, Andrew Rice, Pat Hanson, Brian Dooley, Josh Ahrens, Charles Griplas, Charles Hillier, Paul Dwyer, Marcus Smith, Jacinta Carroll and the founder of *Stories of Hope*, Kerrie Atherton all kept me going with their words of wisdom during some very dark times.

I am also very grateful to the boards of FearLess Outreach and Animal Therapies Limited, whose members have continued to support me during my journey. In particular, I am indebted to my good friend and colleague at FearLess, Belinda Neil, for the incredible enthusiasm she has shown for the book and her very insightful comments.

Getting positive and constructive feedback is essential for any aspiring writer. Therefore, I am very appreciative of the time taken by Belinda, and my friends Bill Crane and Karen Peel, in reading various versions of the manuscript and providing me with such excellent suggestions.

I'm also extremely grateful for the support, guidance, and professionalism provided by the team at Ocean Reeve Publishing. It's been an honour working with you all and I've learnt much from the experience.

In February 2021, I was introduced to one of Queensland's finest young editors and ghost-writers, Roxanne McCarty-O'Kane. I am very honoured and grateful that she decided to work with me on *A Season of Clouds.* Her belief in the book and her capacity to immerse herself into the story was remarkable. Consequently, it is a much better book because of Roxanne's exquisite contribution.

I would also like to thank all my friends and family for their ongoing support and love, especially my wife, Miriam. It is not easy when your husband announces that he is going to write a book that exposes to the world his mental health issues and past love life. But she has accepted my baffling project with grace, dignity, and lots of humour. Thank you so much, Miriam, for believing in me.

Finally, my biggest regret is that our faithful beagle George didn't live long enough to see the book published. He was my best friend and constant companion throughout the three years of writing the book. I shall never forget him. Miss you, buddy.

About the Author

Alex Gerrick is a former army reserve officer, senior bureaucrat, and political adviser who now advocates for PTSD sufferers and men's health in his role as CEO of FearLess Outreach. He holds master's degrees from Deakin University and the National Defense College of the Philippines, as well as several other academic qualifications. *A Season of Clouds* is his first book. Alex lives in Canberra, Australia, with his wife, Miriam. He is currently working on his next book, the second in his proposed *A Season of Clouds* trilogy, *The Search for Martina*.

CPSIA information can be obtained
at www.ICGtesting.com
Printed in the USA
LVHW061201130422
716028LV00011B/508

9 781922 644176